Bolton Council

Please return/renew this item
by the last date shown.
Books may also be renewed by
phone or the Internet.

HO

Tel: 01204 332384
www.bolton.gov.uk/libraries

BOLTON LIBRARIES

BT 188 9890 4

THE PRINCIPALS

THE PRINCIPALS

Bill James

Severn House Large Print
London & New York

This first large print edition published 2017
in Great Britain and the USA by
SEVERN HOUSE PUBLISHERS LTD of
19 Cedar Road, Sutton, Surrey, England, SM2 5DA.
First world regular print edition published 2014 by
Severn House Publishers Ltd.

British Library Cataloguing in Publication Data
A CIP catalogue record for this title is available from the British Library.

ISBN-13: 9780727895448

Severn House Publishers support the Forest Stewardship Council™
[FSC™], the leading international forest certification organisation. All
our titles that are printed on FSC certified paper carry the FSC logo.

MIX
Paper from
responsible sources
FSC° C013056

Typeset by Palimpsest Book Production Ltd.,
Falkirk, Stirlingshire, Scotland.
Printed and bound in Great Britain by
T J International, Padstow, Cornwall.

One

2014

Of course, Martin Moss realized there was bound to be a load of bitchy spite, top-notch rattiness and abiding malevolence about the statue idea. Hang on, hang on. Update. It *began* as about the statue idea – *a* statue idea, singular – but soon became about the *statues* idea, plural, two of them: binary, a term well-known in higher education. Moss thought the second proposed statue could be regarded in a sense as the baby of the first, by a kind of *in vivo* rather than *in vitro* fertilization: out of a living thing, not a test tube. Official minutes, e-mails and memos about the two projects came to be referred to as 'Statue One (L.C.)' and 'Statue Plus (V.T.)'. It was thought that to call the later scheme 'Statue Two' might be to confer on Statue One a hint of precedence – precedence not just time-wise but as to status. No way.

Moss could swiftly and simply describe the origins of the 'Statue One' concept. Those bracketed letters, 'L.C.' were the initials of Lawford Chote, former principal of Sedge University (founded 1885, motto 'Onward Friends Of Learning') during the period of cuts and stringent financial restraints on public sector spending by the third Thatcher Conservative government.

1

Chote had resisted these restraints and cuts and defiantly continued on a programme for Sedge of expansion and expense and galloping debt. Onward friends of learning. He had apparently claimed somewhere that the word 'Positivism' was tattooed on a part of his body not obvious in day-to-day circumstances. He also claimed there'd been plenty of room for an exclamation mark after it, as suggested by the lady tattooist, but Chote had declined this saying it would imply that his positivism was something startlingly unusual, whereas he considered it routine; as natural to him and inevitable as breathing. But, owing to this inveterate free-spending and positivism, with or without an exclamation mark, Sedge in the late 1980s had drifted very, very close to bankruptcy, ruin, total extinction. Onward friends of learning, over the lemming cliff. Martin Moss didn't enjoy thinking about it even so long after.

Utterly against Lawford Chote's wishes, an emergency troop of auditors from the Department of Education and Science had moved in and ultimately, as a result of their findings, it was arranged for Chote to be removed eternally from post. Onward, Chote, to anywhere but here. Half a dozen Treasury people also came from London and assumed temporary control of the university's finances to stop the money troubles getting even worse, the debt vaster. Once some sort of stability had been secured, they would recommend the payment from state funds of a special and hefty salvation grant.

When Sedge seemed likely to die, Chote was

described to Moss by a colleague in the English Department as 'the only man in the world who has single-handedly destroyed a university, a university more than a hundred years old and named after one of its revered and famed Victorian founders.' Chote came in for a fair whack of such vilification and abuse. His drinking, rudeness, half-baked witticisms and gobby, turbulent aggression didn't help his case much.

However, that was 1987. Today, Sedge thrived. Moss was still part of it. That one-off salvation grant, plus a government-driven reshaping of the university's management set-up had worked, and worked so successfully that Sedge might soon be invited to join the select clique of British universities known as the Russell Group, including Oxbridge. On account of this remarkable progress, some influential voices had begun to ask whether Dr Lawford Chote might have been a long-term visionary rather than a reckless, half-daft, giddy, blundering prodigal. Would Sedge be what it was now if Dr Chote hadn't given it a violent, perilous, necessary push-start? Had he shown admirable spirit, doggedness and bravery in standing up to Mrs Thatcher and her philistine, vandal cronies? Had his badger's arse roughness and loud contempt for his enemies been the only means available to oppose Rightist political attempts to curtail the spread of university opportunity for all young people regardless of class and/or low family income? It wasn't as though he stood alone in trying to repulse Thatcherism. Oxford University refused by a plump majority to award her an honorary degree in civil law because of her attacks on research funding. This, despite the fact that she had been a chemistry undergraduate at Oxford as a young woman. And Martin Moss himself had wondered at the time whether Chote's objectives were right, but his ways of trying to reach them sadly clumsy and a turn-off.

So, anyhow, Sedge admirably, gloriously resurgent. And so, also, a statue proposal from the senate and high board and the education press amounted to something more than a formal impulse to commemorate a past chieftain. It was certainly that, yes, but the proposal contained, too, a notable element of apology, of admission that Lawford Chote might have been unfairly punished, even victimised. The statue would be a tangible symbol of regret and of the wish to compensate for timorous, short-sighted error; perhaps, in fact, a symbol of belated love.

Martin Moss still taught and researched at Sedge, but not many other participants in this 1987 crisis were still around: retired, dead, or gone away to other appointments. The contritional statue had to be a corporate matter. It was Sedge itself bringing a plea for forgiveness. As someone on the high board had said, if the statue had a caption plaque, it ought to read: 'They done you wrong, Lawf,' or however that came out in Latin. Leftist members of the present senate and high board – a fair number – cherished retrospective loathing for Margaret Thatcher – as they would have for Mussolini or Genghis Kahn – and were keen to deliver any insult and posthumous kick up the jacksy, such as the statue

4

scheme. Moss wasn't sure about his own attitude yet.

But all this centred only on Statue One. In 1987 the city had two universities, each of them touched by the crisis. And it had two principals, each of them touched by the crisis: Dr Lawford Chote and Dr Victor Tane. Charter Mill and its campus lay a couple of miles away in grounds that still contained the carefully looked-after, historic watermill which had given the university its name. At Sedge, though, it was usually spoken of as 'the leisure centre,' not because the staff and students were lazy but because one of its degree courses was Hotel Management and Leisure Pursuits. Charter Mill had been created from a previous polytechnical college in the 1960s. It offered, as well as traditional university classes, a range of practical, vocational teaching aimed very specifically at preparing students for the careers market: Hotels and Leisure; Journalism; Hairdressing and Beautification; Pop Group Management; Organized Crime And Its Defeat; Secretarial Skills; Advertising; Pin-ball and Fruit Machine Design and Repair. Motto: 'Let Knowledge Be Honoured.'

Charter Mill had been regarded by many at Sedge as OK and, indeed, worthy, but not really what a university should be. Founders of one of the Oxford colleges in the thirteenth century would surely be surprised to discover that a university included a department of hairdressing and beautification. A university's commitment should be to learning for learning's own pure, magnificent sake, not to train students how to

5

land and keep a job, except possibly for a medical or law degree. Chote and many of his Sedge colleagues saw Charter Mill as hopelessly banal, plodding and non-intellectual. It was much smaller than Sedge and, at the beginning of the boodle difficulties Chote had suggested a virtual takeover of Charter Mill. That didn't mean he thought Sedge would benefit by offering a course in hotel management and leisure pursuits, and so on. But he lusted after the mortgageable value of Charter's buildings, watermill and general real estate; and the extra per capita government grant that would arrive for Sedge's increased student numbers.

Victor Tane very competently and solvently led Charter Mill. He had responded swiftly and efficiently to the calls for economising. Charter Mill would be an unburdened asset if merged with Sedge. That's how Lawford Chote had calculated things. Naturally, he would remain as principal of the combined institutions, thanks to Sedge's seniority and distinguished roots. Victor Tane could, perhaps, be taken on as deputy, though without any assurance that he would succeed to the principalship when Chote retired. Although Tane had a First and a doctorate, both in classics, from Oxford, and had won several prizes for the composition of Latin verse there, Chote considered that none of this could adequately offset Tane's connection with journalism production, including tabloids, presumably, pin ball machinery, pop groups and raves.

A merger of the two institutions did in fact take place though not at all as Chote had envisaged.

Soon after the government intervention, Charter Mill took over the tottering Sedge, rather than the reverse, and helped bring about its recovery. Victor Tane became principal of the new place and Lawford Chote was humanely phased out, with no impairment of his pension or requirement to pay back some of the cash he had blown. The city now had only one university. Tane agreed that it should maintain the name, Sedge, and the Charter Mill title was also phased out, though the antique watermill endured. Yes, the reconstituted Sedge had begun to do very nicely. Gratitude to Tane still flourished long after he and Chote had died. As a result came the strong, unyielding lobby from many sources in support of 'Statue Plus (V.T.).' That is, if there were to be statues at all. Would they be sculpted to stand alongside each other like happy equally deserving partners? Or might one of them be slightly the more prominent of the pair? In which fucking case fucking which?

Two

1987

Back more than a quarter of a century, Martin was thinking about a possible second home in Florida while talking in celebratory, milestone fashion to a lecture room full of people about something else. In the front row Mrs Rowena

Chote, the principal's wife, most likely well tanked-up for the occasion, had fallen into a sozzled, uncompromising sleep which required him to raise the volume of his words so they could be heard above the belligerent, intermittent snoring. This intermittent nature of it made things deeply more difficult. In the periods of silence, people could quite reasonably hope it had stopped for keeps and therefore she didn't need to be woken up by a shake or elbow-dig from someone beside her, right or left, or both. She'd remain asleep, perhaps, but, although this might be hurtful and off-putting to the speaker, mere sleeping was not pro-actively disruptive: the opposite.

The principal himself, naturally, had a front row seat, also, but several places away from her, and when the snoring was at its heartiest, noisiest and, seemingly, most entrenched, tried to signal with a hand and leg movement that she should be jabbed or ankle-clogged into consciousness. Then, however, the snoring would pause and those next to her obviously prayed, fingers crossed, that the pause was in fact more than a pause, a finale, making physical intervention by them unnecessary. Although Chote continued to gesture that due force should be used to bring her back fully and fully appreciative to the proceedings, she might resent the treatment and turn loud and very nasty. And the principal personally would possibly in retrospect regret and/or deny, having semaphored the order to intervene. Lawford Chote could be extremely unpredictable and contrary – and exceptionally dangerous. Some described him as 'driven', 'committed', and 'intensely focussed'; others said 'anarchic', 'foolhardy', 'egomaniac', self-contradictory'. There were marginally fewer plus comments about the principal around than minus. If he knew this it would not bother him, Moss thought. Chote would say that positive, thrustful leadership always brought out the sly, miserable, feeble, envious, nugatory backbiters. Their niggles proved he had things damn right. They feared change. Yet he believed that change as directed, powered, by him equated with progress. He regarded himself as the future; and, also, a quite satisfactory present. He would certainly be the only university head in Britain – or anywhere else, most probably – who put a metric tonne of contempt into his voice when he used the standard term for his professional colleagues, 'academics'. He made it sound like a disease, say, 'shingles' or 'piles'. Chote had thick, dark hair that gleamed under electric light, a strong, straight nose, broad neck and shoulders and generally powerful looking, stocky body.

One of Sedge University's traditions that the Principal had decided not to pulverize to date was the kind of inaugural address being given now by Martin Moss in Sedge's Quantum Hall. Moss had recently been promoted to a chair, a professorship, in English and American Literature and it was the rule and practice that those raised to this rank should mark the step up with a discourse about some typical aspect of their work. A congratulatory dinner would follow for selected guests in the newly refurbished staff dining room.

9

Martin Moss's topic was: 'The redundant double-whammy for Sir Clifford in D.H. Lawrence's novel, *Lady Chatterley's Lover*'. Why, he vigorously asked, had Lawrence made the titled Clifford Chatterley unable to get it up and so oblige Connie, his wife, to go for sexual satisfaction from Mellors, the gamekeeper? Surely if Lawrence wanted to portray the upper classes, represented in Clifford, as emotionally narrow and null he should have shown Clifford as like that, not because he'd been paralysed from the waist down by a World War I wound, perhaps received in valorous circumstances, but because the males of his social class were actually born and brought up emotionally narrow and null. Lawrence wanted, as it were, to boot Cliff in the crutch twice, once for being an aristo, and once for being neutered. Did Clifford deserve this extra disability, Martin demanded, his tone fiercely aggrieved?

He pointed the audience towards another novel dealing with impotence but with virtually the opposite tone, though published only a couple of years before *Lady Chatterley's Lover*. This was Ernest Hemingway's *The Sun Also Rises,* renamed *Fiesta* in Britain. Jake Barnes, the hero of this tale, had been similarly incapacitated in the war, but was treated by Hemingway as a tragic, admirable figure, hopelessly in love with the shag-around Lady Brett Ashley. Moss said he would admit, though, that in the novel by British author Anthony Powell, *A Dance to the Music of Time,* failure in the bedroom by the clownish Ken Widmerpool is treated as part of his general, pathetic social ineptitude. Did

American fiction have something to teach the Brits about sympathy and tolerance?

Moss had picked the book for his inaugural because, despite this objection, he liked it overall. It had been unsuccessfully prosecuted for obscenity in 1960 and this acquittal had brought a welcome boost to freedom of expression. Moss had asked a gentle, dreamy girl student in one of his Sedge seminars what she thought of the book. Her reply had been nicely balanced, he thought: 'I can take the fuck and the cunt but am not keen on the shit and the piss,' she'd said. It had seemed a pity she was too young to have offered her opinion at the trial.

In Quantum Hall, Rowena Chote had slumped slightly to the left, her head resting on the shoulder of the university Developments Director, one of the Principal's inner, inner team. The Developments Director didn't seem to mind providing this cushion but, because he knew the Principal so well – his bursts of crazed temper and unforgiving, serial hates – he would find nudging or forcibly jostling her too much. In any case, she had quietened again now. The refusal to act by those sitting near to his wife had probably angered Chote. He'd regard them as craven jerks. It wouldn't please Lawford to realize they must be afraid of him. He'd believe good leadership should enthuse and, yes, inspire, subordinates, not scare them, paralyse them.

Moss continued his address and for a while at the lectern was looking down and reading from his crib sheets. When he raised his head again and glanced towards Mrs Chote and the D.D. to

11

check the current state of things, he felt amazed to see she had opened her eyes, righted herself on the chair, and was staring with vast animation and interest towards Moss. She muttered something and smiled; he experienced a kind of triumphalism. He had broken her deep doze, harvested her attention. How, though, for God's sake?

He had been reading to the audience more or less robotically from the script while his mind went off to calculate what his new salary would justify as a bank loan to buy the Florida property. Now, though, he paused and did a super speed-read of the preceding chunk or two of his notes. He'd been talking about *Lady Chatterley's Lover,* her husband, bodily ruined, and her search for, and discovery of, sexual fulfilment with the gamekeeper; 'not invariably via the dedicated route,' he'd added. And now he thought he could interpret the words she'd muttered a moment ago: 'not invariably via the dedicated route,' she'd repeated. The happy smile had followed. Moss's lecture went well after that.

The staff dining room and bar on the second floor were reached by a wide, curving, azure-blue carpeted staircase. This had been installed lately on the Principal's orders at big expense and despite protests in the senate about extravagance. Dr Chote had declared he wanted a university staircase fit to figure in the kind of university he was making this university into. Impressive staircases gave extra character to their surrounds. The more modest, workaday stairway that had been part of the original building was torn out,

12

broken up and the bits dumped. Moss knew that the Principal considered this as brilliant symbolism: Sedge was on the way up and now had a staircase apt for this ascent. The Principal had also commissioned a revamp of the dining room and bar themselves. They were panelled now in oak and the tables and chairs were also oak. He had said that royalty would most likely visit Sedge in the future to witness directly its outstanding advance, so the décor and fittings should be in keeping.

Dr Chote bought the Developments Director and Martin aperitifs. The Principal, like his wife just now, was smiling. Quite often a smile from Chote could be taken as a genuine, temporary guarantee of friendship and safety. 'Martin,' he said, 'Roy and I were wowed, delighted, at the way you dealt with that situation in Quantum.'

'Absolutely,' Roy Gormand, the Developments Director said. 'Wowed. Delighted.'

'Decisive, tactful, delicate,' Chote said.

'Certainly,' Gormand said. 'Decisive.'

Three

1987

'Look here, Martin, I'm always on the alert for people who will bring inventiveness, subtlety, clarity to what I call my "action group" – Roy, of course, and a few others whom I can trust to

13

see matters as they should be seen, and who will work with me to bring added initiative, merit and distinction to Sedge.' Chote knew he did need people of that kidney, yet their yes-man qualities sometimes bored and irritated him. Sometimes, like tonight, for instance, sometimes did more than bore and irritate him: sickened him. Roy would at least not betray him, desert him, in any battle, though. And there would be battles.

But the kind of help he and others could offer was not very much because (a) they would approve anything as long as it came from him. And (b) people knew the cronies would approve anything as long as it came from him and therefore gave no weight and, or credence, to what came from them. Someone like this young – youngish – Moss would be different. Moss had vision and the striking ability to explain that vision to others. Moss saw that Cliff Chatterley had been treated very poorly by D.H. Lawrence. Roy Gormand would not be capable of such insight. Moss was someone who could phrase a delicate comment about Connie's and Mellors' shenanigans that could wake up and interest Rowena even when she was comatosed and three-quarters pissed. Martin Moss might be of clear-sighted, sensitive use to him.

Clearly Moss was someone with high skills as a communicator. Lawford considered this could be valuable in presenting very soon his case for the proud advancement of Sedge, despite that fucking obstructiveness of Thatcher and her cabinet. Chote felt very glad now that he had

14

not followed an earlier impulse to wipe out the tradition of the new-prof lecture, although he rated some – most – of the twerps who qualified as pompous farts, and very obviously pompous farts when they performed. Not Marty Moss, however.

'Perhaps it's a fault of mine that I haven't given proper heed to your qualities before, Mart,' he told Moss. 'Tonight corrects that. Thank heaven, I say, for Lady Chatterley's acquired taste for rumpy pumpy. Yes, rumpy. We're going to undertake some very testing manoeuvres shortly, I think, Martin, and I believe Roy will agree.'

'Absolutely,' the Developments Director said.

'I know I can count on you for support and help, Martin.'

'Absolutely,' Gomand said. 'I'm sure.'

Lawford thought he'd take Martin Moss out to see Charter Mill. This would be creative principalship. Chote disliked imprecise, woolly talk about his aims for Sedge. If Moss saw the Charter Mill buildings, the old watermill itself, and the playing fields it would give a tangible, touchable form to the general noise about expansion of Sedge. Most of it could be seen from the road: no need to get out of the car. Lawford wouldn't want to be caught spying: some people at Charter would recognize him, including Tane. Awkward speculation about his visit might start. Charter was a couple of miles away from Sedge, but many universities had bits of their campus scattered around a city.

Of course, Marty Moss might already be familiar with the Charter Mill spread. He had

15

lived in the city for almost a decade, first as a lecturer, then senior lecturer, then professor. But Moss would not have looked at Charter with the sort of purpose Chote wanted now: looked at, to be forthright, looked at it as prey; as a potential prize. He wanted Marty to understand – would help him to understand – that, certainly, Charter was fine in its own limited way, but that it would be much safer, more comfortable, more distinguished, if – when – absorbed by Sedge.

Chote would admit that Charter Mill had charm, despite the plainness of the modern architecture – if it could be called architecture – but, surely, Charter could not exist independently and alone in the present tough economic circumstances. Charter *needed* Sedge and it would be only an act of generosity and realism to offer Victor Tane a rescue deal and a lift up to the kind of status implicit in Sedge, natural to Sedge, inherited by Sedge. He thought Moss would see things in this fashion – again, intended to *help* him see things in this fashion – and Chote would be quite interested in Martin's positive response.

At the post inaugural dinner, Rowena Chote had been to tidy up and joined them now in the bar. 'Wonderful, Martin!' she said. 'That D.H. – so smart and comprehensive about sex, isn't he? No wonder Frieda ran off with him, dumping an academic, as it happens, but don't let this bother you, Marty. I love the story of Frieda on horseback calling out that it's *so* thrilling to have something splendidly powerful between her legs. And Lawrence tells her to stop it, she's been reading too many of his books! And then there's D.H.'s *The Virgin And The Gypsy* where Joe Boswell, the sexy traveller, remembers to tell the maidenly Yvette his name after he's been to bed with her, trying to warm her up, both naked, after a flood. Such finesse! Yes, *do* get me a drink, would you, please Lawford?'

Four

1987

Chote moved off to the bar to fetch his wife's bevy. Watching him, she found herself doing what she often found herself doing lately: she'd try to work out what someone like Marty Moss really made of Lawford and the Lawford regime. Of course, Moss would have to respond in agreeable style to Lawford's friendliness: he was the principal, had a lot of clout and knew how to use it, pro or con. Also, he could shout louder than most. He'd had plenty of practice.

She suspected that there were those in Sedge who considered he had grabbed and continued to grab too much influence. They saw him as an autocrat, and non-collegiate. Perhaps he was, a little. Autocrats could keep going, though. As long as they came up with improvements, gains, success; that blue carpet on the new, broad staircase did look fine.

However, universities were inclined to regard

themselves as deeply democratic, their policies decided by committees and votes after civilised, thorough discussion: checks and balances. Lawford lacked affection for committees and votes, and especially for checks and balances. 'Stick them,' he'd bellow. 'Did Julius Caesar have to worry about fucking checks and balances?'

Moss, she reckoned, would be thirty-six or -seven. She thought the views of younger staff like Mart about Lawford's style of leadership could be important. Although Lawford might – did – see himself as the future, the *actual* Sedge future, the calendared days, weeks, months, years and decades, lay with Moss and his contemporaries. The Roy Gormands, nearing retirement, would go along with Lawford at least partly because they wanted a quiet, unstressful rundown of their careers. Why invite aggro so late in the day, so late in *their* day? This might not be the attitude of the Martys.

She regretted now having gin-kipped and probably snored an unmusical bar or two while he did his obligatory, functional spiel. It would be bad if he turned cold and hostile. She felt she ought to demonstrate fast that she'd heard more of his stuff than might be apparent. The shut-eye period could have indicated concentration, an escape from distractions, couldn't it? OK, the snoring, if there had been snoring, knocked this interpretation into the ditch, but it wasn't certain that she'd snored and, if she had . . . if she had she had, no getting around that now.

She tried to recall earlier passages of his lecture, before the jolly section that had roused

18

her, because from then on she'd stayed alert and radiantly wakeful in case he had more of the same on offer. She dredged her brain. Was something said about a hilarious absurdity in the trial? Oh, yes, yes, she could just about remember this.

She turned to him. 'Mart, you mentioned that idiot prosecution lawyer who asked the jury in super dudgeon whether they would allow their servants to read this book. How many jury members would have servants? What was the lawyer afraid of – that one of the housemaids would get hotted-up by envy of Connie's sportif shags and jump the homeowner in the scullery?'

'Order,' Moss said. 'They were scared publication would be a step towards destruction of social order. It was published first in Florence and everyone knew how riotously sexual people around the Mediterranean were. Britain must not accept such a dodgy, subversive import. That was the prosecution's line.'

A middle-aged, dumpy, wheezy-voiced man with a mop of grey hair and a crimson bow tie on a black shirt joined them. He carried a glass of what looked to Rowena like apple juice. 'Greetings, Al,' Rowena said. Alan Norton-Hord was editor of the local morning paper, a graduate of Sedge, and chair of the Former Students' Society. He'd occasionally turn up at a public performance like Mart's inaugural. 'We were just discussing order,' Rowena said.

'There can come times when order will mean repression, wouldn't you say so, Al?' Chote asked. He'd returned with her drink.

'The world has to be run,' Norton-Hord replied.

19

'Roy, what's your view?' Chote said.

'Oh absolutely,' Gorman said.

'Martin?' the principal said.

'An American poet speaks of the "rage for order",' Martin said.

'Wallace Stevens,' Rowena said.

'A possible evil,' Chote replied. 'It can be used to suppress and make us downtrodden, subservient. We must resist, mustn't we, Roy?'

'Unquestionably,' Gorman said.

This was Lawford's gospel. Rowena watched Mart's face but she couldn't read much reaction there. She thought that if Lawford prevailed, the blue stair carpet would be trodden on, but not by people who were downtrodden.

'Talking of resistance, how are things between you and the Universities Finance Centre, Lawford?' Norton-Hord asked.

Rowena switched her attention from Moss to him. His paper was one of a string run by the Roudhouse Gate company, including two national dailies. Now and then rumours, tips, facts possibly drifted down from London to Al Norton-Hord. Rowena wondered whether he'd decided to come tonight with Mart's lecture as a pretext; but in fact looking for a chance to get an unofficial chat with Lawford. A literature prof's prescribed palaver wouldn't rate as news.

'The U.F.C. and us?' Chote said. 'All serene as far as I know.'

'No . . . no signals?' Norton-Hord said. 'Intimations?'

'Signals as to what?' Chote asked. 'Do you know of any signals, Roy?'

20

'Signals?' Gorman said. 'Not that have come my way, I can assure you.'

'Apropos the cuts, the Thatcher cuts policy,' Al said.

'We don't engage in that policy,' Chote replied.

'This is what I mean,' Norton-Hord said.

'*What* do you mean, Al?' Chote said.

Rowena thought his voice might be on the rise.

'We have a university to run,' Chote said. 'We have bright new professors to appoint, haven't we, Mart?'

'You're kind,' Moss replied.

'Some irritation at the U.F.C.?' Norton-Hord said. 'I gather they've already had to deal with a similar situation in Wales – one of the Cardiff principals there being very resistant and bolshy.'

'What happens in Wales is hardly relevant to Sedge,' Chote said.

'Hardly, indeed,' Gorman said.

'Irritation at a seeming failure to comply,' Norton-Hord said.

'Comply with what?' Chote asked.

'Economising. Cutbacks,' Al said.

Lawford stuck his head forward over his glass of ale. He seemed to have decided against shouts, but did a snarl instead. He looked as though he was about to tear off Norton-Hord's bow tie. 'I'm not in the complying vein,' he said. 'Universities do not reach excellence by compliance, by kow-towing to political instructions. Some instructions, some orders are, as I've said, retrograde, defeatist, evil. Torch them.'

'We're being instructed, ordered, to go into dinner, I think,' Rowena said.

Five

The emblematic blue carpet on the stairs to the staff bar and dining room was well over twenty-five years old now. In one or two spots the colour had faded a little and here and there were small, faint traces of intractable staining where someone might have brought in oil on her or his shoes from the car park. But overall it still did what Lawford Chote had required it to do in his spend and spend-again epoch: chime with the qualities of the high-grade university that he had sought to create from the Sedge of his days. The university had, in fact, moved up a fair way towards this glittering status, though not everyone would credit Chote and the hotel-standard carpet for providing lift-off. True, the number tending to think reasonably well of Chote had begun to rise, but it was from a very low start. Sedge had not yet produced a Nobel prize winner to scale the Chote stairway en route to a celebratory bucket of Taittinger. Perhaps very soon, though.

But Lawford Chote wouldn't hear about it. He died within a year of his readily assisted departure from the principalship. The arguments about his influence, worth, strategy continued. Martin Moss, chairman of the recently formed Commemorative Statues Committee had to find a way around these prejudices, doctrinal loyalties and antagonisms and produce a suitably agreed commission for the two sculptures, which could be presented to the senate and then, ultimately, to the high board for ratification.

A couple of times he had dreamt of Chote in full, scarlet trimmed PhD garb, but worn with heavy mountaineering boots, standing halfway up the blue-carpeted staircase, eyes challenging, dauntless, ablaze, and pointing with stretched out, stiff arm to somewhere even further up. Moss had the notion that this somewhere wasn't merely the staff eatery. In fact, on Chote's back, over the PhD costume, was strapped a cheap looking canvas knapsack which might well contain sandwiches and other refreshments for a journey, making the dining room redundant. No, Chote's commanding gesture in the dream urged staff towards brilliant, soaring, stratospheric Sedge achievement, perhaps that longed-for Nobel; or, taking into account Chote's ferocious ambitions for Sedge, the second or third Nobel, plus half a dozen memberships of the Royal Society.

Chote had been a decorated bomber pilot during the Second World War, and perhaps he had brought to Sedge something of the Royal Air Force motto, *'Per Ardua Ad Astra'*, meaning: 'By hard work we'll reach the stars.' Also, Moss recalled reading that when a member of the Black Panther racial equality agitators in the United States was asked by a would-be placator, 'Well, what do you want?' he had answered, 'Everything.' Lawford Chote had wanted everything for Sedge. Post mortem some of it had been secured.

'Height is going to be a problem,' Angela Drape (Environmental Engineering) said, her voice big, accustomed to reaching the back of a lecture room. It was the second meeting of the Commemorative Statues Committee. Several departments had been asked to supply one of their staff for the C.S.C. 'There aren't any actual measurements available as far as I know, but judging from photographs I'd say Victor Tane must have been at least six foot four, as against Chote's five foot eight or even five foot seven.'

'A problem in which way?' Bill Davey (French) asked.

'If they're put alongside each other to suggest equality of achievement – and this, surely, is how it has to be – in such proximity Victor Tane is going to dwarf Chote, make him look like a ballboy,' Angela replied. 'This is hardly the theme we're seeking to display in the two images. The very opposite.'

'We can't have Chote standing on a box to make up the difference, the way they did for Alan Ladd in his movies,' Claud Nelmes (Physics) said. Nelmes liked a joke, a joke always delivered deadpan; and, because most of his jokes were feeble, hardly jokes at all, many people didn't get that what he'd said was one: dead-and-buried-pan.

'But some statues have a plinth,' Bill Davey said. 'Chote could be jacked up a bit on one of those. Watching *Antiques Roadshow* not long ago I saw a statue of the boy David taking aim with his catapult to do Goliath and the kid definitely had a plinth. I got the idea he needed that plinth as much as he needed the catapult.'

24

'Surely most statues have plinths,' Lucy Lane (History) said, putting her nose-picking on hold while she spoke. 'Perhaps all. If Chote gets a plinth it would be an obvious requirement for Tane to get one, too. In any case, if he didn't have a plinth what would Tane's legs and feet actually be standing on? Indeed, plinthless, would Tane be able to stand at all? The point about plinths is that the subject's feet are of a piece with the plinth. Clearly, the feet are not feet in our usual day-to-day meaning of feet and capable of making a platform for their owner, enabling him or her to participate in cross-country or relay sprint races. Neither of the statues will be taking part in that kind of activity, though they were both highly competitive beings! These feet *represent* feet but are, in reality, shaped stone and of the same chunk of stone as is the plinth. This is the essential. Sculpted feet have no separate existence from the stone plinth on which the feet appear to rest, but do not rest in our normal use of that word, because the feet and the stone plinth are integral.'

'Those feet are not made for walking, regardless of the old song,' Davey said.

'I think we have to concede that both statues will require plinths,' Angela Drape boomed. 'Different size plinths would put us back to the same quandary as arises from the variation in height between Tane and Chote. A larger plinth for Chote would be seen as a sort of pitying aid to someone rather stunted. I can envisage the Chote statue coming to be dubbed among undergraduates "Principal Plinth".'

'We need to consider whether the statues have to be painstakingly, rigidly accurate as to height,' Wayne Ollam (Philosophy) said. 'Are we bound to reproduce their physiques exactly as in life?'

'We would possibly need to take advice from the sculptor on this,' Mart Moss said. 'Perspective, scale, contextual background are matters for a professional, I believe.'

'As Lucy very validly pointed out with regard to feet, these sculptures will be *representations* of the two subjects,' Ollam replied ruminatively. 'Likenesses. They will not have blood or bones. So, if they are to dispense with those human properties, are we obliged to try for strict accuracy as to tallness, shortness, fatness, thinness? Why this selective scrupulousness? Where is consistency? The great sculptors might be able to *suggest* blood and bones behind the surface of their work, but it is *only* a suggestion.' Ollam's way with emphases was mild but effective, Mart thought – perhaps *more* effective because the listener would not feel button-holed, bullied and brayed at, and therefore resistant to the message.

'The spectator *infers* the blood and bones but this inference is a tribute to the sculptor's skills; and if there is no spectator – say when a gallery has closed for the night – if there is no spectator to infer the living innards then that statue has no innards. It is stone, end of story. I know some sculptors claim that the finished, statued figure is actually implicit and detectable by them in the block of stone when it is *just* a block of stone. Arty bullshit, I'm afraid.

'Consider Rodin's *Le Penseur, The Thinker.*

26

This is a man seated, sort of crouched forward, his hand up to his chin, as if he's giving some topic a hell of a lot of concentration. But notice that "as if". We – the viewers – have to imagine the statue's brain must be really whirling. We can't *see* his brain, though. We have to take his brain on trust. What we're looking at is a lump of bronze – not stone now – bronze that Rodin has worked on with his chisel so as to make us say, "If this were somebody real he'd obviously be trying to work something out in his head, truly cogitating in an unhurried, plodding fashion." We don't get *into* that head. We have to help Rodin by picking up the hints and doing a deduction from them. We are dragooned by our culture and by habit to supply what Rodin can't – the "thinks" of the thinker. What I'm saying is that statues of their nature, yes *of their nature,* cannot give a full, as it were, account of the person they are meant to resemble and therefore, by extension, the physical appearance of the statue need not be slavishly, pedantically focussed on such banal, virtually random matters as height, girth, general build.'

Elvira Barton (Classics) said, 'I would put this in terms of a syllogism, the medieval style of debate where there are certain assumptions which may be or may not be accepted by both sides; and a conclusion that is deemed valid or invalid. It's like this: all statues are essentially lifeless; lifelessness is clearly not a characteristic of life; therefore, no statue need embody every aspect of the person featured in the statue whether still alive or having been alive.'

'But if Lawford Chote had been a dwarf it would surely be ridiculous not to recognize this in his statue,' Jed Laver (Industrial Relations) said. 'People who remembered him when alive would inevitably have his dwarfdom in mind as one of his most headline characteristics. I do not mean in any respect to mock or malign dwarfs but their stature is bound to be a distinguishing factor. Acquaintances, relatives, friends, even enemies, would definitely feel there was something wrong about the statue if it ignored that basic element. After all, the dwarfdom might have psychological implications – inner resentment that he should fall into this category; perhaps a special vigour and defiance in an understandable attempt to assert he can deal with any problem as efficiently as taller folk can.'

'Why do you pick on Lawford Chote for this unpleasant fantasising?' Gordon Upp (Linguistics) asked.

'No intention at all to denigrate Chote in any way, Gordon,' Jed replied. 'I could just as easily have used Victor Tane's name, though dwarfdom for somebody well over six feet is perhaps more difficult to reconcile, even in a make-believe narrative.'

'And you *didn't* fucking well pick Victor Tane, did you? You reserved your vicious, bilious meanderings for Lawford.'

Martin Moss said, 'I feel we have had a very productive early stage meeting. Certain boundaries and central objectives have been identified and positively, promisingly, touched on. This will set us up very well for our next scheduled session in a fortnight. I have no doubt some informal private discussions will take place in the interim between committee members and we should all return ready to take matters in this supremely worthwhile project a further distance forward.'

Six

1987

'Do I understand him right, Mart?'

'Who?' Moss said.

'Al Norton-Hord,' Rowena Chote said. 'About the signals, or no signals, from the Universities Finance Centre. What did the signals say, if there *were* signals?'

'I'm not sure I understood that myself,' Moss said. The dinner following his inaugural had ended and people were dispersing. Rowena Chote had made her way to him, as if to offer a handshake and hug in final congratulation; but he realized now mainly to quiz him about what the journalist had said. Norton-Hord had already left.

Mrs Chote would be in her late forties. She had a broad, friendly face, alert blue-grey eyes, perhaps refreshed by the lecture room snooze. Mart had been in company with her before and knew she had a big, loud laugh, but only when she found something genuinely funny, not just an attempt to break the ice or indicate a disarming, sociable nature. She wore a blue, two-button wool jacket over a lattice topped white blouse, and blue long-panelled skirt. Her hair was assisted fair-blonde worn at shoulder length. She had a snub, small nose, but, as they all knew now, obviously capable of that noisy, disproportionate snore din; yet also to sniff subconsciously that it was time to wake up and hear some stuff about interesting sex.

'And the comparison with a similar situation in Wales,' she said. 'What situation?'

'Expenditure outstripping income, I imagine. It's happening to most universities to a major or minor degree because of government cutbacks, even Oxbridge,' Moss said.

'And here, at Sedge, it's a *major* crisis, is it?'

'I don't think Norton-Hord said a crisis, did he?'

'No, his tone said crisis, though,' she answered. 'He spoke of signals and the U.F.C.'s possible irritation with Sedge, and presumably with Lawford.'

'It wasn't clear where his information came from. But *was* there information at all, or just a volley of questions?'

'He's a journalist. Most of their information comes from other journalists, doesn't it? Sometimes it's right, all the same. It's how Lawford seemed to take it, wouldn't you say? The signals, the irritation. That's what they appeared to mean to him. Suggestions of trouble – of crisis, yes. He was rattled. We came very near to one of his famous in-depth, state-of-the-nation, rages. I called time – and only just in time.'

'The move into dinner?'

'I have to look after him, Mart. He'll sail daft and determined towards heavy weather. In some ways it's admirable, loveable in him. Courageous. Defiant. But also obsessive, egotistic, vain, suicidal?'

'He does stir up the adjectives.'

'I hope you will help me with this. He's got a good cause, higher learning for anyone who wants it, and thinks this such an obvious boon that as long as he doesn't waver it's bound to convince others and win through. This is a mission with him, a holy grail job. But it isn't bound to. He could get mangled. We must have some *real politik*. My speciality, but I need help with it.'

This made two of them – Mrs Chote and Chote himself – asking for Martin's assistance. He hadn't known that literature professorships at Sedge came with so much baggage. As Mrs Chote had said, Lawford Chote did have a good cause and Moss would back it. But, as she'd also said, not everyone admired this objective, and some of those who didn't were powerful and clever and ruthless and intent on hacking away at public spending, university public spending in particular.

Mart was out for a spin in Chote's office Volvo, the principal driving. He'd asked Martin to come for an excursion with him and take a look at Charter Mill. The invitation had seemed to Moss loaded with a kind of special excitement, perhaps touched by some of that obsessiveness Rowena had mentioned as strong in Lawford. Moss felt

31

it was as if Chote believed the sight of the Charter layout – the actuality of it: brickwork, cement, windows, doors, footpaths, the 'Charter Mill University' name board, gold lettering on black – yes, these undeniable proofs of brazenly being there, would help show Mart that a change was required, urgently required.

Maybe Chote remembered an episode in Boswell's *The Life of Samuel Johnson* where they were discussing Bishop Berkeley's theory of the non-existence of matter. Boswell declares it's hard to refute this. In response, Johnson gives a large stone a hard kick and says this is how he refutes it. Did Chote want to show Mart the reality of Charter Mill and so persuade him that in the present tight national economic circumstances, Charter should be part of Sedge, and part of Sedge soon, for its own good as well as for wider reasons? Chote might believe that almost anyone would be convinced of this, but especially somebody as enthusiastic about higher education as a new, go-ahead, perceptive prof who had detected unconventional hetero-bonking in *Lady Chatterley's Lover* and knew how to talk about it with delicate tact.

'There's much that's admirable about Charter, I would never deny it, Mart, but what's an imperative now is for it to be brought to full fruition. This simple move will benefit everyone. When I consider Charter, I imagine how the great landscaper of the eighteenth-century, Lancelot Brown, might have reacted to it: "This bog-standard little lot has capabilities." The watermill? Of course, living locally, you'll have seen it before today. It has charm. Gimmicky? Yes, but I'd be willing to keep it in place for a year or two. There'd be no real point after that, would there, when the name and identity of "Charter Mill" have been expunged? I don't mind an occasional slip into sentimentality as long as it's *only* occasional.'

Chote was silent for a while, as they drew close to Charter. 'They're putting a gaggle of auditors into Sedge, you know, Martin.'

'Who?'

'Universities Finance Centre, alias the fucking philistine, fascist government.'

'Is that what Norton-Hord was talking about?'

'Of course, they'll come looking for faults and trying to slant things that way,' Chote replied. 'They'll have been briefed – i.e., brainwashed. These people live with figures and know how to cook them to suit whatever the doctrinaire politicos want. Will they get anywhere near under-standing the Sedge-Charter Mill situation?'

'The situation in which sense?'

'The sense that unification, merger, takeover – whatever term we use for it – such benign unification will see the end of any difficulties Sedge might have, or any that Charter Mill might have, too. They should realize – should be helped to realize – that the solution to any troublesome circumstances is right there in front of them, plain and guaranteed. If Norton Hord comes to you for insights on things between Sedge and the U.F.C. it would be best to explain matters to him along those lines, Mart. He's a reasonable bloke. I got somewhat ratty with him the other evening, but he knows that's only the unmalicious knockabout of debate. Healthy. Challenging. Honest.'

But he more or less snarled these terms. He probably despised their comfy, prim harmlessness. 'OK, the Charter Mill property is functional bordering on hideous, and many of the courses offered there are somewhere between workaday and farcical, but I'm willing to take them on, the whole package, Mart. It's necessary for the eventual good. It would be dereliction on my part if I didn't seek to organize rescue.'

Moss felt uneasy. Was he being sucked into croneydom, as others, like Roy Gormand, had been? Did the share-my-pilgrimage-out-to-Charter edict show a wish by Lawford to bring Moss into his select, inner cabinet? It was as though Chote had said, 'Come join with me in sizing up a piece of real estate that we – you, I and others akin to you – will benignly grab for our portfolio, acting out of generous kindness to the Victor Tane combo. And, if you should be talking to Norton-Hord, talk to him as I recommend you talk to him and not as you might have talked to him if I hadn't had a word with you, Mart, about how to talk to him.'

In general, Moss saw the reason for Chote's colonising campaign and thought it right. Some of the detail troubled him, though. Martin knew that no grand, mystical experience would take a hold on him as they ogled Charter Mill. And if that had been what Lawford wanted for Moss, he had failed.

Seven

2014

'Proximity,' Lucy Lane said, her thin face taut with triumph, as though hooking and landing this notion had been a fearsome struggle but, now, here it was, conclusively ashore. 'Have we properly considered whether proximity is essential?' Using a tartan-themed handkerchief, she wiped one of her fingers. This cleansing job went on for more than a minute while she tried to dislodge one super-sticky bit of nose debris from under her index nail.

'Proximity in which regard?' Bill Davey asked. The Commemorative Statues Committee (C.S.C.) was in session again, Mart Moss chairing, as before.

'Are we assuming, without due thought and analysis, that Lawford Chote and Victor Tane – the statues of, I mean, obviously – are we assuming that Lawford Chote and Victor Tane, or to reverse this for impartiality's sake, Victor Tane and Lawford Chote, have to be placed close to each other? What I meant by "proximity". It is this envisaged proximity, isn't it, that gives rise to the height problem? Proximity will invite comparisons; no, will *enforce* comparisons, in fact. Someone short alongside someone tall, or to reverse it, someone tall alongside someone short, is bound to be noticeable. I recall that television sketch about social class, with the tallest man on the left representing the upper class, someone not quite as tall representing the middle class, and someone short representing the lower class. The differences in status are quickly made graphic by these, as it were, symbols. Something similar might occur in people's reactions to the two statues if they are, so to speak, cheek by academic jowl.'

'And yet some might think of the Book of Amos, chapter 3, verse 3,' Elvira said.

'Might they?' Lucy said.

'"Can two walk together except they be agreed?",' Elvira replied. 'This is what's known as a rhetorical question, being, in truth, no question at all because the answer "No" is built-in. The Bible is fond of rhetoricals. Probably the first is, "Am I my brother's keeper", Cain requiring an "Of course not" from God?'

'True,' Angela said.

'Putting me in mind of the three-legged race at school,' Gordon Upp said. 'A pair of contestants have their right and left legs tied together and they must not simply walk but run as a unit, so they certainly need to agree about how to do it or they're liable to pull each other over. Same with coalition governments: some progress possible, but, also, some bad difficulties.'

'At least one statue would have to be parked outside the main building, surely,' Bill Davey said. 'A valuable identifying marker to the people passing in the street, some of whom will not be familiar with the city. The caption plate would give the appropriate name and then, "Principal of Sedge University" and his dates.'

'"Main" is rather a loaded term, isn't it?' Wayne Ollam replied. 'This is, indeed, a university. That title doesn't come without deep implications: all its buildings are of *universal* significance. If we speak of a "main" building we speak also by irresistible implication of a "main" statue and of another building that is not "main", is less than main. This is to cave in to the kind of ranking of the two principals that I think it's accepted we should skirt.'

'If the statues were sited on separate campuses, which I take to be the hinted suggestion by Lucy, taking into account her down on proximity, there wouldn't seem to be much doubt about what Bill calls the "main" part of the university – its proper designation "Humanities" – and the other out at what was Charter Mill, now re-christened as "Life Sciences",' Upp said.

Lucy asked, 'Why do you say—?'

'I know what you're going to query,' Upp cut in.

'What?' Lucy said.

'Why do I say "out" at Charter Mill?' Upp answered. 'What constitutes its "outness"? I was very aware, believe me, of the provocative nature of the word. Yet there is some truth involved, is there not? The Life Sciences block *is* out, in the sense that it's out on the edge of the city, not central, as is Sedge. The watermill has been removed, yes, so that further student accommodation could be constructed on that spot, but there is still something bucolic, something agricultural

37

– perhaps pleasantly bucolic and agricultural, comfortingly rural – about that area. However, if one of the statues were consigned to there, malicious folk might see in it something yokel-like, no matter which of the principals it might be: village idiots could be short or tall.'

'"Consigned"?' Lucy said.

'Freighted,' Upp said.

'If a plurality of statue locations *were* preferred,' Elvira said, 'it would almost certainly mean the Tane figure must go to that erstwhile Charter Mill, now Life Sciences, spread.'

'Why do you say so?' Jed replied. 'Why?'

'This was Tane's home ground,' Elvira said.

'Yes, it *was* his home ground, but he could play away,' Jed replied. 'He very evidently did not remain restricted to that home ground. In due course he was able to make both campuses his home grounds, in fact.'

'He did "bestride the narrow world like a Colossus",' Wayne Ollam said.

'That is why Sedge still exists and comprises the two components; and why we are undertaking these discussions on the duality of statues,' Jed said.

'There's a C.P. Snow novel based on an actual situation called *The Masters*,' Elvira replied, 'about the election of a new head at a Cambridge college – in reality, Christ's. I feel if anyone were writing a tale about *our* proceedings it should be titled *The Principals*.'

'It would be inaccurate, misconceived, unjust, wouldn't it, to send Tane "out" – if I might take

Gordon's word for a moment – out to this far-flung region?' Jed said. 'I think of Napoleon being transported to St Helena. I think of the leper forced to take himself off to the wilderness.'

'Well, that's fucking ludicrous,' Upp replied.

'Would you want the Chote statue, instead, put at Charter, now Life Sciences. Jed?' Lucy asked.

'I'm saying only that it would be an error to ship Tane there, merely on account of his earlier connection,' Jed said.

'Wasn't there some rumour about Tane needing to use staff from the Organized Crime And Its Defeat department at Charter Mill to protect himself when the 1987 situation was at its worst?' Theo Bastrolle (Business Studies) asked. It was the first time he'd spoken at any of the C.S.C. meetings. Mart came to think that Theo often seemed to follow a personal brand of thoughts, not much related to any of the other comments and debates.

'Yes, I heard something along those lines,' Davey said.

'Occasionally, I feel we are ignoring one of the chief sources of information potentially available to us,' Lucy said.

'Oh, which?' Upp said.

'Can I be alone in thinking this?' Lucy said.

'Which?' Upp said.

'Martin,' Lucy replied. 'Our chair. I realize he has to avoid bias in this role, but perhaps that shouldn't prevent him offering some neutral, informal guidance. After all, he has the kind of first-hand experience of the period which most of us lack. I have in mind extra light on the two principals' characters, which might help us with the physical style – styles – we recommend for the statues. For instance, I was away in Cardiff a little while ago and in the shopping centre saw a statue of the great Welsh politician, Aneurin Bevan, and the sculptor had managed to get the impish, belligerent forward crouch I'm told Bevan would adopt when making one of his fierce speeches. I'll have a trawl through the Sedge and Charter archives looking for material that might be useful in this regard. It's quite common knowledge, isn't it, Mart, that you and Lawford Chote were buddies during the crisis months? Nothing reprehensible or even surprising about that. But it could be relevant. I'm not suggesting cronyism, though I expect there *was* some of that: it's endemic in any organisation.'

'Certainly,' Elvira said. 'The disciples.'

Moss said, 'He chaired the panel that appointed me to a professorship. Some contact was inevitable. And then Rowena Chote fell ostentatiously asleep at my inaugural. Comical, really, though I probably didn't think so at the time. I believe Lawford felt he had to compensate – show some extra friendliness.'

'I expect all of us have had snoozers in our lectures now and then,' Elvira said. 'I find the zonk-out rate for Cicero highest.'

'None of it has any bearing on our present task,' Mart said.

Eight

1987

On the way back from their sightseeing visit to Charter Mill, Lawford Chote said, 'That bastard.'

'Which?'

'Tane.'

'What's annoyed you, Principal?'

'Annoyed? That sounds like a carer to some half-witted antique wreck.'

'Angered, then,' Moss replied.

'Enraged,' Chote said.

'What's enraged you, Dr Chote?'

'Damn photography.'

'Photography? Which?'

'He had a photographer out at Charter recording the car. Didn't you see him?'

No, Moss hadn't seen him, if the photographer existed. In any case, if Mart *had* seen him he probably wouldn't have mentioned it. He didn't want to feed any of Lawford's obsessions. 'How could he know we'd be passing Charter to do our survey of the buildings and so on?'

'People at Sedge would have seen us leaving. Some traitor gets on his mobile to Tane.'

'People might have observed us leaving, but they wouldn't know where to, would they, Dr Chote?'

'Why else would he get a photographer in

41

place with a damn sneaky camera? Someone at
Sedge saw the departure and made a guess as to
destination. It's a fairly obvious guess, isn't it?'

'Well, I don't know,' Moss replied.

'But *I* know. Oh, yes – he can't fool me.'

Moss sought some sanity. Had Chote tipped
over? 'What would be the point in photographing
us, anyway, Principal?'

'Don't ask me to read his damn twisted mind.
He gets a picture of you and you're with me.
That might suggest to his poisonous brain some
sort of complicity.'

'But which sort?' Moss asked.

'Oh, yes, he'd be alert in his scheming head
to signs of that category – or to what he could
imagine were signs of that category. He's creating
some kind of dossier.'

'But which kind?'

'Quite,' Chote replied.

Nine

1987

In the projection room at Charter Mill, Gloria
Sondial, head of Organized Crime And Its
Defeat, said, 'Principal, as part of our final year
course we get students to carry out a covert
surveillance exercise – one of the fundamental
skills they'll need in a career with the police
or security services.'

'Certainly,' Victor Tane replied.

'I've asked you kindly to spare some moments this morning, Principal, to look at a film one of our undergraduates took yesterday while carrying out that kind of work.'

'Delighted to, as it were, take part,' Tane said.

Gloria switched off the lights. 'First sequence, please, Alec. This is what we call "a situationer", Dr Tane,' Gloria said. 'It gives us a location, is a kind of context. In a surveillance operation, background can often tell plenty.'

'Right,' Tane said.

The technician started the film. A string of cars moved at speed limit pace across the screen, and then the camera swung away and showed some buildings. 'Oh, we're at Charter Mill, are we? There's the porter's lodge,' Tane said.

'Yes, we give the student a very familiar setting first and then, if he/she deals OK with that we'll put her/him in other, perhaps more complex, surroundings for subsequent tests. We know there are some good, semi-hidden spots to operate from here. Our people have to remain unobserved by the targets. The photos of the vehicles will show us whether the driver or passengers, if there are any, have spotted the camera and are gazing at it. If they do, the student is referred and must have another go at a later date before trying the more difficult stages. This exercise required the student to get a photographic record of six vehicles sequentially. Obviously, in a reality situation the camera would be aimed at one known vehicle only. That's not so in our present version. We go for a random six.'

Tane watched the screen as, first, a silver Ka with a woman driver passed, then a black Mercedes estate, an elderly male driving and a woman in the passenger seat, also elderly. A white Mazda 6 saloon, no passengers, a male driver, followed. None of the drivers or passengers seemed to notice the camera. After a pause a dark red Volvo, two men in the front seats, travelling very slowly appeared on the screen.

'Hold it there, Alec, would you please?' Gloria said, and the film froze.

'Ah, yes, I see,' Tane said.

'I wasn't sure I recognized either of them at first,' Gloria said, 'but I thought I might have seen media pictures of the driver. I know now it was when the TV news showed the Sedge principal with one of their ex-undergrads, later a decorated Falkland war hero, who came back to give a talk to students.'

'Yes, that's Lawford Chote,' Tane said.

'What struck me most about this view of the Volvo and its occupants wasn't so much the half-memory in my mind of one of them, but the way they both seemed to be examining the Charter Mill buildings and grounds – Chote less so than the passenger, of course, since Chote had the wheel, but I got the feeling that he was talking to the passenger, telling him where to look – as though they were on a sort of reconnaissance, sizing up the campus. The passenger is younger than Chote and it seemed to me that the Sedge principal might be introducing a subordinate to the kind of asset Charter Mill is, and accompanying this with some sort of commentary. They

44

move slowly so as to take in as much detail as possible.'

'Yes,' Tane said. He leaned forward in his seat, studying the two faces in the Volvo.

The lights came on. Gloria was holding a clipboard. 'I asked two of our students to discover who the passenger is,' she said. 'This kind of tracking is another skill they'll most probably need in their careers – contributing to dossiers. They've come up with quite a full portrait.' She began to read from notes on the clipboard. 'He is Martin Calhoun Moss, born 1952 in Preston, married 1975 to Grace Shell, divorced 1980, no children. Graduated Cambridge 1973 (First, English Literature). Schoolmaster 1973-9, lecturer at Sedge 1979, prof 1987 – modern Eng and US lit. Address 4A Maliphant Close. Lives alone. Doesn't appear to be in any sexual relationship since divorce seven years ago. Drives a Vauxhall Astra, navy blue, 1981 model. Banks at Lloyd's. Is regarded by other staff at Sedge as a good and reliable colleague; not part of the clique known at Sedge as Chote's Chipper Chums, a kind of elite kitchen cabinet of unswerving henchmen and women, some of whom have been placed in newly created, executive posts by Chote to increase his clout. This does not seem applicable to Moss. His promotion to a chair is the outcome of much published research on Wilde, Lawrence and Auden.'

'Yes, I've read some of his stuff. Bordering on the intelligible.'

Gloria said, 'It's speculation, not fact, Principal, but I'd guess that this Volvo trip is a preliminary to inviting Moss into that elite Chumdom.'

45

'I wondered about it,' Tane said. 'But what do you make of this trip, this "reconnaissance", apart from that?'

'I thought it looked like window shopping,' Gloria replied.

'How I saw it, too,' Tane replied.

Gloria gave him a couple of stills from the surveillance film and, back in his office, he gummed these into a log book he kept of his years as Principal of Charter Mill. He added a short caption for the pictures: names, location, source and date only. He felt that future developments could make any commentary he might have added look very off-beam and foolish. Of course, he had views about the Volvo and its crew – had agreed with Gloria's verdict – but backed off from writing anything down. It would be too committing. Careful, perhaps cagey, that was Tane. Occasionally, his caution bored even himself, but he was stuck with it, and knew this. Tall and unrobust-looking, he walked in a very tentative, doubting style, as if afraid there would be no floor for his next step.

Mart wondered whether Tane had been horrified as a kid by that scene in Robert Louis Stevenson's 'boy' novel, *Kidnapped,* where David Balfour, the hero, is climbing a staircase in absolute darkness and suddenly finds there is no further stair, only emptiness, into which he might have plunged. Perhaps that terror still affected Tane.

His receding, mousy coloured hair was brushed back hard over his ears. For someone who seemed so frail he had a surprisingly craggy face,

46

though, with a wide-nostrilled Roman nose. Mart had heard that Tane spent plenty of mental energy trying to make sure his parents' quirks and foibles didn't in any fashion affect his present outlook on life.

Ten

2014

At the next statues meeting, Gordon Upp (Linguistics) said, 'I hope I'm not running ahead into quite complex, tricky matters before we've properly dealt with all the basics, but I wonder whether we should give some thought to what we might term the psychology – or, rather, *psychologies*, plural – of our two subjects, Chote, Tane – Tane, Chote – as they should be depicted in the statues. By psychologies I mean their mental make-up, their personalities, their spirits, their individual selfhoods.'

Upp would be under thirty years old, probably the youngest member of the committee. His moods swung about between extreme politeness and over-the-top pugnacity. He had a wide, heavy-jawed face. His gingerish eyebrows were much too sparse for this big area, like slivers of garden vegetation in a valiant but hopeless battle against some pesticide. His head hair, of the same colour, seemed comparatively healthy and worn long. He said, 'Lucy's very timely reference to the

47

Aneurin Bevan statue over there in Wales goes some way towards what I'm getting at – *trying* to get at – Bevan's bodily stance as a kind of adjunct to his speechifying. But that is only what the Eng Lit people would term a *persona,* rather than his true unique *personality:* a pose, an assumed, theatrical-like, thesp-like, role, in harmony with one specific act – the speech – in one specific place – a political public meeting. Moments after doing his platform bit, he'd become someone else, not a spiel performer, but a bloke among other blokes and blokesses. I feel sure that each of us would wish the principals' statues to tell us something more profound, more fundamental, more, as it were, inborn than, for instance, Bevan's temporary, *ad hoc,* for-the-occasion, fighting posture. Somehow – and I certainly don't underestimate the difficulty of conveying this in a lump of stone or brass – but somehow the sculptor has to tell us of the differing, discrete qualities of these two men, not evaluations of them – this man good, or goodish, this one bad or baddish – but simply their abiding, congenital essences, their very fibre.

'I say "simply", but it is not at all a simple process. It is a massive challenge, or a pair of massive challenges in this instance. Although we are very wisely concerned to ensure equality between the statues – Tane, Chote – Chote, Tane – and although, also, each statue must tell the world of certain common qualities possessed by the two principals, crucial for men in their kind of leadership jobs – I mean, positivism, creative energy, devotion to learning – I feel it would be a mistake to make their facial expressions identical – both benignly smiling, for instance. A double helping of benign smiles if the statues are close to each other might be read by spectators as the result of a shared spliff or a heavy two-man session on the Jack Daniels. We need, rather, a comprehensive search into their very natures, and a due reflection of such in the statues. The character of Sedge itself should, to an extent, be blazoned in these statues.'

Lucy Lane (History) said, 'I promised last time to do a little browsing in the archives and I think I might have come across something with a bearing on what Gordon has just been talking about in his acute fashion. It is an item which rather directly involves Martin, our chair, too, and he will possibly be able to comment on it in a purely informative, unbiased fashion, without compromising his present office.'

'Oh?' Moss said.

'I'm sure it will activate memories although we are going to move back more than a quarter of a century.'

'Oh?' Moss said.

Lucy bent down and took what seemed to Moss like a large cardboard covered scrapbook from her briefcase. 'Victor Tane kept a kind of log of events in Charter Mill in 1987 and before and after, in what became the new Sedge,' Lucy said. She opened the book at around halfway. 'I think the fact that he did this tells us something about him. The log starts only from 1986, although Tane was in post at Charter several years prior to this. I could find no earlier log. I think his decision to begin the record when he did shows he realized something extremely major was happening, or was about to happen, and that a personal account of it day-to-day could be very to the point. He is perceptive. He is methodical. He is forward-looking. He is intelligently alert and, perhaps, self-protective.

'I'll pass the book around in a moment but I can tell you that it shows Principal Lawford Chote and our Professor Martin Moss in a red Volvo saloon on a piece of road which I thought I recognized. I went out to confirm it as being close to what was then Charter Mill, now one of the Sedge campuses. Chote is driving, Mart has the passenger seat. Although Chote is at the wheel his eyes are off the road ahead at the moment of the photograph. He is gazing at the Charter buildings in what seems to me an almost imperial style, noble and dauntless in its way, but, of course, hindsightedly poignant, ludicrous.'

Ollam said, 'If you're driving a Volvo the only hindsight available is through the rear-view mirror.'

'Imperial in which sense, Lucy?' Angela Drape asked.

'In the sense of colonising, in the sense of taking, of taking over.'

'"*Veni vidi vici*"?' Elvira said.

'"I came, I saw, I mean to conquer", and today I'll give Marty a briefing on it. "*Veni vidi vici*", Moss.' Lucy replied, laboriously deadpan. 'Chote's lips are apart and I think he might have been talking to Martin. No froth visible, but the tone of the messaging looks intense. This is

50

something he should be able to clarify for the meeting soon.'

'What you seem to be telling us, Lucy, is that any statue of Lawford Chote must capture what you term the nobility and dauntlessness, while also suggesting that this seeming nobility, this seeming dauntlessness, are both, in fact, pathetically inappropriate and deeply frail when retrospectively viewed,' Theo Bastrolle (Business Studies) said. He'd be used to seeking a balance. 'I've been doing some archive research myself and have a similar impression,' Theo said.

'That complex mixture will be difficult to get in stone,' Upp said.

'Yes, how exactly does sculpting work?' Angela Drape asked. 'My training is in the actualities, the practicalities. Before he/she starts a bout of shaping does she/he say to himself/herself over breakfast, I'll do some work on the nobility and dauntlessness aspects of the subject this morning? She/he sets off for the studio, gets into dungarees and begins. If we were present would we note that he/she was holding the chisel at a recommended special angle for nobility and dauntlessness and hammering it with a likewise particularly stipulated force for nobility and dauntlessness – perhaps greater than usual, perhaps less – so that after a couple of hours, or days, or even weeks, carving like this she/he has knocked one area into a palpable noble and/or dauntless area, ready to be slotted eventually into the completed statue? Would he/she require a particular type of stone, capable of being banged and chivvied into a nobility and dauntlessness identity? And,

51

even if the stone were absolutely OK for the task, would the noble and dauntless sector have to lie alongside another area or other areas, whose purpose is to show that the incorporated chunks of sculpted nobility and dauntlessness are of only limited account although she/he has spent at least hours and possibly much longer battering and chipping then into that wedge of stone?'

'Was Chote talking to you about take-over potential then, Mart?' Bill Davey replied.

'I think of the devil showing Christ all the glories of the world and declaring that the whole caboodle was there for the taking if only Christ would bow down to him,' Elvira said. 'Gospel of St Matthew.'

'It's a long time ago,' Moss answered.

'Which, the forty days in the wilderness or the cherry-picking trip to what was then Charter?' Jed said.

'In the pic, Martin, you look slightly bemused, guarded, sceptical,' Lucy said.

'Well, if there's ever a statue of me it will have to show that three-layered mélange of attitudes,' Moss said.

'Accompanying the pic is a note by Victor Tane,' Lucy said. 'It's economical to the point of terseness, as though he felt there was no call to explain the photograph, other than to record rock-bottom details – names, origin, date, time – because the faces and the background location would tell everyone that this was some sort of prospecting jaunt. "Care for a little trek Charter Millwards in the Volvo, Mart?"'

52

'I wonder if the word *lebensraum* was mentioned at any stage,' Nelmes said.

'If Tane detected in Chote such an aggressive impulse we might have expected signs of resentment, anger, fear in the handwriting. But no,' Lucy said. 'The captions are very neatly done, label-like, no emotional swirls in the lettering, no screaming triple exclamation marks, no furious dashes or mid-sentence capitalisations. If he felt any menace he does not show it. Is this an indicator of Tane's confidence that, although Chote might turn up to remind himself of the plus elements in Charter, and to show a younger colleague the treats on offer, nothing would ever come of it? Or not that nothing would ever come of it, but that something *would* come of it, but this "something", the utter opposite of Lawford Chote's plan.'

Bill Davey said, 'Tane's statue, then, should radiate his calmness, self belief and contempt for Chote's dream, and Mart's dream, too, if he had become absorbed into Lawford's inner clique.'

'Had you been, Martin?' Jed asked.

'There was no need to take me out to have a stare at Charter. I'd often driven past it,' Moss replied.

'Yes, yes, but this time he probably wanted you to look at it as a possible target, as a potential prize,' Elvira said.

'Well, I can't say what he wanted,' Moss replied. 'You'd have to ask him.'

'It seems to me that ambiguity will be a required facet of the Tane statue,' Angela said. 'Can stone or brass do ambiguity?'

53

'Provenance?' Jed asked.

'Of what?' Lucy replied.

'The photograph. Why was it taken?' Jed said.

'They had a crime and detection department at Charter Mill,' Lucy replied. 'It might just be an exercise and the Chote inclusion simply a fluke.'

'So Tane is loved by Lady Luck,' Nelmes said. 'No wonder he won. Can statues be made to look lucky?'

'What's remarkable about this picture and the log,' Bastrolle (Business Studies) said, 'is that Tane left it for the archive. As you've described it, Lucy, this was a private journal kept by him for his own purposes. I would have expected Tane to take it with him on retirement, instead of which he makes it very accessible to posterity.'

'That's us,' Nelmes said.

'Of course, by the time of his retirement, he was Principal of the enhanced, enlarged Sedge,' Angela said. 'There's a subtle, crowing over Chote in Tane's making the pic, and, presumably, other material, open to inspection at the archive. The seeming neutrality and restraint are a front only, aren't they? He's really saying to anyone using the archive, to Lucy and via Lucy to the rest of us, "Get a look at this barmy, would-be invasive, Volvo-borne braggart, will you please?"'

'He's branding Chote a cunt, would you say, Ange?' Elvira (Classics) said.

'There'll be a need to get irony into the Tane statue, as well as all his other components,' Davey said.

Eleven

1987

'What we have to ask, Martin, isn't it, is who had availability at the specific time this morning?' Chote said.

In his head, Moss tried to analyse the principal's diktat. Mart reckoned he could have led a two-hour seminar deconstructing it. Which 'we' had to do the asking? Ask whom? Why the compulsion of '*have* to ask'? Why the awkward 'is' tangle in 'isn't it, is'? Which 'specific time'? Which 'availability'?

Chote had spoken in a very measured, matter-of-fact, calm, untroubled tone. Probably this meant the principal didn't feel at all calm and was severely troubled, Moss thought. Lawford had put in some excellent work on imitating normality. However, normality was not normal for him: normally he was abnormal. He seemed to sense that what he intended saying next might suggest unease or even paranoia, and he would guard against this. Did he suspect he must have sounded momentarily panicked and crazed about the photographer as they drove back from Charter earlier today and wanted to correct that? After lunch Chote's PA had phoned Mart in his departmental office and asked him to look in at the principal's suite as soon as he could.

Moss searched for enlightenment. '"Availability" in which regard, Principal?' he asked.

'Oh, yes, availability,' Chote replied. 'The very word! You've hit it exactly, Martin! The crux, surely.'

'Available to do what, though? "Availability" suggests there is some task or commitment which the available person, she or he, is available *for*.' He gave that some really dogged, plonking force. 'Availability' was getting the interrogation treatment.

'I'd like to take this matter very step-by-step and very logically, Mart,' Chote replied.

Which sodding matter? But Moss said, 'It's what people would expect of you, I'm certain.' And, yes, there might be some who would.

'This is a university,' Chote said.

Although the principal gave this a slight rise in intonation at the end, Moss took the words to be as a statement, not a question. 'Very true,' he replied. And it plainly was. Eu-fucking-reka!

'That might seem a barmily obvious comment but here's the point, Mart: proper, rational procedures are to be expected in such a setting. Are, in fact, *de rigueur*.'

'Definitely.'

'Thus, applying such rational procedures, I can state that if there were no availability there could be no action arising out of the availability,' Chote explained. 'There cannot be both availability and absence, one word cancelling out the other; and making the idea of possible shoulder-to-shoulderness absurd.'

'Agreed.'

56

'I've referred to step-by-step progress, and this recognition of the vital importance of availability is the first of these steps. Availability is a pre-requisite.'

'Understood,' Moss said.

'But you'll reproach me and say this is mere theorising and wind-baggery. Where is the example of this availability? A fair point, Martin. I admire your vigilance and clarity of thought.'

'Some disputation moves from the particular to the general, some from the general to the particular,' Moss said. 'Each is valid. I think you are applying the second of these, Principal.'

'Absolutely, Mart. What this comes down to, finally, is of course, who? This is a wonderfully brief summation. Who?'

'Who in which particular?'

'Who had this availability that we've so far been discussing only as an abstract notion. The "who?" which we now ask, sharpens the topic, makes it specific. "Who", we inquire, "had this availability at the precise moment, moments." I don't say the answer to the "who?" is simple. We have to try to decide who among several possible whos. Here, then, comes the seminal question: who was available to see us move off in the Volvo this morning and give a call to that aspiring, window-dresser, Tane, informing him we were on our way, so he could get his damn filthy spy camera into place, ready to infringe on us?'

'Ah,' Moss replied, 'I get it, now: by "available" or "availability", you mean someone happened to be in a position to see us leaving in the Volvo.'

Chote's lips went into snarl mode, curling back

over his teeth and showing entirely healthy, richly red, unbulbous gums. '*You* can say "happened" to be present and therefore available, Mart. That's not how I see it.' Lawford's voice was still mild and controlled, but Moss could detect a slight tremor there, perhaps from anger, perhaps from a fixation, perhaps from self-pity.

'We spoke about this in the car,' Moss said. 'No matter who saw us go, he/she wouldn't know to where. This is not like a bus with its destination shown in a frame up front. There'd be no apparent cause to phone Tane. What was there to say? "Principal Chote and Professor Moss have hit the road together in the same car." Well, hold the front page!'

'Let's put it like this, Martin. There was a ruthless plot to film us casing Charter Mill. Right?'

'Principal, this has not been totally established – not whether there was a plot at all, and, if so, a ruthless plot.'

'The creepy photographer is established, isn't he? You say you didn't see him. I did.'

'I accept that,' Mart replied. 'What isn't established is why he was there.'

'He's a photographer. He's there to take photographs.'

'But we cannot be sure why, Principal.' They had courses involving camera work over at Charter. A student might have been told to take some pics of traffic, as an exercise. By coincidence, the Volvo and its driver and passenger were possibly included in that traffic. From this, perhaps, flowed Chote's fierce suspicions.

'Tane told him to be there,' Lawford said,

'and to get shots of me, of us. Tane having been given the word that we're *en route* to do the casing. That's what Tane would call it. *We* might regard it simply as an innocent visit to look at Charter *in,* so to speak, *situ*. He'd say to the photographer – probably a student on one of their Dumbo courses, "Get into position near the entrance to the campus and, if you want to be given a degree here, don't come back without a picture of them – of them both, mind – both gawping at Charter and licking their sickeningly greedy lips."'

'Several imponderables here, if I may say, Principal,' Moss replied.

'Bugger imponderables.' Chote gazed about his office suite, as if seeking a spot uncorrupted by Mart's niggles and quibbles. It was a large room, with dark green wall-to-wall carpeting. The wallpaper also was mainly dark green, a kind of jungle theme: dense vegetation, stalks, fronds, branches, shrubs, possibly William Morris influcnced. Chote sat at a long desk, one end of it containing his computer. Moss had a dark green leather armchair, near him. He felt it was like being in a bower, except for Chote who, to Mart, didn't seem a bower sort of person, even though he'd probably ordered the colour scheme.

'Yes, a plot,' Lawford said. 'And it worked, didn't it? How? Because there was a message from someone here saying that I and Profesor Martin Moss had gone journeying together in the principal's red Volvo. The recipient of that tip-off makes a guess, or a calculation, and decides the pair could be coming to Charter. It

59

would be natural for someone like Tane to suspect this. He's jumpy. He's fearful. Rightly, he feels menaced by circumstances. Nerves savage him. He wants a record of the visit and as extra might get an identifying picture of a possibly new Lawford Chote associate – you, Mart. Tane orders the photo-surveillance and, we must suppose, achieves what he wanted. I would say – and I believe, Mart, that you will come to think the same – I would say that this completeness, this culmination, is the fruit of not just someone who "happened" by sweet fluke to be where she/he could observe our departure, but a someone who was uniquely "available" for that scheme, that plot, through the power of his/her instincts and magical opportunism. Hence my wish, Mart, my resolve, to check on availability.'

Martin Moss saw no 'hence', if hence meant, as it generally did, a reasonable, sane, deduction from what had gone before. Did Chote's apparent trust in instinct and magical opportunism indicate that he had gone full-out unhinged?

'Now, I think you'll grasp why I'm so concerned about availability, Mart,' the principal said. He picked up three A4 sheets of paper from his desk. 'I've done some private research.' He leaned forward and handed the pages to Moss. 'I believe you'll find them thought-provoking,'

Martin studied the top one. It had what appeared to be initials at the head: **R.S.G.**

Beneath these letters was today's date and then a column of figures:

0920–0940
0940–1000
10.00–10.20
10.20–1040
10.40–1100

Against 0920-0940 a typed note said: 'Room 17A, scheduled meeting with Estates Management Representatives.' Alongside the next two sets of figures, 0940-1000 and 1000-1020 was typed: 'Ditto, continuing.' Then, against 10.20 to 1040 and 1040 to 1100 a note said: 'No scheduled entries.' Moss glanced at the other two pages. They were set out in similar format, though the notation alongside the figures was different, and the capital letters at the top also varied.

'Do you see what they are, Mart?' Chote said.

'Well, not exactly,' Moss said.

'Which one are you looking at?'

'R.S.G.'

'Royston Stanley Gormand,' Chote replied. 'Roy.'

'What about him?' Moss asked.

'That's as near to timetabling his movements this morning as we can get. He had the diaried meeting with some estates people in 17A, diaried meaning it was entered in the departmental Appointments section. Availability you see, Mart. We can work out Roy Gormand's availability to some degree at least from his timetable. Such availability could begin at 1020.'

'Roy Gorman's availability as a traitor? But I thought Roy was one of your special—'

'I'm not sure of exactly what time we set out,

you and I,' Chote replied, 'so I've tried to cover the complete 0920-1100 hours. I think we might have left at about 1025 or 30. I don't know if you can make it more precise than that. If you look on page 2, you'll see that C.L.M. – Carl Ivor Medlicott – lectured in B7 on 'Climate Irregularities In The Tundra' from 10 until 11, so, palpably, has no availability in the sense that interests us here. He can be eliminated from our survey, Martin. Contrariwise, Flora Dane Dinah Ellison had a pre-planned meeting with one of her post-grad students from 1000 until 1020, the rest of the period unaccounted for and therefore a possible as to the said availability.'

'But she might simply have been working alone in her room, before and after,' Moss said.

'Absolutely. Non-availability is undoubtedly conceivable. I might get telephone records to see whether she made or received calls during those uncharted minutes. If she did, it could clear her by proving what you've suggested. I want to be entirely fair, yet meticulously thorough.'

Gormand, Medlicott, Ellison: these were three of Chote's praetorian guard, his main and constant support. Moss sat bemused for some seconds, bemused and slightly scared at witnessing whatever it was that had taken Chote over. He had a very pale, long, aquiline face and it stayed pale and orderly now, showed no evidence of mental riot or bitter fantasising. How could that be?

'You're surprised at these names, I see,' Lawford said, his voice kindly, sympathetic. 'But a leader's closest associates know his strengths and weaknesses best and might be more able than any others to use that knowledge to neutralize those strengths, exploit those weaknesses. Think of rulers killed by their bodyguards.'

Mart thought, instead, of the John le Carré espionage novels: the obsessive line on betrayal in the Secret Service, and the hunt for a traitor among seeming colleagues and friends. Lawford Chote appeared to be taking that obsessiveness one stage further: into mania. 'Availability to carry out some action is not the same as actually carrying it out, Principal,' Moss said.

'Of course it isn't,' Chote replied. 'It is a necessary preliminary to that action, though. I must watch these three. Perhaps you will help me in this, Mart? I don't need an immediate answer. But give it thought, will you, please? We are talking about the well-being of Sedge. We may have in our care its safety, its continuing life, indeed. You may keep the papers for study and reference. They might help you realize the seriousness of the threat confronting us. The lists of times look so routine and harmless, yet what might they hide, Mart? Yes, what indeed?'

Twelve

1987

Of course, the injuries and general chaos that ended the banquet to mark Sedge's centenary should have been foreseen. And, to be fair to

63

himself, Mart Moss *had* expected some turbulence there, some joshing and teasing. What happened went way beyond this, though. Surely, nobody would have predicted such violence. Although the setting could hardly have been more dignified, time-blessed and uplifting, this failed to inspire a due response from some of the guests. Moss suspected they had deliberately planned their vandalism in advance. This wasn't just a lark, spontaneous and childish, but well-organized destructiveness.

The banquet took place in the magnificent Plain Parlour of Standfast Fort. This nicely restored and preserved castle dated from Tudor times and stood in the city centre. It was famous throughout the county and beyond for hosting high-grade knees-ups in its Plain Parlour. Standfast had been prominent during the seventeenth-century Civil War, on the Royalist side. At one stage it was, in fact, overrun by some of Oliver Cromwell's troops and most histories of the period said Plain Parlour saw hand-to-hand fighting and even bloody deaths. No deaths now, but some scrappping.

The regrettable behaviour at the Sedge centenary do was not caused by people wanting to re-enact in a playful, modern-dress way those Civil War ructions, but arose out of very contemporary opposed views and lively hatreds. The hiring charge for Plain Parlour, a bar and staffing was already steep. Damage and breakages caused to salvers, tureens and general crockery, to the lighting system, to some mahogany panelling (this disputed), and to chairs used as weapons and/or missiles, pushed the bill higher still. In any case, could it be altogether sane to put on this lavish function now? Martin would concede that it would honour Sedge's one hundred years of existence and achievement, a very worthy aim; but also very expensive. Sedge would be stuck with the complete festive costs at a time when its finances were rumoured to be overstretched, perhaps terminally overstretched. Back at Sedge there might one day be fighting as rough as any ever witnessed in Plain Parlour, but it would be against bailiffs, not Roundheads.

It hadn't happened yet, though, and the jubilee proceeded. There had been several serious attempts to stop it altogether or, at least, to keep it modest and comparatively cheap. Lawford didn't do modesty and despised anything cut-price. But, after all, 100 was no great age for a university: England and Europe had colleges and universities that went back to the Middle Ages. Luther lectured at Wittenberg in the early 1500s. Moss knew about one of these doomed efforts to cancel or shrink the pageantry because he had been involved in it – unwillingly and more or less accidentally involved, but involved just the same.

He'd had a phone call on a Sunday morning at home in Maliphant Close from someone who said he was Ned Lane-Hinkton of the U.F.C. (Universities Finance Centre). 'I'm coming down to Sedge tomorrow, Mart, and I wondered if we could meet up.'

Moss had been startled to get what he assumed was a business call on a Sunday; surprised, too, that he should get a call at all from the U.F.C. This wasn't his kind of terrain. He wouldn't have thought anyone at the U.F.C. could even have heard of him, a non-Oxbridge Humanities prof, let alone address him by his shortened first name and suggest they 'meet up'. Why 'up'? Wasn't it only Americans who met *up*? Brits met.

'To do with what?' Mart had said.

'May I ask you to book somewhere for lunch?' Lane-Hinkton replied. 'Not the famed Sedge dining room, nor anywhere on university ground. Somewhere reasonably discreet in the town.'

'Somewhere secret?'

'Discreet. If poss. Know anywhere like that?'

Moss gave him the name of a dockside pub where he and his wife used to eat now and then before the divorce. He couldn't remember ever seeing anyone he knew lunching there.

Lane-Hinkton turned out to be fat, jolly-looking, his voice confiding. The words arrived unrushed from one side of his mouth, varying right or left, depending not on the political flavour of what he was saying, but simply on where his listener, listeners, was, were. Moss thought Lane-Hinkton – ('Ned, or Neddy, please, Mart') – was abour twenty-seven or -eight, unmoustached, apparently untattooed, teeth his own and well looked after, very dark hair, pony-tailed and bound at the back with a plastic clasp of some sort. He was short, physically slow-moving, blue-black eyes, mouth open more often than not, as if he had trouble getting enough oxygen to his lungs, although his tongue looked radiantly hale. He wore shiny grey leather trousers, a pale red linen jacket, weighty brown, lace-up shoes, most probably advertised as 'water-repellent'. Under the jacket he had on a formal white shirt with ruffles across the chest, a stiff collar and bow tie, one wing of it purple, the other turquoise.

He was already at a table in The Lock Gate when Moss arrived and rose to welcome him. 'Mart,' he said, 'grand to see you.' Moss was to his left as he came into the dining room and Ned's greeting was from that side of his mouth: the bow tie's purple side. 'Lovely place. They've got black-pudding hash on as Meal of the Day, one of my very favourites. Worth travelling from London for. One can get it in smart joints there, yes, but I always feel they're doing it to show they know how to go basic peasant once in a while. Here, though, it seems natural. Quite possibly the black pud is top range Irish, maybe Clonakilty. Unbeatable. *So* eatable.' He held out his hand and Moss shook it. Three other tables were occupied. 'I'd have recognized you anywhere, Mart,' Ned said.

'How?'

'The photo. Damn clear. A professional, I shouldn't wonder. You, gazing very hard at the surrounds, obviously on a kind of survey.'

'Which photo?' Moss replied. So Lawford had been right.

Ned sat down and Martin took the other chair. 'Volvo,' Lane-Hinkton said. 'A copy came our way the way these things will in their own fashion, won't they, Mart?'

'Will they? Which way will they come in their own fashion?'

'In one sense it's the photo that brings me here,' Lane-Hinkton said.

'Which?'

'What?'

'Sense,' Mart replied.

'I can't say it was the black-pudding hash because I didn't know it would be on until I got here.' He laughed mildly to offset the clunking plod of this logic.

'In what sense, then, Ned?'

He had the remains of his chuckle still softening the line of his lips. 'In confidence, Mart, I prefer Neddy. It has that nursery touch about it; a toddler's affectionate cognomen. People feel safe with me. They relax. I can surprise and floor the stupid sods by suddenly turning so fucking uncongenial and ruthless.'

'Right, Neddy,' Martin replied.

'Oh, I don't include you, Mart.'

'Include me in what?'

'As one of those stupid sods who can be fooled by a crude stratagem, viz, sticking a couple of extra letters on to Ned. You'd see through it.'

'Is this another stratagem?' Mart asked.

'Which?'

'To say I'd never be fooled by that cruder stratagem,' Moss said.

'God, Mart, this conversation could go on and on, like the never-ending line of Banquo's ghosts in *Macbeth*. We must focus on our main topic. The ride out to Charter was a special quest, wasn't it? I've said a survey. Inventorying? We are inclined to regard it as one of those rites of passage – you'll know the Golding novel of that title, naturally – something that possibly changes a life in the most profound style.'

68

'Which we?'

'And for a special quest he took a special guest: your very self, Mart. This would seem to proclaim a relationship – not a relationship in the *relationship* usage of *Lady Chatterley's Lover* – about which more later – but a relationship of a work-related, professional, drift.' Lane-Hinkton shook his head. It was severe reproof of himself. 'Do forgive me, Mart, but I seem to be taking charge in a pushy, metropolitan way. Because *I* fancy the black-pudding hash so unambiguously, so vividly, so convinced that the onion-potato ratio of the hash will be perfect, I'm assuming you will fancy it, too. Arrogance! There's liver and bacon, also, which, had there not been the black-pudding hash, I would have gone for. And this might well be your choice. Or they have a vegetarian course, or skate, or lasagne. Don't let me bully you, Mart! I trend in that direction, I'm afraid. On my personnel dossier at U.F.C. there's probably a note: "Ned is inclined to bully re black-pudding hash." Wilt take some ale, or an Old Raj gin and bitters. I checked that they have max alc Old Raj.'

'There's a photo?' Mart replied.

'Well, as I said, Martin, it's the photo that prompted the visit. Geraldine – she and I are the "we" – Geraldine thought I should come and have a word. And, clearly, what Geraldine in her newly enhanced power role at U.F.C. says goes. A moot, a suggestion, is an edict. Also clearly, what she is looking for, what, indeed, the whole of U.F.C. is looking for, is a convenient way to reach this maverick sod, Chote. When I say convenient, what I mean is a mode of reaching him which

69

doesn't touch off all his extreme and negative reactions leading to impasse. The time for impasses has passed, Mart, I think you'll agree. There should no longer be impassible impasses.'

'Reaching him?'

'Get through to him. Get his attention. Get him to hear the warnings and respond rationally to them, not detonate or spit and/or sulk.'

'Which warnings?'

'Geraldine envisages a sort of go-between service,' Ned replied. 'But don't take that as a slight, will you? This would be, will be, a crucial liaison role, with enormous implications. We need someone, and you seem wonderfully well suited, Mart. Cohabitation of the Volvo on that keynote saunter sends us this signal. Geraldine schemes a sort of devious, though legitimate, approach to Lawford. When Geraldine writes her memoirs they'll be titled *The Compleat Wangler.*'

Moss loved lunchtime drinking. Afternoons could be memorably or non-memorably improved by it. He'd come by bus and would get a taxi back. The English department had no teaching on Mondays. Traditionally it was regarded as a wind-down day after the weekend. But, by quick, intelligent adaptation, it could be used, too, as a weekend extension day, if, for example, a good lunch materialized. Ned must realize this about university Humanities departments or he wouldn't have suggested the feed.

He had the kind of teeth that would tell black-pudding hash who was boss. He and Mart both downed Old Raj and bitters to kick off with, then a bottle of Chilean white between them for the first course, kedgeree, and a claret magnum with Ned's black-pudding hash and Mart's liver and bacon. Mart took a half bottle of Sicilian Corvo with the cheeseboard and Ned had a bumper glass of Barsac for the sticky toffee pudding.

During the main, Ned said in very kindly though not sloshed tone, 'There's quite a bit of affection for Lawford at U.F.C., flagrant shit-or-bust arsehole though he might be, Martin. We sincerely wish to help him and Sedge. Swapsies? I'll give you a mouthful of my hash so you may marvel at the ingredients' balance, and I will take a token square of your liver-tinged bacon.'

For a moment Mart wanted to reject this idea, afraid that, when Ned said he would give Mart a hash mouthful, Lane-Hinkton meant his own mouthful. This to be delivered to Moss's mouth by lips contact and a controlled disgorging from Ned's right or left mouth area depending on how he felt it best to approach Mart as to tilt for the transfer – a move something like one motherly aircraft refuelling a small-fry plane in flight.

But Ned meant only a cutlery-based exchange of samples, a piece of black-pudding garnished with hash from him, a strip of liver-boosted bacon from Mart. He'd had the black-pudding hash here on one of his visits with Grace and had found the hash too dense, and still did, though he said, 'Excellent, yes. Oh, yes!' And Ned praised the augmented bacon. Moss thought Neddy might regard this mutual mouthful savouring as a kind of blood-brothers bonding ritual. People spoke of 'breaking bread' with someone as a sign of abiding inter-dependence

71

and friendship. This would be 'breaking black-pudding hash' or 'liver-partnered bacon', but perhaps Lane-Hinkton saw their across-the-table, non-drip forkings as a similar symbolic pledge of shared purpose and comradeliness.

'It's your newness, you see, Mart. This is what Geraldine homed in on. That's one of her attributes – to home in on essentials. She doesn't care for lav language, but if she did she would probably have as her motto "cut the crap". As it is, she speaks of "getting to the inner".'

'Is that where I am?' Moss replied.

'We can't go to Roy Gormand or Flora Ellison or Medlicott, Chote's clique of cliques people, his devotees. They're cowed. We wouldn't be sure they'd do the job in the fashion it needs to be done.'

'Which job? Which fashion?'

'The warnings. Categorical.'

Lane-Hinkton had brought complexities with him, as well as dress style. Chote's clique of cliques, his devotees, were not relied on by Geraldine or Ned to 'reach' him, 'get through' to him, and they wanted Mart for that. But, alongside this, Chote's attitude to his clique of cliques, his devotees, was troubled because he suspected one of them – more than one? – had given the treacherous word that put the camer-aman in place and, apparently, produced a Volvo pic. Mart felt tugged in two directions, one to be Ned and Geraldine's man and 'reach' Lawford; and, two, to be Lawford's man and hunt down the spy or spies, if they existed, which, on balance, he thought they didn't. Mart took a decidedly forceful swig of the claret – though from his glass, not the magnum bottle – a swig to clear his head, or to take him to an afternoon men's spot where he didn't have to worry whether his head were clear or not. Or even whether it was still there.

'This meal, for instance, Mart.'

'Always reliable.'

'Oh, true. But, no, not this one.'

'Which?'

'The Sedge Centenary feast,' Lane-Hinkton said.

'In Plain Parlour?'

'Geraldine thinks it must not go ahead. Or not go ahead on the proposed scale.'

'The thing about things . . . Sorry . . . The thing about events at Plain Parlour, Neddy, is that they have to be of a due grandeur and shape. The surroundings demand it. That kind of setting must be lived up to or the occasion's a contemptible flop. History requires it, surely. The Charles aspect. The Cromwell aspect.'

'This is why I referred to warnings, Martin. I'm not one to look down on history and neither is Geraldine, to my knowledge. The reverse in my own case. But, just as in hash, ratio is so important, and is acknowledged by you as admirable in the present dish, so there has to be a satis ratio between history and the present fucking dark situation menacing Sedge, owing to distortions in the ratio of Chote's splendid leadership flair on one hand, and respect for the dictates of income and cash generally – or their looming lack – on the other. Now, Mart, I don't want you to think I ordered the black-pudding hash merely to make a clever-clever allegorical point about potato-onion ratio and university governance. That would be a disgustingly calculating ploy. The black-pudding hash is brilliant in its own right, in its own Lock Gate right, as appreciatively endorsed by you. But the comparison of the hash and the Sedge Principalship came to me just now as a sudden revelation and I felt duty-bound to mention it. Perhaps I'm using imagery in the metaphysical poets' fashion, where, at first sight the two sides of a metaphor seem utterly unlike, rather than like each other – for instance, the human body as a dungeon, in Andrew Marvell; or black-pudding hash and the principal of a university, here – but on second thought the resemblance is clear and striking.'

Ned got another piece of black-pudding on to prongs and rubbed it gently around his plate to add another hash smear, then offered it as before to Mart, a kind of refresher in the ratio discussions. Moss thought he'd better take it, for fraternity's sake. He had a degree of difficulty in getting his mouth to exactly where the tidbit was but eventually managed this acceptance OK without disturbing any of the other customers too much. He greatly liked The Lock Gate, even though Grace didn't accompany him any longer, and he would hate to be banned. This was the chief reason he'd repressed the impulse to drink straight from the claret magnum just now. Mart reckoned there was something at least impolite and possibly crude about drinking wine from a magnum in a public area. After a while he responded with a bacon-liver montage remnant for Lane-Hinkton. Ned didn't seem able to get a simile of any sort from this part of the menu to put extra light on the Sedge predicament, thank God.

'It's like giving the finger to U.F.C.,' Ned said.

'What is?'

'Plain Parlour. The outlay.'

'Geraldine knows about it?' Mart asked.

'Lawford has asked her to pencil in the date. Naturally, she'll be invited. Obligatory. She is one of U.F.C.'s main figures. The Plain Parlour carry-on will be using U.F.C. money, won't it, Mart, unless Geraldine puts a stopper on funding? This is within her power-range now – why I mentioned the enhancing. But I don't think she'd wish to cut off the boodle like that. Peremptory, Mart. That's how she'd regard such an extreme move: peremptory, contrary to the wholesome ethos of university education in G.B. Consider the likely media treatment of such a disaster. "FAMED CENTURION UNI SKINT", and then a list of distinguished Sedge alumni with grieved and/or angry quotes about the impending death of a fine, beloved *alma mater.*

'And so she'd like you to talk to Chote and highlight the . . . the tensions. Geraldine considers that there is no sexual element in Chote's special attention to yourself. I hope that doesn't disappoint you, Mart. She's had some inquiries made and finds that Lawford greatly appreciated your reaction to Rowena Chote's trumpet-tone dossing during a lecture you gave on Lawrence and the

75

Mellors-Connie shag experimentation. This is what made him interested in you.

'Perhaps Chote had been feeling that his closest gaggle of minions were, are, no longer coming up with sparkling ideas for Sedge's progress; perhaps, even back then at the lecture, he wondered about the loyalty of one of them, or more. Principal Chote is ready to turn elsewhere in his search for major support, and, suddenly, at a standard inaugural spiel about Connie Chatterley's widening romantic experience, sees what he immediately regards as a gifted possible aide, Mart Moss. Now, of course, Mart Moss is not entirely new to him. Mart Moss has moved up the grades over the years to a professorship, and Chote has been Principal there for some of those years. But the night of the lecture brought a revelation to Lawford about said Martin's qualities, Mart.

'Here is someone strong and confident enough to carry on his performance through a snores blitz by the principal's piss-artist wife; a glistening achievement in itself, but, capping this, he has the ability to reach in to the deep recesses of Rowena's kip, and freight her back to lively, fascinated consciousness by flagging up unconventional fuckings among the clucking game bird chicks. Chote possibly blamed himself for not recognising your talents, Mart. This is why, as a kind of reparation, a kind of self-correction, he takes you on the Volvo mission. He believes in you, Mart. Hence, you are someone of serious power and valuable influence. We inevitably recognize that this might be a temporary matter, only. But then, life is only a temporary matter, isn't it? Geraldine wouldn't want to be other than straightforward about this. We've seen what's happened to Gormand and the others. They have their little day and that's it.

'Geraldine wants to avail herself of your favoured position while it is so. She is confident you can persuade Lawford into restraint, into acumen, into self-salvation. Geraldine said she would bet a cool 20p that at no stage during this drive was Chote's hand on your knee or higher, that this was not a wooing or grooming jaunt in the Volvo, but a testament to your harmonising with his professional and business attitude, a harmonising which we dearly want to avail ourselves of, Mart, in an attempt to divert Lawford Chote and the university you all worship from catastrophe.'

They took a couple of Kressmann Armagnacs with their coffees. Ned said, 'From the Condom area.'

'How do you mean? What is?'

'The Armagnac. Condom, West France. And then there's Rowena, of course.'

'Is there?'

'She might feel just as indebted to you as is Lawford on account of disrespectful, ostentatious sleeping while you gave your inaugural. Perhaps she still harbours guilt about that and is keen to make up for it.'

'I haven't ever noticed any sign of guilt.'

'Of course you haven't, Mart, because, as we understand it, she came out of the slumber into sheer perkiness and joy at your delicious exposition of wayward, all-round sex. That's the aspect

77

of her you see. But there could be others. You have captured the esteem of both a wife and her hubby. This is a terrific accomplishment. And now, surely, as well as your direct route to Lawford you can call on Rowena to help in trying to talk him out of mad money-chucking at Standfast.'

'She's said something like that to me, asking for help. My impression of Rowena is she'll always back Lawford in whatever he proposes.'

'That would be her initial instinct, yes. But, Mart, you have her ear. At least her ear.'

Thirteen

2014

'I've been casting my mind back,' Lucy Lane said.

'Well, that's what historians are supposed to do,' Nelmes said with a kindly smile.

'Touch-*bloody*-é,' Lucy replied, also smiling. 'But not very far back – only very, very recent history. Ours. Plinths. The previous discussion of.'

'As I recall it, the plinth matter was left unresolved,' Moss said.

'So it was, Mr Chair,' Lucy said.

'Our discussion was about entitlement,' Gordon Upp said, 'turning on whether one or both rated a plinth. No, "rated" is probably the wrong term – certainly *is* the wrong term, since it suggests

78

a ranking of plinths whereas plinths are really much of a muchness. In any case, the general feeling was that if Chote had a plinth Tane must have one, and of course, contrariwise.'

'Exactly,' Lucy Lane said. 'Now, what I'd like to ask is what was the prevailing, though unspoken, background presumption here?' She put some merriment into her voice, as if running a quiz for primary school children. Lucy left her nose contents undisturbed, probably intent on giving full attention to the poser she'd set; no matter what her nostrils had ready to be fished out, she could not allow this distraction now. Martin thought she might want to escape for a while the 'historian' label just fixed on her and get into the bustling, intriguing present.

'The presumption?' Bill Davey replied. 'It was that each principal deserved to be honoured via a statue.'

Lucy did a brief, minor handclap. 'Absolutely. But I'd like you to note two words there,' she replied. She paused. 'Which two words, you might ask?'

'Or maybe not,' Jed Laver said.

'Well, I won't toy with you, tease you,' Lucy replied. 'The two words are, of course, "each" and "a".'

'Naturally,' Laver said. 'They always bring with them a special glow. They really stand out, "each" and "a". Where would eloquence and oratory be without them? Hearing them we know we're in touch with a vocabulary.'

'OK, OK, take the piss if you must, Jed. What do the two imply, though?' Lucy said.

'Well, they look harmless enough, in the context,' Elvira Barton said. 'We're not going to get a lot of aggro from a word such as "a".'

'"In the context" is so right,' Lucy said. 'What *is* their context, Elvira? Forgive the doggedness, but I feel I must push on towards a worthwhile truth.'

'The context?' Elvira replied. 'Statues.'

'Spot on!' Lucy said.

'And their plinths,' Wayne Ollam said.

'I was taking their plinths for granted,' Elvira said.

'But can we?' Theo Bastrolle asked. 'Plinths are not a simple, subordinate, on-the-nod matter.'

'Plinths don't grow on trees,' Jed said. 'In fact, if anyone can cite a country where plinth trees grow I'll pay a grand to the charity of his or her choice.'

'Bill's observation was that "each principal deserved to be honoured via a statue",' Lucy said. 'The "each" and the "a" refer to single, solo entities, don't they – "each" principal, "a" statue. But if we put them together, as is done in Bill's typically perceptive remark, we have a plural, a duality, don't we? Because there are two principals and each must have a statue, it's clear that there must also be two statues – and, incidentally, two plinths. This is why I mentioned the context as being important. And now, here – a little late, I'll agree – is my point. It seems to me that in our conversations we have always assumed two separate statues and, accordingly, two separate plinths. I want to question this. In fact, we *must* question this.'

'You Cambridge graduates, so driven by rigour,' Wayne Ollam said. Yes, Lucy's light-hearted tone had been displaced now.

'What are you saying, Lucy – that there should be only one statue – singular, not plural?' Elvira asked. 'Surely we all agreed very early on in our meetings that fairness and, indeed, justice demanded there should be two.'

'We did, we indeed did,' Lucy said. She smiled again, plainly about to suggest something that would roughly shake at least some of their previous plinth thinking.

'Well?' Elvira said.

'We indubitably must have two statues,' Lucy said, 'but my mind lately has been relentlessly asking, do we need two plinths rather than one? Do we *have* to think binary? Are two compulsory?'

'But that has also been covered in our discussions on fairness and equality,' Jed Laver said.

'It has, it has,' Lucy replied. 'However, our premise then was that there would be two statues at different locations. In this case, to deprive one principal of a plinth would appear biased, partial, uncivil. There had to be a parity of plinths.'

'Am I reading you right, Lucy?' Angela Drape asked with something of a gasp.

'Are you?' Lucy replied impishly.

'You're putting in front of us the notion that there should be *one* plinth only and both statues should be on it,' Bill Davey said.

'You've got it, Bill,' Lucy said.

'Buddy, can we share a plinth?' Laver said.

'That would require them to be very close to each other, perhaps even touching,' Bill said.

'Our intended theme is unity, isn't it?' Lucy said.

'That's its public face, yes,' Bill said.

'Public faces are what we are concerned with, Bill, the public faces of statues – faces and the other parts of the imitation bodies. We want to preach a grand message of accomplishment through what? Through cooperation,' Lucy said. 'Is there a better way of doing this than to have the two men jointly responsible for this unity and accomplishment standing proudly together, blazoning sculpturewise that superb harmony by their comradely togetherness on a shared plinth?'

'Like Abbott and Costello,' Angela said.

'Who?' Lucy said.

'In a way that's quite a promising comparison,' Elvira said. 'These were two comedy stars in the 1940s and 50s. Their films come on the movie channel now and then. The underlying motif is that neither is complete without the other. They are complementary facets of one personality, facets which are not always in accord, but which are complementary all the same.'

'Sort of Abello,' Laver said.

'Similarly, George Burns and Walter Matthau in *The Sunshine Boys*.' Elvira replied. 'Another vaudeville comedy duo who score off each other in their act, and even in real life, but there is the same sort of implied powerful bond. They need each other.'

'Clown and straight man?' Laver asked.

'Perhaps we shouldn't go too closely into that at this juncture,' Elvira said.

'Which juncture *is* it?' Bill said.

'Speculative,' Elvira replied.

Theo Bastrolle said, 'OK, well let's speculate a bit further. Under Lucy's plan—'

'Well, only an idea for now,' Lucy said.

'Under Lucy's idea the two of them cohabit a plinth. How do they inter-act, given this proximity?' Theo asked.

'They're stone or brass,' Ollam said. 'Limiting for interaction.'

'But they are stone or brass copying life,' Lucy said. 'They are like all art – in this case sculpture – yes, all art seeks to, as it were, capture in one glimpse of the subject, one view of a scene, one record of a facial expression, one attitude of a body, a whole statement about the context – there's that word again – a statement about the context, the setting, that has provided this scene, that facial expression, the bodily attitude. The statues are what Eliot might term "objective correlatives".'

'Ouch!' Laver remarked, 'take me back to "each" and "a".'

'Would they be looking at each other on the plinth in sort of mutual respect, even affection, for each other?' Gordon Upp said. 'Like that song, "Me and my Shadow"?'

'It would certainly not answer the problem if they were shown staring at each other with contempt and/or hatred,' Angela said. 'Too much truth can become . . . well, too much.'

'Or perhaps not looking at each other as plinth passengers, but gazing out in different directions, their bodies, especially feet, inevitably plinth-close but angled away from each other, as if to

83

signal the marvellously holistic nature of universities,' Lucy said, 'their . . . well . . . universality of outlook and aim. Obviously, I think of that line in, I think, a Robert Bridges poem, addressing a handsome, wind-driven vessel: "Whither away, fair rover, and what thy quest?",' Lucy said. 'Each principal having been an intellectual "rover" in his fashion, voyaging forward on his own individual quest, mainsails hoisted, that quest in both cases being the enhanced reputation, glory, continuance of Sedge.'

'But, of course,' Nelmes said, 'neither of them will be looking towards a horizon, if we go for this kind of tableau. They are not aboard that great questing ship with a vast empty expanse ahead of them, just perfect for whithering away into with a full spread of canvas. This is a built-up area. Depending on the nature of their stance they will be as if taking a long glance at certain specific urban features. And the contemporary viewers of the statues should, I imagine, be able to catch something of each principal's character by noting what he is deemed to be gazing at, what interests him. The point with statues, of course, is that once their eyes are fixed on something they have to stay fixed. A statue can't look back over his or her shoulder if worried about being stalked, unless, that is, the statue from the start is of someone looking back over her/his shoulder, not a common statue style, however. Rodin's *Le Penseur* might have thoughts ranging in all kinds of directions, as is the nature of thoughts, but the statue has him facing strictly ahead and a bit downwards.

'So, for instance, perhaps the Lawford Chote would have his eyes settled on the new, executive-style housing estate a little way out of the city centre at Cottle Realm. This might indicate that Chote approved of superior, modern domestic architecture, and admired the self-bettering push that enabled people to shell out for such pricey properties. Or, of course, it could be Tane who felt like that about the estate. The other statue, whichever it might be, could seem very fascinated by the mixed sex Brade Academy playing fields nearby, exciting tourneys of netball, lacrosse and so on. That could be an entirely innocent, wholesome, matter but might tell us something about the leanings of one of them, Chote or Tane or Tane or Chote.'

Angela twitched a bit, then boomed, 'If they were plinth-linked as in Lucy's scheme, we have to ask about location.'

'Location?' Lucy replied.

Angela said, 'Sedge, as it exists now, is one university but with two campuses – what was Charter Mill and what was Sedge. Now, though, Charter Mill as a title is extinct, though the Charter Mill buildings and so on are very much with us; perhaps in one sense more with us than is the original separate Sedge, since the merger became possible only because Charter remained brilliantly solvent, even in its controlled, unflamboyant way, thriving. To continue the maritime imagery, Charter under Tane was the lifeboat that rescued Sedge in its previous, drifting, wrecked form, Captain Chote still on the bridge, the engine room telegraph set at Full

Ahead, but with no engines. Where, then, should any double-item tribute stand – in front of the city centre Sedge complex, on view to many; or at the outlying former Charter unit with its *prima facie* case to be the core constituent of our present day Sedge?'

Lucy said, 'Naturally, I've already considered this difficulty. My thinking is that conjunctive statues on their single plinth might easily be transported between each campus and established at one or the other for, say, a sixth month or annual spell. There could be an impressive ceremony at the arrival of the statues for their stint at this or that site, like the changing of the guard at Buck House.'

'Wouldn't this here-today, gone-tomorrow policy suggest nervousness, even confusion, about the stability of the new Sedge?' Elvira asked. 'How would the statues be dressed? This is a matter we haven't dealt with yet. But if Chote and Tane or, alternatively, Tane and Chote, are going to be in doctoral robes with mortar boards and tassels, carted back and forth on the back of a lorry across the city at switchover dates, they'll look like aristos getting tumbrilled off to Madame Guillotine.'

'There would have to be a recognized resting place for the plinth at each campus, a concrete platform, and how depressingly voided and abandoned that would seem at whichever of the campuses were without the statues for the ordained period,' Angela said.

Lucy said, 'I thought there could be an inscription cut into the concrete: "We shall return" – a slight adaptation of General Douglas MacArthur's

"I shall return" when he escaped from the Japanese in the Philippines during the Second World War. This would be a positive factor, not the reverse. That "we" captures the wonderful conjoint purpose. It is a promissory note sure to provoke anticipation of their assured reappearance in this reserved, designated spot.'

Fourteen

1987

'I know you'll forgive this . . . this . . . well, I think it must be termed subterfuge, or intrusion, at least, Martin. I can't even say it's well-meant. No, impossible to say that. The thing is, we don't feel 100 per cent private, secure, back there in the buildings, as it were. You've probably noticed that a dire sort of atmosphere has, regrettably, begun to prevail, an atmosphere hard to define, but obviously to do with acute anxieties, anxieties bordering on fear, and, in addition, something sickly, something toxic and disabling. We're certain we'd feel inhibited there, given the nature of what we want to discuss with you.

'And so we thought we'd take the chance – see if we could catch you at home. This is presumptuous, perhaps – presumptuous in the sense that it might be deeply inconvenient for you. If it is, Martin, please say so at once. We'll vamoose. We'll not be offended. We quite recognize that it's outstanding good luck to find you here, answering the doorbell to an unannounced call. For us to then go further and demand a slice of your time is beyond presumptuous. It's super-presumptuous.' She paused and for a second put her hand over her mouth, as if to silence herself. 'But, I say, what a spiel this is on your doorstep, Mart! I've gone blabby.'

And, yes, she bloody had. 'Come in, do come in,' Moss replied with gorgeous affability.

'May we, really? We're not a nuisance? I hope you won't think we're ganging up on you – the two of us in a combined, double-pronged approach.'

'Please,' Martin said. He led them into the sitting room. He didn't see how this visit could be other than extensively bad for him. Their need for 100 per cent privacy and security unsettled him. The lavish, galumphing politeness put him on guard. He wished he hadn't made them lucky by opening the door. Yes, he *did* suspect this visit to be a double-pronged approach, a double-pronged attack, the old one-two.

'As you'll no doubt have gathered, I elected myself spokesperson for the early moments at any rate. Well, you might say, it seemed a lot more than moments – yes, elected myself as icebreaker spokesperson,' Flora Ellison said.

'I knew Flora would make a better fist of it than I possibly could,' Roy Gormand said, 'her flair for summing up a situation in a few meaningful words.'

'Comparatively few,' Flora said.

'Summing up and clarifying,' Gormand said. 'No matter how complex that situation might be Flora will provide a simplified version, missing none of the essentials.'

'Such a lovely room – the sense of space and yet also of comfort,' Flora said, doing a panopticon gaze. 'I'm deeply fond of watercolours.'

It was as if she felt scared of reaching the actual reason for their visit. Her nerves drove her to talk, but to talk about nothing that mattered very much; something, in fact, that didn't matter at all – room decoration. Mart thought he could guess what brought them.

'Watercolours, so unvulgar, so unbrash, so gently declaring "pray take me as I am",' she said, 'so true to the moment when the artist spotted his/her topic and set up her/his easel and began. And don't let anyone claim that watercolours are easier to do than oils. Water is . . . well, watery. It's liable to run and needs strict control. So, the watercolourist must have the inspirational element but also management skills or it'll be the day the damn dam broke. I suppose it could be argued that all artistic production depends on such a fusion – you can't reproduce the almost magically created Chopin piece without the mechanical ability to hit the right notes with the right emphases and timing – but the water in watercolours demands special aquatic busybodying. Think of that inscription asked for by Keats to go on his gravestone: "Here lies one whose name was writ in water," meaning insubstantial.

'My mother was in many ways an arrantly stupid cow but she often correctly pointed out that "water always finds its own level"; and that level is downwards as far as it can get, including through gaps in the floorboards. Thus, a water-colour artist has a continuous problem in keeping the water from slipping down her/his legs to the ground.'

Roy said, 'Mothers, despite themselves, can come up with all sorts. I remember a—'

'Then, the room has, too, its armchairs and settee in uncut moquette, infinitely serviceable, an irresistible invitation to relax,' Flora replied. 'Whether *cut* moquette as against uncut would have the same happy effect has to remain moot. We have no example here. I stick to the "settee" name though some find it low-class – probably because it's bracketed with other somewhat snootily regarded nouns, such as "serviette", "kitchenette". It's that "ette" sound. People seem to think it's from the French and fusspotty. But why take against French? Those who would outlaw "settee" tend to prefer "sofa". Well "sofa" is from Arabic and therefore just as much a foreign import as any "ette" word. In fact, "settee" isn't foreign at all, but a development from the old English "settle" – meaning a place to sit, which is, obviously, what a settee is, even in this twenty-first century.'

'Can I offer you both a glass of sherry,' Mart said, 'speaking of matters continental? Tesco's own.' He went to the sideboard for a tray, the bottle and three glasses. Flora was in one of the armchairs. Roy settled on the settle-settee-sofa.

Moss served the wine, then sat down in another of the armchairs.

'Are you sure we're not imposing on you?' Flora said, sipping.

'I imagine you can intuit why we've come,' Roy said, 'and why we'd prefer to talk here rather than at Sedge.'

'Flora mentioned a changed atmosphere there,' Mart said. 'Probably this is in the nature of universities, in fact of many kinds of organisation – a dynamism, an urge to improve and go on improving. A university must constantly move forward, otherwise, atrophy and collapse.'

'It's no fucking improvement,' Flora said. The gushing preliminaries and lavishly decorous admiration of the room's pictures and furniture had obviously been ditched, at last.

'This is a little embarrassing,' Roy said.

'In which way?' Moss asked, though he thought he was beginning to understand which way.

'You're part of it, aren't you, Mart?' Flora said.

'Of what?'

'Of the change at Sedge,' Flora said. 'You're one of them.'

'One of what?' Mart said.

'Changes,' Flora replied.

'But we're not here to blame you,' Roy said. 'That's not at all in our remit. We look upon you, Mart, as—'

'We want to get things into the open,' Flora said. 'There are decisions to be made.'

'We don't consider you the instigator, Mart. You went along. It could be argued you had no real choice.'

91

'Of what?' Moss replied.

'It all began as a totally unplanned incident, didn't it?' Roy said.

'Which?'

'No evidence of devious scheming.' Moss thought he might be getting hard cop–soft cop treatment. Roy said. 'How *could* it have been planned? True, Rowena's supping-up tendency is well-known, but the way things went at the inaugural was utterly unpredictable. Rowena, pissed again, falls asleep. You are shocked but continue, bravely unperturbed, and in due course wake her and win her fascination by recounting what the gamekeeper was giving her ladyship and where. Lawford is unstintingly grateful. Perhaps his own sex life gets a lift and a happy variant or two because of your lecture. At any rate, you're suddenly the inadvertent golden boy, Mart. Most probably you'll get a top-table invite to Standfast Fort for the Plain Parlour centenary banquet.

'That's perfectly all right. Indeed, it's better than all right. Excellent. Lawford sees someone new, of unexpected talents, and wants to avail himself of them. This, surely, can be only a plus, not just for Lawford but for Sedge. It would torpedo an unpleasant belief held by some that the principal is surrounded and propped up by an exclusive cabal or clique – Flora, myself and a couple of others that we needn't name now. On the contrary, Chote has shown himself willing to take support from wherever it comes. There is a transparency and welcome width to his behaviour. And when I say welcome I mean welcomed by all who have the health of Sedge prominent in their minds, including those like Flora and myself, supposedly members of the specially favoured, self-protecting, narrow cluster.'

'Roy is right, up to a point,' Flora stated. 'Naturally, anyone who strengthens Lawford strengthens Sedge and is a boon. Boons are much needed. But there can be side effects – very hurtful, negative side effects. It's because Roy and I came to realize this – independently of each other at first – yes, it's because of this realization that we decided we must talk in confidence, away from the Sedge buildings, to you, Mart. I've mentioned the very deplorable change of atmosphere at Sedge. But I wonder whether you, in fact, are conscious of this, even though you are there as often as Roy and myself. To you, things might seem all tickety-boo: any changes are good changes, making things better than you have ever known them because what Roy and I would see as a darkening, a falling away, you, Mart, might regard as blissful sunshine and triumph. You're suddenly *in* with L. Chote, a success.'

She sipped. 'Potentially, you're our sodding ruin, Moss, or you'd like to be. You sit on your naff, bourgeois furniture, surrounded by wanked-out daubs on the walls, untroubled, snug, smug, while Roy and I are made to feel obsolete, discarded, useless, even traitorous. Yes, that. If you're such a sex guru, why are you here on your own when we call without forewarning? OK, you're divorced from Grace. Don't you have any replacements? And then the sherry? Are we at an Oxbridge tutorial, for God's sake? Do this banal room and your inaugural performance about brisk and saucy coitus, satisfy you now?'

'Well, Flora, I don't think much of that's particularly to the point,' Roy said.

'Doesn't it make you enraged to see such grotesque contentment while we are victimized?' Flora replied. Moss guessed she'd be about fifty. She was middle height, her eyes very pale blue and friendly even while she tore into him and his sitting room. She had a very hearty, unapologetic way of saying 'fucking' and 'sodding', and gave the 'f' and the 'uck' and the 'dd' sounds full wham. This differed from routine cursing: her heart was in it, though her face remained kindly and apparently eager for eternal matiness. There were certain words that Moss liked to mess about with. 'Dichotomy' was one, meaning a difference, a division where one might have expected a unity. If they ever brought in a Nobel prize for dichotomy, Flora would walk away with it: genial, carer's appearance; moody, switchback soul.

Mart considered it would be wrong and cliché-driven to describe her features as mobile. They weren't. They never moved away from expressing total amiability, and this accompanied the initial doorstep civilities just now and the multi-layered contempt she'd directed at Martin and his uncut moquette redoubt. She had on a heavy dark brown duffel coat, untoggled while indoors, over a vividly striped – scarlet, yellow, purple – high-necked blouse

94

and bell-bottom black trousers. Her feet were small in pink, very high-heeled and sharply pointed shoes.

'Think of dear Roy,' she said. 'For at least months and possibly years he has brown-nosed Chote with unwavering diligence and, indeed, relish. You won't find anyone in Sedge who can put as much sincerity and approval into the word "certainly".

'The principal will say something – quite possibly something virtually lunatic – and Roy, with a fine, discriminating smile will reply, "Certainly". He doesn't overdo this in case it starts to sound like mockery. No, he'll adjust with seamless skill to a resounding, "Absolutely", in support of some other blatant Chote crap. There is a benign, Darwinian strategy from Roy here; although Lawford Chote is frequently wrong and farcical he is sometimes right, and right about big, brave, admirably creative proposals for Sedge. Roy has decided that Chote's plentiful barmy ideas and behaviour must be approved so that the principal's confidence remains intact, enabling him occasionally to produce one of these splendid, unique, seminal developments for the university. Roy doesn't fling such endorsements around willy-nilly. They are specifically crafted for use on Lawford Chote, like a made-to-measure suit. Is Lawf aware of it – the brilliant accuracy and thoroughly simulated affection that's gone into this generous kowtowing? Perhaps he *was* once and felt grateful. But now? Roy is cast off, as I, too, am cast off. Why? Because some shallow, flashy, smarmy bastard comes along and uses these slimy qualities to get the approval of the principal's boozed-as-buggery wife and, through her, Lawford Chote's approval, too. You, Moss.'

Roy Gormand began to weep. It was noisy theatrical, unignorable weeping, not controlled, manly, muted grief but recurrent great waves of sobbing accompanied by fitful arm waving. It seemed wrong for someone on an uncut moquette settee or sofa. Mart's house stood in a fairly modern terrace. The walls were not thick and solid as in older style properties and he felt afraid neighbours might hear this heart-broken din and wonder whether something terrible had happened or was happening to him. Flora and Roy had come in Flora's Ford and it stood out front. That might cause people next door – on either side – to suppose a visitor or visitors had brought stress or tragedy to Mart's place, say forcible debt collection or a gangland revenge. He didn't want them thinking he was a crybaby.

Roy had his sherry glass, still half full, in one hand. He stared down at it and then at some indeterminate spot on one of the walls, then back to the glass. It reminded Martin of the way place kickers in rugby went through their ritual: first a glance at the angled ball on the ground; then a longer look at the goal posts; then the attempt to send the ball over the crossbar. Roy seemed about to fling the glass and the sherry to shatter on the selected area of plaster as part of his roaring sorrow display.

Flora obviously interpreted things the same.

She stood quickly, feinted with her right and then switched stance to punch Roy hard with her left on his right cheekbone, just below the eye, a classic straight jab, not a haymaker or upper-cut. Although Roy didn't fall, the blow forced his head around sharply twenty degrees to the right, but Moss thought there'd be no bone splintering. He wondered whether Flora had dealt with him like this at other times of crisis. Mart tried to remember if he had ever seen Roy around the Sedge corridors with abrasions to his face and/or teeth missing. The punch seemed very precisely and knowingly placed so that it would destabilize and bring pain but not knock him out or require surgery. 'Calm yourself, Roy, would you, please, you showy, waistcoated, near-defunct git?' she purred. 'We both feel for you, I'm sure, but this sympathy has boundaries and you'd better recognize them. Blub away if you like. A blub is commensurate with the hurt Chote has caused you. But no vandalising.' She took the glass from him. He did not resist.

He had been sitting crouched slightly forward on the settee, but now moved himself back and straightened, as if this constituted part of a recovery. It was like coming to attention while seated, possibly a drill he'd learned when called up in World War Two. He wiped his eyes with the backs of his hands. He was near retirement age – mid-sixties – with plentiful grey-white hair, nicely cut. He had a square face with brown eyes behind thin-framed glasses, a deep unlined brow, upper mouth false teeth, too white and too immaculately shaped. He was short-legged but stretched out his paces when on his feet, possibly hoping people would think he must be taller, to cover so much ground at one pop.

He wore a three-piece, grey double-breasted suit, the jacket unbuttoned now, the edge of a spectacle case poking out from one of the waistcoat pockets. His lips were full. Mart wondered whether they'd plumped themselves out like that through framing so many concurring, unctuous, comfortable phrases for Lawford. It was hard to think of lips like those saying anything cantankerous or niggardly. Roy's job title made him sound important (Sedge Developments Director) but he had only very minor power; Chote looked after most of that area himself, 'Development is my life-theme,' he'd said in an article written for the *Sedge News* quarterly magazine.

'As you can see, Martin, it's an emotional matter for me. Flora is younger, so although it is an emotional matter for her, too, it is also a very practical matter. Does she want to stay on at Sedge in these changed, shaming conditions, or does she look for a post elsewhere? Also, for me, a room is just a room, so I don't feel the rage that Flora obviously does. For her, this room betokens your selfishness, your indifference to the appalling indignity Lawford has imposed on both of us, and perhaps on Carl Medlicott, also. I'll be gone soon. I don't have to think of a tomorrow and a string of tomorrows here. It's the past I think of, Mart, and my loyalty to him and his cause, all of that now apparently disregarded, spurned.' Gormand seemed about to start sobbing again and slumped a little on the settee.

98

The right cheekbone had a red-black swelling, but Moss felt certain now that the bone was intact.

'Unfailing devotion came from Ray to Chote,' Flora stated. 'This was sucking-up of a quality rarely encountered among educated adults; connivance of an unparalleled purity and enthusiasm. Now, as poor Roy remarks, this wholesome relationship is abruptly and permanently expunged, blotted out.'

Gormand said, 'For instance we hear that Lawford asked for a schedule of our timetable on a specific day and a specific time. The reasons are not clear. Whatever they might be, though, it is unpleasant, chilling, to think we have been spied upon. To what purpose, Mart? Flora's guess is that it's something to do with a photograph she's been informed of by an acquaintance at the U.F.C., a photo of you and Lawford in his official Volvo seemingly on a sightseeing tour around Charter. Flora's U.F.C. pal says that about you there was a—'

'*I* can report what she said, thank you, Roy,' Flora replied. 'Rest while you recover. She reported noting a "complicit" appearance on your face, Mart.'

'What does it look like, a complicit face?' Moss asked.

'Complicit,' Flora replied.

'There wasn't much to be complicit *in,* was there?' Mart said.

'Was there?' Flora said.

'A seemingly innocent little journey but to what purpose?' Roy asked. 'You'll have seen

99

Charter Mill frequently in your goings and comings about the city.'

'And we are not the only ones curious about that journeying, are we?' Flora said.

'Lawford didn't know the photographs were going to be taken,' Moss said.

'Of course he didn't know they were going to be taken. His expedition to Charter had been turned against him, trumped, hadn't it?' Flora said.

'Had it?' Mart replied.

'Despite all his damn slyness he's rumbled,' Flora said. 'Or not just Chote, you as well, Mart. Let me give you the full scene, will you?'

'Which scene?' Moss said.

'The scene as Flora sees it,' Roy said. He seemed pretty well OK now after the punch and talked clearly. He bent and picked up his glass from near his feet, where Flora had put it, and took a drink to help. 'And, generally speaking, the same as I see it,' he added.

'U.F.C. have not only a copy of the photo but the date and time it was taken,' Flora said. 'This would indicate, I think, that it comes from someone in Charter, someone who knew about the filming. As I'd expected, the date and time match the dates and times of Chote's timetabling inquiries, Mart. This confirms that he wanted to know whether one of us, or more than one, might have been around to witness your start in the pictured Volvo – to witness it and to make a call to Tane, or one of Tane's people, to say you were on your combined way.

'So, you'll reply that nobody watching that departure would know where Chote was taking you. This is a naïve reaction though, isn't it? What we can see is that at the Charter end they instantly and rightly assume the Volvo is coming there, and, accordingly, get the camera man or woman into position. I say "instantly" because they wouldn't have much time to arrange for the filming. It's only a couple of miles from Sedge. I say "instantly" for another reason, too. The reaction to that tip-off at Charter is virtually automatic and instinctive. Doesn't it look as if someone there – possibly Tane himself, perhaps one of his team – hear in the call from Sedge that with Chote in the car is someone not normally considered as one of Lawford's particular mates – Roy, me, Carl Medlicott. The swift Charter deduction is that Chote has a new lieutenant and wants to break him in, show him the likely objective in Lawf's colonising dream? The fact that you knew already what Charter Mill looked like is not important to Lawford. He wants you, Mart, to see those buildings and playing fields in a different fashion from previously, see them as an apprentice conquistador might – as a possible prize, as a target.

'Now, as a matter of fact, Roy and I would agree with that assessment of events. You are the new man, Moss. Roy and I are nowhere. That's how he and I might read the situation. Not, though, how Chote does. He believes Roy, Carl and I were not nowhere but very much *some*where – somewhere that enabled one of us, maybe more than one, to watch the Volvo and its passenger hit the road and let Charter know about it. Hence the research into our timetables. He's hunting for a traitor, traitors. Can any of us – Roy, Carl, I – ever work properly with him again after this disgusting slur?'

'If that disgusting slur really does exist, Flora,' Gormand said.

'Of course it exists, you limp oaf,' Flora replied. 'That's what we're here to confirm, Mart. If it's the case, I'm putting myself on the market for a job somewhere else. Possibly even with Tane. This ludicrous behaviour from Chote almost certainly means he hasn't got the kind of brain and stamina that might save Sedge. I'm not going down with the ship. Lawford can, if he wants to. He's the captain, isn't he? Captains do.'

'It wasn't you who rang Charter about the Volvo was it, Flora?' Roy asked.

'Who says anybody rang?' she replied.

'Well, I thought that was your theory,' Roy said.

'Yes, Flora,' Moss said.

'Am I reading the situation right, Mart?' Flora asked.

'I had a ride out to Charter with Lawford Chote, yes,' Moss said. 'The purpose I'm not sure about.' Moss tried to give this a brush-off tone.

It didn't work. '*I'm* sure,' Flora said. Apart from that minor emphasis on the 'I'm' Flora spoke more or less off-handedly, as if Mart's opinion didn't rate. She obviously believed almost everybody would expect her to see and understand matters better than anyone else; and therefore she didn't need to bluster and/or harangue.

'As I mentioned earlier, the thing about Flora is she cuts through to the very core of things,' Roy said.

'Does she?' Mart replied.

102

Yes, Moss could accept that she often did. The Volvo hop-over to Charter had probably been what Flora said: a kind of recruitment device by Lawford to bring Mart into the topmost Chote team, a brief, motorized induction ceremony. But, although that's what might have been in Chote's mind, Moss detested this interpretation of the Charter Mill excursion. He didn't want to be regarded as a principal's stooge, a principal's yes-man, his minion. It had always depressed him to observe how Roy and some of the others in Chote's retinue would slavishly agree with him, defer to him, creep to him. Mart hoped he had a more independent spirit than that and what he'd heard described as 'proper pride' – not vanity, not coxcombery, but decently earned, solid self-esteem. He wouldn't allow Flora's poisonous caricature of him to kill that.

Mart could understand how someone in a leadership position like Lawford might get excited and energized about possibly extending the scope of that leadership, conferring his unique skills and strength on new areas; more or less an obligation. Moss had mentioned atrophy and collapse to Flora just now – the penalties for failing to move forward. Moss didn't know much about capitalism but he had often heard that a business could not stand still. It had to develop or it would be overtaken and crushed by competitors. Same with some public bodies, such as universities? Chote wanted to do the overtaking, not drop behind. Moss regarded this as a reasonable ambition, in fact, a fine, necessary ambition and didn't mind helping Lawford with it, if Mart could.

And he didn't mind having traipsed over to

103

Charter with Lawford to share a reminder of where, if Chote managed matters OK, the Sedge expansion would take place; this was part of that excitement and energy. But to sympathise didn't mean Mart had become Roy Mark Two, he hoped, or would ever become Roy Mark Two, gutted and lickspittling.

'Who chose them?' Flora asked.

'Chose what?' Mart said.

'The watercolours,' she said. 'I imagine it must have been Grace. *You* wouldn't pick such tame, insipid stuff. And not even she wanted them when you split, I guess. You hang on to them out of a quaint sense of loyalty, I suppose?'

'No, definitely not Grace. *I* picked them,' Moss replied.

Actually, Flora was right again and Grace *had* chosen them, then lost interest. But Mart felt he must do a bit of self-assertion on Flora. He didn't mean to answer her questions about Chote's and his own aims and intentions. 'I love the watercolours,' he said. 'Gentle, unobtrusive yet amazingly alive, so intent on their unique, individual identities.'

'What the fuck does that mean?' Flora replied.

Exactly. He didn't say it, though. He found the pictures wishy-washy and lackadaisical and had several times considered taking them down and dumping them on the Salvation Army for one of their raffles. But that would entail buying other works of about the same size so as to cover the faded patches of wallpaper where the watercolours had hung; or getting the room redecorated. He couldn't be arsed.

Fifteen

2014

Mart Moss said, 'At some time reasonably soon the committee will have to go as a body to look at prospective sites for the statues. You'll note I say "sites", not "site", and perhaps you'll also note that I say it tentatively, a slight tinge of query in my voice. But, just the same, I believe I have it right. Despite the suggestion in a previous session that the two figures should share one plinth, and, therefore, obviously, one site, though moveable, I felt that the discussion of that proposal – albeit a thorough, balanced and sensitive discussion – yes, I felt nonetheless that the majority view quite perceptibly favoured separate plinths, and, as a probable consequence, separate sites on the two campuses, giving each statue its own personal, psychologically speaking, autonomous space.

'If anyone feels I have misread the committee's thinking on this, I would, of course, be willing to put the matter to a vote, on the simple question: "Do you favour a unitary plinth per statue or one binary plinth per paired statues?" – abstentions to rate as acceptance of the *status quo,* the *status quo* being the original working assumption of one statue one plinth.'

Wayne Ollam (Philosophy) said, 'No need,

Mart, none at all. I think you've caught the general view accurately. That is, respectful, positive consideration of the solo plinth with double occupancy suggestion, but eventual abandonment of that idea as over-complicated, particularly the inescapable, endless requirement to transport the duo and their close-cohabited plinth across the city at specified intervals. If the statues were visible on the back of a lorry during such trips the general public, although quite unbiased, might feel this arrangement to be laborious, contrived and even slightly farcical. On the other hand, were the plinthed couple moved between locations secretly – say under tarpaulin on the lorry, or in the windowless back of a van, and this became known to the media, we could be knocked, mocked, for behaving sneakily and furtively with the images of two men who, in their time, had stood for transparency, openness, honesty – fundamental qualities of universities worldwide. Also, because of this periodic transfer, requiring time on the road between Sedge and Charter, or, to put it another way, for the sake of equality, Charter and Sedge, there would inevitably be spells when both campuses had no statue or statues at all. Agreed, that might be only a brief break since the distance is not great, but I believe we should strive to establish a completely uninterrupted continuum, symbolic of a steady, strong, unthreatened future for the new, composite Sedge.'

Theo Bastrolle (Business Studies) said, 'And if the statues were single-plinthed and swapped around at set intervals between the two campuses,

106

Sedge and Charter, or Charter, Sedge, like changes of shift, it would similarly look – what were Wayne's words – look, yes, laborious and contrived. There's another demeaning comparison, isn't there: one of those barometers where two figurines came out in turns according to what the air pressure and weather are doing?'

'So, if Victor and Lawford, or Lawford and Victor, are to be mono-plinthed and fixed in their respective locations we come back to the major problem touched on at a previous meeting of who is where?' Lucy Lane (History) said. 'I recognize that the statues could be close to each other, without that implying they're at each end of the same plinth. We have already considered proximity issues such as the height disparity between dumpy Chote and beanpole Tane, or beanpole Tane and dumpy Chote.

'But if there were to be proximity, though not on a single plinth, it would imply that only one of the campuses would get the statues and the high board might not see this as suitable. There would be an acute risk of false appearance. For instance, if both were installed near each other in what used to be Charter, this might be interpreted by some as meaning that they jointly brought the new university into happy conjunction with the older one; whereas it's clear to anyone who reads even the smallest amount of documentation and press coverage of the period that Lawford Chote loathed the notion of a merger, regarded it as a kind of slumming to have any link with Charter, let alone a formal marriage. On the other hand, if both individually

107

plinthed statues were set down not far from each other in the Sedge campus it could be taken as a statement that Lawford had gladly welcomed Vic Tane into his bailiwick as an admired, supportive partner which, of course, is top-of-the-range bollocks.'

Angela Drape (Environmental Engineering) said, 'Had we been thinking of statue placements in 1987 we'd have met no real difficulty. Lawford Chote was installed at Sedge and Victor Tane at Charter Mill, or to put it differently, Victor Tane at Charter Mill, Lawford Chote at Sedge. But, clearly, the problems wouldn't have arisen then because they were both alive, not requiring statues, and actually in their obvious *situs*. Do we now, a quarter of a century later, follow that pattern and put the Tane statue at what is today the Charter Mill campus of Sedge and the Chote statue in what is today the Sedge campus of Sedge University, a title which encompasses both?'

'What this comes down to ultimately, I think,' Elvira Barton (Classics) said, with a let's-cut-the-crap rasp, 'is whether one of the apparent options presenting themselves to us for selection is in truth an option at all. We would never choose it. I refer, of course, to the notion that in the disposition of statues Lawford Chote's could conceivably be allocated to Charter, while Tane's at Sedge is a perfectly feasible concept since he became Principal of the merged Charter and Sedge, or Sedge and Charter. Consequently, he's entitled to be at either site; and – specifically – is entitled to what some might regard as

108

the more prominent, city centre display. There is no such similar obviousness in a suggestion that Lawford Chote's replica should go to Charter. There would be something crazy in any decision to send the Chote image there. Some would put things much stronger than that and possibly talk of Lawford's being dumped out there – "out there" referring to its semi-rural, semi-obscure setting – as a kind of punishment for his mismanagement and presumptuousness, a kind of malign, sneering joke.'

'Like Devils' Island or Alcatraz or Siberia,' Bill Davey (French) said.

'In what sense a joke, Elvira?' Gordon Upp (Linguistics) asked.

'There are still people around – me, for instance – who have heard that it had been Chote's blatant boast that he and Sedge would take over what was then regarded as the lesser, entirely undistinguished institution, Charter Mill,' Elvira said. 'He would probably have gone about slagging off this neighbour for needing a name that blared possession of a charter in order to call itself a university. This, he would have argued, showed it was very shaky – and deservedly so – about its identity and status. Was Oxford or Harvard or the Sorbonne ever mistaken for something other than universities because they didn't have charter or the French equivalent in their titles?

'But then comes the reversal, the cruel, absolute, humiliating reversal and an end to Lawford's braggadocio. Sedge doesn't eat up Charter because Sedge is broke and can't afford that kind of delicacy. Instead, Charter makes a snack of

109

Sedge and spits Lawford out like a lump of irredeemable gristle. To put his statue at the former Charter now would be like saying to him, "You wanted Charter Mill, didn't you? Now you've got it, but only a tolerated bit as big as your plinth, Chotey. Look about you and see the quiet orderliness and solvency that brought Sedge last-minute salvation, but brought it at a cost." If the statue's face showed the authentic Lawford self-satisfaction and arrogance, it would come across, wouldn't it, as an indication of outright madness, as if he couldn't realize what a terminal mess he'd made of things; still imagined he had a future and was on his way to a knighthood or even a peerage for services to higher education. We surely can't allow such gross lampooning of someone who had several genuine achievements in his career. Well, one or two.'

'I think we shouldn't make our minds up until we've done an organized, on-the-spot examination of each potential site, whether in what was Charter Mill or the original Sedge,' Mart Moss said. 'The actuality can be a brilliant help in attaining clarity of vision when things are complex and clouded.'

'Of course, Mart, you would most likely be able to endorse that from your own experience, wouldn't you?' Claud Nelmes (Physics) said.

'Not sure I follow that, Claud,' Moss replied, in fact following it very well. He didn't fancy getting frogmarched into that snippet of history, though.

'I was a research student at Sedge during those run-up months to the merger crisis. I remember, don't I, Mart, that there was a kerfuffle about a picture of you and Lawford in his belligerent Volvo apparently sizing up Charter as a possible target in a Sedge expansion scheme? A Chote expansion scheme. "Come in under my umbrella, Charter, and feel the instant benefit." It seemed both of you wanted to see that "actuality" you've just mentioned. Or re-see. This was the rumour around, anyway. And a copy of the photo reached the Education Ministry heavy mob in London, didn't it, leading to a series of clean-up interventions?'

'All sorts of rumours flying then weren't there, Claud?' Moss replied.

'But this seems to me an example of that actuality thing,' Nelmes said.

'Actuality *thing*?' Mart replied, as if amused.

'You spoke just now about actuality, Mart, referring to it as "a brilliant help" to our thinking and understanding. Contact with actuality, you seemed to say, would be an advance on what so far is only ideas – ideas in this case about the statue sites. You suggested, didn't you, that we should go "as a group" to see, to experience in that *actuality*, the competing emplacements.'

'Ah, we've got a very obvious touch of *esse est percipi* here,' Elvira snarled.

'Absolutely!' Lucy said.

'I've never seen a better case of *esse est percipi*,' Bill Davey said.

'A case of *what*?' Claud replied. 'We've got *what*?'

Of course, Mart had made this comparison himself when actually on the Volvo trip with Lawford, but he didn't say anything about that now and let Elvira give the explanation.

111

'Dr Johnson and his pal Boswell were talking after church one day about Bishop Berkeley's theory that things existed only in the mind – *esse est percipi (*to be is to be perceived),' she said. 'Boswell comments that, although this is blatant rubbish, to refute it might be difficult and perhaps impossible. Johnson lashes out with his boot and kicks a large stone, hurting his foot. "I refute it thus," he says, meaning that the stone had a real, an *actual,* existence, and had it before the kick, and would have it afterwards, not depending on someone's mind thinking about it.

'We, so far, here in our committee, are dealing in ideas – *only* ideas – regarding the statue sites, as Mart would appear to suggest. The statues don't yet exist. However, we have in our minds, certain abstract qualities that they will represent – commemoration, praise, gratitude. The significant phrase here is "in our minds". *Only* at this stage "in our minds". What Mart wants us to do is move forward to the next point – reality, the possible locations themselves.

'Mart would like us to get to the potential sites and perhaps not aim kicks at them but get the feel of the places where a statue, or the statues, might stand and note the nature of the ground under our feet – perhaps grass, perhaps cement, perhaps timber – and experiment with the kind of views available from such sites. This he considers will bring guidance and clarity to our deliberations, and I'm prepared to believe he is probably correct.'

'It would be rather illogical, wouldn't it, Elvira, for us to go about kicking stones given that the statues we have in our minds will most likely themselves be made of stone,' Jed Laver (Industrial Relations) said.

'Interesting,' Moss replied. 'Perhaps on that fascinating observation we should adjourn now.' He'd heard enough discussion of this topic and similar. The Volvo saunter had embodied all the vainglorious absurdities of Lawford's principalship, and Mart would prefer not to be associated with it now. He'd detected a *j'accuse* tone in Nelmes's voice when he asked about Martin's part in that reconnaissance operation with Chote, a reconnaissance that became irrelevant and fatuous almost as soon as it had taken place.

That minor travel episode turned out to be much less important than the series of journeys from London to Sedge that it provoked. In Whitehall, Geraldine Fallows – later *Baroness Fallows* – had learned of the sortie and seen the photograph. Result? Neddy Lane-Hinkton is sent down to vet the local black-pudding hash and to discover what the fuck is going on at Sedge, the first of many nosy, investigative deputies on mission from HQ. Unfortunate truths about the mess-up at Sedge began to emerge and, in a short while, imminent disintegration was diagnosed and emergency treatment begun: i.e., Lawford neutralized and virtually booted out, along the lines of Dr Johnson's treatment of Bishop Berkeley's idealism.

Martin recalled that he'd felt half sympathetic to Chote's aim to expand Sedge; but also half uneasy about his attempt to enlist Mart by getting him to think of Charter mainly – entirely? – as a desirable and available slab of real estate, lecture room, labs, a canteen, playing fields. Mart had often in those immediately pre-crisis days tried to picture what Chote was like as, simply, Lawford Chote; as just another man, not as head of Sedge. But Martin had found that, as far as he was permitted to see, Lawford lived for Sedge; or rather he lived for Sedge with Lawford Chote at the top of it and resolutely eager to be at the top of something akin but bigger. There were good aspects to this. He brought drive and a kind of creativity to Sedge – his kind. And his kind of creativity demanded a lot of money and some luck. At or near the end of his tenure neither of these was to hand.

Now, Moss wished he had been a good deal less than half in favour of Lawford's jinxed ambitions. Although that was only the wisdom of aftermath, it would have to do. It dictated his attitude to the Volvo-Charter-Sedge-Lawford-Moss situation today, and today was where Mart indubitably was at. 'Thank you all very much,' he said. 'Reassemble in a fortnight, same time.'

Sixteen

1987

'I wanted to congratulate you, Vic.'

In his office at Charter Mill, Victor Tane had a call on the confidential line from Geraldine

Fallows at the Ministry's Universities Finance Centre in London. Her voice was steely, in the fashion that voices of executive rank in the Ministry's Universities Finance Centre in London generally were steely, but traces of excitement and faux warmth came over, too.

He'd been handwriting a substantial letter to his mother when the phone rang, describing what he regarded as interesting news about himself, underlining some crucial words, and exclamation marking several of the most startling, to give an ironic flavour. He got a real kick out of penning exclamation marks, which he'd found wasn't the case if he typed the letter on his computer. He felt that the narrow nib imprinting the paper like that was the culmination of a happy trek from his brain, where the decision to use that piece of punctuation was made, then down his arm and fingers and the body of the fountain pen to the very ready surface adjoining the word to be kitted out with the exclamation mark.

His mother had been dead for just over two years but he felt it wise to get in touch like this every few months or oftener. It amounted to more than an antidote to grief; had not much to do with grief at all. He would put his home address including postcode as sender on the back of the envelope and it soothed him thoroughly when the letter was returned with 'NOT KNOWN', or 'GONE AWAY' alongside the franked stamp, usually in pencil, and usually in capitals.

'GONE AWAY' was the inscription he preferred. The 'NOT KNOWN' response seemed an attempt

115

to negate her, claim she didn't exist and never *had* existed. Because Tane knew this to be untrue, he deduced that the 'NOT KNOWN' statement showed nothing about his mother but proved that whoever had written this comment was possibly stupid or slapdash or indifferent. It troubled Victor. He felt that his mother might still be around and potentially active, although not known to some.

This disturbing factor was pleasingly absent from 'GONE AWAY'. He took these words to mean that there had certainly been someone of Tane's mother's name at this address but she had decided to change locations: had voluntarily removed herself from contact with the recipient, recipients, of the letter, and therefore from Tane's reckoning, also. He could confidently reassure himself that she wouldn't be turning up to yell at him in her customary style about the 'poncy uselessness' of his classics degrees, and then go systematically through his letter declaring every paragraph aimed at charming and updating her was shit.

He realized that the people now living at her last house would eventually get sick of returning his letters, and this could make him edgy, as if she must still be present somewhere and liable to accost him suddenly, the pages in her hand, most likely flecked with rage saliva. Or the folk at the receiving end might open the letter and read it, then write to tell him this one and most probably all those they'd sent back as 'NOT KNOWN' or 'GONE AWAY' were rot and full of daft dogs' cocks, as he knew exclamation marks were called in journalism.

'The photograph,' Geraldine said on the phone. 'Maybe I should have rung you earlier with my thanks, but I asked Neddy Lane-Hinkton to do a little prospecting at Sedge and wanted to get his account of things before I spoke to you.'

'Fluke,' Tane said.

'I don't believe in flukes. Some things are beyond our understanding, yes, but that doesn't make them flukes. Consider intuitions. Consider extra-sensory matters. There are more things in heaven and earth, Victor, than are dreamt of in your philosophy, as Hamlet almost says.'

'In this instance shouldn't that be "photography" not "philosophy"?' Tane replied. He hated quotations, except those lifted from limericks on the walls of public lavatory cubicles. He knew thousands of quotations, English, French, Backslang, German, Latin, Greek, but would never use one, and suspected those who did. They needed something to prop up their own thoughts and ideas, so went and filched earlier versions of them, versions that had possibly endured for centuries and so must be strong and safe. *Hamlet* quotes he loathed above all. 'To be, or not to be, that is the question.' Most actors gave the 'that' a real wallop, as if to squash any other questions, especially banal queries such as 'do you take milk and sugar?' Well, perhaps to be or not to be *was* the fundamental question and most people decided to be rather than not to be just yet. Because of this they looked both ways before trying to cross the road. It was so obvious that it wasn't worth going on about. One quote from *Hamlet* Tane did treasure: 'Give it

117

understanding, but no tongue', i.e., think, and keep your trap shut.

'Our Organized Crime And Its Defeat department here runs regular surveillance exercises and tests for students hoping to get into the police or security services,' he told Geraldine. 'We are very hands-on, as they say. One of them did traffic filming and happened to net the Volvo and its two occupants, along with many other vehicles. Nothing planned. A fluke. Gloria Sondial, department head and a sharp lady, skimming through the kid's work to check clarity, focus, composition, realized what we had and let me know about it.'

'That's hardly fluke, is it, Vic? The opposite: she saw the importance. She made a decision to tell you, show you. All very logical.'

'The filming – luck,' he replied.

'I prefer to think mysterious, subliminal hunch,' Geraldine said. 'I prefer to think unexplainable inspiration. Britain needs people like that student, and like Gloria, in MI5 and 6. There's something psychic about this revelatory sequence.'

'I agree that if Chote noticed the cameraman, he'll probably think Charter had been tipped off by phone from someone in Sedge that the Volvo had set out on its way to eyeball Charter, and I ordered the filming. I've heard Lawford can be a bit paranoid.'

'But how would anyone at Sedge know they were coming to you, even if they were spotted leaving?'

'Chote would probably reply, "There are more things in heaven and earth, Geraldine, than are dreamt of in your philosophy."'

'Look here, Vic, we're at a crux situation,' she replied.

'Crux how?' Tane asked.

'It's plain.'

'But how?'

'He was on a shopping excursion, wasn't he?'

'Chote?'

'Chote and his fresh chum.'

'Shopping in which way?'

'Your fucking way. Charter Mill way. I see it as a kind of plea, Vic.'

'See what?'

'The photograph. Or not simply the photograph, but the fact that you should send it to me.'

'It's not a fact. I didn't.'

'All right, all right, you didn't. I think I can work out why you wouldn't want to admit you did. You feel it might make you look weak, sneaky, unmanly. You wouldn't want to be deemed unmanly. You wouldn't want to be thought incapable of dealing with this yourself. I referred to a kind of plea, Vic. You'd probably feel ashamed to be caught making such a plea.'

'What plea?' Tane replied.

'This is the enemy at the gates, isn't it? I'm told we have recognisable bits of Charter in the picture's background. You smell danger. You smell intent. You smell machinations. This is Chote with a new lieutenant. Lawford no longer finds his usual top gang adequate. Forthcoming pressures will be too much for them. I've met some of this special caucus in previous dealings with Sedge, of course – Roy Gormand, Flora Ellison. Gormand at this sunset stage of his

119

career is intellectually frail, feeble, merely a yes-man. I'm not sure he's ever been more than that. Now, he's liable to blub under stress, even negligible stress. Carl Medlicott, frequently unwell. Then Flora – subject to very disturbing mood swings, volatile, epically unreliable, unpredictable, no doubt a splendid, frantic shag if caught at the juicy point in her emotional orbit, but Lawford needs something else currently.

'This replacement, Martin Moss, unfledged in the Sedge-Charter situation and possible – probable – future developments seems to have impressed Lawford somehow. Well, I have a notion how. Neddy did some nosing and comes up with a report that Moss's inaugural as prof seemed to tickle Mrs Chote with its commentary on Connie and the gamekeeper's romantic variants. He decomatosed Rowena. You very prudently – if I may say – very prudently see these changes – Gormand, Flora, Medlicott out, Moss in – as an important indicator. It shows an intensification of the Charter-Sedge tensions. Chote seeks to increase his firepower. So, Martin Moss. Lawford will make his gambit very soon.'

'Which gambit?'

'Lawford has the Sedge centenary celebrations coming up,' Geraldine replied. 'He'll be feeling extremely bouncy, extremely bullish and questing. You very prudently – again, if I may say – very prudently decide to seek support from outside. Nothing abject or craven in that, Vic. It's what we're here for. Hence I get this copy of the photograph. A wholly unnecessary tact means the snapshot is sent anonymously. But its message is apparent. No caption is required, no disclosure of source. I'm ringing now to ask you to let us know at once of any further signs there that Chote or his new aide, Moss, might be contemplating other stratagems. Why I mentioned a crux, Victor. We are very near something now.'

'Near what?' Tane said.

'I'm talking about signs that possibly only you in your position would spot the underlying meaning of – or perhaps with the intelligent help of someone like your gifted, clued-up Gloria Sondial. To most folk the Volvo and its crew would amount simply to a Volvo and its driver and passenger. It takes unusual sensitivities and nous to get behind the obvious and supply a context and a prognosis. I say once more, "Congratulations, Vic," and please pass similar from me to Gloria.'

When she had rung off, Tane continued the letter to his mother. 'As one of the items in "A Day Of Sport" put on by the "Physical Education Sport And Bodily Wellbeing" (PESBW) department here recently a seven mile walking race was featured and it inevitably put me in mind of that sonnet you wrote about a similar event. Do you recall it, dear Ma? I do, every line. But you wrote so much poetry – including those longish parodies of *Paradise Lost* books Five and Nine. Perhaps you forget some of your other works. Let me then close with the aforementioned sonnet. I recited it to some of the contestants after the competition. I don't think they liked it very much:

Preposterous goons, why must you jig
and twitch like this, all elbows, knees
and tortured hips, heel-toe, heel-toe,
contorted, spit-slimed lips? You jerks
reduce to robot jerks the rich refine-
ments of the human frame; you've
turned your bodies into rule-clamped,
comic sites. Now, here's the ref, arrived
to check the rights and wrongs of what
he dubs your styles. 'I've learned to
spot the cheats,' he says, 'sly runners
who pretend to walk, but flap their arses,
lift their feet too high, all discipline
adrift. The sport's grand skills rest only
with a few: between their buttocks stars
could fix a pin, then race, while never
puncturing the skin.'

I'll say farewell for now, mother. Your ever
distant son, Vicky

Seventeen

1987

But Tane's mother didn't hate *all* sports. Although
she despised that kind of walking style required
in racing, and abominated, too, televised tennis
with its scuttling, servile ballboys and girls,
she adored soccer and especially goalkeepers,

'solitary between sticks, like an unmelted sugar cube in tongs,' as she thought of them. It was because of her fervent regard for goalkeepers that one of them came to have what Victor considered quite a notable influence on the Sedge-Charter Mill situation. This wasn't – couldn't be – instant. It evolved over several years, thanks to Mrs Tane.

She'd written a poem about these 'custodians' – heartfelt and full of unbridled praise; none of that towering irritability plain in *Two Views*. It began, 'Oh, goalkeeper, my goalkeeper,' and, as Tane remembered it, this note of excited, all-out reverence was maintained to the end. Several times she'd told Victor that Albert Camus, the great French philosopher and Nobel Prize winner used to be a goalie in a local Algerian team, 'before he started all his seminal stuff about the Absurd.' Mrs Tane believed that goalkeeping helped put him on to this kind of philosophy because there was something comically farcical – absurd, in fact – about the sight of a goalkeeper powerfully, unsparingly, flinging himself to one side when trying to block a penalty, but, as it turned out, the absolutely wrong side. Didn't this glaringly demonstrate that human effort was pointless in a cruelly malevolent world? Oh goalkeeper, my goalkeeper, how noble you might be at times, and how mercilessly exposed.

'Good goalkeepers have courage, agility and undaunted free-spirited self-hood,' his mother insisted, 'this last above all.' Any evidence of serfdom in sport or in life generally always

123

nauseated her – the mad rules, as she regarded them, imposed on contestants in a walking race; the bent-double fetch-and-carry ballboys and girls forced to make themselves more or less invisible, crouched low against the net post between rallies, like dogs waiting to be let off the leash; Victor Tane's sickening subservience to the rigidities of Greek and Latin grammar. Music of all types disgusted her because at the composition stage it was 'just blob notes clinging pathetically to stave lines, resembling hopeless messages stuck by prisoners on the barbed wire, perimeter fence of a concentration camp.'

Tane's father had been a couple of decades older than Amy, Tane's mother, but in his early fifties had persuaded an amateur club near where they lived to let him play in goal for their Thirds so as to please his wife and get at least some of her esteem. Although he bought goalkeeper-type mittens he was useless, but brave. In his first and final game, when he'd already let in four goals, he rushed out, attempting to scoop the ball away from the feet of the opposing centre forward, to prevent his hat-trick, got badly kicked in the head and went into a coma from which he never recovered. Amy had the words, 'In a league of his own' inscribed on the gravestone.

Several years ago, probably 1981, she had come to visit Tane shortly after his appointment as Principal. It was a Saturday and the Charter Mill soccer team were due to play a Sedge eleven in the afternoon on the Charter Mill ground. A vivid rivalry would be on show in the match because of the geographical nearness of the two universities and Tane decided he must attend as a spectator, to demonstrate solidarity and support. He'd guessed his mother might be keen to see the game and mentioned it when they arranged her visit on the phone. Amy brought white wellington boots and thick, grey socks in her holdall. Tane wore his heavy walking shoes.

Lawford Chote, also, had obviously decided this match was a meaningful occasion in the Sedge-Charter relationship and was on the touchline with what Tane took to be a couple of his male staff, maybe from that special fawning coterie Victor had heard rumours of. Poor sods, if they didn't like soccer. But, then, Chote might not, either. It was a duty attendance, perhaps. Same for Tane. He'd have to try to nick some of his mother's enthusiasm. The heavens declare the glory of goalkeepers. As the teams took their positions for kick-off she'd said, 'Burly and tall enough to close off some of the space, admittedly.'

'Who?'

'The Sedge goalkeeper.' she said. 'But burliness and tallness are not necessarily enough.'

'Oh?' Victor replied.

'Although yours – Charter's – himself has some burliness and height, I can read something else there. Let's call it "inherent purpose", shall we, Vicky?'

'What inherent purpose?'

'Goalkeeping.'

'Surely the Sedge goalkeeper would also have that purpose, Ma? It's what goalkeepers do – keep goal.'

125

'Not the same,' she replied. 'But I wouldn't expect someone like you to appreciate this.'

'Someone like me in which respect?'

It had been a fine, cold November afternoon with a mild wind favouring Charter in the first half. There was no seating but a crowd of a couple of hundred, mostly undergraduates, stood around the touchlines, partisan, and noisy.

'It's a destiny, Victor.'

'What?'

'Goalkeeping. Not some drab job at the back given to someone just because of bulk and tallness to help him cope. No, a mission. A disposition. A designated role. A congenital urge. These are the in-built qualities the true goalkeeper has and they are immediately apparent to some of us.'

'Designated who by?' Victor asked.

'By blood, by fate. He has been singled out. He does not wear the striped, buttoned shirt like his ten colleagues but a single-colour, polo-necked jersey. In the Charter case, green. But you'll protest and say the Sedge goalkeeper also has a single-colour sweater, but purple. I don't argue that the distinctive top garment is the *only* exceptional factor. In some instances – such as Charter-man – it is the accompaniment, the, as it were, frame for all those other required factors.'

'Surely, Mother, the goalkeeper wears the heavier garment because this is a winter game and he might be required to stand around doing nothing much and therefore liable to get cold. His mittens would protect only very small areas. The mono-colour of the sweater-jersey isn't really of much relevance.'

126

She'd clearly found this ridiculously naive and had a good-natured, throaty chuckle at it. Then she said, 'Gabby twat.' She wore a double breasted black leather greatcoat which she'd told Tane was of the type used by Swedish army dispatch riders, a grey woollen scarf, tied like a running bowline knot, a navy bobble hat, also woollen, and brown corduroy trousers tucked into the socks and wellingtons.

Charter had made an easy task of drubbing Sedge, as Tane would have expected. After all, Charter had a Physical Education and Bodily Wellbeing degree course. It attracted students who, when they finished, might have a professional interest in sport, and so they devoted most of their university time to preparing themselves for that – skills, fitness, diet, psychology.

But the Sedge team would regard games as merely something aside from their serious work – a break, a relaxation. Charter beat them 6-0, four of the goals in the second half, as though Charter wanted to prove they could triumph just as well against the wind as with it. Psychology. Self-belief. Adaptability. The Charter goalkeeper had only two saves to make throughout, both simple and soft. But Amy Tate yelled 'Sublime!' when he made the first of them and 'Rapturous!' for the second. Tane, scared of seeming indifferent and/or churlish cried 'Bravo!' for each, with credible, robust power.

'I thought "Bravo!" was what opera groupies shouted,' his mother said.

After the final whistle, Chote and his mini-entourage had crossed the field and approached

127

Amy and Victor in genial, brisk style. Tane introduced his mother and Chote introduced his companions, Carl Medlicott and Roy Gormand.

Chote said, 'We must congratulate you, Victor, on a fine win.'

'Yes, indeed,' Gorman said. 'Fine.'

'Deserved,' Medlicott said.

'Oh, certainly,' Chote said.

'Unquestionably,' Gormand said.

'You can see why he's called Victor,' Amy said.

'Indeed, indeed,' Gormand said with a thorough smile.

Tane could tell that his mother was almost into one of her wraths. A Swedish army dispatch rider wearing that type of coat to combat Scandinavian weather would reach his/her destination and hand over the dispatch without any knowledge of its contents or any opinions about the message. Mrs Tane, although in the same kind of coat, was different. She had attitudes, views.

She said, 'You three are totally content to see your lads conclusively squashed. Your words sound gracious and larded with fair's-fairness – gentlemanly, bourgeois, upper-crust English civility – but really it's because you don't give a fish's tit about the game. Victory or defeat are the same for you since in your reckoning a soccer match is but a soccer match, of no significance alongside all the academic, intellectual distinction you believe exists in Sedge. You speak *de haut en bas* and can afford to gush the compliments, patronize Victor and Charter with worthless praise.'

128

'There'd be no point in denying Charter were the better side, Mrs Tane,' Chote replied.

'That was patent,' Medlicott said. 'Our team strove, and strove, but, as Lawford stated, their striving fell short.'

'Unfortunately,' Gormand said.

'Your goalkeeper, dismally ungifted,' Amy Tane replied. 'A big lump of a journeyman, no extra-terrestrial glow.'

'My mother has made a study of goalkeeping,' Tane said, 'the inner qualities needed, not just the obvious ones.'

'This little area of ground behind him or her and immediately ahead is his or hers to patrol, to guard, to launch a counter attack from. If he, she, fails at this she, he is a nonentity, in your case a purple nonentity.'

Later, when the teams had showered and come together for a drink in the pavilion before their meal, Amy had made a path for herself to the Charter goal-keeper to tell him face-to-face how splendidly he performed his designated role and responded to his congenital urge. Tane went with her, but she did the talking. 'And your name?' she said. 'We shall want to follow your golden career. You will be getting many a fan letter from me via whichever top club the media report you as playing for – and I'm sure you *will* make it to a top club.' His name was Bernard Optor. She handed lipstick for him to autograph the outer surface of one of her wellington boots.

And Amy did follow his career, presumably

sent fan letters, and kept the signed boot dry. A couple of years later she had phoned Tane at home to ask if he'd seen the back page of the *Daily Mail*. He hadn't so she read a couple of sentences to him. They said that goalkeeper Bernie Optor had just signed a contract with one of the most famous Spanish sides that would bring him £140,000 a week, beside what he might earn from internationals.

And now, today, the phone rang once more, in his office this time. 'Principal? It's Bernard.' He pronounced it in the American way, Ber*nard,* probably as someone now rather cosmopolitan. 'How's Mrs Tane? Look, I hear a situation has developed there, what with tensions over the future for Charter and Sedge. Charter *or* Sedge. And I wonder if Sedge might be getting ahead on that. We ought to do something. I can't have my *alma mater* going to the wall.'

'What kind of thing, Bernard?'

'Yes, we ought to do something. After all, Principal, we beat them easily enough back whenever it was that afternoon, '81 was it? My final year. And I bet Charter have beaten them every year since. In that game – yes, '81 – I had hardly anything to do and I got almost paralysingly cold.'

'But you had the green jersey on and black mittens.'

'I have to work harder where I am now, I can tell you, Prince.'

Eighteen

2014

Gordon Upp (Linguistics) said, 'What we have here, of course, is a process – the process of arranging, selecting the kind of statues we wish to recommend and their sites or site. Think of the Duke of Norfolk preparing the pageantry for a coronation or Royal wedding. But, also, our statue deliberations are a process that, as it were, looks at itself. It is reflexive.'

'Oh?' Theo Bastrolle (Business Studies) said. Instantly, Martin Moss recognized this 'Oh?' as, in fact, very much a Business Studies 'Oh?' – the kind of 'Oh?' that students in Theo's department would be taught for use in their commercial careers after graduating. For instance, the 'Oh?' should be their response to a sterling, euro or dollar figure demanded from them in some big-time company negotiations for bonds or commodities or easements. It was intended to express shock, disbelief, outrage at the preposterous, rip-off amount asked for. It suggested that the other party should think again and quote a charge not entirely unrelated to the one already cited but divided by two.

This 'Oh?' when uttered as a haggling ploy, said in coded, abbreviated form, 'Cheap! – at half the price.' Theo's 'Oh?' now didn't exactly match that situation, but it contained a similar unwillingness to accept meekly what he'd heard. In this exchange Moss thought the 'Oh?' from Theo might have a slightly different coded, abbreviated form, such as: 'What the fuck does "reflexive" mean?'

But Lucy Lane seemed to have grasped instantly what Upp's 'reflexive' signified. 'Clearly, Gordon,' she said. She was viewing with concentration and affection something in her handkerchief, like a passenger in a train stopped at a station catching sight of a friend in another train that has pulled up alongside; proximity but not overdone proximity.

'What I'm getting at is, we are asked by the present, very current principal, Sir Bert Greg-Peterson, to decide on how the university should honour two past principals, two sequential past principals who had limited respect for each other,' Upp said. 'Thus begins the process I've referred to. It might appear at first to be a straight-forward administrative task. "Pray give me feedback on what we should do with these puta-tive two lumps of stone or brass." Naturally, however, as Greg-Peterson initiates this process he is bound to throw his mind forward into the unknown future, when the present principal, viz, Sir Bert, has himself become a past principal and therefore due a statue in his turn. "The king is dead or retired or gone to a bigger job. Long live the king, as monument." Sir Bert will be interested in this process, as a guide to a similar process in the future, of which he will be the subject; while at the same time taking part himself, now, not as subject but as originator in the present, 2014 process. Some future Sedge principal will request a special working party, comparable with ours in 2014, to discuss the type of statue needed for Greg-Peterson and the most suitable site for it, if it is to be a single permanent site; or a duality of sites, if a rotation is favoured, taking in what will by then be the strongly established single university with paired campuses, which at present might still be lingeringly, wrongly, but forgivably thought of as Charter Mill and Sedge, or Sedge and Charter Mill.

'Admittedly, certain differences between those future proceedings and our own are going to exist. I'll name one: the kind of debate we had over single or double plinth occupancy will not be appropriate then, since the commemorative statue and its mono-plinth would be for one past principal only – Sir Bert – not, as in the 2014 case, Chote and Tane or Tane and Chote, each with formidable *prima facie* entitlement, each requiring and deserving fair play.

'That future planning group would have to take into account that there were already two ex-principal statues on university sites, or *a* university site if, eventually, we decide on a binary plinth for two statues, one at each end of it, Chote and Tane, or, to phrase it differently, Tane and Chote. The present principal will be thinking as he considers our findings on the Tane, Chote, or Chote, Tane statues, how, in that on-coming future, he would like his own statue sited in relation to the already placed – locationed, if you will – statues of Tane and Chote or Chote and Tane.

133

'Several questions would need consideration, the central one being, should the Sir Bert statue be close to or distant from the by then existing Chote/Tane, Tane/Chote statues? If these two are single plinthed and therefore very near each other, more or less plinth-integrated, might the Sir Bert statue seem somehow set-apart if it were deposited close to the pair but not, of course, as close as the two single-plinthed figures would be to each other? Might the Sir Bert image seem excluded, even shunned, by the two in this case? Or, to reverse it, would the Sir Bert statue appear snooty and stand-offish, aloof, as if proclaiming that the other two were elements of an exceptionally messy Sedge, Charter Mill, or Charter Mill, Sedge past, redeemed by the power and brilliance of the masterly, remote, true leader, Sir Bertram?

'If, on the other hand, the 2014 decision is to go for single statues of Chote and Tane or Tane and Chote, should the Greg-Peterson statue be put adjacent to one of them, and, if so, which one would it be? More rotation? Or are further permutations envisaged? Finally, might it be best to unfix Chote and Tane, or Tane and Chote, from their shared plinth and devise a larger plinth able to provide room not just for Tane and Chote, or Chote and Tane, but Sir Bert, also. Clearly this would require skilled stonemasonry, or brassmasonry, so that the two's shoes and feet should not be fractured during the severance, but it *could* be feasible. However, a threesome on one plinth would give rise to additional, obvious contentiousness. Two on one plinth did not suggest any kind of precedence. One end of a plinth represents no superiority or inferiority to the other end. Each statue would be at the end it was, right or left, left or right, simply because it was – no overtones. But triple-plinthed statues must plainly imply a central figure. Might centrality suggest dominance, distinction, as if the other two, one on each side, were aides only or minders? Which statue would occupy this middle position?

'If order of plinth alignment were decided by length of existence and chronology, then perhaps Chote would come first, on the left, because of Sedge's age, then Tane, head of the younger institution, then Sir Bert, as principal of a very new combined entity. This would, accordingly, put Tane in the mid position. There might not be general agreement about that. Tane could be regarded by some as jumped-up. They might argue that the new university under Sir Bert subsumes both previous universities and, there-fore, his statue should dominate, that is, should be at the plinth's core and central. We have to keep in mind that Sir Bert *is* Sir Bert – he has a knighthood, which neither of his predecessors achieved. Perhaps a central spot on a tripartite plinth would be his proper due.

'This is what I mean when I say that the process we engage in now, here, 2014, is more than itself in that our present principal will be virtually bound to use our process as a start-up for thoughts of an imaginary but comparable statue planning committee trying to decide the most suitable style and emplacement for his – Sir

135

Bert's – post-retirement statue, possibly on a unitary plinth share basis, possibly otherwise.'

'But could it not be, Gordon, that the statue creating mode for ex-principals will no longer apply when our present principal, Sir Bert, might be dead or of an age and/or situation that would put him into the potentially appropriate category for the tribute of a statue?' Wayne Ollam (Philosophy) said. 'I feel there is already something of a distaste for the manufacture of statues to mark supposed achievements of a selected figure. Perhaps there's something crazy about representing in stone or brass a person whose life has been characterized by dynamic activity. We have, after all, the phrase "stone dead", meaning very dead. Maybe there is much of that about statues.

'Then again, isn't a statue discriminatory? Of its nature it discounts credit for all those non-statued folk who might have provided essential help for the one acknowledged star. We've heard a while ago about the statue of Aneurin Bevan in the commercial centre of Cardiff, the Welsh politician who helped create the National Health Service. But, obviously, doctors, nurses, consultants, administrators, other politicians were involved in that. Do any of them get statues in a shopping mall? No. And by the time Sir Bert qualifies public disenchantment with statues might have become even stronger. The principal we are visualising – i.e., not Sir Bert but the one who comes after Sir Bert, and is therefore faced by the Sir Bert statue problem – this new principal might be of a socio-political academic background and averse to the creation, indeed the proliferation, of statues on the kind of democratic grounds I have just referred to: elitism.'

'Widmerpool questions whether a statue is the right way to commemorate a great man,' Elvira Barton (Classics) said.

'Who?' Bill Davey (French) replied.

'Kenneth Widmerpool,' Jed Laver (Industrial Relations) said. 'He's already been mentioned – a comical, plonking, rather dangerous character in Anthony Powell's twelve-volume novel *A Dance To The Music Of Time.*'

'Yes, in *A Buyer's Market* – second book of the sequence – people at a dinner party are discussing what would be the right sort of statue to honour Earl Haig,' Angela Drape (Environmental Engineering) said.

'A dinner at the Walpole-Wilson's in Eaton Square, London, I think,' Claud Nelmes (Physics) said. '*Circa* 1928.'

'Haig led the British Expeditionary Force in the Great War. Butcher Haig as he was sometimes known, because of the millions of soldiers killed,' Elvira said. 'Powell is mocking this kind of lumbering, slightly zany conversation – should Haig be shown on a horse, or in a car or at a desk? Someone suggests a *papier mâché* model of a horse to ensure accuracy. Widmerpool says statues could cause traffic problems.'

'But the principals' statues will be on university ground, surely,' Theo said. 'Traffic wouldn't be affected.'

'We are concerned with the principles,' Ollam said.

'Yes, I know it's about the principals – Principal Bert and the other two,' Theo said.

'The principles,' Ollam said. 'The general question of whether statues are the kind of thing wanted these days to indicate worth.'

'There's a town called Widmerpool, in Cheshire, I believe,' Davey said. 'Perhaps this Widmerpool gent thought he, personally, wouldn't need a statue because he had a town named after him. Therefore statues should be phased out.'

'I think it was the other way about,' Jed said.

'Which other way?' Davey asked.

'Powell named the character after the town,' Jed replied. 'The town pre-existed the fictional person. Philip Larkin, the poet, slammed Powell for pinching a name like that.'

'Does Larkin have a statue?' Davey asked.

'He was very tall, wasn't he, maybe as tall as Victor Tane?' Theo said.

'Lucy argued a while back that one or two of our presumptions about the statues might be open to question – the plinth matter, for instance,' Wayne Ollam replied. 'But I want to ask whether our absolutely basic assumption – that there should be statues at all – might have been too hastily arrived at. Should we really be niggling over structural and positional details? Isn't there a case for recommending that there should be no statues at all, neither the Chote, nor the Tane, nor the Tane nor the Chote, let alone the fanta-sized, forecasted Sir Bert?'

Mart Moss said, 'But we've been asked by the principal – in fact, more or less instructed by the principal, Sir Bert – to come up with a plan for installing the statues, Wayne. This would appear to endorse the provision of statues, wouldn't it?'

'Ostensibly, yes,' Wayne replied. 'I would like to ask, though, whether in his thinking about the statues of his predecessors and therefore also speculating mentally about his own, in due course, statue, he will sense that perhaps in the 21st century – and possibly much further on in the 21st century entailing continuous, deep, rapid social change – he might sense that statues will have become *infra dig* and super-naff. He might decide he will not need a statue, that, in fact, a statue would be otiose and vain. And this could cause him to think that even now, at this earlier 21st-century date, statues have become redundant, corny, gross, as well as incapable of showing the actual energy he brought to his career. He'd possibly come to regard statues as objects to stick piss-pots on the stone heads of or to daub with painted ribaldries, such as "Show us your arse."

'He finds himself, however, in the grip of snobbish tradition rather than free to follow his private conclusions, and, accordingly, he commissions us to devise a practicable scheme for the Chote, Tane or Tane, Chote memorials. Does it strike nobody else here that he might wish to be liberated from all those trite pressures and expectations? Might it not be an act of mercy to go to him and say, "Sir Bert, we find after several *causeries* carried out in the best, balanced, higher-education style that we are of a concerted mind which says statues are unholy shit and the Tane, Chote or

139

Chote, Tane project should be finally and irretrievably flushed away."

'There is, of course, one outstanding reason why memorials are regarded with scepticism now, though perhaps we would not put this to Sir Bert. It has an element of controversy about it. I'm sure some of you would understand what I mean.'

'The Jimmy Savile headstone,' Theo said, 'with that appalling inscription, "It was good while it lasted."'

'Exactly,' Wayne replied.

'"Philanthropist", another of the inscriptions,' Theo said.

'The *Sir* Jimmy, O.B.E. headstone,' Wayne said. 'This memorial in a Scarborough cemetery was four feet high and six feet wide. It reeked of praise for a man whose life had seemed devoted to good causes, especially good causes aimed at helping children. In fact he was a rampant, scheming paedophile and used his secret closeness to some children for sex. He had a television spot called *Jim'll Fix It*. This was supposedly concerned with granting selected children something they wished for, dreamed of. It's actual purpose, though, was to fix things for himself sexually. Likewise, he presented a music programme called *Top of the Pops*, which gave him access to young fans of the show.

'When the truth about him emerged after his death the black granite headstone came to be seen as a disgusting, lying monstrosity and it was demolished and sent as landfill by his family. I'm not saying that the statues of Victor Tane and/or Lawford Chote, or Lawford Chote and/ or Victor Tane would get destroyed, but I *am* saying that people looking at memorials these days and, no doubt, in future days, no matter what form they take, wonder whether the tribute is deserved or a cover-up for the remembered one's real life.'

Moss said, 'This will certainly give us something to think over before our next scheduled *causerie*, Wayne. Thank you.'

Nineteen

1987

CENTENARY CONCERT AT
d'BRINDLE HALL
By O.T.O. Jurbb, Music Correspondent

Last night's musical event at the city's brand new d'Brindle Hall marked the opening of three weeks' celebration in honour of Sedge University's centenary year. Some will see a chilling comparison between this ambitious, glittering occasion and the so-said re-arranging of deck chairs on the *Titanic* as she sank. Others might recall Thomas Hardy's poem, *The Convergence of the Twain,* which described the luxurious fitting out of the liner during construction, while the iceberg that would slash the vessel open was also under construction, but meteorological construction, growing bigger and more dangerous at the Pole, ready to 'converge'. A similar sort of grim convergence might have been in the air yesterday evening at the d'Brindle: high, splendid ambition in deadly collision with Sedge's massive debts and near bankruptcy. As E.M. Forster nearly said, 'Only connect the prose of this review and the poverty.'

For the Sedge concert to take place in the d'Brindle Hall could be seen as painfully ironic. The d'Brindle is a magnificent, very recent addition to the Sedge campus and is named after the distinguished British composer and conductor, Harvey d'Brindle, a former student and subsequently professor of music at Sedge, who died a few years ago. His widow, Martha Maud d'Brindle was present last night. She heard one of her husband's most famous works, the gigue, *Cumulus Resurgent*, played with reasonable vim and competence by a section of the orchestra.

The unpaid builder's account for d'Brindle Hall is one of the university's major debts. To a cruel degree it typifies the kind of cash difficulty afflicting Sedge. The fine new, acoustically perfect venue, is very much the brainchild and darling of Dr Lawford Chote, Sedge's principal.

142

He, unquestionably, provided the original impetus for creation of the d'Brindle and has diligently guided and nursed the project through the not-always-positive and/or helpful intricacies of governmental and/or academic bureaucracy. The d'Brindle is, in some ways, a tribute to Dr Chote as much as it is to Harvey d'Brindle.

But this tribute to the principal comes with a bill. And it is a millions sterling bill. The number of millions has not been disclosed. Guesses range from £4 million to £12 million. At any rate, formidable. Good acoustics don't come cheap. Sedge has so far failed to pay. Sedge *can't* pay. Knowledgeable folk in the audience last night might have been glancing back over their shoulders in case the duns and bumbailiffs arrived with something other than gigues in their minds. The d'Brindle is, perhaps, the most flagrant instance of what can be seen as Dr Chote's heady, audacious, thrilling but devilishly pricey, expansionism. There are others on campus, including an impressive new curved staircase, carpeted in azure blue, leading to the grandly refurbished staff dining room and bar, a stairway to the stars, or to the cliff's edge.

Dr Chote is himself an accomplished amateur musician, specialising in percussion and particularly the cymbals. At the concert he gave a short, cameo performance of a piece from Wagner's *Tannhauser.* As he clashed those two shining brass discs together at pretty well exactly the right dramatic moments one could see the challenging sound as defiance, a sort of Bronx cheer, aimed at those who regard his principalship as disastrous, and want him kicked out while there might still be time to save Sedge under a new chief and a more sane regime.

Dr Chote is not a big man and has a sensitive, pale, aquiline, nunnish sort of face, but the force he could get into smashing those two cymbals together seemed ferocious. Your critic half expected him to stick his tongue out at any enemies in the hall between each ultra-decibelled bang. His features showed no feelings, though. He remained virtually deadpan except for a scarcely perceptible, flickering hint that he kept an orderly, vindictive pack of hatreds kennelled within him and might turn it loose at any time he'd regard as appropriate and/or destructive.

Reading this review in the local daily, Martin Moss wondered whether O.T.O. Jurbb was an alias for Alan Norton-Hord, editor of the paper, who'd seemed so investigative and clued-up about the Sedge predicament in the grandly refurbished bar and staff dining room, immediately after Mart's inaugural spiel about rural rogering as a newly promoted prof. Editors sometimes took pen names so that personal views should not be regarded as the views of the paper. There were *people* called Jurbb? But in a multi-cultural country there might be.

Mart couldn't remember ever having seen this by-line in the paper before. He'd noticed Norton-Hord at the concert last night, but he might have been attending as a civic dignitary, not as critic and reporter. Was Norton-Hord the kind who would flourish his familiarity with Thomas Hardy and Morgan Forster? As an ex-Sedge student, would he write so bluntly about the university being near-fatally hard-up? Would he spray the faint praise around: the performance of *Cumulus Resurgent* done with 'reasonable' vim and competence; the timing of Lawford Chote's interventions with the cymbals at 'pretty well exactly the right dramatic moments' in the *Tannhauser* clip? Would O.T.O. Jurbb?

Mart Moss didn't go much on classical music so he couldn't judge whether the performance of *Cumulus Resurgent* was only just up to scratch; nor whether Lawford Chotc had the timing of his cymbal flurries right. Watching Chote with the instruments had reminded Mart of some B.B.C. television archive material re-broadcast lately in a programme on changing comedy styles. A small, baby-faced, bald performer called Charlie Drake had done some cymbal bashing with an orchestra and after each echoing, metallic boom looked totally dazed, as if the din had morphed into solid form and clobbered his head. Jurbb, in his column, had called Chote's appearance at those aftermath

145

moments 'deadpan'. Martin thought 'concussed' more to the point. But he would agree with Jurbb's suggestion that the clangour caused by Lawford carried a message of defiance, contempt, war, for those who wanted his humiliation and defeat. There might be a further show of defiance when the centenary celebrations culminated in the Plain Parlour banquet at Standfast Fort.

Cymbals in Lawford's hands might also have been useful in keeping Rowena awake. She had a front row seat. Mart was some way behind and could not see her face, but she hadn't slumped and seemed to do a little shoulder dance during a movement from one of the Mozart symphonies. Moss reckoned music started to fall away after the seventeenth century, and definitely by the time Mozart started. This didn't mean Mart would go along with Jim Dixon's description of Wolfgang Amadeus in *Lucky Jim* as 'filthy Mozart'. What people should remember about Mozart was that he had to write much of his stuff for paying patrons who might be laid up at home with gout and/ or a double dose of pox. They wouldn't object that a composition was full of phoney joyous, scampering, bubbly riffs. To be reminded of joy, and the ability to scamper, and/or something bubbly in any form would be a plus for them. But Mart preferred, say, Henry Purcell's neat, unshowy, purposeful songs and anthems about a hundred years earlier, and British with it.

Moss read some more of Jurbb.

Although several of the items on the centenary concert menu were executed with no more than workmanlike efficiency, we have to be grateful that the musicians turned up and played at all when, most probably, they had no assurance there would be a cashable cheque to follow. Despite all the rumours – and more than rumours – about impending disaster, the combined names of Sedge and Lawford Chote have been enough to make a function like last night's possible and to a not inconsiderable sense successful. Although Sedge and Lawford Chote are perilously short of cash, they still have charisma.

Yes, Mart could say 'Agreed' to this.

Twenty

1987

Rowena and Lawford Chote also read the O.T.O. Jurbb review next morning. It gave them a few good laughs. They were in bed. They had a pre-breakfast daybreak routine. Soon after the newspapers had been delivered, she or he – an alternating duty – would go downstairs to pick them up, then return, snuggle under the duvet again and for half an hour or so read bits to each other and perhaps view some of the more striking photographs together. If there were exciting pictures of, say, the return of otters to a stretch of river somewhere, or a seascape, or an arboretum, or a starlings' flight-swarm, they might take a break from the press for a while and make leisurely love, so as to link up, as it were, with nature. Breakfast could be delayed for a while. She thought more of nature than Lawford did, but he wasn't actually anti and would go along with Rowena.

It would have been wise before starting sex if they'd folded the newspapers and put them on the floor or a bedside table. But both felt this would seem too calculated and unimpassioned, as though they had to abide by an etiquette book *diktat:* 'Always clear away surplus items before coitus.' If they wanted a sort of inspired link with thousands of soaring, swooping starlings they couldn't take time out to make some press sheets dailies tidy. As a result pages could get badly crumpled and even torn because of the threshing about. If they were smoothable-out afterwards Rowena or Lawford would smooth them out. Torn pages might be repairable with transparent sticky tape. They kept some of that in the bedside table drawer along with scissors and a stiff-backed copy of the proper, King James version of the Bible. Now and then they'd enjoy a joint reading of a Psalm, one doing the first, strong line of a verse, the other coming in with the backup. A favourite at present for Lawford, as could be expected, was: 'Plead my cause, oh Lord, with them that strive with me: fight against them that fight against me.'

The concert review didn't set them off hormonally but did produce major non-sexual chuckles. 'Yes, Ro, I think it does what we wanted,' Lawford said, 'that sort of back-handed praise: nothing too lavish and sloppy. So, only *reasonable* vim and competence given to *Cumulus Resurgent*. And then, my *pretty well* timed cymbal wallops.'

'The *Titanic* references work OK, I think, don't you?' she replied. 'They'll get through to people's feelings. Decent, sensitive folk will say we had that terrible tragedy all those years ago, so why haven't we learned from it?'

Lawford giggled. 'I liked "acoustics don't come cheap". Slangy but terse-effective. And then those in the audience who couldn't concentrate on the music because they were afraid the bums were about to arrive and strip the place! A hoot.'

They both had guffaws at this idea, and, possibly, at an imagined glimpse of Lawford sticking his tongue out and/or giving a raspberry to his opponents between clashes on the pretty well-timed cymbal detonations. Sitting up in bed they did a duct of fart noises with their lips.

'How's my charisma looking today, Ro?' he said.

She put her head under the duvet. 'Seems fine to me,' she replied.

Lawford went through the review again. 'The "stairway to the stars" that turns into a lemming-drop. Great, Ro! And the internal hate kennels! "Cry Havoc! and let slip the dogs of war." Wonderful!'

'It wasn't easy, you know, Lawf.'

'I can see that.'

'I didn't want it to sound abject and self-pitying

149

yet to be, in fact, an appeal for understanding and sympathy.'

'You hit that. It will help us.'

'And not biased – not biased in favour of you and Sedge. I had to promise Alan Norton-Hord that, before he'd let me do it. He wants to help Sedge – past chairman of the students' union and so on. But he's editor now of a respectable provincial paper and has to seem to be fair and impartial.'

'Maybe.'

'I had to phrase things here and there to sound blunt and dogmatic – "Sedge has so far failed to pay. Sedge *can't* pay." But my review's overall objective was to make people – especially government people – yes, the objective was to make them ask whether it was sane to let Sedge go under like the *Titanic* because the university's finances couldn't keep up with the principal's noble, life-enhancing, splendiferous, aims.'

'The "O.T.O.", Ro? What were Mr or Mrs or Miss or Ms's Jurbb's first names?'

'"Only This Once". The gender and family ranking are immaterial.'

Twenty-One

2014

A couple of weeks later they had a vote on Wayne Ollam's proposal to recommend a no-statue, no-statues policy, and he was the only one in favour He took the thrashing without any obvious sign of disbelief or rage. He was a philosopher and knew about stoicism and the dominance of naffdom and knee-jerk in others. Wryly, almost graciously, he said, 'So sodding be it.'

But some of the committee seemed sorry for him, embarrassed for him. Ollam had a round, jolly-looking, schoolboyish, snub-nosed face under blondish curls, and Mart could see that some committee members felt it brutal having to humiliate him. As a sort of compensation several people became more bolshy-aggressive than usual, perhaps to prove they were no pushovers; not slavishly choosing to carry on with the project because they thought the principal wanted it. The sniping began after Theo Bastrolle had floated a new idea.

He said, 'Something at first sight extraneous, but actually quite to the point, I think, has startled me. Startled and baffled me. I wondered if other members had felt the same.'

'The same as what?' Angela Drape (Environmental Engineering) said in her curt, barrack-square bellow.

'It's very simply put,' Theo replied.

'Put it,' Angela said.

'Here goes then. I suddenly noticed that we have no member of the music department among our number,' Theo said. 'Am I the only one who has spotted this grave lack? I doubt it.'

'Grave?' Lucy Lane (History) said.

Theo said, 'Oh, I recognize that someone might reply, "So what, there are several departments unrepresented here. No Chemistry. No

151

Geography. No Maths. Omissions are inevitable or the meetings would become unwieldy." Fair enough. But I regard Music as very much a special case.'

'In what respect, Theo?' Jed Laver (Industrial Relations) asked. 'I don't see it. What is so precious and unusual about Music?'

'A building,' Theo replied.

'Yes, yes, there's a building, d'Brindle Hall,' Jed said. 'Nobody can deny that. Yet I still ask, why should we give particular attention to Music, d'Brindle or no?'

'It's not "or no," though, is it, Jed? It is very much an emphatic "Yes".' Theo said.

'Why "emphatic"?' Bill Davey (French) said.

'I lived through that period here, so think I might see what Theo means,' Martin Moss said.

'Oh?' Lucy Lane replied.

'Thank you, Chair,' Theo said.

'Thank him for what?' Davey said.

'To do with d'Brindle,' Mart said.

'What about it?' Jed replied.

'We have to think of our purpose here. Our *raison d'être* as a committee,' Theo said.

Gordon Upp (Linguistics) said, 'Oh, *d'être* and d'Brindle! What *is* this?'

'Remember that old song, "It's delightful, it's delicious, it's d'lovely"?' Elvira (Classics) asked. 'Cole Porter?'

'What it is, Gordon, and what we are,' Theo stated, 'is a committee established to discuss and eventually recommend the most suitable – in our view – the most suitable siting for, and nature of, a statue or, more likely, statues, as a tribute

152

to two distinguished past principals. We act at the behest of our present distinguished principal who may or may not be thinking of how his own period of office might be commemorated when his time at Sedge is done one way or the other.'

Mart said, 'Theo, like the majority here, has moved away from the option that there should be no statue, Gordon. He has returned to the basic requirement of our committee – to choose a site or sites. And, since the d'Brindle is a building with some lawn in front – is, in fact, potentially a statue site – he is wondering why this has not come previously into our reckoning.'

'Thank you, Chair,' Theo said.

'Oh, is this a put-up job?' Claud Nelmes (Physics) said.

'Is what a put-up job?' Mart replied.

'You two.' Claud made his voice slimy, grovelling. '"Thank you, Chair." Have you agreed *sub rosa* beforehand that you'd back each other up – tout the Music department's case jointly?'

'There's no backing up, Claud. I summarized what I took to be Theo's standpoint,' Martin said.

'Summarized it favourably,' Jed replied. 'Where's the chair's impartiality, Chair? Why can't Theo speak for himself? You've pre-worked out a scenario between you, yes? You've decided that from now on all major decisions should be made by the chair, because that will seem unbiased and, authoritative?'

'I've been looking at the d'Brindle papers in the Sedge archive,' Theo replied.

'To what purpose?' Angela said.

'We've heard from various sections of both

153

archives, Charter's and Sedge's, or Sedge's and Tane's, but I don't think anyone has looked at the d'Brindle file,' Theo said. 'The Sedge papers show very clearly that Lawford Chote was the main force in getting the d'Brindle built,' Theo said.

'I can endorse that,' Mart said. 'Many of us at Sedge then knew it.'

'Ah!' Lucy said. 'Deduction: he should have his statue placed in front of the d'Brindle. That your argument, Theo?' Her thin face seemed to grow even sharper when she reached this question.

'A sort of Euterpe figure,' Elvira said.

'A what?' Angela said.

'The muse of music,' Jed said. 'My parents were going to call me that if I'd been a girl. But I wanted to go for industrial relations, anyway.'

'Chote himself was an amateur musician, apparently,' Theo said.

'Playing what?' Lucy said.

'Cymbals,' Theo said.

'Do we recommend a statue of Chote banging a couple of them together in front of his chest?' Davey asked.

'There's a review of a centenary concert in the file,' Theo replied. 'Chote actually took part. A piece from *Tannhauser* required cymbals. The review's slightly snooty – implies Lawford didn't quite get the timing right during the performance.'

'Cymbals sticking in a shattering sound at the wrong spot could fuck up the whole item,' Angela said.

'The New Testament has a "tinkling" cymbal,' Nelmes said.

154

'*Tannhauser* would want something stronger than a tinkle,' Davey said.

'Who wrote the notice?' Jed asked.

'An O.T.O Jurbb,' Theo said.

'Otto, do you mean?' Davey said. 'Like Klemperer and Bismark.'

'No, O.T.O.,' Theo said. 'He or she makes a meal of the contrast between the glittering social occasion and Sedge's desperate lack of funds. There are comparisons with the *Titanic*.'

'The *Titanic*? That's cruel, heartless,' Claud Nelmes said. 'The reviewer would know the *Titanic* went down. He or she couldn't have the same certainty at the time of the concert that Sedge was about to sink. At least, Sedge as it had existed for a hundred years up till then.'

'This was supposed to be a critique of some music, wasn't it, not an attempt at clairvoyance,' Elvira said.

'What you said, Claud – "cruel", "heartless" – is possibly correct but it was also a warning. I think, and a disguised cry for help,' Theo replied.

'A very subtle piece of journalism,' Bill Davey said.

'I'll have it copied and circulated,' Theo replied. 'Tucked in with the newspaper review I found two reports by accountants showing a debt on the d'Brindle building and fitments of between £9 and £10 million,' Theo said. 'Incidentally, other considerable unpaid bills were for new student accommodation blocks as part of Chote's expansion programme. But, regardless of these enormous shortfalls, what comes over in the concert review, and what the contemporary reader

155

would sense, is the fine, positive, determined, effort through this concert to take forward Sedge's reputation as a top-class creative, cultural university. One feels these debts were . . . would it be foolishly exaggerated to say *noble* debts? I get the feeling that Lawford had contempt for the strictures of finance.'

'"Tax not the royal saint with vain expense",' Lucy replied.

'Who said that?' Angela asked.

'Wordsworth, a sonnet, about King's college chapel, Cambridge, founded by Henry VI,' Lucy said. '"High-heaven rejects the lore/Of nicely calculated less or more".'

'Whitehall didn't though,' Angela snarled.

'The review ends with a powerful accolade to Chote's and Sedge's charisma,' Theo said.

'How do we get the sculptor to give us charisma in stone or brass?' Upp asked. 'We've already fretted over how to portray ambiguity.'

'Are we talking now about a Chote statue either with or without cymbals installed at the d'Brindle?' Nelmes asked.

'Victor Tane would have nothing to balance,' Jed said.

'Balance how, what?' Theo asked.

'Nothing equivalent to the cymbals held by Chote, if they were,' Jed said. 'Tane might appear deprived, comparatively untalented as to cymbals and possibly music generally.'

'If we go for two statues on the one plinth, Chote and Tane will look not so much like muses as a couple of duetists because of the d'Brindle Hall, Music department background,' Upp said.

'Ah, such as the old Bing Crosby-Bob Hope record?' Elvira said. She would often go out of her way to show she could handle more than the Classics and other heavy stuff, such as the Book of Amos. Mart learned today that Cole Porter and Bing and Bob were also on call when it suited, or, as now, when it didn't.

Elvira crooned effortlessly, in two different voices, one tenor, one alto, beating time with her small hands, her pale blue eyes alight with joy as she fondled the irrelevant melody: 'We're off on the road to Morocco, de-dum-de-dum, I'll lay you eight to four we'll meet Dorothy Lamour, de-dum-de-dum, Like Webster's dictionary we're Morocco bound.'

'Tane, of course, has no real connection with the d'Brindle,' Lucy said.

'Tane helped turn its finances around,' Angela replied. 'And so the d'Brindle is still there, still housing good concerts.'

'I went online to the Newspaper Archive in London and Googled for an O.T.O. Jurbb around in the 1980s. Nothing,' Theo said. 'I tried anagrams in case this was a pen name only: Rob Jobut, Jo Burbot, but blank.'

'No, I'd never read anything previously by him or her at the time,' Mart said.

'Rob Jobut – there's a name to conjure with,' Davey said.

'And what do you get when you conjure?' Theo asked.

'O.T.O. Jurbb,' Davey replied.

Twenty-Two

1987

Victor Tane read the review of last night's Sedge centenary concert a couple of times at breakfast and then passed it to his wife, Ursula. She was a lawyer, trained to see behind what people said and wrote. She had a lively, squarish face very ready to go into a grin but ready, also, to turn combative if antagonized by something or somebody. She was middle-height, neat-breasted, and slim. She'd gone auburn lately, a good, restrained but rich shade, worn as a fringe across her forehead and gathered into a clasped bunch at the back. 'O.T.O?' she muttered. 'Is that supposed to be Otto, like Klemperer and Bismark?'

'Not sure. I've never heard of a writer called O.T.O Jurbb, nor Otto Jurbb.'

'Nor me. Weird surname, too. Might the two bits – O.T.O. and Jurbb – be an anagram of the writer's real moniker?'

'I've considered that.'

'Jo Burbot?' Ursula said.

'Rob Jobut?' Tane replied. 'Names to conjure with.'

'What do you get when you conjure, Vic?'

'O.T.O. Jurbb.'

Ursula forked in scrambled egg while she read. She was thirty-five, Tane's third wife. He was her second husband. Tane had an adult son, a TV director, by his first wife. 'Clever,' Ursula said. She swallowed carefully, thoroughly, then grinned one of her big, jolly grins, no egg traces on her teeth or lips; Ursula was not the sort to allow that kind of facial unkemptness. Tane thought her grin would be part in admiration of the cleverness, whatever it was, and part in admiration of her own cleverness in seeing through the cleverness, whatever it was. Ursula had a flair for making him feel stupid. He'd wondered sometimes whether she'd done the same to her previous husband, which might have helped towards the divorce. He had been an MP. The job itself could have made him feel stupid and he wouldn't want that at home as well. Anyway, if Tane wished to ponder the reasons for a divorce he realized he should consider his own two; and he didn't fancy this.

'Clever?' he replied.

'The *Titanic* pushed up to the front like that. Necessary first sentence to tell us where we're at, then straight into catastrophe.'

'Tactical?'

'The sea-worm,' Ursula replied.

'Which?'

'The one in the *Convergence* poem. We did it at school. The *Titanic* is on the seabed and over its luxury bits and pieces "The sea-worm crawls – grotesque, slimed, dumb, indifferent."'

'Dumb? Don't sea-worms talk to one another?'

'Sets a tone from the outset.'

'What tone?'

'Hardy's a nasty piece of work, isn't he?' she replied.

'Is he?'

'Getting a smirk out of the disaster. This was a fine ship. Brave funnels. OK, it had luxurious, lavishly, ostentatiously costly fittings and good deckchairs, but so what? Is it an offence to do things in style? Yes, he gets a smirk and/or a snigger at the thought of all this flagrant privilege going to the bottom because of a ripening berg. That title.'

'*Convergence*? Bad?'

'It's loaded with septic irony, Vic. Normally, it would be a neutral, map-reading term. Here it means two mighty big items both trying to get on the same spot at the same time. Procrastinated doom: for ages, the berg has been preparing itself for this jostle by making sure the deadly seven eighths of itself below the surface is all present and malicious. In other words, Vic, those *Titanic* references seem to mock Sedge but actually indict others – Whitehall, the Ministry – for threatening to bring destruction to it. And then the Forster quote tacked on: the prose of the review wants to highlight Sedge's poverty and induce those able to put all that right, to put it all right – Whitehall, the Ministry. I wouldn't be surprised if someone close to Chote wrote this, with his connivance.'

'I gather he's got a new acolyte over there. We have a picture of them in a Volvo. Him perhaps? If he's on the Humanities staff he might have the literary allusions ready – Hardy, E.M. Forster.'

'Maybe. Or possibly Rowena. She would have to seem detached, even harsh, but the real intent is something different. She'd use unfriendly

160

phrases like "devilishly pricey expansionism" and "vindictive pack of hatreds" as a kind of camouflage to conceal her authorship.'

'Rowena?'

'She's smart enough and had an education. She gets in a slab of praise for Lawford Chote – creating the d'Brindle, his "brain-child and darling", but then has to spout a virtual retraction so as to seem objective – the "millions sterling bill" which "Sedge *can't* pay". Doesn't someone who could conceive the d'Brindle deserve a handout? That's the message. And then that brilliant contrast.'

'Which, Ursula?'

'Between Harvey d'Brindle and Lawford Chote, of course.'

'How does that work?'

'We have Harvey d'Brindle, more or less a genius, known worldwide, especially for his gigues e.g., *Cumulus Resurgent*; as against Chote doing his approximate best with the cymbals but not at all a gifted star like d'Brindle. Chote makes his well-meant but faulty contribution to *Tannhauser*, an opera about a singing competition, and one he'd ruin with his mistimed cymbals. interventions. But the review is saying that as an undergraduate and graduate even the natural prodigy, H. d'Brindle, needed opportunities to develop those in-born qualities, such opportunities being provided by somewhere like Sedge, headed by one of Chote's predecessors as principal. This is a debt d'Brindle acknowledged by joining Sedge's staff and making some of his talent available to new generations of students.

161

'The review's point, surely, Vic, is that even a wonderful composer and performer like d'Brindle, can do with the guidance and backing of a Sedge-type apprenticeship. To let the university dwindle and perhaps die because of a temporary shortage of boodle is, O.T.O. Jurbb believes, an example of idiotic, short-sighted vandalism. He/she is telling the Education Minister, "Cough up, you fucking philistines." Those benighted Whitehall people would send in duns and bums because – to go poetic – Lawford Chote has no regard for sums. But not even those low-grade, disgusting terms can do irreparable harm to Sedge and Chote because their "charisma" still works, and will go on working for as long as the miserable, workaday banalities of special funding are taken care of. The fact that the musicians agreed to play even though they might not get paid showed the pulling power exercised by Sedge and Chote.'

Ursula went off to appear in a court case. Tane could linger for another half hour. He washed up and took a cup of coffee to his study. He felt like writing to his mother. 'Ursula sees a real crisis for the other university here at Sedge, Ma. She sort of deconstructed a review in the local paper and found it to be a rather sneaky, roundabout demand for more money from central government to keep Sedge afloat, saving it from foundering like the *Titanic*. I don't believe the money will arrive. This has obvious implications for Charter Mill and myself. Part of me feels quite sorry for the principal over there, Lawford Chote.'

If his mother had still been alive and received

162

this he thought she would probably reply something like: 'Which part of you feels quite sorry, you gaunt and gangling twerp? Remember, I'm the one who gave you all your parts and none of them should show weakness. Stop patronising. Be a winner. Come out from between your goalposts, surge through the astonished opposition and score the clinching goal that ensures promotion.'

Twenty-Three

2014

Her voice gentle and considerate, Elvira Barton (Classics) said, 'Wayne recently asked us to look at, and pronounce upon, the very existence of the statues theme and decide whether we should recommend abandonment of the project, which would put us out of existence also! We gave an answer, and, what I believe it's fair to term, an unambiguous one, an answer which Wayne has honourably accepted. I'm sure we would have expected nothing other from him.'

'Here, here,' Angela Drape (Environmental Engineering) said.

'*Absolument*,' Bill Davey (French) said.

Seated between Gordon Upp (Linguistics) and Lucy Lane (History) Wayne Ollam (Philosophy) gave a small nod-bow in acknowledgement and some curls fell forward on to his brow, like rounds from a disturbed sliced loaf. Unhurriedly, he pushed them back with the spread fingers of his ringless right hand. The whole exchange had a simple, but emphatic dignity. To Mart, those fingers looked for the moment like fingers which knew they were among top-grade stuff, even if the curls belonged to someone crash-ball annihilated in a vote not long ago.

'And, despite the way our moot went then, I feel I have learned something from Wayne's boldness in scrutinising the very fundamentals of our duties,' Elvira said. 'He humbly included himself in his suggestion that we might have been hasty and careless in not questioning why the statues committee had come into being. Perhaps our vote negated that criticism. But it taught me that this is the kind of head-on confrontation we should practise with all aspects of our musing and mulling. For instance, and this brings me to my point, the matter of equality. Now, equality is a very fine thing. None of us would deny that, I'm sure.' She stopped. Mart thought some talented pre-planning, even rehearsal, had gone into this.

'Well . . . no . . . I'm *not* sure!' she said, the 'not' categorical, aggressive.

Martin recognized one of the standard tricks by lecturers to stop students dozing off: the deliberate error, followed by a wake-up-at-the-back-there correction.

'This uncertainty is why I'm badgering you with my spiel now,' she said. 'It is the kind of re-think that Wayne's courageous initiative has caused me. Slavishly – and a little farcically at times – we have striven to avoid giving either of the universities and either of the principals any sort of precedence, any sort of priority. And so the laborious recitation of, say, the universities' names: if in one phrase we refer to "Sedge and Charter Mill", we immediately have to reverse this in the rather tiresome and pathetic avoidance of notional favouritism and add, "Charter Mill and Sedge". Likewise "Tane, Chote" has urgently to be back-to-fronted, "Chote, Tane".'

'Oh, but come now, Elv, that is mere politesse, isn't it?' Theo Bastrolle (Business Studies) said. 'My parents told me about a weekly comic radio programme in the 1940s called *It's That Man Again* where one of the running jokes was a pair of characters about to pass through a door and saying, "After *you,* Claud." "No, after *you,* Cecil." Isn't the Sedge, Charter, Charter, Sedge and Chote, Tane, Tane, Chote like that?'

'It is deception. It is pretence,' Elvira replied. 'It is blind-eyeing.'

'In which respect, Elv?' Theo asked.

'You very kindly furnished us all with a copy of the centenary gig review in d'Brindle Hall, Theo,' she said. Elvira waved her copy. Other committee members studied theirs.

'Yes,' Theo replied.

'I'd like to ask the Chair – ask Martin – what kind of reception that review got at the time,' Elvira said. 'We are lucky to have someone who was well-placed in Sedge when so many of these events took place.'

'Reception?' Mart said. 'Receptions varied, like receptions of any opinion expressed in a newspaper.'

165

'How did *you,* personally regard it?' Elvira said.

'Regard exactly what, Elvira?' Mart said.

'Take this sentence about the *Tannhauser* interlude,' she replied, reading from her copy: '"As he clashed those two shining brass discs together at pretty well exactly the right dramatic moments one could see the challenging sound as defiance, a sort of Bronx cheer, aimed at those who regard his principalship as disastrous, and want him kicked out while there might still be time to save Sedge under a new chief and a more sane regime."' Elvira looked up from the article and gazed around the room, taking in everyone. 'Now, what do we make of that?' she asked.

'Well, what do *you* make of it, Elvira?' Martin replied, with a Claud and Cecil intonation. He wondered whether Elvira, also, had seen the historic tape of Charlie Drake half concussing himself with the cymbals din. He thought he could detect which way her questions were headed, though. He didn't want to be an accessory to bloodletting, and was glad to fall back on the excuse that a chair had to be all-round non-partisan. 'It's too long ago for me to remember what I felt then and I'm not allowed to have feelings now, except to exercise a casting vote if necessary, which it isn't.'

Elvira gave him a ten second you-fucking-fuckface stare then said, 'This is ridicule masquerading as praise, isn't it?' She waved the copy and returned to the text. 'We hear he did his banging bit at "pretty well exactly the right moments". What does "pretty well exactly"

166

mean? It means not quite exactly. It is a boot in the balls phrased urbanely, but still a boot in the balls. To be slightly off with his cymbals contributions is as bad as being a mile off. It would rupture the *Tannhauser* excerpt.'

She lowered her eyes towards the end of the review then hopped about willy-nilly to make her points. 'He has charisma, yes, but no money to match it and make the charisma of some use. Childishly he can give a Bronx cheer but it damages nobody. "Red hat, no drawers" as the folk wisdom goes about mere show. Although Mart, for his own reasons, refuses to endorse this, the impression given in 1987 by the review is of a leader struggling frantically, pitiably, to lead, but barred from doing so any longer because he lacks the wherewithal. Almost everyone must have observed this. Mart, through what I suppose might be deemed respect for the conventions of his present role and a failure of memory, declines to say so, but probably knows that this is how things were.'

'You mustn't tell me what I'm thinking, Elvira,' Mart replied.

'And it is here that we come to the question of equality, and its relevance to the statues,' Elvira said.

'Relevant how?' Jed Laver (Industrial Relations) asked.

Theo said in a definitive, boardroom voice, 'What you're telling us, Elv, is that the review probably got the picture of Chote right, despite its snide tone here and there. You think he was generally regarded as a runaway nincompoop:

massive, even glorious, ambitions, no genuine ability to achieve them. You believe this should not be tactfully, sentimentally, ignored, "blind-eyed" now. You think what would stick damningly in the reader's mind back then is the mention of his kennel of wild hatreds; and the notion that he should be kicked out and a new chief and more "sane" regime established while there was still time to save Sedge. Out of this analysis you would bring a demand that, in the matter of statues, Victor Tane's should, in some way or ways, indicate a superiority to Chote, Tane being the one who would soon have the task – and complete the task well – of repairing the appalling damage done by Lawford Chote.'

'Along those lines, Theo, yes,' Elvira said. 'This review offers vision. I'll say why it must have been effective. It's this: it has balance. Certainly it mocks his cymbals clumsiness, and is unkind in the *Titanic* comparison. But it also delivers admiration for him. It recognizes his inspired doggedness and positive imagination in creating d'Brindle Hall, a beautiful building and brilliantly acousticked concert centre. Jurbb saw that Chote refused to be domineered by money, or its shortage. Like some warrior hero he was facing fearful odds and *would* face them. But his defeat is treated as almost inevitable. The fearful odds are justifiably, accurately, fearful. He is blatantly unable to handle the basic task – running Sedge, or saving Sedge by the time O.T.O. wrote.'

'We still don't know who this Jurbb, capable of so many penetrating insights, really was, do

168

we?' Angela said. 'Mart has admitted he can't help on this.'

'Jurbb is – or, at least was – Jurbb, as far as I could discover. I did wonder about the then local editor, Alan Norton-Hord, possibly choosing to hide under a pen-name, but that was only speculation,' Martin replied.

'He/she is by-lined as Music Correspondent. Did she/he review in the paper regularly?' Angela asked.

'Not to my knowledge,' Martin said.

'Those extraordinary initials,' Upp said.

'If they *are* initials,' Bill Davey said.

'How do you mean, Bill?' Lucy asked.

'We spoke of anagrams previously, taking up all the letters,' Davey said. 'The O.T.O. would be part of the hidden name – Jo Burbot, Rob Jobut. We called them "names to conjure with". Well, we've tried to conjure and the trick doesn't work.'

Elvira took charge again. 'Theo, with his business expertise, will be able to confirm what I'm going to say now. In management there is a theory dubbed The Peter Principle. Its originator argues that people in top jobs will frequently get promoted to a position one stage above their abilities. A vast muck-up results. Nixon would be an example, and Anthony Eden. And Lawford Chote. I gather that he had a brilliant academic and administrative career before Sedge. I wholly accept this. His CV must have been irresistible. But past form is only that – past. Sedge turned out to be a fatal bit too much for him. He valiantly, foolishly, made his wager against those fearful odds and lost, though unwilling to admit

169

he'd lost until compelled to by the Universities Finance Centre. Happily, though, this, was not the end of the game. Someone else – Victor Tane – stepped in and ultimately secured recovery.'

'"A second Adam to the fight and to the rescue came,"' Upp said. 'Cardinal Newman?'

'Doesn't this rescue require special, obvious recognition?' Elvira replied. 'In universities we do not champion equality, and we certainly do not champion flagrant failure, nor the purblind determination not to acknowledge that failure, causing further chaos. We are *higher* education, in fact, the highest. We are the top, and this implies there is much below. We exist to recognize and encourage merit. There are First Class degrees and there are Third Class degrees. Thereare first class institutions. There are seventh or tenth class institutions. There are staff who get elected to the Royal Society. And there are others who don't. It would be dishonest and intellectually sloppy and perverse to pretend that each ex-principal deserves exactly the same quality memorial and similar prominence. We must have distinctions. That's what I've been getting at today.'

'What about the plinths?' Upp asked.

'Plinths are important, though not of the essence,' Elvira replied. 'But, yes, it might be appropriate to differentiate statues' status by plinth variations.'

'Plinths are very eloquent in their own stony way,' Angela said.

'Perhaps at that interesting contribution we should break,' the chair said.

170

Twenty-Four

1987

Eligible under a special civil service protocol, Mart was invited to join them when Geraldine Fallows and Neddy Lane-Hinkton travelled from London to Sedge for a meeting with Lawford Chote in his suite there. Neddy had telephoned Martin in advance to tell him of the arrangements. 'Geraldine remains very anxious, Mart. Well, "anxious"? Perhaps that's not the word. It makes Geraldine sound nervy, which she ain't. Perhaps "watchful" would be more like it. Yes, very watchful.

'We had this Volvo pic, with its unclear, possibly disquieting implications; and now our press cuttings service here have put the O.T.O. Jurbb piece in front of her. They've been asked to look out for anything to do with Sedge and, or Charter Mill. You'll have seen the article, of course. *Jurbb* – who the fuck is he or she with a name like that? Sounds like a belch. Is it a misprint? We've done all the searches, but nix, Mart. And those initials. Is that another misprint? Should it be Otto? Are the sub-editors all pissed on that paper? We wondered if it was a real name anagrammed as cover. But we got only Jo Burbot, who'd be female, and Rob Jobut or Bob Rojto. Nothing on these, either.

171

'You'd have been at the concert, I imagine. Did you see anyone who looked like a Jurbb? Is that an absurd question? Probably. But what I mean is, he or she could be foreign. Possibly Jurbb is as commonplace as Smith in some other country. She or he might be black. There are probably some good music colleges over there in Africa, say, Malawi or Kenya. He or she could have been trained at one of those and then come to Britain looking for journo work. Music is very international. Just think of Aaron Copeland or Edith Piaf. There is often some quite interesting ethnic hullabaloo stuff on the BBC Radio Three programme late at night. Would someone like that know *Convergence Of The Twain,* though? It's unquestionably a bit of a puzzler, Mart.

'Perhaps he or she at the concert, white or black, would be making notes to remind herself/ himself of the *Titanic* witticism, and of Chote off-kilter on the cymbals. She or he possibly had one of those small torches used by theatre critics in the stalls when jotting down her/his reactions to the acting and sets. I wonder if you observed any little gleams like that?

'The *Titanic* stuff: that's savagery against Chote, and perhaps partly justified, but, it smears Geraldine as well, doesn't it? Smears all of us in her bailiwick. Implies negligence, indifference. Chote's ship is going down while Geraldine and her department busy ourselves elsewhere with flimflam. I mean she's our expert on university finances, and we're talking serious finance here, aren't we? As I remember it, there's a sea-worm in that poem excitedly waiting in the depths for

172

a look at itself in one of the state room mirrors. This is a dark fate for a fine vessel. Not a pretty comparison, Mart.

'Ger didn't object to his staging the centenary concert – or, at least, she didn't object at full Geraldinish whack. Sedge is Sedge and to date still there, occupying its ground, educating its intakes, offering places for next year. She considered it reasonable for the birthday to be marked, despite everything. There's a sensitive side to Ger, not always on view, though. But then this fucking O.T.O. Jurbb is let loose on the event. We did inquiries and found that the editor of the paper is . . . hang on . . . I've got the name and details here . . . yes, the editor is an Alan Norton-Hord who was actually an undergrad at Sedge and held student union office. Him? Or him a party to it, although, plainly, he can't be anagrammed into Jurbb?

'But Ger says she thinks she divines a woman's hand and mind in the review. Don't ask me why – something to do with the use of adverbs, I gather. Geraldine's sharp. The fact that the initials are the same if read from the front or back like the word "kayak", infuriates her, more than the double "b" in Jurbb, though it's a near run thing, as Wellington said after Waterloo. She asks, what kind of parents would send a kid out into life with initials like those? It's an invitation to mockery and bullying, in her opinion. That is, if the O.T.O. Jurbb name is genuine. You're a prof. Have you ever heard of a word ending in a double b?'

'It's not the kind of thing that would come up

173

in English Literature studies, or American. There's Bob Cratchit in *A Christmas Carol* where there are two "b"s and one is at the end, but it's separated from the earlier "b" by the "o",' Mart said.

'We might imagine that boob would be given two, with the round, base bit of the "b"s imitating a pair of knockers,' Neddy replied, 'but not so. Why is the second one necessary in Jurbb? No, not "necessary". That's my whole point. "Indulged in" rather than necessary. Utterly *un*necessary. The pronunciation is the same whether it's double or single. Geraldine is not against double "b"s *per se*. Clearly, she sees them as acceptable and even obligatory within the body of words like "Scrabble", and "rubble" and "babble." A single "b" in these instances would produce a different and possibly confusing pronunciation: "Scrabble" would sound like "Scrayble", "rubble" like "rouble", "babble" like "babel". Sorry, Mart, am I, as it were, babbling on a bit? But for the repeated "b"s to be tacked on to the end, as in Jurbb, Geraldine regards as a kind of affront to readers of the paper and to all those associated with Sedge.

'Ger can see that the review might in a devious way be trying to support Sedge by lobbing some praise at Chote for getting the d'Brindle done, an acoustics paradise. ("Lobbing", there's another allowable double "b"! It would be the alternative "o" pronunciation if only one "b": lobing, maybe to mean earholing, eavesdropping.) Geraldine believes that Chote's enemies – the iceberg, metronomes, accountants, bailiffs, ministries

174

– are depicted as evil persecutors of a decent, conscientious chap, if, admittedly rather head-strong. But she doubts whether this is the message most people will carry away from O.T.O., or may we call you O?

'Geraldine thinks there'd better be some head-to-head stuff – her head and Lawf's. She's talked to Tane, so has one side of the situation fairly clear; and she doesn't think it would be wise to wait for you to report back after my visit and our conclave at The Lock Gate. That was to ask you to keep us briefed. She doesn't believe there's time for this any longer. Urgency has taken over. She possibly thinks, too, that you might not feel comfortable about offering insights on Chote because you have a certain admirable loyalty. Maybe she's right. I haven't heard anything from you since our lunch, and neither has she.'

Neddy paused, apparently hoping Mart would comment – attempt an explanation. He stayed silent, though. He supposed he *did* have a sort of loyalty to Chote off-and-on, even if he thought Chote often ludicrously and perilously wrong. Things were too complicated to be dealt with in this phone session with Neddy. And, anyway, Mart didn't feel like putting himself into a situation where he was offering excuses to someone like Ned, who had no boss status over him. Neddy had been a good lunch companion. This was the whole story.

Lane-Hinkton said, 'But she hasn't a down on you, Martin, because of your possible unwilling-ness to give us insider glimpses. She understands

175

that you possibly don't wish to spy – to turn informant. Perhaps you consider that kind of thing contemptible. Regardless, she would like you to sit in along with myself when she sees Lawford. This will be what's known in our splendidly astute bureaucracy as a "Preparatory Parameters Survey (U)" the U standing not for Upper Class as usual in terms like "non-U", meaning prole, but for "Unminuted".

'The natty convention is that the two main, official figures – here, Geraldine Fallows and Lawford Chote – confer directly, armchair to armchair, or across a desk. But, so as to establish the meeting's informality and casual nature, two other people should be present, each linked to one of these chief participants, though having no designated connection with the topic or topics discussed; in this case, you, Martin, and myself. You're an academic, not an administrator, more interested in Pinter than in policy; and I am only a sort of Premier League office boy and gofer at Universities Finance Centre. The essential nobodies – that's us. But we are both allowed to join discussions – are not mere clerkly background, on call with appropriate stats and bottled water. In fact we are *required* to join in. However, the meeting or meetings has, have, no executive power because of our non-executive role in it, them. By contributing we invalidate. Think of the crazy, impregnable logic in Joseph Heller's famous novel, *Catch 22*. The rules and conventions for these "unminuted" sessionss are not quite up to that mad standard, but let's say they form a *Catch Twenty-One-And-A-Half*. The

176

reasoning Byzantine but almost flawless. A meeting of this sort might not get known about except to those involved. But even if it does, never mind, because such get-togethers can be passed off as simply idle chin-wagging with no binding outcomes, full of sound and hooey, signifying nothing much.

'Geraldine is especially agitated by the closing Jurbb thought, Mart.' Neddy spoke at his accustomed slow pace and Martin tried to guess which side of the mouth the talk was coming from. Mart thought that if he could get another hearing of a multi-syllabled word like 'agitated' he might be able to diagnose the left or right source. It wasn't vital to know, but would help Mart keep Neddy's jolly type of face in his mind, bringing some lightness to a fairly clunking conversation so far.

'Did you say "agitated", Neddy?' he asked

'Yes, agitated.'

Mart found he could visualize this word laid out like a patient etherized upon a table and, looking hard at it, as a surgeon might, felt it was most probably from Neddy's lips angled for ouput from the left. This verdict was instinct only. Mart realized that. He couldn't have pointed to any evidence, but he would have bet a bundle it was left. It came to him as a kind of revelation.

'Charisma, Mart,' Neddy said. 'The sort of pay-off for the review, a conclusive thumbs up.'

'Charisma *is* mentioned, at the end, yes.'

'What especially troubles Geraldine and probably persuaded her to decide on a personal trip

177

to Sedge and Lawford, is the yoking together of Sedge and Chote's charismas, or should it be charismae?'

'Yoking?'

'I have the final sentence in front of me, Mart. "Although Sedge and Lawford Chote are perilously short of cash they still have charisma."'

'Yes, that's the last line.'

'I think you'll see why this would disturb Geraldine. Perhaps, in fact, it's already troubled *you*.'

'In which respect, Ned?'

'You don't see it?'

'See what?'

'The identification charisma-wise of Sedge and Chote.'

'Identification?'

'The marriage – the assumption as Geraldine sees it, and as I'm inclined to see it myself, I admit . . . yes, the assumption seems to be that they are interdependent for charisma – if one of them has it then the other must, too. Now, Mart, Sedge obviously does have charisma. It is a university 100 years old which, although by comparison with Oxbridge or the Sorbonne might seem trivial, is *not* trivial for provincial, red-brick and breeze-block places.

'And Sedge has alumni in distinguished posts right across the main professions, in business and the creative arts. True, Charter Mill has an international goalkeeper among its most successful former students, who's probably earning more than any Sedge graduate – and three times more than the Charter Mill principal's

178

and senior academics' combined salaries. But we are not talking loot here, are we, Mart? We are not talking goalkeepers. We are talking intellectual renown earned over the decades. We are talking genuine charisma. The danger, as Geraldine views it, and I don't disagree, is that Lawford, being of the awkwardly indomitable, egomaniac kind we know him to be, will decide that if Sedge has charisma, the principal running Sedge at present, i.e., Lawf, must also have charisma. Geraldine fears, and I share this apprehension, she fears that Chote, on reading O.T.O. Jurbb, will deduce that all he has to do is carry on as ever in his job because the way he conducts this has brought him charisma and will continue doing so after a few local difficulties about money and debt have been dealt with and forgotten, just as the inept cymbals interlude will be. He's not going to kowtow to accountants and their talk of black holes in the Sedge account books. His view is that charisma will cancel all those piddling anxieties.'

'"Tax not the royal saint with vain expense",' Mart said.

'"High-heaven rejects the lore/Of nicely calculated less or more",' Neddy replied. 'But there's another aspect to it.'

'I *did* wonder.'

'It could be that some harsh things will be said at this meeting and some harsh decisions confirmed. Although Geraldine can be very understanding and sweet-tempered, clearly she isn't coming on a crisis trip from London by train just to dispense understanding and sweet-temper.

179

It's true she sees my expenses sheets, of course, so is aware of our pleasant, refreshing snack at The Lock Gate, and might feel it worth a visit. She wanted to know if it was up to snuff – can't believe any eatery outside London is a goer – and I naturally referred to the black-pudding hash. But I don't think this, on its own, accounts for her determination to travel. For all I know, Mart, she isn't into black-pudding hash. She didn't indicate one way or t'other.

'In any case, she'll probably want to lunch in the Sedge staff dining room. She's heard of the lavish upgrading and might feel a duty to look at it and the deluxe carpeted approach. No, the black-pudding hash is probably not a motivator. She has a well-defined, serious purpose. This is why I spoke of possible harshness arising. The meeting will begin, most likely, in a very civilised, even amiable, style. In fact, Geraldine would see this as essential. It ties in, Mart, with another reason for wanting you present. If matters reach an abusive, end-of-the-fucking-road, ultimatum stage, Ger will require someone present who can report to the rest of the Sedge staff that Lawford was given every consideration and kindness from the outset but would offer no concessions, no decent response; behaved, in fact, as if he were in a morality play representing the quality of pig-headedness. She wants head-to-head contact but not with a pig.

'This is where you'll be invaluable, Mart. Colleagues know that you and Lawford are friends, and if you have to admit he behaved in a negative, blatantly uncooperative style they

180

will accept this as almost certainly a fair and honest judgement. Geraldine or myself might be suspected of bias. She has to keep in mind that even when the Sedge situation has finally settled she will still need workable relations with Sedge and all of Britain's universities, never mind what shape Sedge emerges in after these troubles. She will not want to be regarded as a bureaucratic bully. Such a reputation would spread far and fast. It might appear that having kicked her way through what is known as the glass ceiling, hindering women from reaching a major job, she'd developed the kicking habit and had given some toecap to Lawford when he was down – though Lawford would never have admitted he was down, of course. Down is not his habitat.'

'You spoke of an ultimatum, Neddy,' Martin said.

'Oh, yes, there could be an ultimatum.'

'Of what nature?'

'Geraldine is sure to bring documents already part prepared, in case. She wouldn't necessarily produce them. She probably wouldn't *want* to produce them. She'd prefer another route. But that route might not be open. It would be a matter of judgement at the time.'

'Documents for what?'

'We're talking *aide memoires*.'

'Are we?'

'This is one of the things about Geraldine – preparedness: she's famed for it. Geraldine could have mentored Lord Baden-Powell, founder of the scout movement with its motto, "Be prepared",' Neddy replied. 'I've had her a few

181

times as you'd expect and she makes all the arrangements – no possibility of discovery and interruption; champagne, vintage brut from an ice box; cork double-thumbed out by her in one explosive, decisive move and jetting off to some safe corner of the room or car or garden shed; the wine poured at exactly the right angle into the flutes, preserving the liveliness, but with no wasteful and messy bubbling over the sides and perhaps chillingly on to her body; biting only in areas normally hidden by garments; the cork recovered afterwards by Ger and disposed of in a public waste bin with the bottle and any of its paper-bag shreds so as to leave no evidence of a high-jinks, multi-cum occasion.'

'Preparedness to do with the ultimatum?' Martin replied.

'The documents ready for close interrogation if utilized. Not for signature yet, obviously. No signed agreements can come out of a Preparatory Parameters Survey (U), because the meeting has no power or acknowledged status: might not even be known about generally. It is irrevocably (U). The procedure she'd be hoping for is discussion involving all four parties – herself, Chote, you, me; verbal agreement on the required major points; agreement, also, on the date of a formal, officially diaried meeting; signatures, then; minutes then. No invitation for us this time because our presence in an apparently policy-making session would disqualify its proceedings and render the signatures worthless.'

'Agreement on what, Ned?'

'The terms would have been set out in the *aide*

memoire I mentioned, but need not be referred to, let alone shown, if the parties at the (U) settle everything by conversation and handshakes. The pattern for this would be each of us shakes hands with the other three, although, technically, the handshakes you and I provide would add up to bugger-all, especially as one of the handshakes would be *between* you and me, who have utterly no rank, and so whose handshake rates as bugger-all squared. The handshake between Lawford and Geraldine would also amount to bugger-all at that stage since the meeting had no standing because you and I were there, Mart.

'However, the Lawford–Geraldine handshake will – if it happens – be of a promissory kind, resting on the honour of the two. She'd be entirely willing to accept this commitment from Chote, although unbacked by paperwork at that juncture. I've heard Geraldine call him by all kinds of abusive, filthy and blasphemous terms, but I have also heard her pronounce him straight – straight in the sense of undevious and trust-worthy, not anything to do with sexuality.'

'But what would she and he be shaking hands *about*, Neddy? What would the *aide memoire*, if ever brought forward, aid them to remember?' Mart replied.

'I don't think this sounds anti-woman, but to treat a handshake as something more or less sacred we would normally take as being between males, I believe, wouldn't you say so, Mart? But for Geraldine, who has kicked her way through the glass ceiling, this, in a heartening way, seems to free up her hands as well as her feet so she can get in on the shake procedure, as if it were absolutely normal for females. But she certainly remains all woman, Mart. I can assure you she won't black mark you for seeming to be very much of Chote's inner gang. Are you keen on brut champagne at all? I can't recall what we sipped at The Lock Gate.'

'You ought to keep an *aide memoire*, Neddy.'

'And the biting, although forceful, is nicely controlled to draw no blood; perhaps more a suck with tooth backing rather than an authentic bite,' Lane-Hinkton said. 'The redness soon fades but, obviously, for a day or two you have to be careful when undressing at home or with someone else. This is only standard decent manners.'

Twenty-Five

1987

'Thank you, thank you, thank you!' Victor Tane yelled. He waved graciously to the crowd of spectators lining the pavement. It was the kind of wave he'd seen performed by a Caesar to the masses in a film on TV lately, probably *Ben-Hur*. The imperiousness of it didn't quite fit in with all the thank yous. Caesars wouldn't lavish gratitude on their subjects. But Tane wasn't a Caesar and thought he'd better go half-and-half: part grand and aloof, part affable and populist.

Although skinny, he had a big, refined voice, the sort of voice you might hear if the colonel himself were commanding a Coldstream guard of honour for some visiting head of state. A jazz band banged brassily away fairly near in the procession but Victor could be heard above it. He was standing on the back of a slow-moving, open lorry. 'Thank you for supporting our charities,' he shouted. Students in a range of comic costumes and masks – Bo-Peep, Red Riding Hood, Cruella de Vil, Micky Mouse, Oliver Hardy with a padded stomach, small moustache, braces, black bowler – they moved among the bystanders with collecting boxes. 'Give, give, give!' Tane bellowed. 'It's Bounty Week.'

'Yes, folk, be generous. Dig deep,' Bernard Optor shouted. He had a big voice, too, and was built for it. He'd have had plenty of practice, cursing referees or his defensive backs for mistakes that left him exposed. He was alongside Tane, wearing the usual kit when in goal for his club or country: navy woollen bobble hat, polo-necked green sweater, brown woollen mittens, navy shorts, football boots. Behind him, reduced size imitation goal posts with netting had been rigged up on the lorry. His bulk would have made it more or less impossible to get a ball past him into that net.

Tane himself had on a yellow-and-black striped football shirt. Ursula said it made him look like a tall wasp. He wore also a blue ski hat, black shorts and red-and-white trainers. He was a good deal over six feet in height, slight and gawky, bordering on the wispy. He'd known he wasn't at his best in sports gear, or any gear involving shorts, but Optor had phoned a while ago to say he'd thought of a way to help Tane and Charter Mill, and Victor had agreed to his scheme. His scheme required shorts.

Tane's acceptance of the plan was in some sense posthumous kow-towing to his mother, her orders unspoken and, in fact, non-existent, of course, but envisaged as very true to her character, if only she'd been alive: *'Victor, cherish, heed and obey this glorious goalkeeper.'* From his days as an undergraduate at Charter, Optor apparently remembered the traditional Bounty Week, when the two universities put on a combined carnival parade through the city centre to raise money for a handful of charities. Optor had said, 'We'll do a footy theme for one of the lorries, eh, Principal? But I suppose I can call you Victor now, or even Vic, after so many years and since we're buddies, but it does feel cheeky.' Optor explained the ins and outs of the project and said he'd 'pop over' from Spain to take part.

He'd told Tane his agent, Loriner Vone, was vastly enthusiastic about it. Vone had said that such a pure, unmaterialistic labour of love carefully publicized was worth its weight in pounds sterling or the equivalent in pesetas, i.e., numerically a lot more. He didn't think he'd ever come across a smarter PR gambit. Not just the local media would be interested but national, too – the great Bernard Optor journeying back to his *alma mater* on a good, utterly selfless mission; loyalty of a magnificently high order. Vone considered this was the kind of generous gesture guaranteed to help improve the general reputation and image of professional soccer. It would consolidate the link with the game's fans, help build a fine relationship with them, almost certainly pushing up attendances. In particular, this example of the 'sweeter' and 'more wholesome' aspect of players' behaviour off the pitch might encourage more women to support the game. The extra following for Optor and his club would, naturally, be reflected in fatter transfer fees if he moved in the future. Although Optor played for a Spanish team the favourable impact of his Bounty Week contribution would certainly reach the media there as well as throughout the UK and pile more value on to Bernie.

Charter Mill would not be called on to pay any of the costs for Optor's travel, accommodation and other expenses, Optor told Tane. Vone had explained to Bernie that such outlay could be set against tax because the benevolent, spontaneous gesture by him in supporting Charter Mill would be very germane, if not essential, to developing his celebrity profile as not just a soccer star but a citizen who cared in a positive, practical, deep style about the community. He wasn't someone who simply stood between the sticks blocking or fisting out balls. He shone with responsibility in the widest of contexts. Loriner had said this could be deftly yet sensitively utilized.

Bernie told Tane that Loriner Vone believed the 'community concept' was an infallible switch-on for the media, national and local, and the kind of coverage Optor would get was sure to be a plus, both for himself and 'the education place in question'. And for the charities. People in Whitehall would be impressed by Optor's obvious splendidly strong bond with the past 'education place in question' because it proved that this 'education place in question' was brilliant. Optor had said he might be able to bring one or two other famous footballers with him to boost the lorry's cast.

And Optor had, in fact, brought a couple of top players – Pierre Pajot and Sean Nuseby, both in club gear. Their expenses, also, would be an allowable tax break for Optor. On the back of the lorry now they mimicked shots at Optor's goal and all three of them frequently bent over the sides of the vehicle to sign autograph books of fans who trotted to keep pace while Optor and his friends scribbled. Although Tane had felt obliged to get into soccer kit himself to maintain tone, he didn't expect anyone to want *his* autograph.

It was part of the Bounty Week tradition that both principals should be personally involved in the cavalcade and a little way ahead, next in line to the jazz lorry, Victor could see Lawford Chote apparently garbed in breastplate armour and occasionally wielding a sword. He was clearly meant to be Shakespeare's Macbeth. He wore a pink plastic crown. Near him three staff members dressed and made-up as witches sat around a big metal cauldron that simmered over a paraffin heater. It gave off occasional puffs of steam. Most probably the witches would be muttering their creepy spells, though Tane could not hear any of that from this distance. Would they predict for Lawford what was going to happen to Sedge and Charter? The early witches' scene in *Macbeth* had a mewing brindled cat referred to. Maybe Chote would see some sort of link to the d'Brindle Hall. Which sort, though?

Victor thought one of the witches might be Chote's Volvo companion, now in rags, his face smeared with what could be black boot polish, and with a wig made of what seemed to be a mixture of grimy cord and rope bits.

Twenty-Six

1987

As the Sedge *Macbeth* float trundled the last stage of its journey, Chote seemed to get bored with the play-acting. He sheathed the plastic sword in its glinting plastic scabbard and put it on the floor. He came and squatted down with the witches at the cauldron and said to Martin, 'So what kind of future do you see, Third Witch? "If you can look into the seeds of time/And say which grain will grow and which will not?" We see her tactics, don't we, Mart?'

'Whose?'

'Geraldine's.'

'Tactics?'

'There's to be a meeting, isn't there – Geraldine, Lane-Hinkton, you, me? Why does she require you in on it? I'll tell you: she's trying to concoct an appearance of fairness. Geraldine's bringing Lane-Hinkton for various services, so she'll balance that by inviting you. She wouldn't want, say, Roy Gormand with me. He's near the end and seeks a calm and sedate life from now on. Entirely understandable. He would do his customary act of backing me absolutely on whatever, wherever – not so much loyalty as serfdom. She believes that wouldn't be so with you, Mart. The main part of your career is still to come, isn't it? You'd like Sedge to survive in its present state to help you along with that. Also entirely understandable, Mart. Geraldine believes she and Lane-Hinkerton can convince you that what they're going to propose is the correct and, in fact, the *only* feasible policy for Sedge. She's sure they can win you over and sure, also, that you will then help them to persuade me into cooperation with them. Blandishments – you'll get blandishments, and they'll expect you to give *me* blandishments. It's why I ask how you see the future, Mart. Will they be able to recruit you?'

'Ned Lane-Hinkton phoned and spoke of an ultimatum, but didn't specify what it was,' Martin Moss replied.

'Oh, I can tell you: they'll demand I cut Sedge expenditure for at least a spell of years. "Do it our way or we slash all government funds to Sedge immediately. You wouldn't be able to pay the staff or put the lights on."'

'That would be extreme, wouldn't it?' Mart replied.

'Geraldine *is* extreme when she wants to be.

Lane-Hinkerton would copy. She's his boss, *inter alia.*' Chote waved to some spectators and adjusted his breastplate which seemed to be giving him discomfort. He became silent, head bent forward a little. Mart went quiet, too.

Second Witch, Jasper Dunning (Archaeology), and often a deep-dyed nuisance, said, '"Stay you imperfect speakers, tell me more." That's a Macbeth line, but Witch 2 has borrowed it.'

'Sod off, Jasper,' Chote replied.

'You mentioned the future, I think, Principal,' Dunning said.

'Yes, the future for Sedge, now, starting at 1987 and going on into the 1990s and eventually into the new millennium as far as we can see,' Chote said. '2001, 2010, 2020 etcetera.'

'But you've pissed on that, haven't you, Principal? Never mind the new millennium and thereafter. Is Sedge going to reach even the start of the 1990s so my students can get their degrees?'

'There are more important matters than one year's student degrees,' Chote said. They were talking to each other across the cauldron, the steam blotting out one face for a while, then the other.

'My classes don't think there are more important things than their degrees,' Dunning said.

'I've worked to make places available for many more students to get their degrees,' Chote replied.

'And you've made a fucking mess of it, Chote. You're going to sink Sedge solo.'

Chote stood. He picked up the scabbard and sword and moved fast around the cauldron towards Dunning.

191

Twenty-Seven

2014

Theo said, 'Before the break Elvira was talking about the need to put a precise, personal value on each of the two principals, not simply and tritely regard them as equals. She suggested that any difference in worth – and she saw a mighty difference – yes, this difference should be reflected in the debate about statues. It means we've had a pair of very fundamental proposals before us lately. First came Wayne's outright, even sweeping, declaration that there should be no statues at all, because many would consider such memorials elitist, backward-looking, stonily lifeless while pretending to be alive. I think the word "naff" was also used, though I wouldn't like to attempt a definition. Wayne's submission was, of course, well-expressed and structured, but not favoured by this group.

'Elvira's subsequent claim that it is intellectually slipshod and even dishonest to treat both principals as of the same merit, and that Victor Tane's statue should somehow indicate this, is almost as deeply challenging. I don't believe she would go so far as to say that there should be only one statue – Tane's – though some might think this is where her argument must lead.

Bill Davey said, 'It surely would. What occurred

in 1987 was a crisis involving two universities and two principals. One of those universities was in real danger of disintegration because – it could be convincingly argued – yes, because of the policies followed by one of those principals, Lawford Chote. But, absolute disaster was prevented, and here we are today in a healthy, distinguished university formed from the merged Charter Mill and Sedge, or Sedge and Charter Mill. One of those two principals was hugely influential and, indeed, instrumental, in bringing about the 1987 rescue act: Victor Tane.

'Suppose we went along with Elvira's premise, there would plainly be something absurd, in the full, philosophical, chaotic universe, sense of that term, if the architect of catastrophe – Chote – were commemorated at all, let alone in some statue inferior to Tane's. Could any sculptor indicate in his/her works that one principal had been a wondrous, resourceful saviour while the other was a bonkers, money-chucking, fuck-up, though well-intentioned?'

'It might be possible to get statues from two separate artists, one specialising in happy, ebullient-seeming likenesses, the other in those less happy and ebullient,' Angela replied.

'*Yellow Pages*?' Jed asked. '"Jolly Statues Ltd. Monumental Cheeriness. At Your Personal Service." Or "Morose Statues, Free, Miserable Home Delivery in the UK".'

'Tane's scrimshank, spectral body-form wouldn't easily be made to appear ebullient,' Gordon Upp said.

'I want to bring to the meeting some other

archive material unearthed in my searches,' Theo replied. 'It might have a bearing on our present discussions. Well, no "might" – it *does*, certainly have a bearing. There was then, in 1987, as there is now, in 2014, a Bounty Week devoted to raising funds for charities. The 1987 Bounty Week turned out to be exceptional because a famous soccer goalkeeper, Bernard Optor, plus two other international footballers, appeared with Victor Tane on one of the Charter Mill floats in the annual motorized parade. Archive papers show that Optor was a Charter Mill graduate. He must have dutifully come back to give Tane and Charter some *réclame* at a critical time, and it worked.'

'Bernie Optor?' Gordon Upp said. 'Played most of his club soccer in Spain? Wasn't he involved in a let-goals-in-for-a-fee scandal?'

'Later,' Theo replied. 'In 1987 he was close to sainthood. Because of Optor and his pals the Bounty Week back then got a lot of press coverage, national as well as local.' He brought copies of some newspaper cuttings from his briefcase and put them on the table to be passed around. 'Most of the attention is on the three players, and particularly Optor. You'll see pictures of young kids scampering alongside the lorry to get autographs. In the background one can spot Victor Tane in soccer gear – a yellow-and-black striped jersey.'

'He looks like a tall wasp,' Lucy Lane said.

'There'd obviously been a decision to pick soccer as this float's theme and attract publicity for Tane and Charter. Note the imitation goal posts and netting to Victor's left. The aim evidently was to make Charter and its head look successful, strong, popular at that time of massive tension in the city's universities. Optor is praised in all the papers for faithfully taking time to help his *alma mater*. There must have been a briefing to let reporters know he'd graduated from Charter Mill. This was a skilfully planned operation. The media had been managed. Soccer agents would be very experienced at that.

'For fairness, the Sedge main float also got mentions, but usually well down the columns. Chote was there apparently as Macbeth with breastplate, sword and dagger at his belt, and, no doubt, the occasional warlike scowl.'

'I was a witch,' Martin said. 'We made up some curses about Charter Mill to chant and boiled murky water in a big metal tub to give off sinister fumes.'

'There are several interesting paragraphs about that,' Theo said. He read from one of the cuttings. '"When the Sedge float was passing through Highbridgc Road a fight seemed to break out on the back of the lorry between Chote and one of the witches, a man but supposed to be female. Eyewitnesses said Macbeth had put his sword away in its scabbard earlier as if tired of the game, but there was what looked like a heated conversation between him and one of the witches, and suddenly he picked up the sword, still in its scabbard, moved fast around the cauldron, and began to beat the witch with it.

'The witch had on only Y-fronts and a sort of in-character, unfetching sleeveless smock, probably made from old potato sacks. Although the weapon used by Macbeth was only plastic, it could most likely give quite painful blows on the witch's poorly protected body. The witch didn't defend himself very well, as if shocked and confused by this onslaught. As a tip-top warrior, Macbeth was sure to know the value of surprise."'

Theo said, 'The writer leaves straight reporting and does some speculation now. "But, while Macbeth was naturally capable of such very sudden physical aggression, nobody expected it from the principal of a university. Macbeth would have been proud of Lawford Chote – the sword hidden away until the exactly proper moment. Some of those watching this burst of violence couldn't decide whether it was a real dispute or something staged – what used to be called 'a happening' to amuse spectators.

"'Red weals and dark bruising could be seen on the witch's neck and shoulder, though, which should have proved to spectators that it must be a genuine in-house spat. The witches' bowl or cauldron was tipped over during this fracas and some people watching got soaked, perhaps scalded, by the hot, filthy water. Several men shouted curses and for a while it looked as if they might get aboard the float and hammer Chote and possibly the witches, though the witches couldn't really be blamed for the mishap. None of this was derived from the play. Shakespeare's Macbeth never attacked a witch or witches with his sword, either in its scabbard or not; and the witches' cauldron was not spilled, it just went on simmering."'

'It wasn't you he went for, was it, Mart?' Lucy asked.

'No, Second Witch. I was Third. The episode lasted only a minute and a half. Some of it made the local TV news. Lawford apologized all round and offered to pay for any dry-cleaning needed and/or ointment and painkillers for the folk scalded.'

'In some ways this must have made the whole attempt to resemble the play hopeless,' Gordon Upp said. 'I mean, there'd be no dry-cleaning available in those days, nor ointment, though I think certain leaves were believed to have an analgesic influence.'

'Dry-cleaning and ointment were not needed in the play,' Elvira replied, 'because the cauldron stayed upright and bubbling OK with bits of all sorts in it – a thumb, a newt's eye, a dog's tongue, a lizard's leg. Probably they wouldn't have had any of those on the Sedge lorry, except for thumbs. And Macbeth didn't clobber one of the witches.'

'Macbeth gets terminated, doesn't he?' Jed asked. 'It's a tragedy, yes?'

'Some actors won't mention the play's name because the plot is so dark,' Wayne said.

'Fucking precious thesps,' Elvira replied.

'Yes, it's dark,' Theo said. 'Maybe that's why Chote picked this role. It's an aggressive-defensive, do-your-worst, kind of choice.'

'But what's your point about the statues or statue, Theo?' Upp said.

'What do we learn from this age-old, back-of-a-lorry, stuff?' Elvira asked.

'Well, Elvira, isn't there, on the face of it, a sort of equality, despite what you've just told us?' Theo asked. 'Both principals, were willing to make a spectacle of themselves for the charities' sake, each recognising the force of the Bounty Week tradition and cheerfully ready to uphold it. That is a very basic, very substantial, resemblance, as is the fact that they were both major scholars, whatever their qualities as managers might have been.

'However, I'd say that if we're going to put differing values on them the nobler, more worthwhile figure is Lawford, although we know he would tumble before the year ended. There's a magnificent, basically flawed grandeur to him, as there should be to all tragic heroes and heroines, or heroines and heroes, in the theatre. He stands alone with his plastic sword, dagger and breastplate and will confront whatever comes. Just like Macbeth at Dunsinane he wouldn't lose his nerve even if a forest started to move against him.'

'Why did he attack Second Witch, Mart?' Jed asked.

'Second Witch was a Sedge lecturer called Jasper Dunning (Archaeology), ever a troublesome, sniping sod, recently knighted for the quality of his digs in Wales and France. He said something Chote didn't like. I forget what now.'

'Lawford's reaction shows he wouldn't take any insult or insubordination,' Davey said.

'Staunch, as I've already pointed out,' Theo replied. 'I regard Tane as a lesser figure, who had to make use of help from elsewhere – from a

198

supposed celebrity, and a tainted celebrity, as he would become subsequently. There are three time lines running in our discussion: 1987, now, but also the quarter of a century and some between. It's my conviction that there must be two statues. Tane's should have about it somehow a spruce aura of achievement, because his success in making the amalgamation possible is plain and undeniable. But there should be a hint that his success came via a dubious, meretricious route. Possibly the sculptor could get some shifty, conspiratorial quality into his eyes. Chote's statue should also have an aura, but of non-surrender, tenacity, valour and error – firmness in the face of those previously mentioned fearful odds; the fearful odds that refused to change in his favour and, in fact, grew worse.'

'You'd say we get a generous dose of catharsis from Lawford?' Lucy asked. 'Tragedy is supposed to bring that, isn't it?'

'I used to know what catharsis meant,' Upp said. 'Something emotional?'

'Release,' Elvira said.

'Yes, good,' Mart said, standing.

Theo began to gather up his cuttings, but remained sitting. 'A postscript, if you don't mind, Chair. It might have a bearing on the statues mission. In my search of the archives I found some very well maintained secretarial diaries. They were handwritten. Nowadays, of course, they'd be in some computer's memory bank. Normally, the entries give time and place of meetings and a short title of the business carried out, the names of those present, duration, and sometimes the outcome if

199

a policy decision were reached. But I came across a May 1987 occasion in Chote's suite without any of the customary detail. The diary note said only: "Principal's conference area engaged from 1420 to 1647".

'The date could be significant. It's very close to the crux stages of the Chote–Sedge crisis, isn't it? I had a really thorough hunt for anything further, particularly names of those who might have attended, and the subject for consideration. Nothing, though.'

Martin sat down again. 'Yes, this would have been a "Preparatory Parameters Survey (U)",' he said.

'Oh, what's that when it's at home?' Elvira replied.

'It's a meeting that existed, but also didn't,' Mart said. 'The bracketed U indicates the type of Preparatory Parameters Survey: the unminuted genre. There will be no list of those participating, no labelling title, no statement of results. It happens that I was at this one plus Geraldine Fallows – Baroness Fallows now – Neddy Lane-Hinkton and Lawford Chote. The fact that I, or rather Neddy and I, were included means that this session could not have taken place.'

'I don't get it,' Angela said.

'It's a beauty, isn't it?' Mart replied.

'But the diary reports that it *did* take place,' Lucy said.

'No, it says that the conference area was engaged for a measured period,' Mart said.

'Engaged with what, if it wasn't a meeting?' Wayne asked.

200

Mart said, 'What I was present at *felt* like a meeting – four people coming together to talk, two having travelled from London specifically to be there – but I was told with great firmness that reference to a meeting having taken place was perverse and foolishly deluded.'

Gordon Upp said, 'This reminds me of that nonsense poem by Hughes Mearns:

"Yesterday upon the stair
I met a man who wasn't there.
He wasn't there again today.
I wish, I wish, he'd go away."'

'But Martin *was* there,' Elvira said.

'And because I was it couldn't have taken place,' Mart said.

Twenty-Eight

1987

'Good legs,' Ursula Tane said.

Vic Tane didn't much like this. His own legs were not good – between bony and emaciated – and they'd been displayed on the Bounty Week float. 'Hell, Ursula, if I said that, but about a woman, you'd go into a flaming jealous spasm.'

'When a man praises a woman's legs he's not really thinking about the legs but where they start from or lead up to, and how welcoming they would be when apart. A woman's legs might be lovely, but they are not the complete agenda.'

201

Ursula had lovely legs, but Tane would admit they were not the complete agenda.

'Whereas,' she told him, 'when I note Lawford Chote's "good legs" it just means what it says, legs that seem strong and well shaped. Normally, his legs wouldn't be on show, but when he's doing a Macbeth in breastplate over short jerkin, there they are, bare and obviously serviceable.'

They were watching the late evening local TV news coverage of the Bounty Week parade, and Chote's sudden, all-out, frenzied attack with his scabbarded sword on one of the witches. The film showed most of the tussle including the tip-up of the cauldron, dowsing some onlookers with what looked like very mucky water. They were obviously cursing and threatening Chote and the witch, but viewers needed to lip-read because the sound had been edited out on grounds of hygiene.

Vic Tane adored television. They had four sets in Kule House, the eighteenth-century, semi-rural, six-bedroomed mansion that came with the job at Charter Mill. It had been already furnished but Tane added more. This signalled a kind of compulsion. They were in what was called the East Study where the largest TV stood, a very over-furnished, small room. As well as the television it contained a three-piece suite of two ample easy chairs and a lengthy settee in pale mauve velveteen, a sideboard, a round, rose-wood table, two nests of small mahogany tables, an archery target on its stand for use in the grounds fairly often when Ursula and Victor competed against each other, Victor almost always the winner. This was important to him, even vital. Ursula could sometimes make Tane seem stupid in argument, but he had the drop on her as to bull's eyes. He would mock her: 'We'd never have won at Agincourt if our longbow troops were like you, Urs.' She liked this ugly shortening of her name because it sounded similar to the French for a female bear – *ourse* – and made her feel cuddlesome, like a teddy.

'The other two witches don't do anything to help their sister,' Ursula said. 'Poltroons. Where's solidarity?'

'Despite the rope wig and rough garments, I think I recognize one of them from a photograph taken a while ago, a non-witch picture. He was in Chote's Volvo then, not on the back of a lorry, and seemingly a new member of Lawford's special clique. He probably wouldn't side against Macbeth here.'

'He can't survive this,' Ursula said, pointing at the screen.

'Who? The witch? Lawford's sword and scabbard are only toys. The witch hits back. He's taking most of the blows on his arm.'

'Chote.'

'Survive it?'

'This publicity will finish him. I mean, Vic, this is the principal of a university. OK, a provincial university but still a university with a boss who ought to behave with some decorum. The police are sure to be involved and the safety people – antics on the back of a lorry and chucking hot water over what are known as innocent bystanders, that is, bystanders whose innocence means they don't need a wash, especially not in foul water. Was he drunk, or high on something? In a way it's hilarious, of course: a procession admirably in support of charities becomes a venue for thuggery.'

'But in a way it's also sad, of course,' Victor said.

'Has he flipped because of the Sedge troubles?'

'Flipped?'

'Overheated brain, trying to think of a way out of the Sedge agonies when there probably isn't one – or not one he could accept,' she replied. 'The only one he *would* accept, most probably, is Sedge's debts written off and a new tranche of Education Ministry boodle for him to squander.'

'I think the witch must have said something to him. They seemed to be chatting normally near the cauldron, the way any two people might chat near a witches' cauldron, and then abruptly he goes ape.'

'Said what?'

'Obviously, something offensive.'

'What sort of something?' she said.

'Oh, about Sedge and the mess he's made of it. They'd be doom-laden words and coming from a witch who, don't forget, Urs, has second-sight into the future.'

'It's not a witch, it's a bloke doing a turn for Bounty Week, as you did.'

'But Chote's in a bad state,' Victor replied.

'Pissed?

'Has strain made him deluded, so he can't tell the difference between street-theatre and fact, fantasy and the back of a lorry?' Victor found

204

some of it unbearably embarrassing to watch and let his eyes wander from the screen and move around the East Study. What he liked about cramming so much furniture in was the way this corrected how things had been at home when he was a youngster. His mother and father were minimalists by nature, long before the word and style became commonplace. Some rooms in the house had only a couple of basic items in them, though they were used daily, not abandoned.

'Victor, I must have space!' his mother had bawled at him one day, when standing in the middle of what she and Tane's father referred to as the Nominal Room, because they'd gone in there during Mrs Tane's pregnancy to decide on what the coming child should be called. The room could offer then, as it probably could until the house was sold, two straight-backed kitchen chairs and an ottoman with a padded hinged lid where sheets were kept.

His mother had told Vic that she and his father sat opposite each other on the chairs for hours going through names. Eventually they'd settled on Victor Horace, and Madge Emily for a girl. 'So you see, Victor Horace, what I mean when I state in all humility I must, absolutely *must*, have space,' his mother had said that day when he was in his teens, touching with a kind of awe and reverence the chair she'd been on when choosing Victor Horace and Madge Emily.

Vic Tane hadn't, in fact, seen why she should demand space because of the naming slog and to counter what he saw as the barminess of his mother's supposed logic he went in for loading

205

rooms at Kule with gear so that he could prove to himself, and to anyone else who inquired, that he was not for ever bound by his mother's thinking, even though she and his father had spent so long in an uncomfortable, mean-looking room naming him and the girl who didn't come.

Tane enjoyed sending her photographs of the East Study and descriptions of the layout there. Of course, she was dead and no effective retaliation from him to her was possible, but taking the pictures and listing any new stuff, such as a flagrantly surplus nest of mahogany tables, gave him an authentic, malicious pleasure. Sometimes the letters and photographs would come back to the return address he'd put on the back of the envelope, and sometimes they disappeared, presumably thrown away by the people now in the house. He liked to imagine them, perhaps angered beyond by the continuing flow of mail for her, opening the envelope in protest and reading the furniture inventory and enjoying the back-up photographs of, say, a bookcase, hatstand, pouffe.

That kind of unintended, random contact with people whom he didn't know delighted Tane. It gave him the same sort of thrill as television. Watching programmes, he often felt a kind of link between him and performers on the screen. He had the conviction that if one of those professional broadcasters stepped out into the East Study, as the actor does in that Woody Allen film, *The Purple Rose Of Cairo,* he/she would warm to all the homely clutter and excess. This was a lived-in room not some poky, inhospitable cubicle for picking babe names.

He liked to make love to Ursula on the mauvish settee while the television was on a couple of metres away. It was part of that longing for a link with the great outside and elsewhere. He had bought the mauve suite because of its long settee. He was six foot four inches tall. The settee had to provide a suitable and safe site. He'd read somewhere that Eva Braun, Hitler's mistress, used to have a good giggle when distinguished visitors came and sat on a sofa that only recently she and Adolf had used for romance. Tane felt the same when they had guests and some of them took places on the convenient settee.

Ursula had unzipped his trousers and eased her hand inside. Tane said, 'Yes, Lawford might have lost touch with the actual. He was hallucinating? Think of Macbeth seeing the ghost of Banquo just after Macbeth has had him murdered. Lawford believes that if he can beat the witch into silence he'll have some peace. Perhaps he sees the witch as Satan. The trio do come across as evil in the play, don't they?'

The TV news finished and a food programme built around some smirking, amiable chef began. Tane reckoned that a lot of TV shows were obviously constructed to encourage a special sense of intimacy. In many of them, the people taking part worked damn hard to make themselves really likeable. They charmed via the camera. This was how they got to be on the screen at all. They'd have undergone tests in likeability and were then let loose to practise their happy flair in transmission. Programmes that broadsheet critics would label rubbish often had this special matiness and geniality towards the viewer. Tane loved *Top Of The Pops* for instance, presented by that ever-smiling, brilliantly chirpy Jimmy Savile.

Television brought life to Vic and also took him into life. He hadn't ever got that sensation from his time with the classics at Oxford. There was even less chance of it happening now. Who the fuck cared about Apollo wandering around the world looking for somewhere to leave his oracle? No wonder the nymph of the spring at Telphusa tells him to scram and take it to Pytho. He saw staff and students, of course, but felt this was a very enclosed corner.

Ursula had been quiet for a little while concentrating on intelligent finger movements. 'Chote hallucinating?' she said now. 'But does he realize that witches can be vengeful if badly treated? There's one in the play who's so enraged because a woman munching chestnuts tells her to aroint – meaning sod off – when the witch asks her for one that she's going to take it out on the woman's husband who's over Aleppo way. Distance no object, see, when it comes to payback from a witch?'

Vic said, 'There might be some special, transcendental link between witches and chestnuts. Shakespeare knew a lot about that kind of folklore thing. If the witches foresee disaster they've got it right for Macbeth, haven't they, and that's what scares Lawford into antic action?' He paused, knowing that what he intended saying next might be dangerous. 'I feel a kind of shame, Ursula, having watched the awfulness, the deranged, tormented behaviour of Chote in that clip.'

'Shame? How so?'

'Am I one of the causes?'

'Causes of what?'

'Have I helped drive him crazy?'

'Of course you're not and of course you haven't,' she snarled. 'He's done it solo, and gloried in doing it solo. You just happen to be there at the other end of the city. You've done nothing to damage him. In fact some would say you've been insipidly docile. Your only fault is no fault at all – you just happen to be there.'

'Being there is what I mean. By being there I scare him. Whitehall might look on me as a possible top man in a merger. Has this pushed him towards mental breakdown?'

'Oh, stop being so fucking noble and selfless, Vic.' She pulled her hand back. 'This is a kind of grandiosity: you imagine you're so influential.'

'While he's engaged in that idiocy with the sheathed sword and the upset cauldron, I'm calm and safe on another float, surrounded by imported, here-today-gone-tomorrow figures who ensure I get lots of lovely attention and reflected prestige. There's something disgusting about it, something shoddy and sly. Yes, shame, I'm ashamed, Urs. I feel like going over to Sedge in the morning and telling Lawford we should consider proposing the two institutions must join, he the Number One, me his deputy. He's older and I could move up when he retires. He was probably thinking of that kind of change when he came prospecting in the Volvo with the witch. I think the idea would be very acceptable to him.'

'Of course it bloody would. But if you do anything like that you can say goodbye to me, Vic. Or you won't have time to say goodbye, I'll be gone. Screw your courage to the sticking place and we'll do OK out of this crisis. I'm a lawyer and I'm trained to win. I wouldn't want to be linked with some soft-centred, infirm-of-purpose prat who's too decent and limp to grab a chance when it's offered on a plate. All hail Victor Horace Tane! That has to be our battle slogan.'

'You remind me of someone when you talk like this and with those kinds of words,' Tane replied. 'You know how much I hate quotations.'

'They're not from *Hamlet*.'

Twenty-Nine

1987

Probably because Neddy Lane-Hinkerton almost always came over as such an amiable, good-humoured type, Geraldine must have told him to do the introductory bit at this Preparatory Parameters Survey (U) meeting. Mart could see and understand that a friendly tone, at least as starters to such a difficult conference, was vital.

It could be a softening-up tactic. But, also, a university, more than any other brand of institution, ought surely to offer a decent show of tolerance, politeness and civility. Geraldine would probably feel it only proper to abide by some sort of token respect for that kind of pious thinking. Neddy wore a pale green summer-weight jacket, a bow tie, one wing purple, the other yellow with silver stars, and scarlet trousers, also summer weight. His shoes were costly looking black lace-ups; Mart thought Neddy appeared relaxed, unreproachful, light-hearted.

Getting unhurried, joyous stress on to each key word, and speaking from the decidedly left side of his mouth, Ned told Chote, 'On the train, Principal, Geraldine and I realized we both revelled in the chance to get away from London, and come to spend an all too short a time, but welcome, nonetheless, in this gorgeous part of the country where Sedge lies.' He lingered especially on the two different 'g' sounds in 'gorgeous'. There was a nice rhythm to the whole statement. Ned might look flashy in his gear, but he knew how to manage a complicated sentence.

'Yes, Sedge fits in to its good surrounds very well,' Chote said.

To Mart, this seemed sweet and banal enough, yet he thought he detected some Lawford-style arson there, too.

'Oh, certainly,' Geraldine said, with a sort of congratulatory smile, *her* sort of congratulatory smile, meaning it might or might not be truly congratulatory.

211

'That bastard Dunning deserved what he got, and he knows it,' Chote replied. 'I wish I could have done more. Bruises suit him.' It sounded as though he were answering a reproach, though none had been made. There was no forerunner. He would choose the agenda and decide what came first.

'You mean the incident on the lorry?' Geraldine said. 'We heard something of that – a moment or two of it on television news.'

'They networked it – regarding it as *so* funny and quaint,' Chote said.

'Oh, I wouldn't say that, Principal,' Ned replied.

'Wouldn't you, wouldn't you?' Chote barked.

'When you tell us he deserved it, what exactly do you mean, Lawford?' Geraldine said.

'Did he go to the police?' Chote said. 'No, he didn't. The police went to him, though, and he sent them away, said he didn't want to make any charges. The police themselves told me this. They'd asked him about what you call the *incident* and he'd said it was all part of the Bounty Week show, with me as Macbeth, the great warrior, acting as great warriors did in those ancient times, wielding their sword. The police said there were still red marks on his neck and the side of his face, and probably on the clothed parts of his body, but he insisted these were all according to the scenario and for the sake of authenticity in the *Macbeth* sketch. The sergeant termed it "virtual reality" and commented that we'd both taken our roles excellently in the interests of charity.'

'But that's not really what the onslaught was about?' Geraldine asked.

'Of course it's not what it was about,' Chote said. He spoke crisply, like one who lived among great spiritual and visionary matters and who knew very few others capable of such insights. His pallor seemed to intensify, as though he wanted to assure people that he felt no red rage at Geraldine's need to ask her superfluous question. Mart thought Lawford probably did feel the red rage, but he wouldn't want his skin suffused and mottled at this point. 'It was about something profound, something of massive significance,' Chote said. 'This is what I'm getting at when I say he deserved the beating. He's ashamed, and rightly ashamed, about how he provoked it. We should note what Lane-Hinkerton said during his intro.'

'Which part of what I said, Principal?' Neddy asked.

'The way Sedge has made itself an integral part of this city, part of its, as it were, fine context,' Chote said.

'Well, yes indeed, I definitely stand by that,' Neddy said with slow earnestness.

'And I definitely agree,' Geraldine said.

'Jasper Dunning had questioned Sedge's position,' Chote said.

'In what particulars, Principal?' Neddy asked.

'This would be at our conversation near the cauldron,' Chote replied. 'He spoke as though Sedge would soon be no part of that context, that pleasant local background, because there would be no Sedge.'

Mart saw Neddy glance at Geraldine. They both stayed brilliantly deadpan but Martin guessed they

213

were at Sedge to pronounce pretty much the same thing. 'That's absurd, Lawford,' Geraldine said. 'Sedge will endure.'

'Dunning said this likely extinction resulted from my policies as principal,' Chote replied. 'He's an archaeologist and accustomed to looking for evidence of what brought certain organisations and systems down.'

'I can assuredly understand better why you would have attacked the subversive sod,' Neddy said.

'Thank you,' Chote said.

'It's a blatant, cruel insult,' Neddy said.

'It is, it is,' Geraldine said. Mart waited for her to add something like, 'And yet, and yet,' but for the moment she kept that locked away. This was still only the opening minutes of the P.P. Survey (U). Pleasantries had temporary charge.

Chote, though, did speak. 'Oh, yes, you two see it as a blatant, cruel insult, don't you, but correct, just the same? It's why you're here.'

Soft-voiced and reeking of reasonableness, Geraldine said, 'But that's such a negative manner of looking at things, Lawford, not at all like your usual forthright, confident self.' Mart interpreted this as: 'your usual blunt, arrogant, bullying self.'

In Chote's office suite, they were sitting with coffees around one end of the conference area's long oak table, nobody at the head in the bigger, heavier, boss-man's chair. Mart knew Chote would find it not just unnecessary but pathetic to advertise his suzerainty by taking this spot. They were on his territory, still his territory, and

214

anyone should be able to sense that immediately without a prompt from furniture. Those who couldn't ought to be sent on a course in sensitivity. As to Geraldine's word, 'negative', he would have regarded it as hopelessly negative to show lack of faith in his own inborn and instant, deep impressiveness.

Geraldine said, 'We – and I speak not just as Ned and myself, but also the minister – we see nothing at Sedge that cannot be put right.'

'Put right?' Chote replied. 'This means you see something, some *things,* wrong. It's as I said – you agree with Jasper Dunning.'

'Yes, can be put right,' Geraldine said. She was obviously used to ignoring what she didn't want to hear, and sticking to her line. 'Yes, can be put right,' she repeated.

'Nothing, but nothing, is in an irreversible state,' Ned declared. If Geraldine could say something twice, he would, too.

'Well, we are glad of that,' Chote said. Mart noticed that 'we' parodying Geraldine's. Mart assumed it meant Lawford and himself. Chote obviously thought of the meeting as two camps, Sedge's insiders, Sedge's malevolent incursers. Mart wasn't sure what he felt about that. Often these days at Sedge he wasn't sure what he felt about a clearly important issue except that it was clearly important. He'd begun to sympathize with that betwixt-and-between, but-on-the-other-hand, character, Sir Thomas More, in Robert Bolt's play, *A Man For All Seasons.*

'You're here about the banquet, aren't you?' Chote said.

'The banquet is inevitably part of it, yes,' Geraldine said.

'And the banquet is one of those things that you would like to "put right",' Chote said.

'We believe that discussion about the banquet could be useful,' Neddy said.

'You think plans for the banquet are not . . . what was your term? Not "irreversible",' Chote said.

'The banquet is a minor issue when seen against the general Sedge debts schedule as revealed in the recent audit,' Geraldine replied.

Chote said, 'But the banquet has become a . . . what's the word, Martin?'

'A touchstone, a symbol or emblem,' Mart said.

'Exactly,' Chote said.

'We feel – that's the minister, as well as Ned and myself – that the banquet should be abandoned,' Geraldine said. 'We advise this with great reluctance. And, of course, we see the difficulties. The invitations will have gone out long ago and the number of acceptances is known and provisionally planned for. But perhaps *very* provisionally. The audit's alarming discoveries were, naturally, private, but rumours about Sedge's financial state have been in the air for a long while. Ned heard some of them when on his earlier visit. The management at Standfast might well have heard them, too.' She struck her forehead with the base of her thumb. 'But, of course, of course, they've heard them. These are smart business people who run a successful company, not the sort to miss crucial whispers and hints. Lawford, we see an alarming danger that *they,*

216

not Sedge, might cancel the booking, out of fear the cost will be unmet. And I have to tell you that such fear is very reasonable. No, I don't have to tell you because you've probably thought it for yourself already – and have decided you'll gamble on Standfast not pulling the plug.

'Have you thought what the result would be if your bet turned out wrong? This would be very damaging publicity – bad not just for Sedge and yourself, but for universities generally, throughout the UK. The higher education sector would look paupered. Now, you might reply that if the cancellation came from Sedge, and not from the Standfast Fort management the publicity would be bad, also. But at least a cancellation by you and Sedge would show that you have wisely, honestly, dutifully identified the problem and willed its solution, not had that solution arbitrarily imposed by others. This is existentialism on the job, Lawford – the acceptance that things are as they are, and acceptance also of personal responsibility to do something about them. I'm sure you'll be thinking of that de Vigny poem, *La Mort du Loup* (Death of the Wolf).'

'Will I?' Chote said. 'Thanks for letting me know.'

Geraldine quoted: '"Gémir, pleurer, prier est également lâche.

Fais énergiquement ta longue et lourde tâche

Dans la voie où le sort à voulu t'appeler.

Puis, après, comme moi, souffre et meurs sans parler."'

Geraldine continued, 'Happily, of course,

217

we're not dealing with death in your case, Lawford, but it's the qualities of the wolf's response that I think could match yours, I'll translate: "Groaning, weeping, praying are all equally cowardly. Get on energetically with your long-lasting and heavy task, in the path that fate has called you to. Then, afterwards, like myself, suffer and die without a word."'

'"Without a word",' Neddy said. 'This was before those "It's good to talk" ads by the telephone firm. And before the "let it all hang out" philosophy.'

'People would see merit as well as defeat in that decision,' Geraldine said. 'They would recognize this resolute behaviour as typical of Lawford Chote.'

'What's the euphemistic military term for what they are proposing, Mart?' Chote replied.

'Strategic withdrawal,' Mart said. This *mot justing* for Chote seemed to be his only role. He didn't mind that. '"Live to fight another day".'

'Except there wouldn't be one,' Lawford said. 'I don't think I'm exaggerating when I say it takes a while for centenary functions to come round again. Mart can tell us exactly.'

The jocoseness was infantile but Mart played along: 'I think it's every hundred years,' Martin said. 'That's the usual way with centenaries.'

'See?' Chote asked Geraldine and Lane-Hinkerton.

Yes, Martin deduced that his only part in this P.P. Survey (U) confab was going to be as a stand-by dictionary and phrase-maker for Chote. Mart wouldn't even get a mention in the minutes, because of (U). As well as feeling a resemblance to slippery Thomas More, Mart also saw a similarity between himself and Nicholas Jenkins, narrator of Anthony Powell's *A Dance To The Music Of Time* novels. He too is more an observer of others than a participant.

'We have pride at Sedge,' Chote said.

'Certainly, you have, and very justifiably,' Geraldine replied. 'And that pride was clearly demonstrated in the centenary concert at the d'Brindle Hall, where you performed on the cymbals yourself. I wish I could have been present. We received several very fine reports of the occasion.'

Mart reckoned she would be late thirties; she was tallish, narrow-faced but not beaky, with very dark hair cut into jagged stooks, smoky blue eyes, nicely rounded chin, good teeth. She had on an amber cotton jacket with wide lapels over a cerise, high-necked blouse, white, slim-cut trousers, black silver-buckled shoes with middling high heels. She wore a thick-band wedding ring.

'Our feeling is that the concert was an appropriately distinguished function to celebrate Sedge's birthday,' she said. 'We understand that the musicians – your fellow players on the night – remain entirely confident that they will, in due course, get paid.'

And so, Martin thought, the meeting moves into its brutal stage – the agonising contrast between Sedge pride and Sedge bankruptcy made explicit, and made explicit without much subtlety or compassion.

219

'They'll get their money,' Chote said.

'Yes, they will,' Geraldine said, 'if you can accept the proposals, the very constructive proposals, we – that's Ned and myself, on behalf of the minister – the proposals we bring to the survey (U) today.' Lawford had accidentally given her the cue for listing the demands they brought. She had a small, grey canvas travelling bag with her, acting as a briefcase. Geraldine produced some papers and shuffled them to the right page. 'The proposals, then: they are that, with your permission – and, as matters stand for the present nothing can happen without your permission—'

'Your permission is regarded as not merely desirable but obligatory, Principal,' Neddy said.

'Yes, that with your permission a recovery team of eight or nine people will take over the running of Sedge's finances and general admin for a set period of three months and put right what palpably needs to be put right. That would include the payment from special Ministry funding, of the fees and expenses claims of the concert orchestra, including, of course, the fee of the star cymbalist! The concert will be treated as entirely in keeping with the Sedge celebrations and therefore worthy of exceptional, one-off, concert-designated support. Although the team are mainly financial experts they can appreciate and respond to the larger, wider aspects.

'You'll probably say, Lawford, and quite reasonably say, that, on the face of it, at least, there's an absurdity about bringing in this team, with all the extra costs involved – travel, hotel bed and board – when their task is to reduce and eventually eliminate debt. But those costs will run into thousands only, whereas the team will have as its objective the saving of millions. Its members would be salaried by us, of course. Some of your finance and administrative people could be stood off temporarily and continue to draw their pay from Sedge – a kind of suspension, with no implication of criminal or incompetent behaviour. "An organisational re-jigging", that's how the moves could be described. The team might require one or two of your people to stay on to answer any queries and speed matters up by explaining on the spot how the various offices have been functioning.'

Mart thought she'd already have a statistically documented view on 'how the various offices have been functioning'. Catastrophically. The audit said so. But she wouldn't pre-judge anything further. Or not aloud, anyway.

Lawford stroked his long, deceptively sacramental face with the plump, short fingers of his right hand. 'So, what do we make of it, Mart?' His voice was warm with fellow-feeling.

Oh, God, this went further than providing lexicon help, Chote was asking for commitment. 'Make of what, Lawford?' Martin said.

'Geraldine's existentialist proposal.'

'I don't think I've ever understood the proper meaning of existentialist,' Mart replied.

'To put it another way, then: Geraldine and Lane-Hinkerton would like me to vote for my personal extinction *"sans parler"* like the wolf,'

Chote said. '"Kindly get lost, Lawford, and keep your mouth shut about the circumstances."'

'I don't think that's at all fair, Lawford,' Geraldine said. 'In fact, it's fucking ungrateful and perverse.'

'They move their holy "team" in for a strictly measured period of three months,' Chote said. 'But, once they're in and, after those three months, Whitehall decides this is not quite an adequate period to work the required miracles, how are they to be got out? Geraldine and Lane-Hinkerton dodge off again from the boredom and rush of London, poor dears, and they arrive to announce that the squad needs another three, or six or twenty-six or sixty-six months.

'And, Mart, there's another issue. The take-over group will establish their own pattern of running things during those three months or more. That's why they would be here, isn't it? The team's own pattern of running things will be deemed successful, or at least promising by the minister, Geraldine and Lane-Hinkerton. They would have a career interest in declaring it good, and they'll see one major consequence of this. The new style of management will most likely be very different from the previous style of management, meaning mine. They will believe – they will choose to believe – that I could never adapt to the changed, splendid system and should therefore be force-fed early retirement, eased out, kicked out, replaced.'

'This is a totally distorted version of things, Lawford,' Geraldine said. 'We are here to help you.'

'That so?' Lawford replied.

'Our aim is to prevent development of a situation where all funding to Sedge stops. I mean the most basic, regular funding. You'll probably not be able to pay staff or keep the lights on.'

'As to *"sans parler"*, Principal, I would say that, on the contrary, there has, in fact, been a great deal of discussion, not *"sans parler"* in the least,' Lane-Hinkerton stated.

'What we've had is a long diktat from Geraldine and we don't like it, do we, Martin?' Chote replied. 'Geraldine, you say you need my permission to move in your gifted, encroaching platoon. We do not give it. We refuse them entry, do we not, Mart? I'm applying my existentialist right and duty to take responsibility for my unique selfhood.'

Mart thought Chote might be taking responsibility not just for *his* own unique existentialist selfhood but for Mart's also, and Mart didn't really care for this.

Thirty

2014

Mart reckoned he must have done the chairing job of the statues committee pretty well because there was unanimous agreement that he should pose as both Lawford Chote and Victor Tane, or Victor Tane and Lawford Chote, when they all

223

moved out into the grounds of the Sedge and Charter campuses, or the Charter and Sedge campuses, to select and test possible sites for the statues. They moved between the two campuses in a convoy of seven cars like some head of state arriving at a conference with his administrative and security back-up.

The group's all-round approval showed Martin that he had been right from the start to avoid commitment and partisanship; and, particularly, to resist any invitation to inner-circle croneydom from Lawford Chote. Mart saw that the committee trusted him, and he felt grateful. Even when they were considering what might be the most suitable ground for the mooted double statue on a single plinth they wanted Mart to represent both Lawford Chote and Victor Tane, or Victor Tane and Lawford Chote. Logistically, this involved shifting just short of a metre from his position as, say, Lawford, to the other end of the imagined plinth where he would become Victor, or vice versa.

Members accepted that there were hints in what people had said during the several indoor meetings which might indicate a special affection or a special hostility towards one or other of the pair and that this could result in favouritism when picking what were regarded as the best site or sites and who should occupy it or them. Mart thought of that unpleasant tiff between Jed Laver (Industrial Relations) and Gordon Upp (Linguistics) because Upp thought Laver had denigrated Lawford Chote and protected Tane.

Martin recalled that there had been a lot of profound discussion in committee sessions about the feet of the two statues if the ultimate choice was for the double statue on the single plinth, rather than an individual plinth for each. Someone had very perceptively pointed out that the feet were not really feet at all according to the normal definition of feet, but only part of the same stone entity as the rest of the statues. Martin went along with this analysis and felt it would be stupid to pretend he had to free his feet at one end of the plinth – e.g., the Lawford end – in order to move and become Victor Tane at the other end, or to free his feet at the Victor Tane end and become Lawford Chote. Instead, Martin believed he should step fluently and easily across the gap and turn into a stone Victor Tane, if he had been a stone Lawford Chote up until this point, or around the other way. The possible double occupancy of a plinth did make some difficulties but Mart thought common sense could deal with them. The committee – and Martin himself – should surely keep in mind continuously that the statues and their feet and footwear were, when one came down to it, all from the same chunk of stone or brass. The feet and their shoes did not stand on the plinth in the usual meaning of the word 'stand'. The feet and shoes were *of* that plinth, not *on* it.

As to height, at five foot ten inches Martin came somewhere between Chote and Tane, or Tane and Chote, but this did not trouble the committee. They could supply the plus or minus inches in their imaginations, a plus if Mart was

225

Tane and a minus if Chote. After all, when the actual statues rather than Mart were in place, people looking at them would have to make a much bigger imaginative jump than was required to see Mart as someone taller (Tane) or shorter (Chote). They would have to see stone or brass as living flesh, bone and blood – quite a step. In the kind of university teaching of English Literature that Mart did there was a theory summed up in the phrase 'The author is dead.' This didn't necessarily mean the author was dead, although, obviously, many of the writers studied *were* in fact dead. But what the phrase signified as a piece of critical theory was, once the author published his/her work he/she had no further control of it. The reader was supreme and could make of the item whatever he/she liked. She/he could say, 'I love this poem because when I first read it I'd just had one of the best liver and bacon dinners ever.' This might seem irrelevant to many, but it is not irrelevant to that particular reader. Similarly, the matter of Mart's height or lack of it could be adjusted to the correct measurements in the imaginations of the committee.

Using what was known as 'The Method' style of acting, Mart tried to think his way into the very differing minds of each principal and convey their personal qualities by the way he held his head as he gazed forward on his notional plinth, and his styles of stance. When he was Lawford he set his face to show general belligerence, some contempt for most of humanity, but also a determination to give as many components of that humanity as he could the boon of higher education. It wasn't easy to get this mix of curmudgeon and philanthropist. Mart attempted it by shaping his lips as for an imminent foul-mouthed snarl, arranging his shoulders as though to help with the delivery of a concussing left fist punch, yet softening his eyes into a gaze proclaiming not just goodwill to all men, but super goodwill to all men, and women.

For Tane, Martin went for a look of quiet orderliness and decency but coupled with a resolve to see himself on top in the long run. This was largely a chin matter. Mart didn't make it jut like a reckless challenge but he endowed it with four-square solidity and strength. Also Mart put one of his feet slightly forward of the other signifying the likelihood of a sudden, unexpected dash to victory, despite seeming until then only a runner-up to Lawford and Sedge. This potential spurt forward was akin to, but not the same as, the move Mart made when changing ends of the double occupied solo plinth.

Undergraduates on their way to and from lectures of course noticed the cluster of women and men at the various selected sites on the two campuses staring at Mart in one of his transfigurations and judging its suitability as against other nominated sites.

'What's it about?' a girl asked. She had on short purple shorts, a detached stiff white shirt collar fastened around her neck by a stud, but no shirt, only a black singlet, and a denim waistcoat. She carried a laptop and a half full water bottle.

'It's about the future,' Elvira said. 'But in the past.'

'What future?' she said.

'You,' Elvira replied.

'Me? How?'

'This is Lawford Chote,' Elvira said.

'Lawford who?' the girl replied.

'He had you in mind.'

'How could he? He doesn't know me. I'd remember if I'd met someone called Lawford. And Chote.'

'We're talking about 1987,' Elvira said.

'1987? I wasn't born then,' the girl replied.

'That's why I said he had you in mind. You were the future.'

'So the future is now, is it?'

'It was then,' Elvira said.

'Then? But this is not 1987 and he's here. You're all gawping at him. He's the present, not the future nor the past.'

'These are merely technical points,' Elvira said.

'The course I'm on is technical,' the girl said. 'I.T. Information Technology. There's nothing mere about it.'

'He'd be pleased to hear you argue back like that.'

'Well, I can tell him, can't I?' She yelled at Mart, 'Hey, Lawford or whatever. I'm technical.'

Mart liked the look of the purple shorts and wished he could have smiled in appreciation. But this would have been wrong for his present embattled Chote self.

Thirty-One

1987

Martin had another phone call from Neddy Lane-Hinton. 'As I believe I said, Mart, a little while ago, I have what could, I think, be reasonably termed a special extra mural relationship with Geraldine.'

'Yes, you did mention something along those lines.'

'It puts me in a particularly influential position vis-à-vis her.'

'Yes, I can see it might.'

'A screwing arrangement as simply that – a screwing arrangement – would surely strike both Geraldine and myself as slightly, or more than slightly, degrading. Animal-like.'

'Yes, I understand.'

'Well, you would, you would, Mart. We've heard how you've made yourself something of a specialist in that general area as mentored by *Lady Chatterly's Lover.* But Geraldine and I talk. There is mind-contact as well as bodily. I don't say one is superior. They can comfortably co-exist, not at all like Marvell's *A Dialogue Between The Soul And The Body* where each is sniping at and thuggishly berating the other. The soul calls the body a dungeon and the body calls the soul a tyrant. Foolish polarisation. Ger and I avoid that.'

229

'This happy acceptance of the two modes I can understand, too.'

'In one sense, of course, she is a boss figure.'

'She's the sort who'll probably qualify for a damehood in due course.'

'Possibly. I don't think I've ever had it off with a baroness. I'm very keen on that gear they wear in the Upper House.'

'She might let you try it on,' Mart said.

'So, at any rate, there are times when our conversation is complete and utter business, and therefore in the nature of orders, instructions, to me, the tone and message unaffected by our extra, unofficial and personal connection. That's as you would expect. But occasional topics arise which, although clearly business items, can also be influenced in some measure by that sweeter, fleshly link we've established.

'For instance, Mart, Geraldine versus Chote in the barren (U) meeting that never took place. She was altogether serious when she told him that if he didn't accede to the proposed takeover of Sedge management by a Ministry team she would cut off all funding to him and Sedge so there would be no money for basics, including wages. She could probably find in the articles of British university governance a ruling to be implemented by someone of Geraldine's rank, that if the behaviour of a principal, president, provost or chancellor became flagrantly chaotic and damaging, there would be not only an option to stop further waste of taxpayers' money, but a directive to do so, an absolute duty.'

'Yes, there is an impression of power about her,' Mart said.

'There is power, but there is also a tenderness, something which I can occasionally reach mainly on account of the exceptional closeness we achieve from time to time outside the parameters of usual university polity. For instance, Mart, the Sedge wages.'

'I get no word from the bank that mine have been discontinued.'

'Nor will you, Mart. Not so far, anyway. Why am I so sure?'

'Yes, why, Neddy?'

'I intervened.'

'In what sense?' Mart replied.

'I made an appeal to that tenderness I mentioned just now, and which I knew was present, though not immediately detectable.'

'You have a special "in" with her?'

'Yes, it could be put like that, I suppose. When a stopper on Sedge funding was first considered as leverage against Lawford Chote I naturally thought of that delightful as it were bonding lunch at The Lock Gate. Although you took something other than the black-pudding hash, I felt a real and rare harmony existed between us immediately.'

'Certainly,' Mart said. 'I meant no disparagement of the black-pudding hash. It was just that my taste buds on that day, and specifically and limited to that day, required something different.'

'There's no accounting for taste buds. The occasion remains in my memory as a brilliantly pleasant

231

one, and, consequently, I found I could not go along with Geraldine's plan to activate a general curse on Sedge. I tried to envisage the impact of the sudden block put on your pay. It would not be simply a matter of withheld money. No, such withholding indicates a unilateral destruction of contracts. It is uncivilized. It is anti-civilized. The foundations of good order are shaken, perhaps terminally shaken. This is not the kind of pain one wants imposed on a good friend with whom one has, so to speak, broken bread. I described my reaction to Ger. She knew, of course, that we had made such a fine occasion of that visit to you. I said I didn't wish to be a party to such undeserved punishment of someone I had come to think of as a chum – and I hope I'm not presuming, Mart.'

'Not at all,' Mart said. 'A feeling shared.'

'Thank you, thank you,' Neddy replied. 'Many a boss would grow angry and dismissive to have his/her plans brazenly resisted in such outright fashion by a subordinate. But this is where that tenderness aspect began to tell. She could look sympathetically on the kind of sound relationship established by you and me at The Lock Gate. Why? Because, Mart, she knows from our own – hers and mine – relationship that I am one who prizes such strong and warm affection between two people. I don't mean she thinks there's a gay element linking you and me. No. But she can appreciate the worth of simple, heartfelt camaraderie and companionship. She and I have that, though boosted by occasional vivid, intemperate sex. The sex is fine but not essential, Mart.'

'I think I follow, Ned.'

'She listened to my objection and for a while grew silent, obviously weighing its worth. Her head was on my chest and I could trace the twirls and ridges of her left ear via my skin. As a matter of fact we were just winding down after a very charming love passage on a Turkish rug in the sitting room of her exceptionally stylish home in Highgate, London. Her husband was on a fishing trip in Scotland and their son away at Eton. As you probably know, even a top-quality rug can scorch knees during this kind of vigorous set-to, but Geraldine had, has, a conscience about taking me into any of the beds there. I could appreciate such nice delicacy and still do, Mart. To invite a man to follow her up the stairs surely indicates calculated intent, whereas to yield to sudden, ungovernable desire on an imported, beautifully handwoven floor covering gives a touch of inevitability and *jeux d'esprit* adultery. Of course, unless she's on top *her* knees don't suffer. But that's simply one of the privileges of high office.'

'Adaptability is a splendid quality,' Mart replied.

'I think I mentioned previously the biting.'

'Yes. You spoke of its controlled nature.'

'There was none this time, controlled or uncontrolled.'

'Did you deduce something from this, Neddy, like the dog that didn't bark in the Sherlock Holmes story, this silence giving the great detective an important clue?'

'Her mind, preoccupied to a degree. Do you remember what was said about President of the U.S.A. Gerald Ford – that he couldn't chew gum and think at the same time?'

'Gerald and Geraldine similar?'

'She had some thinking to do, yes, after what I'd said. She seemed to feel it would be inappropriate – sort of tapas behaviour – to nibble at my neck skin and/or nipples, given the circs.'

'Well, yes, there has to be a protocol about that kind of thing,' Mart replied.

'My body was naturally confused. It is used to a certain sequence and the biting figured in it as a major component. She raised her head off my chest and I thought she was about to get back on track with the tooth work. Not at all. Although we were on a damned expensive Turkish rug and had been drinking some decent brut champagne she was plainly unsettled, Mart. Moving up a little so that her breasts rested reassuringly on mine she said that OK, she would accept my line about the potential pay freeze, and its impact indiscriminately on all Sedge staff, you included. Instead, she would closely focus her reaction to where she could now see it should have been focussed from the outset.

'Geraldine thanked me for helping her to think more clearly and equitably. She detailed a new plan. Possibly through Rowena Chote, who was more likely than Lawford to appreciate the realities of their situation, Geraldine would offer Lawford a U.F.C. package that would compel him to take early retirement, early meaning immediate. This could be managed without too much humiliation for Chote and little loss of dignity. She said the Sedge debts were only a part of the trouble, though the major part. She couldn't ignore reports of that Macbeth idiocy on the charity float, and

234

the soaked spectators. Nor did she like the rumours about staff quitting Sedge and unease among Sedge students as to the worth of their degrees – if, that is, Sedge was able to continue courses and award degrees. So, Victor Tane would be appointed at once to a joint principalship of the two merged universities and would host the Standfast Fort Banquet backed by further moneys from the U.F.C. She says merger she says.

'I realized, Mart, that although she hadn't got her teeth into me she had into Lawford Chote, regardless of what she'd said about only minor humiliation and loss of dignity. She stood and retrieved the champagne cork. I said I'd get rid of it and the bottle in a public waste bin on the way home. She said, "Good" and came and snuggled down again with me on the rug in front of the imitation coal gas fire on at full blaze to prevent the absence of clothes leading to a chill. Anyone looking in would have regarded this as a very homely tableau. "I'm glad all that's tidied, Ned," she said.'

'I expect she was,' Mart said.

Thirty-Two

1987

But Martin loathed some parts of Geraldine's revised campaign, especially her plan to drag Rowena into the crisis. Geraldine would ask for her help in convincing Lawford that he should chuck the Sedge principalship immediately and disappear, pension and severance lump sum gorgeously intact, though not his reputation. Ever since he brought Rowena out of her booze-aided snooze at his inaugural, Mart had felt a strong, subliminal link with her. They had chimed. This was big. He wanted her well-being, her lifelong well-being. He didn't think Geraldine's 'tidying' scheme would secure that. He had to protect Rowena. Theirs was a unique, mystical connection established by *Lady Chatterly's Lover,* and Mart's commentary on its sex theme. Rowena depended on him, even though she didn't know it. He owed her. He had words that could rout her gin coma.

There were two possible outcomes if she did what Geraldine required. Neither was good for Rowena and/or her marriage. If she succeeded and Lawford eventually agreed to cave in, he would always, in his eminently paranoid way, think he had been pressured, betrayed, by a traitor. Hadn't Mart seen that kind of crazy, elaborate suspicion take hold of him on the day of the Volvo reconnaissance to Charter Mill? Such mistrust could permanently put a shadow over his relationship with Rowena. Alternatively, if he rejected Rowena's advice and refused to leave, his notion that she belonged to a conspiracy against him could be even more powerful. He would see her for ever as a turncoat. And when by some other means Geraldine got him out of his job he might still regard Rowena as one of the gang against him and not want her in his life any longer.

Mart went back to that phrase, 'by some other means'. He did accept now that Lawford could not stay much longer in the principalship. Neddy had told of Geraldine's switch of tactics against Chote and accounted for it by describing her essential, inner tenderness towards Mart himself and all the rest of the Sedge staff. Maybe. But what Martin gathered from the phone chat with Lane-Hinkton was that if one scheme for getting rid of Lawford had to be abandoned, she would find another: she'd give up the idea of cutting off Sedge's money, but she'd trawl for some substitute way of making him go – Rowena's pleas perhaps. Geraldine's 'tenderness' rested on an adamantine backup. Perhaps, too, she had an Education Minister driving her to fix an end for Lawford, regardless of how. Mart, for so long chary, even afraid, of commitment now knew he had to get committed. He must tell Lawford direct, with no involvement of Rowena, that he could not win in this battle with Geraldine and Whitehall. He should agree to what sounded like excellent terms from Geraldine and move, with little publicity and embarrassment, into an enjoyable and peaceful retirement. Rowena would bear no taint of treachery. Mart thought he'd give Lawford a ring on the internal phone and try to fix an appointment. Most probably, Chote would be shocked and possibly hurt to get such a recommendation from him. This Mart regretted. Perhaps he, not Rowena, would be regarded by Lawf as the rat. Up till today Chote had seemed to value Mart's opinion on all topics. Now, that esteem would inevitably be withdrawn. Never mind. Martin sought only the best for Rowena and Lawford – particularly Rowena – and had come to believe that the best was for both of them to bow out.

Mart's intention to ring for an appointment turned out to be unnecessary, because it was Chote who arranged the get-together. Mart was giving a lecture to undergraduates on what he called 'The Destruction Of Language For The Sake of Meaning' in some Shakespeare sonnets such as: 'When my love swears that she is made of truth/I do believe her, though I know she lies.'

He thought he heard a door open behind him and realized that most of the students were looking at something to his right. Mart stopped his commentary on the word 'believe' in the sonnet – which meant its opposite – and turned his head to see what the disturbance was. Lawford Chote stood a few metres away. He came forward to the lectern. 'Please allow me to interrupt for a moment, would you, Professor Moss?'

'Of course, Principal,' Mart said. Of course, of course.

'Something has happened which I need advice on, not simply from you, Professor, but from a representative sample of Sedge students, such as your class here today. By a striking coincidence the theme of your lecture has a bearing on what I wish to discuss.' He edged Mart away from the lectern and stood behind it. Mart went to sit in the front row of the hall.

'Recently, a meeting took place in Sedge which did not take place, just as in the poem he believes his mistress but doesn't. It couldn't have taken place because you, Professor Moss, were present and this makes the existence of the meeting impossible.'

'Yes, I had that outlined for me,' Mart said.

Chote was in shirtsleeves. He had on the waist-coat, but not the jacket, of a grey suit, with a gold watch chain across half his midriff. The shirt was white with narrow crimson stripes. It was open-necked, with no tie. What looked like a couple of inches of cream thermal vest showed behind it. His face radiated combativeness as it often did, but Mart also saw there a lurking sadness, even despair. Perhaps that was to be expected, though Mart wouldn't have expected it from *him*.

Chote said, 'At this meeting which didn't take place there was a discussion which didn't take place, either, as Professor Moss could explain to you all if the meeting and discussion had occurred.'

'Certainly,' Mart said.

'One of the points that couldn't have been made at this non-meeting was a warning from a Ministry of Education official that if I did not give up my principalship of Sedge at once all funding to the university would cease. We would be put into a state of siege. Obviously, this would have been worrying if the threat had been voiced. I would have rejected it and subsequently decided to ask a typical Sedge group – say, Professor Moss's class and Professor Moss himself, whether I would have done the right thing in dismissing that proposal and threat with maximum, principal-style disdain.'

'Disdain is the only possible response,' Samantha Colley, a red-haired girl at the end of a row, said. 'Oxford showed it to Thatcher. We have a precedent.' Sandra had been in one of his seminar groups last year.

'Could I call for a vote: Stay or Go?' Lawford said.

Every student in the room raised a hand for Stay.

'Thank you,' Chote said.

'But the professor didn't vote,' the girl said.

'I think he should go,' Mart said.

Thirty-Three

1987

Among the student attack group that broke commando-style into the centenary banquet at Standfast Fort's mahogany panelled, high-windowed, historic Plain Parlour, Mart spotted a few of his own English Literature undergraduates, including Sandra Colley, the red-haired girl, today wearing a turquoise jogging outfit and almost matching green mountaineering boots. Mart wondered if they'd had cooperation from someone in the Parlour work force – a cook, a waiter, a sommelier. This, after all, was a fortress and built to keep enemies out. Had someone deliberately left a door unlocked? But why? Perhaps there were Sedge students doing part-time jobs in the kitchen or around the tables

240

and sympathetic to the Lawford cause, grateful for his expansionism that had given them a university place.

The timing of the inrush struck Mart as suspiciously perfect. They entered, yelling and baying, a few minutes into a speech by Victor Tane as newly appointed principal of the combined institutions of Sedge and Charter Mill, following the well-earned retirement of Principal Chote from Sedge.

It would have been kindly, Mart thought, if they could have left two empty chairs at the top table for Rowena and Lawford. Had they been invited? Was there a forwarding address for them? Judging by what Martin knew of Tane, such an invitation seemed the sort of decent, commiserating gesture he might have made. After all, they were a legitimate, renowned part of Sedge's centenary; in some ways more legitimate and renowned than the Tanes. It occurred to Mart that in the future there might be a proposal for some sort of memorial to honour Lawford; say, a statue. If so, a complementary or counter proposal would probably emerge: another statue, but this one, Victor Tane. The duality would almost certainly lead to endless debate about which statue should get the more prominent site; would the Tane statue dominate if the two were close because of his height; would it be necessary to shift the statues around the city so that each had a spell in the Charter campus and a spell in the Sedge; would it be mere sentimentality to give Chote a statue although he'd sunk Sedge in its previous form?

But if a plan for two statues went ahead would they be on a shared plinth or each have his own? Mart had a feeling that the plinth allocation question would entail profound, lengthy disputation. Although some might regard plinths as neutral, uncontroversial slabs, Mart suspected they could become of towering significance then.

Of course, the Chotes would not have accepted an invitation to the Plain Parlour banquet. Lawford would imagine Tane was crowing over him, lording it and being magnanimous in victory. Lawford would probably phrase it as 'being sodding magnanimous in victory the gaping-nostrilled, Latin versifying prat', though.

There were fourteen or fifteen in the assault party, Mart reckoned, nine men, five or six women. They came in four units of four, four, three, three or four. That could mean they'd been smuggled in by instalment as opportunities appeared. It took about two minutes for them to assemble at the far end of the Parlour. Mart thought he could detect clever tactical organisation, like troops in street fighting advancing in small formations, maximising cover. Many of the diners failed to notice the build-up, their attention on Tane's vacuous celebratory words. At first, before things went destructive and dangerous, the students seemed satisfied to stand at the far end of the Parlour and shout and wave cardboard banners with 'Bring Back Lawford', 'Lawford's The Lad',

'Lawford We Love You' in crimson letters. 'Hail to Lawford', they shouted. 'We want Lawford'.

'Tane, get back to your fucking Mill,' Sandra Colley screamed. The lettered message on her banner read: 'Chote IS Sedge, and Sedge is Chote', like Rod Steiger as Napoleon in the film, *Waterloo*: 'I am France and France is me'. 'Foul Betrayal', another banner mourned and another said: 'Down with the Thatcher Lapdogs'.

Apart from a pause or two and a few sentences that didn't quite add up to good sense, Tane bravely kept going. At the end, there was unfervent but respectful applause. Then, while they waited for the desserts and toasts, Tane, at the top table with the minister, the Lord Mayor and Lady Mayoress, Ursula Tane, editor Alan Norton-Hord and other persons of interest, seemed to fall into vigorous conversation, possibly about the grand prospects for the new double-unit Sedge. Somehow, Tane seemed even stringier in formal garb. The polarities of black jacket and bow tie on a white shirt appeared too definite and strong for his wispy frame. But he had doggedness and, for a moment, Martin thought that by ignoring the bellows and snarls, he might have triumphed. The banners were lowered suddenly and chucked aside.

Martin soon saw why, though: the protesters wanted their hands free to snatch missiles from the feast remnants and, crockery, cutlery, glass on the guest tables. These opening salvoes were reasonably harmless items – fruit, various types

243

of cheese, leftover slices of sticky toffee pudding, and gateaux, bread rolls. The targets were all on the top table. Again Mart sensed a battle briefing pre the offensive, its objective clearly stated. Geraldine, in an elegant navy blue boardroom suit was hit by a half orange on her lapel. Something wettish and murky lodged itself in Tane's scarce hair. Ursula got half a ripe Camembert under her right eye and clawed the bits off and hurled them back, hissing, 'I'll kill the rioting jerk.'

Despite Roy Gormand's forecast that Mart would be on the top table, he was, in fact, seated in the body of the hall at a very ordinary spot and remained untroubled.

Standfast had security staff, male and female, and several of them came into the Parlour at a rush now and moved fast towards the invaders. This was when the missiles became more dangerous as some serious fighting began as security tried to drive the students out. Crockery, cutlery, glass and even chairs were hurled. A china tureen shattered on the flagged floor when half a dozen wrestling guards and intruders barged against it. Several diners, some of the students and some of the security posse, were cut about face and head, and Sandra fell, concussed by a flying chair. Someone phoned for the police and ambulance service.

After about half an hour the Parlour was in something like working order again. Sandra recovered, the rest of the intruders were cleared from the big, handsome room, some possibly arrested, some possibly treated by paramedics from the ambulances. Tane, still with whatever it was darkening his hair, resumed his speech, saying that some birth pangs were unavoidable during the creation of the changed institution and that the 'little recent unfortunate turmoil was, in fact, a heartening sign of vigorous life'.

Thirty-Four

2014

'"Dear Professor Moss".'

Mart read aloud to the statues committee a handwritten letter he'd received from Rowena Chote apparently living now in Hastings on the south coast. She'd obviously decided in view of what was coming to say that she should shun the familiarity of his first name.

Word has reached me here of a proposal to erect a statue of my late husband, Lawford Chote, at Sedge University. Information is sometimes slow in arriving to this area and I hope I am not too late to declare in the strongest terms that the proposal should be rejected outright. Lawford would detest the idea. He was devastated when, Professor Moss, you announced that you thought he should step down at once from his

245

post as principal. He regarded this as incontrovertible evidence of his defeat. He laid great store on your opinion in any controversy following the happy incident at your inaugural lecture upon being promoted to a professorship. Lawford would maintain, if still alive, that vanquished leaders should not be commemorated in any form. He'd consider such a seeming accolade as meaningless and grossly hypocritical. He would find it especially obnoxious, Professor Moss, that you, after your base defection, should now have the unholy impertinence to chair a committee whose ostensible purpose is to decide the form of a monument to him.

Whatever his faults might have been – and there certainly were some – Lawford believed in absolute honesty in all aspects of his life. He was made of truth. He would want no statue, of himself. I, similarly, do not want it and abhor the suggestion. May I ask you, please, to do all you can to get this fart-arseing fucking idea negated. I address my appeal to you because you were the one who brought him down and therefore should be aware of the notion's absurdity more than anyone else, though I'm not sure you *are* aware of it or ever will be.

Yours faithfully, R. Chote.

'Blimey,' Elvira said.

'What incident at your inaugural, Mart?' Lucy said.

'So we go for Tane only, do we?' Gordon Upp said.

'Do we?' Mart replied.

The Age of Disunity

by

JOHN KENT

LONDON
EPWORTH PRESS

FIRST PUBLISHED 1966
by EPWORTH PRESS 1966

Book Steward
FRANK H. CUMBERS

SET IN PLANTIN AND PRINTED IN GREAT BRITAIN BY
BUTLER AND TANNER LTD, FROME AND LONDON

To my former students at
Hartley Victoria College, Manchester

Contents

Introduction   ix

1   Methodist Union   1

2   The Doctrine of the Ministry in Early Nineteenth-century Methodism   44

3   Methodism Misunderstood   86

4   Historians and Jabez Bunting   103

5   Methodism and Politics in the Nineteenth Century   127

6   Anglican Episcopacy and Anglican–Methodist Relations   146

7   Federation or Union?   193

Index of Names   207

Introduction

METHODISM is probably the most misunderstood of English religious movements. It has been presented as the almost miraculous creation of an Oxford don on a horse, when it was really a nation-wide religious reaction whose roots ran far back into the seventeenth century. It has been described as an example of the wildly emotional, irrational side of eighteenth-century England, whereas one of the more unusual elements in this upsurge of popular religion was the absence of any Methodist enthusiasm for an allegedly imminent Second Advent, or for the kind of phenomena—such as glossolalia or 'spiritual healing'—which one associates with Pentecostalism. (No one seems to have been struck by the fact that Methodism might be labelled a Holiness Revival manqué, that as such the movement virtually died in the 1760s, and that this early death largely explains the crisis of identity which has been the central theme of Methodist history ever since.)

Or again, Methodism as a whole is usually classed as part of the Dissenting or Free Church tradition, whereas the most significant Methodist group, the Wesleyans, never identified themselves completely with Nonconformity. Anglican historians also misinterpreted Methodism when they implied that nineteenth-century Methodism was a kind of betrayal of the ideas of John Wesley, who intended his followers to remain a society within the Church of England. There is no solid historical evidence, however, to show that Wesley expected events to take a different course from what they did after his death in 1791 or that he would have regarded the emergence of a Methodist denomination as a serious personal betrayal. And so one might go on: the whole picture of the Evangelical Revival of the eighteenth century has been confused by recent church historians who have ignored the doctrinal differences between the Wesleyan Methodists on the one hand and the Evangelical Anglicans and the followers of the Countess of Huntingdon on the other, and who have blended two sharply opposed groups into a non-historical sentimentalized mish-mash.

On a wider scale, few attempts have been made to interpret Methodism against the general background of English history.

Lecky and Halévy still haunt the scene, while more recent historians seem to accept rather uncritically their assumption that 'Methodism' can be treated as a single compact organic historical force, whereas 'Methodism' was split internally in a way which reflected the divisions of Victorian society and supplied reinforcements to both sides of every struggle. This error, a serious methodological one, occurs in the most recent attempt to interpret nineteenth-century Methodism, the chapter which Mr E. P. Thompson included in his book, *The Making of the British Working-Class*. Mr Thompson's approach is psychological—at one point he describes Methodism as 'a ritualised form of psychic masturbation'; at another he says that 'Methodism is permeated with teaching as to the sinfulness of sexuality and as to the extreme sinfulness of the sexual organs'. Such generalizations have their comic side. But Mr Thompson seriously regards Methodism as the transforming power which disciplined the nineteenth-century working-class in England. Methodist conversions produced 'the psychic ordeal in which the character-structure of the rebellious pre-industrial labourer or artisan was violently recast into that of the submissive industrial worker. . . . It is a phenomenon almost diabolic in its penetration into the very sources of the human personality, directed towards the repression of emotional and spiritual energies.'

Two comments might be made. On the one hand, anyone acquainted with religious groups would be aware that 'conversion' only rarely takes place at the level of seriousness which Mr Thompson is here describing, and that if it does so its social consequences certainly cannot be foreseen with the certainty which he implies. Only a minority of Methodist factory workers are likely to have been 'converted' in this sense, certainly not enough to affect the psychology of the English working-class very greatly. On the other hand, of course, the early working-class had to be disciplined before it would accept long hours of work under factory conditions with very brief week-end rests and little annual holiday, etc. But one does not need to invoke Methodism to explain how this was done; Methodism played only a minor role in the process. The employers used beatings (especially of children in the textile mills), dismissal or threats of dismissal, blacklisting of awkward men in a whole area, heavy fines for absenteeism, the break-up of unions, and the building of factory villages in which the owner had large coercive powers, as methods of negative discipline. Incentive payments were the chief positive approach; drinking and swearing were tackled through fines.[1] The employers certainly compelled their labour force to attend church or chapel wherever possible: behind this, however, lay the hope of persuading the workers to accept the ideal of 'respectability'—not Christianity—as a goal to be achieved through regular hard work. Any respectable variety of religion would do; there is little evidence that manufacturers had the enthusiasm for Methodism which one would expect on Mr Thompson's argument.

The essays in this book—written over a period of years—are attempts to get behind some of these misinterpretations of Methodist history. There is an essay on Methodist Union—the first serious study of the subject—which explodes the myth that Methodist Union encountered no doctrinal difficulties, and attempts to see the whole process against the historical background of the period. I have reprinted the short essay on Halévy as a historian of Methodism because it still seems necessary and relevant to point out how fundamentally ignorant Halévy was of even the simplest facts of Methodist history. Taken together, the essays on early nineteenth-century Wesleyan doctrine of the ministry, on Jabez Bunting and on 'Federation or Union', at least show the complexity of Methodist history after Wesley; they contain the first serious attempt to explain the divisions of nineteenth-century Methodism; and a much-needed account of the development of the Methodist doctrine of the Church and Ministry between 1791 and 1932. The final essay, on Anglican episcopacy and Methodism, contains a careful re-examination of the causes of the original separation of Methodism from the Church of England and an attempt to put the present Anglican-Methodist controversy about episcopacy into its historical setting. As such, it is intended as a contribution to ecumenical theology.

John Wesley's personality has overshadowed the idea of Methodism, and interest in him has largely distracted attention from the wider business of studying Methodist history. Students of English history in the nineteenth century still invoke 'Evangelicalism' as the solution of almost all their religious problems.

---

[1] See an interesting article in the *Economic History Review*, December 1963, by Sidney Pollard, 'Factory Discipline in the Early 19th Century'. Mr Pollard (*pace* Mr Thompson) thinks that sexual irregularity was of no great interest to the factory owner.

Evangelicalism, like the Feudal System, never existed. As an important element in the religious world which is given this vague label Methodism deserves more serious attention than it has commonly received.

I am grateful to The Association Press, 291, Broadway, New York 7, for allowing me to use material from a shorter version of the essay on *Methodist Union*; to Darton, Longman & Todd for allowing me to reprint *Bishops and Society*, from *Anglican–Methodist Relations* edited by W. S. F. Pickering (1961); to the Oxford University Press for the quotation from Lord Fisher of Lambeth's *Anglican–Methodist Conversations and Problems of Church Unity* (1964); to Constable's for the extract from Donald Mackinnon's lecture in *Objections to Christian Belief* (1963); to the Editor of the *Proceedings of the Wesley Historical Society* for permission to reproduce *Methodism Misunderstood* and *Historians and Jabez Bunting*. *The Doctrine of the Ministry in Early Nineteenth-century Methodism* consists of the Wesley Historical Society Lecture for 1955, published by Epworth Press as *Jabez Bunting: the Last Wesleyan*.

I should also like to acknowledge how much I have owed over the years to my wife's help and encouragement.

JOHN KENT

ONE
Methodist Union

METHODIST UNION in England, as Sir Robert Perks was never tired of pointing out, went back to the day in 1878 when lay representatives at last became part of the Wesleyan Conference, the governing body of the Old Connexion. This step removed the biggest single constitutional difference between the English Methodist denominations, and involved a definite break with the traditional Wesleyan view of the Ministry.[1] According to this view, the Ministry was charged with the *episkope*, or oversight of the Connexion, and must therefore have the authority to carry out its pastoral responsibilities, which ranged from a monopoly of legislative power to control of admission to and exclusion from the local Societies.

---

[1] For the benefit of non-Methodist readers it may be pointed out that the denominations which united in 1932 were the Wesleyan Methodist Church, whose traditions ran back directly into the eighteenth century to John Wesley himself, and whose membership at the time of union was about 500,000; the Primitive Methodist Church, which had grown steadily since about 1807, was originally largely rural or mining in background, but had become more urban after about 1870 (membership 225,000); and the United Methodist Church, membership about 140,000. This last body had been set up in 1907; it contained three older groups, the Methodist New Connexion, a small but significant secession from Wesleyan Methodism in 1797; the Bible Christians, a small body rather like the Primitive Methodists, but almost entirely limited to the south-west of England, where it began about 1815; and the United Methodist Free Churches, which was founded in 1857 by various groups of seceders from the Wesleyan Methodist Church. After 1857 there were no further serious divisions in British Methodism from an institutional point of view; it is often forgotten, however, that the Salvation Army was not only created by ex-Methodists (George Railton, the most important formative influence on the movement after the Booths themselves, had, like them, been Wesleyan Methodist), but also drew some of its early support from Methodists who had become discontented with the comparative respectability of late nineteenth-century Methodism. The Holiness Revivalism of the early Army was a conscious throw-back to an allegedly 'primitive' Wesleyanism. In this way the Army, which had no close institutional contacts with the Methodist Churches at all, masked what was perhaps the last stage of nineteenth-century Methodist fissiparity.

Their use of these enormous powers had repeatedly brought the Wesleyan Ministry into conflict with the laity. This is not the place to explain how the situation gradually changed, but during the nineteenth century Wesleyan Methodism, partly because of external pressure from the Anglican Oxford Movement, moved closer to the other English Methodist Churches. As a result, the older Wesleyan view of the pastoral office was slowly replaced by a vaguer 'representative' theory, according to which the minister, although still described as 'called of God', was thought of chiefly as a 'representative' of the laity, with no kind of authority which the laity did not already possess. In all the Methodist churches the idea of pastoral 'oversight' was largely replaced by the idea of the minister as a 'leader'; the idea of a 'call to the Ministry' often took second place to that of the minister as a kind of full-time layman, a professional executant of the priesthood of all believers. Once the Wesleyan Ministry had adopted this view it was possible to admit laymen to the Wesleyan Conference, and for many Wesleyan ministers after 1849 the admission of lay representatives took priority over everything else. The practical price in division and secession of upholding the original Wesleyan constitution had become unendurable. Memories of the older Wesleyan view of the Ministry lingered on, however, to complicate the negotiations about reunion.

Several other factors help to explain why Methodist Union became practical politics toward the end of the first World War. (Wesleyan Methodism had set up a committee to explore the situation as far back as 1913, but it was not until 1918 that a united Committee, Wesleyan, Primitive and United Methodist, was given powers to draw up a draft Scheme of union.) One of the most important of the background factors was the transient idealism which affected so much English thought and action for a few years after 1918. It seemed as though the vast human sacrifice of the war might possibly be justified if there were some marked improvement in human relations, both personal and international. The naïve (or compulsive) optimism of the post-war period acted as a vigorous stimulus to the movement for the reunification of the Churches. Advocates of reunion emphasized the need to have a new Church to face an allegedly new Era, and they often seemed to take it for granted that a unified Methodism would have an increased moral influence on the nation. This prophecy was not fulfilled. The attempt to advocate Methodist union as 'progressive',

2

however, only half-veiled the sense in which the movement was a consolidated retreat: what the leaders hoped to recover was the power and influence which the English Free Churches had briefly possessed in the later nineteenth century and Edwardian Age.[2]

Doctrinally, the post-war period was also propitious. The few printed references to the negotiations (see, for example, *Something to Remember* W. J. Noble) suggest that there were no significant theological differences between the negotiating bodies. Strictly speaking this is inaccurate for, as we shall see, the main obstacle to union was disagreement about the proper doctrinal standard for the united Church, and about the doctrines of the Ministry and Sacraments. But such comments reflect the fact that the negotiators could assume that most people in their respective denominations accepted what they called 'evangelical doctrines'. This assumption was less important than it might seem, because the discussions were taking place in the trough of the wave of liberal theology, which in 1920 still had enormous prestige as the 'progressive' point of view. There was a general feeling that Biblical Criticism had freed men (and especially ministers) from the dead hand of creeds, official doctrinal statements, and the past as a whole. This attitude was so strong that A. S. Peake, the distinguished Primitive Methodist scholar who did so much to persuade his generation to accept Biblical Criticism, said quite openly at an early stage in the negotiations that he would have preferred to omit any reference to John Wesley's writings from the doctrinal statement of the united Church. (It must also be remembered that while the Wesleyan Methodists saw this reference as a necessary act of piety, the non-Wesleyan representatives saw it as suggesting that Methodism was a sect.) The negotiating Committee

---

[2] It was characteristic of this state of mind that one of the first practical attempts of the Methodist bodies to work together in the 1920's took the form of a plan to revive the Temperance movement, a revival which was also stimulated, of course, by the apparent triumph of Prohibition in the United States of America. The British Temperance movement had lost its impetus during the first World War; the disastrous failure of American Prohibition, unforeseen in England in the early 1920's, completed the transformation of Teetotalism from an expanding, aggressive social phenomenon of some importance into a dwindling, defensive sectarian attitude. In this and in many other ways Methodist Union was to encounter the fact that the manipulation of Christian institutions could not in itself reverse the social tendencies of the period.

never acted on the idea, popular in a few quarters, that it should draw up a list of specific doctrines, but pointed instead to vague but respectable terms like 'evangelical', or 'the Reformation'. This was certainly wiser than the unfortunate Anglican attempt to draw up an agreed syllabus of doctrines in the 1930s.[3]

Other more purely Methodist factors were also involved at the institutional level. There was, for example, a general hope that unity might help to check declining membership. In 1921, for example, Aldom French, the secretary of the Wesleyan section of the Union Committee, made a public statement along these lines. He said that since 1907 the Wesleyan Church had suffered a loss of thirty-five thousand members; that the Primitive Methodists had lost ten thousand members; that the United Methodists had lost nine thousand members. There was some dispute about his figures, but in the case of Primitive Methodism this only led to the conclusion that if the membership was taken as 205,307 in 1907, it was 200,177 in 1920—which was certainly a decrease. In all three cases the figures suggested that the origins of the decrease went back well before the outbreak of the first World War and began to show statistically about 1907. Luke Wiseman had been investigating the decline in Wesleyan Methodism, and had reached the important conclusion that in the circuits proper the decline could be traced back to the 1890s, but that this had been obscured for a short time by the initial success of the Central Missions, an institutional innovation which dated from the 1880s.[4] Moreover,

---

[3] *Doctrine in the Church of England* (London, 1938).

[4] An official investigation had been made into Wesleyan Methodism, which reported to the Conference of 1918. This stated: 'For eleven years in succession the membership returns show a decrease, amounting in the aggregate to no less than 28,571 members. During the last thirty years the net addition to Church Membership is 47,000. Merely to keep pace with the increase of the population we ought to have added 60,000 more. The Central Mission movement, which commenced about thirty years ago, has added some 25,000 members, chiefly during the first twenty years of the period. It would seem, therefore, that while the period recording net decreases began eleven years ago (1907), decline in the Circuits had set in much earlier. Very significant is the fact that decrease is most marked in the counties where Methodism had formerly its strongest hold. Cornwall and Lincoln Districts each return over 3,500 less members than they had thirty years ago, and the four Yorkshire Districts an aggregate of nearly 7,000. During the decade of decrease (1908-18) our Church had received into fellowship no less than 337,000 new members; in the

the fall was more serious than the figures suggested, for there was
no longer the margin of uncommitted hearers which had been a
fruitful field of evangelism in the past. Unity did not effect this
train of development: the days were not so very far distant when
the congregation would normally be smaller than the membership
at most services. Aldom French suggested that union would help
to solve this problem by making Methodism as a whole more
efficient.[5] He quoted the example of the United Methodist

previous decade 459,000 (1898–1908). In the same periods over 186,000
and over 216,000 respectively were returned as "ceased to meet". Removals in the last ten years have resulted in a net loss to the Church of
86,000 members.' The Central Missions of the Forward Movement were
put in on top of the normal circuit system; it was hoped that they would
feed members to the circuits; the Manchester Mission was begun in 1885,
the West London Mission shortly afterwards. As the inquiry showed, the
Missions produced only a temporary increase in the overall membership
figures, and their chief importance lay in their social welfare work. The
Report to the Conference of 1918 had few suggestions to put forward to
explain the movement of the statistics: much was made of the struggle
between capital and labour 'today the opinion is widely entertained
among the workers, and sedulously fostered by opponents of Christianity,
that the Church is an affair of the middle classes . . . and therefore has
no sympathy with the aspirations and ideals of the workers in their
struggle for economic and social freedom'. Rather more unexpected is the
willingness of the Committee to say that some witnesses had attributed
the decline in part to 'slackness of the ministers'. The Report commented
that the standard of diligence depended entirely on the individual minister, but made no recommendations about the oversight of the Ministry.
No mention was made of the highly political role of the Free Churches
(almost as a branch of the Liberal Party) between 1880 and 1914, and the
reaction which probably took place against the Free Churches because of
it, and because the political stance of the Free Churches began to look
increasingly old-fashioned. One comparison is significant: in 1918, on the
basis of a total membership of about 469,000, the Wesleyan Methodist
Church took in 23,876 new members; in 1963, on the basis of a membership of about 719,000, the unified Methodist Church received 24,188
new members.

[5] How irrelevant these arguments were may be seen from the actual
movement of Wesleyan Methodist membership statistics in the following
years:

1920 Membership 462,625 decrease of 2,814
1921 ,, 464,945 increase of 2,320
1922 ,, 468,540 ,, 3,595
1923 ,, 475,598 ,, 7,058

(Contd overleaf)

Church, which since its formation twelve years before had been able to dispense with 150 ordained and ninety-three unordained ministers, as a financial saving which he put at £50,000 a year.

Another internal factor which made Methodist union feasible was that the social pattern of England was changing steadily, and that the social differences between the Wesleyan and the other two bodies had largely disappeared. In the later stages of the negotiations it was sometimes said that snobbery was all that held the hard core of Wesleyan opposition together, but even this attitude was more often based on a preference for the fixed Wesleyan order of Holy Communion as compared with the free orders popular in the other Methodist bodies, than on social distinctions. A simple example of the degree to which the three groups had come to resemble one another is the stipends of the ministers. In 1924 these were:

	Wesleyan M.	Primitive M.	United M.
Superintendent	£270	£250	£250
Others	£240	£220	£240
		(£240 after 6 years)	
Probationers	£160	£160	£170

This close approximation enabled the Financial Committee which reported in 1924 to propose that in the United Church all ministerial stipends should be established at the highest of these figures. (It is not possible to say how far one would have expected, even

---

1924	Membership	484,134	increase of	8,536
1925	„	490,118	„	5,984
1926	„	495,113	„	4,995
1927	„	497,487	„	2,374
1928	„	499,283	„	1,798
1929	„	498,809	decrease of	476
1930	„	499,014	increase of	430

The years 1921–8 turned out to have seen the last flicker of expansion of modern Methodism. The increase was chiefly concentrated into the years 1922–6; it was the product of intense effort along traditional lines; much use was made of the ageing Victorian revivalist, Gipsy Smith, who had been born in 1860, served part of his apprenticeship under William Booth of the Salvation Army, had often led missions in the United States, and who had been employed in the opening years of the century by the National Evangelical Free Church Council as its special missioner. The Gipsy's prominence symbolized the sense in which this evangelistic drive was backwards looking; he had published his autobiography as far back as 1901.

in 1924, that a Wesleyan minister might have some private means; it is clear that one would not have expected this to be true in the case of the Primitive Methodist ministers.) Wesleyan manses would normally have been larger and better furnished.

A third internal institutional factor underlines the similarity between the three denominations at the local level of organization. In 1924 nearly half the circuits of Methodism as a whole were what were called 'single-minister stations', that is, only one minister was appointed to them. The actual figures were these:

In Wesleyan Methodism 756 circuits, of which 133 were single-minister stations.

In Primitive Methodism 684 circuits, of which 486 were single-minister stations.

In United Methodism 330 circuits, of which 250 were single-minister stations.

The total was thus 1,770 circuits, of which 824 were single-minister stations.

Thus for the whole of Methodism in 1924 almost every other circuit was a single-minister station, almost every town of any size had at least one minister who worked in virtual isolation from his brethren. The figure was high even for Wesleyan Methodism alone, but if one takes the two smaller bodies the result is still more shocking: out of 1,014 circuits 691 were single-minister stations, about sixty-nine per cent, or two in every three. This showed how deeply local particularism, the real danger to sound Christian polity whatever Karl Barth may say to the contrary, and highly characteristic of the Anglican parish system, had bitten into Methodism since the Disruption of 1849–57. It would be an exaggeration to say that by 1924 Methodism had repudiated its cultural heritage, but there was something very non-Methodist about a situation in which so many ministers worked largely by themselves, almost independent of any hierarchy. This had been the great attraction of the system in the United Methodist Church, and it is important to recall that the two smaller bodies cherished a traditional dislike of the Wesleyan custom of dividing the Connexion into Districts, each with a ministerial Chairman, who possessed a degree of oversight (*episkope*) over his brethren. In the case of Primitive Methodism the evidence suggests that the single-minister circuit was a comparatively late innovation. In an article on the subject in the *Primitive Methodist Leader* in 1926 it was stated that 'a generation ago the denomination was captivated by the idea of the pastorate, and although the ideal was impracticable with us (because the number of societies, some of them very small, far exceeded the number of ministers) yet the Church went as near to it as possible and broke up the old circuit system, which usually was large, into circuits which were small. . . . This has worked out . . . that without adequate experience ministers too early in their career have been compelled to undertake arduous tasks. . . . In London especially there were calamitous results.' The writer added that in the larger towns single-minister circuits 'are not as a rule the most progressive areas of the Church'. Thus the Primitive Methodist single-minister circuit developed partly as another of those late-nineteenth-century institutional experiments designed to cope with the troubles of the Church in the welter of urbanized England. But the use of the word 'pastorate' is important. It implied a more settled Ministry, in which the bond between pastor and church was closer, than had been the ideal of Methodism in the past. Once again Methodist unity did not close the chapter, though it changed the conditions. A new flight to the solitude of the pastorate has developed since 1932, although this time a 'pastorate' would be defined as the care of a single large society *within* a circuit. This may at times come closer to Independency than the single-minister circuit, in which a group of half a dozen or so country chapels were often linked with a single, stronger, urban society. Nevertheless, one of the greatest institutional blessings of Methodist Union was that it led to the abolition of a large majority of these 'single' stations and a return to a more Methodist way of working; something like three quarters of them have disappeared. On the other hand, the existence of so many of these 'single' stations helps to explain the stubborn resistance to circuit amalgamation and to effective union which was one of the features of the generation after 1932. This factor, in other words, is involved deeply in the whole complex issue.

Such were some of the factors which made Methodist union practical politics by about 1918. The Wesleyan acceptance of the principle of lay representation in the Annual Conference mattered more than anything else, because it vastly simplified the institutional side of the negotiations. This, however, lay in the background. The catalyst which brought popular opinion into the issue on the side of union was the emotional aftermath of the first World War. A. W. Harrison, a distinguished Wesleyan minister, recalling this post-war mood for the Ecumenical Methodist Conference of 1931, said:

There was a phase of violent emotional disturbance, unrest dangerously near to revolution, with a deep sense of exasperation at the disappointments of peace. These were days when there was much talk of reconstruction, with little to satisfy the dreams of the idealists. If we could sum it up again in one expression, it would be in the aspiration of the younger generation, 'Let us tear the whole rotten structure down and begin again!'

The negotiations went ahead quickly in response to such an atmosphere immediately after the war; they bogged down as the mood changed to one of depression, the mood which in a more general social sense culminated in the General Strike of 1926. At this early stage the absence of wide social or doctrinal differences between the three Churches helped to sustain the process.

The negotiations ran into very few snags of an institutional nature; what held up the scheme from 1920 to 1933 was the opposition of a powerful Wesleyan Methodist minority strongly concerned about the doctrines of the Church, Ministry and Sacraments. Institutional differences presented so little difficulty that the compromise arrived at in 1920 was hardly altered in succeeding years. This was not entirely what was expected at the time. Despite the changes indicated at the beginning of this essay, the Ministry still had more authority in the Wesleyan than in the other Methodist constitutions. Thus in the case of Wesleyan Methodism, the Annual Conference, the real source of authority in all forms of Methodism, was divided into two sessions, the second of which, known as the Pastoral Session, consisted only of ministers; in Primitive and United Methodism there was no such division, and the Conference was in each case made up of representatives of the ministry and the laity. In an itinerant system like Methodism the Committee which stations ministers plays a vital role: in Wesleyan Methodism final decisions about the stationing of ministers had been in the hands of the Pastoral Session, whereas in the other two Churches laymen had shared in this responsibility. Another unique feature of the Wesleyan Conference was the Legal Hundred. This was a body of one hundred ministers, elected by their brethren, according to rules which were constantly being reviewed, who were permanent members of the Conference, and therefore provided an element of continuity theoretically independent of both the departmental officers and the constantly changing elected representatives. This was regarded by the Primitive and United Methodists as highly undemocratic—and 'democracy' was a word to conjure with in 1920—although there were very small permanent groups in the other Conferences. Finally, in the non-Wesleyan Churches the highest offices in the Connexion, such as the Presidency and the Secretaryship of Conference, had been regarded as open to laymen, though laymen were not often elected to them; in Wesleyan Methodism such appointments had always been purely ministerial. This openness of the Church as an institution to the laity was characteristic of the non-Wesleyan bodies. Perhaps the most striking example is ministerial training. At Hartley, the Primitive Methodist theological college in Manchester, the dominant personality on the staff was A. S. Peake, a layman, who also held a professorship in Manchester University, and there is no question but that it was he who moulded the Primitive Methodist ministry between 1900 and 1930; no layman on the other hand was ever appointed to the staff of any of the four Wesleyan theological colleges.

Out of this rather unpromising material a rough compromise emerged quickly, probably because most of the Wesleyan leaders no longer held the view of the pastoral office which was still implied by some parts of the Wesleyan constitution. The President, for example, was always to be a minister, but there was also to be a Vice-President, who was always to be a layman. The non-Wesleyan bodies regarded this introduction of a lay Vice-President as an important concession on the part of the Wesleyans; they felt that the Vice-Presidency was a guarantee that the rights of the laity would be respected in the new Church. It can hardly be said that the office has been as important as some supporters of the idea expected, but in 1920 the change played a big part in the institutional compromise. This does not mean that everyone accepted the situation happily. The Conferences of 1923 received the comments of their circuits on the Union as it existed in draft: forty out of the 760 Wesleyan circuits still objected to a lay Vice-President; out of 686 Primitive Methodist circuits 102 voted that the Presidency ought to be open to a layman.

The negotiators also quickly agreed that there must be a Pastoral Session. For a short time this was a lively issue, especially as the first draft scheme suggested that the Pastoral should follow the Representative Session, as was the Wesleyan practice. When the Primitive Methodist District Meetings considered the scheme in 1921 fourteen out of twenty-five voted that the Pastoral Session should come first, in order to make sure that the Representative Session should have the last word. This alarmed many Wesleyans, who thought that what mattered was that the Representative Session should have the first word. The point attracted so much discussion that in June 1921 Sir Robert Perks, perhaps the best-known Wesleyan layman at the time, actually wrote an article along these lines for the Primitive Methodist denominational newspaper, *The Leader*. He said that when the Representative Session was first introduced in 1878 it had followed the Pastoral Session, just as the Primitive Methodists were now suggesting. But by 1887 the Wesleyan laity were already asking that the Representative Session should have priority. J. H. Rigg, almost the last convinced exponent of the old Wesleyan doctrine of the ruling ministry, had opposed this, saying that it would deprive the Pastoral Session of its initiative. Rigg had said: 'I ask who are the prime guardians appointed by the Master. That sacred interest ought to come first.' (This, whether Sir Robert Perks liked it or not, and he didn't, was the authentic voice of the Wesleyan tradition.) Dr Rigg was defeated in the Representative Session by 178 votes to 117, but from 1889 the experiment was tried of sandwiching the Representative Session between two meetings of the Pastoral Session. This lasted for ten years, but in 1899 the Representative Session once again requested priority, and this time the Pastoral Session accepted the change by 172 votes to 154. Perks concluded: 'There can be no doubt that by this great change the initiation of legislation, and also the more effective control of the administrative work of the Wesleyan Methodist Church, passed from the hands of a purely clerical body and became vested where it ought to be, in a Representative Assembly of ministers and laymen chosen by the Church.' Since this conclusion was precisely what the non-Wesleyan critics had in mind this letter really settled the issue. I have dealt with it at length for two reasons: in the first place it illustrates once more how the development of Wesleyan Methodism facilitated Methodist union; it also shows how much in common

Wesleyan and non-Wesleyan laymen might have in their general attitude to church polity. It is a fascinating fact that the Methodist Conference of 1960 agreed to reverse the order of the sessions once more, and one of the reasons given would have made Sir Robert Perks's hair stand on end; if the Ministerial Session wished to give a lead to the Representative Session in any important matter it could only do so, as matters stood, by reporting to the next Conference.

The Primitive and United Methodists had conceded a point in accepting the idea of Pastoral Session. They did so on various conditions. The most important of these was the disappearance of the Legal Hundred, whose origins went back to John Wesley himself. The non-Wesleyan negotiators were anxious to make the new Conference as 'democratic' as possible, and regarded anything like permanent membership as improper. The Hundred was a rather glaring example of permanency, and ministerial permanency at that. It had never been quite clear whether a member of the Hundred was obliged to withdraw when he retired from the active ministry, and not all did: a Wesleyan Committee which was discussing this point while the union negotiations were going on, hesitated to say that a supernumerary should be compelled to give up his place in the Hundred. Now the whole system was abolished, which may not have been the wisest solution. An attempt was made to provide some continuity to Conference membership. In the 1920 Scheme it was suggested that the Conference itself should elect thirty ministers and thirty laymen for six years, five of each group retiring every year. But the idea was unpopular, even when laymen had been added to the ministers who comprised the Legal Hundred. In the 1922 Scheme the length of term was reduced to three years, ten of each group retiring every year. In the present Standing Orders of the Methodist Church the process has gone a stage farther: twenty-one ministers and twenty-one laymen are elected for three years, seven of each group retiring every year. The intention of the original negotiators was to spread membership as widely as possible, and it is significant that Primitive and United Methodist advocates of union claimed that the proposed constitution was even more democratic than what already existed in their Connexions. The Primitive Methodists were not all convinced of this, however, because in their Conference the laymen outnumbered the ministers by two to one, which seemed to them very democratic indeed, whereas in the proposed United Conference ministers and laymen were to sit in equal numbers.

From these examples it should be obvious enough what was the basis of the institutional compromise. The non-Wesleyan Churches were prepared to accept certain features of the Wesleyan constitution (such as the Pastoral Session and the District Chairman), as long as the Wesleyans in their turn agreed to such modifications of Wesleyan practice as would make quite clear that they accepted a 'representative' doctrine of the Ministry. Almost the last traces of what early nineteenth-century Wesleyans approvingly called 'pastoral supremacy' disappeared: ministerial 'leadership' and Connexional 'democracy' were the watchwords.[6] This was true in the

___

[6] It is important to grasp accurately the theological 'moment' at which the negotiations took place. By 1938, for example, when the climate had changed, Dr Newton Flew could write with complete assurance: 'In this world of space and time Christianity must always take form as a visible community, and therefore the idea of the Church is essential to Christian theology. "Just as you cannot say Citizen without implying the State, so, the New Testament teaches, you cannot say Christian without implying the Church." But in the course of the nineteenth century this truth was often neglected or obscured. . . . Indeed, the doubt was entertained whether the Church could be regarded in any sense as a deliberate and direct foundation of Christ' (*Jesus and his Church*, p. 23). It was in some such terms that ecumenical conferences after about 1937 celebrated their own 'rediscovery of the Church', as it was usually called. How far the indictment of the past was valid is a difficult problem. Dr Flew, in the preface to the book quoted above, said that 'the conviction that Christian people in the last two centuries had given insufficient attention to the doctrine of the Ecclesia was widely shared at the Oxford and Edinburgh World Conferences of 1937'. Such a conviction was badly worded from a historical point of view. In fact, the nineteenth century had spent a great deal of time on the doctrine of the Church, and what theologians of the 1930s really meant when they criticized their predecessors was that they didn't agree with the doctrine of the Church which Harnack and others produced. This late-nineteenth-century attitude emphasized that the visible, institutional ecclesia was of human origin; Christ might be supposed to have had an ideal Church in his mind's eye, but the New Testament gave no definite clues as to what sort of institutions this ideal implied. This kind of attitude affected all the negotiators who worked for Methodist Union in the 1920s, and explained why some of the strongest opponents of lay administration of the Holy Communion, for instance, found it hard to produce a logical defence of their own position. It was natural, however, to suppose that if Christ had not laid down the kind of Church order *all* denominations must follow, then men might change the

case of the Stationing Committee, which was 'democratized' as far as possible in make-up and methods of work, and also (though this is in part jumping to another aspect of the subject) in the case of the administration of the Holy Communion. From the start the negotiators assumed that administration of the Holy Communion by laymen would have to be permitted in the new Church, however tightly it might be restricted, and despite the fact that this had not been the Wesleyan custom. Some compensation for this major Wesleyan concession (without which it is certain that no scheme would have been successful) may be seen in the non-Wesleyan acceptance of the office of District Chairman, but there is no suggestion in contemporary records that this was thought of as a momentous step. The Chairman was conceived as the 'representative', not the ruler, of his fellow ministers in the District, and was expected to give them 'leadership', rather than pastoral oversight.

Some comment must be made on this institutional compromise. At the higher level it worked very smoothly. There was no drastic change of system. Final authority in the new Church still rested in a representative Conference, and if everybody was not familiar with a Pastoral Session, at least the term was self-explanatory, whereas the true system of the old Wesleyan Conference, the Legal Hundred, had been abolished. No important new organs of power were created. There was nothing in the history of the office of the District Chairman to suggest that its wider adoption would prove revolutionary as long as the Chairmen remained simultaneously superintendents of large circuits. All the uniting Churches had possessed central departments which handled such matters as Finance, Youth Work, Social Questions, and so forth; these were fused. In the case of ministerial training a fusion of the two non-Wesleyan Colleges produced the present Hartley Victoria. The biggest financial difference between the three Churches had been that the Primitive Methodists made much less use of invested funds, but a change here had no striking consequences.

This leads one to ask whether the process was not a bit too easy, whether the new Church was not too like the old? Little serious

---

institutional structure of the ecclesia from time to time to suit the changing political ideals of their society without breaking any divine law. About 1920, democracy, with its corollary representation, was believed to have a high moral value; how could it be wrong to work out a Church order in terms of these ideas?

effort was made to take the chance offered by the negotiations to devise a form of Methodism more suited to the present century. If the Chairman, for example, had been immediately freed from circuit responsibilities and had been specifically charged with the job of making union a success on the local level, it is possible that in the first excitement of coming together much might have been achieved. The introduction of Separated Chairmen twenty-five years later was not at all the same thing.[7] In any case, the success

[7] This may seem rather unrealistic, but in fact the special Home Mission inquiry which reported to the Conference of the Wesleyan Methodist Church in 1918 had concluded that: 'The growing demands upon the time, strength, and attention of the Chairman of the District, especially in view of the unwieldy size of many of our Districts, render it impossible that he should properly discharge the double office of Circuit minister and Chairman of District.' The Committee recommended the setting up of Separated Chairmen immediately; the Conference set up a committee to consider this which reported in 1919. This committee suggested a radical change in the duties of the Chairman, who was to 'visit every Circuit in his District at least once a year for the purpose of inquiring into the state of the work of God in the Circuit, to advise on questions of policy or any other matters affecting the well-being of the Circuit; and if he deem it desirable, to attend the Quarterly Meeting . . .'. This was a more considerable authority than has been conferred on the Chairman of the unified Methodist Church, and would have cut deeply into the independence of the Circuits. The Conference of 1919 wanted an experiment, and so arrangements were set on foot in the East Anglia, Cornwall, Bristol and Bath, Liverpool, and Scotland Districts. The scheme met a divided reception, however; the Conference of 1926 was told that, however desirable, the plan could not be followed connexionally for financial reasons; Districts were given the option of asking for a separated Chairman if they wanted one, and could meet certain financial demands. More significant was the changed definition of the separated Chairman's duties: '*By arrangement with the Superintendent* to visit each Circuit in the District at least once a year: inquiring into the state of the work of God, advising on questions of policy or other matters affecting the well-being of the Circuit, and *if it should be deemed advisable*, attending the Quarterly Meeting. . . .' This wording has only to be compared with that above and it is obvious that the original plan for a firm, bold leadership given to the District from above had been weakened considerably; there were only about half a dozen Separated Chairmen in the Wesleyan Methodist Church. Nevertheless, it is a pity that at the time of union no statesman emerged who could persuade the uniting denominations really to experiment with the possibilities of church organization; as it is, the powers of the Separated Chairmen who were finally appointed in the 1950s were less than those which the Wesleyan Committee had suggested as far back as 1919.

of the institutional merger at the top was not paralleled by a successful merger at the circuit level, that is, at the level where ordinary Christians met one another. Such a statement may sound unnecessarily controversial, and it is therefore worth while making a long quotation from an article published by Dr Eric Baker, in which he summed up his experiences as President of the Methodist Church in 1959/60. As Secretary of the Conference for many years, Dr Baker was well qualified to speak on institutional matters:

There is widespread impatience, especially on the part of our younger people, at the continued tolerance on the part of the Conference of the redundancy which is steadily strangling our effectiveness. . . . Let me give two examples which are typical, not exceptional. There is one city which contains within its boundaries fifty-nine Methodist churches, considerably more than the Church of England possesses. Congregations are small, and we could well do with half of them. I visited a town recently with a population of 17,000 where there are four large Methodist churches, none of which has an average congregation of fifty. . . . Methodist union took place twenty-eight years ago. When Conference then decided that union at the circuit and society level would be a matter for local action, they could never have dreamed of such a sequel. The laity of the three Churches ought never to have voted in such numbers for union unless they intended to consummate it locally. Ministers, of course, voted for it too, but not in such large numbers, and they are itinerant anyway. What can be done? I do not know. Conference has done everything in its power short of coercion, and unless new powers are sought from Parliament . . . can do no more. In area after area, the appeal and often the direction of Conference has been flouted. Worship of bricks and mortar has supplanted worship of the living God.

Now I think it would be a big mistake to suppose that there was much specifically Methodist about such wickedness. It is more than possible, of course, that in many cases both ministers and laymen voted for the scheme because they did not intend to consummate it locally, and because they knew that nothing in the scheme itself would compel them to do so. The negotiators drew back from any attempt to determine in advance what should happen at the local level; there were no teeth in the scheme, and it is difficult to see how there could have been; from an institutional point of view all churches are voluntary associations, you can *ex*-communicate, but you cannot bind *in*. There is a danger in such negotiations that a tide of opinion flows so strongly that in the end no one can withstand it: many ministers and laymen voted for the scheme because they felt they *ought* to do so, but once the vote for righteousness had been given they lost interest; numerical majorities are not always the best guide in church affairs. Although gradually at the local level many ex-Wesleyan, Primitive and United Methodist circuits joined together in what were called 'amalgamated circuits', this usually meant that all the chapels involved remained open, and that the opportunities for efficiency and effective evangelism were not faced. In fact, union made the problem of redundancy worse, because situations which could be dimly defended in terms of one of the three uniting Churches became monstrous in terms of the one united Church. To some extent, moreover, the financial benefits of union helped to support redundancy. The conclusion seems to be that in any future organic union in a country where overlapping is as considerable as it was in the case of the three English Methodist Churches, the important step is to deal with the problem of local organization before union is implemented. The sequel of Methodist union is a warning against the assumption that in such a case the unification of ministries and of central departments will be sufficient to guarantee effective union where it really matters, where the Christian meets the non-Christian. This would obviously be true of any plan to unite the Free Churches of Great Britain. No Methodist minister could face a repetition of the problem of redundancy as he has known it in united Methodism. Nor is this just a counsel of perfection. The failure of union at the institutional level has had repercussions on the supply of candidates for the Ministry. One might quote Dr Baker again as saying that 'we cannot expect our ablest and most devoted young men to offer for the Ministry when they see before their eyes the frustrating and unnecessary conditions under which many ministers are forced to work'.

A word of warning is necessary here, however: Methodism must be studied in the general context of Church History; it would be absurd to limit the explanation of the comparative failure of Methodist union to Methodist factors. The question of the number of candidates for ordination provides an instance of this general background; rough comparison with the state of affairs in the French Roman Catholic and the Anglican Churches brings out what I have in mind.

In the case of the Church of England, ordination figures from 1872 to 1961 may be found in Table 36 of *Facts and Figures About the Church of England* (1962). This table shows that the highest number of ordinations occurred in 1886, when it was 757; the figure then fell rather quickly—in 1895 it was 658, in 1899 it was 587, and in 1901 it was 500. Between 1900 and 1914 the total showed a tendency to rise, touching 640 in 1911; it was 610 in 1914. After the first World War the figure for 1920 was 258, from which level a slow climb brought it back to 503 in 1930, 585 in 1932, and 589 in 1939; in 1946 the figure was 158, and since then the total has risen through the 1950s (when it was often below 500) to about 650 in 1963. Some Anglican observers suggest that the totals since 1945 are not strictly comparable with those before 1914, because a lowering of overall standards has been partly responsible for the number of ordinands; other Anglicans would dispute this, and one suspects that it is the social level of the candidates which has changed since 1914, rather than their intrinsic ability.

In France, the number of ordinations to the Roman Catholic priesthood was 1,753 in 1901; 825 in 1913; 830 in 1930. After a tremendous effort in the 1930s, a total of 1,350 ordinations took place in 1938; after 1945, however, the totals fell once again to between 800 and 900. (In both countries the total number of priests fell by about a quarter in the first half of the twentieth century.) In both countries there was a tendency for the total of ordinands to stabilize at a level well below what was common in the later nineteenth century; in both countries the fall began well before 1914, and cannot be attributed, therefore, to the baleful effects of the first World War. It also looks as though the Roman Catholic Church made in the 1930s the effort to restock the priesthood which the Church of England has been making since the early 1950s; if this is so, one would expect that within the next few years the Anglican total would fall again at least as far as about 500; one effect of the negotiations between the Anglican and Methodist Churches, however, might be a temporary increase in the number of candidates for ordination; this, however, as we shall see, did not happen in the case of the Union discussions among the Methodists in the 1920s.

Methodist figures for ordinands are the figures of men recorded in the *Minutes* of the Conferences as 'received into full connexion'. From 1908 it is possible to calculate the Methodist total by adding together those received into full connexion by the Wesleyan, Primitive Methodist, and United Methodist Churches. In 1908 the total was 165, and this bears a similar relation to the later figures as the Roman Catholic 1,753 and the Anglican 757. In 1911 the total was 136; in 1914, 116; in 1920 it was 90, and it seems to have touched rock bottom, in consequence of the lean years of the first World War, in 1923, when it was 34. The total then ascended to 86 in 1929, and the frantic efforts to refloat Methodism made in the early 1920s bore fruit in 124 ordinations in 1930 and 136 in 1932. Union itself, however, didn't provide an additional spur: in 1936 there were 100 ordinations and in 1939 as few as 90. After the effects of the second World War had receded totals lower than this were recorded in 1954 (81), 1955 (77), 1956 (86), and 1958 (82). The 1960s saw an improvement to 127 in 1963; this, of course, reflected the intake of five to six years before: it looks as though the figures for the period 1964–8 will fall to the level common in the 1950s.

These figures have certain things in common with those quoted above for the Roman Catholic and Anglican Churches. Once again the fall in vocations began before 1914: from 165 in 1908 to 116 in 1914. Once again an effort was made to check the fall, and in 1932 the number of ordinations, 136, reached the level of 1911. After the second World War the figure oscillated violently, but showed a long-term tendency to settle down at a total in the region of 70–90; this resembled the movement of the Roman Catholic figures.

One other comparison may be made: the Wesleyan Methodist Church became so anxious about the supply of candidates for the Ministry that a Conference Committee was appointed in 1925 which reported to the Conference of 1926. This Committee stated that 'whereas in the first ten years of the present century the average number of candidates recommended by the Synods was 151 per annum, in the next quinquennial period (1911–15) the average had declined to 114, and in the following period (1916–20) to 54. The decline had already commenced in pre-war days, but was naturally intensified in the years of war. While the numbers have improved during the last five years, the average being 91, we are still considerably below the standard of twenty years ago.' The significant comparison here is with the number of candidates offering in the Methodist Church in recent years: 1960—106, 1961—101, 1962—109, and 1963—123. At the beginning of the century the Wesleyan Methodist Church alone was receiving more candidates for the Ministry than the Methodist Church itself in the early 1960s.[8]

* * *

The second part of this essay is concerned with the doctrinal factors which provided the real difficulty of the negotiations. Although these factors were intrinsically important, concentration on them helped the neglect of more detailed problems. In this sense the Wesleyan opposition to union, although it did good work in clarifying and broadening the doctrinal statements, was looking in the wrong direction; in the long run the mistakes at the local level proved more important than the improvements obtained at the doctrinal level.

What we are considering here is the section called 'Doctrine' which stood at the beginning of the various draft schemes of Union. The first paragraph of the section was meant to be the doctrinal standard of the united Church. In the 1920 Scheme the original draft of this paragraph ran:

That the evangelical doctrines for which Methodism has stood from the beginning, as held by the three Conferences, and as generally contained

---

[8] The Primitive Methodist total ordinations follow a similar pattern to that described above. In 1900 the figure was 27; in 1905 it was 20; in 1907 it reached its highest point of 47. In 1908 and 1911 it was 36; by 1914 the usual decline had set firmly in and it was 24. In 1920 (43) and 1921 (32) survivors from the war were mopped up; after that the figures read 1922 —17; 1923—17; 1924—17; 1925—23; 1926—22; 1927—27; 1928—21; 1929—17; 1930—33; and 1932—25. In this case only a slight recovery was made after the end of the first World War. The United Methodist Free Church figures were similar: in 1908, when the new denomination was properly launched, the total was 37; in 1909—23; 1910—20; 1911— 24; 1912—24; 1913—18; and 1914, lower as usual, 13. In 1920 and 1921 the total was 8; in 1922—1; in 1923—3; 1924—2; 1925—8; 1926—11; 1927—8; 1928—16; 1929—10; 1930—17; 1931—19; 1932—32. In the case of Wesleyan Methodism the figures of those received into full connexion (not candidates) were: 1900—62; 1901—52; 1904—61; 1905— 60; 1908—92; 1909—79; 1910—83; 1911—76; 1912—98; these were figures which often equalled the number ordained in the Methodist Church after 1932. In 1913 and 1914 the figures were 78 and 79. In 1920 and 1922 they were 51; in 1923 the total was only 14; 1924-47; 1925—34; 1926—52; 1927—39; 1928—45; 1929—59; 1930—74; 1931—74; 1932 —79. In the pre-1914 period the Wesleyan Church was turning down a large proportion of the candidates who offered; in the later period there was a smaller number of candidates.

in John Wesley's *Notes on the New Testament* and the first four volumes of his *Sermons*, shall be the doctrinal basis of the Methodist Church.

This must have seemed mild and natural to some; to others it looked like a road-block; they had been encouraged to base their preaching on the findings of Biblical Criticism, and now they were sent back to Wesley's *Notes on the New Testament*. One Primitive Methodist critic wrote: 'Frankly, many of us *don't* believe what John Wesley believed.'

By the February of 1920 A. S. Peake, himself both a biblical scholar and a member of the Union Committee, thought it wise to write a public article on the subject. He appreciated the difficulty about the *Notes on the New Testament*. 'I confess that I should have greatly preferred the omission of this reference [but] the loyalty of the Wesleyans to their great founder is such that the inclusion of the reference seemed to be imperative.' Peake underlined the importance of the word 'generally': of course Wesley must be criticized, his exegesis of the New Testament must sometimes be rejected, his interpretation of the Book of Revelation 'is radically unsound'. However, in 1919 the Wesleyan Conference itself had adopted a series of resolutions on doctrine, one of which said that the *Notes on the New Testament* and the *Forty-Four Sermons* 'were not intended to impose a system of formal or speculative theology on our preachers', and, A. S. Peake suggested, this would be a reasonable basis for their interpretation in the united Church.[9]

[9] Cf. *Minutes* of the Conference of 1919, Special Resolutions, *Unity of Doctrine*, p. 264. There had been considerable discussion as to the value of John Wesley's writings in view of the later development of Biblical Criticism. The Special Resolution said that the *Sermons* and the *Notes* were intended to set up 'standards of preaching and belief which should secure loyalty to the fundamental truths of the Gospel of Redemption'. How far this could be distinguished from a system of formal theology it would obviously be difficult to say. In 1919, Wesleyan ministers were still required to answer, once every year, at the District Synod, the question: Do you believe and preach our doctrines? The Special Resolution went on to say that this question was to be understood in the light of the question asked in the Ordination Service: 'Do you believe that the system of doctrine therein contained is in accordance with the Holy Scriptures?' Thus in one paragraph the resolution said that the *Notes* and *Sermons* didn't contain a 'system' of doctrine, and in the following paragraph implied that they did. In the final Scheme of Methodist Union this second paragraph did not appear. A. S. Peake was probably reassured by the concluding section of the Special Resolution which said that the Holy Spirit

It is clear, however, that Peake was not entirely satisfied, for when the Union Committee met in the first week of March 1920, it appears that he had arranged in advance with Maldwyn Hughes, one of the Wesleyan leaders, to make a significant addition to the paragraph. He proposed:

That the evangelical doctrines for which Methodism has stood from the beginning, as held by the three Conferences, and generally contained in John Wesley's *Notes on the New Testament* and the first four volumes of his *Sermons, subject to the authority of divine revelation recorded in the Holy Scriptures,* shall be the doctrinal standard of the Methodist Church.

In view of his earlier article it looks as though Peake's intention was to conciliate his own radicals by the introduction of the Bible as the decisive factor in the definition, for the new wording meant that anything which could be squared with the Bible need not be squared with the *Notes on the New Testament.* This left Biblical Criticism the arbiter rather than Bengel modified by Wesley.

So much for the liberal attitude to the question of standards, which might be summed up under two heads: (*a*) an anxiety about the freedom of critical inquiry in the new Church; and (*b*) the fact that in Primitive and United Methodism little emphasis had ever been placed on John and Charles Wesley, they were thought of as almost a peculiarly 'Wesleyan' possession. A sociologist might find it worth his while to try to ascertain why the Methodists have been so uninterested in their own history—even the Wesley Historical Society was only founded in 1893.

More important than the liberal reaction, however, was that of a powerful wing of the Wesleyan Church. The leaders were ministers like J. E. Rattenbury and Amos Burnett, and laymen like Sir Henry Lunn and Kingsley Wood. They could count on the support of about one third of the Ministry and laity. They claimed to care especially for the links between Wesleyan Methodism and the Church of England, links which had been partly broken in the later nineteenth century, and which had no emotional appeal at

---

would preserve the purity and safeguard the development of doctrine within a faithful Church; and that it was essential to spiritual freedom that the living Church should interpret its own standards; this mention of *development* was what the non-Wesleyan Churches required to balance the implication that Wesley had set down the system of Evangelical truth once and for all.

all in the non-Wesleyan Churches. (The Primitive Methodists and United Methodists did not find much to satisfy them in the Anglican Book of Common Prayer and inherited a rather contemptuous assessment of Anglicanism.) Rattenbury and Lunn, however, did not really hold the Wesleyan theory of the Ministry which had been associated with these sentiments in early-nineteenth-century Wesleyanism and therefore lacked a completely coherent position; this was just as well, because they would have found even less sympathy than was the case if they had advocated a high view of the pastoral office. What they fastened on in the first paragraph of the section called 'Doctrine' was (a) its satisfaction with a statement about Methodism quite divorced from any setting in the Catholic Church, and (b) the absence of any appeal to the historical standards of the faith, either to the Historical Creeds, or to such seminal epochs as the Reformation. Such omissions, the Wesleyan opposition said, would make any future reconciliation of Methodism to the Church of England much more difficult. Of course, the mention of Creeds was anathema to many non-Wesleyans, who were not in any case very concerned about union with the Establishment. Their attitude was also deeply affected by what seemed at the time the unchecked progress of the Anglo-Catholic party in the Church of England; the Methodist negotiations took place during the unsuccessful campaign for the 1928 Prayer Book, a campaign which temporarily reawakened the old bitterness of Dissent. The 1920s were not the best time at which to advocate union between Methodism and the Established Church.

Two other points in the doctrinal section disturbed the opposition. In Scheme A the statement on doctrinal standards was followed by a very brief reference to the nature of the Ministry. No definition was offered. It was simply stated that 'the office of the Christian minister depends upon the call of God. . . . Those whom the Church recognizes as called by God, and therefore receives into its Ministry, shall be ordained by the imposition of hands, as expressive of the Church's recognition of the minister's personal call.' Such a rationalization of the laying-on of hands hardly justified laying them on at all, but of course the Wesleyan introduction of this form of ordination in 1836 did not rest on any profound belief in its theological necessity, but on an anxiety to assert the reality of the Wesleyan Ministry against the criticism of such Anglo-Catholic leaders as Pusey himself. Behind the rather vague brevity of this paragraph lay both the tumultuous history of nineteenth-century Methodism, in which the claim of the local preachers to be equal in status to the ordained minister played an important part, and also the growth of the popular picture of the Free Church minister as a cross between a highly rhetorical lecturer (W. M. Punshon), a business-man (C. H. Spurgeon), and a political leader (J. S. Lidgett). Here, however, the Wesleyan opposition was on weaker ground, for they had no very definite alternative doctrine of the Ministry to offer in place of the 'representative' theory. They knew that they felt a strong hesitation about what they were offered, but they could not help seeing the problem in the terms used by their opponents.[10]

[10] The Wesleyan opposition would probably have accepted the statement made by the Methodist Conference in 1960, when it said, in the course of a long official definition of *Ordination in the Methodist Church* that 'The Methodist Church is committed to the view that the ordained minister does not possess any priesthood which he does not share with the whole company of Christ's faithful people. But the doctrine of the "priesthood of all believers" is that we share, as believers, in the priesthood of our great High Priest, Jesus Christ Himself. As our High Priest he sacrificed Himself, a faultless offering, in utter obedience to God and infinite love to man, for the cleansing of our sins and our reconciliation to God; His sacrifice was made once and for all, but it is for ever efficacious, and He for ever makes intercession on our behalf. Into that priesthood of Christ we are taken up by faith, and we in our turn, and in self-identification with Him, offer ourselves in utter humility and obedience as a living sacrifice to God. We are "priests unto God", and therefore "take upon ourselves with joy the yoke of obedience", as we are enjoined in the Covenant Service. So the doctrine does not mean that every Christian has the right to exercise every function and administer both sacraments. For it is not an assertion of claims, but a declaration of our total obedience. A Methodist minister is a priest, in company with all God's faithful people; but not all priests are ministers.' Rattenbury and his friends were certainly looking for ways of making just this kind of distinction (whether the paragraph quoted above does more than assert such a distinction is another question, and the claim that laymen can administer Holy Communion in certain circumstances does not stand or fall with a particular definition of the doctrine of the priesthood of all believers, a doctrine for which no authoritative definition exists). Rattenbury was fighting against the stream in the 1920s, when a majority of the negotiators would have probably agreed with the *Dissentient View* published in the *Final Report* on the Anglican-Methodist Conversations (1963); the Dissentients said that the Methodist reference to the priesthood of all believers was not intended 'to obliterate the distinction between minister and laymen; but

The same difficulty oppressed them in their resistance to the last paragraph of the section on Doctrine. In this paragraph the negotiators tried to escape from the difficulties which surrounded lay administration of the Holy Communion by a standstill agreement; the 'general usage' of the uniting Churches, it was suggested, might continue. This could not be a final solution, because such a step meant federation rather than union. The subject was very complicated at the circuit level, however, because there were wide differences of practice in the actual service, which even affected such details as whether the communicants received the elements sitting or kneeling, from the minister or from a lay poor steward, or stewards. It was clear that without an agreement to allow most of these distinctions to continue for the time being no scheme of union would be accepted; none of the schemes mentioned the actual order of the service. And even apart from this strong practical argument in favour of lay administration, opposition to it would have had to be based on a doctrine of the Ministry in which the opposition did not really believe.

One may illustrate the situation from the intervention of the Mesopotamian chaplains in February 1920. Four Methodist chaplains, stationed in the Far East, F. W. Beal and J. J. Cook, who were Primitive Methodists, and H. A. Hindle and R. Newton Flew, who were both Wesleyans, discussed the questions of union together, and sent an eirenical letter to the Methodist Press. In this they said that 'according to the tradition of all branches of

---

the distinction is to be sought where Methodism has always looked for it —in gifts, graces and fruit, and specifically in the call of God to prophetic and pastoral work. . . . The normal officiant at the sacraments will be a minister, not because he is a special kind of priest but because the sacraments are bound up with preaching and pastoral work . . .' (op. cit. p. 61). The Conference statement of 1960 was prepared to make the positive statement that every Christian has not the *right* to administer both sacraments; the Dissentients of 1963 wished to insist that the minister would only be the *normal* officiant. In theory, the two positions could easily be reconciled, but in practice they depend on basic temperamental attitudes to the idea of the Ministry. The problem that Rattenbury faced, however, was also historical: neither the Primitive nor the United Methodists saw any objection to the frequent administration of baptism by laymen, for instance, and it is difficult to find a passage in the New Testament which specifically forbids laymen to baptize; traditional usage did not constitute ministerial *right*, it would have been argued in such quarters.

Methodism our Ministry is prophetic'; after ordination, which is the Church's confirmation of the preacher's personal call, 'the preacher has a more representative character than before'. The chaplains then considered the administration of Holy Communion and said that—(i) administration was almost entirely confined to ministers in Methodism as it was; (ii) the cause of general reunion in the future was better served by confining the duty to ministers; (iii) it was expedient that the one who presided at the Table of the Lord should be as representative as possible; and therefore (iv) 'laymen may forgo their claim to administer'. It was not easy to make a case for the total abolition of lay administration in the new Church if one's argument came so close to pure expediency: suppose there were a principle at stake.

For a few months there was considerable optimism about the 1920 Scheme and people talked as though union were imminent. But early in May 1921, the Wesleyan synods met and discussed the Scheme. Only the Sheffield and Cornwall Districts voted against it outright; at Leeds a similar resolution was lost by only two votes; but the thirty synods which passed affirmative resolutions did so in very cautious terms, and optimism vanished. Burnet, Rattenbury, and Lunn were encouraged to raise the principle of union at the meeting of the Union Committee on 2nd June 1921. Their defeat, by 108 votes to 12, was decisive; after that, the opposition could never hope to do more than amend the Scheme. This was also evident when the opposition raised the issue at the Wesleyan Conference in July 1921. J. E. Rattenbury and Sir Kingsley Wood moved an amendment in favour of some scheme of Methodist federation, but were defeated by 332 votes to 151. The Representative Session then accepted the 1920 Scheme as a basis for further discussion by 341 votes to 57, which left a large block of neutrals. In the non-Wesleyan Conferences there was no vote of any consequence against the Scheme.

In the debate in the Wesleyan Conference both Rattenbury and Lunn referred with approval to a speech on the doctrine of the Ministry which A. S. Peake had made at the Primitive Methodist Conference, and which had been published afterwards. The two Wesleyans said that if they really thought that Peake's speech represented the state of opinion in Primitive Methodism—it is perhaps worth while pointing out here once more that Peake was a layman —they would have had little hesitation about the Scheme. As it was, Rattenbury actually said that if the Scheme was adopted 'the religious life of the Methodist Church would be lowered'.

Peake had begun by saying that 'there is no strictly defined doctrine of the Ministry in the Methodist Church'. His own views, he thought, resembled those of G. G. Findlay, a Wesleyan. What then was the source of the ministerial commission and what was its significance? 'It comes to you through the Church and can only come in that way. Never forget that the divine source of your call does not render you independent of the Church. . . . You do not derive your ministry from the ministry by any succession which goes above the head of the Church and behind its back to Christ, for in all this He wills to trust His mystical body with the amplest powers and the fullest responsibility. You are therefore chosen representatives of the Church, possessing no privilege, no authority, which she does not possess, exercising no function which is not within her right, charged with no spiritual gift which is not already hers. . . . You have your ministerial significance only in so far as you are the accredited representatives of the Church, holding her commission, dispensing her gifts and graces. You are priests, but so is every Christian, and your priesthood is not intrinsically different from that of your lay brother.'

It is perhaps a sign of how much things have changed since the eighteenth century that John Wesley would hardly have accepted the limits set by Peake. He would have agreed with the rejection of the Anglo-Catholic position; he would have agreed that the pastor is the servant, not the master, of the Church of which Christ is the Head; but he would have seen an unnecessary confusion in Peake's use of the word 'Church'. He would have said that within the meaning of this concept there exists a fundamental relationship between pastor and flock, and that this cannot be satisfactorily described by saying that anything the pastor does, a member of his flock may do, or that the pastor is the 'representative' of the flock. To say that the Ministry has no authority which the Church does not possess is neither here nor there: the minister has authority *within* the Church. For Wesley, however, this authority was given by God; in extreme cases the layman might withdraw from one pastor and join himself to another, but as long as he remained with him he was bound to accept the pastor's authority. The situation was a little like that of the Byzantine ruler whose despotism was limited by his subjects' right of revolution.

Any Methodist theory of the Ministry must cover the early history of Methodism; an early itinerant like Christopher Hopper certainly appealed to Christ for his authority over the head of the visible Church as he knew it; Wesley himself would surely have hesitated at a definition which identified the Church so completely with the visible institutions of the Methodist world in the 1920s.

The negotiating committee set to work again and produced a second scheme which was presented to the Conferences of 1922. Little was done to quiet the doubts of the Wesleyan opposition, though the Wesleyan Conference was itself obliged to draw official attention to the loose drafting of the paragraph on the Sacraments in the section on 'Doctrine'. It is interesting to compare this paragraph with the similar passage in the answer which the Wesleyan 1922 Conference made to the Lambeth 'Appeal to all Christian People'; the Wesleyan Conference there affirmed its acceptance of the Apostles' and Nicene Creeds—'while claiming reasonable liberty of interpretation we heartily accept the substance of the teaching contained in both these venerable documents'. The Conference also said that Christ instituted two sacraments for His Church. In Scheme B this was put more loosely. 'The Methodist Church recognizes two sacraments . . . which from the beginning have been observed in the Church and of which it is the privilege and duty of members to avail themselves. . . . According to Methodist usage the sacrament of Baptism is administered to infants.' There was no actual statement of dominical institution in either case, nor any clear suggestion to parents that they were under any kind of obligation to bring their children for baptism. There is no need to suppose anything very significant behind this unhappy piece of drafting; but the rather casual attitude to doctrinal questions implied by all this helps to explain the alarm which some critics felt about the doctrinal statements.

At the Conference of 1923 statistics were produced which gave a clearer picture of what the laity of the three Churches thought of the prospect of Union. In Wesleyan Methodism there were 760 Quarterly Meetings. Of these, 341 voted for Scheme B as it stood; another 193 wanted amendments to the Scheme without claiming that they were essential. It was not so easy to analyse the remaining figures in the form they are given in the *Wesleyan Conference Minutes*, but it seems that 89 circuits voted against the 1922 Scheme, and 85 against the idea of organic union. About a fifth of the circuits were lukewarm or hostile. The actual votes in the Quarterly Meetings are given, and amount to 20,835 in favour of union and 9,682 against in the two groups cited above. These are small numbers, compared to the 1923 membership of Wesleyan Methodism, which stood at about 475,000, but the members of the Quarterly Meetings were the body of lay office-holders, especially class leaders and stewards, who mattered most in the denomination. One meets here straightaway the fact that about thirty per cent of the Wesleyan laity were either lukewarm or hostile to Union.

In the Wesleyan Methodist Church the local chapel trust also voted. Of 7,748 trusts 4,264 voted for Scheme B, and another 21 for the Scheme with amendments. Against Scheme B there voted 343 trusts, and against Union 1,343. In actual votes this amounted to 25,000 votes in favour of union and nearly 11,000 against. About 1,000 trusts did nothing at all, which suggests that they were not enthusiastic. In the case of the Trusts one can analyse the geographical distribution of the returns.

The biggest resistance was found in the Cornwall District, where there was a majority of 94 trusts to 60 against union, and in the Oxford District, where the majority in favour of union was only three—79 to 76, with 46 trusts which did not vote on the subject. These were both southern Districts, and in the three London Districts taken together the majority in favour of union —327 trusts to 142—was not much more than two to one. Elsewhere in the south, opinion ran more strongly in favour of union: Bedfordshire and Northamptonshire 150 to 51, Kent 77 to 28 and Portsmouth 124 to 39, were three to one in favour, while Devonport 125 to 31, Exeter 148 to 36, and Bristol 207 to 55 with 61 abstentions were as high as four to one. In East Anglia the trusts voted in favour of union by three to one—127 to 46—and this looks like a proof of friendly relations, for there were more Primitive than Wesleyan chapels in East Anglia, an unusual situation in England as a whole, but this area had the largest number of non-voting trusts, 66.

In the Midlands the Lincoln District voted heavily in favour of the Scheme, 195 to 44, and Notts and Derby only a little less so, 235 to 71, but the Birmingham area resembled London, for the majority in favour of union, 182 to 99 with 40 abstentions, was less than two to one.

None of the Northern districts produced a majority against the idea of union, which is all the more interesting because after 1932 some of the most stubborn local resistance to co-operation was to be found in Yorkshire and Lancashire, but six Districts were much more evenly balanced than the southern ones. Majorities similar to those found in the south occurred in Bolton 159 to 48, Halifax and Bradford 150 to 47, Whitby 196 to 42, and Carlisle 147 to 27, nor were there many trusts which did not vote in these Districts. But in the Manchester District 112 to 102, Sheffield 110 to 76, Leeds 104 to 78, York 118 to 79, Macclesfield 129 to 83, and Hull 92 to 62 with 59 abstentions, one sees a pattern of considerable tension.

The Primitive Methodist laity voted more heavily in favour of union. Out of 686 circuits 248 voted for the Scheme as it stood and only 26 voted against the Scheme or against union altogether. What probably added to the alarm of the Wesleyan opposition, however, was a fiery cluster of amendments proposed by the circuits. About 102 Primitive Methodist circuits still suggested that the Presidency should be open to a layman, and 125 would have liked to abolish the Ministerial Session of the proposed Conference; 60 circuits thought that in principle every official meeting should be free to elect its own chairman, and many circuits thought that a local preacher should be able to administer the Sacraments.

In the case of the United Methodist Church 45 out of 361 circuits accepted the Scheme as it was, the remainder simply submitting their favourite amendments. Eighty-one circuits sought the abolition of the Ministerial Session, and almost as many thought that laymen should occupy all the offices of the Connexion; 36 circuits, which contained ten per cent of the membership, asked for the omission of the reference to Wesley's *Notes* and *Sermons* in the proposed Standards, and 29 circuits, with about 10,000 members, objected to ordination by the imposition of hands. That there was very strong opposition to any interference with the principle of lay administration of the Sacraments becomes obvious when one puts together three groups of circuits. All accepted the principle of lay administration: 64, with about 23,000 members, thought that the local quarterly meeting should appoint suitable people; 34 circuits, with more than 17,000 members, thought that local preachers should be regarded as automatically qualified; another 20 circuits, anxious to safeguard the principle, proposed that each church should continue with its present practice. The total membership of the United Methodist Church at this time was 138,947 members. This feeling about lay administration never reflected itself in hostility to union, because the proposals covered the practice of United Methodism from the start; but the size of the group helps to explain why so many Wesleyan ministers thought that there was insufficient agreement on the subject to justify union, and even a chance that this point of view might spread, through union, into Wesleyan Methodism.

The Scheme which was submitted to the Conference of 1924 showed the influence of these figures. The most important point was that no great alteration was made to the section on doctrinal standards; there was still no mention of the Historic Creeds or of the position of Methodism in the Church of Christ. The issue of Baptism, raised by the Wesleyan Conference, was settled rather neatly by the insertion of the phrase 'of divine appointment and perpetual obligation' after the reference to the two Sacraments. The phrase was taken from the Foundation Deed Poll of the United Methodist Church (1907), in the circumstances an unimpeachable source. The article on lay administration, however, had grown extremely vague: 'The general usage of the three uniting Churches, whereby the sacrament of the Lord's Supper is administered by ministers, shall continue to be observed. Exceptions to the general usage may continue until the Conference, with fuller knowledge of the needs and resources of the United Church, is able to determine how to provide for all the Methodist people to partake of the Sacrament with "regularity and frequency".' As a formula this guaranteed the *status quo* for the time being, left the final decisions in the hands of a united Conference, in which the non-Wesleyan Churches would be strongly represented, and conceded to the opposition the usage, rather than the principle, of ministerial administration.

At the same time one new paragraph made its appearance, an attempt to define the Ministry. 'Christ's ministers in the Church are stewards of the household of God and shepherds of His flock. Some are called and ordained to the sole occupation, and have a principal and directing part in these great duties; but they hold no priesthood differing in kind from that which is common to all the Lord's people, and they have no exclusive title to the preaching of the Gospel or the care of souls. These are ministries shared with them by others, to whom also the Spirit divides his gifts severally as he wills.' This was taken from a Wesleyan Methodist statement on Church Membership (1908). It is a good illustration of the historical truth that the Methodist idea of the Ministry differs from the Anglican partly because it has always been affected by two institutional facts of some importance, the offices of the class leader and of the local preacher, the first concerned with the care of souls and the second with the preaching of the Gospel. In Methodism these offices existed from the start, so that any discussion of Methodism must mention them, whereas the Anglican lay reader is a recent innovation.

The circuits were now asked for a straight vote for or against the 1924 Scheme. This was done in 1924/5 and revealed a rather similar situation in each Church. In the case of Wesleyan Methodism the figures were 650 quarterly meetings in favour, 101 against, and eleven ties, this meant that 85·3% were in favour of union. When this was converted into actual votes, there were 27,230 in favour and 11,564 against, which meant that about 70% of the laity consulted were in favour. In the case of the trustees meetings, about 69% voted for this third Scheme, and the votes were 29,135 in favour (69%) and 13,086 against. The Primitive Methodist figures were much the same: 578 (86·3%) quarterly meetings voted for C Scheme, 92 against, and there were eleven ties. This represented 11,627 votes for the scheme (75·5%) and 3,769 against. In the United Methodist Church 280 quarterly meetings (80%) voted for Scheme C, 69 against, and there were seven ties; there were 7,963 votes in favour (70·74%) and 3,294 against. But although these figures implied an opposition of about 25 to 30 per cent in each denomination, the Wesleyan Conference was the only one in which this minority was represented at anything like full voting strength. The broad similarity of all forms of Methodism at this time is confirmed by the fact that 70 per cent of the Wesleyan laity was prepared to vote for Scheme C.

It was clear to the United Committee, however, that concessions must be made if success was to be certain in the Wesleyan Conference, all the more because it was agreed in 1925 that before legal powers were sought to consummate the union a vote of 75 per cent in favour would have to be obtained in each Conference. A sub-committee was set up to discuss the doubtful points, and it reported to the executive of the Union Committee in March

1926. Its proposal justified the delaying action fought by Rattenbury and his friends up to this stage. At the head of the section on
Doctrine a completely new paragraph was inserted, which established Methodism in the continuity of the historic Church. 'The
Methodist Church claims and cherishes its place in the holy Catholic Church which is the Body of Christ. It rejoices in the inheritance of the Apostolic Faith, and loyally accepts the fundamental
principles of the historic creeds and of the Protestant Reformation.
It ever remembers that in the Providence of God Methodism was
raised up to spread Scriptural Holiness throughout the land by the
proclamation of the Evangelical Faith. . . .' This gave the 'other
side', as they were sometimes called, most of what they had asked:
mention of the Catholic Church, the Apostolic Faith, the Historic
Creeds, and the Reformation tradition; the reference to Holiness
was a welcome return to the first principles of Methodism in a
period prone to accept the nineteenth-century heresy that the doctrine of assurance is the primary doctrine of Methodism. It is not
so clear what was meant by the appeal to the 'fundamental principles' of the Protestant Reformation; the term 'Reformation'
covers a wide variety of attitudes, and in England the Protestant
tradition had been predominantly Calvinist, until the Wesleyan
reaction gave a new respectability to the word 'Arminian'. This
point was actually raised in the full Committee by one of the
United Methodist representatives, J. T. Newton.[11]

[11] This all helps to explain the difficulties in which the later Anglican
and Methodist negotiators found themselves when working toward the
Final Report of 1963, which produced a scheme for the stage-by-stage
unification of the Anglican Methodist Churches. One of the negotiators,
Canon Kemp, wrote that 'whereas the Church of England has a number of
more or less official statements of its position in regard to various theological issues, and its Prayer Book, Ordinal and Articles occupy a special
position as guides to doctrine, the Methodist Church has no such body of
formularies. There are certain statements in the Deed of Union and there
are some documents which have since then been issued by the Methodist
Conference, but these are few in number and not widely known.'—*The
Anglican–Methodist Conversations, a Comment from Within*, E. W. Kemp
(1964), p. 30. In discussing Stage Two of the proposals made in the *Final
Report* Canon Kemp said that one of its problems would be as to 'what
doctrinal basis, if any, in addition to the Scriptures and the Creeds, shall
be adopted for the United Church? What is to become of the Thirty-
nine Articles and the Methodist Deed of Union?' (Ibid. p. 27). One cannot help feeling that the Scriptures and the Historic Creeds, both of which

To balance these additions the sub-committee proposed to add two sentences to the definition of the Ministry which had first appeared in the 1924 Scheme. The purpose of the insertion, according to Dr J. S. Lidgett, was to convince the non-Wesleyan representatives that the Wesleyans had nothing 'sacerdotal' in their minds. 'The Methodist Church holds the doctrine of the priesthood of all believers and consequently believes that no priesthood exists which belongs exclusively to a particular order of men. But in the exercise of its corporate life and worship special qualifications for the discharge of special duties are required, and thus the principle of representative selection is recognized.' These sentences seemed to express the view of the Ministry contained in the statement by A. S. Peake already discussed above.

Finally, a change was made in the approach to lay administration. This was important, because the institutional and theological cross at this point. The new section said once more that the 'general usage' of ministerial administration would continue, and then went on: 'Where, however, it can be shown that any Church is deprived of a reasonably frequent and regular administration through lack of ministers, the Circuit concerned may apply to Conference for the authorization of persons other than Ministers to administer the Sacrament.' Two points arise: (a) for the first time in the Schemes it was implied that lay administration was simply a solution to a problem caused by a shortage of ministers. Since union was being recommended on grounds of increased efficiency this was also to imply that the practice of lay administration would soon become unnecessary in the united Church (for it was unlikely that there would be any drastic increase in the frequency of Methodist Communion Services). The new paragraph therefore favoured Rattenbury's point of view, in so far as it

---

figure in the official statements of both Churches, would make a suitable basis; to draw up a new doctrinal basis would be to invite either a report like that on Anglican Doctrine issued in 1938, or the victory of one theological party over another, with the inevitable withdrawal of the defeated. Canon Kemp writes as though somehow the possession of plentiful official statements has been an advantage to the Church of England, but its history hardly bears him out; at any rate, the Methodists could only accept the Thirty-nine Articles 'with the same liberty of interpretation' that is notoriously a fact in the present Establishment. The very general terms of the Methodist statement make qualifications much less necessary.

seemed more important to stop lay administration than to show its theological impropriety. In 1960, however, there were still 156 lay dispensations. (b) The section referred to 'persons other than ministers'. This did not rule out the possibility of women administering the Lord's Supper. In fact, of the 156 dispensations granted in 1960, 38 were granted to deaconesses; there were 243 deaconesses at work in England of whom 62 were in pastoral charges. In 1958 the number of deaconesses with dispensations was 28. It is unlikely that anyone quite foresaw this development in 1926. Certainly the non-Wesleyan negotiators were satisfied. The United Methodist leader, Dr Brook, told his Conference in July 1926 that the section guaranteed 'the fact that there is no difference between the ministerial and lay administration' of the Holy Communion. The President of the Primitive Methodist Conference of 1926, A. L. Humphries, said in his address: 'What matters is not the hands from which the bread and wine is received, whether they be those of an ordained minister or a godly layman, but the realized presence of Christ, and that faith in the communicant which enables him to receive with the bread and the wine the grace of which they speak.'

There is no need to carry the story much farther, for this Scheme was the final compromise, its effect delayed until 1932 by the continued resistance of the Wesleyan minority. In the Wesleyan Synods of 1926, one Representative and eight Pastoral Sessions voted against the Scheme; in the Representative Sessions the vote in favour was 66% and in the Pastoral Sessions 57%. J. E. Rattenbury, J. H. Rider, and W. H. Armstrong now felt driven to persist. In the meantime the Primitive Methodist Conference met in June 1926; it passed the new clause on doctrine by 168 to 9 and the clause on the sacraments by 172 to 9; the final vote in favour of the scheme was 167 to 26. At the United Methodist Conference, which met in July just before that of the Wesleyan Church, the majority in favour of the new clauses was 263 to 7.

The majority party in Wesleyan Methodism made a great effort. At the July Conference J. E. Rattenbury's plea for further delay in view of the Synod results was rejected by 399 votes to 138 in the Representative Session; the resolution to go forward in terms of the 1926 Scheme was carried by 414 to 125. On this occasion the minority was reduced to less than 25%, the lowest in the whole struggle. It is very obvious that at this stage the Wesleyan laity was forcing unity on the Wesleyan Ministry; Hornabrook told the Pastoral Session, which accepted the Scheme 377 to 159, that the Representative Session of the twentieth century would never sit down to a blockade by the Pastoral Session. Even so the resources of the minority were not exhausted, and the leaders were themselves horrified when in 1927 the Wesleyan Representative Session carried by only 400 to 166 the resolution which would have initiated the legal consummation of Scheme D. This was less than the 75% majority which had been fixed as a target. Hastily, the leaders of the minority, including both J. E. Rattenbury and Sir Henry Lunn, came to terms with the advocates of union; they did so because they had no further positive demands to make, and because they could hardly carry on what was rapidly becoming a civil war in Wesleyan Methodism. A compromise which did not effect the content of the 1926 Scheme made union possible by 1932.

This seems to be a convenient point at which to look again at the question of the social causation of Methodist union in England. One important factor would be the gradual decay of the rural community after the agricultural distress of the years after 1870. Village Methodism slowly ceased to be a source of strength to the Connexion and became a financial embarrassment instead. Rural depopulation diminished the number of Methodists; the sudden disappearance of such ancient centres of independence as the windmill, the growth, in the twentieth century, of industrialized farming, all added to the problem. As the power of the Established Church in the countryside lessened, the necessity and the desire for a religious counterpoise weakened as well, and rural Nonconformity lost part of its *raison d'être*. The clerical magistrate and the rural Methodist political leader declined together. On the other hand, the various branches of Methodism gained little from the later tendency of southern and midland villages to become middle-class dormitories to the nearest large town: the chapels already belonged to 'the village', with which the commuters mixed much more superficially than they realized; if the 'new villagers' remained Christian at all they usually attended the Parish Church. Many villages retained from the later nineteenth century three rival Methodist chapels, each weakening the other two. In the union negotiations centralizers and rationalizers hoped to reduce the financial drain which all this involved. Rasher prophets talked as though union would make possible the Methodist colonization of the several thousand villages which had no Nonconformist chapel; realists knew that with luck unity might facilitate the strategic withdrawal of Nonconformity from rural England. That such a withdrawal was widely necessary showed that a considerable change had taken place in the pattern of rural society. After union, however, village Methodists proved deeply attached to their traditions and were often unwilling, in over-chapelled villages, to join together in worship. Thus rural depopulation and decline weakened all three denominations and made their leadership ready for union (the brief Wesleyan Methodist gains in membership in the mid-1920s were largely urban); in the countryside itself, however, union tended to cause further decay.

Another social factor which was deeply involved was the problem of status. In the early 1920s the Wesleyan Methodist Conference passed resolutions which would have meant a substantial rise in ministerial stipends; within twelve months the administration had to confess that many circuits could not meet the new scales, and the plan dropped. The brief affluence of the 1920s, and the rise in Wesleyan membership made little difference to the situation. As a result, the post-war social status of the Methodist Ministry (which depended largely on the prestige of the Wesleyan Methodist Ministry) fell: already in the 1920s the Wesleyan Conference was deploring in its public *Minutes* the lack of first-class candidates for the Ministry. It was said (and the statement was one which was heard again in the 1950s) that many suitable men were entering the teaching profession instead, a fact for which the lowered status of the Ministry was partly responsible. A wider pattern was operating here: the status of the Protestant Ministries had been declining in America and England since the early nineteenth century: it corresponded to the rise of the highly organized professions, whose skills became more highly valued by the community as a whole. Protestant Ministries moved towards one another in the struggle for social survival; this was one of the famous non-theological factors in the ecumenical movement.

Nevertheless, the question of social status probably helps to account for the opposition to union in Wesleyan Methodism. Many Wesleyan ministers must have been sensitive to the social decline of their caste and have clung hard to the traditions and independence of Wesleyan Methodism as a source of strength—this process seems to have repeated itself in the opposition to union between the Methodist and Anglican Churches in the 1960s: the virtual disappearance of Methodism would mean a similar loss of identity for many Methodist ministers. In the 1920s this Wesleyan ministerial opposition interpreted the union schemes as meaning the absorption of the non-Wesleyans by the Wesleyans; they regarded such a step as a dilution of their own order; bringing in United Methodist and Primitive Methodist ministers could only, as they saw it, further depress the social level of the whole new group. Any group whose status is falling will think any change is for the worse. (In all three groups some institutional friction occurred because men who had had hopes of promotion in the existing denominations were likely to stay unpromoted in the major body.)

The causes of this sense of social dilution (often expressed in terms of religious dilution) were various. The instance of the Wesleyan and Primitive Methodists is instructive. Primitive Methodism had originally emerged as the religious expression of what has been called 'the revolt of the field', the effort of the nineteenth-century rural worker to achieve recognition as a human being, equal in every respect to the worker in the towns. This struggle, symbolized by the erection of country chapels and the foundation of agricultural workers' unions, had ended by about 1914—in fact, a further source of decline in the case of Primitive Methodism was a split between pietist and political activists which resulted in the withdrawal of most of the political activists in the Edwardian period. Nevertheless, the main strength of Primitive Methodism lay outside the larger towns, and the whole process left in the mythology of the other Methodist groups an image of the Primitives as poor, under-educated, and rural. In reality, in Durham and other parts of the north-east the Primitive Methodists had been miners; in railway boom towns like Swindon they worked on the railway and in railway factories; on the coast, as in East Anglia, they often worked part of the year as fishermen. After 1914–18, however, groups like these, as well as the farming industry, dwindled economically; this damaged both the social image and the actual strength of the Connexion.

In Cambridge, for instance (itself in a rather backward agricultural county), the head chapels of the Wesleyan and Primitive Methodist circuits were both examples (at the time of union) of what is best called Late Victorian Builders' Ecclesiastical, less a style than a way of indicating 'here is what you will recognize as a Nonconformist chapel without actually having to enter it'. The Wesleyan chapel was much larger than the Primitive one, however, and had been supplemented by a second, even larger chapel built in an Anglican-looking style with a centre aisle, shallow transepts, and a rather wide chancel. In Manchester, the Wesleyan Methodists had proved elastic enough, through the Forward Movement, to replace their once-famous urban chapel in Oldham Street with a Central Mission on the same site (1885) to which was added the non-architectural Albert Hall (1910). The Primitive Methodists, on the other hand, had no powerful church in central Manchester, and in the 1920s had to borrow the Albert Hall when they wished to hold their Connexional Conference in the city. In Wiltshire, one of the scenes of early Primitive Methodist triumph, Swindon had prospered as a railway town. A leading Primitive Methodist layman of the 1920s was a business man in Swindon, but the chapels were closely identified with the railway (the old Great Western) and the other prominent local layman was a trade-union leader who stood as a Labour candidate for Parliament on a number of occasions in the county. On the whole, the middle-class laymen produced by Primitive Methodism after about 1880 failed to stamp their image on either the connexional or the larger ecclesiastical map; when Wesleyan Methodist official statements in the 1920s deplored the middle-class image of Wesleyan Methodism and said that it estranged the working classes from the body, they still thought of the Primitive Methodists as existing on the working-class side of the social fence.

The United Methodist Church was much less homogeneous than the Primitive Methodist. It contained some very old New Connexion societies, a south-western Bible Christian element whose traditions were anti-Anglican rather than anti-Wesleyan, and a large group of formerly Methodist Free Church societies (Baillie Street in Rochdale would be the perfect example) which traced their origin back to direct conflict with Wesleyan Methodism. Wesleyan ministers thought of the United Methodist Church largely in terms of this last group; they inherited a strong historical prejudice against them as seceders from the Wesleyan Connexion at some time between 1827 and 1857. Although almost all Wesleyan Methodist ministers had abandoned the attitude to the Ministry which had been a major cause of the conflict of 1849 they still thought of the United Methodist Church as one in which the Ministry was denied its proper authority. An accession of United Methodist ministers and laymen would, they believed, mean a further weakening of the traditional importance of the Wesleyan Methodist Ministry. Taken together, this complicated pattern of social and historical prejudice goes a long way to explain why there was so much resistance to union in the Wesleyan Ministry.

Another factor which made for union was a steady decrease in the number of people whose lives were entirely bound up with the existence, survival, and rewards of the Methodist denominations. The demand that a man should completely identify himself with his particular Free Church, should live every aspect of his life, from marriage to politics, through *its* life, and should make heavy economic sacrifices for its sake, became common in the course of the nineteenth century, and in the end over-reached itself. Reaction against this excessive demand for attention probably explains the rapid contraction of the English Free Churches after about 1910 (and also explains why the Church of England, which has normally demanded less of its laity, has done less badly in the same period). All ministers, including Anglican and Roman Catholic, tend, consciously or unconsciously, to try to create a church-centred laity of this kind; they buttress the attempt with theological word-pictures of the Church, identifying their particular institutions with the Body of Christ. It looks, however, as though the great nineteenth-century success of the attempt to create such an intensively loyal laity was due chiefly to particularly favourable social circumstances. There were the Dissenting disabilities (and the whole social situation which they implied); the social and cultural isolation of the kind of rural group often attracted to such bodies as Primitive Methodism; the ethnic and political isolation of certain groups of Roman Catholics, for that matter. Social change in the present century destroyed many of the old patterns of isolation on which denominational loyalty largely depended; the leadership of the Methodists, if not the rank and file, found themselves living in a far more open society. Here the demand for excessive attention, which was still being made out of force of habit, had two effects.

Reaction against it made Methodists who remained attached to their denominations more willing to achieve union. On the other hand, much of the *local* resistance to union, a resistance that in the end nullified much that seemed to have been accomplished in the exultation and self-congratulation of 1932, came from the surviving groups of people whose lives were totally identified with the older denominational structure and who could not adapt their lives to a new one. Such people were naturally not often represented in the leadership of the connexions; they might even have voted for union on a national scale; but at the local level their lives were so moulded by the form of the local society which had been their essential environment that they could not make their votes effective, however hard they tried. One further point that emerges here is that when denominations with a tradition of demanding excessive attention shrink they tend to become more obstinately independent and more difficult to attract into schemes of union: this is because the majority of people who actually belong to this kind of shrinking body are those whose personal happiness virtually depends upon its continued existence. In countries where the uniting bodies do not overlap this presents much less of a problem, since the sacrifice of the local society is less likely to be asked for immediately by a reunion scheme. In other words, it is vital to unite Methodism and Anglicanism before Methodism contracts beyond the point at which such a union can usefully take place at all. In some parts of the country this point has been passed already.

This list of social factors is not exhaustive. It would require a special essay to discuss the impact on Methodist particularism, and then on the very existence of Methodism, of the rapid abandonment of Methodist (especially Wesleyan) day-schools after 1870. Almost all the social factors after 1900 were working towards the destruction of the foundations of the Methodist denominational system as part of the environing Free Church system: in this sense Methodist union was only a stage in the dissolution of Methodism. Union created no new constituency, did not in itself alter the social situation in which the new denomination existed. A denomination must presumably serve either a social or a religious purpose, or both. The Free Churches, including the Methodist Church, seem to have lost their social justification; they could survive if they had a religious justification: the Brethren, for instance, can probably survive almost any degree of social irrelevance to the total community. In the 1920s the Wesleyan Methodist opposition to Methodist union fought for religious points, but could not find a religious ground for the continuing separation of Wesleyanism from the other Methodist Connexions. They had to yield to the social realities. In the same way the defenders of the *Minority Report* have to find a religious ground for the continuing separate existence of the Methodist Church in the 1960s before they can hope to defy the social realities of the situation. In the present disintegrating state of theology their success in persuading people that they *had* a religious ground would be an ecclesiastical disaster, for success could only mean that they had invented a sect.

CONCLUSION

At first sight there was little to divide the three branches of English Methodism, and yet the struggle was intense, especially in Wesleyan Methodism. Why was this? The answer seems to be that for the Wesleyan minority, at any rate, the 'Church' meant the traditional kind of institution which they knew best through Anglicanism of the older, plainer, less Anglo-Catholic kind; an Anglicanism in which the relation between the minister and the people was taken for granted rather than worked out theologically. It was psychologically impossible for a Wesleyan brought up against this background to imagine himself receiving the elements from the hands of a godly layman, and to tolerate those who did seemed a kind of treason. In the non-Wesleyan Churches, on the other hand, there had evolved a very different ecclesiastical pattern; here the 'Church' meant a community wide open to the laity at all points. A Primitive Methodist of this generation might almost have been persuaded to accept episcopacy, provided the episcopate was open to the laity. A lay bishop was precisely the idea behind their lay vice-president. The Wesleyan minority felt that the non-Wesleyans would destroy any sense of order in the Church; the non-Wesleyans felt that the 'other side' wanted to impose an ecclesiastical order for which there was insufficient theological justification. The flaw in the position of the Wesleyan minority was that they had no basis from which to attack lay administration in principle; general consent to lay administration in practice, however restricted, made union possible.

The weakness of the non-Wesleyan position lay in a flabby doctrine of the Holy Spirit which assumed that the 'spiritual' must always be the spontaneous, the unrehearsed, the unwritten and the unread. Behind this again were two forms of social organization, the one emphasizing the need for hierarchy, the other content with something more like a permanent 'frontier' conception of society. At Methodist Union the two groups united only the negative aspects of their respective principles. The clash was fundamental because the one tradition emphasized that the Holy Spirit normally worked through a social and ecclesiastical hierarchy, whereas the other preferred to think of the Holy Spirit as more probably cutting across existing social and religious institutions.

On the whole, this study suggests that the usual picture of Methodist Union in England is misleading. It is usually implied that doctrinal factors were unimportant; in fact, they presented the major difficulty that the process struck. The general pressure in favour of union was so strong, however (and here the all-pervasive indifference to theology was probably decisive), that the Wesleyan minority was forced to abandon its hope of preventing any form of lay administration of the Eucharist. At the same time, however, the apparent agreement on the institutional level was a little illusory; it worked all right at the departmental and college level, but became much less obvious at the equally important level of the local churches. This would have mattered less in a country where the uniting denominations had flourished largely in separate areas geographically (as was the case with Methodist union in the United States just before the second World War), but the three uniting Churches were represented in every English town of any importance, and sometimes in even quite small villages. The resulting problem was one of human relations, rather than Church relations. In so far as these problems have solved themselves since 1932, the major cause had been the steady growth of a common English culture, based on prosperity.

TWO

The Doctrine of the Ministry in Early Nineteenth-century Methodism

I—THE EXTRAORDINARY MESSENGERS OF GOD

'The Conference is the living Wesley'—JABEZ BUNTING

'CHANGE is not Reform', said John Randolph of Roanoke, the Virginian disciple of Edmund Burke. The central theme of this essay is that the present Methodist view of the Ministry differs widely from that held in Wesleyan Methodism in the early nineteenth century by the conscious successors of John Wesley, men such as Richard Watson and Jabez Bunting. The secessions from Wesleyan Methodism which were such a marked feature of the period between Wesley's death and 1857 are best explained as the clumsy, human, and unfortunate way in which the movement from the earlier to the later doctrine of the Ministry took place. Jabez Bunting himself figured so largely as the leader of men who believed that they drew their ideas and values straight from John Wesley, that it seems reasonable to call this head of a superseded party the Last Wesleyan. For few people nowadays recognize his name, and fewer still would recognize his point of view as Methodist.

The intention of this first section is to supply the background against which the later debates about the nature of the Methodist Ministry must be understood. To do this it is necessary to go back to the early years of the Revival when, if we may still quote Professor A. J. Toynbee, John Wesley was hard at work 'evangelizing an English underworld to which an eighteenth-century Established Church had heartlessly turned a blind eye'.[1] In the first phase of the Revival there was naturally no suggestion of a specifically Methodist Ministry, since John Wesley, himself an Anglican, thought of the early Societies as a means of stimulating, and even perhaps of reforming, the Church of England, and so did his best to keep within the limits set by the regulations of his own Church

[1] *A Study of History,* IX.459.

44

Preaching, sacramental worship, and discipline were all at first in the hands of the small group of evangelically minded clergymen who felt that God was prepared to accept such canonical irregularities as their itinerancy, and their willingness to preach in market-place and field without episcopal permission.

But their successful preaching of the Gospel meant that here and there a layman like John Nelson, the mason of Birstal, found himself led little by little into what amounted to preaching. There is nothing astonishing in this; the previous century had grown familiar with men who felt that the Lord had given them a special message for their generation. But it did create what rapidly became a unique situation. The spread of the Revival through the country was the work of laymen as well as of the recognized clergymen, and the harvest was soon too great to be handled by the episcopally ordained ministers alone. Nor was there much hope of additional pastoral assistance from the Church of England; for if official Anglicanism was suspicious of Methodist doctrine, John Wesley himself had a poor opinion of the doctrines held by many of the parish priests to whom he would have had to commit his people. This remained a constant factor in his reasoning, as is obvious in his correspondence with Samuel Walker of Truro. (It is a significant comment on Walker's own position that the Societies he laboured to keep within the parish system seceded after his death, because of the attitude of his successor.)[2]

Wesley's reaction to this situation was definite without being dogmatic. He believed that the converting power of the lay preachers was more significant than their standing in the eyes of a Church which had always frowned on the unordained—and therefore normally untrained—preacher. He saw that in the actual circumstances of the Revival it would be extremely difficult to stop these men from saving souls by sending them home to silence, as he was often advised that he ought to do. He never attempted to deny the faults and even excesses of some of these men, or to conceal their lack, in many cases, of a formal education. But he refused to sacrifice their usefulness to the indifference of the bishops and the strait-jacket of rules; because he realized that if men like John

[2] See *The Early Cornish Evangelicals*, G. C. B. Davies, S.P.C.K. (1951). The writer sympathizes with Walker, and does not see the significance of the fact that the Truro Congregational Church was founded by Walker's followers in 1770.

Nelson were controlled and taught, their value might be immensely increased. It seems to me one of Wesley's major triumphs that he so largely succeeded in the difficult task of giving the Methodist preachers a common voice and a common loyalty—a triumph which has often been ignored in Methodism, because it is so frequently taken for granted that a man is sufficiently equipped for his ministry by the original call of God. Wesley, as the *Minutes* of the eighteenth-century Conferences show, laboured all his life to encourage in the itinerancy habits of disciplined living, of hard study, of convinced assent to certain fundamental doctrines, and in this way sought to create a preaching order which God could effectively employ. In the first stages of the Revival, when a permanent denomination was the last result which Wesley must have expected from his work, there was no reason why he should believe that he was seriously trespassing on the traditional privileges of the Anglican Ministry by giving these men his personal authority to preach. The theory that an unordained man ought not to mount the steps of a pulpit has always had a somewhat artificial, institutional look about it, although it has the commonsense value of making a congregation less likely to suffer subjective revelations in the best Fifth Monarchy style. But Wesley knew what his preachers, local and itinerant, were saying; he believed that their doctrines were the very essence of the Church of England's standards, and so he was the less disturbed at the offence which was technically taking place. (Methodists often forget that although Wesley himself held that a man could preach the Gospel without episcopal permission, the Church of England did not.)

But the very fact that Wesley accepted, trained and directed the itinerant preachers made it more likely that they would develop into a formal Ministry. An individual wandering preacher made no serious inroads into the authority of parson or bishop, and might be ignored, unless he seemed a public nuisance. But a disciplined band of men with no ecclesiastical sanction beyond what Wesley gave them, and no loyalty other than their personal loyalty to him and to the Societies which they served, was another matter altogether. By the middle of the century, as Wesley told them in 1769, they had become 'one body', and 'acted in concert with each other, and by united counsels'.[3] Perhaps one of the grounds for their rapid itinerancy was a desire to mark the dis-

[3] *Minutes of the Wesleyan Methodist Conference* (1862), I.87.

46

tinction between them and the settled parish priest of the eighteenth century, but the system added enormously to their sense of being a group apart, of being dedicated men whether or not they were ordained, of being 'the Methodist Preachers', a title of honour as well as of notoriety. And the character of their office was still further impressed upon them by the *Rules of an Assistant* (1744), of which the first set the tone for all the rest:

Be diligent; never be unemployed a moment. Never be triflingly employed. Never while away time. Neither spend any more time at any place than is strictly necessary.[4]

In the development of the Methodist Ministry, nothing is more important than the authority which John Wesley felt himself able to exercise. How he justified his position to himself may be seen from the *Minutes* of 1745, where he discusses the origin of Church government:

Christ sends forth a preacher of the Gospel. Some who hear him repent and believe the Gospel. They then desire him to watch over them, to build them up in the faith, and to guide their souls in the paths of righteousness. Here then is an *Independent* congregation; subject to no pastor but their own, neither liable to be controlled in things spiritual by any other man or body of men whatsoever. But soon after some from other parts who are occasionally present while he speaks in the name of Him that sent him, beseech him to come over to help them also. Knowing it to be the will of God, he consents. Yet not till he has conferred with the wisest and holiest of his congregation, and with their advice appointed one or more who has gifts and grace, to watch over the flock till his return. If it please God to raise a new flock in the new place, before he leaves them he does the same thing: appointing one whom God has fitted for the work to watch over these souls also. . . . These are *Deacons*, or servants of the Church, and look on the first Pastor as their common father. . . . These congregations are not absolutely *independent*: they depend on one Pastor, though not on each other. As these congregations increase, and as their Deacons grow in years and grace, they need other subordinate Deacons or helpers: in respect of whom they may be called Presbyters, or elders; as their father in the Lord may be called the Bishop, or Overseer of them all.[5]

It would not be fair to Wesley to press the details of this passage too closely, but in it we can see how the course of the Revival had seemed to him to justify the fundamental step of using the

[4] Ibid. p. 24.   [5] Ibid. p. 26.

full-time but unordained preachers to do the essentially ministerial work of overseeing the congregations. There was first the suggestion of a natural link between converting people and having authority over them in the Gospel, an idea which he would no doubt have defended by referring, for instance, to the relationship between St Paul and his converts in the churches of North (or South) Galatia. A man who receives this basic authority, which depends upon Christ, may, in consultation with the wisest and holiest of the people, appoint someone to look after his people when he is evangelizing elsewhere. The deacon's status was subordinate, as his name was meant to imply, and his authority was entirely derivative; but to do the task which he was set he must obviously carry out the duties of the Ministry. This was in accordance with what Wesley had decided in 1744. He had said that an Assistant was to be used 'only in cases of necessity' (for he was still anxious to conform to Anglican custom as far as possible), but that 'in the absence of the Minister, (he is) to feed and guide, to teach and govern the flock'.[6]

One may be permitted to find the explanation of his personal authority which Wesley implied in this sketch of the origin of ecclesiastical government more persuasive than that which he later adopted from Lord King. It was more closely relevant to the historical realities of Wesley's own position, whereas a discussion of the relative status of presbyter and bishop was neither inspiring nor very conclusive. But Wesley's concern with the possible episcopal powers of presbyters sprang from his later need to make a case for the ordinations which he saw must come; in this earlier, more fluid situation, he took a broader, less technical view of the matter. It is one which may be used to establish an excellent general justification of the existence of the Methodist Ministry.

But this was not, of course, what Wesley had in mind in 1745. He was not apologizing for a claim on the part of the Assistants to ministerial status; he himself did not think of them as ministers. He was anxious to explain the fundamental point, that his authority derived from his being sent by Christ to preach the Gospel. In the actual day-to-day circumstances of the Revival the pressing problem was how to build up the people who had been brought from darkness into light, and who had for the first time become a people in the Methodist Societies. As a true minister of Christ,

[6] *Minutes of the Wesleyan Methodist Conference* (1862), I.23.

Wesley felt a tremendous responsibility for the spiritual welfare of those who had come into the Church, for there clearly had to be a sense in which they belonged to Christ's flock. The parish priests, however, would not often help, but often willingly hindered, and there remained this host of souls crying out for oversight, for guidance, for knowledge, for government.

Wesley's profound conviction was that in such a moment God Himself is not limited by the rules of His Church, but is free to act through His chosen servants; when Christ's messengers find themselves at a loss, He Himself empowers them to turn from the normal pastoral system and themselves choose and appoint men to do what must be done. This is not in the first instance to create a new Ministry; only with the passage of time could such deacon-assistants become presbyters, and Wesley added as qualifications growth in wisdom and grace. But in the meantime, Christ's government of the Church must be carried on. Thus the origin of the Wesleyan Assistants was to be found not only in the command of God to preach, but also in the necessity of pastoral oversight. This twofold source was apt to be forgotten in the nineteenth century, when a deal of time was wasted in trying to show that there was no difference between a local and an itinerant preacher.

In this evangelical necessity, then, lay the origin of the Assistants; and in Wesley's original qualification, that they were to be used 'only in cases of necessity', can be seen the tension in his mind as to what he was doing. So far as organization was concerned, Wesley spent his life trying to reconcile the contradictory demands of his loyalty to the Church of England and his loyalty to the Revival. He could say that the Assistants possessed no ministerial status, because they were unordained, did not administer the Sacraments, and drew their authority to preach and teach from his own authority as a Pastor and Overseer in the sense of the *Minutes* of 1745. Their continual movement prevented them from presenting the appearance of settled ministers. But the success of their preaching and of their pastoral work meant that they grew in popularity and in *de facto* authority as the years went by; and the personal dependence upon Wesley became less obvious, less all-important as the Connexion expanded. The movement toward ministerial self-consciousness started early, but was never likely to reach its natural conclusion as long as Wesley lived. He himself always preferred the mental compromise which he worked out in the 1740s. In the famous Korah Sermon,[7] which he preached in 1789 (and which was once a favourite with High Church writers who sought to question Wesleyan orders), he sharply rebuked some of the Assistants who thought that they could administer the Sacraments in virtue of the original authority which he had given them. In that sermon he described the itinerants of the 1740s as 'extraordinary messengers of God', called to provoke the ordinary Ministry of the Church to jealousy and emulation, and so to make the office of Assistant unnecessary in the long run. This perfectly summarized Wesley's attitude for many years. But when he preached the Korah Sermon he had already been ordaining since 1784, and the sands of that compromise were running out.

Enough has been said to show the tradition of which Jabez Bunting became the heir. It was the tradition of an *extraordinary mission*, which was gradually developing into a settled Christian community. We may exaggerate the slowness of the change after 1791. However much the 'virtual ordination theory' is open to criticism (see an article 'Ordination in Methodism', by A. Raymond George, in the *London Quarterly and Holborn Review*, April 1951), the young men who were received into Full Connexion in the years after Wesley's death did not regard themselves as entirely without ministerial status, though it must also be said that a feeling of inferiority to the Clergy did persist for at least a generation. The introduction of ordination by the imposition of hands in 1836 was at once evidence of this, and of the growth of a complementary self-confidence. Bunting said to the Conference of that year that he thought of himself as having been ordained 'in essence'. He normally meant exactly what he said, and it was certainly not his intention to cast doubts upon the validity of his own ministry. There was no suggestion in 1836 that the men already in Full Connexion should be 'reordained'; instead, the new departure took for granted the 'virtual ordination' of the Conference. Forty-five years after Wesley's death there seemed no hope at all of obtaining episcopal approval from the Establishment, now in the throes of the Tractarian controversy. Indeed, the Conference of 1836 welcomed the introduction of the laying-on of hands, as a gesture of reply to the now renewed Anglican doubts about the validity of Wesleyan sacraments, and about the propriety of Methodism in general.

[7] *Wesley's Works* (1860), Vol. VII, Sermon 115.

Yet the question of ordination was vital, because a form of ordination would be the recognizable bridge between an extraordinary and an ordinary commission. Wesley had done his best to persuade some existing, orthodox Ministry to confer its regular authority by the imposition of hands. The failure of his efforts is well known, and the Conference made no attempt to continue the succession of ordinations which Wesley himself began. But by 1836, after all the refusals and evasions, it had become clear that the Methodist itinerants could become regular ministers only through an act of their own. And the decision to introduce ordination by the imposition of hands was the necessary proclamation of conscious maturity. For the fundamental question was still one of authority and not of ceremony. Whether the hands were those of John Wesley or those of the President of 1836, Jabez Bunting himself, could make no difference in the eyes of those who insisted that the hands must be episcopal, nor has official Anglicanism ever accepted the view that a presbyter may ordain as well as a bishop. In an ordination charge, delivered in 1829, Bunting said: 'You do a solemn thing when you take the pen and cross out the name of one who is no longer esteemed worthy of a place in the visible Church.'[8] It was the growth of the conviction that the fruits of the extraordinary mission had taken their place within the One Church of Christ which gave the Wesleyan itinerants the confidence to proclaim their Ministry. Their action was based on the conviction that God, acting through an earthly succession of events rather than of bishops, had made them presbyters.

II—THE OFFICE OF A BISHOP

'It is no sin for a man to think that our discipline is wrong, provided that he quits us'—JABEZ BUNTING (1835)

On 27th August 1828 a new Methodist body, styling itself the 'Wesleyan Protestant Methodists', was formed in Leeds. A pamphlet was published, to 'clear their conduct from those unworthy, secular, and political motives, which have been falsely attributed to them'. The Tenth Protest perfectly summarized the impression

8 *Bunting's Sermons* (1862), II.363f.

which Jabez Bunting's view of the Ministry made on many Wesleyans, and the fury with which they reacted against it:

They protest . . . against submitting any longer to the unlimited authority of the preachers, as being contrary to the principles of Christianity, the practice of the Primitive Church, and the privileges of English subjects; and from the experience they have had that such power has been perpetually on the increase, is still increasing, and is unworthily exercised; and because there has been no instance in the history of the Christian Church in which spiritual tyranny has not been fatal to the interests of religion, the character of its ministers, and the undoubted rights and privileges of the people.[9]

Vigorous language! Though it is mild enough, if compared with some pamphlets that we might have quoted. What then was this view of the Ministry, which its opponents called 'spiritual tyranny', and protested against as 'unlimited authority'?

What James Everett loved to sneer at as 'Buntingism' was simply the claim by the Wesleyan ministers that they had reached a point in their development at which they were entitled to the prerogative which John Wesley had regarded as essentially ministerial. There was no trace of the layman left in the itinerant, who had become a true minister of Christ, as Richard Watson said. And a true minister of Christ possessed great authority, because he was entrusted with great responsibility; moreover, it was felt that God was no respector of 'the privileges of English subjects'.

The theory of Bunting and his friends began with the assumption that the Ministry was of divine institution. Alfred Barrett, for example, opened his *Essay of the Pastoral Office*[10] by showing how Jesus instituted the Ministry through the apostles, who in their turn gave directions for its perpetuation, and for the superintendence and instruction of the Church, guided by the Holy Spirit which they received at Pentecost. The minister, however, was not called simply to do the work of an evangelist, in the sense of being only a preacher and teacher. The Ministry existed by a divine commission, for the purpose of enforcing specific morality as well as of preaching specific doctrine; and the carrying out of these responsibilities could not be made dependent on the opinions, the will, or the votes of the people to whom the Ministry offered itself. It would not be far wrong to say that, in the true Wesleyan

[9] The Protestants protested vigorously; this was the Tenth and concluding Protest.   [10] London (1839).

52

theory, the Ministry as a whole had the same significance for the Church as is possessed, in Anglican thinking, by the episcopate.

Bunting believed that God himself placed the local Methodist congregation in the charge of the pastor, who would have to answer for the souls of his people in the Last Day. And since Methodism was Connexional (and it is very important to remember that Connexionalism itself was looked upon as a New Testament principle), the ministers were found to meet together for their mutual advantage; and when they did so, their authority was of the same kind as that of the individual, but could be applied on a wider scale. Thus the annual ministerial Conference had the same kind of responsibility for, and oversight of, the whole Connexion as the individual minister exercised in the local Societies. For the duration of the Conference, a united Ministry accepted the burden of the whole laity.

The language of the day spoke of the authority inherent in the pastoral office, and of the obedience which Christian people owed to those who had the rule over them. In more recent terminology, we may prefer to speak of the place of '*episkope*', in the sense of oversight, in the life of the Church of Christ. We must speak of life rather than of structure, because this was most emphatically not the kind of reinterpretation of 'episcopacy' which accepts it as a form of Church government which may be expedient in particular historical circumstances—a point of view which sometimes suggests that the Church of Christ is like any secular corporation, which needs a chairman and a book of rules before it can function happily. *Episkope* was understood by Bunting to mean the minister's oversight of the Christian well-being of the souls committed to his charge by God, so that Church government was not a 'thing indifferent' to be settled by compromise in a spiral of committees but a fundamental relationship established in the Church by Christ Himself as supreme head. Oversight as a part of the Church's very being had been driven deep into the consciousness of early Methodism by the behaviour of John Wesley himself, who rode about England not only as an evangelistic preacher but also as the overseer, the Superintendent, of the Methodist Societies. On occasion he virtually disbanded a society which failed to satisfy his conception of the conduct proper to members of the Church, and this power of oversight was never subjected to any degree of popular control.

We may pause here to consider the relevance of other theories of episcopacy to this position. The word 'episcopacy' itself is constantly used with different meanings, and it is well to remember that in the early nineteenth century, Wesleyan ministers like Jabez Bunting, deeply perturbed by the growth of the Oxford Movement, firmly repeated John Wesley's own denial of the all-importance of the historic succession of bishops. Alfred Barrett, for example, was at great pains to show from the Pastorals that a minister must be 'blameless', one who walks not after the flesh, but after the Spirit. Without this, apostolic ordination was useless:

If he be brought into ever such an unbroken line of succession from the apostles, it is all in vain; no power on earth can ordain a man who upon the principle of St Paul has no right to be viewed as a candidate for pastoral office. . . . The first person in the line of ordination who, when he was inducted, could not be called a faithful man, broke the claim oɪ that time, as such, to the authority of Christ and of the Holy Ghost, and the true Ministry was perpetuated only among its faithful living links . . . .[11]

So far as the system of diocesan episcopacy was concerned, Barrett followed Richard Watson in the opinion that the superiority of the Bishop came about *iure humano*, with the common consent of the presbyters, and rested on no higher foundation.[12]

But the existence of diocesan episcopacy was a reminder of the need for oversight on the ministerial as well as the congregational level. The natural way in which to discharge this responsibility was through some form of hierarchy. Barrett, for instance, pointed out that in circuits where several ministers were stationed, one was called Superintendent, 'which word is a literal version of Bishop';[13] within the district there was further subordination to the Chairman, though this was by compact, 'and does not arise from any original distinction in ordination: he is an elder who rules';[14] while the principle of subordination was further exemplified in the President, who was 'eminently the bishop of the general church'.[15] But the hierarchy did not really culminate in an individual, whether at the presidential or the District level; the real apex of the hierarchy was the ministerial Conference, for the

[11] *Essay on the Pastoral Office*, pp. 38–9.   [12] Ibid. p. 73.
[13] Ibid. p. 115. Bunting often called the Superintendent 'the Angel of the Church'.   [14] Ibid. p. 116.   [15] Ibid. p. 120.

actions of any minister, whether superintendent or chairman, were never thought to be guaranteed by their own authority, but required the approval of the following Conference. In other words, when people draw a particular analogy between the office of an Anglican bishop and that of a District chairman, their implied emphasis is foreign to the Wesleyanism of the age of Bunting. He boldly claimed for Wesleyan Methodism the 'oversight of a true, primitive episcopacy',[16] but he did not advance the claim on the strength of the District system alone. When he used the word 'episcopacy', he was thinking less of individuals than of a work of oversight in which the whole Connexion shared. *Episkope* was less a matter of being something, of status, than of doing something, of active oversight. Although the fundamental responsibility for the care of souls remained on the hearts of the Ministry, Bunting had not forgotten the existence of the lower terms of the hierarchy —the class-leaders, the local preachers, the prayer-leaders, and the various stewards—whose share in the actual oversight of the Connexion was no less real for being closely circumscribed. To quote from Alfred Barrett again:

The utmost latitude is allowed for their co-participation with the Conference in the government of the societies, and only stops short of the line of co-legislation. One does not necessarily imply the other. The subordinate offices of the Church are created by the ministry: let that cease, and the rest will fall.' [17]

Apart from these spiritual offices, Bunting himself introduced the policy of associating laymen with all the general financial administration of the Connexion, and with those bodies, like the Committee of Privileges, which acted on behalf of the Connexion on political and allied questions. It was usual to compare all these lay offices with that of the New Testament deacon, who was allegedly the assistant of the pastor and the servant of the Church. Thus there was a hierarchy of responsibility which stretched from the Conference to the class-leader, and constituted a government of whose efficiency Wesleyans were proud, especially when it was compared with a diocesan machinery which seemed as inadequate to cope with the problems of Tractarianism, as they believed it had been to cope with the problems of the Methodist Revival.

---

[16] *Sidelights on the Conflicts of Methodism*, B. Gregory (London, 1898), p. 361; said in 1844.   [17] *Essay on the Pastoral Office*, p. 131.

Three years before Jabez Bunting laid claim to the true, primitive episcopacy, he had said:

Unless the Church of England will protest against Puseyism in some intelligible form, it will be the duty of the Methodists to protest against the Church of England.[18]

The section of Wesleyan Methodism which held views on the Ministry quite different from these we are describing always suspected that Jabez Bunting wanted to introduce episcopacy in the Anglican sense into the Connexion. For this belief many irrelevant factors were responsible. He successfully resisted the proposal to prohibit the wearing of gown and bands; he openly advocated the use of liturgical services; he opposed himself to the most popular visiting American evangelist of the period, James Caughey; and all this was apart from his insistence on the general prerogatives of the Ministry as he understood them. He made no public answer to these suspicions, which were groundless in the conspiratorial form which the grumblers gave them, but his most likely reply would have been that such a revolution would simply be playing with words. Episcopacy in its primitive form of pastoral oversight ran through the Wesleyan system as he advocated it, and might be summed up in the picture of the superintendent guiding and watching over the societies and ministers committed to his charge; episcopacy in the Anglican sense he followed Wesley in rejecting. The *name* of bishop was neither here nor there: 'I have been so called,' he remarked on one occasion. But in any case, according to his doctrine of the Ministry, *episkope* was of the essence of the Ministry itself, as well as of the Church: any true minister was ordained to act as an overseer in the congregation of Christ's flock, and so any circuit superintendent was as much a bishop as the Anglican bishop of the local diocese, because *both* were *ministers*. Bunting would have said that episcopacy, expressed through a Ministry (not necessarily a three-fold one), was of the *esse* of the Church, because Christ exercised his own supervision of His Church through such a body of men. There was no question of the introduction of episcopacy; as a part of the true Church, Wesleyan Methodism already had it. We may repeat here that this pastoral responsibility was for specific doctrine as well as for specific morality, and could not be adequately discharged by a

[18] *Sidelights on the Conflicts of Methodism*, p. 317; said in 1841.

sentimental yearning over people. To the Conference of 1835 Bunting said:

Christ has given the members to the Pastors in a sense in which they are not given to the Leaders. . . . The leaders cannot naturally care for the flock. They have no special call of God for such work.[19]

We must turn from these general considerations, however, to see how the theory was applied in practice. First of all, here is the list of powers which were generally regarded as inherent in the Ministry in the light of the New Testament:

(1) The power to receive candidates into Church fellowship, having first judged of their fitness for the privilege.

(2) The power to remove from the body the disobedient and incorrigible.

(3) The power to inflict censures in the case of less flagrant offences.

(4) The general power of appointing officers in the Church.

To these may be added further powers, to which the ministerial Conference laid claim:

(5) The oversight of candidates for the Ministry, together with sole authority for their final admission into Full Connexion (and after 1836 the power of ordaining them by the imposition of the hands of the presbytery).

(6) The oversight of the Ministry itself.

(7) An authority to station the preachers, that was held to be absolute in the last resort.

(8) The power to elect the President.

(9) Power to legislate for the Connexion as a whole, which had no more than a possible advisory capacity.

Such a list may provoke the kind of comment which Alfred Barrett half expected when he came to his chapter on 'Pastoral authority':

Ministerial authority, nevertheless, by persons who have had their minds prejudiced by worldly politics, has been smiled at as the mere invention of a superstitious age. A minister is by them considered as a

[19] *Sidelights on the Conflicts of Methodism*; composite quotation, see pp. 191 and 210.

speaking brother, and nothing else; an individual maintained to preach and pray for the solace and instruction of believers, and the awakening of sinners. All acts which are different from these, such as the admission of candidates for membership, and the censure and expulsion of offenders, say they, are passed and performed by the vote of the assembled Church.[20]

And in fact the Wesleyan Ministry had never governed quite as absolutely as the table of its potential authority would suggest. It was admitted that ministers did not necessarily make perfect rulers, and that whatever the Methodist Societies might have been, they were no longer the chapters of an order. Bunting usually spoke of the introduction of 'safeguards' for the people; his apologists about the need for 'checks' on the pastoral office. It was one of the tragedies of the period that precautions had been taken as long ago as 1795–7, but the Constitution, as it was often called, was patient of more than one interpretation. The germ of the *Rules* of 1797 may be seen in a statement made in a Conference letter to the Societies published in 1794, which said that the spiritual concerns of the Connexion should be managed by the preachers, 'who have *ever* appointed Leaders, chosen stewards, and admitted members into and expelled them from the Society, consulting their brethren the Stewards and Leaders'.[21] By 1797 this vague statement stood in need of further definition, and the secession which culminated in the foundation of the New Connexion compelled the Wesleyan Conference to meet the dissentient laity half way. At this time the growth of the Wesleyan Ministry was not complete, and so the Conference made what it thought of as concessions to the Leaders' meetings; but unfortunately the rules were to prove more ambiguous than they appeared on paper.

So far as the oversight of the local minister was concerned, the 'Constitution' said:

(1) The Leaders' Meeting shall have a right to declare any person on trial improper to be received into the Society; and after such declaration the Superintendent shall not admit such person into the Society.

(2) No person shall be expelled from the Society for immorality, till such immorality be proved at a Leaders' Meeting.

(3) No person shall be appointed a Leader or Steward, or be removed from his office, but in conjunction with the Leaders' Meeting; the

---

[20] *Sidelights on the Conflicts of Methodism*, p. 189.
[21] *Minutes of the Wesleyan Methodist Conference* (1862), I.314.

nomination to be in the Superintendent, and the approbation or dis-approbation in the Leaders' Meeting.[22]

It was of these rules that the Conference of 1797 said: 'We have given up to you far the greatest part of the Superintendent's authority.'[23] To these same rules Jabez Bunting's critics appealed, convinced that they gave to the Leaders' Meeting a co-pastoral authority. Above all, the opposition claimed that the second rule meant, in effect, that no one could be expelled without the agreement of the Leaders, and this gradually expanded into a claim to a general right to help to decide on the sentence.

Jabez Bunting never denied the existence of the 'Constitution', but denied that its effects were so far-reaching. The interpretation which he accepted was that offered by Richard Watson when, during the troubles at Leeds, he published *An Affectionate Address to the Trustees, Stewards, Local Preachers and Leaders of the South London Circuit*, who sympathized with the malcontents there. (At this time—1828—Richard Watson had a great reputation in Methodism as a theologian, and his general standing was almost as high as Jabez Bunting's.) Watson agreed that the rules on admission and expulsion were meant to act as checks on the minister's authority, but not that they subtracted from his power. In the last resort the power was still there, and 'should a church refuse to admit into its communion persons brought to God under his (the Pastor's) ministry, and on whom he enjoins the scriptural obligation of Christian communion, and that without any reason but a factious opposition; or should it resist the expulsion of persons notoriously wicked, and proved to be so on unquestionable evidence, from laxity of moral feeling on the majority of the members, or from the same factious spirit; the rightful scriptural exercise of his ministry is asserted',[24] and the misguided laymen ignored. The Leaders, in other words, might sound an alarm bell to warn the minister that in their opinion he was about to make a mistake; but there was no question of co-pastorship, since that, to quote Watson again, would give to the Leaders' Meeting, 'in all cases, no matter how unfounded, the power to forbid us to receive members into the Church, to restrain us from expelling immoral members'.[25] Watson genuinely believed that whatever the rules of

[22] Ibid. p. 391.
[24] *Watson's Works* (1835), VII.95.
[23] Ibid. pp. 393–4.
[25] Ibid. p. 97.

1797 might appear to say, the men who drafted them did not mean to surrender the superintendent's authority to such a degree, 'for certain powers are inseparable from the duties of the Ministry, and cannot be transferred or put into commission with those who have not this calling'.[26] The same attitude was taken by Joseph Beecham, whose *Essay on the Constitution of Wesleyan Methodism* appeared in 1829, and was a full-scale defence of Bunting's point of view. Beecham said that it was incontrovertible that

in 1795 and 1797 the power of the pastor was not taken away from him and given to others, or even shared with them; that all the privileges then conceded by the Conference were only so many fences and guards thrown around the pastor to prevent him from using his power injuriously; and that by means of the Special District Meeting, and right of appeal to Conference all cases of difficulty, which cannot be settled in the ordinary way, are determined by pastoral authority—that the final decision of extraordinary questions is not with the people, but is what it ought to be—it is *pastoral*.[27]

Lest Beecham's blunt authoritarianism be thought too typical, let us remember Alfred Barrett's advice to the Ministry that 'the obligation to administer discipline should be calmly assumed';[28] 'do not attempt to bully a man, by telling him that you are God's minister and have a right to his obedience, but take it for granted, and stick to the biblical principle which is in view in the particular case; "Official vanity is a source of perpetual disquietude".'[29]

But the temper of Beecham's words, and the warning which Barrett felt necessary, both underline the temptations and dangers of the theory in practice. The first and last of the three rules of 1797 gave the Leaders' Meeting no more than a negative influence; they could not propose candidates either for membership or for office; and therefore Bunting's critics concentrated on the rule about expulsion. But against the background of the Leeds Organ Case (1827–8), and the agitation against the Theological Institution (1834–6), this rule showed itself thoroughly unsatisfactory. The real problem of the superintendents in those years was how to deal with men who persisted in agitating the Societies in favour of reforms which, in the eyes of both parties, would to a large extent abolish the pastoral office. Were they to allow resolutions

[26] *Watson's Works* (1835), VII.95. p. 98.
[27] *Essay on the Constitution* (London, 1829), p. 111.
[28] *Essay on the Pastoral Office*, p. 236.　　　　[29] Ibid. p. 238.

condemning the existing state of Methodism to be moved, discussed, and perhaps even carried in their Leaders' Meetings?
Were they to tolerate the holding of 'unofficial' meetings (they
were often called 'illegal' because the superintendent was not in
the chair) to debate and promote such opinions? When did such
behaviour, and the kind of language often associated with it,
especially in the pamphlets of the time, constitute a breach of the
bonds of the Connexion? For after all it was not easy to put your
finger on a precise law which was being broken. And if the superintendent decided that a particular would-be reformer had gone
beyond all reason and must be brought before a Leaders' Meeting,
he might be faced with a further difficulty, in the shape of un-
sympathetic Leaders who either refused to agree that any genuine
offence had been committed, or took the line that the charge had
not been proved. It was all very well for Richard Watson to say
that in the face of such factious opposition, the rightful, scriptural
exercise of one's ministry was asserted; all very well to be told by
Barrett to take one's authority for granted; but here the text-book
came to life in a flesh-and-blood opposition which often had considerable local standing. The whole difficulty was that in some
circuits (and in 1849–57 it was in many), the powers of the pastoral
office had themselves become the subject of such violent disagreement, that compromise seemed impossible, and some ministers
were provoked into ill-considered action, which called their
authority further into question.

When actually faced with a recalcitrant Leaders' Meeting, superintendents interpreted the law about expulsion in various ways,
according to their view of the powers of the pastoral office. Some,
either out of sympathy or moderation, left the matter there. Others,
however, on the ground that the law did not say in so many words
that a man must be given a trial before the Leaders' Meeting before
he could be expelled, refused members their class tickets without
bringing the cases to a Leaders' Meeting at all. This certainly
meant that the final decision was pastoral, but also that it was often
unpopular. Others gave a somewhat sophistical twist to the part
of the rule which spoke of the immorality being 'proved at a
Leaders' Meeting'. The rule said nothing about the charge being
proved to the Leaders' satisfaction, though Bunting himself said in
1835 that such was the proper way to understand it. Provided they
themselves were satisfied of a man's guilt, some superintendents

were ready to over-rule a contrary opinion in the Leaders' Meeting, and return a verdict of guilty. Then there was the question of what constituted 'immorality': it was not unusual for a minister to insist that attendance at a public meeting in support of Dr Warren, or, later, James Everett, was itself an offence, while the Leaders vehemently denied that any ground existed for a charge. Finally, the law of 1797 did not state clearly whether the Leaders should have a voice in deciding what was to be done with a man who had been found guilty of a breach of Connexional discipline, and the vast majority of superintendents simply refused the Leaders any share in the passing of sentence.

In 1835, at the height of Dr Warren's agitation, Jabez Bunting himself made a tremendous effort to settle these confused questions. In his long career he wrote and published little more than a few sermons, but we know that the Conference regulations of 1835 were almost entirely his personal work. It is unfair to judge Bunting only in terms of his fiercely repressive actions at Leeds in 1827-8; the rules of 1835 were the product of a more mature attitude, despite greater provocation. Nevertheless, Bunting was not ready to yield at the vital points, but was anxious to set out clearly the rights and duties of both parties.

Indeed, the new legislation was introduced by the statement that 'with respect to the essential principles and fundamental regulations of our established discipline, we are unanimously and deliberately resolved . . . to make no change whatever'.[30] But in the declaratory sense there was much that was new. Bunting had always opposed any codification of the laws of Methodism, because too much written law interfered with the free action of ministerial prerogative; but he now tried to describe the limits within which the prerogative was to work and in doing so sought to provide a definition of 'immorality' in the rule of 1797. In a section called 'The Law of God contained in the Holy Scriptures', Bunting said that 'any conduct in a man professing godliness, which can be shown to be decidedly condemned by the precepts and principles of the New Testament, is surely sufficient to justify, if persisted in, the application of a suitable ecclesiastical censure, or other penalty, to such an individual'.[31] He did not try to show in detail what the laws of the New Testament were, but instead referred generally

[30] *Minutes of the Wesleyan Methodist Conference* (1835), Q.xxiv.A.
[31] Ibid., Special Address, sect. 2, art. 6.

to the scriptural laws of courtesy, brotherly kindness, mutual charity, peace and godly quietness, and to the requirement of 'reasonable submission, on the part of Church members, to those who are over them in the Lord'[32]—by which was meant the ministers. Against this background, Bunting gave his verdict on such agitations as Warren's, and declared that anyone who remained in Wesleyan Methodism when he really disapproved of either its doctrine or discipline, and did not remain silent but used his position for purposes of opposition and strife, 'was guilty of a flagrant transgression of that morality of the New Testament, the observance of which was a principal condition of his admission into our society',[33] and might properly be expelled. This meant that the superintendents were entitled to rule that open support for the reforming point of view constituted an offence worthy of ecclesiastical death.

With this broad definition of the kind of law which ran in the courts of Methodism, Bunting turned his attention to the question of the law of expulsion. He made it clear, to begin with, that a superintendent could expel a man on his own authority, but it was now put down in writing that if a man asked to be tried before a Leaders' Meeting, then his request must be granted. In such a trial, the Leaders must be satisfied—Bunting accepted the criticism of the reformers so far—that sufficient proof was given 'of a wilful and habitual negligence, or of the violation, of some Scriptural or Methodistical rule'.[34] But once the Leaders' Meeting had given its opinion to that effect, it had 'discharged its whole part of the painful duty to be performed'[35]—in other words, it was now made definite that only the Ministry could decide the sentence. In a few phrases, Bunting tried to show why this was necessary. The minister was especially concerned with the sentence 'in his pastoral character as the person whose peculiar call and province it is to "watch over that soul" as "one that must give account" '.[36] At the same time Bunting introduced a new tribunal, a Minor District Meeting, to provide for the situation in which a Leaders' Meeting brought in a verdict 'notoriously inconsistent with the facts proved', or with 'the laws of God, or of our own body'.[37] Bunting's anxiety to find a middle position was obvious in the provision that either layman or superintendent could appeal from the decision

[32] Ibid.   [33] Ibid., art. 9.   [34] Ibid., art. 4.
[35] Ibid.   [36] Ibid.   [37] Ibid., art. 6.

recorded in the Leaders' Meeting, but the opposition noted sourly that the new court consisted entirely of ministers: the chairman of the District, and four others, two chosen by the layman, and two by the superintendent of his circuit. The decision of this court of appeal was therefore as pastoral as Beecham had said it ought to be, and the reforming party did not accept the impartiality of such a meeting. Yet Bunting himself was not unaware of the danger of superintendents being as impetuous as he himself had been on occasion: and it was decided that they must not pass sentence until at least a week after the Leaders' Meeting; that the case must be discussed in the weekly meeting (*sic*) of the circuit ministers; and that if the superintendent were still dubious as to his proper course of action, he was to make private inquiries to satisfy himself.

How far Bunting was from surrendering anything which he thought fundamental to the pastoral office may be seen in the adverse comment made on the law of expulsion by Robert Eckett, the able leaders of the Wesleyan Association: ' . . . the preachers have absolute power as to the exercise of discipline over the lay officers and other members of the Connexion.'[38] Eckett was equally unimpressed by the changes which were proposed and made by Bunting in the way in which the ministerial Conference exercised its legislative powers. Bunting was absolutely opposed, of course, to any kind of lay delegation, because, apart from anything else, he disliked the intrusion of political language and ideas into the field of ecclesiastical polity. The demand for lay delegation arose largely from the theory that as a legislative body the Conference ought to represent the governed. Bunting liked to close the argument at this point, with the reply that it was an inevitable consequence of his view of the Ministry that the laity were already represented in the Conference through the Ministry. The Conference, properly understood, was not a legislature of a political kind, a concentration of the power of Methodism as an organization into a small group of hands, but rather a spiritual assembly of the divinely called and appointed overseers of the Church, met together in counsel for the better discharge of their common responsibility. With such business the laity had nothing to do except through their pastors. As Alfred Barrett said:

Is it needful to have the suffrage of delegates to determine whether

[38] *The Conference and the Fly Sheets Condemned* (London, 1849), p. 14.

intemperance, dishonesty, or impurity be sin? or whether such sin should be visited with censure and excision? Could they judge better than the regular convened members what stations were fittest for ministers, whose talents and qualifications are as various as can be imagined? Can the Societies be more than represented [he meant through the Ministry]? Not unless they become their own pastors, and this would be transgressing the scripture lines, and very soon would be the destruction of order, of efficiency and peace; and then, immediately after, the destruction of the Church itself.[39]

Bunting entirely agreed that the layman could not be his own minister, and he would no more accept lay delegation to Conference than he would have admitted lay delegates from the circuit to the weekly meeting of circuit ministers. So far as the government of the Church was concerned the laity must accept, on scriptural grounds alone, limitation to an advisory capacity. Throughout the Connexion ran the principle of ministerial responsibility, and just as only a minister could actually appoint a leader or steward in the sense of bestowing upon him the power of his office, so only the ministerial Conference could appoint a layman to one of the great Connexional committees. Bunting did not care if as a result his enemies said that he filled these committees with his friends or sycophants; what mattered was not to concede to the laity at any point in the Connexional system the right to elect either an official or a representative. For implicit in the right to elect was the power to confer authority, and so far as the oversight of the Church was concerned, the laity had no authority to confer.

Just how completely Bunting rejected everything which lay delegation implied may be seen in the slight concessions which he made on this subject in 1835, when he described the idea as 'dead and buried'.[40] Reluctantly, and hedging about the permission with numerous administrative restrictions, the new rules consented to the calling of a Special Circuit Meeting, once a year only, in time to decide whether Conference should be petitioned either to change an old law or to make a new one. But this new body was put firmly in its place before it could even meet. First of all, it was told that the 'local affairs of any other Circuit or Circuits'[41] were excluded from its scope, the limiting effect of which was

---

[39] *Essay on the Pastoral Office*, pp. 219–20.
[40] *Sidelights*, p. 209.   [41] Special Address, sect. 3, art. 4.

obvious to those who remembered that the Leeds Organ Case had been defined as local business. Secondly, requests for new legislation must be confined

to such changes only as are consistent with the essential principles of Wesleyan Methodism, and within the pale of our established constitution. The Conference cannot fairly be required to receive any propositions of a manifestly revolutionary character, or which are wholly subversive of that system of doctrine or discipline which has been confined to them by Mr Wesley as a sacred deposit, and which, as they believe, has also been committed to their keeping by the provision and grace of God.[42]

Lay delegation, of course, was subversive of the system. And finally, the Special Circuit Meeting was not to concern itself with 'the disciplinary jurisdiction of the Preachers over each other, and their rights of regulating among themselves all that relates particularly and specifically to the Christian Ministry and the Pastoral Office'.[43] Robert Eckett dismissed this meeting as 'utterly impotent',[44] and from the point of view of the Wesleyan Association one can quite see why. From Bunting's point of view the restrictions were inevitable, because the Conference was going beyond what it strictly should permit, and could only do so by taking elaborate care that no fundamental pastoral right was sacrificed in consequence.

In this chapter we have considered the Wesleyan Ministry in terms of the vast pastoral responsibilities which its development called it to exercise. It seemed worth while to do this because of the changes which have taken place in British Methodism since the crash of 1849. But the Wesleyan minister of the period cherished as well his place in the very human, though inspired tradition of aggressive evangelism, personal preaching, and domestic austerity which stretched back to the earliest of the itinerants. Let us close with a quotation from this Ministry at its best, from the Conference Address of 1842, when the Puseyite movement had driven Wesleyan Methodism to complete self-awareness:

While we wish to stand in a friendly relation to that Church from which our fathers were compelled to separate . . . we claim, both for our sakes and yours, all the rights of the true scriptural pastors. . . . Denying the

---

[42] Special Address, sect. 3, art. 4.   [43] Ibid.
[44] *The Conference and the Fly Sheets Condemned*, p. 20.

sacerdotal character of the Christian Ministry, we claim no Priesthood, because we know, and the New Testament knows, no Priest but the one in Heaven: we claim not to offer sacrifice at the altar for we know of no altar but the Cross, and of no atoning or propitiatory sacrifice but the Saviour's blood: but being inwardly moved by the Holy Ghost to take upon us the office and Ministry of the Christian eldership, and being outwardly called thereto by those who were in the Ministry before us, even to Mr Wesley's days, and separated unto it from all worldly employments by ordination and prayer, we do claim to be, in all necessary aspects, the true Apostolical Pastors of the charge which God has committed to our trust, and the successors of those who in former ages have been similarly actuated and appointed. . . .

Whatever the faults of the Wesleyan Ministry under Jabez Bunting, those claims were true.

III—PASTORS AND PEOPLE

'Lay Delegation is dead and buried'—JABEZ BUNTING (1835)

Although Bunting claimed that his view of the Ministry and the Church expressed Wesley's own position, it must not be supposed that this claim was universally admitted; in fact, the early nineteenth century saw division after division in the ranks of the Methodists. The New Connexion, the Primitive Methodist Connexion, the Bible Christians, the Leeds Protestant Methodists, the Wesleyan Association, and the Methodist Free Churches—not to mention the personal followings of such individual ministers as Rayner Stephens the Chartist, Joseph Barker the arch-doubter, and Tabraham the teetotaller—shared a general approach to the nature of Methodism and the Ministry quite different from the prevailing Wesleyan view. Not that Wesleyan Methodism enjoyed unanimity of outlook: when Jabez Bunting said that 'Ours is, and always will be, Wesleyan Methodism', he was confessing that in the Conference itself there existed two opinions.

These two general attitudes may be distinguished as High and Low Methodism. The chief characteristic of Low Methodism was a reluctance to follow the line of development taken by Wesleyan Methodism after 1791. (Indeed, the New Connexion, which seceded in 1797, may almost be said to have been a protest in anticipation of that development.) Wesleyanism without Wesley placed a growing emphasis on the importance of the Connexional principle, and of the itinerants themselves. In Low Methodism, on the other hand, emphasis fell on the *local* elements in Methodism, and on the part played by *laymen* in its pattern. (Methodism, after all, began as a number of local societies united by their personal link with John Wesley, and the itinerants were originally laymen who owed their authority to preach to his commission.)

This different emphasis inevitably affected the attitude of Low Methodism to the Ministry, which it saw far more in a local than a Connexional context, and with the lay aspect of the itinerant predominating. For Primitive Methodism, for the Bible Christians under O'Bryan's leadership, as for the more curious Leeds Protestant Methodists, the Ministry existed simply as the agency of a special mission, and required no complicated background of 'ordination' or 'succession'. The minister was essentially an itinerant evangelist, to be compared unfavourably, at times, with such experts as the Americans, Lorenzo Dow and James Caughey; his business was to preach the Gospel, and he could be distinguished from the local preacher by his full-time service. The leaders of the non-Wesleyan bodies, men like Hugh Bourne, William Clowes, William O'Bryan, James Sigston (the Leeds schoolmaster), and Robert Eckett (the London builder who guided the Association in its early years), rose to authority while still self-consciously laymen, and were bound to feel that the traditional view of the Ministry exaggerated the formal elements, especially over such questions as ordination. Their picture of the itinerant, as still what Wesley originally called him, the 'extraordinary messenger', helps to explain why both the Bible Christians and the Primitive Methodists readily employed women as itinerants. Bourne, it is true, did his best to prove that the Bible encouraged the practice, but what really convinced him was the marked ability which some of them showed as evangelists. Bourne's whole idea of the itinerant was bound up with his passion for evangelistic results; in the early days of the movement a man remained an itinerant as long as he made converts and kept the finances of the local Society in a healthy condition; once he failed to do so, he was sent back home. Nothing more perfectly illustrates how Low Methodism tended to perpetuate an image of the 'minister' as a 'missioner', with no other special authority in the Church.

This point of view, with its emphasis on the local and congregational aspects of Methodism, was partly produced by the dissenting background of many of the later converts to Methodism. But it also appealed to many who saw in the course taken by Wesleyan Methodism after 1791 a betrayal of the Revival; what to Bunting was the badly needed consolidation of the gains of the eighteenth century was to these critics a hardening into unevangelical respectability. One may trace back into the eighteenth century the belief that what was unconventional, irregular, or even to some tastes shocking, was the hallmark of genuine Methodism. To such an outlook the 'normal' Ministry which Wesleyan Methodism was developing seemed flat and uninviting. Somehow the pace of the early triumphs ought to be maintained, and failure to sustain it was a proof of spiritual decline. Bunting felt that there was a certain truth in this last position, but whereas he held that part of the answer was sounder organization and a better trained Ministry, his critics, on the other hand, asserted that what was needed was a freer constitution, and the ministry of plain men, unpolished, unlearned, but the passionate advocates of a simple gospel; for in such men, they maintained, had lain the secret of the Revival's success. During the controversy over the Theological Institution this attitude appeared in another form: the Warrenite pamphleteers declared again and again that God had raised up Methodism with a special mission to the poor, but that the Wesleyan ministers had forgotten that such people existed, and visited only the rich. The argument was unfair, and confused the 'lower orders' of the stable society of the eighteenth century with the urban, industrialized masses of the disorganized nineteenth-century society; but it nevertheless pointed to the same unwillingness to admit that perhaps circumstances had changed more than Methodism. When the same critics quoted the successes of the Bible Christians and the Primitive Methodists, they forgot that these triumphs were largely secured in districts of rural England where the Establishment was highly unpopular, and where the atmosphere of the previous century yet lingered—so much so that preachers of the Gospel could still be stoned or ducked in village ponds. Nevertheless, a strongly formative influence on the Low Methodist conception of the Ministry was a rejection of the Wesleyan point of view in favour of a past which was already becoming romanticized, and in which John Wesley would hardly have recognized himself. His subtle 'irregular Anglicanism', as we have called it, could be given more than one interpretation; the Low Methodists often interpreted his elasticity as Dissent. In the end they developed a more than dissenting antipathy to gown and bands, and a religious horror of anything in the nature of a Prayer Book (except at weddings and funerals). They were convinced that Bunting was an innovator when he supported such habits of worship, and although he struggled to defend his more accurate picture of the past, his chief reward was the persistent belief of many that he and his fellow administrators had necessarily lost their evangelical fervour. One notes here that nagging narrowness of the Protestant tradition, which is always eager to credit the spiritual deadness of everybody except the members of the critic's tiny clique.

Low Methodism, then, was prepared to use the minister as an evangelist, but recoiled from the way in which the eighteenth-century Wesleyan itinerancy was growing into a formal Ministry with widespread powers. This recoil corresponded to an emphasis on the local and the lay, and we must now consider how this emphasis affected the question of the oversight of the Church. What is immediately evident from the constitutions of the non-Wesleyan bodies is that they refused to consider any suggestion that the oversight of the Church was something for which the Ministry was uniquely responsible. This is not to say that Low Methodism in the early nineteenth century rejected the need for discipline itself; in fact, the Church courts were more commonly used than they are now, for what one might almost call the Protestant tradition of interference lingered on. But it was assumed that the laity naturally provided themselves with a quasi-democratic self-discipline, through such organs as the Class, the Leaders' Meeting, and the Quarterly Meeting. These meetings owed their existence to John Wesley, but he had intended them to advise, and not to govern, with the itinerant as the responsible person. In any case, he never meant them to act as more or less independent entities, free from any kind of external control; the very presence of the minister in these meetings was a reminder and a guarantee of the authority of the Connexion in the background. Methodism was born Connexional, and inasmuch as, after Wesley's death, the symbol of the Connexion became the Conference, which was composed of ministers, the Ministry itself became the standard of reference throughout Methodism. Now the Low Methodists rejected this aspect of the itinerancy altogether, and said that disciplinary authority belonged to the local meetings of the circuit. As early as 1797 the New Connexion said that members should be admitted to and expelled from the society 'by the concurrence of the members in the place where they live',[45] who either voted themselves, or treated the Leaders as their representatives. This was all the more possible, since the same set of rules said that a Class had the right to elect its own Leader, quite free from external interference. These rules did not even mention the minister, nor was there any suggestion that in virtue of his office he had both special authority and special responsibility for such business; in practice, he was reduced to the status of a customary chairman. The Low Methodist outlook took quite calmly what horrified Jabez Bunting: the picture of a Leaders' Meeting hearing a charge against a member, arriving at a verdict, and inflicting what it thought the appropriate penalty, all without any reference to the minister at all. At this primary level of the oversight of the local Society, the High Methodist view of the Ministry was already made impossible, and the minister's status diminished to that of a potential example or standard. One says 'potential' of necessity, because he was not always thought of as even that; but it remained true (as long as the preservation of the itinerancy in its turn preserved the various non-Wesleyan Connexions from a lapse into pure Independency), that the minister might be regarded as the embodiment of that larger Church by the side of which any local Society ought to be willing to measure itself. But the means to be more than an example had been shorn away at a fundamental point, never to be recovered.

It was natural that there should be a similar revulsion against the collective oversight exercised in the Wesleyan Connexion through the purely ministerial Conference. A Ministry of the kind which we have been describing was unlikely to be given the sole legislative authority in a Connexion, or even to desire it. Nor was it likely in terms of the historical background of the bodies concerned. The Bible Christians and the Primitive Methodists were the product of genuine religious revivals, under the guidance of strong, lay personalities, and the itinerancy grew up among them simply as a by-product of their general evangelistic enterprise; only at a very much later stage in the growth of the movements could a self-conscious Ministry have asked for the prerogatives

[45] *Minutes of the New Connexion Conference* (1798).

possessed by the Wesleyan Ministry. In the New Connexion, the Wesleyan Association, and Leeds Protestant Methodism, bodies more theoretically minded, each with bitter memories of its own secession from Wesleyan Methodism, there was in any case a resolute determination never to be ruled by a 'Ministry' again. Hence the eagerness with which the Wesleyan Association said in 1837 that a local preacher was competent to exercise all the functions of the Christian Ministry; hence also the suspicion which Robert Eckett showed toward the alleged authors of the *Fly Sheets*. Despite a temporary setback during the Napoleonic Wars, the dominant preference in this period of English history was for government that was more and more broadly based (a preference which should not be confused with the modern enthusiasm for democracy, which in the 1830s meant government by the uneducated, underfed, and overworked proletariat). It became a commonplace in Low Methodism that the principles of civil and religious liberty were the same, and operated through the same kind of machinery. When such thinking was applied to the problem of Methodist government, this principle gradually emerged from the dust of a thousand pamphlets: that the Church was a voluntary association of Christian people whose primary right was self-government. In Victorian England, the middle—and Methodist—classes strongly objected to being ruled, and a government of parsons was regarded as clerical despotism; Ebenezer Elliott, for example, called the Legal Hundred 'the hundred Popes of England's Jesuitry', and Jabez Bunting must have grown weary of seeing himself described as the Methodist Pope. Good men, and all instinctive Nonconformists, resented the suggestion that the Wesleyan ministerial Conference had a peculiar responsibility for their souls; they wanted to take care of themselves in religious as in civil affairs. And when the ministerial Conference dared to pronounce on political and social matters, acquiring a rather unfair reputation for unadulterated Toryism,[46] the need for self-government seemed to be proved.

[46] The 'Toryism' has been exaggerated. The famous 'no politics' rule was observed equally in the non-Wesleyan bodies. Bunting supported a Whig Government over the Tolpuddle martyrs. In the 1840s Wesleyan Methodism continually opposed the policy of Peel's Tory Government. In reality, the political opinion of Wesleyanism was at this time much closer to what was later called the Nonconformist Conscience than is sometimes suggested.

In the half-century under discussion, lay control of the government of the Connexions extended only gradually. The general principle of self-government implied that the minister was God's representative in the pulpit, no one's representative in the Leaders' Meeting, and only a possible popular representative in the Conference. But the New Connexion, for example, founded in 1797 under the shadow of the recently departed Wesley, still treated ministers as somehow different from other men; as a special body, they received representation equal to that of the laity. This balance of 'interests' was in the spirit of the eighteenth century which the New Connexion preserved, and its apologists recommended the formula as a cure for all constitutional troubles. But in practice the Connexion gave less power to the Ministry than this might suggest, for when awkward decisions had to be taken, they were passed to the circuits in the form of a referendum, and the last word was given to the votes of the membership. Thus in 1838 the New Connexion abolished the rule by which circuits had been expected to make reports on the conduct of their ministers, after a referendum in which twenty-one circuits, containing more than half the total membership of the Connexion, had voted in favour of the change. In the Bible Christian and Primitive Methodist Conferences the itinerants were outnumbered two to one, and they were only given a definite representation because of the practical importance of their work, not because of any right to it inherent in their office. By the time that the Wesleyan Association was formed, the implications of the representative theory could be carried to their logical conclusion: the Association left the circuits free to send as many or as few ministers as they pleased, and the early Annual Assemblies—'Conference' sounded too Wesleyan for the Association—had lay majorities. In all these mixed Conferences there was no question of a separate ministerial session, nor was the oversight of the Ministry left to the ministers alone. The principle of lay delegation was extended to District Meetings and Committees, as these were instituted, but the antipathy of Low Methodism to government was such that for years the district system was suspected of being an administrative device to give the central offices of a Connexion increased control over the circuits.

Writing from the High Methodist point of view, William Vevers, in his *Defence of the Discipline*, said that Low Methodism believed 'that the authority of a Christian pastor [was] derived from the people; and they therefore [wished] to treat pastors as mere servants'.[47] We may see from what has been said how far this summary was accurate. But to appreciate why Jabez Bunting regarded Low Methodism as such a serious threat to any proper conception of the Ministry, we must consider what was implied by the constitution set up by the men who seceded from Wesleyan Methodism at Leeds in August 1828. The famous Organ Case left a permanent mark on Methodism, for it was then that a knowledge of the extreme which he was opposing led Bunting into an open demonstration of how great a prerogative he was prepared to assert on behalf of the Wesleyan Ministry. To defend the very nature of Wesleyan Methodism as he understood it, he undoubtedly broke its written constitution; and though he was successful at the time, his action gave rise to forces of recrimination, vengeance, and misunderstanding which reached their violent climax in 1849. Bunting's only defence was the nature of what he was fighting, and that only became clear in the curious form of Methodism which was created by James Sigston, the Leeds schoolmaster who directed the secession.

The First Draft of the *Rules of the Leeds Protestant Methodists* was published in Leeds in August 1829, and the final version appeared after the Yearly Meeting at Leeds in September 1830. Like most contemporaneous attempts to reform Methodism, the system took as its basis the Circuit Quarterly Meeting, which was defined as the trustees, stewards, leaders, and local preachers of the circuit. The oversight of the local Societies was in the hands of this meeting, which possessed the power of expulsion. Up to this point the apparatus had a familiar Methodist appearance, even if some of the pieces might seem slightly displaced. But Sigston and his friends were so determined to destroy the power of the Wesleyan Ministry that they almost destroyed the Ministry altogether; for instead of ministers, the chief officials of the circuit were elders, so called, elected by the Quarterly Meeting. The number of elders varied, but seven was considered sufficient for the Leeds Circuit, which was the largest in the body. An elder held office for a year at a time, and was eligible for immediate re-election; but since he might not be chosen to serve again, there was no question of his giving up his secular employment during

[47] *A Defence of the Discipline of Methodism* (London, 1835).

his term of office. There was little point of comparison, therefore, with the separated Wesleyan minister, though the elders made the plan, issued the class-tickets, and from 1830 administered the Sacraments. From the elders was chosen a Presiding Elder, who was a kind of antithesis of the Wesleyan Superintendent. He normally took the chair at circuit meetings, but if he refused to put to the vote a motion properly moved and seconded, he had to resign the chair for the time being. This rule was a direct result of the situation in Wesleyan Methodism, where superintendents asserted a general power to decide what subjects a Leaders' or Quarterly Meeting could legitimately discuss.

In these rules the bias in favour of localism is apparent, and the creation of the lay eldership meant the end both of the Ministry and of the itinerancy. It is significant therefore that in 1830 the final version of the rules set up a Missionary Committee—really a *Home* Missionary Committee—which could employ full-time preachers to open up fresh fields of evangelism. The Missionary obviously corresponded to the idea of the minister which we said at the beginning of this chapter was most common in Low Methodism: a man set apart by God and the Church to preach the Gospel. The Connexional emphasis was evidently not quite dead, and the rules gave the Missionary authority to administer the Sacraments. But there was to be no question of any revival of either ministerial status or power. The Missionary, though himself technically an elder, was subordinated to the elders of the circuit in which he was working, and he was forbidden to hold the office of Presiding Elder. One Wesleyan commentator, Daniel Isaac (in *The Rules of the Leeds Protestant Methodists brought to the Test of the Holy Scriptures* [Leeds, 1830]), said that the Leeds Methodists had deliberately turned the scriptural order of the Church upside down, by making the part-time lay elder superior to the full-time Missionary. Isaac was more than generous in his identification of the Missionary with the Wesleyan itinerant; for the inversion was quite conscious, there was no question of ordination, and the task of the Missionary was only too often to do propaganda work for the reformers' cause in the local Wesleyan Societies.

Finally, the *Rules* of 1830 set up a Yearly Meeting, for the Leeds Methodists anticipated the Wesleyan Association in the rejection of the very name of Conference. The Yearly Meeting was highly representative, as was possible in a small community. (In 1830 the Protestant Methodists numbered 3,997 members, spread thinly over Yorkshire and Lancashire, apart from 402 in London.) Each circuit sent to the Yearly Meeting its Presiding Elder, an ordinary member chosen by the Quarterly Meeting, and a local preacher chosen by the Preachers' Meeting; the missionaries were also represented. The powers of the meeting were vague, but it could alter the rules. It provided another example of the hold which Connexionalism had on even the most Congregationalist of Methodists. But quite clearly not a shadow of the Wesleyan Conference remained; instead there was one of the most completely non-ministerial systems of ecclesiastical government which could possibly be devised.

In all times of ecclesiastical disagreement there are those who hope to find a compromise, but Bunting saw no room for accommodation between such an idea of the Ministry and his own. He said that those who shared Sigston's views were not Wesleyan Methodists, and he denied their right to agitate the Connexion in favour of 'reform'. They had, he said, two courses of action open to them: they could suffer in silence, or join one of the non-Wesleyan bodies. But if they remained within Wesleyan Methodism and disturbed the Connexion's peace, then the Connexion was entitled to expel them. And this was the course that he took at Leeds in 1827-8. It was one of the greatest grievances of the Low Methodists within Wesleyan Methodism that any attempt to advocate their opinions was regarded as an offence against the general law of the Connexion. But the constitution of the Leeds Protestant Methodists makes it clearer why Bunting was so obdurate; he would not tolerate his opponents, in case toleration should lead, by easy stages, to change in the direction they desired. Bunting could imagine nothing worse; but it was what actually happened.

IV—THE LAST WESLEYAN

'Ours is, and must be, to all eternity, Wesleyanism'
—JABEZ BUNTING (1837)

Our present-day picture of Jabez Bunting depends too much upon the impression that he has made on historians who were less concerned with religious than with social values. Historians such as

Elie Halévy interpreted his defence of what he believed to be the true Wesleyan theory of Church and Ministry as merely a part of the general European struggle between the Children of Light and the Children of Darkness, the friends and enemies of Liberty. The Wesleyan Reformers who took as their motto 'A Free Church and a Free Ministry' already misunderstood him in this way, and regarded his eclipse as a triumph of the Spirit of Progress. Yet Bunting was not a denominational dictator, and much of the evidence that said that he was, emanated from sources corrupted by the stealthy jealousy of James Everett. Nor was he in any sense original, and Benjamin Gregory, in the *Sidelights*, distracts the reader from the truth when he presents Bunting's principles as though they were peculiarly the product of his personality; it is misleading to say that Bunting 'stamped the impress of his individuality upon the institutions which he fashioned'.[48] Bunting was above all the representative figure and executive spirit of a general movement of the Wesleyan Ministry toward what it believed to be John Wesley's own conception of the pastoral office. A later generation saw this movement in the light of the catastrophe of 1849, and found a natural, but too simple explanation of the Connexion's troubles in the masterful character of the man whom his enemies nicknamed the 'Methodist Pope'. But Bunting's power in the Conference had its source in the fact that he personified the positive element in the Wesleyan tradition, which still worked throughout this period to determine the Church-form of the Wesleyan Societies; his personal authority was another matter, and we have heard too often of the solitary occasion, in 1844, when he attempted to assert a doctrine of Presidential prerogative. We must distinguish between the creative forces which worked through Bunting to put into practice the theory of pastoral oversight, and his own at times ungovernable will to govern, which often lent the theory such an unattractive colouring. For the Wesleyan Ministry was developing naturally along the lines laid down by the eighteenth century, until the events at Leeds in the late 1820s; after that, its growth was more and more hampered, until the calamity of 1849 convinced the Connexion that the traditional conception of the Wesleyan Ministry must be radically changed.

This strange combination, that he was at once the Wesleyan of the Wesleyans, the normative man of the itinerancy of his day,

[48] Op. cit. p. 540.

and at the same time the individual whose logical but autocratic leadership was to imperil everything that he most venerated, is part of the ground which we take in calling him the Last Wesleyan. But there is a further ground: we have only to compare what we nowadays accept as Methodism's doctrine of the Ministry with what we have here described as Bunting's standpoint in action, to see how the generations which followed him honoured his name far more than they honoured his teaching. 'The genius of Methodism is not the genius of democracy—the two can never harmonize',[49] he said in 1838, but twenty years after his death it already seemed reasonable and Methodist—but *could* it be called Wesleyan?—to admit laymen to the newly formed Representative Session of the Annual Conference. Hugh Price Hughes might urge the adoption of the title of Wesleyan Methodist Church, but Bunting would have challenged the right of the Societies to use it. 'So long as the rightful authority of the Pastorate is secured,' he said in 1829, 'all other ecclesiastical arrangements are mainly matters of discretion.'[50] But while it might be a matter of discretion to alter the name of District Meeting to District Synod, the same could hardly be said of changes which had taken away, little by little, the responsibility of the minister for admission and expulsion; and there was little room in later Wesleyanism for Bunting's insistence that 'a Methodist minister has the right, though not to expel a member from the society, yet to forbid him the Lord's Supper, without the formality of a Leaders' Meeting'.[51] What Bunting would have said about a lay Vice-President one can only imagine.

Such changes must be kept in perspective, however. A movement toward greater lay participation in the government of the various English Churches was characteristic of the later nineteenth century, and has by no means disappeared since. In 1885, for example, the Convocation of the Province of Canterbury resolved to form a House of Laymen, elected by the various Diocesan Conferences within the Province, to confer with the members of the Convocation. Not long afterwards a similar House of Laymen was constituted by the Convocation of the Province of York. In 1904 was formed the Representative Church Council, consisting of members of both Convocations sitting together with the Houses

[49] Gregory, *Sidelights*, p. 258.
[50] Ibid. p. 82   [51] Ibid. p. 505.

of Laymen of both Provinces. This body had no legal authority, nor could it claim to be really representative of the laity of the Church of England; but it was the root from which representative bodies within the Church, possessing definite legal powers, soon afterwards sprang. The creation of the Church Assembly between 1919 and 1929 was the conclusion of this process. We must remember of course that the creation of the Church Assembly does not mean that the bishops and clergy have surrendered the direction of the Established Church to the will of a mixed majority and nothing more, but the whole pattern of events does mark a growing sense that every member should feel his share in the government and life of the Church. When Anglican Convocations were prepared to confer with a House of Laymen, it is less surprising that Wesleyanism gradually diminished the concentration of authority in ministerial hands. It may emphasize the degree of the change to remember that in the Centenary Year Jabez Bunting had said: 'The Kilhamite practice of proposing members at the Leaders' Meeting is one of our abominations.'[52]

This essay is obviously not the place to sketch the largely unwritten history of English Christianity in the nineteenth century. But once we have established the fact of change, that we should not give the young men in our theological colleges Alfred Barrett's *Essay* as their textbook on the Pastoral Office, we are bound to consider one or two factors peculiar to Methodism which help to explain the kind of discontinuity which is implied in what we have said. There was, first of all, the criticism which embodied itself in the seceding movements, the last of which, the United Methodist Free Churches, started its separate life in 1857. Though they made the worst of their case, not least by their efforts to prevent the raising of money for the support of the Wesleyan Ministry, the seceders did convince many people (not all of whom quitted Wesleyan Methodism) that what they regarded as a deliberate usurpation had bred a ministerial oligarchy insufficiently protected against the temptations of its own position. Any Ministry which acts in the name of the One who washed His disciples' feet must be convincingly humble, and few things are more easily misunderstood than a readiness to remove people from the list of Church membership. The seceders reminded Wesleyan Methodism that although the theoretical authority of the Ministry, and

[52] Ibid. p. 266.

79

the line of ecclesiastical ancestry which it claimed, were both important, what mattered as much to the congregation and to the Head of the Church was the spirit in which the oversight of the Body was carried out.

This was all part, however, of a larger problem. Wesleyan Methodism had become by 1830 a highly developed organization for the pastoral oversight of the laity, but in the meantime had neglected to provide equally for the efficient oversight and spiritual direction of the itinerancy. This was not because the Conference was unaware of the difficulties caused by superintendents who relied on their prerogative, instead of working patiently toward agreement with their Leaders' Meetings; nor was it because the problems of the isolated itinerant were ignored. But the tendency was to apply traditional remedies, and in practice it was not enough to set up courts in which a minister could be tried if he broke the rules of the Connexion or offended against Christian common sense. (Methodism was in any case too litigious by half in the early nineteenth century, which makes a curious comment on the general grasp of evangelical Arminianism.) Indeed, the problem of the proper oversight of the Ministry was one of the underlying causes of Methodism itself, for the eighteenth-century Revival had been in part a sharp protest against the flabby spiritual state of too many Anglican parishes—itself the result of a partial breakdown in the oversight of the Ministry. The weakness of the Anglican episcopacy went much deeper than a theological inability to welcome Methodism with open arms.

The need for proper discipline within the more fully developed Ministry was made all the greater by the strains imposed by the parallel growth of the connexional system. Bunting was the second great ruler of Wesleyanism, and as Everett said, 'he . . . kept his eye fixed on the working of the whole of the machinery, while others have attended to the rotatory motion of a single wheel'.[53] He wanted Wesleyanism to be free from dependence upon the somewhat artificial revivalism which was then creeping in, and which led him to say in 1837 that 'we may excel in getting revivals, but we have yet to learn how to manage them'. He saw London as the natural centre of a national body, and a network of powerful committees as the most efficient form of administration. It was almost inevitable that in and out of the conference a ministerial

[53] *Wesleyan Takings* (1840), p. 12.

executive should emerge, and also that Bunting should dominate it. But the contrast with the past was grave, and Bunting could be all too masterful. James Everett stalked him patiently for years, because, as he said in 1840, 'he is great in mind, and great in influence—too great to be forgiven; if he were less so, it might be borne'.[54] Everett himself was the stuff of which Piltdown forgers are made, and if he did not write the *Fly Sheets*, he must have been sick with envy of the man or men who did. He would certainly not wish us to think that he did not write them. The *Sheets* ignored the deeper problems of the nature of the Methodist Ministry; they concentrated venomously on Bunting the Connexional Engineer, and attacked the whole principle of centralization, together with the personnel of the existing committees. Their author could see no farther than a repudiation of the administrative gains made since the Plan of Pacification. But in any case anonymous slander was no way to purge the Ministry of its faults; nor was the answer of George Osborn, that each itinerant must sign a declaration that he abhorred the *Fly Sheets*, any more effective. The loss of tone and temper which all these events implied helped to discredit the High Wesleyan theory of the Ministry, though it was hard to believe that anyone was really to blame for James Everett.

Thus there was a double strain, between pastor and laity, and between minister and minister. In this almost tragic situation (and 1849 had its cathartic aspect) one feels above all compelled to murmur, *Quis custodiet ipsos custodes?* This is the side of *episkope* which the Protestant tradition has increasingly neglected, and in modern ecumenical discussion it seems too often to be taken for granted that there is no serious need for improvement from this point of view. It was of the oversight of the Ministry that Bunting was thinking in 1844, when he said:

If the time of my departure were at hand, and I was requested to say what is best to be done, I would say, strengthen your executive; whether we feel the want of it or not, our people do.

But the Wesleyan itinerant retained too much independence, and the non-Wesleyan bodies had very little of a constructive nature to propose. They solved the problem by the negative method of stripping the Ministry of all but the most circumscribed powers, so

[54] Ibid. p. 6.

that whether in a circuit or on a Connexional committee a minister's authority depended upon his personality. The Rev. Daniel Jenkins, himself a Congregationalist, has recently said that in the Reformed Churches a minister

is not simply a president of the Assembly, nor yet a clerk, who reads and speaks on behalf of the congregation what anyone of ordinary competence is equally capable of reading and speaking.[55]

That he thought this worth saying at all must have been because he was aware of how often in the past hundred years the average Free Churchman has asserted what he here denies.

Our first general explanation of the change then is that circumstances and secession enabled the critics of the High Wesleyan view of the Ministry to carry their chief point. Whether or not historians should moralize on man's experiences, practical men do so, and it was the considered verdict of the majority that the policy of putting so much authority into the hands of a small group of ministers had not justified itself. They were impressed above all by the obvious fact that Methodism's contribution to English society had been immensely reduced by the divisions. They knew that secession is not necessarily the work of the Holy Spirit because the seceders are sincere and devoted to principle. And those who looked forward to eventual reunion saw that the High view of the Ministry could not, in the light of the past, form a basis for it.

We have suggested that the divisions of Methodism greatly reduced the value of the movement as a whole. But behind the eclipse of Jabez Bunting, and the change implied in Methodism's doctrine of the Ministry, lay the far-reaching effects of the more fundamental separation which parted Methodism from the Church of England. The cost of divisions within the Body of Christ is always very high, whatever the gains, and the history of Methodism suggests how hard it is to establish a new Ministry of Christ. Not that a permanent new Ministry of Christ was originally a conscious aim; John Wesley's activity set the itinerancy in motion, but he constantly urged the Methodists to hold fast to the Church of England. From Jabez Bunting's point of view, however, a new Christian community existed. He told the Conference of 1841 that

When Mr Wesley was alive something ought to have been done; but

[55] *Congregationalism* (London, 1954).

not now: we must now maintain a separate and distinct position, and yet hope that the time may come for a more formal union to be effected.

It seemed natural that the Ministry of this new body should approximate to the Anglican ideals of its founder. This was all the more true because the separation was not, as in the United States, a confident breach with a feeble Anglicanism, but a reluctant parting with a reviving Establishment. In the course of the 1834 debate on Rayner Stephens, who was charged with supporting the agitation for disestablishment, Bunting could still remind the Conference that 'when we gave our people the sacrament in our own chapels, we publicly guarded against its being taken as a sign of separation',[56] by which he meant that Wesleyanism had no tradition of what he called 'fierce, formal Dissent'.[57] It was only in the 1830s that the Oxford Movement hardened the hearts of the Wesleyan leaders, and made them doubt the value of an establishment which provided security for Puseyism.

But the uneasiness caused by Anglo-Catholicism came too late to affect the issue deeply. So far as the development of the Wesleyan Methodist Ministry was concerned, what mattered was the fact of an independent existence, at least from the time of the Plan of Pacification. But a new 'Church', and especially a new branch of the Ministry, cannot be created in a few decades, however dynamic the Revival from which they spring, and however tenacious and well informed the leadership. Church reformers usually see themselves as restoring the lost image of the Primitive Community, but their actual achievements often involve simultaneously a break in the continuity and wholeness of the Church. No care for successions of the hand-to-hand variety can prevent the impoverishment of bodies which weaken the more subtle connections between them and the main stream of the Church's life (which is not to be found, of course, in any single 'Church'). I take it that this was what the Rev. Dr R. Newton Flew had in mind when he said that 'the Church of England itself, as a reformed Church, broke continuity in the sixteenth century with the Church system of which it had until then been a part: that is, it reformed itself at the cost of schism'.[58] In the case of Wesleyan

[56] Gregory, *Sidelights*, p. 155.   [57] Ibid. p. 162.
[58] *The Approach to Christian Unity*, a series of sermons preached before the University of Cambridge in 1951. See pp. 45–50.

Methodism, what took place in the 1790s severed many of the delicate nerves which led back into the Church's past. A Ministry of the kind for which Jabez Bunting struggled could be maintained only against the background of a long tradition, which bred in ministers and people an accepted knowledge of how they should behave toward one another. The tremendous weight of responsibility which the theory of pastoral oversight thrust upon the Wesleyan Ministry overwhelmed men who could not rely, in themselves or in others, on the invisible but potent support of the long-tested practices and habits of a Christian community. Roman and Anglican, with many of the advantages of such support, were not infallible; deprived of much more, it was the less surprising that the Wesleyan Ministry went astray. If there had been only a little more lay support for the ideals of High Wesleyanism, all might have been well. But the undercurrent of disagreement was too strong, and tested the Connexion too sharply in 1827, when Jabez Bunting himself was unable to rise above the average and handle events with vision as well as logic. And the lay support could never be uncompromising, because Wesleyanism had absorbed other elements, especially the Class Leader, the Leaders' Meeting, and the Local Preacher, which were imperfectly reconciled with the High Wesleyan view of the Ministry.

Unfortunately, the tangle of interests, opinions, and ideals was not a very fertile one. After 1857 the tendency seemed to be for everyone—reformers, seceders, continuing Wesleyans—to fall back upon the simple expedient of taking for granted that there was such a thing as the Ministry, and not asking awkward questions about its nature or purpose. The gap has been filled by an individualism of interpretation, which 1932 inevitably increased. But in the process Methodism has lost two kinds of continuity. One was with the past of Methodism itself. But the deeper loss was with the past behind her own. The impoverishment was not fatal; that is shown by the enthusiasm with which Methodism has welcomed the Ecumenical Movement. But one of our chief needs in that work is precisely a positive doctrine of *episkope*, a belief that oversight, whether of pastor or people, is a necessary part of the one Church of Christ. It is convenient sometimes to sit lightly to Church order. But even with regard to the college system of training the Ministry, the principal gain in this field which Bunting passed on to later Methodism, it is taken too much for granted that three or four years in a college is sufficient in itself to support a man throughout the long years of his ministry; the assumption has often cost both man and Methodism dear. Jabez Bunting once said: 'My friends overstate my case; I could state it better myself.' Let us therefore allow him to sum up in his own words:

My opinion is that the Lord Jesus has left his Church very much at liberty, but He has laid down principles . . . the plan of Presbyterianism is nearest to the New Testament at first, but it was found to need some form of episcopacy.

In his last illness, he sent to the Conference of 1857 a message[59] which may still make us pause to wonder how we should give a valid reason for the Faith and Order which we in our turn have inherited:

Tell the Conference I die in the true faith of Evangelical Arminianism. I do not say Arminianism, because that alone leads to legality in experience, and to something like Socinianism in doctrine—but Evangelical Arminianism, that is, the true Gospel . . . .

I regard my policy, that is, the course which I have seen it my duty to pursue, to have been right. It was the best for Methodism. *I am a true Methodist. . . .*

---

[59] *Life of Jabez Bunting*, by T. P. Bunting (London, 1887), p. 742.

THREE

Methodism Misunderstood

ONCE UPON a time students of early-nineteenth-century English history simply ignored Methodism. That they no longer do so with such complete equanimity was largely due to the French historian, the late Elie Halévy. His *History of the English People in the Nineteenth Century*, the first volume of which appeared in French as far back as 1913, and of which an English translation began to come out in 1924, has recently received the accolade of a paperback edition.

It would be a pity, however, if either Halévy's facts or his opinions about Methodism were to be taken for granted by yet another generation of students, as though his *History* offered that historical rarity, an entirely reliable secondary source. For although Halévy deserved credit for seeing something of the relevance of Methodism in the social pattern of the 1830s, he was not a trustworthy source of fact where Methodism was concerned, and this in turn affected his value as an interpreter of the importance of Methodism. A good example is his treatment of the effect on Methodism of the passing, in 1829, of the Bill for Roman Catholic Emancipation, as it is usually called.

In his second volume, Halévy described Catholic Emancipation as 'a victory of Liberalism over Evangelicalism, and Evangelicalism suffered from the defeat'. As a result, 'the powerful Methodist body . . . was forced to register, if not, as in 1820, an actual decline in numbers, at least a marked diminution in its growth'.[1]

From 1827 to 1838 the gains or losses of the Wesleyan Methodist Societies in Great Britain were as shown on page 87.

Between 1829 and 1831 there was in fact a check, though it was compensated for by the tremendous increases shown in 1832–4. Halévy's explanation is both vague and misleading. He said: 'In 1829 the report (the Annual Address of the Wesleyan Methodist Conference to the Societies) ascribes the disappointingly small increase to "the distress of the times" and to "various other causes which have been in active and injurious operation". This guarded

[1] *History of the English People, 1815–30* (London 1926), p. 276.

86

language refers to the disputes occasioned by the question of emancipation, on which the report preserves absolute silence.'[2]

```
1827—gain of  6,194
1828—  „   „   7,995
1829—  „   „   2,235
1830—  „   „   1,749
1831—  „   „     527
1832—  „   „   6,553
1833—  „   „  22,898
1834—  „   „  12,009
1835—loss of    951
1836—gain of  2,000
1837—loss of    439
1838—gain of  4,108
```

As the Annual Address in question covered the year from midsummer 1828 to midsummer 1829 it was hardly likely that there would have been an official comment on a subject on which no official action had been taken. The phrase 'various other causes', however, though it may include some reference to the debates about Emancipation, is much more likely to be a reference to the internal troubles of Wesleyan Methodism during and after the Leeds Organ Case.[3] The Conference of 1829 debated memorials from many circuits protesting against the way in which the Organ controversy had been settled at the previous year's Conference. Halévy makes no mention of the Organ Case at all, nor does he seem to be aware that there was no full-scale discussion of the emancipation of the Roman Catholics at the 1829 Conference.[4] There can be little doubt that at the time, the Address was understood as referring to the debates and actual divisions which had taken place over the strenuous refusal of Jabez Bunting to make

[2] Ibid.

[3] For further information about the Leeds Organ Case see the preceding essay. The affair by no means confined itself to Leeds, the London South Circuit becoming heavily involved.

[4] It is inconceivable that Gregory would have omitted from the *Sidelights* any reference to a *lengthy* debate; he was not shy of the Catholic question; it is just possible, however, that he was so prejudiced against Jabez Bunting that he ignored a *short* discussion on the subject, because he would have been obliged to show Bunting in what would have seemed by the 1890s to be a favourable light.

any concession to the demand for a greater lay share in the government of the Wesleyan Methodist Societies. These controversies had naturally checked the work of preaching the Gospel. It was characteristic of the writer of the Address to avoid any direct mention of the troubles in Leeds; the same reticence marked the Addresses published between 1834 and 1838 when two actual decreases in membership were recorded.[5] National events of some importance took place between 1834 and 1838 but it would be safer to ascribe these actual losses to what has normally been called the Warren Controversy, a second round in the contest between the anticlerical and paternal tendencies in Wesleyan Methodism.[6] Halévy was jumping to conclusions, without considering the internal history of Wesleyan Methodism.

This is borne out by the third volume of Halévy's *History*, in which he reveals a surprising misunderstanding of the whole matter of Methodism and Roman Catholic Emancipation. He said that in 1829 'the Conference had not had the opportunity of making any official pronouncement on the question of Catholic Emancipation, for the Bill had been rushed through Parliament in the interval between the two Annual Conferences'.[7]

It is unlikely that the timing of the Bill was affected by an anxiety by a desire to avoid a clash with Jabez Bunting; the Wesleyan Methodists themselves hardly realized their potential political influence until the education controversies of the 1840s. This is a minor point, however; what Halévy appears to suggest is that the Wesleyan Methodists were incapable of political action unless the Conference happened to be in session at the time of a national crisis. This is an error of fact: from the days of Lord Sidmouth's sudden attack on the Methodist Societies Wesleyan Methodism had possessed machinery to cope with political emer-

[5] Cf. the table given *supra*, p. 87.

[6] The Warren Controversy was on a larger scale than its predecessor; it lasted from 1834 to 1837. I have used 'anticlerical' and 'paternal' here because not all the defenders of 'pastoral supremacy' were Tories in politics, and not all the laymen who asked for change were politically liberal; to reduce the struggle to political terms, as between 'authoritarian' and 'liberal' may be misleading, and commits one automatically to the 'liberal' position. An anticlerical need not be an anti-Christian: he may simply believe that priests are the last persons to be allowed to govern, whether in Church or State.

[7] *History of the English People, 1830–41* (London, 1927), p. 166.

gencies. The powerful Committee of Privileges, which consisted of the most prominent preachers and laymen in the Connexion, was able to act on its own authority subject to the approval of the next Conference, an approval normally given without much hesitation.

Halévy clearly found it difficult to explain why the Wesleyan Methodists made no public pronouncement on the emancipation issue. He said that 'it was common knowledge that the majority of Wesleyans were opposed to Emancipation'.[8] In fact, the reason for this public silence was quite simple: no pronouncement was made because the Committee of Privileges met, discussed the problem, and failed to come to an agreed decision. Or rather, they agreed only that they would not act in the matter. For this there is first, the testimony of the Rev. Joseph Entwisle, which may be found in a *Memoir* published by his son in 1848.[9] Entwisle had received a letter from the Irish Methodist minister, Adam Clarke, in which Clarke, a strong anti-Roman Catholic, asked: 'How is it that our President and our Heads of Houses do not call upon all our people to petition both houses, and carry, if necessary, our remonstrances against those Papists even to the foot of the Throne.'[10] Entwisle agreed with Clarke on principle, but made this note on 14th March 1829:

Received a letter from Mr Mason, as Secretary of the Committee of Privileges. They have met and come to the following resolution: 'That with respect to the Bill for the relief of His Majesty's Roman Catholic subjects, now before the House of Commons, the Committee of Privileges do not think it their duty to take any proceedings in their collective capacity: but every member of the Methodist Society will, of course, pursue such steps in his individual capacity on this occasion as he may think right.' A wise conclusion, in my opinion: for, as a religious body, I trust the Methodists will never move collectively on any civil or political question.[11]

There was no doubt about what Entwisle did himself: he signed petitions against the Bill in Bristol as an ordinary citizen, and he wrote to his son after the Act was passed that 'we must submit, but I feel as if part of my birthright were gone'.[12] Another example of the contemporary Wesleyan ministerial attitude was that

---

[8] Ibid. p. 166
[9] *Memoir of the Reverend Joseph Entwisle*, by his Son (London, 1848).
[10] Ibid. p. 436.   [11] Ibid.   [12] Ibid. p. 440.

of Daniel Isaac, then stationed in Hull. Isaac had shown himself moderately liberal in Connexional politics, but in 1829 he wrote:

You know, I believe, that I was formerly favourable to popish claims. I thought the political character of popery had undergone a favourable change. The conduct of the Priests, and of the Association, in Ireland, has convinced me that I was mistaken. Concession has been made very liberally of late years; but, instead of conciliating them, they have grown more violent. Their violence is the reason assigned by Ministers for granting the claims. The Association has repeatedly stated that they have objects beyond seats in Parliament; and these statements being in perfect accordance with the letter and the spirit of their religion, are entitled to full credit. As they have succeeded hitherto by menace, it is foolish to suppose that they will not use it to gain their ulterior objects. We must, therefore, give them all they want, which, unquestionably, is popish ascendency, or meet their threats with the bayonet. As no real protestant can agree to grant them all they ask, I think we had better fight it out, before the possession of political power shall have nerved their arms for the combat. If Ministers fear them while they are besieging the constitution, what will they do after the enemy is admitted into the citadel? For the first time in my life I have signed a petition against them.[13]

There would have been plenty of support, in other words, for more direct action by the Committee of Privileges, but in fact the Committee circulated a noncommittal resolution, and this formed the basis of the advice given by superintendent ministers to the laity. Clark, Entwisle, and Isaac all signed petitions against the proposed change, but did so as private citizens. It so happens that evidence had survived which explains how it was that the Committee of Privileges behaved in such an unexpected manner, and why the Wesleyan Connexion did not protest officially against Catholic Emancipation.

This evidence is to be found in the autobiography of the Rev. Thomas Jackson.[14] The key to the situation was that Jabez Bunting was President of the Wesleyan Methodist Conference in 1829, and so able to add the prestige of the highest office in the Connexion to his own personal power, then perhaps at its zenith.

[13] *The Polemic Divine*, by James Everett (London, 1839), pp. 273-4. Daniel Isaac was 51 in 1829; he died in 1832.

[14] *Recollections of My Own Life and Times*, T. Jackson (London, 1873). For a modern appraisal of Jackson, see *Methodist Patriarch*, by E. G. Rupp (1954).

Bunting was actually in favour of Catholic Emancipation, a fact of which Halévy was obviously unaware, and which he might not have expected in view of his normal picture of Bunting. From Jackson's account it looks as though Adam Clarke[15] joined with several other ministers and laymen who 'deemed the measure fraught with permanent mischief of the worst kind' to call together a meeting of the Committee of Privileges in the vestry of the City Road Chapel in London. They appear to have done this without informing Jabez Bunting although, as President of the Conference, he was an ex-officio member of the Committee. If he was informed, the notice was probably sent as late as possible, in the hope that he would not make the journey from London to Manchester. Thomas Jackson continues:

Dr Bunting, who was then stationed in Manchester, received intelligence of this meeting, and in the midst of its deliberations, unexpectedly appeared, asking for what purpose the Committee had been called together. On being informed, he said that the Committee had no authority to meet for any such purpose; and that, if it should pass any resolution in opposition to the Catholic claims, or propose to send any petition to Parliament against the Bill which was then pending, he would inform the Government that the Committee was acting against authority, and would enter his protest against its proceedings in the public papers. The consequence was that the meeting broke up, its members deprecating a public dispute between the President of Conference and one of its most important Committees. Those Methodists who were on principle opposed to the measure affixed their names to petitions drawn up by Christians of other denominations.[16]

Bunting was bluffing—or at any rate exaggerating for a purpose the powers inherent in the Presidency of the Conference—when he said that the Committee of Privileges had no authority to act in the circumstances: all he meant in practice was, that the Committee had no authority from him to act. But as Thomas Jackson commented:

That Dr Bunting had a right to his opinion on this occasion, no one will deny; but that he had a right to control the action of his brethren in the manner now stated, I for one was never convinced. If the Committee of Privileges was not appointed by the Conference to petition Parliament

[15] Adam Clarke's last years involved him in several clashes with Jabez Bunting, the effect of which on later Methodist history has not been fully appreciated.   [16] *Recollections*, p. 407.

against the admission of Roman Catholics to legislative power; did the Conference, on the other hand, appoint him to issue what was, in fact, a prohibition; and to hinder the congregations and societies generally from publicly expressing their conscientious judgement on a question which affected the dearest interests of the nation, and that in perpetuity?[17]

Perhaps the simplest answer to Jackson's essentially rhetorical question was that the Committee submitted to Bunting's unexpected assault; their weakness partly arose from being caught in the rather childish act of solemnly holding a meeting behind their President's back. The result was, as Jackson said, that the voice of Methodism was not heard at a moment when 'the British Legislature was being divested of its Protestant character, and the adherents of the most hideous tyranny that ever existed were admitted as the makers of laws for free men'.[18] Jackson's version of the story is all the more convincing because he normally acted in concert with Jabez Bunting, was himself President of the grim Conference of 1849 when Bunting's wounds were avenged (not entirely according to his desire) on the persons of his principal tormentors. In his autobiography Jackson said that Catholic Emancipation was the one issue on which he thought that Bunting had been mistaken —for Jackson, as is obvious from the above passage, deeply hated Roman Catholicism. There can be no doubt, however, that Bunting prevented action against the Government virtually single-handed in 1829. His feat may not have been devoid of historical significance, for, as was to be seen in the later battles over education, Wesleyan Methodism in protest could muster considerable political weight; the absence of an organized protest in 1829 may have been a vital negative factor in the Bill's safe passage. Finally, Jabez Bunting's position shows once again why the Conference Address of 1829 made no comment on the subject: he would have resisted any unfavourable declaration; his enemies in the Conference would hardly have tolerated the added thrust of an approving one.

From this subject one may turn to the question of Wesleyan Methodism's alleged Toryism. In his *History of the English People, 1830–41*, Halévy insisted on the Toryism of the Wesleyan Connexion as a whole.[19] He pointed out that when the disestablishment issue became acute the Wesleyan Methodist Conference adopted

[17] *Recollections*, p. 408. [18] Ibid.
[19] Op. cit., p. 156.

the same attitude of 'unfriendly neutrality' which had characterized its rare reflections on the Reform Bill. He continued:

This attitude was by no means acceptable to certain members of the local congregations. . . . A Wesleyan minister in Lancashire, the Reverend Joseph Rayner Stephens, without referring the matter to his superior, accepted the position of Secretary of a Church Separation Society. He was suspended from the Ministry. This was the signal for the revolt that broke out among the Lancashire Methodists. A considerable body of laymen, led by a minister named Warren, took possession of the local chapels and refused to accept the authority of their Superintendents.[20]

There is considerable confusion here. There was no real connection between the Stephens affair and the Warren controversy. Stephens's suspension was debated by the Wesleyan Methodist Conference of 1834; he was expelled from the Ministry; but no popular movement in his favour took place in the north. He gathered a personal following which supported him as an independent minister for the rest of his life, but that was all. So far from coming to Stephens's assistance at the head of an army of rebel laymen, Warren actually took part in the Manchester District Meeting which suspended him. He described his attitude in the Conference debate:

I proposed at the District Meeting that we should not deal with Mr Stephens as a culprit, on the express condition that he should give up his secretaryship and abstain from attending anti-State meetings in the future. I endeavoured to show him the propriety of this by pointing out that he had broken our law. But Mr Stephens was inflexible. The only point about which I demurred was the extremity of the sentence.

Mr Squance: When Mr Stephens refused to assent to the prohibition of the Meeting, Dr Warren lifted up his hands and said: 'It is impossible to save him.' [21]

In other words, at the time of the District Meeting, Warren was only concerned to protect a young man, if possible, against the consequences of his folly; at a later point in the debate he said that 'in the present state of things we should be as neutral as possible, and maintain our middle position between Church and Dissent'.[22] This was the strict Wesleyan position in the 1830s, and Jabez

[20] Ibid. p. 157.   [21] Gregory, *Sidelight*, p. 152.
[22] Ibid. p. 138.

Bunting might have used the same formula. There was no question of Warren sympathizing with Stephens in his attack on Establishment; a few years later, when he had become weary of the ex-Wesleyan radicals with whom circumstances, not principle, had associated him, he left them in order to become a clergyman in the Church of England.[23] One cannot see Rayner Stephens choosing that as his exit line from history. Halévy assumed much too easily that the closeness in time of the two disturbances meant that there must be some practical link between them.

Even if one leaves personal factors out, there is no truth in the statement that the suspension (or even the virtual expulsion) of Stephens gave the signal for a Wesleyan rising of the north. This later episode had two main sources: the proposal to set up a college in which to train Wesleyan ministers for their job—this brought Warren himself into the field and alarmed many Wesleyans who felt that the training of ministers should be left to a more indirect working of the Holy Spirit; and the dissatisfaction in towns such as Liverpool, Rochdale, and Sheffield with the way in which the Leeds troubles had been handled. Some of those who joined the Wesleyan Association were opponents of Anglicanism, and there was a tendency to interpret the proposal for a college as the kind of step towards the Church of England which the middle-of-the-road Wesleyans disliked, but it is safe to say that the issue of disestablishment played no part in the contest, in which Stephens himself was not, significantly, a partisan. Many members of the Association had supported Parliamentary Reform, but there is no concrete evidence that the attitude of the Conference Address towards the Reform Bill was a specific grievance; indeed, the political comment on the Reform Bill printed in the *Wesleyan Methodist Magazine* had been quietly on the side of moderate change.

The climax of the struggle in which Warren was involved came in 1835. At the Conference of that year Bunting made what he thought of as concessions to the laity; he tried, as he believed, to make it easier for them to bring complaints about Methodist affairs to the Annual Conference. Halévy's account sounded rather

[23] Warren was the nominal head of the Wesleyan Association, formed during the internal struggle of Wesleyan Methodism between 1834 and 1837. Members of the Association were predominantly anti-clerical; Warren really shared Jabez Bunting's theoretical view of the Ministry.

different. In his third volume he said that in 1835 'the entire organization of the Methodist body was revised so as to give the lay members a limited control over the chapel funds, but on the other hand to preserve unimpaired the spiritual authority and the exclusively clerical character of the Conference'.[24] The first part of this sentence was misleading, because the funds in question were the Contingent Fund and the Auxiliary Fund; no drastic revision was needed for this change, which was simply the final development of a long-accepted policy, that laymen should be associated with ministers in the financial control of the Wesleyan Methodist Connexion. These were, in any case, *Connexional* funds, strictly speaking; *chapel* funds, to which Halévy actually referred, were *local* funds which had been largely in the hands of laymen for some time before 1835.

Halévy expanded the second part of the sentence in his fourth volume, in which he said that 'the obligations placed on the Superintendents to consult at regular intervals the leading laymen of the Connexion was so minutely regulated by the enactment of 1835 that it was rendered to a large extent ineffective. Jabez Bunting remained the "Methodist Pope". When he persuaded Conference to found a Theological College, he had himself appointed President and distributed the teaching-posts among his partisans.'[25]

Much of this information was misleading. The obligation referred to (only an annual one) was to discover if a majority of local lay officials in each circuit (hardly the 'leading laymen of the Connexion') thought that the circuit was dissatisfied with some existing law, or wanted some new law to be enacted. The aim of the law—or this part of it—was not to reduce the power of the superintendents but to provide a legitimate channel of communication between the circuits and the Conference. The objection of the Wesleyan Association was that this law was a substitute for lay representation in the Conference itself, and that nothing short of lay representation would end what the Association regarded as a priestly tyranny. It is true that Jabez Bunting was sometimes called the 'Methodist Pope', but to those who supported the Association the title was only a convenient way of talking about what they thought of as a Wesleyan ministerial oligarchy. It was usually

[24] *History of the English People, 1830–41*, pp. 157–8.
[25] *History of the English People, 1841–52*, pp. 328–9.

95

other Wesleyan ministers who sneered at Bunting's personal power; the laity objected to the collective power which the Wesleyan ministers shared through the Conference machinery. When ministers complained about Bunting they usually meant that they were not receiving what they regarded as their fair share of this collective authority; when the Associationists complained, it was on the ground that they had no share of the power at all. This is another reason why one cannot simply describe the internal Wesleyan situation in the political terms of the day: many a Wesleyan layman who was a Tory in politics might still feel that he ought to have some share in the legislature of Wesleyan Methodism.

The last sentence of my quotation from Halévy gives a wrong impression of what happened over the 1834 proposal for a Theological Institution. It may be supposed that Halévy, who normally relied on secondary sources for his Methodist data, had not read the account of what happened in the 1834 Wesleyan Conference; perhaps it was just as well, because the event did not entirely bear out his version of Bunting's omnipotence. (The fact that Halévy mentions the Institution in connection with the laws of 1835 makes it look as though he was also vague as to when the proposal was made.) In the form in which the proposals reached the floor of the Conference, Bunting was designated both as General Superintendent of the Institution and as Theological Tutor (and Warren's anxiety to hold the second position probably determined his sudden onslaught on the scheme, for which he had voted in the preparatory committees). This double appointment aroused so much distaste that in the course of the discussion the proposals were dropped: another minister was nominated as Theological Tutor, Joseph Entwisle[26] was chosen as 'House Superintendent', and Bunting reappeared on the list as the 'Visitor', a title which was so disliked by members of the Conference, apparently because of its Anglican associations, that it was later altered to 'President' by general consent. If Hannah (the Theological Tutor) might be said to depend on Jabez Bunting, the same could hardly be said of Entwisle. He was twelve years senior to Bunting in the Wesleyan Ministry, had attended forty-eight Conferences, four of them in the lifetime of John Wesley himself, had sent three sons into the Wesleyan itinerancy, and was chosen for the obvious reason that he incarnated the original Wesleyan tradi-

[26] See *supra*, p. 89.

tion, which so many of the Institution's critics felt that the new training would inevitably destroy. To call Entwisle one of Bunting's partisans was to misread the situation seriously; it was at least an exaggeration to suppose that the appointments to the Institution showed Bunting at his most imperial. His anxiety to dominate the Institution played into the hands of his critics; in this sense his actions weakened him, summoning more sympathy for the critics of the training-scheme than would otherwise have been available.

In his last volume Halévy made one very remarkable omission in his discussion of Methodism. He described the agitation and disruption of 1844–9 without any reference to the famous *Fly Sheets*. His account developed straight out of the statement that Bunting distributed among his partisans the prizes of the Institution. 'The voice of complaint, therefore, was not silenced. . . . In 1846 the discontent came to a head. . . . An independent Press came into existence among the Methodists, which opposed Bunting's political views.'[27] There was, of course, no reason for saying that the discontent came to a head in 1846 (this might have been a printer's error in the original, but after what had already happened, one wonders) for the explosion occurred three years later, in 1849. The question of the newspapers was much more complicated than Halévy implied. The use of the Press as a weapon in Connexional warfare dated at least as far back as the Warrenite controversy of 1834–7, when John Stephens, the brother of Rayner Stephens, employed his *Christian Advocate* to defend the Wesleyan Association and to criticize Jabez Bunting. Largely through Bunting's own efforts, *The Watchman* was launched as a semi-official Wesleyan paper intended to put the official side of the case. It provoked the *Watchman's Lantern*, an irregular paper of the Wesleyan Association, which lasted through 1834–5. As the tension increased in the 1840s other papers superseded the *Christian Advocate*, but were not over successful; by the end of 1848 the *Wesleyan Record* and *Wesleyan Chronicle* had withdrawn from the field. The *Fly Sheets*, whose effect on the critical side was much greater than that of the ordinary newspapers, were anonymous tracts—the first appeared in 1844, and others followed in 1846, 1847, and 1848; until 1849 they circulated only among the Wesleyan Methodist ministers. *The Watchman*, which never overcame

[27] Halévy, *History of the English People, 1841–52*, p. 329.

a certain ponderousness, was no match for these vigorous invectives, and on 1st January 1849 the official Wesleyan Book Room itself went into the field of anonymity, publishing what it called *Papers on Wesleyan Matters*—these were pamphlets, similar to the *Fly Sheets* in size, but superior in intelligence and savagery. The *Wesleyan Times*, the latest and best of the opposition papers, first appeared at almost the same time. It was also in 1849 that Samuel Dunn and William Griffith began to publish the *Wesley Banner* (1849–54), an opposition monthly. In the case of *The Watchman* and the *Wesleyan Times*, the editors were known; the *Papers* and the *Fly Sheets* were anonymous.

The most political of these papers was the *Wesleyan Times*, which championed the strong tendency of Wesleyan Methodism to move closer to the older Dissenting Churches. The *Wesleyan Times* had strong views on education policy: many Wesleyan laymen supported the idea that the Churches should educate the children of the poor without any kind of interference from the Government: the decision of the Connexional leaders to co-operate with the State and to allow State inspection of Wesleyan dayschools cost them dear in 1849. (One reason why Benjamin Gregory is not a good guide to the conflicts of Methodism in the early nineteenth century is that he ignored issues like education completely; so also, of course, did the *Fly Sheets*.) This dramatic reversal of policy was carried through in a small committee without reference to the majority of Wesleyan laymen: the consequent sense of powerlessness added point to the gibes in the *Fly Sheets* about Bunting's dictatorship (though in fact, of course, the new education policy of the late 1840s originated in the mind of John Scott, who could hardly be described, in Halévy's phrase, as a 'partisan' of Bunting). The more one studies the 1840s the more important the education issue seems to be in crystallizing a demand for lay representation in the Annual Conference: it was one thing for the Wesleyan Ministry to express unpopular political opinions —no one exaggerated the importance of the ministers' opinions; but it was quite another when the ministers showed themselves able to take vital political steps in an area where they could translate opinion into action. Few people resent the political parson when he stands on his soap-box in St Paul's; few people welcome him, however, when he accepts political responsibility.

The *Fly Sheets* had no political opinions. The first (1844) made a sharp attack on the internal economy of Methodism; the second (1846) set the theme of the following three years. Its aim was to make Joseph Fowler, the hope of the more restive ministers, President of the Conference, and to break the custom of re-electing Presidents at intervals of eight years, a custom according to which Robert Newton (who shared Jabez Bunting's general attitudes) was bound to be chosen as President in 1848. The campaign failed; Newton became President in 1848; the campaign began again in terms of 1849.[28] The *Papers on Wesleyan Matters* naturally attacked Fowler, though his name was not mentioned. *The Watchman* also ran a campaign against him. The argument, however, rarely touched political issues at all; the *Fly Sheets*, the *Papers*, and *The Watchman* represented divisions in the Wesleyan Ministry rather than in the Wesleyan Connexion: the *Fly Sheets* could not be called 'liberal' for they did not even advocate lay representation in the Wesleyan Conference.[29]

Halévy's description of the controversy was not very enlightening. He said that 'in 1846 the gain in membership for the whole of the United Kingdom was only 310, in 1847 there was a loss of 5,000. Bunting and his supporters laid the blame for this on the malcontents, who, they said, were bringing the Society into discredit by shaking the authority of its rulers.'[30] Presumably the reason for the mention of the 'United Kingdom' was that the loss of 5,000 in 1847 was made up of 2,913 in Ireland (really a quite separate issue) and 2,089 in Britain. The Conference of 1847 discussed the state of the Connexion briefly in its closing stages: the main themes were the career of James Caughey and the damage

[28] Benjamin Gregory was obliged to defend Joseph Fowler's reputation, since it was Fowler's diaries which he used for the *Sidelights*. He published enough to make it clear that Fowler was very critical of Bunting, and it is hard to believe that Fowler gave no encouragement to writers of the *Fly Sheets*.

[29] The *Wesley Banner* supported the *Fly Sheets* in general; its peculiar ingredient was strong support for Revivalism, to which Jabez Bunting and others were said to be opposed. It was through the influence of the *Wesley Banner* (and the memory of the American Methodist revivalist, James Caughey, whom the Conference had finally silenced in England in 1847) that opposition to Bunting was for a time identified with a claim to preserve the old evangelistic enthusiasm of the Wesleyan past. Halévy was unaware of the existence of this tension.

[30] *History of the English People, 1841–52*, p. 329.

done by revivalism in general. When Jabez Bunting offered explanations of the decline of the 1840s he usually mentioned Socialism, the wealth of the societies, insufficient pastoral visitation of the members, the new, somewhat artificial revivalism, and sabbath-breaking. Fowler's diagnosis, recorded in 1843, on the eve of the first of the *Fly Sheets*, was more parochial. He thought that most of Wesleyan Methodism's troubles came from building outsize chapels endowed with heavy debts: this meant the employment of fewer ministers, which affected the whole pastoral oversight of the people; he also attacked what he called 'popularizing', by which he meant the way in which some ministers competed for Connexional prestige by travelling all over the country preaching special sermons. This last point certainly reminds one of the *Fly Sheets*, which returned to this issue again and again.[31]

Halévy continued: 'The latter (the malcontents) retorted the blame on Bunting and his partisans, who, according to them, had isolated the Society from the mass of the nation.' In practice, as has just been illustrated, the disputes centred on more definitely internal questions. Halévy failed to distinguish the three parties in Wesleyan Methodism: civil war existed in the Ministry, while a large section of the laity was alienated from both ministerial groups. The alliance between these laymen and some of the *Fly Sheets* party was more fortuitous than Halévy thought. Of course, there were political overtones to the struggle, though it should not be forgotten that in this essentially ecclesiastical warfare, a favourite way of denigrating one's opponent was to accuse him of political (and therefore base) motives. But if one of the principal complaints about the Wesleyan leadership was its decision to co-operate with the State in education, one can hardly dismiss such leadership as Tory obscurantism: in taking this decision John Scott and his 'partisans'—among whom Bunting might presumably be numbered—were showing a proper sense of responsibility; it was the lay opposition that was behind the times.

Halévy concluded his account of the controversy—in which he had not really mentioned the *Fly Sheets* at all—by saying that 'Bunting took the bold step of expelling three ministers for col-

[31] For Fowler's comments, see Gregory, *Sidelights*, p. 346. At the Hull Conference of 1848 Robert Newton was elected to the Presidential chair by 197 votes to Fowler's 83. It was not often that the runner-up received so many votes.

laborating with the opposition Press'.[32] This was not at all exact. The campaign against the anonymous authors of the *Fly Sheets* was led by Thomas Jackson and George Osborn—the latter seemed to have a personal and passionate mission to unmask the authors of the *Fly Sheets*. Bunting, who was ageing rapidly, sat in the background and hardly influenced the Conference. The expulsions were the work of a bitter and often quite hysterical Conference, which was maddened by the stubborn refusal of James Everett, Samuel Dunn, and William Griffith to say whether or not they had written the *Fly Sheets*. They refused to answer the question at all, and Everett, whose expulsion mattered much more than that of the two others, was expelled for contumacy, because he would not answer. One has to realize the almost universal conviction of the Wesleyan Ministry that Everett was the anonymous author before one can understand the decision.[33] Dunn and Griffith were expelled on the ground that they published the *Wesley Banner*, and wrote for the *Wesleyan Times*. Griffith admitted that he sent reports of Conference meetings to the *Wesleyan Times*, but defended himself on the ground that other 'conservative' ministers reported the Conference for *The Watchman*, which was quite true. The accounts of the 1849 Conference, however, make it quite clear that Dunn and Griffith were the other two ministers most suspected of writing the *Fly Sheets*, and in a sense the charges on which they were expelled were substituted for a lack of evidence on the major charge. Whether they would have been believed if they had denied any hand in the *Fly Sheets* is another question.

Halévy said that the chief point of the subsequent battle was the freedom of the Press. '*The Times* declared that the decision of the Conference was a threat to the liberty of the Press and gave its blessing to the attempts made by the victims of an irresponsible tyranny to reform the constitution of a Church whose political conservatism it pronounced detestable. With this powerful support the rebellion spread.'[34] This led him inevitably to the conclusion that the formation of the United Methodist Free Churches in 1857 was due 'not to a doctrinal, but a political issue'.

Historians are often tempted to arrive at such dogmatic

[32] *History of the English People, 1841–52*, p. 329.
[33] Everett had a long history of anonymous writing and was a well-known personal enemy of Jabez Bunting.
[34] *History of the English People, 1841–52*, p. 329

conclusions: it was not so-and-so, but so-and-so which settled the fate of the nation. Halévy did not know enough about the internal history of Methodism to allow for anything but a political motive in the struggle which lasted inside Wesleyan Methodism from about 1825 (if not 1797) to 1857. The freedom of the Press made a fine, emotive issue in the debate which raged from 1849 to 1857, but the central themes were internal to Methodism. Hosts of tracts were written about the laws of 1835, about the *Fly Sheets*, about the Brotherly Question, the powers of superintendent ministers and of the ministerial Conference. No doubt, if Halévy was right, the authors lived in a dream world, transforming their under-lying political animosities into religious statements. Nevertheless, Methodism, as a society, had still, in the 1850s, a much greater historical autonomy than Halévy grasped. It contained thousands of people for whom life was a Wesleyan creation, who saw the sur-rounding world through Wesleyan spectacles, for whom the future of Wesleyan Methodism mattered far more than the fate of secular empires far away in a different dimension. These were the people who struggled to define and dominate the Wesleyan soul. To the outside, it seemed supremely unimportant whether the authority of a Wesleyan minister derived from his congregation, or whether he possessed an authority come down from heaven, which his con-gregation could neither give nor take away; but one cannot leave out this element in the controversy (to which it supplied a great deal of the emotional force) or transform it into a 'political' disagreement by drawing the obvious analogies between power in the Church and power in the State. Bunting and Thomas Jackson were not just the ecclesiastical equivalent of Derby and Disraeli; when they claimed absolute responsibility for their laity they stood in an ancient tradition as ministers of the Church; and in the same way the opposition to their claims had lay traditions which ran back far beyond the genesis of nineteenth-century political liberalism. Halévy's misunderstanding of Methodism can be traced to a failure to see that Methodism still remained, even in the noonday sun of the nineteenth century, a religious organism, not quite cut off from its eighteenth-century origins, but filled with anxiety about its own nature and its own future. It was after 1860, in the era of Hugh Price Hughes, that Wesleyan Methodism began to be tempted to identify its nature with a political programme. Jabez Bunting was many things, but he was not a Hugh Price Hughes.

FOUR

Historians and Jabez Bunting

MORE THAN a century after Jabez Bunting's death it seems
worth while to consider what he has suffered at the hands of
historians. Bitter controversy surrounded him throughout his
career, and it has never quite ceased since his death. This essay
does not pretend to be an absolutely exhaustive review of the
literature on the subject, but only to indicate tentatively the main
lines which interpreters of Bunting have followed.

One cannot decide how wide a public was reached by Wesleyan
studies of Bunting in the nineteenth century. Almost in his own
lifetime he had occupied the central place in the third and final
volume of Dr George Smith's *History of Wesleyan Methodism*.
Smith had known Bunting personally, and had written in his defence in the *Fly Sheets* controversy. By 1861, however, three years
after Bunting's death, when Smith was finishing his task, he felt
free to be more critical, and his general conclusion, that what
seemed to him the failure of Bunting's career had its roots in personality, rather than policy, established one of the major themes
of the later interpretation of the last Wesleyan.

Smith's work, however, seems to have had very little influence
on the later Free Church summaries of Wesleyan nineteenth-
century history. This was probably because Smith wrote before
the introduction of a lay representative session into the Wesleyan
Conference: he was both free and willing to defend the ministerial
Conference, and his book accurately represented the mind of the
majority in mid-Victorian Wesleyan Methodism. Smith had no
doubt that the policy followed by Bunting was right. He could
speak 'from a lay standpoint and . . . with perfect independence',
and he set out the conservative case without qualification:

God has laid on the ministers of Christ spiritual responsibilities which
require the possession of the highest spiritual power in His Church.
This is the first principle in Wesleyan Methodism, and we trust it will
always be maintained. The Christian Church is a spiritual kingdom, of
which Christ is the Supreme Head. He hath appointed 'as it hath

pleased Him', persons to stations of trust and responsibility in sub-ordination to Himself. The separated ministry, according to the uniform teaching of the New Testament, is the first in responsibility, and, of course, should be so in authority. The supreme administrative and executive power in the Church must centre either in the minister or in the laity. To speak of its being equally divided between the two, is vain and misleading. In seasons of tranquillity and peace, it has almost always been practically exercised conjointly by ministers and officers; but in times of excitement and strife, the ultimate court of appeal must be composed either of the ministry, or of the laity. There can be no effective co-ordinate authority between these two classes, when the laity outnumbers the ministry by a hundred to one; nor is there a vestige of authority for such a co-ordinate jurisdiction, *in spiritual matters*, in the New Testament.[1]

Smith meant every word of this, and judged Bunting accordingly; Bunting was right in his aims, but wrong in his methods of secur-ing them, especially at the time of the setting up of the Theological Institution in 1834.

Dissenters naturally disapproved of such ideas about the Church and the Ministry and gave cordial encouragement to the Wesleyan Reformers in 1849. There was nothing new in this: a tradition of Dissenting hostility to Wesleyanism ran back at least to the begin-ning of the century. David Bogue and James Bennett, for instance, the Dissenting historians, said of Wesleyanism about 1800 that 'great praise is still due to their persevering efforts to call sinners to repentance. But the want of competent knowledge in the great body of their preachers has nourished errors and enthusiasm among the people, and too fully justified the heavy censure which has been passed on this communion, as containing a greater sum of ignorance of the Scriptures than was ever found in any body of Protestants since the Reformation.'[2] The theological decline of the Independent and Presbyterian Churches in the eighteenth cen-tury hardly bears out this condemnation, but the hostile attitude it represented might also be found in H. S. Skeats's *History of the Free Churches*, first published in 1867, later than Dr Smith's trilogy. This popular *History* was reprinted at the close of the century with an additional chapter by Edward Miall, once the great prophet of a

[1] George Smith, *History of Wesleyan Methodism*, III.506-7.
[2] *History of the Dissenters from 1688 to 1808*. D. Bogue and J. Bennett (4 vols, 1812). The quotation comes from IV.392.

disestablishment which never came, and the Wesleyan *London Quarterly* sharply criticized the weakness of the section on John Wesley. Miall made no attempt to modify Skeats's original comments on the *Fly Sheets* controversy either in the light of Smith's work or that of any later Wesleyan writer. He said: 'In 1849 another secession took place, originating in the arbitrary proceedings of the Conference. For some time previous to this a few persons had expressed their dissatisfaction with the government of the society which was then principally lodged in the hands of one successfully ambitious man—the Reverend Jabez Bunting.' The expelled ministers of 1849 were said to have declined, when challenged by the Wesleyan Conference, 'to be parties to a proceeding which savoured more of the Inquisition and the Star Chamber than of any modern or Christian court'.[3] This savoured of the style of the more intemperate Wesleyan Reformers; no attempt was made to put a case for the Wesleyan Conference. Instead, their conduct was described in the same sort of language as another popular Free Church historian, Sylvester Horne, was to use in 1903—'the arbitrary rule of a clerical body'.

It was the more significant that the friendliest of Free Church historians in the nineteenth century did make use of Dr Smith's *History* as the principal source for the Wesleyan part of his narrative. This was John Stoughton, whose *Religion in England, 1800–1850* was published in 1884. Stoughton did not assume that the Wesleyan Reformers, as honorary Congregationalists, were always right; instead, he pointed out how difficult it was for an outsider to understand Wesleyan law; not least, he added, Wesleyan 'common law'. This hesitation prompted him, unlike other Free Church writers on the period, to offer some explanation for the actions of the Conference of 1849. Methodism, he said, 'constituted a sort of family, for the existence of which more than the usual confidence is necessary. Questions, it is said, may be asked in a household which are not admissible elsewhere. . . . How far such a policy was wise is a question which will probably be viewed differently now by many Methodists from what it was then.'[4] Stoughton quoted, as an explanation of the final disaster, Dr Smith's

[3] Skeats, *History of the Free Churches* (1868 edn), p. 622.
[4] Stoughton, *Religion in England, 1800–1850*, II.316. Stoughton was probably speaking from personal acquaintance with many prominent Wesleyans.

argument that the new rules of 1835 came too late, and should have been introduced after the secession of the Leeds Protestant Methodists (1827–8). Stoughton omitted any set description of Jabez Bunting, but eulogized his son, William Maclardie Bunting, who by no means always agreed with his father. Stoughton's calmer view of Wesleyanism partly resulted from his having grown up among the Norwich Wesleyans: he has a charming chapter about them in his autobiography.

Stoughton's book, however, never vied in popularity with Skeats or Horne, and the popular historian is perhaps the one who matters most, because he creates or invests with the power of print a mythology about the past: in later Methodist history one has to remember that many Methodists were probably drawing their ideas about Jabez Bunting from Congregational sources. An equally important illustration of the influence of non-Wesleyan accounts of Wesleyan history can be found in the Church of England. The Bampton Lectures of 1871 were given by the Principal of Lichfield College, G. H. Curteis. *Dissent in its Relation to the Church of England* reached a sixth edition by 1885. Curteis summed up Wesleyan history as a chain of secessions and, perhaps remembering Pusey's sharp but shallow description of Wesleyanism as a 'degenerating heresy', added that the last of these secessions had not yet been seen. 'Interior decomposition', he wrote, 'has set in. And its destructive agency knows no limit, until every atom shall stand apart and separate from its fellow—until, in short, Congregational Independency is reached, or even Unitarianism, where every individual claims his own personal freedom to the uttermost.'[5] Curteis attributed this sad decline to the 'neglect and disobediency' with which Methodists had treated John Wesley's injunction not to separate from the Church of England.

An examination of Curteis's sources reveals no direct quotation from any Wesleyan book on Wesleyan nineteenth-century history. Abel Stevens's not very remarkable *History* was used for the lifetime of John Wesley; the English editions of Stevens (who was an American) available to me, all stop at the centenary year of 1840. Curteis quoted Skeats, on the other hand, as an authority throughout his *Lectures*, and it was with a quotation from Skeats that he supported his argument that it was when John Wesley 'accepted

[5] *Dissent in its Relation to the Church of England* (London, 1871), pp. 381–2.

this foreign notion of the "new birth" ' after his experience in Aldersgate Street that 'the unhappy present decadence of the Wesleyan revival into a mere additional form of English Dissent becomes not only accounted for, but natural and logical'.[6] Thus failure to communicate to the world outside the nature of either the Wesleyan Connexion or of Bunting's policy meant that later nineteenth-century Anglicanism could be quite ignorant of the significance of recent Church history.

Smith wrote before the great decision was taken in 1877–8 to admit lay representatives into part of the Wesleyan Conference. *Sidelights on the Conflicts of Methodism* was not published until 1898. Towards the end of *Sidelights*, Gregory, not uncharacteristically, suggested that no answer had ever been given to the question: What was Dr Bunting's policy? In fact, he had himself answered this very question at some length ten years before in a *Handbook* to Wesleyan Methodism to which reference will be made later. This, however, did not prevent Gregory from continuing in his best style:

Scattered and unconsolidated intimations and fragmentary, disjected materials for an answer may be picked up on the tide-left beach of controversial chronicle; but these *disjecta membra* have not been pieced together into a recognizable, a realizable, and a vital unity.[7]

In reality, between 1877 and 1898 a group of Wesleyan writers, whom we might for convenience call the Evolutionary School, and among whom Gregory might properly be included, had attempted to put a more positive case for Bunting. In their work the emphasis was shifted from Bunting's personality to his policy, and an important underlying motive was the need to show, if possible, that the introduction of laymen into the Conference did not involve any drastic breach with John Wesley's ideas of Methodism. Thus J. S. Simon, in an article in the *London Quarterly Review* for October 1893, expressly denied that 'the agitators of 1835 had the misfortune to live before their time, that they have been justified by subsequent events, and that the Conference has since conceded all the reforms for which its antagonists contended'.[8] It was Bunting, and not his opponents, the Evolutionary School maintained, who worked in harmony with the forces of his age. But the influence of this group was small. When Sylvester Horne wrote his *Popular*

History of the Free Churches in 1903, he still stated that Bunting's weakness was a 'fatal insensibility to the significance of the greatest movement of his time alike in State and Church',[9] by which Horne meant the growth of the democratic spirit; and the late Albert Peel made no attempt to alter anything that Horne had said when he reissued the book with an additional chapter in 1926. One reason for the comparative failure of the Evolutionists was the publication of Benjamin Gregory's *Sidelights*.

Much of the evolutionists' material came out in 1887. Public (but unofficial) speculation about the possibilities of Methodist reunion had caused a brief exchange of books. An able New Connexion minister, Dr J. C. Ward, had defended Alexander Kilham against J. H. Rigg in *Liberal Methodism Vindicated*, and J. S. Simon had backed up Rigg and, incidentally, George Smith, in a reply called *Wesleyan Methodism Defended*. At this time the long-awaited final section of the standard biography of Jabez Bunting also appeared, to be greeted in the *London Quarterly Review* by a long, anonymous, and important article, called 'The Middle Age of Methodism and its Greatest Man'. This certainly expressed the views of J. H. Rigg. Between 1887 and 1893 J. S. Simon wrote a series of articles in the *London Quarterly Review* which were never, I think, reprinted as a book, on the history of Wesleyan Methodism between 1827 and 1835; these were mainly narrative, but reflected the same general desire to find connecting links with the past and so justify change by showing as wise reformers commonly do, that their most daring innovations are but a return to the traditions of the fathers. In 1888 Benjamin Gregory brought out his official *Handbook of Scriptural Church Principles and of Wesleyan Methodist Polity and History*, such as 'might be put into the hands of our intelligent young people and the conductors of more advanced classes for religious instruction'—an odd compilation, in catechetical form and Gregory's own inimitable prose. Much later, when in 1908 Dr Rigg wrote a brief biography entitled *Jabez Bunting, a great Methodist Leader*, he used much of the *London Quarterly Review* material, followed this same general attitude, and made no attempt to grapple with the *Sidelights*. And finally, if one turns to the pages on Jabez Bunting contributed to the *New History of Methodism* by J. R. and A. E. Gregory, one finds that the interpretation of Bunting runs along the same familiar lines.

[9] Page 294.

Despite Benjamin Gregory's certainty that the question about Jabez Bunting's policy was not even put, much less settled, in the standard biography[10] a fundamental passage for this picture of Jabez Bunting occurs there:

'It was his policy . . . to promote simultaneous improvements in all directions. Let the entrance to the ministry be still diligently guarded: let all the ancient usages of mutual inquiry and supervision, of itinerancy, and of sustentation, be sacredly preserved; let the standard of literary, theological, and religious attainment be made higher and more uniform; in short, let the ministry be such as should command, without controversy or reluctance, the recognition and confidence of the people. But at the same time respect *their* rights; secure their services in every department not assigned by the New Testament exclusively to the ministry or to the pastorate; relieve the clergy from a burden which was greater than they could bear, and from wretched suspicions, ill-natured insinuations, and bitter calumnies; and pour the light of noon-day upon the smouldering fires of faction, so putting them out for ever. These two lines of action, so far from being diverse, were the two component parts of one complete and comprehensive system; and, as each was steadily and prudently pursued, it promoted and secured the other.'[11]

Of course, everything turned on the question as to whether Bunting did respect the rights of the laity, not least at Leeds, and the word 'prudently' would have made others pause, but here at any rate was a positive approach.

In the *Handbook* already mentioned, Benjamin Gregory showed, not for the last time, the ambivalence of his attitude to Jabez Bunting. He first developed, at rather greater length than George Smith, the difficulties caused by Bunting's powerful personality Then he switched to the question: 'What were the main characteristics of Dr Bunting's policy?' His answer reads as though it might have been framed very largely in terms of the paragraph just quoted, and which he summed up in the sentence: 'The two poles of Dr Bunting's policy were Pastoral Rights and Responsibilities on the one hand, and Popular Rights and Responsibilities on the other.'[12] He expanded the second point in a way which

[10] Cf. *Sidelights*, p. 495.
[11] T. P. Bunting, *The Life of Jabez Bunting*, pp. 331–2.
[12] Gregory, *Handbook*, p. 237.

seems strange to those accustomed to the late Elie Halévy's picture of Bunting as a kind of ecclesiastical Metternich:

... by his simultaneous development of the prerogatives and powers of the people he was the champion, the protector, and the evolver of the popular element in our polity. . . . The culminating legislation of 1876 was, to most minds, the logical deduction from, and the natural sequence of, the adjustments and amplifications which were the handiwork of his constructive genius.[13]

One cannot resist quoting the next question in the catechism: 'Is there any great name in English history of which you are reminded by the genius and career of Jabez Bunting?' The answers were William Pitt, and 'the greatest of American statesmen, Alexander Hamilton'.[14] Making similar comparisons in the *Sidelights*, Gregory deserted English history and added Pericles for good measure.

So much by way of assertion; for supporting argument one may turn to Dr J. H. Rigg's *Comparative View of Church Organizations Primitive and Protestant, with a Supplement on Methodist Secessions and Methodist Union*. Rigg said that from 1797 there was a steady growth of lay power and influence, in connexion especially with the District Committees, the Connexional Committees of Management, and the Annual Committees of Review, 'the development having been chiefly guided and worked out under the master hand of Dr Bunting, who until feebleness of age began to touch him was the great and truly liberal and progressive leader in Connexional legislation'.[15] Rigg pointed out that the system of mixed committees favoured by Bunting (and greatly strengthened by him in 1835) led naturally to a stage, about 1820, when these committees began to hold meetings preparatory to the Conference. By 1840 these meetings were being reported in the Methodist Press, and officials used them to give an account of their stewardship; inevitably, these gatherings, the Committees of Review, influenced the Conference. Moreover, the laymen were not all the nominees of Bunting: the rules of 1835, for example, said that the fifteen laymen who were on the Committee of the Contingent Fund should be chosen by the circuit stewards of the Districts most contiguous to the place where the Conference was being held. The extension of this principle of representation was a slow process, but that such a process took place was undeniable, and it

---

[13] Op. cit. p. 238.   [14] Ibid. p. 239.   [15] Op. cit. p. 257.

was possible to say, as Benjamin Gregory said in his *Handbook*, that the Representative Session 'seemed to most minds the logical development of the Committees of Review, of which the representative element was the lay element, and which exercised such a powerful and salutary effect on Methodism'.[16] In the *New History of Methodism* it was boldly claimed that the constitution of Wesleyan Methodism, like that of the United Kingdom, has 'slowly broadened down from precedent to precedent'.[17]

The advantages of the position taken by the Evolutionary School were obvious. On the grounds indicated above it is possible to argue that the admission of laymen to the Wesleyan Conference was not the victory of the Reformers over the defenders of 'clerical absolutism', and over Jabez Bunting in particular, but the logical outcome of his policy, which would have taken place without a single agitator or secession. And this point of view was reinforced by J. S. Simon in the *London Quarterly Review* for 1893, in an article in which he analysed the demands of the opposition in 1835. He pointed out that most of the leaders of the reforming movement were nervous of any kind of central governing body, however elective and representative its make-up. What they wanted, like the Leeds Protestant Methodists, was a system of circuit independency, the circuit existing in a federation so loosely held together that no kind of pressure could be brought to bear on a single circuit by the will of a majority of the other circuits. Looked at from this point of view, the case for Bunting's attitude became much stronger. If the primary issue was not lay representation, Bunting could not be accused of denying the right of the laity to any share in the government of the Church. Instead, he could be seen as the great defender of the right of Wesleyanism to remain a Connexion, of the very principle which seemed to his contemporaries the explanation of the amazing success of the Methodist movement. At the same time, Simon's article, in which Bunting was hardly mentioned, shifted the emphasis away from the defence of the pastoral office to a defence of the traditional Wesleyan idea of a Church. From this standpoint Simon could criticize the *Fly Sheets* very sharply, for the anonymous authors showed no interest in lay representation, and little in the character of the pastoral office, but interpreted Wesleyan politics largely in terms of the replacement of one ministerial cabinet by another, the Ministry of Jabez

[16] Page 242. [17] Edited by H. Workman, I.402.

Bunting by (in reality) the Ministry of James Everett. Once again Bunting emerged as much more statesmanlike than his critics. Simon, moreover, had found an effective counterpoise to the Wesleyan seceders' use of the idea of 'liberty': they favoured freedom and Bunting hated it. In fact, Simon implied, what the seceders fled from were the restraints of a properly organized New Testament Church; their 'freedom' was not worth the price they paid for it.

In the period under discussion, however, the most remarkable piece of writing about Wesleyanism was undoubtedly Dr H. B. Workman's introductory essay in the *New History of Methodism*. Much of the *New History* is now as faded as the gold letters on its spine, and there was a natural tendency to smooth over the troubles of the Wesleyan nineteenth century in view of the friendlier relations which had developed between the Wesleyan and non-Wesleyan bodies after the first Methodist Ecumenical Council, which met in London in 1881. Workman's attempt to decide on 'The Place of Methodism in the Life and Thought of the Church' is still very much alive, and by no means limited by denominational frontiers. Dr Workman elaborated the medieval parallels to Wesley and Methodism which had suggested themselves to Southey and F. D. Maurice (parallels the exact value of which it is difficult to decide—have they more than a literary interest? are we betrayed into them by a passion for championship tables?), but he had less to say about the nineteenth century. When Tyerman published his *Life and Times of the Rev. John Wesley*, James Dixon, then superannuated and blind, wrote to him and said: 'I used to think as you do up to 1849, namely, that Methodism was the most glorious development of the grace and truth of God ever known in the world; but the horrors of that dreadful time shook my confidence, which, I am glad to say, your book has very much revived.' Dr Workman stood a long way from 1849: he felt able to assert that 'the virtual suppression of Evangelicalism as a governing force in the Church of England has made Methodism more conscious of itself as the representative Evangelical Church of the country'. The development of the Anglo-Catholic movement had meant that 'even the Wesleyan Methodist Church, which at one time was regarded as a sort of poor connexion of the Establishment, has drifted into complete separation', and allied itself with a nonconformity prepared to resist hotly the alleged intention of those whom Workman was still calling the Tractarians to 'undo the work of the Reformation'. Workman did not mention Jabez Bunting, or 1849, or the transformation of the Wesleyan Conference; it is equally important that he had laid positive emphasis on the Methodist doctrine of Assurance and said in comparison little about the Methodist doctrine of Perfect Love. For him the meaningful changes in nineteenth-century Methodism were: first, the altered relationship of Wesleyanism to other ecclesiastical bodies; second, the acceptance—general, if not universal—of the itinerant as a full minister of the Church. In fact, Workman's summary of nineteenth-century Methodist history makes one wonder if, when he claimed for Methodism 'a definite place in the progress and development of the one Holy Catholic Church' he was not actually pointing to the fact that denominationalism had at last found a place in the life and development of the Methodist Societies.

This might have implied a drastic criticism of Jabez Bunting— and for that matter of Hugh Price Hughes—but Dr Workman seemed to regard what had happened as the inevitable and welcome outcome of Anglo-Catholic pressure from outside, coupled with internal changes best covered by the word 'progress'. Methodism had become ecclesiastically mature. Workman's treatment of the changed status of the Wesleyan itinerant took the rather odd form of the assertion, based on the uncertain authority of Harnack and the dubious evidence of the Didache, that 'the chief office of the Early Church revived by Methodism was that of the apostle'. The Wesleys (Charles at any rate until he married), Whitefield and Coke were 'apostles', together with Asbury. In a sense, however, 'the apostolate died with Wesley. The one remaining "apostle", Coke, with his roving commission, was always jealously regarded by the prophets and presbyters, who succeeded to Wesley's authority but not to his office'. All this is romantic rather than historical: there is no sober ground for suggesting that Methodism revived any office of the Early Church, nor would present-day scholarship pay much attention to the Didache as a source of information about what the Early Church was like.

Dr Workman seems to suggest that the development of Methodism conformed to a pattern set by the Early Church: just as the Primitive 'apostle' found himself superseded by the jealous 'episcopos' or bishop, so Coke's 'apostleship' was never really accepted

by his fellow itinerants. One cannot, however, successfully interpret the period 1791–1830 in terms of an attempt by Jabez Bunting and his fellow '*episcopoi*' to overthrow or supersede an 'apostolate'. Their policy was to improve the status of the itinerants,
to lift them to the position of universally recognized ministers of the
Catholic Church; the struggle which was the core of the Wesleyan
history of the period arose from the stubborn resistance of many of
the itinerants to any such change. They wanted to remain 'Methodist
preachers'; they did not want to become ministers in a more or less
Nonconformist sense. They felt little jealousy of the power of the
Wesleys or of Asbury, though they resented the idea that Coke was
really on a level with such men: their hero was Adam Clarke,
himself not without some right to the title of 'apostle' as Workman
defined it. Although they would have agreed with Dr Workman's
second, and somewhat contradictory suggestion, that whatever the
nature of Wesley's position it perished with him, they did not
make this the basis of further claims about themselves—and this
was the extraordinary development, on which Workman's analogy,
for it could not possibly be regarded as more, threw no light whatever. Symbolically, the Wesleyan itinerants, as soon as John
Wesley died, called a halt to the Wesleyan ordinations, repudiat-
ing their Father in God at what was surely his most 'apostolic'
point, the point at which he attempted to pass on the authority
which Dr Workman (and more recently Edgar Thompson, in
Wesley, Apostolic Man) was anxious to claim for him.

There was also the additional contradiction in Workman's thesis
that he appeared to approve entirely of the nineteenth-century
development of Wesleyan Methodism. The question which James
Dixon raised with Tyerman, and which clearly haunted Bunting in
the last years of his life, was whether a subtle tragedy had not taken
place in which both sides in the Methodist Disruption were the
losers—a tragedy whose profoundest mark was the paucity of
Methodist theology about Perfection in the nineteenth century,
and for which it was small compensation to be able to say that
Wesleyanism was no longer the poor relation of the Church of
England. This question Dr Workman did not touch; indeed, the
general attitude of the *New History* to the divisions of the nineteenth century was to emphasize that they were not 'doctrinal',
and therefore, somehow, not important. Even in the restricted
sense that it would have for patristic students this was not quite

accurate: the doctrines of the Church, Ministry and Sacraments were deeply involved in the controversies of the period. Such minimizing comment always implied that the diseased personality of Jabez Bunting (though it was really James Everett's personality which was more evidently diseased) must take the blame for the Disruption.

Dr Workman made a more direct attempt to throw light on the period in his section called 'Methodism and Puritanism'. There he attributed some of the characteristics of Methodism to its alleged inheritance from the seventeenth century of a dualistic attitude to life. This had shown itself in Methodism inasmuch as 'the cultivation of the ugly', the opposition to the Theological Institution, and a widespread suspicion of culture, together with indifference to social and political issues, could all, he thought, be traced to this Puritan background.

Dr Workman's first instance seems rather dubious, and one's confidence is not increased by his comment that the cultivation of the ugly was 'aggravated by the Philistinism of the Georgian age'. When Matthew Arnold talked about Philistinism he meant a brute indifference to the arts, whereas the Georgian, whatever a late Victorian might have thought of his achievements, consciously aimed at cultivated taste. For Workman, Methodist Gothic was evidently an improvement on Methodist Georgian, but that either style was evidence of a dualistic attitude to life one may doubt. Methodism simply followed the taste of the age, as it has done in the present century, adopting a style best called Light Industrial. In all three cases beauty was the aim, but Workman left out two points: a good architect is both rare and expensive, and in the hierarchy of English society Methodism long occupied a place subject to a cultural time-lag.

The second case is equally doubtful. The opposition to the plan put forward by Bunting for a Theological Institution was based on an explanation of the success of Methodism worked out in terms of its actual history, not in terms of an abstract attitude to 'culture'. John Wesley had told Samuel Furly that of all men a clergyman 'should imitate the language of the common people throughout', and this at once defined both the manner and the audience of Methodist evangelism. If many Methodists in the 1830s dreaded the results of 'culture' in ministers, it was also because of their long experience of university-raised Anglicanism in the parish pulpit. The universities themselves had not risen far from their eighteenth-century squalor, as the mid-century Royal Commission was to prove, so that nervousness about 'young men gathered together into institutions' was more reasonable than it seems today. It was unfair in any case to accuse the Puritan of a suspicion of culture; Puritanism proper was a university movement, in revolt against the illogicalities of old-fashioned thought about education, politics, and the Church settlement. Methodism, it is true, was affected by the Pietism of the later seventeenth century, but this was a distinct growth, whose rebellion against the contemporary scientist and biblical critic was, as A. N. Whitehead saw, an ominous event in the intellectual history of Christianity. In Bunting's lifetime the representative of this tradition was the Anglican Evangelical: he, not the Methodist itinerant, spent his leisure at meetings of a Prophetical Investigation Society, or speculated as to the costume which Louis Napoleon would wear when he was revealed to an astonished world as the Antichrist. It was in the second half of the nineteenth century that Methodism fell seriously out of step with the environing world of thought, substituting, one might almost say, Pietism for perfectionism. But that a suspicion of culture, caused by a dualistic attitude to life, was a reason for the attack on Bunting's scheme for a theological College one may doubt. The plan was the occasion, not the substance, of the secession: on its substance this analogy threw no light.

In the third instance Dr Workman covered himself against possible objection by saying that indifference to *all* political and social issues was possibly more ostentatious than real. Nevertheless, the use of the word 'all' gave the statement the air of exaggeration, or suggested that only certain issues counted in the mind of the writer. There has been a constant tendency to criticize the Methodism of 1815–50 because it did not choose the social and political issues that later generations have felt they would have chosen as fields of action. The 'no politics' rule, to which Workman presumably referred, was accepted out of political partisanship, not political indifference: there was great anxiety lest the prestige of the Connexions (for the Primitive Methodists worked the same rule) should be thrown on one side of the party war. As long as the major subjects of politics were secular this could be achieved by formal indifference: the few occasions when Bunting broke bounds were significantly seized on and handed down to posterity. When, however, as in the 1840s, the subject-matter of politics lay in fields where religion and the State encountered each other, and once the policy of Sir Robert Peel's Government had united the Wesleyans against the Tory Party, the complaints about Bunting's political activities ceased, the political importance of the *Connexion* became great, and the 'no politics' rule dropped into the background. Here, if anywhere, the dualism to which Workman referred might have been supposed to operate, but not as a generator of political indifferentism: the 'come-outer' spirit, as American Church historians sometimes aptly call it, worked to promote a vigorous and successful interference in national politics, the defeat of Sir James Graham's education bill in 1843. Taken as a whole, Dr Workman's use of this concept of dualism betrayed his conviction that nothing tragic had happened. He made this assumption clear when he went on to say that Methodism had now virtually outgrown this 'Puritan' streak, thanks to the influence of John Henry Newman and his school.

In studying this interpretation of Bunting one has to remember that Dr Workman wrote in the flood-tide of Nonconformist self-confidence. He lived, as may be seen from his references to Harnack and to the Didache, at a time when it was possible not only to believe in the results of modern criticism, but also in the results of modern history. In both cases, this confidence has become difficult. The results of modern research are in danger of cancelling one another out; the publication of a new commentary on the Old or New Testament is no longer an important event in the history of Christian thought. Workman's straight contest between an Evangelicalism championed by Methodism and an Establishment dominated by Anglo-Catholicism has disappeared. Workman could say that the dissidence of dissent had given way to a nobler conception of evangelical solidarity 'the end of which is not yet'— present-day spectators of the Free Church Federal Council may feel, however, that the end is not far off. Methodism has reached a point in the 1960s when it seriously considers union with the Church of England itself. From Workman's point of view his judgement on Bunting—that he was an unfortunate interruption of the natural development of the century—was natural enough. At the same time one is tempted to say that Dr Workman's approach to Methodism, through analogies drawn from earlier centuries and other cultural systems, was unfortunate as a historical method. There was even a touch of the comic about his anxiety to show that Methodism was respectable because things rather like it had happened before. Closer attention to the career of Jabez Bunting would perhaps have compelled him to admit the historical awkwardness of Methodism, the permanent challenge which it presented to orthodox ways of describing the Church.

From Dr Workman it is now necessary to turn back to Benjamin Gregory, to whom so many references have already been made in the course of this essay. Popular opinion—rarely very accurate—imagines that his Sidelights on the Conflicts of Methodism[18] was an important book which produced immense quantities of hitherto unknown facts about Jabez Bunting and first enabled us to understand him. Gregory has often been treated not just as the rather rambling editor of Joseph Fowler's notes on the debates of the Wesleyan Conference between 1828 and 1849, but also as a reliable interpreter of them. Quotations from the Sidelights have become almost a variety of historical scripture upon which no higher criticism may be practised. There is nothing new in this: the infallible source is a recurrent feature of historical study—Horace Walpole's Letters, for instance, have sometimes been greatly overvalued as sources of eighteenth-century history. In fact, however, Gregory's book was not the foundation of the study of Bunting but the rock on which that study nearly foundered. For what resistance his garrulous text did not wash away he overcame by a luxuriant concentration on personalities which shifted the interpretation of Bunting back to where it began—in the pages of George Smith. Gregory's bland suggestion that no one had really coped with the problem of Bunting before proved enough to throw many off the scent; the work of the Evolutionary School disappeared, leaving no trace in later studies.

The unwary reader assumes that the subject of the Sidelights is the personality of Jabez Bunting. In fact, the book was just as much an apologia for Joseph Beaumont—an attempt to explain

[18] Sidelights on the Conflicts of Methodism during the second quarter of the nineteenth century, 1827–52. Taken chiefly from the notes of the late Rev. Joseph Fowler of the Debates in the Wesleyan Conferences. By Benjamin Gregory, D.D., President of the Conference, 1879. The dedication was dated December 1897, 'in the centenary year of the Plan of Pacification and the Leeds Regulations'.

the Disruption of 1849 purely in personal terms. Although Gregory supported moderate revision of the Wesleyan constitution after 1850, he did not think that the reformers had any case in principle; he believed in concession for the sake of peace, on the ground that the behaviour of the old order of superintendents had made any other course impossible. There are moments when Gregory reminds one of Indian Army officers at the time of what Hindus now call the First Freedom Struggle (1857), who were so often unable to believe that *their* sepoys could revolt: the Disruption 'laid waste some of the fairest and most fruitful circuits in Methodism, on which I or my father or grandfather had looked with exultant thankfulness, and had laboured with success and shouting, bringing our sheaves with us'.[19] There could have been nothing wrong internally with these circuits, nor with the system that produced them: poison must have been injected from outside. The source of this poison Gregory found within the annual Conference, and in the notes of the debates taken by Fowler he possessed just the kind of evidence that he needed to support this idea.

His position really rested on another and much larger assumption, never stated explicitly, and not always consistent with some of his comments. Gregory—unlike every other student of the period—saw no more than a superficial continuity between the quarrel over the Theological Institution in 1834, and the renewed agitation for reform in 1849. He seems to have thought that the earlier withdrawal of the Wesleyan Association, and its absorption of such other seceding bodies as the Leeds Protestant Methodists, had drained off most of the restless laity, provided a home for those who still wanted change, and left a situation which could have been calmed completely by judicious government. This underlies his conviction that if Everett alone had been expelled in 1849 the Connexion would have accepted his dismissal as just. Instead, the agitators, he felt, were made a present of a solid case on which to renew their demands—by the reckless handling of Dunn and Griffith, as well as of the author of *Wesleyan Takings*. This mistake occurred because the Conference of 1849 was swept by an extraordinary mood of hysteria, which had been growing since 1840, and which was caused by a clash of personality inside the Conference for which Gregory held Jabez Bunting only partly responsible.

[19] *Sidelights*, p. 494.

Thus Gregory confused the personal quarrels only too common in a public body with the deeper contradictions in the Wesleyan system which made the renewal of the reform movement inevitable in the long run. There was, of course, a distinction between those who thought that the expelled ministers were treated unfairly and those who were reformers on principle, but this does not account for what seems the fact that people seized on the actions of the Conference of 1849 as symptomatic, that they scented the hysteria to which Gregory bears witness, but that they attributed this inflamed state of mind to the principles rather than to the personalities of the Conference majority. It was characteristic of the position of James Everett that he reached the same conclusion only several years after his expulsion: the Everett of 1849 certainly did not want to set up the Methodist Free Church.

Gregory's standpoint had important effects on his use of Fowler's record of the Conferences. He sought to guarantee the picture which he gave by printing on the title-page of the *Sidelights* Bunting's alleged comment on Fowler's activities: 'I have great, confidence in one individual who has been accustomed to take from year to year copious notes of the proceedings of the Conference.' It is worth underlining that Bunting spoke of the notes as copious: within the pattern of the whole he was prepared to take his chance. Now, where something like this copiousness was reproduced by Gregory, Bunting's confidence was not misplaced: for example, in the long account of the debate which preceded the withdrawal of Rayner Stephens in 1834 there is a complete refutation of the secular historian's assertion that Stephens was ruthlessly expelled on political grounds by a fanatical assembly. Bunting did not mean to guarantee a selection from Fowler's material not even made by Fowler himself; still less would he necessarily have welcomed Gregory's part-publication of the notes, half buried under a magisterial commentary. The *Sidelights* shattered the attempt to understand Bunting's policy; once again, but in greater detail than ever before, Bunting's character became the subject.

One sees in such a book as William Redfern's *Modern Developments in Methodism* how wrong Bunting had been if he supposed that Fowler's notes would conciliate the Wesleyan Reformers. William Redfern was a prominent minister of the United Methodist Free Churches, and he wrote *Modern Developments* as part of a series called 'Eras of Nonconformity', edited by Silvester Horne, to which Samuel Chadwick contributed a volume on eighteenth-century Wesleyanism. The series was sponsored by the National Council of the Evangelical Free Churches; *Modern Developments* came out in 1906, a time at which Wesleyan Methodism stood as close as perhaps it ever did to the older Free Churches. Redfern, not unnaturally, seized on the *Sidelights* as his principal source.

Redfern saw the history of nineteenth-century Methodism as the conflict of two ideals. 'On the one side there was the clerical ideal, which insisted on the supremacy of the Pastoral Office, which was rooted in the High Churchmanship of Wesley, and which had been strengthened by Methodist institutions and traditions. Opposed to it was what, for want of a better word, may be called the Scriptural ideal, which insisted on the brotherhood of the Church, was rooted in spiritual experience, and strengthened by all the liberal and progressive tendencies of the nineteenth century'.[20] (What a century the nineteenth was in its radical heyday!) Redfern's position was clear; he made no bones about his support of the second ideal. He regarded Bunting as the 'ablest champion' of the ideal of pastoral supremacy, and no one, he added, understood Bunting who had not studied the *Sidelights*. There Gregory 'furnishes an absolutely trustworthy and unanswerable indictment of Bunting's policy and conduct in the Wesleyan Conference'.[21] The weakness of this assertion was the suggestion that Gregory indicted Bunting's policy as well as his personal conduct: on page 163, Redfern quoted J. H. Rigg as telling the Methodist Union Committee that in Wesleyanism the power of the pastorate 'has not been changed one iota', and in 1896 at any rate Gregory would have agreed. But while Redfern does not represent an important link in a literary chain of influences, he is a typical example of the conclusions that men drew from Gregory's *Sidelights* right down to the somewhat perverted account of Wesleyanism given by Elie Halévy.

This is not to say that Redfern's use of the *Sidelights* was always beyond criticism. For example, on page 131 he dealt with the question of the *Fly Sheets*. He defended their anonymous publication on the ground that the writers would have been 'connexionally exterminated' if they had given their names—'the Conference simply revelled in the exercise of its despotic power'. He offered to

[20] *Modern Developments in Methodism*, p. 131.   [21] Ibid. p. 101.

prove this by four quotations from the *Sidelights*. The first of these was that the Conference deposed one man for 'maladministration which had caused disturbance'. Redfern, however, omitted the next sentence in the *Sidelights*, in which Gregory said that 'Dr Bunting objecting to the sentence, was in a minority of one'.[22] Anxious to show the tyranny of the Conference, in which he no doubt sincerely believed, Redfern, one guesses, left this out as unduly favourable to Bunting. Gregory, however, made his comment for exactly the opposite reason, to imply that even when the Conference unanimously decided against a superintendent, Bunting, always on the side of authority, defended his man. Neither Gregory nor Redfern was anxious to underline the possibility that Bunting, even occasionally, was in a minority at all. Since Gregory gave no facts about the case in the *Sidelights*, it would have been a fair assumption that the Conference, in this case at any rate, acted justly. The absence of detail was the significant aspect of Redfern's next instance, also from page 424, where Gregory wrote: 'A brother was charged with having "spoken against certain members and acts of the Conference". His defence was: "I thought I had a right to take which side I pleased." ' Redfern quoted this accurately, apart from the addition that the defence was 'given innocently enough'. Two comments suggest themselves: that Gregory again gave no details, and that he also did not say what, if anything, was decided about the case. Redfern followed the general implication and introduced the adverb 'innocently', but little seems left of the despotic power.

The third instance also came from this unlucky paragraph. Redfern reported that 'another man was censured for having allowed his beard to grow. He was told either to shave or to resign.' Gregory actually wrote: 'Another brother was reported to be afflicted with "a strange idiosyncrasy—he declines to use a razor". It was decided he should be sent for and conversed with by selected ministers. This committee recommended that he should either shave or sit down. This reads very strangely after the lapse of seven times seven years.' In a paragraph like this Gregory was paraphrasing, not reporting Fowler in full. The decision to appoint a committee suggests that this was not simply a matter of Conferential whimsy: the minister concerned may have been ill, or the victim of a doctrinal aberration which does sometimes occur. Gregory

[22] *Sidelights*, p. 424.

left the story incomplete; Redfern, perhaps too easily, accepted the implication of despotism.

These three instances all come from the account of the Conference of 1848, which Redfern chose no doubt as the nearest to that of 1849, to show that the attitude of the '*Fly Sheet* Committee' was justified right to the end of the play. But the choice was not very fortunate. For this was a Conference at least so much at liberty that Joseph Beaumont could return three times to open attack of Bunting, putting down an interrupter in a style which Gregory thought never surpassed except by 'Professor Huxley's terrible retort to Bishop Wilberforce of Oxford at the British Association of 1860'.[23] On the following page Gregory added of Bunting that 'under Dr Beaumont's strictures the working of his facial muscles told plainly of severe and steadfast self-suppression'. The final quotation given by Redfern was not from a report of a Conference, but from notes on a meeting of the Book Committee later than 1843.[24] The instance was more material, but once again the absence in Fowler's notes of any detail to show that disciplinary action was *not* justified is the weak point in the argument. On the whole these passages do little for the anonymity of the *Fly Sheets* except contrast it with the open warfare of Beaumont.

Redfern, of course, would have defended himself by saying that he tried to give the impression which *Sidelights* made upon him as a whole. The point which neither he nor some of his successors have always kept clear is that Gregory was using Fowler's notes only to show that there was a deep-seated division within the ministerial Conference, for which he held Bunting's will to power partly responsible. Redfern quite sincerely misused this picture as evidence of the soundness of the Reformer's criticism of pastoral supremacy over the laity, a matter with which Fowler's notes have little to do. Gregory had no sympathy with the Reformer's attitude to the pastoral office: his intention was the much more limited one of showing that the ministerial opposition to Jabez Bunting in the Conference both existed and had a valid case to make against him.

In the twentieth century, secular historians tackled nineteenth-century Methodism for the first time. They were not very interested in the internal history of the various Methodist denominations, but were concerned about the relationship between Methodism and political and economic issues. The most famous of these,

[23] *Sidelights*, p. 430. [24] Ibid. p. 518.

the French historian, Elie Halévy, I have commented on elsewhere.[25] His interpretation of Jabez Bunting as an ecclesiastical authoritarian who was not only himself a Tory in politics but also anxious to prevent other Wesleyans from being at once openly Liberal in politics and Methodist in religion, reappeared in Dr Maldwyn Edwards's *After Wesley* (1935),[26] among Methodist studies, and again, but with a peculiar note of vituperation, in Mr E. P. Thompson's *The Making of the English Working-Class* (1963).[27] In another essay in this book I have tried to show that the Wesleyan Connexion was not quite as 'Tory' in politics between 1820 and 1850 as it often assumed.[28]

Much more interesting from the point of view of this essay was Mr E. R. Taylor's book, *Methodism and Politics, 1791–1851*, which was published in 1935. Mr Taylor summed up his interpretation of Bunting in terms of a comparison with John Wesley:

The churchmanship of both John Wesley and Jabez Bunting brought upon them charges of 'popery', but they were 'Popes' of very, very different types. Both men were autocrats, but, whilst Wesley's authority held his societies together, Bunting's produced a loss of 100,000 members in five years (1850–5). Those facts point to the chief difference between the two men. Wesley claimed loyalty to himself as the 'Father of his People'; Bunting to the system of which he was the directing genius. Wesley, though spiritually a High Churchman, was content to throw aside the system, and 'to be more vile' in order to save souls;

[25] Cf. 'Methodism Misunderstood', p. 86, *supra*.

[26] Dr Edwards was careful to say, however, that at least until 1830 Bunting's views represented those of the Methodist people, and that after 1830 the opposition to Bunting was always a hopeless minority (p. 158). This in itself rather weakens the suggestion that Bunting was a kind of tyrant. Presumably any Wesleyan leader in the period would have had to say similar things.

[27] 'In Bunting and his fellows we seem to touch upon a deformity of the sensibility complementary to the deformities of the factory children whose labour they condone. In all the copious correspondence of his early ministries in the industrial heartlands . . . among endless petty Connexional disputes, moralistic humbug, and prurient enquiries into the private conduct of young women, neither he nor his colleagues appear to have suffered a single qualm as to the consequences of industrialism' (op. cit. p. 354). This refers to the period 1805–14. Moreover, Thompson added, the Methodist leaders weakened the poor from within by adding to them 'the active ingredient of submission' (ibid. p. 355).

[28] *v. i.*, p. 127.

Bunting, without Wesley's spiritual depth, and with a less adequate conception of the Church, wished to mould Methodism according to a concrete model. The real difference between the two was a difference between a spiritual and a material High Churchmanship: Wesley's was the ascendancy of a saint, Bunting's the ascendancy of a masterful ecclesiastic. Jabez Bunting has no true place beside John Wesley in the 'Wesleyan Reaction'.[29]

In some ways all this is only too true, but one may still wonder whether Mr Taylor wasn't letting John Wesley off a little too lightly. Elsewhere Mr Taylor spoke as though Bunting modified the Wesleyan Reaction by introducing a doctrine of clerical supremacy on a paternal model, in which all authority flowed from the local superintendent, who must have absolute power because he was absolutely responsible to God for the souls committed to his charge.[30] It was this modification, Mr Taylor said, which 'not only undermined the Reaction, but which, by canalizing and "materializing" the theory, prevented the evolution of that "High Protestantism" which Methodism was particularly qualified to produce'.[31] He thought that Methodism might have united its Catholic elements with the doctrine of the priesthood of all believers, have allowed lay administration of the sacraments and so have developed 'a really Catholic Free Churchmanship'.[32] According to this interpretation Bunting would have misunderstood the Wesleyan Reaction and have ruined it by the introduction of a form of Church and Ministry alien to its nature: such an understanding of the period would justify the main body of Wesleyan seceders who would then have to be seen as struggling to preserve the original genius of Wesleyanism against a clerical distortion of it.[33]

There is much to be said for this view, but one qualification must be added. One finds it difficult to see Bunting as an innovator where the Wesleyan system was concerned. He added such

---

[29] Taylor, op. cit., p. 129.　　[30] Ibid. p. 122.
[31] Ibid. pp. 122–3.　　[32] Ibid. p. 110.
[33] If one accepted this thesis, I think that one would still have to distinguish between the lay opposition, which often protested in terms like those which Mr Taylor uses, and the ministerial opposition in the Conference (and this includes James Everett) which did not seek to reduce the theoretical power of the itinerants; it was the manner, not the authority, they disliked. Mr Taylor seems too complimentary to the *Fly Sheets* when he says that they were intended to lead on to a demand for lay representation.

institutions as the Theological College but he did not remould.
John Wesley may have asked for loyalty as the Father of his People,
but he also expected obedience as a clergyman of the Church of
England. Bunting's paternal clericalism depended upon Wesley's:
the mind of the man in the tomb behind is law for us, as Bunting
once said. He saw himself as obliged to maintain what Wesley had
established, obliged above all because the system had worked so
amazingly well. Wesley himself would not have agreed to lay administration of Holy Communion; Wesley himself believed in
paternal clericalism; he drew in the idea with the Anglicanism in
which he was reared. He did not, as is often implied, learn a lesson
about authority in Georgia. He changed the demands which he
put upon his flock, but he still expected his demands to be obeyed.
He disapproved of Independency quite as much as Bunting did.
The ministerial Conference was invented by Wesley, not Bunting,
and if it was a bad system of ecclesiastical government and in some
ways the ruin of Wesleyan Methodism, Wesley must take most of
the blame. Historian after historian repeats the platitude about his
genius for organization. Even his manner was not quite always the
manner of the saint, any more than Bunting's was invariably that
of the despot—those who baulk at this should recall Wesley's disastrous handling of the American Methodists at the time of the
American War of Independence. And Bunting's politics could
easily be justified from Wesley's political writings. It would be
difficult to prove, one feels, that Bunting seriously misunderstood
Wesley.

Even so, one senses that Mr Taylor had put his finger on the
right spot. The argument of the 1820s and 1830s was an argument
about the nature of Methodism and such an argument was bound
to polarize itself. The Wesleyans invented Bunting in order to keep
up the illusion, possible while Wesley lived, that there was someone who knew what Wesleyanism was, someone whose definitions
would always guide a Connexion in distress. For with whom were
they in connexion once Mr Wesley died? Wesley himself had said,
'The Conference', and what Bunting did was to try to give meaning to the theory which Wesley had bequeathed to his people.

FIVE

Methodism and Politics in the Nineteenth Century

IT MAY FAIRLY be said that the standard interpretation of Wesleyan Methodist political attitudes in the nineteenth century is misleading. Much has been written on the subject. There is Mr E. R. Taylor's excellent book,[1] which sought to prove that Wesleyan Methodism fulfilled its destiny by coming gradually closer to the Liberal Party. There are the studies by Dr Maldwyn Edwards[2] and Dr R. F. Wearmouth,[3] for both of whom Wesleyan Methodism in the first half of the century showed distressing signs of a complacent, almost unchristian Conservatism. In the late Elie Halévy's famous volumes[4] a striking picture is drawn of Wesleyan Methodism, which the French historian saw as a kind of unconscious stabilizing factor in a potentially revolutionary British society; if Dr Edwards implied that Wesleyan Methodism might have saved England by being more Radical, Halévy thought that Wesleyan Methodism actually saved England, without really intending to, by remaining Conservative. Of course, one cannot deny that for various social reasons it was broadly true in the earlier part of the century that when members of the non-Wesleyan Connexions chose their political allegiance they were perhaps more likely to choose the Whig or Radical groups than were members of the Wesleyan Methodist Societies. But the gap between the two Methodist groups, even on questions of secular politics, can be exaggerated.

For example, it would be easy to assume that in the case of the Reform Bill of 1832 the non-Wesleyan bodies would be joyfully in favour of sweeping measures of reform, but that the Tory-minded Wesleyan Methodists would heartily oppose all changes in

[1] *Methodism and Politics, 1791–1854* (1935).
[2] *After Wesley* (1935).
[3] *Methodism and the Working-class Movements, 1800–50* (1937). See also *Some Working-class Movements of the Nineteenth Century*, by the same author (1948).
[4] For M. Elie Halévy, see the essay on the subject of this historian's writings on Methodism, p. 86.

the Constitution. In fact, such a judgement would greatly exaggerate the extent to which Wesleyan Methodism officially opposed the Reform Bill. As early as June 1831, 'Christian Retrospect', the Connexional magazine's political commentary, regarded the passing of the Bill as a foregone conclusion, since the nation had expressed its will at the polls. No attempt was made, in the magazine or elsewhere, to rally Wesleyan Methodist opinion against the Bill. By February 1832, the writer of 'Christian Retrospect' was saying firmly that one had to be positively obtuse to say that changes were uncalled for. He suggested that the more level-headed of the opposition should now stop trying to defeat the measure altogether; the longer the fight lasted, the more extreme the demands of the Radicals would become. One can hardly object strongly to the fact that by July 1832, the magazine was warning its readers that they should not expect a new heaven and a new earth just because they had a new franchise—all power was open to the temptations of evil, and no one would benefit much from the redistribution of political authority unless the public mind was also subjected to moral influence. As I shall show, this was not the only occasion on which early-nineteenth-century Wesleyan Methodism anticipated the later Nonconformist Conscience.

Those who think of Jabez Bunting's Wesleyan Methodism as peculiarly Tory usually do so in terms of what has been called the 'no politics rule'. In theory, this meant that as a religious corporation Wesleyan Methodism should keep aloof from the great secular political issues of the day—from issues, that is, like the Reform Bill of 1832. It is said that in practice the 'no politics rule' meant that the Wesleyan Connexion was committed to Conservative positions, because it made almost any organized Wesleyan support for Radical reforms impossible. The basis of the rule might be found in John Wesley's acceptance of the view that the Scriptures demanded obedience to the rightful rulers of a nation. In one of the rare formulations of the rule, in the *Minutes* of 1792, in answer to the question, 'What directions shall be given concerning our conduct to the Civil Government?', the Conference actually said that 'none of us shall, either in writing or in conversation, speak lightly or irreverently of the Government under which he lives: we are to observe that the oracles of God command us to be subject to the higher powers, and that honour to the King is there connected with the fear of God'.

This passage, and the very similar letter of the Conference of 1793, are not adequate evidence for the general view that the Wesleyan Methodists were indifferent to abuses in the Constitution. After all, the resolutions were passed at a time when the French Revolution had made the British governing classes very uncertain of the permanent loyalty of those whom they governed. The Conference meant to be understood in simple, patriotic terms: it was not giving a guarantee that Wesleyans would never in the future support demands for political reform in England. When Lord Sidmouth tried to crush the Wesleyan Societies in 1811 there was no question of immediate submission to the higher powers, but savage, successful resistance. Moreover, it is necessary to remember that in the early 1790s the itinerants who made up the Conference were having to tread very carefully because of the 'Church Party', the section of the Wesleyan Methodist laity which still viewed with disfavour any move to introduce the administration of the Sacraments by the preachers. The Conference Letter of 1793 was written as an answer to a circular sent out by trustees belonging to this 'Church Party' in which the trustees (who did not want the Societies to become effectively independent of the Church of England) suggested that some of their opponents were politically disloyal. No doubt the Conference wanted to reassure anyone in Government circles who studied Methodist literature; but the more important aim of the Letter was to prevent the 'Church Party' Trustees winning the internal Methodist struggle by making use of political prejudice.

From the point of view of secular politics the important aspect of the 'no politics' rule was that it was not just a Wesleyan Methodist idea, but was accepted by the non-Wesleyan Connexions. The Primitive Methodist Consolidated *Minutes* of 1836, for example, forbade the itinerants to make speeches at political meetings or at elections, and gave the local preachers a broad hint that if they did so they should at least be discreet, and not begin every paragraph with the phrase, 'Speaking as a Primitive Methodist. . . .'[5] Similarly, the Wesleyan Association stated in 1837 that in the discharge of their ministerial duties the preachers should carefully avoid allusions to all subjects of a political character.[6] This did not

[5] See the *Primitive Methodist Consolidated General Minutes*, published by James Bourne in 1836, under the heading, 'Removals'.
[6] Wesleyan Association Annual Assembly, *Minutes* of 1837, section x xiv.

prevent political preachers emerging: they existed in each denomination. One of the best known was William Griffith; but measured by Griffith's career were the activities of these political peachers really so impressive? Griffith,[7] says Mr Taylor, held that he could not separate religion and politics, and therefore ignored the 'no politics' rule, while he was a Wesleyan itinerant, but was the reason perhaps that he could no longer tell the difference? Griffith was the kind of Nonconformist who derived inordinate pleasure from being rude to a bishop; he was a pacifist, and said that the sight of a soldier was as abhorrent to him as the sight of a murderer; when Queen Victoria was made Empress of India, he sent a one-man petition of protest against this breach of his republican principles.[8] Chew's biography does not suggest that Griffith's political behaviour was very significant, apart from the undoubted satisfaction which he drew from it. Now the 'no politics rule', when strictly interpreted, did not forbid a Methodist preacher to hold all the eccentric opinions held by Griffith. It simply said that he should not create strife within his own denomination over these secular political issues. There might well be disagreement as to what was a secular issue, but within the limits of common sense the rule was not unreasonable, and Griffith's career was not a very substantial argument for dispensing with the safeguard.

In Primitive Methodism, the 'no politics rule' was administered as far as Hugh Bourne could reach, 'for the idea of anyone introducing politics into his preaching was almost as dreadful to him as the preaching of "flat Popery" was to Oliver Cromwell'.[9] Bourne, like Jabez Bunting, emphasized the difficulty of preserving spirituality of mind in the midst of political agitation, and he thought that

[7] For William Griffith, see *William Griffith: Memorials and Letters*, by Richard Chew (London, 1885). He was the son of a Wesleyan pastor, like Rayner Stephens, and similarly highly strung in his youth. He was born in 1806, and received into Full Connexion in 1836. After his expulsion from the Wesleyan Conference in 1849, he settled almost permanently in Derby.

[8] He wrote in 1876: 'Our worthless royalty will remain, a burden as it is to the nation, as long as our miscalled aristocracy exists. The two cheats will live on so long as the practical hypocrite of a State Church lifts its ... head towards high heaven. The fall of either one will be the death-knell of the other two' (Chew, op. cit. p. 187).

[9] *The Life of Hugh Bourne*, by William Antliff, revised by Colin McKechnie (London, 1892), pp. 160–1.

if politics and religion were mixed in the Church and in the pulpit, it would be religion that suffered. A clear instance of his attitude occurred in 1821, when he entered the Hull Conference and said, pointing at one man: 'That man shall not be in this chapel.' When asked why, Bourne answered that the man was 'a speeching radical, a man that is employed in speaking in public against Government'. He went on to tell a not altogether enthusiastic Conference that the Scriptures required them to be subject to the Government under which they lived, that George IV was favourable to liberty of conscience, and that they must do nothing which might tempt the Government to stop the camp-meetings. In the end he had his way, and the man was expelled.[10]

The Wesleyan Association often sounded the same warning. For instance, the Annual Address said in 1839:

Whatever may be your political opinions, never introduce them into the Church of Christ, nor suffer them to interfere with your religious duties, or unduly to occupy your attention. Never substitute the Newspaper for the Bible, or the company of political partisans for that of the followers of the Lord Jesus Christ, or political meetings for the means of grace.[11]

This was surely not so very different from what the Wesleyan Methodist Conference said in 1831, when the fate of the Reform Bill hung in the balance, and the conduct of politics was by no means as quiet and rational as might have been desired. 'Let not worldly politics engross too much of your time and attention', said the Wesleyan Conference;

Avoid all undue eagerness and anxiety on subjects which, however much their importance may be magnified by the men of the world, are only of moment in the estimation of the Christian, as far as they can be rendered subservient to the best interests of mankind. Should you acquire any additional civil rights, you will, we trust, consider them as talents entrusted to your care, to be employed in promoting the interests of humanity and religion.[12]

[10] Ibid. p. 180, et seq. See the parallel account in John Walford's *Memoirs of the Life and Labours of Hugh Bourne* (London, 1856), II.101. Walford said that Bourne was in private favourable to reform, 'both in Church and State' (p. 103).

[11] Wesleyan Methodist Association Annual Assembly, *Minutes*, 1839; Annual Address.

[12] Wesleyan Methodist Conference, *Minutes*, 1831; Annual Address.

There was a clear community of feeling here with the attitude of the New Connexion. The Kilhamites were naturally inclined to favour the Reform Bill a little more openly, but the Address of 1831 added that as far as the pastors were concerned, 'we presume that they never take part in political discussions, remembering their Master's declaration, "My Kingdom is not of this World" '.[13] In the fiery year of 1848, when it seemed for a few months as though the old world was coming to an end, the Association stated in its Address: 'We do not say: "Cease to take an interest in the progress of public events which have a bearing upon your social, commercial, or political interests"; but we say, "Take care lest your minds be overcharged with these things".'[14] Was there so much difference between this and the warning of the Wesleyan Conference in 1832, another time of troubles: 'We affectionately advise you to take care how you listen to any solicitation urging you to become political partisans', for 'can you, with perfect security to your religious character, become the ardent agents of political parties?' Wesleyan or not, all Methodist bodies made these formal recognitions of the social rules of Evangelical Pietism.[15]

It is fair to say, therefore, that while Methodism was affected by the secular political divisions into Whig and Tory, or Liberal and Conservative, yet the object of the 'no politics rule', in practice, was to prevent the Connexions being internally divided upon such issues as Parliamentary reform.[16] Even though the rule was frequently broken, both by Radicals and Conservatives, both sides knew that they were falling short of an ideal, so that Jabez

[13] Methodist New Connexion Conference, *Minutes*, 1831; Annual Address. The Address of 1832 commented: 'Thank God the storm has blown over; the voice of moderation has obtained in the councils of the nation; the rights of justice have prevailed, and the happiness of our beloved country, we trust, has been secured.'

[14] Wesleyan Methodist Association Annual Assembly, *Minutes*, 1848; Annual Address.

[15] Wesleyan Methodist Conference, *Minutes*, 1832; Annual Address.

[16] Or the agitation for the repeal of the Corn Laws. Ebenezer Elliott, the Chartist poet, hated the Wesleyan Connexion for its refusal to allow its prestige to be used officially in this question. Bunting, however, not unnaturally, held that pastors had other things to do than go up and down the country advocating Repeal. He let it be known, however, as early as 1841, that he was not opposed to the measure in principle, a point not always remembered by his critics.

Bunting himself usually attempted to find some excuse for his conduct.[17] The 'no politics rule' was an essential part of the Evangelical Pietism which was the controlling element in the Methodist attitude to society.

Mr Taylor, however, describes the rule as involving a political neutrality which meant a practical support of reaction. He says: '. . . throughout the period covered by this essay (1791–1851) there was no official political attitude of the Connexion except one of neutrality. Yet there were within Methodism, even at the time when the "No Politics Rule" was most rigidly enforced, men unwilling to be robbed of their political birthright. . . .' There was certainly no official attitude to *secular* politics, though a layman was not likely to be disciplined for supporting the Reform Bill. The Connexion, however, did adopt an official attitude to religious politics, questions which were then more prominent than they are now, and it may be argued that apart from certain questions relating to the Established Church (and these only before the rise of the Oxford Movement) this policy was widely accepted even outside Wesleyan Methodism. Some critics have gone farther and said that Wesleyanism ought to have shown more sympathy towards the aspirations of the working classes.[18] Such criticism often seems to imply that no decent Christian could have been a Tory in the 1830s.

Wesleyan ministers like Jabez Bunting did not come from an elevated social background; they had no stake in the old order of things; their interests were bound up with those of the newer industrialists of the North and Midlands. Nor should the Wesleyan respect for the order and stability of the eighteenth century be dismissed as an improper love of authority. A man like James

[17] As Mr Taylor says, Bunting was one of the worst offenders against this rule, and, what was worse, objected to others breaking it. We must observe, however, that the clashes of this kind recorded in Gregory were usually over religious, and not secular politics. In such matters, Bunting was determined that only the voice of the Conservative majority should be heard outside the Conference. During the Tithes controversy of 1837, for example, he told Galland, his principal opponent, that 'Ours is and must be, to all eternity, Wesleyanism' (Gregory, *Sidelights*, p. 238), and denied that Galland had any right to express publicly the Dissenting point of view.

[18] Dr Maldwyn Edwards, for example, in *After Wesley* (1935), and E. S. Thompson, in *The Making of the British Working Class* (1963).

Dixon, who hated the private domination which he believed Bunting to have secured in Methodism, was just as much a political Tory as his opponent, because he regarded the Tories as the bulwark between England and the triumph of revolutionary violence. (He had no idea that one day a French historian would see *him* as part of the bulwark between the Tories and revolutionary violence.) 'I seem to stand alone,' he said, 'no earthly being seems to speak the language of my old friends, the Tories. Let it be so, to them belongs the honour of having saved the country from the mania of the French Revolution; and if they cannot save us from the second, they may perhaps have it in their power to break the force of the dashing and foaming waters let loose upon the country by men who ought to have had the sense and manliness to have stemmed the current, rather than given it increased force and agitation.'[19] One might disagree with him, but this was a position that an intelligent man could hold in the 1830s and 1840s.

After 1832, the middle classes were genuinely afraid of the lower-class passions which they had stirred in order to secure the passage of the Reform Bill, and they knew little of Chartism and Trade Unionism, except that they feared them. One must remember that their determination that the social order should not collapse was not confined to Wesleyan Methodist Conservatives, or to political Tories. Though the Whig and Conservative parties fought one another for possession of the new electorate created by the Reform Bill, they were prepared to combine against the threat from below. This was illustrated in the case of the Tolpuddle Martyrs. There is no question of seeking to palliate the conduct of Bunting or of Melbourne,[20] but when Dr Edwards says that Bunting lent his weight to the Government on this occasion,[21] it is worth remembering that this was a Whig government, and not a Tory one. By 1840 most Wesleyan Methodists were ready to educate the poor,

---

[19] *The Life of James Dixon*, by R. W. Dixon (London, 1874), p. 177. The quotation comes from a letter written in 1832. Dixon, however, wanted to support in Methodism 'the great Tory principle of local independent action' (ibid. p. 473).

[20] Both Whig and Tory landlords disliked agricultural unionism, and in fact no efficient rural union existed until long after many urban trades were well organized.

[21] *After Wesley*, p. 157.

to give them clothes so that they might come to chapel,[22] to en-encourage them to save money and to seek after the salvation of their souls, but they discouraged any dabbling in the radical regions of politics. This attitude was not as unreasonable as Dr Edwards suggests, for no one in the middle classes could seriously be expected to believe that England would be better off in the hands of the Irish egoist, O'Connor. The lower classes were poorly fed, poorly paid, poorly housed, and poorly advised, and they wanted some solution to the problems which life had brought them. One may say that the Methodists should have given them better advice (and the economic side of Methodist political think-ing was its weak spot), but one can hardly be surprised at the fact that they resisted the form which the working man's aspirations actually took. But this kind of Conservatism was found as often among the new mill-owners, who detested the Unions, as among the land-owners who feared rick-burning, and we must not blame Bunting too much if he did not detect in the Dorsetshire labourers the coming glories of the Trades Union Congress.

Bunting's Toryism, moreover, did not go as far as the Tory Radicalism of Richard Oastler and Rayner Stephens. Oastler's chief Methodist support in the north of England came from the Primitive Methodists, who were themselves on the other side of the social gulf. Stephens and Oastler reached a very violent mood by 1836, and this was bound to cost them official Methodist sup-port. Nevertheless, these men had much in common, for Oastler and Stephens, like Bunting, believed in the reconciliation of classes and not their conflict; all three had little room for 'democracy', in the universal suffrage sense; they all thought that social salvation ought to come from above, and not from below. What Oastler could not understand was how Bunting could tolerate the suffer-ings of the factory children; but of these sufferings Bunting had no real experience. This was, after all, the time when Baines of the *Leeds Mercury* could say quite seriously that machinery had alle-viated the physical toil of the masses, and Baines was no political Tory. Nevertheless, in the 1840s, when the fear of violence had begun to die down, the *Wesleyan Methodist Magazine* was pre-pared to support Ashley against Sir Robert Peel on precisely the

[22] In the Royal Commissions of the period, poor people were often quoted as saying that they would go to chapel if only they had decent clothes to wear.

same kind of *moral* grounds which Oastler had used ten years before. The complexity of the time is shown by the fact that both Peel and Ashley were lukewarm in their attitude to Trade Unions. The greatest contribution that Methodism made to the final victory of the Factory Agitation was the degree to which it stimulated the sensibility of people, and so helped to make possible the wave of sentimental feeling which led to Ashley's victory. This kind of 'Toryism' was found in all branches of Methodism,[23] except those which were by nature on the working-class side, the Primitive Methodists and the Bible Christians, together with the dissident poor in the other Connexions. The Primitive Methodists, however, who could hardly be suspected of Bunting's Toryism, worked hard in Durham,[24] for example, to create a trade unionism based on moral force, and shared the horror of the other Connexions at atheistic socialism and social violence.

There is an excellent illustration of this in the records of the Primitive Methodist Norwich Second Circuit. On 11th September 1839, the Meeting preparatory to the Quarterly Meeting stated that it did not consider that

Bro Bowthorpe's conduct was justifiable on the 30th of June in walking from Ringland through Drayton to Norwich in the rain then [sic] stand up in the open air near our chapel to the ingery of our cause to make a speech for the Chartists, moreover, as there are complaints made against Bro Bowthorpe's new fashioned way of preaching in every part of the Branch where he as spoke this Quarter and as this meeting is deeply conscious of the ingery that the Society has sustained by his late proceeder if Bro Bowthorpe do not express his sorrow for the past and

[23] The Annual Address of the New Connexion, for example, in 1843, referred to the strike in the North Midlands, 'when the unemployed masses, misguided and inflamed by political demagogues, plunged into turbulent excitement, which was attended, in some cases, with the loss of life and property. We congratulate you, brethren, that you were not found either among the leaders or participators of those disturbances, while not a few of you were commendably active in the protection of property and the restoration of order. We trust that you will ever be that which our history proves you hitherto to have been, and which our principles and religion alike require—faithful to the throne, constitution and the laws of our beloved country—the exemplars of order, loyalty and patriotism.'

[24] Cf. E. Welbourne, *The Miners' Unions of Northumberland and Durham* (1923).

promis to do better in futer this Bord must for the sake of God's cause take cognisance of his conduct at the after period of the meeting.

In the Full Meeting it was decided that 'Bro Bowthorpe's Plan with his intention to resine be received as he say his arm shall drop from his body before he will recant or be sorry for the past or promis to do better in feuter'. To this was added a further resolution, that 'Sister Maria Bowthorpe's Plan with her intention to resine be received as she is dtermend let the consequence be what it may to do as her Brother does and to go where he goes'.[25] This incident illustrates the two sides of a single process: Methodism was both producing men who revolted against the established order and also disowning them, if their activities seemed to imperil the religious society's existence.

So much for secular politics, but although the 'no politics' rule was intended to prevent people from importing into the different Methodist denominations the kind of secular political quarrels which divided them outside, this did not mean that organized Methodism took no part in politics. There was another side to nineteenth-century politics. Mr Taylor says that Jabez Bunting 'in spite of his thoroughly Tory sympathies could only be drawn into political controversies when he saw them as religious questions'. Mr Taylor excluded these questions, which were chiefly matters concerning education and the relation between Church and State, from further consideration, but this makes too sharp a distinction between 'secular' and 'religious' politics. And in fact, even in the sphere of 'religious' politics Jabez Bunting, as he grew older, actually ceased to support Tory political positions at all. It is this gradual change of position which makes the normal criticism of Wesleyan Toryism so misleading when one considers the causes of the Wesleyan Schism of 1849, for instance, disagreement about educational policy must rank high in the list, but it has not been clearly emphasized (if indeed it has ever been mentioned) that the policy which John Scott (supported rather than directed by Jabez Bunting) was following in educational matters was one of co-operation with the State, whereas the Wesleyan Reformers clung obstinately to the already hopeless and sectarian voluntary principle. The simple traditional contrast between the Wesleyan Reformers, understood as lovers of liberty and progress, and the

[25] MS. in the possession of the writer.

Conservative Wesleyans, understood as reactionary authoritarians, does not fit the facts.

The political existence of the Church of England certainly played upon these divisions in Methodism and the gap between the two Methodist groups never quite closed. In the earlier part of the century, for instance, the Wesleyan Association was always ready to declare its support for societies and conferences dedicated to disestablishment;[26] while on the other hand the forced resignation of Rayner Stephens in 1834, or Bunting's attitude to the Tithe controversy of 1837, reflected the opposite, Conservative, opinion. At this date Bunting's feelings towards the Church of England, and the Anglican background of the Tory party, clearly supplemented one another, but from 1833 the rise of the Anglo-Catholic movement caused a sharp change of feeling among the leading ministers in the Wesleyan Connexion. The opposition of the Wesleyans to the education clauses of the Factory Bill of 1843 was an open declaration that they distrusted an Establishment which tolerated Puseyism. The Annual Address of the Wesleyan Methodist Conference of 1843 said:

It has been publicly stated, that *one* ground of our strenuous opposition to the lately projected measure of public education was its obvious tendency to give to the Clergy of the Established Church, an unfair and undue control over the religious teaching in the schools which it would have established, We think it right to confirm this statement, not out of any hostile feeling towards the Established Church as such, for this has never been the feeling of our Body, but with a view to bear our own distinct and solemn testimony against those *grievous errors which are now tolerated within her pale*. . . . Opinions concerning the insufficiency of Scripture as the sole authoritative and universal rule of faith and practice, the exclusive validity of Episcopal Ordination, and the neces-

[26] In 1844, for instance, the Wesleyan Association Annual Assembly passed the following resolution: 'This Assembly, believing it of very great importance to the purity and the extension of the Kingdom of Christ, that the alliances subsisting between Christian Churches and civil governments should be dissolved; it therefore most earnestly desires success to all Christian and lawful means employed for liberating State Churches from the degradation, bondage and corruption, necessarily resulting from their union with, and dependence on, the support of earthly governments; and therefore most heartily wishes success to the operations of the 'British Anti-State Church Association'. The Bible Christian Methodists of south-west England were especially strongly opposed to state churches.

sarily saving efficacy of the Sacraments, which can only be distinguished from Popery by an acute and practised observer, and which in their necessary consequences lead directly to Popery, have been revived when they were almost extinct, have spread with fearful rapidity, and are now held by a large number of the Established Clergy.

The Address added that Wesleyans need not be alarmed, 'the doom of Babylon is sure'.

The depth of the change was brought out when the Wesleyan Conservatives actually supported Thomas Chalmers and the seceders from the Scottish Establishment in 1843. It was true that the Wesleyans were able to tell themselves that Chalmers was the last hope of Evangelicalism in the Church of Scotland, but the fact remained that they were really supporting the men who founded the Free Church of Scotland. Without any very conscious change of theoretical position the Wesleyan leaders reacted so violently against the development of Tractarianism that they moved much closer to the position of the non-Wesleyan Connexions, and so into opposition to the Church of England. In the first half of the century they did not break so completely with the past as to advocate disestablishment, but they were convinced that the State ought not to subsidize the Anglo-Catholics. By the end of the century many Wesleyan leaders were looking forward with hope to the eventual disintegration of the Church of England as a result of the constant strife of Anglo-Catholic and Evangelical. They took the same view of the various State attempts to give the Roman Catholic Church money for educational purposes: they held that both forms of Catholicism were morally wrong, and that to subsidize them could not be politically right.[27] In such opinions there was evidence that the Wesleyan schism of 1849 was not profoundly affected by the relationship between Jabez Bunting and the Church of England, for even the most revival-conscious of his enemies could hardly have expected him to attack the Pope and Puseyism more bitterly than he did.

In the 1840s, moreover, the Wesleyan Connexion was almost continually at war with Sir Robert Peel's Tory ministry. The clash

[27] Apropos of a proposal that legal provision should be made for the Roman Catholic clergy in Ireland, a reviewer in the *Wesleyan Methodist Magazine*, May 1835, said (having shown, as he felt, that Romanism was an undiluted evil) that 'it is a question of morals and religion; and that which is morally and religiously wrong can never be politically right'.

between the policy of the Tory Party and his own religiously based political ideas was no doubt painful for Jabez Bunting, but he did not hesitate to break with Peel's Government when he thought that its policy was incorrect. The struggle went so far that in 1845 William Bunting said: 'I, who have taken some pains to lift the present Conservative party to power will, in my own place, as a Minister of religion, do my very best to help them out of power'.[28] He said this in the course of the inter-denominational Conference called together to protest against the Tory Government's plan to subsidize a Roman Catholic College in Ireland. The Wesleyan Methodists had a meeting of their own on the same subject on 25th April 1845, at which a Resolution was passed which said that 'all Wesleyans possessing the elective franchise, should on this occasion forget merely party and political bias, and should unite with all of every religious community, like minded, to further in every legitimate way the return of those Candidates at the next Election who, rising with the greatness of the crisis, above a time-saving expediency, shall be determined to support the integrity and perpetuity of our National Protestantism'. Jabez Bunting was in the Chair at this meeting. In committing himself with such direct-ness he was not breaking the 'no politics rule', nor was he propos-ing for Wesleyan Methodism a political course of action with which his normal Wesleyan critics disagreed: he was adopting as a role of Methodism in politics an attitude with which his Wesleyan opponents profoundly sympathized.

This does not mean that the Wesleyan Conservatives would not have liked to remain Tory in politics, or that they were always baffled in the attempt, but it does mean that the union of interests between them and the Tory Party was neither as considerable nor as durable as has sometimes been imagined. When one recalls that all the Methodist Connexions in the early nineteenth century shared the 'no politics rule' and were generally agreed in their attitude towards working-class political movements, and adds the fact that they often united in opposition to Sir Robert Peel, one may suppose that there was a Methodist political philosophy, and that politically speaking Methodists of all Connexions were not simply divided by other people's secular political ideas.

[28] *Proceedings of the Anti-Maynooth Conference of 1845*, ed. Rev. A. S. Thelwall (London, 1845), p. 164. William Bunting was Jabez Bunting's son, and a distinguished Wesleyan minister in his own right.

This was true even in the second half of the century when the Wesleyan Methodists joined the other Methodist groups in allegiance to the Gladstonian Liberal Party. In fact, Wesleyans as vigorously political as Hugh Price Hughes were never as deeply attached as they themselves sometimes imagined to the Gladstonian political philosophy. It was not a political accident that in 1899 a majority of Wesleyan Methodists sided with Lord Rosebery and supported the South African War. It was social interest rather than Liberal political philosophy which bound later nineteenth-century Wesleyans to the Liberal Party, and in their turn they tried, especially between 1890 and 1914, to make the party the vehicle of a political programme which had its real origins in the Wesleyan political understanding of Evangelical Pietism: such a policy did not appeal to the professional politicians of the Liberal Party, and this explains some of the internal contradictions of the Liberal Government of 1906.

This Methodist political philosophy naturally had a religious basis. Justification, sanctification, and the conversion of others were the proper ends of life. Living in the world of the ordinary affairs of men constituted a major problem, and the redeemed had to remember that strictly speaking they had died to the world. The final outcome of such an outlook was a kind of Evangelical sectarianism. For the private life of the individual member of the group could not remain his own concern. It became increasingly the affair of the Connexion and of connexional courts which tried hard to make sure that he fulfilled certain standards. The political thought of Methodism, and also its political programme, originated when the Connexions began to seek to apply this moral oversight not only to their individual members but also to the society in which Methodism existed. Here, in the early nineteenth century, one strand in the Nonconformist Conscience began. From the early years of the century, Methodists had said that no one had any moral right to own a slave; they helped to compel society as a whole to accept this point of view. The demands made upon society in these early years were not very great; little imagination was put into working out the consequences of the theory, and the slave-owners, for example, lived in the West Indies and could be comfortably sacrificed by people living in Britain.

In the 1840s and 1850s teetotalism became a factor of growing importance, but the new attitude had to subdue the Evangelical world itself before its enthusiasts could launch a Dry Campaign against the world outside. It is not easy to find in secular political divisions an explanation of the fact that leading Wesleyans opposed teetotalism for years, not only in Jabez Bunting's time, but for long afterwards. Teetotalism, however, certainly began as a working-class movement of dissociation from other people's ways of life. It was only after 1860 that many middle-class Pietists adopted teetotalism as a new means of moral and social aggression against the surrounding non-Pietist society.

All this might be summed up in the Address of the Wesleyan Conference in 1840, which said:

Endeavour to close your domestic affairs, and complete your domestic arrangements, in such time that Saturday evening may be a season of hallowed preparation. Rise early, and follow our old custom of attending the early morning prayer meeting. . . . In your attendance at the House of God, be punctual. . . . Improve the intervals of worship by Scripture reading and religious conversation; and, either in the afternoon or evening, catechize and pray with your children. Suffer neither newspapers, history, nor books of science, to form any part of your Sunday reading. Sacredly abstain from trading-journeys and pleasure excursions; and neither read nor write letters of business. Discountenance Sunday visiting, and shut out political conversation. If any of you are connected with Railroad or other Companies, who prostitute the Sabbath to purposes of worldly pleasure or gain, we charge you, before God, to take the first opportunity of protesting against the impiety. The loss of money must not be put into comparison with the favour of God. We are strongly impressed, that the present unparalleled commercial distress is an intimation of the divine displeasure, and is designed to turn us from our national sins, of which Sabbath-breaking is one.

The weak link in the chain of ideas was economic, for Evangelical Pietism gave insufficient attention to the economic element in human society. There was a strong feeling, inherited from medieval Christianity, that a Christian ought not to be very much concerned about money. The feeling that Providence exercised a vague but definite control over commercial affairs, causing booms and slumps, which were intended to encourage or punish society, was very widespread. The Methodist New Connexion, for instance, was following in a long tradition when it referred in 1848 to the 'long continued commercial depression with which it has pleased Divine Providence to visit our native land'. The Annual

Address added that whereas 'a blind unbelief and sceptical philosophy looks no further than the perceptible instruments of our calamities, let us reverently acknowledge a divine agency in all that is brought upon us, at the same time betaking ourselves to prayer, that the indignation of heaven may be turned away from us'. As an instance of religion, Methodism may or may not have facilitated the rise of capitalism, but it certainly did not necessitate it.

Methodism, in fact, committed itself to something very close to the medieval idea that a man might have as much money as was necessary for his station in life, that rich and poor existed by the will of God. This led in the 1840s to vigorous warnings against attempts to increase one's wealth by speculation. This, the Wesleyan Conference said in 1840, obviously implied a making haste to be rich, a want of contentment with such things as one already had. 'If they are undertaken with our own money, we cannot be said to glorify God with the substance so employed . . . but, generally speaking they are undertaken to a great extent with the property of others; and when this is the case it implies a manifest breach of the love we owe to our neighbour.' Once again Wesleyan and non-Wesleyan Connexions shared a common point of view. In 1842, for instance, the New Connexion's Annual Address stated that the peculiar situation in which many were placed in regard to business, the hazard connected with it, the fearful vicissitudes occasioned by the critical state of the commercial world, demanded more than ordinary circumspection and integrity if the cause of Christ was not to suffer from their indiscretions. According to Protestant tradition older than Methodism, a man who went bankrupt forfeited his Methodist membership.

Warning the rich not to try to get richer, sympathizing with the poor in their poverty, this about expresses the economic thinking of the Annual Addresses. Methodist writers did not often suggest that poverty was a crime or that it was a punishment for sin. General commercial distress was interpreted as a judgement on society, but individual poverty was often seen as a challenge to individual philanthropy. A more obvious criticism would be that Methodist writers were not really alarmed if a man was poor, because they felt that his poverty was also the work of God, and would no doubt have its compensations. Methodists, that is, felt no special call to alter the economic framework of the society in which they lived. It can hardly be said that the Chartists had a much clearer idea of the problem involved, or that their revolt expressed more than a natural dislike of the poverty of the 1830s and 1840s. Moreover, if one compares the Methodists with other Christian thinkers and considers the writings of the so-called Christian Socialists of the mid nineteenth century, Charles Kingsley, Thomas Hughes, John Ludlow, and F. D. Maurice, one is chiefly struck by the inappropriateness of the word 'Socialism' as a description of their ideas. They protested, as the Methodists of all Connexions failed to protest, against the competitive nature of the mid-Victorian capitalism; but their remedies were flavoured with the same middle-class paternalism, and their careers reflected a similar dislike of the emergence of the working class as an independent political and social force. It is true that no prominent Wesleyan minister closely resembled Charles Kingsley, who in the crucial year of 1848 stammered out the bold assertion that he was a Chartist parson; on the other hand, the opposition of the Wesleyan leaders to Chartism was at least as much a matter of objecting to the use of political violence, and of defending Christianity against the attacks of Socialist lecturers, as it was a question of propping up a social system which Kingsley himself was not criticizing in a constructive manner. [29]

There was, however, some development of Methodist economic thought even from the theoretical point of view. In 1844, for instance, Sir James Graham, the Conservative Home Secretary, was debating with Lord Shaftesbury the wisdom of restricting the hours of child labour in factories. Graham was prepared to accept a limit of twelve hours, and Shaftesbury was arguing for ten. Sir James Graham thought the ten-hour proposal inexpedient, because it would cost the nation, considered as an economic machine, two hours of daily labour for every person concerned, and also reduce the wages of the adult workers. A commentator in the *Wesleyan Methodist Magazine*[30] said that in the abstract those who fought for complete freedom in commercial affairs held a position from which it was difficult to dislodge them. Graham, however,

[29] Contemporary Methodist documents contain little suggestion that poverty was a crime, or that it was a punishment for sin. General commercial distress seemed to be a judgement of providence, but individual distress a call for philanthropy.

[30] *Wesleyan Methodist Magazine*, May 1844, 'Christian Observations', an article identical in kind with the earlier 'Christian Retrospect'.

had abandoned this position when he agreed to the restriction of child labour to twelve hours, and his sole reason for objecting to ten hours was 'pecuniary loss'. Therefore, the Wesleyan commentator said, all Sir James Graham was really saying was: 'I should be glad to apply the remedy; but, though it be morally right, yet, as tending to pecuniary loss, it is commercially and politically wrong: it is therefore inexpedient and I must oppose it.' The commentator then maintained that a statesman should first decide what was right and then do it, trusting in Providence, for 'right is the true measure of expedience, not expedience the rule of right'. He concluded: 'If the protection for which Lord Ashley contended is right, let it be granted; and in granting it, let the legislature do homage to that never-failing Providence which ordereth all things in Heaven and Earth. If it be wrong, let it be shown so, and let not an argument of justice and humanity on one side be met with an argument of pounds, shillings and pence on the other.'

A Tory Government was opposing the Ten Hours agitation, and the Manchester Liberals could hardly be in favour of it, but a Wesleyan commentator who wrote like this was not absolutely committed to either party. What is equally significant is the instinctive anticipation of the slogan so popular in the 1890s, that what is morally wrong cannot be politically right. The evidence for any drastic change in Wesleyan Methodist political attitude in the nineteenth century can easily be exaggerated. The change which did take place, perhaps as early as 1843, was the discovery that the Connexion was now sufficiently powerful to impose its will from time to time on the environing society. This formed the root of the later social aggressiveness of Wesleyan Methodism in the form of the Nonconformist Conscience. I cannot entirely agree that Methodism's political mission was to add strength to the Liberal Party. There was always a clash between Victorian individualism, which counted for so much in liberalism, and the societary instinct of Methodism. Of course this organic life could become what Matthew Arnold said it was, provincialism. At its worst, this meant the rather vulgar Liberal imperialism of Sir Robert Perks and Hugh Price Hughes. At its best, it meant the more generous Christian Socialism of S. E. Keeble.

SIX

Anglican Episcopacy and
Anglican–Methodist Relations

SECTION ONE

THE RAPID secularization of Western culture has deeply affected the position of Anglican bishops in English society. In the eighteenth and early nineteenth centuries the connection between bishops and the State still remained fundamental to Anglicanism, whereas Wesleyan Methodism never formed a part of the apparatus of government, but had a socially determined tendency to drift into opposition circles. The discovery that the old order was changing came slowly: the Oxford Movement—itself a protest against secularization—began for a High Churchman like John Keble when he realized that the links between Church and State were so relaxed that the State was now willing to abolish Anglican bishoprics and even to allow financial support to Roman Catholicism. Indeed, one outcome of increasing democracy has been a growing unwillingness on the part of English politicians to sacrifice potential Roman Catholic votes to either Anglican or Wesleyan sympathies. In the seventeenth century, Stuarts and bishops had fought side by side, and Laud had died for the dynasty as well for Catholicity; in the eighteenth century the bishops still mattered to the Government's majority in the House of Lords; but in the nineteenth century it became quietly clear that in a secularized society a bishop was no longer an important cog in the machinery of government. It was certainly significant that by 1867, when Walter Bagehot published *The English Constitution*, he could write a long chapter on the House of Lords without any reference to the bishops at all. For a political romantic who set great store by symbol and ceremony, and who looked to the House of Lords to save an idealized past from an uncomprehended future, this meant much. The medieval system withered away locally as well as nationally, and a secular civil service dispossessed the Anglican clergy of the jobs that they had often done as the agents of Royal and Parliamentary commissions, or as inspectors of education. Brilliant and unforeseen as the Anglo-Catholic offensive was, the ground lost could not be regained.

On the other hand, as the State became more secular the Church of England became more ecclesiastical, even more religious. To sketch the whole of that development as it affected the episcopate would take far too much space, but the salient features were these. The bishop, prompted by such men as Blomfield of London, Wilberforce of Oxford, and Thompson of York, strove to become the active religious centre of the diocese. He circulated more regularly for confirmation services, increased the severity of ordination examinations,[1] and surrounded ordination itself with a more imposing atmosphere; he encouraged the building of new churches and of houses for the clergy; in his charges he wrestled with liturgical and other topical problems. The bid was made, in fact, to give reality to the idea of the bishop as the natural source of leadership and authority. But at the same time this New Episcopate suffered heavy reverses, quite apart from the decline in social and political prestige which has continued right down to the present. In the first three quarters of the nineteenth century almost every English bishop must have put himself on record as believing that such characteristically Anglo-Catholic practices as aural confession, life vows for men and women, and reservation for other purposes than the communion of the sick were without

---

[1] One must not exaggerate the pace of the change. W. S. Swayne, later Bishop of Lincoln from 1920 to 1932, gave this description of his ordination at Farnham by Harold Browne, the Bishop of Winchester, in 1885: 'There was nothing in the nature of an ordination candidates' retreat, but one of the chaplains on the Friday evening did give us an Address in chapel on the Societies of the Church of England, the National Society, the SPG, the Incorporated Church Building Society and the great Missionary Societies. We listened dutifully, but were aware that this was not precisely what we wanted. On the Saturday evening the Bishop addressed us mainly on the practical duties of the pastoral life. I remember that he told us that agricultural labourers were often deaf. We must therefore learn to speak clearly and intelligibly in church. This was sound and practical advice . . . but again I was aware that this was hardly the word which we needed from our Father in God at such a time. I had a brief interview with the Bishop, and he discussed with me how far infidelity was prevalent among the present generation at Oxford. . . . On my return to Oxford, Charles Gore examined me somewhat narrowly as to the circumstances of my ordination at Farnham. When I had told him my story, he groaned'—*Parson's Pleasure* (1934), pp. 84–5.

doubt un-Anglican.[2] Yet all these innovations became permanent, and Tait's Public Worship Regulation Act of the 1870s was an abject failure.[3] If the Church of England became more Catholic

[2] All the bishops agreed to a statement issued in 1873 according to which the formularies of the Church of England did not authorize ministers of the Church 'to require from any who may resort to them to open their grief, a particular or detailed enumeration of their sins, or to require private confession previous to holy communion, or to enjoin, or even to encourage, any practice of habitual confession to a priest, or to teach that such practice of habitual confession or the being subject to what has been termed the direction of a priest, is a condition of attaining to the highest spiritual life'. In 1899 certain of the bishops asked for a ruling on the lawfulness of the use of incense and of processional lights in public worship. The two archbishops, of whom Temple was the more important, said that 'they were obliged to come to the conclusion that the use of incense (and of processional lights) in the public worship, and as part of that worship, is not at present enjoined nor permitted by the law of the Church of England'. Later in 1899 Frederick Temple issued another formal statement which said that 'the Church of England does not at present allow Reservation in any form'. Temple's statements did not represent opinion in the Church of England at the time they were uttered —he was seventy-five when he became Archbishop, and ought never to have been appointed—but they summed up the general opinion of Victorian bishops pretty accurately. Temple was born in 1821, and it is significant that Bishop Westcott, who was born in 1825, agreed with him about Reservation in 1899, apart from a hesitation about the possibility of communicating the sick with bread and wine taken straight from a celebration. There is no evidence that Temple's decisions carried any weight in the controversy.

[3] This Act, passed in 1874, and broadly agreed to by all the Bishops, was meant 'to check lawlessness and extravagance in Ritual on the one side, and negligence in the performance of the offices of the Church on the other', in other words, to balance limitations on Anglo-Catholic innovation by criticism of Evangelical practice. When Disraeli, however, said in the House of Commons that the measure was meant 'to put down Ritualism', he described its psychological effect. When A. C. Tait, by then Archbishop of Canterbury, spoke on the Bill in the House of Lords he referred to the use in some Anglican Churches of altar-cards which contained prayers which implied invocations to the Virgin Mary and the Twelve Apostles, to be said in a low tone during the celebrating of Holy Communion. He continued: 'I call upon those who glory in the name of members of the Church of England, who have no feeling for Puritanism in any form, but who have often fought the battles of the Church of England against the Church of Rome on the one hand, and against Puritanism on the other—I call upon them to come forward and declare themselves manfully against such a desecration of the Holy Communion as all Churchmen

it did so against the will of the overwhelming majority of the New Episcopate itself, who found themselves defied by an appeal to what was allegedly the traditional law of the ecclesia: Anglo-Catholic presbyters, moreover, normally assumed that they were not obliged to accept an episcopal interpretation of this body of law, but that they had as much right as a bishop to decide what was meant.[4] This presbyterian claim to define the teaching of the

---

ought to unite in condemning'—*Life of A. C. Tait*, R. T. Davidson and W. Benham (1891), p. 201. While the Act was passing, Tait noted that 'Lord Houghton met me on the steps of the Athenaeum—"You are as triumphant as Laud in his worst times: I hope it is not to end in the same way" ' (ibid. p. 234). Tait was well equipped to protect Liberal Anglicans against the frequent, rather unholy alliance of Anglo-Catholics and Evangelicals; he lacked, however, enough sympathy with 'Ritualism' himself to see that the time was not yet ripe for the kind of 'comprehensive' Anglicanism which he believed possible.

[4] Take, for example, this exchange between A. C. Tait, then Bishop of London, later a very remarkable Archbishop of Canterbury, and the Rev. E. Stuart, one of the original founders of the English Church Union, then incumbent at a London church. Tait wrote, 5th March 1858: 'I must therefore lay my commands upon you to discontinue the practice you have introduced without any authority in St Mary Magdalene, Munster Square, of lighting the candles on the Communion Table in broad daylight, except when they may reasonably be considered necessary or convenient for purpose of light. I cannot hold it to be a good reason for the lighting of them at the celebrating of Holy Communion in our Reformed Church, that lighted candles were, in Roman Catholic times, or even during the short period of transition before the Reformation was fully settled in England, placed before the Sacrament on the high Altar at the celebration of the Mass. . . . The point beyond which a private clergyman must not go, in following his private judgement in the forms of public worship must surely, in the very lowest view of Episcopal authority, be settled by the Bishop, and I cannot but hope that when your Diocesan, having given his best attention to the law and customs of the Church, forbids an innovation, you will drop the practice objected to . . .' To which Stuart replied: 'I must respectfully decline to obey this command, as I believe that in issuing it you have (unintentionally, of course) transgressed the limits of that authority which the Church of England had committed to her bishops. I believe you have done this by forbidding what the law of the Church distinctly allows. . . . I must deprecate the use of such a phrase as "setting you at defiance". It is simply impossible for a priest of the Church of England to set at defiance any lawful exercise of the authority of his Diocesan, since the Church has given abundant power to her Bishops to compel obedience in such a case; but a matter of advice implies of necessity a discretionary power in the person advised. . .' *Life*

ecclesia seems to me to be a more complete break with Anglican tradition than John Wesley's assertion of a presbyterian power to ordain in special circumstances. In any case, the prestige of the bishops suffered, for despite the claims made for the office, it remains that the enormous changes which took place in the Church of England were dictated by the intransigent Anglo-Catholic clergy in the face of often almost united episcopal resistance. Only overseas, as the British Empire reddened the maps of the Pacific and Africa, did the bishop enjoy a further lease of importance as a symbol of the State and a founder of Churches.

But this extension of the Anglican episcopate outside England was very important. In a sense it was only in the nineteenth century that the post-Reformation Church of England grasped the religious possibilities of the bishop. The idea of a bishop who actually lived in the colonies was comparatively new. The *Interim Report on the Methodist–Anglican Conversations* (1958), commenting on the fact that when John Wesley ordained preachers for North America there was not a single Anglican bishop resident in the area, said that

The responsibility for the failure to consecrate resident bishops for North America rested squarely on the ministers of State, who had rejected a series of projects put forward by the archbishops, bishops and the S.P.G. Under the existing conditions of establishment the Church of England could not act independently of the State. Yet even here Wesley's commissioning of Thomas Coke antedated by only a short space the inauguration of an Anglican episcopate in America in the person of Bishop Seabury.[5]

But a body which asserts that episcopacy is of the esse of the ecclesia (and would like to believe that its eighteenth-century episcopate held this position too) can hardly be allowed to take cover behind Ministers of State when asked why it did not provide for the confirmation of Anglicans born in the American colonies from the early seventeenth to the late eighteenth centuries. Either these things matter or they do not matter, yet to speak of American

---

of *A. C. Tait*, by R. T. Davidson and W. Benham (1891), I.220–2. Any anxious Methodist who is afraid of episcopal despotism should study the history of the Anglo-Catholic party: he will find a whole arsenal of techniques for frustrating the will of the duly constituted authority.

[5] Op. cit. p. 12.

Anglicans as episcopal at all in this period seems rather difficult, unless the concept of *episkope* is first evacuated of all meaning which could not be expressed by the Bishop of London's vague tutelage, which usually amounted to the ordination of such Englishmen as were willing to go to America, and of such Americans as could afford to travel to and from this country. There was certainly an American Anglican demand for a resident episcopate. New Jersey Anglicans, for example, were so keen on having a resident bishop that they persuaded the SPG to buy an episcopal 'palace' in February 1711–12; the empty house burned down in 1747, but the land remained on the Society's hands until 1785. But they wanted a 'spiritual' bishop, one, that is, not limited by what the *Interim Report* called 'the existing conditions of establishment'. The distance which the concept of a bishop has travelled may be seen in the resolution of the New Jersey convention of 1765, which asked that the proposed American bishops should be authorized

only to exercise those powers which are essential to the office, with Jurisdiction over none but the Professors of the Church. Altho' this is less than reasonably could be expected in a Christian Country, as we know of no Instance since the Time of Constantine in which bishops have not been invested with a considerable Share of Civil Power; yet we shall be glad to accept it. . . .[6]

To describe Seabury's ordination as the 'inauguration of an Anglican episcopate' is technically correct, but as far back as 1722 John Talbot had obtained non-juring consecration on his own initiative only to be disowned by the SPG, and first reactions to Seabury's private action suggested that English attitudes had not altered. It was an integral part of the historical situation that Seabury acted on his own initiative—just as John Wesley did. From the point of view of this essay it is also important to note Wesley's clear recognition that the American Wesleyans needed superintendents—men set apart to the oversight of preachers and people, as well as to ordain ministers.

Fifty years transformed the Anglican attitude and the colonial bishop became a commonplace, so much so that the centre of the Anglican Communion shifted ever so slightly. The close links with

[6] Cf. *The Anglican Church in New Jersey*, by N. R. Burr (Philadelphia, 1954), p. 351.

the State—though still often passionately defended in England—
ceased to be a fundamental of Anglicanism, since the Anglican
bodies which developed outside England were voluntary, gathered
Churches, joined, as time went on, by the Irish and then Welsh
Establishments as involuntary sacrifices to Nonconformity. Moreover, the pressure for the first Pan-American Conference came
from North America, whereas the greatest reluctance was shown
by the bishops of the English Northern Province of York, who
did not even attend the first meeting in 1867 (they had the dubious
advantage of the support of Dean Stanley). This really meant
that the Anglican episcopate outside England was not willing to
leave the English bishops—even with Convocation restored to a
semblance of life—to make by themselves decisions which would
inevitably affect the future of the Anglican episcopate as a whole.

The result of these changes was obvious in the Lambeth Conference of 1958. Take, for example, the committee which provided
the newspapers with their largest headlines when the report of the
Conference was made known: *The Family in Contemporary Society*.
The work of this committee was very important because it broke
with the largely negative attitude of previous conferences towards
the use of contraception by Christians. There were thirty-eight
bishops on this committee, and their spread is interesting. From
the British Isles ten—seven from England, two from Ireland, and
one from Scotland; from North America seventeen—one from
Canada and the remainder from the United States; from other
areas eleven—two from West Africa (one of whom was D. R. Oye-
bode of Ibadan), two from the Far East (including J. Amritanand
of Assam), three who were extra-provincial (including D. Dent
Atong, Assistant Bishop of the Sudan), and one each from
Australia, New Zealand, South Africa, and the West Indies.

I do not want to imply that this proves more than a simple
matter of fact, that bishops with close English connections were
probably in a minority, but I would like to emphasize how incredible the simple fact would have seemed to the episcopate of
the *ancien régime* still firmly established in the lifetime of John
Wesley. The point is so important that it is worth while comparing
the composition of this committee with that of another, just as
important, the committee on 'Church Unity and the Church
Universal', which had to guide the attitude of the Lambeth Conference to the Church of South India, for example. This was a

much bigger committee, for it had seventy-one members. Of these, seventeen came from the United Kingdom—twelve from England, two each from Wales and Ireland, and one from Scotland; and twenty-nine from North America—six of them from Canada. From the Church of India, Pakistan, Burma, and Ceylon there were six. Of the remaining nineteen, seven were extra-provincial bishops, including N. A. Cuba'in of Jordan, Lebanon, and Syria, and F. H. Olang', Assistant Bishop of Mombasa; four came from West Africa, three of whom were Africans; there were three from Australia, and one each from Central Africa, South Africa, New Zealand, the West Indies, and Japan (M. H. Yashiro of Kobe). Here the number of those with and without close English connections was probably about equal. I have laboured this point because I do not think that the average Methodist is aware of this immense modern extension of the Anglican episcopate, or of the sense in which these changes have increased the institutional value of episcopacy to the Church of England.

For there would be some point in suggesting that a New Episcopate was created in the nineteenth century, quite apart from the new tradition of the bishop as the diocesan dynamo which was inaugurated by such men as Samuel Wilberforce of Oxford and Winchester. The growth of the Lambeth Conference enabled Anglicanism to retain a Cyprianic sense of unity in the oneness of its whole episcopate, and to embody this unity in the decennial gatherings. This elasticity was further exhibited at the 1958 Conference. The Committee for Church Unity pointed out that the success of schemes like that for the United Church of South India would deprive the Lambeth Conference of the fellowship of the bishops from many parts of the world; would similarly cut these bishops off 'from the inspiration which comes from the enriching experience of sharing in this Conference'; and would involve the risk that small united Churches, such as that proposed in Ceylon, would become isolated from the main stream of Catholic tradition and the life of the Church universal. The committee therefore suggested

that when any church belonging to the Anglican communion decides, with the encouragement and goodwill of the Lambeth Conference, to join a united Church, the bishops, or representative bishops, of the united Church should be invited to attend the Lambeth Conference as members. It is recognized that there will be occasions when matters of

Anglican policy are under discussion and when it may be desirable for decisions to rest with those who have jurisdiction in Anglican dioceses.

What is important here is the simplicity with which episcopacy can be used to foster unity across the barriers set up by the success of the Ecumenical Movement. (Of course there is nothing to prevent the Methodist World Conference from asking the Church of South India to send representatives to the decennial meetings of the Assembly; and perhaps this is the kind of action which ecclesiastical leaders ought to be thinking of at the present time.) Nor did the formation of the Church of South India sever all its ties with the British non-episcopal communions whose mission districts accepted episcopacy. But one suspects that such representatives would tend to be regarded as guests rather than as full members; whereas for Anglicans episcopacy still carries with it a distinctive character which gives a canonically appointed bishop a status independent of the very existence of the province in which his diocese lies. One might put this in the Ignatian epigram that where the bishop is, there is the ecclesia also. Of course, as Lightfoot said, what Ignatius probably meant by this was that 'the bishop is the centre of the individual church, as Jesus Christ is the centre of the Universal Church', and one hardly thinks of the modern Anglican bishop in relation to the 'local church'. For although English bishops retain titles which are based on the picture of the bishop as the head of the local church, they actually administer much wider areas, and the contrast between the title and the see was even greater before the nineteenth century inaugurated the division of dioceses. A historical critic might say that the prestige of the office depended upon two factors which have now largely disappeared: first, the combination of wealth and political influence which bishops retained until the end of the last century; the other, the picture of the primitive bishop enthroned in his basilica, flanked by his presbyters, facing his laity, a picture which has been cleaned and re-hung since the beginning of the last century. Nevertheless, when bishops meet—and not only Anglican bishops—they do so trailing these clouds of ancient glory, at once religious, political, and romantic, and so a meeting of the kind envisaged by the Lambeth Report would take place on a level far removed from the simply representative and would involve—for Anglicans—an embodiment of unity. And if one asks

154

whether an episcopal *conversazione* constitutes more than a super-ficial kind of unity, whether it means anything in terms of the Evangelical and Anglo-Catholic 'local churches' scattered up and down the various dioceses, then perhaps it is proper to reply, in an essay on episcopacy as an institution, that the anxiety to achieve more than this symbolic unity, this contact of the Heads of Houses, so to speak, sometimes arises from an unnatural dislike of differ-ence. The old passion for uniformity makes an unattractive page in the history of all established Churches: the moderate fashion in which the Roman Catholic authorities have handled the Liturgical Movement has been a far better advertisement for hierarchical unity than the foot roughly stamped on the worker priests.

The significance of this kind of unity must not, however, be exaggerated. The 1958 Lambeth Report said in the section on South India that 'no Church or Province of the Anglican com-munion is bound by the action of another. Nevertheless, the common traditions of faith, order, and worship which unite the Anglican Churches inevitably dispose them to give due weight to each other's actions' (2.26).

Thus the possession of a common episcopacy does not prevent the authors from speaking of 'Anglican churches': the Methodist is bound to wonder if this is not an illogical and insufficient under-standing of episcopacy as he has been asked to take it into his system. What the Lambeth Conference meant was made clear by its resolution about the Church of South India. Since 1948, of eight Churches or provinces five had acknowledged the bishops and episcopally ordained presbyters and deacons of the Church of South India to be true bishops, presbyters, and deacons in the Church of God, while the Episcopal Church of the United States seemed on the point of following suit. Two—the Church of the Province of the East Indies and the Church of the Province of South Africa—had in effect accorded recognition only to former Anglican clergy serving in the Church of South India and had permitted them to exercise their ministry within the Province concerned (when on leave, for example), provided that they did so in the Anglican churches only.

To a Methodist the important comment would seem to be this: that it must matter both from an institutional and from a theo-logical point of view that in a case which concerned the fundamental definition of the ecclesia the Anglican episcopate was unable to come to a united conclusion. It does not seem sufficient to reply that bishops can hardly be expected to provide a quick answer to every question put to them. In this case the difficulty arose because two groups came to clear but contradictory conclusions, not because the problem itself remained dubious and intractable. The Resolution of the 1958 Conference underlined this clash of interpretation. The formula adopted did no more than endorse the report of the committee which discussed the situation; the committee went no farther than the belief—it is true, with 'an increased sense of assurance'—that words used in 1948 could be repeated: 'We look forward hopefully and with longing to the day when there shall be full communion between the Church of South India and the Churches of the Anglican communion.' In other words, in so far as practical action was taken on grounds of principle, the principle had been decided by the Churches or provinces and not by the united episcopate at all; moreover, the decision of the 1958 Conference to leave the question where the 1948 Conference had left it—in suspense—meant in effect that in the Conference the minority had carried the day. I realize, of course, that the Conference could not make a law which would bind the minority; but the real issue was one of truth, not ecclesiastical politics. And here, in a matter which centred on the fundamental definition of the ecclesia, we do not find a united episcopate behaving as the guardian of tradition and sound doctrine, but instead two groups of bishops whose disagreement was stitched together in a negative, if possibly expedient, statement. This also suggests a conflict between two different passages in this section of the Report. The Committee said, as I have already mentioned, that 'no Church or Province of the Anglican communion is bound by the action of another'; but a little earlier the committee had already said that it 'would emphasize the important part which it believes the Lambeth Conference must continue to play as a bond of unity holding together the various parts of the Anglican communion' (2.24). But unless the Lambeth Conference is something more than a register of contemporary opinion—and at some times and on some subjects the general opinion of the ecclesia is perhaps better kept dark—then one cannot help wondering if it is wise to hold it at such regular intervals or whether, as has always been the case with councils, the Conference should meet only in time of absolute necessity. Evanston suggested that something similar might be true about the Assembly of the World Council of Churches.

The Methodist comment may be compared with the criticism of the Lambeth Conference made by Dr E. L. Mascall in his pamphlet, *Lambeth 1958 and Christian Unity*. Dr Mascall appears to have been deeply distressed by the way in which the Conference commented on the schemes for union in North India and Ceylon. He therefore raises the whole question of the authority of the Conference itself:

We cannot ignore the fact that, while no formal or canonical authority whatever attaches to the Lambeth Conference and its resolutions, they have, as has been stressed on many occasions, immense moral effect throughout the Anglican communion and even outside. This is an extremely dangerous status for any institution and its pronouncements to acquire, for it tends to separate power from accountability; it gives enormous influence to policies and programmes which cannot be canonically questioned since they have no canonical existence.[7]

Dr Mascall therefore pressed the fact, stated by the Archbishop of Canterbury in a letter to *The Times* (26th August 1958), that no vote was taken on any resolution except that which dealt with nuclear warfare; Dr Mascall said in effect that a majority of ninety-five per cent was often more impressive than complete unanimity. One may agree with this, yet still wonder if Dr Mascall would have raised the issue if he had agreed with the resolutions of the Conference on the unity schemes. But in the concluding part of his pamphlet his first point was that the bishops ought not, out of loyalty to the Conference or for the sake of prestige, to feel bound to maintain a façade of unanimity, but to express with complete frankness their personal convictions about the resolutions. And his second suggestion underlines even more what one may call a scepticism—amusing but not without parallel in such High Anglican quarters—about the value of episcopal decisions.

We must do all in our power to ensure that before the Ceylon and North India unions are inaugurated, the Scheme and the Plan in their final form are brought before the synods of the various Anglican provinces, not for hasty acceptance under pressure from above but for careful consideration in the light both of the theological principles involved and of the likely repercussions upon the life of the Anglican Churches.[8]

[7] Op. cit. p. 4.　　　　　　　　[8] Ibid. p. 17.

This appeal away from the larger, international, to the smaller, local unit may be looked at in many ways. I cannot avoid the impression that for an Anglican it is not really legitimate as a criticism of the Lambeth Conference understood as an episcopal encounter. Institutionally, however, it is difficult to have much faith in international decisions. One also knows from experience how quickly the representatives of the larger unit come to feel themselves the trustees of a larger truth.

Some tentative conclusions may now be suggested as to what has happened to Anglican episcopacy since the eighteenth century.

The first is that Anglicanism, having discovered itself as a worldwide communion, has at last broken through the cocoon of Establishment, which is quite irrelevant to the growth of the body outside England. Anglican episcopacy has shown itself adaptable to the altered circumstances, and in some parts of Africa, for example, the bishop has emerged in something closer to his primitive role.

The second is that since the eighteenth century the English bishop has become a much more obvious religious figure, and as such he grates far less on Methodist susceptibilities.

But there is contrast between what has happened in England and what has happened abroad. One is bound to suggest that the nineteenth-century drive to create a more dedicated episcopate, fully and freely in control of the whole life of the Church of England—a movement which may be clearly distinguished from Anglo-Catholicism—has not been by any means a complete success. For example, from a Methodist point of view, and despite the apologies offered in the various Anglican Reports of 1917, 1935, and 1949, it remains true, as a Free Church Federal Council Commission on Church and State put it bluntly in 1953, that the political control of episcopal appointments 'is fundamentally wrong in principle and potentially disastrous in practice'.[9] Whether the system works well in practice is a matter of opinion; that those who had been chosen by it should approve of it is hardly surprising. One can see no way of reconciling this machinery—especially the Anglican tolerance of the *conge d'élire* itself, which surprisingly has produced no martyrs—with the normal Anglican descriptions of episcopacy. To a Methodist, however, nursed on the idea of succession in doctrine rather than succession through

[9] *Report*, p. 60.

ordination, the Anglican capacity to combine great emphasis on Apostolical Succession with attachment to the political method of selection is not very sympathetic.

A second negative point also emerges if the bishop is to be thought of as institutionally responsible for the spiritual life of the ecclesia. The movement which led to the setting-up of the Church Assembly might be described as an attempt to reconcile three different things: the idea of the New Episcopate as the natural government of the Church of England, the modern trend towards an increasing lay participation in Church government, and the concept of Establishment as actually practised in England. Success was bound to be difficult, and the fate of the Prayer Books of 1927–8 showed that supporters of the scheme had been unduly hopeful: a political body still controlled the worship of the Church of England, and therefore in this respect the bishops as well. In this case the kind of apology made for the political appointments of bishops is invalid, for the Prayer Books were rejected outright against the clearly expressed wishes of the hierarchy. The present revision of the Canon Law raises the same general problems.

This brings one to a third and less negative point. The value of an institution may be measured in terms of its efficiency. Differences in doctrine are not taken as seriously now as they were in the eighteenth century—the original Wesleyans would certainly look with horror at a Church of England which permits monastic orders for men and women, encourages the use of private confession, and has replaced in many churches the kind of pictures and images which were removed in the sixteenth and seventeenth centuries. What matters here is the failure of the nineteenth-century bishops to prevent these changes, their inability, which surely amounted to inefficiency, given the strength of their convictions, to enforce the discipline which they wanted. One is reminded of Samuel Wilberforce, then Bishop of Oxford and regarded as a High Churchman, contemplating what Liddon, as Vice-Principal, had made of Cuddesdon Theological College by 1859:

Then there are things in the actual life I wish changed. The tendency to crowd the walls with pictures of the Mater Dolorosa, etc., their chimney pieces with crosses, their studies with saints, all offend me and do incalculable injury to the College in the eyes of chance visitors. The habit of some of our men kneeling in a sort of rapt prayer on the steps of the communion-table, when they cannot be *alone* there; when the visitors are coming in and going out and talking around them. . . .

When I first wrote this essay I thought and said that 'this inefficiency seems a large mark against episcopacy and makes one wonder what guarantees exist for the future under such a system of church government. . . . If it is suggested that at least the nineteenth-century bishops followed a course which prevented outright schism, well and good, but in that case their activities have to be interpreted in the light of this, and presented as the work of skilful leaders of an ecclesiastical body'—it could hardly be maintained that they had successfully defended, or guarded, a tradition. The practising Church of England in 1900 differed immensely from that of 1800, in doctrine as well as in ritual; it would be no answer to say that the formularies remained unaffected. And I summed up: 'in fact one may distinguish a polite from an actual history of episcopacy in recent times'—a polite history in which the bishops are the great men who deserve massive biographies—'but it would be truer to say that in a struggle about the definition of what was Catholic the opinion of the presbyters proved more lasting than that of the bishops'.

I am still of the opinion that nineteenth-century Anglican bishops as a body showed themselves remarkably unsuccessful in preserving what they believed to be 'the Anglican ethos', but I am no longer so sure that this is a black mark against episcopacy. The more one studies the position of Christianity in modern culture the more one realizes that freedom of opinion is essential to the healthy life and continuing influence of the Church. The nineteenth-century episcopal reaction to Anglo-Catholicism was perhaps the last significant Anglican attempt to enforce uniformity, and it was vital that it should fail. The tradition for which the New Episcopate stood has not entirely vanished, however; one contribution to a strongly Evangelical symposium on the 1963 *Majority Report* said this:

Ministerial subscription to orthodox doctrinal formulations is one of the foundation-principles of the reformed Church of England; in a doctrinally disunited Christendom it remains today as necessary as ever it was; and it is one of the richest contributions that Anglicans can make to a future united church.[10]

[10] *The Church of England and the Methodist Church*, ed. J. I. Packer (1963), p. 55.

And a few pages later the same writer adds that one fundamental of reunion in England would be 'ministerial subscription to a doctrinal confession corresponding to the substance of the Thirty-nine Articles'.[11]

This sentiment has a very Victorian ring about it. One can think of no policy less likely to restore the intellectual respectability of Christianity in twentieth-century England—or one less likely to lead to reunion, for that matter. In view of the continued existence of such groups, however, which still believe passionately in the value of uniformity, it is reassuring to remember that the Victorian bishops failed completely to carry out such a policy. At the same time one has to remember when reading a report like Leslie Paul's *Deployment and Payment of the Clergy* (1964)—which is concerned with administrative efficiency and not with the definition of doctrine—that any increase, in the name of efficiency, in the power of bishops over their clergy is likely to have some repercussions in the field of the guardianship of doctrine. It is very desirable that twentieth-century bishops should not be tempted to resume their nineteenth-century predecessors' habits of passing official sentence on works of scholarship, or of imprisoning clergymen for their taste in ritual.

SECTION TWO

Nevertheless, episcopacy in the Anglican sense played only a small part in the eighteenth-century separation of the Methodist Societies from the Church of England. In view of the publication, in 1963, of the *Majority Report* proposals for union between the Methodist and Anglican Churches it is important that we should come to a clear understanding of what led to division in the eighteenth century. I don't think, however, that an analysis of what happened in the eighteenth century produces the results which some historians have encouraged their readers to accept in recent years. Two characteristic interpretations have developed since the first World War. In one case the intention seems to be to justify the claim of Evangelicalism to be Anglican—a purpose which sounds more necessary to some Anglicans than it may do to a Methodist—while in the other case the idea has been to facilitate reunion by minimizing the differences between Methodism and Anglicanism,

[11] *The Church of England and the Methodist Church*, p. 59.

161

reducing them if possible to the purely institutional, and so increasing the chance that a scheme of constitutional episcopacy might prove acceptable.

I doubt whether either lesson is the appropriate one to draw from the events of Wesley's lifetime: what emerges much more concretely is the difficulty which any Church structure has in adapting, or in attempting to adapt, to the changing social structure of a country so as to include all kinds and classes of people within its communion. The Church of England faced this problem in the eighteenth century—it was bound to if it were to justify its title—and failed to solve it successfully; it might be added that Methodism faced the same problem in the nineteenth century, and that its own internal divisions to some extent reflected another failure to cope with the pressure of society on the external forms of the Church. The eighteenth-century material also underlines the dangers inherent in concentrating ecclesiastical power in the hands of a professional ministerial class, especially when authority in that group is still further concentrated into the hands of a small, in this case episcopal, *élite*, which may be more out of touch with the changing national social structure than the working parsons in the parishes, and yet unwilling to accept what would amount to leadership from below. Such criticisms would matter less if the ecumenical architects of our time were not determined to unite all the present English Protestant denominations into a single body; this has become so conscious an aim that a former Archbishop of Canterbury, Dr Fisher, even criticized the idea of union between the Methodist and Anglican Churches alone on the specific ground that it would—as he thought—make a total union in England less likely.[12] If such a national body were set up, however, it could only be regarded as successful if it proved to be socially all-embracing: as it is, the existing disunited Churches

[12] *The Anglican–Methodist Conversations and Problems of Church Unity*, by Lord Fisher of Lambeth (London, 1964). 'It is far too early yet to foresee what shape the finally reunited Church of England (including all the Free Churches, the Roman Catholic Church in England, and the Orthodox Church in England) will take. For the Church of England merely to absorb the Methodist Church would benefit nobody . . .' (p. 41). This is no more than a version of the traditional last-ditch argument that we must not do anything unless we can do everything; Dr Fisher feels that Anglicanism is paying *too high a price for* organic union with Methodism.

seem relatively confined in their social appeal to the British people. In fact, it is hard to say whether in this sense an 'ecumenical' Church is socially possible, with or without bishops. This raises such questions as how far Christians have ever succeeded in imposing any Church structure on to society; how far the Church structure has always derived from the underlying social structure; and how far in the twentieth century the only widely acceptable forms of Christianity would turn out to have virtually no institutional structure whatever.[13]

When one tries to account for the eighteenth-century separation between Methodism and Anglicanism, one may certainly put aside the almost traditional view according to which John Wesley was the *fons et origo* of the whole eighteenth-century revival, both inside and outside the Church of England. At one time Anglican Evangelicals like Venn and Romaine were thought of as 'Wesleyans who stayed in the Church of England'. One of the more famous— and misguided—advocates of this view was Dean Church, who dismissed the Evangelicals of Newman's day as 'not inheritors of Anglican traditions, but of those zealous clergymen and laymen who had sympathized with the great Methodist movement'. This

---

[13] One has to recognize that at present there is a gap between Christian institutions and many people who would regard themselves as Christians. Or, to put it another way, the visible Church represents, or contains, only a proportion of the religious feeling and thinking of the country. It might even be said that the religious institutions we have help to maintain this gap: Archbishop Fisher's complacent statement that the Coronation of Queen Elizabeth II brought the whole Commonwealth nearer to the Kingdom of Heaven threw some light on why the two groups remain divorced. If one turns to the Continent, Bonhoeffer's theology was expressed against a firm institutional background to which his prison writings make little explicit reference. The popularity of the prison writings in England, however, has depended to some extent on this absence of the ecclesiastical note, on a resulting ethos which might suggest the ideal of a Quaker Meeting dissolved in suburban society. Bonhoeffer was not popular because he changed the mind of a generation theologically; his popularity arose because he reflected accurately the actual religious content of the consciousness of a whole generation, which had not previously admitted to itself what its real, as opposed to its verbal, religious feelings were. But at the point at which even Quakerism seems burdened with institutions the movement back to a radical individualism may be said to be far out; no one who wishes to understand the religious history of the 1960s can afford to ignore the presence of this strong impulse to retreat from entanglement with the institutional Church.

combination of anathema and compliment is found in much
Anglican writing, and is analogous to the equally unhistorical
picture of a sixteenth-century struggle between Puritanism and
Anglicanism, where one would more naturally see a struggle between two groups of Anglicans for the control of the Establishment.

It is not surprising therefore, that attempts should have been
made to provide Anglican Evangelicalism with a more respectable,
a more Anglican pedigree. Recent studies of Cornwall by G. C. B.
Davies and of North-east England by Dr John Walsh, have shown
how some Anglican centres of revival developed on a more or less
Calvinist basis without any obvious link with Wesleyanism at all.
Indeed, the correspondence between Samuel Walker of Truro and
John Wesley may be seen less as a negotiation between potential
allies than as a representative encounter between two distinct
groups, with widely differing attitudes to the message and mission
of the ecclesia. At the same time, brilliant American writing about
Jonathan Edwards has enabled us to see that the New England
revivalism of the eighteenth century had direct precedents in the
seventeenth, and that in the eighteenth century there was taking
place in the Anglo-Saxon world a kind of Calvinist recovery
against the movement of the general stream of Protestantism—a
recovery which had less in common with Wesleyanism than is
supposed.[14]

---

[14] Among John Wesley's earlier associates, William Grimshaw illustrates this background very well. Grimshaw (1708–63) was essentially a
seventeenth-century character. He was convicted of sin by reading
Thomas Brooke's *Precious Remedies against the Devices of Satan* (1652)
and converted by John Owen's *Doctrine of Justification by Faith* (1677).
He often drew up covenants with God in the Puritan fashion. He shared
their passion for strict parochial discipline, and frequently dispatched
parishioners to the Archdeacon's Court. What he did at Haworth closely
resembled the New England revivalism of Solomon Stoddard, in the late
seventeenth century, and has to be interpreted in that light; what attracted
him to John Wesley was a common passion for evangelism—in most other
senses his outlook belonged to a world that was dying when he and Wesley
were born. His old-fashionedness may partly be explained by the fact that
he was brought up in the depths of agricultural Lancashire, the child of
a man who was little better than a labourer; the Cambridge to which he
went in order to enter the Church of England was not calculated to change
him very much; once he had been ordained he returned to the countryside, reigning in his heyday over the remote corner of Yorkshire which

These new patterns of research and interpretation have not yet undermined the belief, however, more commonly held by Anglicans than by Methodists, that even if Wesleyanism and Evangelicalism had very different origins, they were essentially alike. One may instance *Simeon and Church Order* (1940) by Canon Charles Smyth as the best Anglican example of the view that all that finally separated the Wesleyans from the Establishment was a series of comparatively trivial points of Church Order. This view is followed in recent Methodist books by Dr A. S. Wood, in his biography of Thomas Haweis,[15] and by Dr C. W. Towlson in his study of *Moravianism and Methodism* (1957). Dr Towlson, however, also thought that the revival split on account of the clash of too many strong personalities. Perhaps the best summary of this new orthodoxy is a review by the Rev. M. Hennell (himself the biographer of another Evangelical, John Venn), of Dr Wood's book about Thomas Haweis. He said: 'Dr Wood is surely right in seeing the Evangelical Revival as a wide movement, of which the Wesley's revival was a tributary, not the source; the other main tributary being Anglican Evangelicalism. He is also justified in following Canon Smyth and Professor G. C. B. Davies in asserting

---

served as a background to *Wuthering Heights*. It is not surprising that in 1760 he should have strongly opposed those of Wesley's itinerant preachers who already wanted to break with the Church of England; he belonged to a tradition which saw Dissent as an admission of failure. One may call Grimshaw a Methodist, but hardly a Wesleyan. For information about him, see *William Grimshaw*, by Dr F. Baker (Epworth Press, 1963).

[15] *Thomas Haweis, 1734–1820*, by Arthur Skevington Wood (London, 1957). The author quotes Charles Smyth with approval on p. 14: 'the fundamental divergence between evangelicals and Methodists came over the problem of Church order'; on page 18 he distinguishes between Romaine, who was 'clearly on the evangelical side of the fence' because he left the Countess of Huntingdon when she licensed her chapels under the Toleration Act, and Grimshaw and Henry Venn, who itinerated and who built preaching-places in their villages as safeguard against future High Church incumbents—'these irregularities make it impossible to classify Grimshaw and Venn as pure Evangelicals'. I don't think that Grimshaw can in fact be classified satisfactorily in purely 'eighteenth-century' terms; but in Venn's case the use of conformity to Church Order as a test produces rather an unlikely result. Moreover, the assertion that 'we are at least justified in regarding regularity as the touchstone, and in accounting as Evangelicals, even if not always as thoroughbred specimens, those whose sympathies inclined to the parochial rather than the itinerant ministry' would make an Evangelical out of Charles Wesley.

that the real question of difference between the two was Church Order—Wesley and Walker representing the two extremes. Dr Wood correctly points out that many Anglican Evangelicals were not as rigid as Walker and indulged in itinerancy, but he fails to show that the leaders of the next generation—Henry Venn and John Newton—were prepared to accept and practise irregularity only as an expedient for a limited period; they were not prepared to allow their followers or themselves to be pushed into Dissent; they valued what they called Church principles too highly.'[16]

This interpretation of eighteenth-century events has this advantage: it suggests that it would be natural for Methodism to 'rejoin' the Church of England, because the separation had taken place for institutional reasons, such as John Wesley's ordinations and his employment of 'irregular' preachers. A characteristic expression of this point of view is that all might still have been well if the bishops had acted with more initiative and imagination—a view which in any case probably exaggerates the contemporary significance of episcopacy. The *Interim Report* of the conversations between the Methodist Church and the Church of England (1958) was inclined to take this attitude: 'It was not the case that the spread of Methodism was frustrated or hindered by episcopal action' (p. 11)—an odd apologia for the historic episcopate that it did not actually prevent anyone from doing the work of evangelism. The statement is not very easy to prove; the single late quotation offered from Charles Wesley in 1785 may be compared with the two letters written by John to Pretyman Tomline, Bishop of Lincoln, in which Wesley accuses Tomline of driving the Methodists out of the Church of England. Finally, another possible reason for holding this general point of view may be a desire to find for modern Evangelicalism a pedigree as distinguished as that of the Oxford Reformers, setting off John and Charles Wesley, Henry Venn, and Daniel Wilson against Keble, Pusey, Liddon, and Gore.

I am not convinced that this explanation of the separation of Wesleyanism from the Church of England is a valid one, or that the conclusions which may be drawn from it about episcopacy are correct. I should like, very tentatively, to suggest (*a*) that so far as the actual separation was concerned, Wesley's ordinations had no significance as a cause of schism; (*b*) that the current explanation of the separation overestimates the importance of institutional

[16] *Theology* (1957), p. 472.

factors and pays far too little attention to the doctrinal divergencies between Wesleyans and Evangelicals; and (c) that the biggest single cause of the separation was the actual religious pattern of the Wesleyan movement, and that in so far as episcopacy is concerned this pattern is a healthy reminder of the questionable value of the present Anglican system of large-scale dioceses.

(a) The question of ordination had no significance as a *cause* of separation. John Wesley ordained because a separation had already taken place. This is especially clear in the case of the United States: it does not seem a historically likely supposition that if Wesley had delayed his action until after the ordination of Seabury as the first Anglican bishop in America he would have been able to persuade Asbury to accept his oversight. In England Wesley's action was so irrelevant to the form that the separation was actually taking that as soon as he died, the Conference called a halt to ordination by the imposition of hands which lasted in England until 1836, more than forty years after Wesley's death.

Nor, I think, did Wesley consider ordination a serious theological issue. It is true that one may point—and many have—to the fact that he read Lord King's book on the Primitive Church in 1746, and was prepared to quote him as an authority for the right of presbyters to ordain. But the importance of this alleged change of mind has often been exaggerated. It was because Wesley was already practising a form of organization more radical than anything to be found in King's treatise that he was willing, at the theoretical level, to adopt King's arguments. But so little had ordination to do with his real problem in 1746 that he did not feel compelled to translate his opinions into action until the 1780s. To an evangelical like Samuel Walker the Methodist problem was a matter of the itinerants. This was a problem of Church Order, of ordination. If they could not be ordained they should be sent home, and so he told John Wesley. Wesley did not see this as his problem at all. He took for granted that the existing bishops would not ordain more than a handful of his full-time preachers; at the same time, despite Lord King, and despite the pressure put on him from inside Wesleyanism in the 1750s and 1760s, he was clear that he would not ordain them himself. This restraint was essentially practical, not theological: he told the American Methodists in 1784 that he had refused to ordain hitherto 'not only for the sake of peace, but because I was determined to do as little as possible to violate the established order of the National Church to which I belonged'. In other words, he reduced the question of episcopal ordination to a matter of formal obedience to the laws of the Established Church of England, laws which in the very nature of the historical process could not always be left with the last word. This suggests that he took an institutional view of episcopal ordination; that he thought one might accept the normal practice with a good conscience, but that whether there was any absolute necessity for ordination to be episcopal was quite a different question, to be decided by practical considerations. And this remains a position open to the modern Methodist, who may reasonably argue that the time has now come when historical considerations suggest that episcopal ordination ought for the sake of unity to be introduced into Methodism, without prejudice to any meaning which might be found in the ceremony itself. A. S. Peake, for example, in his Free Church Council Address of 1928, said that provided episcopacy was constitutional, with room for the laity and the presbyters, and provided that no theory that episcopacy was of the essence of the Church was demanded, he would be prepared to accept it as a matter of expedience.

But this was only half the problem as Wesley faced it. From the 1740s he had to justify the use of his full-time itinerants not only as preachers but as pastors of the Societies. He solved this problem on what may be called the evangelical level: that is, he placed the need to supply the Societies with men who would preach what he regarded as the full Christian Gospel above the need to supply clergymen ordained in a particular way; in other words, as he told Walker, he would not send the itinerants home because to do so was to leave the Societies to parish priests who if not in earnest would be positively dangerous, and who if in earnest would probably be Calvinist. Thus he placed continuity in doctrine before succession in orders, and this seems to me to be his fundamental position with regard to Orders. The position should be distinguished from both the Presbyterian and the Anglican position, both of which often encourage the assumption that a particular mode of appointment guarantees continuity in doctrine, and this is no more attractive in the Presbyterian than the episcopal form. The Church historian, in particular, knows that no such doctrinal guarantee can be given. Nor I think can a

Church historian accept the late E. W. Thompson's invocation of the non-historical notion of Wesley as an 'Apostolic Man' in order to justify the ordinations of the 1780s.

The intention of Thompson's argument is to free Methodism from any obligation to assert, at any rate on John Wesley's authority, a presbyterian doctrine of the Church and the Ministry. John Wesley was mistaken, Thompson wants to argue, when he supposed (and stated in public) that he could draw from Lord King's famous book on the Primitive Church authority for his own right as a presbyter to ordain. As Thompson interprets King's treatise and Wesley's situation in 1784 the appeal to the treatise is null and void, and the ordinations remain quite indefensible from an Anglican point of view. There is, however, according to Thompson, a better way of explaining and defending Wesley's ordinations for America. Wesley's whole career is then invoked to justify the assertion that he possessed a kind of essential apostolicity, a quintessence of what the Anglican bishop claims to have—and Thompson goes to great lengths to emphasize Wesley's personal superiority over the Georgian bishops as a body: 'If the office of a Bishop may be known by its exercise who in all England was worthier of being a Christian bishop than John Wesley'.[17] Wesley's spiritual odyssey is held to have elevated him into 'an Apostolic Man',[18] and by what is little more than a play on words Thompson shifts from this general idea of an Apostolic Man to the specific authority to set up a new Church Order and to ordain ministers to superintend it—for Wesley, after all, did more than just ordain men to act in an already established Church. 'Wesley's authority', Thompson sums up, 'to ordain and consecrate rests securely, not upon ancient precedents but upon his extraordinary divine commission to preach the Gospel and to shepherd the flock of Christ. God is the great consecrator and nearness to Him—Christ is the great Shepherd and partaking of His mind, is what matters most in the consecrating minister'.[19] If Thompson's arguments were correct it would mean that Anglicans need not worry unduly about John Wesley's ordinations: these were justifiable only because they were extraordinary (Thompson does not seem quite to have faced the question of whether they were also repeatable, whether a succession could really rest upon this kind of

[17] *Wesley, Apostolic Man*, 1957, p. 60.
[18] Ibid. p. 74.   [19] Ibid. p. 81.

foundation) and therefore not a real contradiction of the Anglican theory properly understood; in a sense the ordinations were even Apostolic, since John Wesley was an 'Apostolic Man'. It would also mean that Methodists need not be held back from a present-day acceptance of an Anglican kind of episcopacy by John Wesley's apparent leanings towards a Presbyterian understanding of ordination in his later years, since the validity of his ordination did not depend on the correctness of his appeal to Lord King on the rights of Presbyters, but on this allegedly 'apostolic' power. This saves the face of both parties and paves the way to mutual recognition.

Something must be said about the idea of the 'Apostolic Man' and about Thompson's interpretation of Wesley's dependence upon Lord King's authority. The argument about the 'Apostolic Man' seems to confuse metaphor with fact. One could say that John Wesley was *like* an apostle, inasmuch as he devoted his life to preaching the Gospel, travelling thousands of miles and suffering all sorts of hardships, etc. But this does not mean that one could say he *was* an Apostle in any technical sense, and so able to claim powers of ordination of the kind that an Anglican might suppose the Apostles proper to have possessed. The whole point of the Anglican position is that one cannot safely begin the foundation of the Church all over again, that one needs the restraining hand of tradition and continuity if one is to be truly catholic, that the sects go astray because they are too eager to snap these links with the past under the impulse of some imagined authority. Without actually intending to do so, Thompson was making this kind of sectarian claim on Wesley's behalf, that here was the great exception in whose case one could do without the normal procedure and go straight back to God for one's authority. It seems to me very significant indeed that Wesley did not make for himself the kind of claim which Thompson wants to make for him, but instead founded his authority to ordain, as far as he possibly could, on an appeal to Anglican tradition, to continuity, and on a presbyterian right of ordination which he asserted already existed in the Primitive Church. Wesley might treat his itinerants as extraordinary messengers, but he never forgot for a moment that he himself was a regularly ordained presbyter of the Church of England.

One further point affects the question of the 'Apostolic Man'. The emergence of a new Christian denomination, with its complex of institutions, is the product of a field of sociological forces among which the personality of the charismatic leader such as John Wesley functions only as one. Thompson argued that God ratified Wesley's act of ordination 'by manifest signs and tokens from heaven. The Methodist Episcopal Church of America is the most signal demonstration in history of Hooker's principle—the test by fruits or results. This Church today numbers nearly fifteen million adherents.'[20] Hooker or no Hooker, such an argument is valueless. It is obvious that given the circumstances of America after the War of Independence the Methodists there were bound to organize themselves into a denomination independent of Britain; as Thompson's own evidence shows, a similar play of forces compelled the American Anglicans to act for their own preservation when the English episcopate showed itself as indifferent to their fate as it was to the fate of the American Methodists. The later history of the American Methodists is not a comment on Wesley's ordination of Coke; it is a comment on the greatness of Asbury, perhaps; but essentially both men's careers are footnotes in the history of American Methodist expansion.

The other side of Thompson's argument is his rejection of John Wesley's appeal, in support of his ordinations, to the authority of King and Stillingfleet. Here again, the wider context is important: the right of presbyters to ordain did not depend either on the writings of King, or on the concession made by the essentially episcopalian Stillingfleet, who said that presbyters might reasonably be prevented from ordaining in practice if it were granted that they possessed the power to do so in theory. When John Wesley said that Lord King's book converted him to the view that presbyters might ordain he did not mean that he was therefore strictly limited to the version of this theory which Lord King happened to set out. Part of the evidence for this is contained in the Conference *Minutes* of 1745, where Wesley set down a theory of the development of Church government which owed nothing to King (whom he had not then read), but which clearly foreshadowed the possibility that the Methodist Societies might develop until they reached a point at which a Ministry constituted itself naturally, from the inside, a point which Wesley seems to have tacitly marked by setting up the Legal Hundred. Thompson prints this 1745 passage in full on p. 77, and adds that 'this is a very defective account of the origin and growth of the Christian

[20] *Wesley, Apostolic Man,* pp. 73–4.

Church. . . . One obvious defect is that it fails totally to account for the Church Universal. Up to a point it might explain the united Methodist Societies, but it is no explanation of the Catholic Church.' In fact, of course, the passage in the 1745 *Minutes* was Wesley's meditation on the origin of Church government in the light of the growth of the Methodist movement; it was the Methodist movement he was concerned with, and he foresaw with remarkable precision the direction which that growth would take if it continued, as of course it did. Thompson criticized Wesley on the ground that he began his account: 'Christ sends forth a preacher of the gospel.' 'Christ did not send forth one preacher of the gospel,' says Thompson, 'but many'[21] (p. 77), and goes on to talk about the 'glorious company of the Apostles'[22]. Wesley, however, was musing about his own case, as he did in the more famous account of the rise of Methodism to be found in the *Minutes* of 1766, which begins, 'two or three persons *desired me* to advise and pray with them. . . . Here commenced my *power*. . . '. Thompson was bound to dismiss the 1745 passage because it did not suit his theory at all to find that Wesley could produce—*before he could have read Lord King's treatise*—a description of the origin of Church government which seems largely unaffected by traditional Anglican ideas about episcopacy and the Church. I cannot agree with Thompson's further suggestion that 'it is difficult to find that the plan of development traced (in 1745) was ever put forward again; and for this reason that it was not really characteristic of John Wesley'.[23] In fact, in his classic self-defence in the *Minutes* of 1766 Wesley established the foundation of his authority on the same basis as he had indicated in 1745: people willingly gave themselves up to his direction, either because he had converted them or because they hoped that he would convert them, and from this fundamental relationship there developed the ecclesiastical superstructure of the united societies. The power to ordain was the power to recognize what had already taken place.

The unimportance of King can be illustrated more directly, however. Thompson naturally quotes Wesley's comments on his initial reading of King's book in January 1746:

I was ready to believe that this was a fair and impartial draught; but if so, it would follow that bishops and presbyters are (essentially) of one

[21] Ibid. p. 77.   [22] Ibid. p. 78.   [23] Ibid. p. 77.

Order; and that originally every Christian congregation was a church independent of all others.

Thompson continues:

I am quite at a loss to account for this deduction from King in the concluding phrase of Wesley: for in the context of the eighteenth century an 'Independent Church' could mean none other than a Church consisting of a 'gathered congregation', which was regarded as self-contained and recognized no authority beyond itself. This was the polity of Independence, but nothing resembling it can be found in King.[24]

Of course there was nothing of this in King, but Wesley was a good deal less interested in King than people have assumed. If one turns back to the *Minutes* of 1745, composed about six months before, one finds John Wesley saying, quite clearly and unequivocally:

The plain origin of Church government seems to be this. Christ sends forth a preacher of the Gospel. Some who hear him repent and believe the Gospel; they then desire him to watch over them, to build them up in the faith, and to guide their souls in the path of righteousness. *Here, then, is an independent congregation, subject to no pastor but their own, neither liable to be controlled in things spiritual by any other man or body of men whatsoever.*

In other words, the orthodox story of how Wesley's attitude to Church government was profoundly altered by reading King's book is very much exaggerated: what Wesley found in King was an Anglican authority whom he could use on his side of the controversy. When he read King in 1746 he simply interpreted what he read in terms of what he already believed in broad outline, and what he believed was bound to be re-enacted in Methodism as a revival of primitive Christianity. The idea that Christian congregations were originally independent did not frighten Wesley nearly as much as it did Thompson, perhaps because Wesley was living in the eighteenth century.

In detail, Thompson's argument can be summed up in his statement[25] that when John Wesley defended his ordinations for the United States he did so with a reference to Lord King's book, saying that according to King 'bishops and presbyters are of the same order and consequently have the same right to ordain'—to which Lord King would have been bound to reply, according to

[24] *Wesley, Apostolic Man*, p. 78.　　　　　[25] Ibid. pp. 28–9.

Thompson: 'Presbyters have no right to ordain, except by the bishop's permission.'[26] We know, of course, that John Wesley had no episcopal (Anglican) authorization for his American ordinations: the case is therefore proved, and Wesley's reference to Lord King is valueless.

One cannot help feeling that in propounding an argument of this order Thompson seriously underestimated Wesley's self-awareness, his capacity to defend himself. He was a brilliant debater, who had been over this ground many times before; he was familiar with all the traps and safeguards. Thompson has his eyes too much on Lord King, as though the slightest deviation from King's text leaves Wesley with no defence of his ordinations whatever apart from the idea of the 'Apostolic Man'; he hasn't looked sufficiently at the form of Wesley's explanation of his action in his Open Letter to the Americans. The reference to Lord King is important, but it is also brief and passing, it is there to protect Wesley from the criticism that he was now setting up as the supreme arbiter in questions of Church Order: King, also, Wesley implied, had had these ideas, before ever Wesley was born. In fact, John Wesley based his case for the American ordinations on a wider ground, from which he could still invoke the help of King and Stillingfleet. He made his position clear in a letter written to one of the itinerants, Barnabas Thomas, in March 1785, in which he said that the Bishop of London had peremptorily refused to do anything about the American Methodists, and that 'all the bishops were of the same mind, the rather because (they said) *they had nothing to do with America*' (italics mine).

This was the core of 'The Letter to the American Brethren', dated 10th September 1784. It contained six points. The first was that independent States now existed in North America. The second referred to his acceptance of Lord King's *Account*, and added significantly that Wesley had not used the authority which he believed a presbyter possessed 'because he was determined as little as possible to violate the established *order* of the National Church to which he belonged'. The third point was the vital one:

But the case is widely different between England and North America. Here there are bishops who have a legal jurisdiction: in America there are none, neither any parish ministers. So that for some hundred miles together there is none either to baptize or to administer the Lord's

26 Ibid. p. 29.

Supper. Here, therefore, my scruples are at an end; and I conceive myself at full liberty, *as I violate no order* and invade no man's *right* by appointing and sending labourers into the harvest [italics mine].

The fourth point described what Wesley had done; the fifth simply said that he had not seen any workable alternative. In the sixth point, however, he turned to the most obvious objection to what he had said, that he should have waited for the English bishops to ordain itinerants for the United States. He deals with this objection much more sweepingly than is often allowed, and by no means only on the practical grounds of delay and episcopal vacillation. At the same time he is expanding the third point:

As our American brethren are now totally disentangled both from the State and from the English hierarchy, we dare not entangle them again either with the one or the other. They are now at full liberty simply to follow the Scriptures and the Primitive Church. And we judge it best that they should stand fast in that liberty wherewith God has so strangely made them free.

Here Wesley quite deliberately disposed of Thompson's chief argument; Lord King's *Account* required that a presbyter have the bishop's permission to ordain. In America there was no bishop's permission to obtain; the English bishops themselves admitted it, insisting that they had no power over the American rebels; as Seabury was to discover, the English bishops had no intention of providing for the oversight of the stranded American Anglicans, let alone the Methodists. And in this Wesley and the English bishops shared a typically eighteenth-century view of the Church of England: they felt, as much as thought, of it as a *National Church*, which could not really be exported from the United Kingdom. It was left for the nineteenth century to invent the 'missionary bishop'.

Thompson's attempt to brush all this aside[27] is unconvincing. 'Our conclusion then is this that King's book does not justify Wesley's consecration of Coke. It is only by taking the case of North America *out of the circumstances of the Primitive Church*, as described by King, and regarding it as one not contemplated by King, for which he makes no provision, that Wesley's action can be understood and approved' (italics mine). It was Wesley's whole contention in 1784 that the American Methodists were 'by a very

[27] *Wesley, Apostolic Man*, p. 30.

uncommon train of providence' in the circumstances of the Primitive Church as described by King (and, of course, by the neglected *Minutes* of 1745), and that they ought to retain the liberty which God had given them. In matters of ecclesiastical order (as of doctrine) this liberty entitled them to go back to the Scriptures and the Primitive Church and construct a Church Order purified from the additions which history had made to the ecclesiastical machines of other countries. Such a view was fully in accordance with the principles of the *Minutes* of 1745. It might be a romantic view of the circumstances of the American Methodists —though it was supported by the concrete situation, in Wesley's opinion—but it was certainly not more romantic than the idea of Wesley as an 'Apostolic Man'. And it fitted neatly into the pattern suggested by King and Stillingfleet, inasmuch as Wesley could plead that he didn't need the permission of any existing bishop, and was bound to act as a matter of 'necessity'.

To sum up:

(1) Despite Thompson's criticisms, Wesley was entitled to use King and Stillingfleet as Anglican authorities in his own defence; they said that in certain circumstances a presbyter might conceivably ordain, and it was an act of his kind which Wesley had to defend.

(2) By his appeal to the allegedly 'primitive' state of the American Methodists Wesley allowed in advance for the criticism that he ought to have waited for the English bishops to act, and for the argument that he was going outside what Peter King permitted.

(3) The appeal to King and Stillingfleet is valueless, however, for the much simpler reason that neither author was ever accepted as an Anglican authority on the issue involved, and it was in the eyes of the Church of England that John Wesley had to justify himself, since this was the Church which he obstinately insisted that he belonged to, and from which he was actually breaking away. The idea of the 'Apostolic Man' is just as irrelevant from the point of view of Anglicanism properly understood. From one point of view it involves a misunderstanding of a metaphorical way of speaking; from another it is a tautology, for it amounts to saying that Wesley ordained because Wesley ordained.

The most important fact about Wesley's ordinations—and this has also commonly been ignored in discussions of the subject—

was that the Conference of 1791 repudiated them: it forbade itinerants whom Wesley had ordained for work in England to ordain itinerants in their turn; this decree deliberately cancelled the possibility of a 'succession' from Wesley himself. In doing this the Wesleyan Conference in effect rejected the picture of Wesley as an 'Apostolic Man'. For what the Conference grasped intuitively was what Wesley himself had set out in 1745, that a new denomination ought not to rest its authority on the acts of an individual, however remarkable. Only the virtually unanimous consensus of a large body of Christians with an already settled tradition could hope to justify the departure which Wesley had wanted to initiate. In England it was not until 1836 that this sense of 'being a part of the one Church' had become so strong that the Wesleyan Conference was prepared to introduce ordination by the laying-on of hands; this, however, was the act of Conference, as representing the whole body of Wesleyan Methodists, not the act of an individual. The same kind of consensus is felt to be necessary in the 1960s, when it is proposed to take the 'historic episcopate' into the modern Methodist system.

Wesley, however, did not mean to act with the touch of finality which characterized the Conference of 1836. He thought that Methodism must continue for the moment, because its continuance was the one guarantee—as he saw it—that the full Christian Gospel would be preached to the Methodist Societies. In another important letter to the preachers in America, written in October 1783, he had said:

Undoubtedly the greatest danger to the work of God in America is likely to arise either from preachers coming from Europe, or from such as will arise among yourselves, speaking perverse things or bringing in among you new doctrines, particularly Calvinism. You should guard against this with all possible care; for it is far easier to keep them out than to thrust them out.[28]

He therefore ordained, not with the idea of giving Wesleyanism a permanent structure, or of creating a permanent new denomination, but of providing the institutional basis from which in the immediate future his successors could guard the doctrinal deposit which he regarded as vital. The emergence of the Oxford Movement in the 1830s would, I fancy, have convinced him that he had

[28] *Letters of John Wesley*, VII.191.

acted rightly, just as it drove his followers farther away from the Church of England than ever before.

(b) This interpretation of Wesley's attitude to ordination has already touched on doctrine. One cannot assess the reasons for the separation accurately if one neglects the doctrinal factors, as is fashionable at the moment. A post-liberal age seems to find it difficult to believe that men could have separated over doctrine at all. Yet some of the coolness towards the *Interim Report on the Conversations between the Methodist and Anglican Churches* arose from this source. When the Rev. Professor C. K. Barrett spoke at the Methodist Conference of 1958 he challenged the section of the *Report* which dealt with doctrine—'Common Ground'—and asked:

Are we agreed upon the authoritative place of Scripture over against tradition, however ancient? Are we agreed upon what happens in the Sacrament of Baptism? Are we agreed upon the meaning of the Lord's Supper? Are we agreed upon the way in which sinful man is laid hold of by divine grace, and himself lays hold upon Christ the Redeemer? Are we agreed upon the relation between the Ministry and the Church? What is the good of agreed doctrinal statements which carefully avoid the really divisive issues?

What Dr Barrett had in mind may also be seen in a paragraph from the *Dissentient View* which was appended to the *Final Report* of the Methodist–Anglican negotiating committee in 1963:

It may be said that it is possible for catholic and protestant (or evangelical) elements to exist side by side in one church; the example of the Church of England is often cited in proof of this. It is indeed true that there are questions of minor importance on which divergent opinions may properly be held in one body, but there are also matters of great moment where divergent opinions can only be a sign of weakness and doctrinal levity. The Methodism we have received from our fathers professes the 'evangelical faith' (Deed of Union, 30), and when it claims its place in the 'Catholic Church' uses the word in the twin senses of universal and authentic. Methodists love their catholic brethren, in the Church of England and elsewhere, but there are vital matters where they are bound to think them in error, and where union will only become possible on the basis of (mutual) reformation. Some of the differences between catholic and protestant represent reconcilable differences of viewpoint; in others, one must be right and the other must be wrong. In these circumstances, to move from a Church committed to the evangelical faith into a heterogenous body permitting, and even encouraging, unevangelical doctrines and practices, would be a step backward which not even the desirability of closer relations would justify . . .[29]

This passage, to which Dr Barrett gave his name inasmuch as he signed the *Dissentient View* from which it comes, has a rather eighteenth-century ring about it. Its argument, moreover, is confused. For example, the terms 'catholic' and 'protestant' are used so as to imply to the casual reader an opposition between Protestant and Roman Catholic; 'protestant' is also equated with 'evangelical' so as to produce a division, allegedly within the Anglican Church, between 'evangelical' and 'catholic'. One might quote Dr Fisher, the former Archbishop of Canterbury, on this analysis: 'The Church of England never was, and certainly is not now, properly to be described as a duality having side by side two distinct groups or parties of equal authority, one "Catholic" and the other "Evangelical" . . .'[30] It is a mistake to equate 'Anglo-Catholic' with 'Roman Catholic', and to narrow the meaning of 'protestant' so that it is the equivalent of 'evangelical'. It is even less fair to treat 'evangelical' as though the term covered both Anglican Evangelicals and Methodists, as though they had in common a doctrinal system which neither shared with the Anglo-Catholic. Indeed, the whole weight of the passage is not so much a criticism of the *Majority Report* proposals for union between the two Churches as a protest against the very existence of the Church of England, since it already unites 'Evangelicals' and 'Anglo-Catholics'—'a step backward which not even the desirability of closer relations would justify'. In effect this becomes a protest against the existence of Methodism as well (despite the confident reference to the Fathers), for the Dissentients would have to admit that there are many Methodists who feel more at home in the parish churches of the 'catholics' than they do in the churches of the extremer 'evangelicals'. One cannot really compare a 'Church committed to the evangelical faith' with a 'heterogeneous body' and seriously expect to be understood as comparing the existential realities of Methodism and Anglicanism; the day is over when one could usefully compare and define denominations in

[29] *The Dissentient View*, p. 62.
[30] *The Anglican–Methodist Conversations and Church Unity*, by Lord Fisher of Lambeth (London, 1964), p. 36.

such hard-and-fast dogmatic terms as are assumed in such a use of the words 'catholic' and 'protestant': the significant divisions of the Church run through the existing frontiers of the 'churches'. The Dissentients had the misfortune to write when Pope John XXIII had already shown that one ought not to dismiss 'catholicity' with quite such old-fashioned scorn.

Even in the eighteenth century not everyone was as rigid as the Dissentients: it was felt either that the Thirty-nine Articles ought not to exist—the position at bottom of the clergy of the Enlightenment who were anxious, until the Jacobins made them nervous, for some relief from the milder terrors of clerical subscription; or that there existed one truly Anglican interpretation of the Articles, the monopoly of either the High Church or the Evangelical clergy. John Wesley's own views cut across the fixed lines of these groups, and it is important here not to be misled by H. B. Workman's well-known essay on *The Place of Methodism in the Catholic Church*. As I have pointed out, Workman was mistaken in his assertion that the distinctive Wesleyan doctrine was that of assurance. Workman was following a weak nineteenth-century tradition which had largely abandoned the effort to realize Wesley's infinitely flexible and social idea of holiness. Holiness was the truly Wesleyan emphasis, and it was on this rock that the various attempts to unite Wesleyans and Anglicans came to grief. Both groups accepted a Pietist (not Puritan) belief that in order to become fully Christian one must live among a specific (small) group of people with a particular ethos, but differed strongly as to what ethos was desirable. An excellent example of the stress which Wesley put on doctrine in general, on holiness itself, on the importance of the Christian community, and on not spending too much time among the Evangelicals, may be found in a letter which he wrote to John Fletcher, the man whom he would have liked to succeed him if only Fletcher had not died. The letter was written in March 1768, before Fletcher had decided to join Wesley—

Dear Sir—Yesterday Mr Easterbrook informed me that you are sick of the conversation even of those who profess religion, 'that you find it quite unprofitable if not hurtful to converse with them three or four hours together, and are sometimes almost determined to shut yourself up as the less evil of the two'.

I do not understand it at all, especially considering with whom you have chiefly conversed for some time past—namely the hearers of Mr

Madan and Mr Romaine (perhaps I might add that of Mr Whitefield). The conversing with these I have rarely found to be profitable to my soul. Rather it has damped my desires, it has cooled my resolutions, and I have commonly left them with a dry, dissipated spirit.

And how can we expect it to be otherwise?—For do we not naturally catch their spirit with whom we converse? and what spirit can we expect them to be of, considering the preaching they sit under? Some happy exceptions I allow; but, in general, do we gather grapes of thorns? Do they gather constant, universal self-denial, the patience of hope, the labour of love, inward and outward self-devotion, from the doctrine of Absolute Decrees, of Irresistible Grace, of Infallible Perseverance? Do they gather less fruits from Antinomian doctrine? Or from any that borders upon it? Do they gather them from that *amorous* way of praying to Christ or that way of preaching His righteousness? I have never found it so. On the contrary, I have found that even the precious doctrine of the Salvation by Faith has need to be guarded with utmost care, or those who hear it will slight both inward and outward holiness. I will go a step farther: I seldom find it profitable for *me* to converse with any who are not athirst for perfection and who are not big with earnest expectation of receiving it every moment. Now, you find none of these among those we are speaking of, but many, on the contrary, who are in various ways directly or indirectly opposing the whole work of God. . . .

After a sidestroke at 'genteel Methodists', who are little better, Wesley recommends Fletcher to

persons clear of both Calvinism and Antinomianism, not fond of the lucious way of talking, but standing in awe of Him they love—persons who are vigorously working out their salvation, persons athirst for full redemption, and every moment expecting, if not already enjoying it. Though it is true these will commonly be poor and mean. . . .[31]

Of course there were Evangelical answers to all this, and one section of Henry Venn's far from *Complete Duty of Man* was a vigorous attack on 'the conceit of personal perfection',[32] The popular mythology about the eighteenth century says the Wesleyans and Evangelicals began the period as enemies because of the breach between George Whitefield and John Wesley, but closed it as a happy band of reconciled old men. Dr Walsh has shown, I think, how irrelevant this picture is. In fact, the hostility of Evangelical parish priests towards local Wesleyan Societies increased sharply in the last quarter of the century, especially after

[31] *Letters of John Wesley*, V.84.   [32] Chapter 13, § 5.

the outbreak of the Revolutionary Wars. I myself would be prepared to suggest that this Evangelical hostility was quite as much a cause of the final separation of the Wesleyans from the Church of England as the indifference of the bishops. To a historian this serves as a reminder of the complicated nature of the origins of Wesleyanism: one can move too easily from a simplification of the past to a simplification of the present. It seems to me meaningless to talk about the sin of division at this point. After all, the Lambeth Conference of 1958 felt itself obliged to accept a resolution which almost certainly meant that a new independent Anglican diocese would be set up at Nandyal within the borders of the Church of South India, in order to provide for the pastoral care of those Anglicans who felt unable to join the CSI. The separation arose on doctrinal grounds, the institutional step followed. The parallel is obvious, but in this case the use of the historic episcopate concealed the nature of the departure to some extent.

(c) This brings us to the final point: the biggest single cause of the schism was the religious pattern of the Wesleyan Societies. In the eighteenth century the societary nature of Wesleyanism made the split inevitable. If one takes a strictly institutional view of the local Wesleyan Society, if one envisages it as an item of evangelical technique, or if one sees the class-meeting as a method of penetrating the world outside the ecclesia, one makes a crucial error. The Society and the class-meeting were evidence of a movement already in existence, not of a movement in search of existence. Wesley established them as little pockets of people he could mould and direct into the pursuit of the gift of holiness. He did not form the Societies as the ground-plan of a new denomination; even at the time of his death Wesleyanism remained a connected group of Societies, not a loose union of independent 'churches'. The distinction is vital because it meant that Wesleyanism was as unlike Dissent as it was unlike the Church of England. This sense of unity, of 'connexion' as the early Methodists called it, was foreign to eighteenth-century Anglican ideas of the ecclesia, which were dominated by the congregationalism in the parish system and the lay patron.

The tendency of Anglicanism to disintegrate into its constituent parishes is important: disintegration at this level was one cause of the Civil War in the seventeenth century. In the eighteenth century the problem of the proper oversight of the parish priests was one of the causes of Methodism, for the revival was in part a sharp protest against the flabby spiritual state of many Anglican parishes —itself the result of a partial breakdown of the episcopal oversight of the Ministry. In the nineteenth century the story of Anglo-Catholicism was of a running fight between parish priests and bishops which ended in the twentieth century when the bishops fell quietly into step with the more moderate of the rebels. It is not necessarily a mistake to make unity depend upon a single, central person like a bishop, but the kind of unity which results may be rather thin, especially when the Christians are in the minority but lack the advantage of being, as Indian Christians are, forced together by the pressure of other more or less hostile religious communities. It is difficult to take entirely seriously the way in which men believe that they can be the Father in God of thousands of laymen and hundreds of ministers. Thring, the Victorian headmaster who created Uppingham, thought that no school should be so big that the headmaster did not know each boy personally; otherwise he could not perform what Thring really thought was his chief function, that of protecting the boys against the masters. His ideal figure was about four hundred boys.

What this means in England may be seen by looking for a moment at the example of what the Church of England does about the admission of divorced persons to Holy Communion. For the ideal version of what happens I quote from a former Archbishop of Canterbury, Dr Fisher:

The Church of England, while observing a clear rule that no divorced person shall be married in Church (thus upholding the evangelical principle), feels that it has a pastoral duty to those who have been divorced and marry again. If a priest or other responsible person thinks that there is a spiritual need for such a person to be admitted to Communion or prepared for Confirmation, he refers the case to the bishop. The bishop in the exercise of his pastoral discretion is free to authorize readmission or preparation for Confirmation. He may use his discretion imperfectly, but he has been given freedom by the Church to use it, and seeks to use his discretion by the grace of God.[33]

How the system works it is not for me to say, but how it may look

[33] Fisher, *The Anglo–Methodist Conversations and Church Unity*, pp. 39–40.

to an Anglican layman we can see by referring to Professor D. M. Mackinnon's essay in *Objections to Christian Belief*:

It can hardly be denied that a widespread obsessional preoccupation with the alleged great evil of the remarriage of divorced persons creates the impression that the core and centre of Christian moral teaching is a particular interpretation of the indissolubility of marriage; on this view it is taken as putting an appalling stigma on these second unions, of which we have all met examples, and know to have been more abundantly justified by their fruits than the frequently tragic human distress they replaced. It is impossible to escape the impression, that to certain sorts of clergy, the effective exclusion from sacramental communion of divorced persons who have remarried is the highest form of the Church's moral witness. The cynic might well be tempted to say that the heartless zeal frequently displayed in the bearing of this particular testimony, is a way in which ecclesiastics compensate for their unwillingness to engage with other besetting moral issues of our age.[34]

If Professor Mackinnon is right, his words make a serious criticism of the former Archbishop's ideal picture of the bishop in action. Nor is he without some wider support. In 1946 the American Episcopal Church passed three canons which had the effect of bringing within the scope of nullity as many marriages as possible which have been civilly dissolved, so that remarriage may take place with the blessing of the Church. The American bishops have to decide on how a particular case should be settled; but each bishop is provided with a panel of advisers which significantly, and rightly, includes a physician, a psychiatrist, and a lawyer, in effect, three laymen trained in the subject with which they are dealing. The appointment of such a panel compares favourably with Dr Fisher's rather naïve view of a bishop 'who may use his discretion imperfectly' but who tries to use it 'by the grace of God'. Whether Christ ever intended His Church to manipulate the Communion Service as a means of punishment; whether even the American tribunal—for such it really is—is anything more than a monstrous invasion of human privacy; whether the laity of the churches have not been right, in Roman Catholic as well as Protestant countries, to insist that the alternative of civil marriage was opened to them—these are different questions altogether.

This kind of criticism of what one may call the institutional

[34] Page 14.

ineffectiveness of episcopacy is naturally shared by some Presbyterians. The Rev. A. C. Neil of Didsbury, Manchester, suggested in *The Manchester Guardian* that

an adult Church should not need a hierarchy, and it is questionable whether, with episcopacy, the Church is free to realize its potentialities as 'the body of Christ'. . . . We ask whether a Church, which reserves substantial areas of authority to a higher order of priests deriving their standing in a special way from the Apostles can ever give to the laity the place which is their due. There is a stage in a Church's life when direction from above is helpful. It was so in the early centuries and it may well be so in India now. But the day arrives when it will stifle the life of a maturing Church.

At the institutional level this seems to me very important. The protagonists of an extended episcopate present the case for the bishop as—ideally—a humble man of God, the father of Christ's flock, the *pastor pastorum* who builds up the life of the Churches, maintains faith and order, and represents the unity and universality of the Church.[35] The ideal is generous, but does it add up to more than a man of many committees? On the small scale of the primitive ecclesia such a concentration of responsibility may have been natural, but is it so under modern conditions in the West? May not the logical conclusion of the position be that of the Roman Catholic Church, in which the local bishops have in effect handed all final responsibility for such matters over to the single Bishop of Rome? What perhaps ought to be distinguished here are the two ideas of *episkope* and episcopacy in its modern form. That both the New Testament and the Primitive Church attach great value to *episkope*—the oversight of the Ministry and laity—can hardly be questioned. There is no primitive warrant (if that is the final authority) for an ecclesia of autonomous individuals, settling every problem for themselves by an appeal to the allegedly Reformation principle of the right of private judgement (which seems to be much more a principle of the Enlightenment). On the other hand, nothing in the early records seems to make it imperative that this *episkope* should always be discharged by a single individual: the root principle seems to be that *episkope* is of the esse of the ecclesia, but not necessarily in the modern form of diocesan episcopacy. For in practice the modern bishop is father of Christ's flock only in the most general sense, for the presbyters carry out

[35] Cf. The *Interim Report*, p. 36

the chief burden of the oversight; he does not maintain faith and order except in the same general way, for in the long run this is the responsibility of the occasional theologian of genius; he does not, more than others, among them many faithful laymen, build up the life of the Churches; he can only represent the unity of the Churches in so far as that unity exists, and we should hardly be negotiating if it did: a division of *episkope* is inherent in the situation, and if the idea which most easily attaches to the bishop is that of a *pastor pastorum* it may be that with reasonably sized dioceses this is the natural function for the bishop to perform. Any attempt, however, to draw all the offices of the ecclesia into the office of the bishop in order to justify the more general adoption of episcopacy in its present form seems forced and unconvincing.

With all this in mind let us for a moment return to the eighteenth century and complete the exposition of why separation was inevitable. Wesleyanism was at first an organized laity in which the *episkope* was shared out among the members of the body. Everything, from the job of looking after the money to the work of preaching the Gospel, was done by men and women who thought of themselves as lay people, and if *episkope* means oversight of the whole body in the interests of doctrinal fidelity and moral discipline then Wesleyanism was episcopal through and through, for a carefully graded oversight ran through the whole Connexion from the Great Superintendent Mr Wesley down by way of the itinerants and class leaders to the stewards, local preachers, and ordinary members. This oversight was lay, in a world when men sang, prayed, recounted their spiritual experience, and sometimes endured persecution, *together*. Moreover, Wesley made more use of women than was common in other religious bodies of the period; one has only to read his correspondence to realize how much he trusted women with the spiritual direction of their sex, and in his later years he permitted a few women to preach. (He did not employ them as itinerants, this development took place among the Bible Christians and the Primitive Methodists.) The ethos of early Methodism was societary—everyone sharing in all the exercises of religion, not in the style of a sect but in the atmosphere of a society, in a deliberate effort to realize something of the fullness of the Body of Christ. It is perhaps an offshoot of their concern with justifying the stress laid upon diocesan episcopacy that Anglican writers, also influenced by Anglo-Catholicism, should so often seem so obsessed with the importance of frequent communion that they all admit no other evidence for the presence of what the New Testament calls *koinonia*, the fellowship of believers in the Holy Spirit. But something must be granted to the style of a century: in an age as lacking in sympathy for elaborate liturgical worship as was the eighteenth century it is perhaps too readily assumed that Christianity did not exist if it did not exist eucharistically.[36] In fact, Wesleyanism was filled with a need to express the sense of fellowship in the Holy Spirit and did so through new, unexpected channels. No one would suggest that the Enlightenment so dominated the period that only one attitude to life was possible; in the same way it would be a mistake to assume that the only possible alternative to Latitudinarianism was Ritualism.

If one compares the Wesleyan Society with the Anglican parish the causes of separation become obvious. Eighteenth-century Anglicans had inherited a liturgical conception of corporate worship rigidly defined by the Book of Common Prayer. The Evangelical parish priest did his best to convert his parish, but when his converts sought a means of religious self-expression he was bound to offer them what to him was the normative pattern, attendance at Matins and Evensong, and at the perhaps monthly Lord's Supper, together with the use domestically of such a book as Venn's *Complete Duty of Man*, designed by its author to drive out of the parish the *Whole Duty of Man* and unfortunately successful. (The writers

---

[36] Both J. C. Bowmer (*The Sacrament of the Lord's Supper in Early Methodism* [London, 1951]) and J. R. Parris (*John Wesley's Doctrine of the Sacraments* [London. 1963]) repeat the idea that the early Methodists 'were urged to attend the Church and communicate as often as possible, even when the local minister was hostile to them' (Parris, op. cit. p. 63). This is often misunderstood by those who don't realize that the typical village parish church of the eighteenth century had very few celebrations of the Eucharist, quite often as few as three or four per annum. If the typical country Methodist in the eighteenth century had communicated regularly at his local parish church he would have received communion less often than his twentieth-century counterpart who attends the service once a month in a Methodist chapel. Of course John Wesley celebrated more frequently than this; for one thing he was obliged to provide for the Methodists (as he went round the country) for whom the local parish church was not providing. I don't mean that Wesley did not value the Eucharist; but one must not assume that the religious experience of the eighteenth-century Methodist, even when he remained a loyal Anglican, included what would now be recognized as frequent communion.

of modern text-books who slavishly repeat the traditional Venn-derived criticism of the seventeenth-century book have clearly never read it.) But the Evangelical disapproved of the Wesleyan love-feasts, class-meetings, band-meetings, watch-nights, and so forth, in which laymen did most, if not all, of the talking. In a world where the parson always prayed from the book how could a layman possibly pray publicly at all? It was not really part of the Evangelical experience—as the parson understood it—that he should want to. And so in a very real way the feelings of becoming part of a religious community was missing in the make-up of the typical Anglican of this school. For some individuals this became what Dr Walsh neatly called 'the problem of the eloquent convert' for whom the only solution was to become a clergyman if he could, and an independent pastor if he could not. To the eighteenth-century Evangelical the layman's part in religion was essentially passive—in the awakened parish he might look up in the assurance that he would be fed. One of the reasons why the Irish revival of 1859 failed to spread to England (despite some modern propaganda to the contrary) was the suspicion with which traditional Evangelical parsons still looked at laymen who combined secular employment with a personal call to evangelism.

Of course there lay behind all this horrified memories of what claims to direct inspiration had done among the seventeenth-century Nonconformists, but I am not considering why parish priests held these views, only the fact that they held them. In this specific historical setting it was not in fact the least likely that Wesleyanisms would remain within the margins of the Church of England. The problem was far more than one of episcopal ordination, whatever Samuel Walker of Truro might have thought. (The point usually forgotten about Walker's defence of the parish system was that after his death his Anglican followers seceded and founded the Truro Congregational Church: his successor was not an Evangelical.) It was not just the itinerants who had to be grafted into the Establishment: for this alone, episcopal action might have sufficed. But Wesleyanism as a whole would have had to be reconciled with Anglicanism, the horizontal with the vertical, and in this specific historical situation, Wesley being dead, the historic episcopate, for all its claims to represent unity, proved no help.

A further point must be made here about the itinerants themselves. The growth of the itinerancy produced a small group of men who valued one another highly but who quickly resented any claims to superiority among the brethren. The Wesleyan Ministry was to retain, and share with the Ministries of the other branches of Methodism, a profound dislike of any scheme which suggested that there was more than one order of Ministry—and that order the extraordinary, missionary, mobile, poor, largely self-educated Ministry created by John Wesley under God.

At first sight, then, one's conclusions would seem to be that the reasons which led to the separation of the Methodists from the Church of England in the eighteenth century throw little or no light on our twentieth-century problems. The *Majority Report* did not, after all, propose the reunification of eighteenth-century Methodism and eighteenth-century Anglicanism. It proposed the gradual association of two laities—and of two Ministries for that matter, but they are not so important—both of them radically different from what they were in the eighteenth century. Methodists and Anglicans in the twentieth century are living in a new situation, in which they have the freedom to choose without regarding too closely their denominational past.

This is true, at any rate, at the theological level, but when one turns to the institutional issues which are raised by the idea of organic union between the Methodist and Anglican Churches one finds eighteenth-century habits of thought reasserting themselves stubbornly, not least on the Anglican side. The two instances will suffice, the parish system and the Church establishment.

I have already mentioned the reaction of the 'more extreme' Evangelicals to the *Majority Report*. One of the contributors to the Evangelical symposium, C. O. Buchanan, tried to describe the kind of organic unity which he would be able to accept, and wrote:

Surely the only end worth seeking is that of a wholly parochial system on the present Anglican pattern: one church to each parish and a parish to each church.[37]

And in an earlier essay in the same book G. E. Duffield said that 'now the Anglican clergy were no longer hostile to Methodist "enthusiasm" the conflict over the parish system is largely a thing of the past'.[38] Neither writer seemed aware that the parochial

[37] *The Church of England and the Methodist Church*, ed. J. I. Packer, 1963, p. 56.   [38] Ibid. p. 54.

system has been under heavy Anglican criticism for many years; or that the Methodist circuit-system amounted to rather more than a device for coping with hostile parish priests. For an Anglican comment on this Anglican attitude to the parishes one has only to turn to Leslie Paul, who has made two major points about them. First, that 'the greater the density of the population the more areas become mission areas against the problems of which the traditional parochial forms appear largely ineffective'.[39] The second, that 'the ancient parochial system, historically justified when the parish priest was the spiritual member of both the local and national establishments, no longer protects and shows forth the *persona*, but maroons him socially and spiritually'.[40] I cannot help suspecting that the kind of isolation to which Paul refers rather attracts the kind of man who often prefers the Evangelical interpretation of Anglicanism; in any case, this deeply sincere attachment to the most characteristic of all Anglican institutions reminds one immediately of the eighteenth-century Evangelical, who defended the system with equal passion against John Wesley's often bitter criticism. The clash then took the form of conflict between a highly pragmatic view of the Wesley Societies and a virtually congregational conception of the Church of England—only it was parochial rather than strictly congregational and it was the parson who enjoyed the Independency rather than the parishioners. It is a matter of historical fact that the parochial system proved ill-adapted to the initial strains which the Industrial Revolution put on English society in the eighteenth century and early nineteenth century; nothing in Leslie Paul's *Report* suggests that the present parochial system is better adapted to the strains of an even more mobile twentieth-century society.

My second example of the survival of eighteenth-century habits of mind is the question of Establishment. Here, Dr Fisher's little book, *The Anglican–Methodist Conversations and Problems of Church Unity* (1964), makes an excellent example. Dr Fisher's purpose in writing was to protest against any scheme for organic unity between the Methodist and Anglican Churches in the foreseeable future. Intercommunion, he felt, was enough for the time being; for the next generation at any rate conversations might proceed with the other Churches in England—and he mentioned the

[39] L. Paul, *The Deployment and Payment of the Clergy*, p. 137.
[40] Ibid. p. 138.

Orthodox and Roman Churches as well as the Protestant Free Churches. The concluding pages of his book made clear that the former Archbishop thought that the Church of England was paying too high a price for what he regarded as the 'absorption' of Methodism: he protested with obviously passionate sincerity against the dark hints of the *Majority Report* that the present system of Church Establishment in England would have to undergo a radical overhaul, perhaps even be abolished altogether, in Stage Two, the process of organic integration. In a mood more reminiscent of the eighteenth century than he perhaps recognized Dr Fisher pressed his case:

The Church of England has been in partnership with the Crown and later with Parliament from the very beginning of England's national history. Every partnership has its periods of strain and stress. The Church of England could not have gained its freedom at the Reformation without the co-operation of Crown and Parliament. Both Church and nation have belonged to each other through fair weather and foul. The partnership, however unsatisfactory, has never been intolerable: and recent years have shown that it is flexible and is still able to contribute something Christian to the well-being of the nation. . . . It seems a pity, just at this time when stability in tried values is of great importance for the nation, for the Church of England to seek to run away from the duties and responsibilities which fall upon it as the Established Church. It should be anxious to serve until the nation wishes to discharge it from its national service.[41]

Such language drives Methodists back to their origins in an eighteenth-century world in which Anglican bishops were more concerned about maintaining good relations with the Hanoverian State than they were about keeping the Methodist Societies inside the Church of England—or, for that matter, about providing episcopal oversight for Anglicans stranded in the United States after the War of Independence. The past seems repeated in Dr Fisher's words; one feels a rejection of Methodism as irrelevant to the ecclesiastical problems of the day: 'The absorption of Methodism by the Church of England would benefit nobody.' One concludes that the former Archbishop regards the preservation of the Establishment as a more fundamental objective than unity between the Methodist and Anglican Churches.

Considerations like these form a more formidable barrier to

[41] Fisher, op. cit. p. 43.

organic unity than the question of episcopacy. The Methodist recognizes the values for which in general Anglican episcopacy stands. He agrees that doctrine should be safeguarded against the constant tendency to whittle it away; he agrees that obedience is a Christian virtue, that both the laity and the Ministry should be subject to discipline; he agrees that confirmation should be a solemn act (the word 'confirmation' is now used in Methodism)—though in this instance he is probably very sceptical of the diocesan claim to monopolize its administration; he agrees that the pages of history ought to show the Ministry continuously proclaiming the same message of salvation: though here again he is probably sceptical of any assertion that bishops have been uncommonly successful in guaranteeing such an unbroken succession of witnesses. It is true that the Methodist also suspects that the Anglican shares with the Roman Catholic the illusion that authority is easily come by; for himself, he might go no farther than the fact that the existing Churches are conscious of their need for authority and grope after it, sometimes accepting false authority as absolute, never able to identify a form of authority which cannot be disputed by others.

Nevertheless, through a medium like the Service of Reconciliation of the *Majority Report*, which does not require him to reject his own interpretation of the Ministry or formally to accept someone else's interpretation of the Ministry, the Methodist can accept episcopacy: he has, from his own point of view, always had it. The parish as an Ideal and the Establishment as an Absolute are no more sympathetic than they were in the eighteenth century. Fortunately, there is plenty of indication that both ideas have lost their glamour for many Anglicans also. The local church is not likely to be the chief unit of Christian advance in the next hundred years; Establishment is going to look more and more peculiar as the secularization of society progresses. One wonders whether, just as the royal broadcast on Christmas Day is slipping into obscurity so the great television broadcast of the Coronation of Queen Elizabeth II may not have been the last occasion when the nation showed any marked interest in the links between Church and State? By a strange chain of Providences Anglicanism and Methodism are being set free to choose their future: this is the kind of freedom which living institutions rarely know throughout their history, and we ought not to throw it away through looking too deeply into the past.

SEVEN

Federation or Union?

IN HIS BOOK, *Church or No Church?*, Reginald Kissack has offered us far the best presentation so far of the only positive alternative to the plan for organic union of the Anglican and Methodist Churches on the basis of episcopacy. This alternative would take the form of some kind of federal union of the British Churches: out of a federal dialogue of Churches a deeper and more perfect form of unity might emerge than could ever result from the more political kind of marriage which is envisaged (as he understands it) in the present negotiations. In practice, his policy would mean that the British Churches would continue to negotiate in the hope, on the Methodist side, that the intransigent episcopalianism of the Church of England would weaken with the passing of time. Mr Kissack also argues that his federal view of Church unity is in accordance with the development of Methodist tradition. Why does one nevertheless reject what is at first sight a very strong case, one which appeals to one's sense of the Methodist past? How can I, as a good Methodist, defend the achievement of Church unity on the basis of episcopacy?

I would say, first of all, that in taking episcopacy into its system Methodism would be accepting very much less than Mr Kissack believes. Anglican theories about episcopacy are not as clearly defined (or as authoritative) as he imagines, they are more in a state of flux, and are certainly not unchangeable to all eternity. (The danger of assuming that Churches can *never* change, that we know not only what they think now but what they always will think, is illustrated by the slow but definite abandonment by the Church of Rome of its total opposition to birth control. No Church is as absolute, no episcopate is as powerful, as we sometimes fear.) Nor does Mr Kissack seem to me to put the situation quite accurately when he says, towards the end of his argument, 'What will be the effect on the Ecumenical Movement as a whole if the Methodist Church accepts the Anglican conditions, and assumes the historic episcopate and alien ideas of priesthood?' Here Mr Kissack is taking it for granted that what is going to happen is, to use his own words, that a church of the left, such as the Methodist Church, would be accepting 'what is in essence the position of the right for the sake of unity'. Obviously, a wholesale surrender of that kind would strike at the basis of the Ecumenical Movement, because such a surrender would be insincere. Those of us who favour the *Majority Report* and are prepared to present ourselves for the Service of Reconciliation do *not* regard episcopacy as essential to the existence of the Church. We do *not* hold Anglo-Catholic ideas of the priesthood, we do *not* have doubts about the ministerial existence of the Congregationalist pastor across the street. But we also deny that the acceptance of episcopacy *now* means that the new united 'Anglican-Methodist Church' would be bound to have bishops for ever and ever; or that all 'Anglican-Methodist' ministers would be obliged to adopt Anglo-Catholic opinions; or that 'Anglican-Methodists' would have to remain sadly for ever out of communion with their Congregationalist neighbours across the road. We intend to take very seriously the condition which the Methodist Conference has laid down and from which it has never budged, that we must be allowed as much freedom in our interpretation of episcopacy as exists, and always has existed, in the Church of England. A federal theory of Church union would limit us to an outsider's criticism of Anglican episcopacy; it would be more profitable to attempt to reform the Church of England from inside, in concert with the powerful Anglican forces which have struggled for years to alter its structure, and to whose efforts is attributable the publication of the Paul *Report*.

My chief hesitation about the argument of *Church or No Church?*, however, arises from Mr Kissack's presentation of his federal theory as one which is closely in line with the development of the Methodist doctrine of the Church. The Methodist doctrine of the Church has developed by the assimilation, at times almost entirely unconscious, of other people's ideas, rather than by deliberate intellectual construction. It has reflected surrounding history, its centre of explanation has always lain in the present rather than in the past, or in any tradition of the past. It is therefore very difficult to say that there *is* a *Methodist* doctrine of the Church, or a Methodist doctrinal tradition about it. Mr Kissack recognizes this himself when he points out that nineteenth-century Wesleyan writers like Alfred Barrett or Benjamin Gregory would certainly have disagreed with the doctrine of the Ministry and Sacraments which is to be found in the foundation documents of the present Methodist Church. 'One looks in vain', he says of the Deed of Union, 'for that high concept of the Pastoral Office elaborated by Bunting, Barrett and Rigg. Indeed, one reads instead an extended declaration of principles to which they offered stolid resistance.' In the same way he has to admit that the statement on *The Nature of the Christian Church According to the Teaching of the Methodists* (1937) simply rejects the nineteenth-century Wesleyan Methodist idea of the ministry out of hand. I think that Mr Kissack is quite right in these judgements (although I suspect that Dr Newton Flew, the main author of the 1937 statement, did not intend to go so far). But if Mr Kissack is right in pointing to a breach of continuity in the Methodist tradition this must make it difficult for him to present his federal theory of Church unity as in line with the whole of Methodist tradition as such. In fact, as I shall hope to show, his federal theory is itself a by-product of a late-nineteenth-century abandonment of the Wesleyan Methodist understanding of the doctrine of the Church, and the substitution for it of ideas rashly borrowed from the other Free Churches, ideas which have failed to stand the test of time and experience. A sketch of the historical process involved would seem to be in order.

One cannot quite say at what point after the death of John Wesley the Wesleyan Methodist itinerants first became certain that they were full ministers in the Church of Christ. The process had certainly completed itself by the time that ordination by the laying of hands was introduced by the Conference of 1836. Throughout that period, and down into the 1870s, Wesleyan Methodism was governed in accordance with the constitution which it had inherited from John Wesley, and which Wesley had based on the largely unconscious assumption that his itinerants had achieved full ministerial status. In this constitution, Wesley gave the itinerants all the powers which he thought that a true minister should possess. A purely ministerial Conference had absolute legislative authority over the Connexion, even in financial matters. The local superintendent had a similar kind of absolute authority over the spiritual welfare of the laity. Superficially, this authority was based on the theory that if a minister had to answer to God for the souls committed to his charge he must have power to control their spiritual development. In fact, however, the underlying origin of this high doctrine of the ministry was the constitution of the Church of

England as John Wesley understood it, a constitution in which the parish priest enjoyed almost complete independence, and in which not even Convocation, let alone a body in which the laity were properly represented, ever met to criticize, still less control, the policy or the behaviour of the bishops. At the local level, the parish priest was the Church; at the national level, the Bishop was the Church: Wesley approximated the institutions of his societies as far as was possible to what he believed Anglicanism to be. Neither he nor Jabez Bunting gave the Wesleyan superintendent any more authority than they understood the Anglican parson to possess, and they specifically rejected, time and time again, the Free Church or Dissenting theory that authority in the Church comes from the whole body of believers, including the Ministry, and that the minister is therefore the agent of this common mind, if it can be established, the representative of this common body.

Such was the Wesleyan Methodist tradition, which collapsed in the later nineteenth century. It collapsed for two main reasons. On the one hand, the Wesleyan laity would not remain content with permanent exclusion from Church government. It is instructive to notice that there took place a similar movement of a quasi-democratic kind in the Church of England in the same period, 1850–1919. The creation of the Church Assembly after the first World War was a belated Anglican recognition of the place of the layman in the Church. Unfortunately, this recognition was half-hearted: Convocation, which has no lay element, was not abolished.

In the second place, Wesleyan Methodism was deeply affected by the appearance in the Church of England of a new theory of the Ministry, or the reappearance of an old, but greatly invigorated, view. The rise of Anglo-Catholicism demolished the easy relationship between the Wesleyan and Anglican traditions; the effect can still be seen in Mr Kissack's book, in which Anglicanism is almost always described through Anglo-Catholic eyes. The early Tractarians denounced Wesleyan Methodist ministerial orders, and so the theory that the Wesleyan doctrine of the Ministry was only an indirect way of stating the Anglican doctrine ran into trouble. (Wesley himself had rejected what he called the 'divine right of episcopacy' at least as far back as the Minutes of the Conference of 1747, when he said that if this plan was essential to the Church then all the foreign Reformed Churches would not be parts of the Church of Christ, a consequence, as he said with his uncommon directness, full of shocking absurdity. It is important to realize, however, that when he said this Wesley was speaking in line with *Anglican* tradition himself, he was not just falling back on Nonconformist opinions picked up from his ancestors. Point had been given to the tradition in which he spoke in the earlier years of the century, when there were present in England large numbers of French Protestant pastors driven into exile by the Revocation of the Edict of Nantes: if these men were not only to be persecuted by Louis XIV but also unchurched by Anglican theory then indeed of all men their lot was the most miserable.)

As the nineteenth century developed the Wesleyan Methodist ministry inevitably had to re-define its position. And so one finds James Rigg, that very representative Wesleyan, publishing in 1866 an essay in which he sought to make clear what Wesleyan Methodists were thinking about the Church of England and the Free Churches. Rigg wanted to destroy the impression, always common in the Church of England, that the Wesleyan Methodists were only waiting for the chance to rejoin the Established Church. He therefore denied the statement, often made by Anglican ministers, that the separation of the Wesleyan Societies from the Church of England was a violation of the original principles of Methodism itself, and a repudiation of what Wesley wanted. Wesley in his later years, Rigg said, had watched events moving towards a separation without doing anything material to prevent it; most of his ecclesiastical actions, including his ordinations, had actually speeded the process. The effects of Wesley's personal Anglicanism were dying away; times had changed since the 1830s.

There may be yet some ministers [he said], chiefly if not exclusively, among the seniors of the Conference, who retain towards the Established Church much of that filial instinct of admiration and reverence which John Wesley cherished until his dying day . . . There have been Wesleyan ministers, I am not sure but that there are still a few such, who have felt such a reverence for the formularies of the Church of England that they would be more unwilling to consent to any change in them whatever than almost any Churchman of enlarged and moderately liberal views. . . .

Once he had made the point, however, that Anglicans must not think that they still had some kind of historical claim on the Wesleyan Methodists, that they could not afford to treat them as though they were a sort of lapsed Anglican, Rigg was even more

o

anxious to dissociate himself from the consequences which might seem to follow from what he had maintained. In the struggle which was going on in the 1860s between Dissent and the Church of England the Wesleyan Methodists had followed a policy of virtual neutrality, and Rigg now tried to clarify the position.

The Wesleyan Methodists dissent [he said], at least most of them do, from the discipline and dominant power of the Church of England. They dissent, also, utterly, from High Church doctrine. But *Dissent is no part of their ecclesiastical creed. They are not educated in it as a principle.* They would like to mend the Church of England, if they saw clearly how. . . . But until they see clearly what is to be done for its amendment they are generally content to sit still and say very little. . . . They cannot see that it is a law of nature, or of morals, or of the Gospel, that all Church endowments are necessarily unlawful. And they find it difficult to distinguish between the endowments of dissenting chapels and a considerable proportion, at least, of the endowment of the Church of England. They have a sort of obscure idea that the best thing would be to remove from the constitution and administration of the Church of England whatever is unjust in itself, or inconsistent with the spiritual freedom and efficiency of the Church; that if this could be done, and the Church as a whole could be brought to work manifestly well as a Christian and a national institution, the abstract question of endowments would be hardly worth discussing.

And he concluded his argument by saying that 'we are as independent of the Church of England as those who call themselves Dissenters, or as we are from the Dissenters themselves. We have been smitten on the cheeks by both parties . . .'.

The problem which Rigg's generation encountered, however, was how to define this middle area which, as they said, Wesleyan Methodism occupied. They were agreed in rejecting Anglo-Catholic doctrine, but what they needed was a positive Wesleyan doctrine of the Church, Ministry, and Sacraments. On the one hand, the rise of Anglo-Catholicism obscured the Anglican sources on which they had been accustomed to draw; on the other, the rapid success, in the 1870s, of the drive to obtain lay representation in the Wesleyan Methodist Conference helped to cut them off from their Wesleyan sources as well. A flirtation with the New Testament followed, as Mr Kissack illustrates in his account of Benjamin Gregory, but the attempt to erect a church order on the basis of the New Testament references to the subject can never be satisfactory; the material is so small, and has already been interpreted in so many different ways that one is conscious all the time of the stock answers to the positions one is laying down.

Between about 1880 and 1914, therefore, Wesleyan Methodist writers on the doctrine of the Church did two things. They wrote refutations of the Anglo-Catholic position, defences of their own ministerial existence. They also experimented—and this meant a complete break with the Wesleyan tradition as it had descended through Jabez Bunting, Alfred Barrett, James Rigg, and Benjamin Gregory—with the Free Church doctrine of the Church, Ministry, and Sacraments as a new source for assimilation. H. P. Hughes was the most remarkable Methodist leader of this period, and whilst I don't entirely share Mr Kissack's admiration for his famous predecessor at Wesley Memorial Chapel, Oxford, no one could deny his ability to persuade Wesleyan Methodism to change its direction. As a result, however, it seems to me difficult to speak of a Wesleyan doctrine of the Church at all in this period. What was happening was that a conscious effort on the part of men like H. P. Hughes to assimilate late nineteenth-century Free Church ideas was constantly coming up against obstinate reminders of the much older and quite different Wesleyan tradition proper. The real pressure on the Wesleyan consciousness came from an Anglicanism which seemed to have betrayed Anglican traditions, and in doing so had bereft Wesleyan Methodism of the tradition on which it normally drew for inspiration. Hughes was one of the two chief architects of the Free Church Federal Council of 1895: its creation perhaps represented for Wesleyan Methodism its furthest point of recoil from the Church of England, for whatever fine speeches greeted the foundation of the Council, it organized and directed between 1895 and 1914 a tremendous attempt by the Free Churches, dragging Wesleyan Methodism in their wake, to impose on the nation as a whole the Nonconformist conception of Evangelical Pietism, to do successfully, in fact, what Cromwell (who was significantly a hero of this period, whereas it was Jacobitism that Wesley was suspected of) had failed to do in the days of the Commonwealth. In his address to the first Evangelical Free Church Congress, held in 1896, Hughes said that whereas the Roman Catholics were one only in the Pope, and the Anglicans one only in the Crown, the Evangelical Free Churches were one in Christ. No doubt the applause was deafening but the argument was thin, for

Anglo-Catholic and Anglican Evangelical had quite as much right to claim that they were one in Christ as had the Wesleyan Methodists and the Baptists.

I am not concerned here, however, with the differences between the Wesleyans and the Baptists, but with the gulf that was opening in the late nineteenth century between the Wesleyan Methodists and their founder. When Hughes talked proudly about the Nonconformist Conscience one may say in extenuation that he knew not what he said, but the phrase underlined the change that was taking place. Wesley might have appealed, just conceivably, to the Anglican Conscience, as he constantly appealed to the Anglican sources of Methodist doctrine; but he would not have thought of the Dissenting tradition as a proper basis on which the Methodist could establish his conscience. This may seem a hard judgement to some people, but what I mean is that the Federal view of Church unity which Hughes advocated was not based on Wesleyan tradition as such, but rather on the assimilation of Free Church tradition, and a modern Methodist has a right to judge it in terms of its origins; he is not obliged to accept this view of Church unity on the ground that it is specifically the Methodist traditional view. Hughes was a great man, but he did not entirely understand the past of Wesleyan Methodism; indeed, he almost succeeded in changing what he found out of all recognition. The older outlook broke the surface at critical moments, however, as when the Wesleyan Methodist Church refused officially to commit itself to the ill-judged campaign of 'passive resistance' to Balfour's Education Act of 1902; and in the continuing reluctance of Wesleyan Methodist official bodies to pass resolutions condemning Church establishment as such.

By about 1914, therefore, Wesleyan Methodism might be seen as in search of a doctrine of the Church, Ministry, and Sacraments, rather than as securely in possession of one. Wesleyan writers were inclined to assimilate the Free Church view that authority in the Church was vested in the 'priesthood of all believers', and to accept the Congregationalist conception of the local Church; at the same time, however, they were haunted by memories of an older, more Anglican interpretation of the Connexion and its various constituent parts, according to which the local Methodist Society was *not* a local Church, and the local minister was not a representative of the priesthood of the whole body, but a member of an order (whatever name one liked to give it, or an order with no name at all, which perhaps was preferable) charged with responsibility for guiding, teaching, and governing the laity. And if it is true (as Mr Kissack sometimes seems to suggest) that the logical outcome of the episcopalian position is some kind of submission to the authority of the Bishop of Rome, it is perhaps just as true that the logical outcome of the Free Church point of view was the delightful anarchy of the Society of Friends. There have been many Methodists whose spiritual affinities were closer to George Fox than John Wesley, but Wesley's idea of Methodism was not that of a loose federation of local independent Christian 'churches'; it was to be a tightly knit organic connexion of Christians, whose Christianity expressed itself locally in societies. Hughes undoubtedly hoped that the federation of the evangelical Free Churches would grow into a united Free Church of England; in practice, no such process occurred. In one sense, the Free Churches in this country are now further apart than they were in the 1890s, for the agreement on Christian ethical standards which produced the 'Nonconformist Conscience' has collapsed; resolutions on practical matters passed by the present Free Church Federal Council carry little weight with individual Methodist ministers. This inner disintegration is quite as important as the often-mentioned fact that the theoretical intercommunion which the Free Churches enjoy among themselves has not brought about any serious steps towards organic union, or even particularly close relations without organic union.

However, as Wesleyan Methodism assimilated Free Church attitudes so the gap between the Old Connexion and the other Methodist bodies lessened and Methodist union took place in 1932 on the basis of an almost aggressively Free Church platform. Mr Kissack recognizes this when he says that the 1932 official statements on the Ministry (with their almost entirely negative emphasis on the priesthood of all believers) differed widely from what earlier Wesleyan Methodist writers like Alfred Barrett and James Rigg would have expected. They would have said that the statements contained no proper protection for the minister's pastoral authority over the laity, that it was one thing to assert that Methodism cherished its place in the Holy Catholic Church and quite another to make good that claim in institutional form. They would also have been unhappy at the decision to permit the administration of Holy Communion by selected laymen. Mr Kissack, however, draws no particular conclusion from this clash between the present and the past, nor does he really face the fact that since 1932 these statements about the nature of the Church, Ministry, and Sacraments have become more and more unsatisfactory in the eyes of many Methodist ministers and laymen (though by no means all). He mentions a feeling among Methodist ministers that they have not enough 'authority', but he can only account for it by saying that 'this is less the fault of the theology of the Deed of Union than of the practice that gives the laity a perhaps overweighted share in the stationing of ministers'. He is clearly not entirely satisfied with this explanation himself, for in a footnote he adds that 'one might also ask whether the sense of lack of authority in the Methodist Ministry and Conference does not also root in a serious decline in a concern for holiness in the Church in general'. Both these suggestions have their point, but they are subordinate to the major cause of uneasiness. Modern Methodism is suffering from the inner contradictions which evolved its present constitution, contradictions which arose in the generation of Hugh Price Hughes and Scott Lidgett, the contradictions between the Wesleyan Methodist tradition proper and the half-assimilated Free Church tradition which influenced so profoundly what was written into the Deed of Union. Experience has made many Methodist ministers dissatisfied with the limited kind of ministerial role which is often allotted them, and with the Free Church conception of the Ministry which underlies it, and so with the whole federal attitude to internal and external Church relations.

The ghosts of Bunting and Rigg are walking among us—it is fascinating to meet them in this book, for Mr Kissack has called them up himself—and their view of the Methodist tradition is challenging the view which for the time replaced it. (In recent years one example of the process has been the acceptance of a tougher attitude to redundant churches, a refusal to admit that the last word must necessarily be said by the local trustees.) I do not mean that one can simply replace the new with the old. Both Bunting and Rigg talked too much in terms of authority, pastoral prerogative, and rights of government to sound either intelligible or sympathetic to the modern liberal mind; their point of view, however, can be restated in less legalistic terms. They envisaged the minister as the theological and devotional expert—they would have regarded the ordained social gospeller, the political parson, and the would-be ministerial psychiatrist as doing jobs which Christian laymen actually can do better, and I think that they would probably be right. The minister's business is to understand the nature and development of Christian experience in the individual and in the surrounding environment, and to watch over the Christian development of the adult as well as the young, making it clear that he has the authority of Christ, knowledge and experience to govern his people in their spiritual lives. (They would also say, I imagine, that much of our talk about secularizing the Gospel misses the point so far as the Church is concerned: our laity do not need secularization, they are secularized, and even young ministers flatter themselves if they imagine that they can teach the average layman about secularity. My experience would be that the typical candidate for the Ministry at the present time needs more contact with Christian spirituality if he is to have any surviving usefulness, rather than more contact with the famous Protestant peep-show, 'the world'.) Nothing is rarer in contemporary Protestant experience than for one man to go to another and say, 'Tell me as frankly as you think I can bear what seems to be wrong with my spiritual development.' The pastor understood as Bunting and Rigg understood him cannot always expect obedience: their weakness was that they did not allow sufficiently for the necessary freedom which ought to exist even in a relation of obedience. Sometimes one feels obliged to disobey one's orders and, less often, one is right. The Church may be militant but it is not an Army. Jesus did not use that metaphor. No minister should expect the kind of obedience which was flogged into the backs of Victorian infantry. Indeed, the Protestant Ministry will not recover its authority over an educated laity until it realizes that the western world has outgrown military definitions of the virtue of obedience. But whether they were right or wrong, men like Bunting and Rigg were pleading for a coherent view of the place of the Ministry in the Church, for a view which gave a sense of purpose to the ministers themselves, and if this view can be expressed in terms of episcopacy then many Methodist ministers and laymen will welcome it. For the bishop comes into the system as the natural guardian of the spiritual health of the Ministry—indeed, he ought to want no other function.

When all this has been said, however, one has still to face the question why since 1932 so many Methodists have lost their enthusiasm for 'Free Churchism' without necessarily substituting Anglicanism as an alternative. The decline in Methodist membership since 1932 is often quoted as though it were evidence that 'liturgical services' and 'biblical criticism' have ruined Methodism, but it would be quite as logical to regard the decline as a criticism of the type of Methodism with which our fathers hopefully, but perhaps mistakenly, saddled us.

The deepest explanation of the feeling in favour of the *Majority Report* lies in a dimension which Mr Kissack does not explore in his book and which I think that he ought to have explored, because without this dimension all talk about the union of the Churches remains thin and unimpressive. This is the situation of the churches in the main streets, the side streets, and the backstreets. In a typical area of a northern industrial town, for example, there are between forty and fifty thousand inhabitants. As one moves from north to south through a densely built-up area, with two main shopping streets, scores of sidestreet corner shops, and patches of almost shopless housing-estates, one sees quite a number of churches. Six of these are Methodist, with a paper membership of about seven hundred and fifty, and actual attendance of not more than six hundred. These six Methodist churches are all on one circuit, are grouped in two clusters of three, and one pair is ripe for closure. There are three ministers, only one of whom has a society with more than two hundred members; one other church of the six may be called 'lively'.

The area is contained in six Anglican parishes, changing in character from working class to middle class as one goes further from the centre of the town. They also vary from extreme Evangelical to mild High Church. Since in general Anglicans outnumber Methodists by about four to one, one might expect an Easter Communicant attendance of well over two thousand, but in such industrial areas this would be an exaggeration. There are six Anglican parsons; at least one of the Anglican churches is superfluous by Methodist standards of redundancy. There are also open in the area one more or less derelict Baptist church, two Congregationalist churches, one alive and one dead, and an English Presbyterian church whose function is to give religious expression to the residual national feeling of a colony of Scottish exiles. The four Free Churches have about five hundred members between them. This makes a total Protestant population of perhaps three thousand five hundred, leaving out of account Sunday School scholars, whose numbers diminish steadily. There are actually two Roman Catholic churches, but their popularity resembles that of the Presbyterian church: they form the social and effective centres of large Polish, Hungarian, and Irish colonies and their religious function is hard to disentangle from this context. The whole religious population (one can't seriously call it a community or any word which implies community, this is part of the illusion of federalism) might amount to ten per cent of the population of the area. Two of the parish churches are about five minutes' walk apart on the same road; two of the Methodist churches lie about the same time-distance apart on a sidestreet at right angles to this. One can see the Congregationalist church from the Presbyterian church, and vice versa: between them stands another parish church.

There is some variety of worship among the six Anglican churches (though less than popular legend might make one suppose), but virtually no variation in the worship of the Free Churches, apart from the slight difference of their respective hymn-books and this affects the tunes more than the words, since the denominations have for many years tended to ignore the more characteristically denominational of their hymns and to occupy a middle ground, made up of the popular hymns often found on television and radio programmes. The two groups of churches have only slight contact (the ministers meet one another much more than do the laity) and there is not much contact between the Methodist and the other Free Churches. The Free Church Council and the British Council of Churches both exist in local form, but these again affect the ministry rather than the laity.

In fact, I do not think that there exists among either the laity or the ministers any real sense of living as part of a general Christian community—that sense of belonging to a Spirit-filled, beleaguered, suspect race apart which may be supposed to have characterized the Christian community living in the Roman Empire in the days of persecution. (And how much longer are we to go on pretending that because the Church of England is in some sense established we live in a country in which Christianity is culturally dominant?) So far from living as Christians committed to one another by the Spirit to live as part of the Body of Christ in the world, the Anglicans, Baptists, Congregationalists, and Methodists accept their distinctness from one another just as they accept the endless class divisions of English society, and take it for granted that they must remain as separate from one another as if they were a set of Great Religions, each complete with its own Revelation and distinct Eschatology. The truth is—and this is the final answer to all those who object to schemes for organic union between the members of the Christian remnant trapped in the present age—that there is no longer any point in becoming a Christian if one can only become (and in such an area) either an Anglican, or a Methodist, or a Presbyterian, or a member of some other fragmentary vision of the truth in Christ Jesus. If it is through this chaos of almost unassociated Churches that ministers have to strive for the evangelization of England is it surprising that they grow weary and turn to school-teaching as a more direct way of influencing society? If it is in such walled-off communities that Christians gather is it surprising that fewer and fewer people care to shut themselves up from the world in an almost lifeless federation? Leave this dimension out, and it is bound to seem incredible that a generation of ministers and laymen should have appeared in Methodism to whom the old slogans no longer appeal and to whom it seems a waste of time to worry overmuch if there are Anglo-Catholics in the Church of England. We need one another more than we need fear one another. The world needs us; but not as we are, only as Christ is in us. And Christ is more than the President of a Federal Republic of Christian Associations; He is the Head of the Body which is His Church.

Index of Names

ANTLIFF, WILLIAM, 130
Arnold, Matthew, 115, 145
Asbury, F., 113, 114

BAGEHOT, W., 146
Baker, E., 16, 17
Baker, F., 165
Barker, Joseph, 67
Barrett, Alfred, 52, 54, 55, 60, 61, 64, 79, 194, 195, 199, 201
Barrett, C. K., 178–9
Barth, K., 7
Beaumont, Joseph, 123
Beecham, John, 60–4
Bonhoeffer, D., 163
Bourne, H., 68, 130–1
Bourne, J., 129
Bowmer, J. C., 187
Browne, H., 147
Buchanan, C. O., 189
Bunting, Jabez, passim
Bunting, W. M., 106, 140
Burr, N. R., 151

CAUGHEY, JAMES, 68, 99
Chadwick, S., 121
Chalmers, T., 139
Chew, R., 130
Church, R. W., 163
Clarke, Adam, 89, 91, 114
Clowes, W., 68
Coke, T., 113–14, 150, 171, 175
Curteis, G. H., 106

DAVIES, G. C. B., 45, 164
Disraeli, B., 148
Dixon, James, 112, 114, 134
Dixon, R. W., 134
Dow, Lorenzo, 68
Duffield, G. E., 189
Dunn, S., 98, 101, 119

ECKETT, ROBERT, 64, 66, 68
Edwards, Jonathan, 164
Edwards, Maldwyn, 124, 127, 133–4
Elliott, Ebenezer, 72, 132
Entwisle, Joseph, 89, 96, 97
Everett, James, 52, 62, 72, 77, 80–1, 90, 101, 112, 115, 119–20, 125

FISHER, LORD, 162, 163, 179, 183–184, 190–1
Fletcher, J., 180–1
Flew, Robert, Newton, 13, 25, 83, 195
Fowler, J., 99–100, 118, 119, 122
French, E. A., 4–5

GALLAND, T., 133
George, A. R., 50
Gore, Charles, 147, 166
Graham, Sir James, 117, 144–5
Gregory, Benjamin, 55–8, 77, 87, 107–11, 118–23, 133, 194, 198–9
Griffith, W., 98, 101, 119, 130
Grimshaw, W., 164–5

HALÉVY, E., 77, 86–102, 121, 124, 127
Hannah, J., 86
Harnack, A., 113, 117
Haweis, T., 165
Hennell, M., 165
Hooker, R., 171
Horne, S., 105, 107–8, 120
Houghton, Lord, 149
Hughes, H. P., 78, 102, 113, 141, 145, 199–202

ISAAC, DANIEL, 75, 90

JACKSON, THOMAS, 90–2, 101–2
Jenkins, Daniel, 82

KEBLE, JOHN 146, 166
Keeble, S. E., 145
Kemp, E. W., 33–4
Kilham, A., 108
King, Lord, 48, 167, 169–76
Kingsley, Charles, 144
Kissack, R., 193–206

LAUD, ARCHBISHOP, 146, 149
Liddon, H. P., 144
Lidgett, J. S., 24, 34, 202
Lightfoot, J. H., 154
Ludlow, J., 144

MACKINNON, D. M., 184
Madan, M., 181
Mascall, E. L., 157
Maurice, F. D., 112, 144
Miall, E., 104–5

NEIL, A. C., 185
Nelson, J., 45
Newman, J. H., 117, 163
Newton, J. T., 33
Newton, Robert, 99–100
Noble, W. J., 3

OASTLER, R 135
O'Bryan, W., 68
Osborn, G., 81, 101

PACKER, J. L., 160, 189
Parris, J. R., 187
Paul, Leslie, 161, 190
Peel, Albert, 108
Peel, Sir Robert, 117, 135–6, 139–140
Perks, Sir Robert, 1, 11, 12, 145
Pusey, E., 23, 83, 138, 166

RATTENBURY, J. E., 22, 25, 26, 27, 33, 35, 36
Redfern, W., 120–3
Rigg, J. H., 11, 108, 110, 121, 195, 197–9, 201–3
Romaine, W., 181

SCOTT, J., 100, 137
Seabury, Bishop, 151, 175
Shaftesbury, Lord, 144
Sidmouth, Lord, 129
Sigston, J., 68, 74, 76
Simon, J. S., 107, 108, 111
Skeats, H. S., 104, 106
Smith, George, 103, 104, 107, 108, 118
Smith, Gipsy, 6
Smyth, C., 165
Southey, R., 112
Spurgeon, C. H., 24
Stanley, A. P., 152
Stephens, R., 67, 83, 93, 94, 97, 120, 130, 135, 138
Stevens, A., 106
Stillingfleet, 171, 176
Stoughton, J., 105, 106
Stuart, E., 149
Swayne, W. S., 147

TAIT, A. C., 148–50
Talbot, J., 151
Taylor, E. R., 124–7, 133, 137
Temple, F., 148
Thelwall, A. S., 140
Thompson, E., 114, 169–76
Thompson, E. P., x, xi, 124, 133
Thring of Uppingham, 183
Tomline, Pretyman, 166
Towlson, C. W., 165
Toynbee, A. J., 44
Tyerman, J., 112, 114

VENN, HENRY, 165–6, 181, 187
Vevers, W., 73

WALFORD, J., 131
Walker, S., 45, 164, 167, 168, 188
Walsh, J., 164, 181, 188
Ward, J. C., 108
Warren, S., 62, 88, 93, 94, 96
Watson, R., 44, 52, 54, 59, 61
Wearmouth, R. F., 127
Welbourne, E. W., 136

Westcott, Bishop, 148
Whitefield, G., 181
Wilberforce, S., 123, 147, 153, 159

Wilson, D., 166
Wood, A. S., 165–6
Workman, H. B., 112–18, 180

CLAIMING MY UNTOUCHED MISTRESS

CLAIMING MY UNTOUCHED MISTRESS

HEIDI RICE

MILLS & BOON

First published in Great Britain 2019
by Mills & Boon, an imprint of HarperCollins*Publishers*
1 London Bridge Street, London, SE1 9GF

Large Print edition 2019

© 2019 Heidi Rice

ISBN: 978-0-263-08262-3

MIX
Paper from
responsible sources
FSC www.fsc.org   FSC C007454

Printed and bound in Great Britain
by CPI Group (UK) Ltd, Croydon, CR0 4YY

To my gorgeous husband, Rob,
whose love of Texas Hold 'Em finally
became useful in my writing career!

CHAPTER ONE

I STRUGGLED TO control the tidal wave of panic surging through me as I read the sign on Dante Allegri's Monaco casino.

Welcome to The Inferno

The glitter of lights gave the building's imposing eighteenth-century façade a fairy-tale glow in the Mediterranean night—making me feel like even more of a fraud in the second-hand designer gown and uncomfortable ice-pick heels my sister and I had sourced online. What I was about to do could make or break my family.

Please God, don't let Dante Allegri be in the house tonight.

I'd seen photos of Allegri, and read myriad articles about him in the last month as I prepared for this night. He scared me as a competitor but terrified me as a woman.

Allegri was famous for his ruthlessness, having risen from the slums of Naples to create a billion-dollar empire of casinos in Europe and the US. If I had to play against him, and he figured out the system I had developed, he would show me no mercy.

A sea breeze from the marina below the casino lifted the tendrils of hair off my neck which had escaped the elaborate up-do my sister had spent hours constructing from my unruly curls. Shivers racked my body, but I knew it wasn't the warm summer night that was making me feel so cold inside—it was fear.

Stop standing here like a dummy and move.

Lifting the hem of the gown, I walked up the marble stairs to the main entrance, making an effort to keep my back straight and my gaze forward. The million-dollar bank draft borrowed from my brother-in-law's loan shark stashed in the jewelled clutch purse on my wrist felt as if it weighed several tons.

'You want to throw good money after bad, that's your choice, Ms Trouvé, but I'll be here tomorrow to collect, whatever happens.'

The words of Brutus Severin, Carsoni's muscle man, echoed in my head and the chill spread like a frost.

This was my last chance to free us from the threats and intimidation, the possibility of losing not just our family home, but also our dignity and self-respect. Something my sister Jude's husband Jason had stolen from us twelve months ago—after losing a fortune at Allegri's roulette tables.

Failure simply was not an option tonight.

I approached the security detail standing guard at the entrance and passed them my ID card. I prayed that Carsoni's forger had done the job we had paid him for. The guard nodded and passed it back to me. But my panic refused to subside.

What if my system didn't work? Or had more tells than I had anticipated. I wasn't sure if I'd had enough time to test it properly—and I had never had the opportunity to test it against players of Allegri's calibre. How did I know it would stand up to scrutiny? I was a maths prodigy, not a poker player, for goodness' sake.

The buy-in for tonight's game was a staggering one million euros. And it was one million euros I could not afford to lose.

If Allegri was here, and decided to play—
as he occasionally did, according to my research—and he beat me, not only would Belle
Rivière be lost for ever, but I would owe Carsoni an extra million euros I couldn't repay. Because the sale of the property, now we'd already
mortgaged it and sold all our other valuables
and most of the furniture, would only cover the
balance of Jason's losses and the astronomical
interest Carsoni had been charging us since the
night Jason had disappeared.

*Please, I'm begging you, God. Don't let Al-
legri be here.*

The door guard signalled to a tall, good-
looking man standing at the entrance to the
main floor. He joined us.

'Welcome to The Inferno, Miss Spencer,'
the man said. 'I'm Joseph Donnelly, the casino
manager. We have you listed as one of tonight's
club buy-ins.' He sent me a quizzical look, obviously not used to having someone of my age
and gender join the casino's exclusive weekly
poker tournament. 'Is that correct?'

I nodded, trying to channel my inner elite,
entitled heiress—something I had never been,

even though my mother had been the grand-daughter of a French count.

'I've heard The Inferno's game is one of the most challenging,' I said. 'I was hoping Allegri would be here tonight,' I lied smoothly—playing the pampered rich girl to the hilt. If life with my mother had taught me one thing, before she died, it was how to appear confident when I felt the opposite.

'Appearances are everything, ma petite chou. *If they think you are one of them, you cannot fail.'*

The casino manager sent me an easy smile, and I waited for the words I hoped to hear—that my research had paid off and Dante was in Nice this evening, wining and dining the model he had been linked with for several weeks in the celebrity press.

'Dante's here tonight; I'm sure he'd relish the challenge.' Donnelly's words didn't register at first, and then they slammed into me.

No. No. No.

I pasted a smile on my face, the same smile I had worn at my mother's funeral to receive the condolences of journalists who had hounded her throughout her life, while coping with the body blow of fresh grief.

My movements were stiff though, as Donnelly led me to the teller's booth to deposit the stake I had borrowed at two thousand per cent interest. The stake I couldn't afford to lose.

I ran all the possibilities over in my mind. Could I back out now? Make up some fictitious excuse? Pretend I was sick? Because that wasn't a lie—my stomach was churning like a storm at sea.

Allegri was one of the best poker players in the world. Not only could I lose all the money but if he figured out my system he could have me banned from every reputable casino. So I'd have no chance of ever recovering Jason's losses.

Even as my frantic mind tried to grasp and dissect all the possibilities though, I knew I couldn't back out. I'd taken a chance Allegri wouldn't be here and I'd lost. But I had to go through with tonight's game.

Before I had a chance to handle the visceral fear at the thought of facing Allegri with so much at stake, a deep voice reverberated down my spine.

'Joe, Matteo tells me all the players have arrived.'

I swung round and came face to face with the man who had haunted my dreams—and most of my waking hours—for months, ever since I'd begun working on this scheme to free our family from debt. To my shock, Allegri was even taller, broader and more devastatingly handsome in the flesh than he had been in the numerous celebrity blogs and magazines I'd been monitoring.

I knew he was only thirty, but the harsh angles of his face, and the unyielding strength of muscle and sinew barely contained by the expensive tuxedo, made it clear that the softness and inexperience of youth— if he had ever been young or soft—had left him long ago. Everything about him exuded power and confidence, and a frightening arrogance. No, not arrogance. Arrogance implied a sense of entitlement beyond one's abilities. This man was fully aware of his abilities, and was ready to use them with complete ruthlessness.

His vivid blue gaze flickered over my face— and one dark eyebrow raised a fraction of a centimetre. The tiny tell vanished as soon as it had appeared. His intense gaze took a quick tour down my body. The provocative dress became instantly transparent while at the same time squeezing the air out of my lungs, as if the thin satin had turned to cast iron and was tightening around my ribs like a piece of medieval torture equipment.

Unlike the looks I had experienced from Carsoni and his men over the last year though, Dante Allegri's perusal didn't cause revulsion but something much more disturbing. A heavy weight sunk low into my abdomen and sensation prickled over my skin as if I were being stroked by an electric current. His attention was exhilarating and enervating, pleasurable and painful all at the same time. My reaction shocked me, because I couldn't seem to control it. My thighs trembled, my breasts swelled against the bodice of my medieval torture equipment and it took an effort of titanic proportions to stop my breathing from speeding up.

'That's correct, Dante,' Joseph Donnelly replied to his boss. 'This is Edie Spencer,' he added, wrenching me out of the trance Allegri's presence had caused. 'She's just arrived and is hoping to play you tonight.'

I winced at the amusement in Donnelly's tone, my panic increasing to go with the inexplicable aches all over my body. As if it wasn't bad enough that I had tossed myself into the lion's den tonight, I had decided to poke the lion with that foolish boast.

Allegri didn't look particularly impressed as his intense gaze roamed over my face.

'Exactly how old are you, Miss Spencer?' he asked, addressing me directly for the first time. His English was perfect, the accent a mid-Atlantic hybrid of American and British with barely a hint of his native Italian. 'Are you even legally allowed to be here?' he added, and I bristled at the condescension. It was a long time since I'd felt like a child, let alone been treated like one.

'Of course—I'm twenty-one,' I said in a show of defiance that probably wasn't wise, but something about the way he was looking at me—as if he actually saw me—and the disturbing conflagration of sensation that look was setting off all over my body made me bold.

He continued to stare at me, as if he were trying to see into my soul, and I forced myself not to break eye contact.

The noise from the main floor of the casino, as Europe's billionaire elite tried their luck at roulette and *vingt-et-un*, faded to a distant hum under his intense scrutiny—until all I could hear was the thunder of my own heartbeat thumping my ribs.

'How long have you been playing Texas Hold 'Em, Miss Spencer?' he asked at last, mentioning the variety of poker all professional players favoured.

With five 'community' cards turned face up in the middle of the table, and two 'hole' cards dealt face down to each player, Texas Hold 'Em required the greatest amount of skill in calculating probabilities and assessing risk as you formed your hand from your two 'hole' cards and the five 'community' cards, and the least amount of dumb luck. And that's where my system came in. I had developed a mathematical formula to assess the betting behaviour of the other players, which would give me an advantage as the game went on. But if I was spotted using the formula I would be in trouble, just like players who were caught counting cards when playing Black Jack.

Once the casinos figured out how to spot those players they were banned for life, their winnings forfeit—even though what they were doing wasn't strictly speaking cheating. I couldn't risk either of those scenarios.

'Long enough,' I answered, forcing myself to pretend a confidence I didn't feel.

My mother had been right about one thing. Appearances were everything now. If I wanted to win, I couldn't show this man a single weakness. Appearing confident and in control was as important as *being* confident and in control. In fact, letting him believe I was over-confident would also work to my advantage—the ultimate double bluff, because then he would underestimate me.

His devastating face remained impassive, but the glitter of heat in his irises and the tiny tensing of his jaw, which drew my eyes to a scar on his upper lip, suggested that my cocky statement had hit its mark. I would have felt more triumphant about his reaction if that quickly masked tell hadn't increased the weight in the pit of my abdomen by several hundred pounds—and the prickle of awareness coasting over my skin by several thousand volts.

What was happening to me? I had never had a response like this to any man.

'I guess we'll see about that, Miss Spencer,' he said, then turned to his casino manager. 'Escort Miss Spencer up to the Salon, Joe. Introduce her to tonight's other Millionaire Club players.' He glanced at his watch, all business again, even though the vibes coming off him—of heat and animosity—were turning my legs to jelly.

'I need to speak to Renfrew but I'll be up in thirty minutes,' he added. 'We can kick off then.'

'You're joining the table tonight?' Donnelly asked, sounding mildly surprised.

'Yes,' he said, that deep voice stroking the hot spot which had started to throb at my core. 'I never back down from a challenge, especially one issued by a beautiful woman.'

It took me a moment to realise *I* was the beautiful woman, probably because the glare he sent me before he walked away suggested he didn't consider it a compliment.

But as I was led away by the casino manager

towards a bank of elevators, I couldn't take my eyes off Allegri's retreating back. His broad shoulders looked indomitable, and yet terrifyingly alluring in the expertly tailored designer evening suit. The crowd parted to allow his dark figure to stride through the room.

I had to win tonight, no matter what the cost—my family's future depended on it. But as the inexplicable heat continued to throb at my core, my senses thrown into turmoil by that one brief encounter, I had the agonising suspicion I had already lost.

CHAPTER TWO

EDIE SPENCER WAS an enigma I couldn't solve, and it was driving me nuts.

We'd been playing for over three hours now and I couldn't figure out her system. I was even finding it hard to read her tells—those insignificant physical responses every player had which they were unaware of, but which made them an open book when it came to assessing their next move. And the reason why I couldn't figure out her tells was as simple as it was surprising. I couldn't concentrate on the game— because I was too busy concentrating on her.

While her winnings had been modest so far, they had been building steadily, unlike every other player at the table, who had the inevitable troughs that came with a game of chance. I'd managed to dispose of all but one of the other players, so there were only three of us left at the table. But while my friend Alexi Galanti, the Formula One owner who sat beside her, was down to his last million, Edie Spencer was sitting with a tidy pile of chips in front of her that matched my own.

I knew she had to be using a system which was even more ingenious than mine. But my desire to figure it out was a great deal less urgent than my desire to peel her out of the provocative dress she wore. The lace that covered her cleavage was doing nothing to distract me from the tempting display of soft female flesh beneath.

'Raise, two hundred,' Alexi said as he tossed a couple of hundred thousand euro chips on the table, raising the stake after the blind bids.

I stifled my frustration as I watched Edie's slim fingers lift her hole cards on the table to study them again.

I wanted Alexi out of the game so I could play Miss Spencer alone. But Alexi was a good player. So I needed to concentrate on the play, and not the provocative display of cleavage across the table.

I stifled the visceral tug of anticipation, and the swift tug of arousal, at the prospect of having her all to myself. Mixing sex with poker was never a good strategy. But as I watched her

I had to admit it wasn't just her beauty that had been driving me nuts for hours.

I'd seen a spark of fire downstairs, when I'd questioned her about her age, and it had excited me. For the first time in a long time, I'd found myself relishing the challenge of playing a stimulating game with a stimulating woman. But ever since that moment downstairs, I hadn't been able to tempt that spark out of hiding again.

Her skin had remained pale and unflushed, her hands folded demurely in her lap when she wasn't betting or checking her cards, her breathing even. Her bright green gaze, which had captivated me downstairs, hadn't connected with mine since.

And while that lack of eye contact was frustrating enough when it came to reading her play, what was a great deal more frustrating was that I was becoming even more turned on. Not less so. And even more desperate to see that flash of green fire again.

I didn't like it. I never let physical desire distract me at the table, but what I liked even less was the fact I didn't understand what it was about her I found so hot.

For starters, she was only twenty-one years old. And she looked even younger. When I had first seen her, I would have placed her as nineteen, twenty at the most, the revealing dress and heavy eye make-up making her wide emerald eyes and slim coltish figure look for a moment like a child playing dress up.

Young women were not to my taste. I preferred women older than me as a rule, women with lots of experience, who could match my appetites in bed, provide stimulating conversation out of it—and didn't get over-invested in the relationship, or over-emotional when I gave them an expensive bauble to send them on their way.

I had also never had the desire before to pursue a woman who was not sending me clear signals she was interested in a little bed sport too. The truth was, when younger women bought into the high stakes game they were usually looking for a little of both—the chance to test their skill at the table and test their skills in my bed. A temptation I had found it very easy to resist up till now.

But not this time.

Of course it was more than possible Miss

Spencer's demure behaviour was all an act, intended to intrigue and entice me. If that were the case, I had to give her credit for trying a new tactic. But that still didn't answer the question of why it was working so effectively.

Was it simply the enigma of her? Or that momentary spark of defiance? Or maybe it was the challenge she represented? How long had it been since I had found a woman this hard to read?

As I studied her debating her play, unable to detach my gaze from her, I forced myself to focus.

This girl was no different from the many other heiresses I had met over the years while I was setting up my business. The spoilt, entitled daughters of millionaire businessmen and aristocrats, European royalty and Arab sheikhs, who had never had to work a day in their lives and didn't know the meaning of want. They played the tables to imbue their lives with the excitement their pointless existences lacked—without realising that if money had no value, the risk and the pay-off of gambling with it would have no value too.

But despite my determination to dismiss and

rationalise her unprecedented effect on me, my gaze continued to roam over her, the embers of my fascination burning in my abdomen.

Her skin glowed with youth in the subtle lighting, the plunging V of her gown beneath the lace highlighting full firm breasts flushed with an alabaster softness. The ruched peaks of her nipples, outlined through the satin, were the only response she seemed unable to control.

I would have taken some satisfaction from that… But the increasingly relentless desire to ease the edge of her gown down, expose those peaks and feel them swell and elongate against my tongue wasn't making me feel particularly impressed with my own control.

'Fold,' she said, passing her hole cards to Alexi, who was dealing—and eluding my attempts to force her to break cover, again.

I bit down on my tongue to stop the curse coming out of my mouth, like a damn rookie. But, as if she had sensed my frustration, her gaze flicked to mine.

It flicked away again almost immediately. But in that moment, as our gazes locked, I saw that flash of fire. A jolt of heat eddied through my system.

Her chest rose and fell and then stilled as she regained her composure. But the pebbled outline of her nipples became more prominent against the satin.

Desire flared in my abdomen like a meteor shower, as I finally solved at least some of the puzzle. The veneer of composure was just that—a veneer.

Whatever system Edie had devised, she had just exposed one major weakness.

Maybe she was still an enigma in some ways. But one thing I knew now with complete certainty—she was as hungry for me as I was for her. And for some reason she wanted to hide it. Which gave me the upper hand, because it was a weakness I could exploit.

Hot blood surged in my groin.

In fact, it was a weakness I was going to take great pleasure in exploiting.

Game on, bella.

CHAPTER THREE

HE KNOWS.

I had made a terrible mistake. I knew it as soon as my gaze met Allegri's and held for a nanosecond too long.

I'd been avoiding eye contact all night, that penetrating blue gaze turning my stomach to molten lava and making my nipples tighten every time it caught mine.

I didn't understand my reaction to him. The only thing I did know was that I couldn't let him see it—or I would be completely at the mercy of it, and him. But the more I tried to control my physical responses, the harder they became to hide. And the more difficult I found it to keep my mind on the game.

I should have bet on that hand. I knew the probability he had a better one was fractionally greater than mine, given the way he had betted during the blinds, but if I never tested him, never lost, he would begin to suspect I had a system. The problem was, I had been avoiding going head to head with him all night, the fear of exposing the strange currents gripping my body too great to risk it.

But as soon as I'd folded again, and saw his jaw tense, the rush of exhilaration at frustrating him was like a drug, intoxicating me. As a result I had been incapable of stopping myself from lifting my head and staring directly at him.

He remained calm, the tensing of his jaw easing, and then his lips curved in a sensual smile that fed the rush of adrenaline.

I ripped my gaze away before he could see more. But I knew it was already too late. The giddy longing must have been written all over my face.

My breathing stopped. It just stopped. I had to fight for the next breath, but as I forced my lungs to function in an even rhythm again, my nipples became so hard they felt as if they were going to poke right through my dress.

I listened to the play continue around me, as Allegri finished off Galanti. The motor-racing entrepreneur subsided with good grace, throwing his pair of aces down with a hollow laugh

when Allegri turned over his winning hand—
a two to match the pair of twos already on the
table.

'Damn it, Dante, one of these days, I swear
your luck will run out,' Galanti said.

'Keep dreaming, Alexi,' Allegri said as he
began methodically stacking the pile of chips
he'd won.

Galanti cast a look my way as he knocked
back the last of his whisky. 'Maybe Miss Spencer has your number?' Standing to leave the
table, he offered me his hand. 'You've been an
impressive and beautiful opponent, Edie,' he
said with deliberate familiarity, the look in his
eyes flirtatious.

'Thank you, Mr Galanti,' I said. As we shook
hands, I tried to figure out why I had no reaction to this man and yet was finding it so hard
to control the one I had to Allegri.

'Good luck,' Galanti said. 'Maybe we could
meet afterwards for a drink?' he added. 'I'm
going to try my luck at the roulette table next,
so I'll be around to celebrate with you when
you beat this bastard.'

The vote of confidence surprised me, but
the invitation surprised me more—I made an

effort to make myself invisible whenever I was around men. Both Jude and I had learned instinctively to shy away from male attention, thanks to the endless stream of lovers my mother had brought into our lives as teenagers.

The decision to decline Galanti's invitation was instant and unequivocal. But as I opened my mouth to cry off, Allegri spoke.

'Get lost, Alexi. Miss Spencer is out of bounds—she's all mine now.'

Galanti laughed and left, apparently unaware of the subtle edge in Allegri's voice. But I'd heard it, along with the hint of possessiveness.

She's all mine now.

What was that supposed to mean?

I made the mistake of looking at him again, and my blood pressure spiked on cue. He was watching me, the way he had been all night. But, instead of frustration, all I saw now was satisfaction, and challenge, daring me to react to his outrageous remark.

He finished shuffling the cards, his strong wrists and capable fingers flexing in practised motion, never taking his gaze off me.

The tension in the room increased as the

door closed behind Galanti, leaving us alone in the plush salon. The huge mullioned window gave us a spectacular view of the bay, the boats moored in the marina adding a sprinkle of lights to the dark sea, but the overwhelmingly masculine space, luxuriously furnished in leather and mahogany in accents of green and brown, suddenly seemed dangerous... And exciting.

Allegri had dismissed the serving staff over an hour ago. At the time it had seemed a generous gesture—it had been past midnight. But now we were alone together I was wondering if he had planned it.

For the first time, the strange melting sensation at my core and the panic it caused was joined by a spark of anger at his proprietary comment to Galanti.

I'd spent the last year of my life being bullied and belittled by Carsoni and his hired muscle— I didn't like it.

'I'd prefer it if you didn't make decisions for me, Mr Allegri,' I said, in as placid a voice as I could muster while I was burning up with indignation.

'And what decision would that be?' he asked, cutting the pack one-handed.

'The decision to have a drink with Mr Galanti,' I huffed, indignation getting the better of me.

'As you had already decided to give him the brush-off,' he said, 'I hardly think I took the decision away from you.'

He cut the cards again, and smiled that sensual smile—which did diabolical things to my heart rate. The arrogant comment rattled me, but it infuriated me more, loosening my tongue.

'Actually, I hadn't decided to give him the brush-off,' I lied.

'Yes, you had,' he said with complete confidence. The slight curve of his lip unsettled and confused me—was he amused by my futile attempt to misdirect him?

And how the heck did he know I had been planning to give Galanti the brush-off?

'How could you possibly know that?' I blurted out.

His blue gaze darkened and, to my horror, an answering heat hit my chest and spread across my collarbone like a rash.

'Because he's not your type, *bella*,' he said.

The gruff tone, and his easy use of the endearment, made the rash spread up my neck and hit my cheeks. 'I am.'

CHAPTER FOUR

THE DESIRE I had been trying and failing to control for hours shot through my system like a fine wine, but I was through caring about it as Edie Spencer's gaze finally flashed the green fire I had witnessed downstairs.

Welcome back, bella.

Satisfaction joined with the intoxicating jolt of power and passion as I saw indignation flush her pale skin. The challenging light heated her eyes to a sparkling emerald. She really was exquisite. Provocative, fearless and, from the system I had yet to fully fathom, also wildly intelligent. Whatever game she was playing, she was proving to be a worthy opponent. Not something I was used to when it came to the spoilt children of the rich.

I was going to have a great deal of fun winning this game—and then mining the sexual chemistry we so clearly shared. If she was anywhere near as hot in bed as she was at the table, this was liable to be a very entertaining night.

'You're extremely arrogant, Mr Allegri,' she said, but I caught the catch of breath in her throat as she said it. 'Perhaps you should concentrate on the game, instead of my fictitious attraction to your charms.'

'I happen to be very good at multi-tasking,' I replied as I placed the pack on the table, suddenly less interested in dealing the cards than I was in dealing with her. 'I can play and read your responses at the same time—which is how I know it's me you want, not Alexi.'

'What responses?' she said, her chest rising and falling again in an erratic rhythm. 'I don't have any response to you, whatever your ego might be telling you.'

I decided not to argue the point. I simply let my gaze drift down to her nipples and watched them swell against the satin. I could only imagine how desperate she must be now for rclief. The peaks begging for the sharp strong tug of my lips. Some women were extremely sensitive there; I would hazard a guess she was one of them from the way the flush she'd kept at bay for three hours spread across her collarbone under my examination.

'How about we test that theory,' I said, 'and take a recreational break?'

She stiffened, but the blush was out of control now. And all the more arresting for it.

She didn't respond so I added, 'We've been playing for three hours—and I'm starving.' I let the implication hang in the air that it wasn't just food I was hungry for—while enjoying her attempts to stifle the now livid blush rioting across those pale cheeks.

I saw her debate my request, unsure whether to take the bait or not. If she knew anything about me at all—and I would hazard a guess she had done more than her fair share of research on my habits from her play so far—she would know I frequently played for twenty-four hours straight without the need for sustenance. I didn't get hungry during a match, all my focus on the turn of the cards. But right now I was distracted, so why not run with it? After all, that delectable flash of temper and heat in her eyes was even more challenging than her play.

I wondered exactly how bold she really was. Would she play it safe and decline my offer?

Keep her cards close to her chest and continue to deny the chemistry making both our bloods boil? Or would she take the risk of exposing her own hunger, to get the upper hand in the game of cat and mouse we were now playing?

I was hoping it would be the latter, but had I overestimated her daring?

I thought I probably had when she looked away and I saw her throat move as she swallowed.

But then, to my surprise, she turned back to me and those mesmerising emerald eyes sparked with defiance—and a steely determination.

'I'd love a supper break,' she said, the tiny quiver in her voice contradicted by the thrust of her nipples and the flagrant colour still flaring on her cheeks. 'But only because I'm hungry and I need all my energy to concentrate on beating you.'

'*Touché, bella.*' I chuckled, enjoying her audacious threat, and the sparkle of green fire. I picked up my cell-phone and texted Joe to get a meal up here pronto. She hadn't just taken the bait; she'd swallowed it whole then spat it back out again.

Why that should make me relish bedding her even more than beating her was probably a little perverse—as a rule I never slept with an opponent, however tempted—mixing poker with sexual pleasure could get complicated fast... But, right now, my goal was a simple one. Stoke the hunger between us until she gave up all her secrets.

Then I could make quick work of defeating her at the table—and we could both reap the rewards.

CHAPTER FIVE

HAD I COMPLETELY lost my ever-loving mind?

Why had I agreed to stop play and share a meal with Dante Allegri? It was stupid and reckless to the point of being extremely dangerous—especially if you factored in the pheromones rioting through my body every time he so much as glanced at me.

But I didn't realise how dangerous my situation was until I was sitting opposite him at a table in the adjoining salon, set with sparkling crystal, fine china and antique silverware. His devilishly handsome face—illuminated by the flicker of candlelight—looked more savage than suave as the prickles of sensation all over my skin refused to subside.

It was as if my body had a death wish.

He lifted my plate to serve me from the banquet displayed on a sideboard which had been brought up from the casino kitchens by a troop of waiters who, to my dismay, had disappeared again almost immediately.

'What's your pleasure, Miss Spencer?' The formal address sounded ridiculous, given the way I could feel his voice caressing my skin as he spoke my name in that husky, amused tone.

Wake up, Edie. This isn't real...he's not interested in you... He's a practised seducer trying to use his industrial-strength sex appeal to weaken all your defences.

I shouted the mantra in my head as I fought the strange sensation—a mesmerising mix of lethargy and fizzing urgency—which had taken over my body and drawn me into this perilous position.

I should have resisted the urge to challenge him, to provoke him and to accept the gauntlet he'd thrown down, but I was here now and I couldn't back down so I'd just have to play out this hand to the best of my abilities. Maybe I'd had some vague notion of playing him at his own game but, as the intimacy drew in around me and my ribs contracted around my thundering heartbeat, I realised the recklessness of that knee-jerk decision. I had no experience at all of men, especially not rich, powerful, sexually magnetic men who exuded the kind of confidence and charisma Dante Allegri did without even trying. I might as well have been a mouse, trying to impress a lion.

I breathed in the delicious aroma of the food as I concentrated on choosing a selection but, as my mouth watered and my stomach grumbled, I'd never felt less like eating.

I picked a few dishes from the lavish array of French cuisine—which I noted was plentiful enough to have fed me and my sister for a week—only to find myself entranced by the play of his strong capable hands as he ladled the fragrant samples of delicately spiced fish and lightly steamed vegetables, the rich gratin and colourful salads onto a gold-rimmed fine china plate.

He had wide callused palms and long fingers and blunt, carefully clipped nails. His skin looked darkly tanned against the pristine white cotton of his shirt. He'd lost the tuxedo jacket several hours ago but before serving me he had rolled up his shirt sleeves, giving me a disturbing view of the corded muscles in his forearms, the sprinkle of dark hair, as he placed my plate on the table.

He proceeded to serve himself a large helping, then sat down opposite me. He lifted a bottle of wine out of the ice bucket set next to the
table and uncorked it in a few efficient strokes,
then tipped the bottle towards my glass.

'Some wine? I assure you this white goes well
with Argento's skate *au beurre noir.*'

Drinking probably wasn't a good idea, but
with my heart battering my chest at approxi-
mately five hundred beats per second I had to
do something to slow it down, so I nodded.

He poured me a shallow glass, not enough to
get me drunk, I realised with relief, but as he
served himself I noticed the bottle's label. A
Mouton Rothschild Blanc from the turn of the
new century. I took a generous gulp to hide my
surprise, letting the fresh, delightfully fruity
taste moisten my dry mouth.

I wondered why he hadn't boasted about the
wine, which I knew sold for thousands of euros
a bottle, because one of the many things we
had been forced to do after my mother died,
to pay off her debts, was auction everything in
her wine cellar.

'Buon appetito,' he said, nodding to my plate
before picking up his own cutlery.

I scooped up a mouthful of buttery fish and creamy potatoes, but I could barely taste it as I swallowed. He was still watching me. Assessing my weaknesses, I was sure, with that focused, intensely blue gaze as he devoured his own food.

'Where are you from, Miss Spencer?' he asked finally. He leaned back in his chair and lifted his wine glass to those sensual lips.

I watched him swallow and took another sip from my own glass as I gave up trying to eat the food and attempted to come up with a convincing answer.

Unfortunately I hadn't prepared for this eventuality, having convinced myself Allegri wouldn't even be in the house tonight.

'A small town north of Chantilly. Lamorlaye,' I said, mentioning a town close enough to Belle Rivière that I would know the details, just in case he knew the area too.

'You're French?' His eyes narrowed as his brows rose up his forehead. 'And yet you speak English without an accent.'

'I'm half-French, half-British,' I clarified, my heartbeat stuttering under that inquisitive gaze. I knew it was always best to keep as close to the truth as possible, because then it was harder to get caught out in a lie, but I didn't want to give him information that might make it possible to track me down after I won tonight's game... *If* I won tonight's game.

The jolt of panic had me taking another sip of my wine to calm the nerves that were jiggling around in my stomach with Argento's skate.

'I live most of the year in Knightsbridge,' I said, plucking the most expensive area of London I could think of out of thin air. 'But the city is so stifling at this time of year,' I continued, lying through my teeth now to put him off the scent. I needed to sound urbane and cosmopolitan and a little bored to keep up the pretence that I was a rich heiress amusing herself for the summer. 'So I prefer to stay at my parents' estate in Lamorlaye from May to September... The social scene in Chantilly is so much more exclusive and refined than Paris, and our chateau has a pool and a tennis court and a cinema so I can keep in shape and entertain myself when I'm not socialising or making flying visits to Monaco, or Cannes, or Biarritz.'

'You don't work?' He sounded both suspicious and unimpressed.

I slipped my hands off the table and rested them in my lap, rubbing the calluses on my palms I'd been hiding all evening. The last thing I wanted him to know about was the night-time cleaning jobs I'd taken on in the last year—along with the accountancy work I'd been doing for local businesses ever since my mother died four years ago. If he knew how desperate I was to win this game, it would only make me easier prey.

'Work's so overrated, don't you think?' I said. 'And anyway, I'd hate to be tied down like that. I'm a free spirit, Mr Allegri. I much prefer the danger of riding my luck at the roulette table or the excitement of calculating my odds during a game of Texas Hold 'Em than shackling myself to a boring nine-to-five job,' I continued, the lies floating out of my mouth like confetti at a high society wedding—the sort I'd only ever seen in magazines or on the Internet.

His frown lowered and for a split second I thought I'd overdone the rich airhead act. He had to know I wasn't an idiot from the way I'd played so far. But then the crease in his brow eased and a cynical, knowing smile curved those wide sensual lips. But while my panic at being caught in a lie downgraded, what I saw flicker across his face for a split second had my heart bouncing back into my throat.

Disappointment.

When he spoke again, his voice rich with condescension, I was convinced I must have imagined it. Surely, like all the rich men I'd ever met, he preferred his women pretty and vacuous—the way my mother had always taken great pains to appear when trying to attract a new 'protector'.

'From the way you play poker,' he said, faint praise evident in every syllable, 'I'd say your time has been very well spent.'

Picking up my glass, I toasted him with un-steady hands. *'Touché,'* I whispered, repeating the provocative phrase he'd uttered earlier, in an attempt to sound more confident and pro-vocative.

He toasted me too and knocked back the last of his wine. But when his gaze fixed on my face again, while it still prickled over my skin, ablaze with an intense, focused desire that still disturbed me on so many levels, something crucial had been lost—his regard for me as a worthy opponent and an intelligent woman. He was looking at me now as an object of desire and contempt, not as an equal. The way all my mother's 'protectors' had always looked at her.

Anxiety and inadequacy twisted in my stomach, wrestling with the confusion and longing that was already there. I tried to dismiss the feeling of regret that he despised me now.

It was stupid to care what he thought. I wasn't here to impress him. I was here to win this game by whatever means necessary. And who was he to judge me anyway? A man who had made his fortune by ruthlessly exploiting the addictions of poor, deluded fools like my brother-in-law until they forgot about everything that mattered. And betrayed everyone who loved them.

I pushed the contempt I felt for myself and this necessary charade onto him. If I looked at it that way, Dante Allegri was as much to blame for my family's disastrous circumstances as Jason was. Maybe more so, because Jason had always been weak and easily led, unlike Allegri, who must have come out of his mother's womb with a well-developed sense of entitlement and a complete lack of compassion and empathy or how would he ever have been able to achieve what he had?

Unfortunately my growing sense of grievance against Allegri did nothing to temper the huge surge of adrenaline when he wiped his mouth with his napkin, threw it on the table and then stood and held out his hand.

'Come with me, Miss Spencer. I have something you might enjoy seeing before we resume our play.'

He towered over me. He was a tall man, at least six foot three, and I was only a sliver over five foot four but, with his shirt sleeves rolled up and standing over me, it wasn't just his height that was intimidating. This close, I could see how toned and powerful his body was beneath the tailored shirt and trousers. All lean muscles and coiled strength, he looked like a bareknuckle fighter who would be completely merciless in his pursuit of the win.

The enormity of what I was trying to achieve—beating Allegri at his own game in his own casino—hit me with staggering force but, instead of my flight instinct kicking in, as it probably should have done, the surge of adrenaline, and the rising tide of anger, at all my family had suffered as a result of this man's cold-blooded business practices, had my fight instinct kicking in instead.

Whatever happened now, I would do everything and anything to beat this man.

I took the hand he offered and forced what I hoped was a seductive, confident smile onto my lips. 'That sounds intriguing,' I said, pleased when my voice barely quivered.

But when he folded my arm under his, tugging me close to his side—until all I could feel was the bunch and flex of his strong body next to mine and all I could smell was the clean scent of cedar soap and the devastating scent of him—my fight instinct blurred into something volatile and dangerous.

He escorted me to the mullioned window which looked out over the bay and let go of my arm, to step behind me.

'Over there,' he said as he pointed into the inky blackness over my shoulder.

'What am I looking at?' Was he about to show me his yacht? I wondered. I wanted to believe he was vain and conceited, even though all I'd seen so far was passion and purpose—and an arrogance that he had clearly earned.

But just as I became far too aware of the masculine scent surrounding me, and the warmth of his body against the bare skin of my back, a red glow burst over the edge of the horizon, grabbing all my attention.

I gasped, shocked by the flagrant beauty of the natural light show as it spread and shimmered across the night sky, turning from red to pink to orange and myriad shades in between.

'It's beautiful,' I whispered.

I'd never seen the Northern Lights before. I didn't even know you could see them in Monaco, believing them to be a phenomenon of the Arctic Circle. My heart leapt into my throat. How had he known they would occur at this very moment? It was almost as if he'd conjured them especially for me.

I struggled to dismiss the foolish romantic thought, recognising it for what it was, a notion borne out of an overpowering physical response that I had not prepared for. But then he rested a hand on my hip and the gentle brush of his palm spread the fire in my belly through my body with the same intensity as the conflagration on the horizon.

I stood all but cocooned in his arms. I knew

I should step away from him, the deep drawing sensation in my abdomen far too compelling. But the huff of breath against my ear, the intoxicating scent of soap and man, the strength of his restraint as he tensed behind me had the last of my caution flying out of the window.

We stood there together for several minutes, watching the show—and the drawing sensation in my stomach heated and spread. The mass of contradictions he stirred within me became harder and harder to explain. Why did he excite me so much? How could I enjoy standing so close to him when I knew how dangerous he was?

I shifted and turned as the lights began to fade.

His face was lit by the dying embers of the Aurora Borealis and a passion so fierce and all-consuming it terrified me. But it exhilarated me more.

It wasn't terror I felt when he brought his hand up to cup my cheek then drew his thumb down my neck in a slow glide, to settle against the rampaging pulse on my collarbone. It was longing.

'Don't look at me like that, Edie,' he murmured, using my Christian name—and the only real name I'd given him—for the first time. 'Unless you want to share my bed once the game is over.'

It was supposed to be a warning, but to my dazed mind and the pheromones hurtling through my body it sounded more like a promise.

A promise I didn't want to refuse.

I lifted shaking palms to his stubble-roughened cheeks. He clenched his jaw and tried to pull back, but I refused to let go.

Just this once, I wanted to go with my instincts and to hell with the consequences.

'Damn it,' he swore softly, but then he dragged me into his arms.

Joy burst through me—so inappropriate and yet so intoxicating—at the realisation I had snapped his cast-iron control.

He captured my lips with his. The kiss was firm and forceful, and demanding. Heat swooped into my sex and swelled in my breasts, shimmering through my body like the lights in the fiery night sky. My nipples tightened into hard aching points against the unyielding wall of his chest. My thighs trembled as his hands grasped my buttocks and drew me tight against him so I could feel the full measure of what I'd done to him. The thick outline of his erection ground against my belly.

The size and hardness shocked me, but it thrilled me more.

He wanted me as much as I wanted him. This seduction was real. We were equals.

His tongue thrust deep into my mouth in a relentless rhythm, devouring me. I opened my mouth wider, met his tongue thrust for thrust, the hunger consuming me.

But as the kiss continued, the sensations bombarding me became too strong, too over-whelming. What was happening to me? He was destroying my resistance and every ounce of my will. Why did I yearn to surrender to him?

I stopped massaging his scalp and gripped the silky waves of his hair in shaking fingers to tug his head back.

He grunted but let me go so abruptly I stum-bled.

My survival instinct finally kicked in—sev-eral minutes too late—and I scrambled back, scared that I would throw myself back into that maelstrom of needs and desires if he made any attempt to kiss me again.

But he made no move towards me, his ragged breathing as tortured as my own. He swore, a guttural murmur of Italian street slang that I didn't understand, then swung away and stalked towards the window. The horizon was dark again, the dance of iridescent colours gone.

He thrust his fingers through his hair, then shoved his hands into his pockets. His broad shoulders rose and fell as he heaved out a breath, his big body silhouetted by the sprinkle of lights from the bay.

At last he turned back to me but, with his hair mussed and his movements far from smooth, he was nothing like the man who had faced me across the poker table and then the dinner table. No longer confident and controlled, and indomitable—instead he seemed wild, or barely tame, like a trapped tiger prowling the bars of its cage.

I touched trembling fingers to my lips, the soreness both devastating and invigorating. This new side to him should have scared me more but as he walked back towards me, still struggling to get a grip on the desire which continued to reverberate through my own body, I felt a giddy sense of kinship.

Was he as disturbed by the ferocity of that kiss, and how quickly it had raged out of control, as I was?

'Forgive me,' he growled when he reached me. 'That got out of hand a lot faster than I intended.'

The apology sounded gruff but sincere. And gave me an answer I didn't know how to handle. Dante Allegri, the ruthless unprincipled womaniser, was a lot easier to hate than the man before me, who seemed almost as troubled by that kiss as I was.

'Can we... Can we get back to the game?' I managed at last, surprised by my ability to string a coherent sentence together.

One eyebrow rose a fraction, but then he nodded.

'Yes,' he said.

Lifting one hand out of his pocket, he directed me to precede him into the poker salon. He made a point of not touching me again but, once we were seated at the table and he began to deal the cards, I could see he had regained his composure, and that cast-iron control.

I lifted my hole cards and examined them, but the probabilities I should be calculating as he dealt the first of the community cards and the blind betting began refused to come. My mind and every one of my senses had turned to mush.

My heart shrank in my chest as the play continued and he won the hand.

I tried to get my mind into gear during the next hand, but my judgement was off and my concentration shot. My mind and body were still reeling from the driving needs and inexplicable emotions he had ignited with a simple kiss. A kiss I had encouraged. No, a kiss I had initiated.

I wanted to weep, my panic increasing as he won the next hand. The unrequited need smouldered in the pit of my belly—the memory of his lips on mine, his hands kneading my buttocks, his tongue exploring in deep strokes—a distraction I couldn't seem to conquer...

Long before the final hand was dealt, I knew I had lost and that I had only myself to blame. Because in those giddy moments when I had yearned for Dante Allegri's kiss, then revelled in the stunning way it made me feel and then kidded myself it had devastated him too, I had become the one thing I'd always sworn I would never be... As weak and needy and gullible as my mother.

CHAPTER SIX

'Two fives…' I threw my hole cards on the table next to Edie Spencer's pair of eights. Unfortunately for her, the community cards included another five. 'You lose, *bella*,' I said, grateful that the poker game was finally over.

It had taken an epic force of will and all of my expertise to keep my mind on the cards in the last hour. Ever since that damn kiss. It was a miracle I'd managed to win. After she'd broken off the embrace, I had considered throwing the game to get this part of the evening over with so I could get my hands on her again.

It had been torture, sitting in the chair and struggling to keep my head straight while my blood rushed straight back to my groin every time she worried her bottom lip with her teeth, or the soft mounds of her breasts rose and fell against the lace of her gown.

But I had forced myself to stay focused, or focused enough, to get the job done. Yes, we clearly had phenomenal chemistry, the sort of explosive sexual connection I'd never had with any other woman. And we were both going to have fun exploring it to its fullest potential. But I wasn't going to throw a game to have her—especially as I was pretty sure that's exactly why she had initiated the kiss in the first place.

But her little plan had backfired, because if I had been struggling to keep my head straight and out of my pants after that kiss, she'd been even more distracted.

If she'd ever had a system—something I'd begun to doubt after our conversation over dinner had revealed her to be as spoilt and capricious as every other bored little rich girl who played the casinos on their daddy's dime—it had fallen apart when we'd got back to the game.

She obviously hadn't expected that kiss to go off like a rocket the way it had—which had to be why she'd called a halt to her attempted seduction so abruptly.

But as I raked in the last of her chips, I relished the surge of heat that shot straight to my groin at the thought of what the rest of the night would hold.

She hadn't said anything, and it was hard to tell how she was taking the defeat because she had her head down. But then I detected the tiny tremor running through her body. Impatience and irritation warred with my desire.

Even though I still hadn't figured out why this woman had such a turbulent effect on my usually smart libido, I wanted to take that incredible kiss to its logical conclusion. But if she was going to start crying and try to wheedle a concession out of me because I had beaten her, she could forget it. I'd won the game fair and square and I didn't trade sexual favours—however hot they promised to be—for money.

Sure, I'd had girlfriends in the past whom I'd supported. I liked to treat women I was sleeping with well. And if I was seeing someone on a regular basis I always offered them a generous allowance so they could devote their time to me and had everything they needed. I could be demanding—my lifestyle was expensive and I needed them to revolve their schedule around mine—so it seemed only fair to offer them compensation. I also always gave them a generous parting gift when the relationship reached its natural conclusion. I was a wealthy man, I considered these women friends and I didn't want anyone calling me a cheapskate, so why wouldn't I?

But I wasn't about to be emotionally manipulated by some spoilt young woman because she'd taken a chance with her daddy's money and lost. And I resented the implication that I should.

Despite all that, as Edie continued to sit there, her head bent and her shoulders starting to tremble alarmingly, a weird thing happened. I found myself wanting to take the tremor away. And not just because I had plans for the rest of the night that would become a lot less palatable if she started freaking out about the million euros of her daddy's money she'd lost.

'*Bella*, don't get too upset. I'll sub you a million so we can have a rematch some time.' It was the best I could offer without feeling like a chump. And once I said it I warmed to the idea.

Up until we'd both got distracted by that kiss, I'd enjoyed the challenge of playing with her. Our sexual attraction had added an exciting level of eroticism to the game—like high-stakes foreplay. I would enjoy playing her again, and figuring out if she actually had a system and, if so, what it was, or whether her success in the earlier part of the evening had been down to plain old dumb luck.

Instead of taking me up on the offer though, she shook her head. Still not looking at me.

My impatience and frustration spiked, along with that weird feeling of empathy.

'Look at me, *bella*.' Leaning across the table, I tucked a knuckle under her chin and nudged her face up.

What I saw though—when her emerald eyes finally met mine—was so real it shocked me to my core.

Her eyes were dry, without the self-pitying tears I had been expecting, but also dazed and unfocused—she looked shattered. Devastated.

A stab of something ripped through my chest. And the trickle of unwanted sympathy turned into a flood.

'*Bella?* What's going on?' I said, disorientated and concerned—not just by the haunted look in her eyes, but also by my desire to take her anguish away.

Why did she look so shattered? And why the hell did I care?

'N… N… Nothing,' she stuttered, shaking her head. She stood up. 'I have to go.'

She walked past me, her back ramrod-straight, her face a deathly shade of white, her whole body consumed by tremors now.

I grasped her arm, felt the shudder of reaction. 'Don't…'

Go.

The word got trapped in my throat before I could utter it.

Grazie a Dio.

What was wrong with me? We'd kissed, once. And yeah, it had been spectacular, and unexpected. And I wanted more. But I wasn't about to beg her to stay. So I took a different tack. 'Where are you going in such a rush? Stay and have a drink,' I said, attempting to sound relaxed and persuasive.

I tugged her round to face me, disturbed by the sparkle of moisture in her eyes. I'd been expecting tears. But the sheen of distress looked genuine, something she was making every effort to contain, not use to guilt-trip me about my win.

How could she seem so fragile and breakable now, when she'd been so strong and determined earlier in the evening? And why did I still want her so much? Because her vulnerability wasn't doing a damn thing to stem the tidal wave of longing that had tortured me ever since our kiss.

Surely it was all an act? It had to be. But why couldn't I convince myself of that?

'Bella...' I cupped her cheek, brushed my thumb across the soft skin, stupidly relieved when her pulse jumped against my palm. And her eyes darkened.

She still wanted me too. I hadn't imagined that much, at least.

'It's only money,' I said, certain the cause of her distress had to be her parents' reaction. Perhaps her father would be angry. What man wouldn't be at a million-euro loss, even an indulgent father?

'You're good. Just not good enough on this occasion. But I'll give you a chance to win it back, if that's what you want.'

'Thank you. That's very generous of you,' she said.

'Then you'll stay, join me for a drink?' I hated the element of doubt in my voice. We both knew I wasn't just talking about her staying for a drink—the promise of that kiss was still snapping in the air around us.

'Yes, okay,' she said.

'Good,' I said, more relieved and excited than I should have been at her concession. I placed a light kiss on her forehead, pleased when her breathing stuttered. I forced myself not to take her lips again though, before we were both ready.

She drew away and I had to stop myself from dragging her back into my arms, the desire to stake my claim on her all but overwhelming.

She jerked her thumb over her shoulder. 'Can I go and freshen up first?'

'Of course,' I said, even though I wanted to demand she stay.

I wasn't possessive with women. And I had no idea where the ludicrous desire not to let her out of my sight came from, so I ignored it.

But, as I watched her leave the room, the rush of blood to my groin became all but unbearable.

I poured myself a glass of expensive single malt Scotch while I waited for her, to calm my frustration and my impatience.

Walking to the window, I savoured the smoky liquor as it burned down my throat. Once she was in my bed, and I had begun to tap the heat we had ignited with that kiss, Edie Spencer would soon forget the money she'd lost. And the problem of explaining it to her father.

Hell, if we were as good together as I was anticipating, and that kiss had suggested, I could offer to support her until the fire between us burnt out. She clearly had expensive tastes, no income of her own and enjoyed the thrill of gambling with money she hadn't earned. Perhaps I could employ her as a hostess for the week-long party I was throwing at my new estate in Nice at the end of the month? Edie would be perfect for such a role, smart, beautiful and classy—and well versed in how to charm elite businessmen after her privileged upbringing. Her skill at the table might also be useful.

Of course, I might have a job on my hands persuading her to work for a living. But after her reaction tonight to losing her father's million euro stake, I didn't think it would be that hard to persuade her to take the job. I was a generous employer. Plus taming that free spirit of hers could be enjoyable for both of us.

I bolted back the last of the Scotch, finally feeling more like myself. The burn in my throat matched the warm weight in my gut—a weight which I understood now and knew would be easily resolved once Edie returned.

I glanced at my watch, surprised she was taking so long.

My cell-phone buzzed. I lifted it out of my pocket and read Joe Donnelly's text.

We've got a problem. Call me.

I sighed, tempted to ignore the request. It was four in the morning and Edie would be back soon.

But my innate professionalism took over. Joe wasn't the hysterical type, so if there was a problem he couldn't fix it must require my attention.

I clicked on the call button.

Joe picked up instantly. 'How's the game going?' he asked without preamble.

'I won ten minutes ago, why?'

Joe cursed, the Irish slang he never used unless he was rattled.

'Is Edie Spencer still with you?' he asked.

'She's freshening up,' I said, but already the hairs on the back of my neck were going haywire.

'So she's not actually in the room with you?'

'No... What's going on, Joe?' I asked, but I already knew something was very wrong, the twisting pain in my gut one I recognised from a very long time ago.

'The bank draft she paid us with—it's forged. And so is her ID. The accounting department figured it out ten minutes ago, when they noticed a shortfall in the night's takings in the casino's accounts.'

The pain sharpened, turning into the hollow ache that had crippled me as a kid. She wasn't coming back.

'The good news is we think we might have figured out who she really is.' Joe was still talking but I could barely grasp the meaning of the words, the blood rushing in my ears, the tremble of reaction in my fingers a combination of fury and something far, far worse. Helplessness.

'Who is she?' I asked, fury burning in my gut now, obliterating the distant echo of an anguish I had once been unable to control.

'Ever heard of Madeleine Trouvé?' Joe asked.

'No,' I said, resisting the urge to shout at my friend as my head began to pound. 'Is that her real name?' I said, keeping my voice low and even, although it was the opposite of how I felt. Edie Spencer had tricked me, made a fool of me. Made me relive a moment in my life I had spent a lifetime overcoming. And she would pay for that. As well as the money she'd just swindled me out of. 'We need to track her down,' I said.

Something I intended to do personally. She owed me a million euros. But I knew it wasn't just the money. My fingers clutched so hard on the whisky tumbler it shattered in my fingers.

'Madeleine Trouvé was *the* French It girl of the nineties,' Joe continued. 'Famous for the high-profile affairs she had with a string of rich, powerful and mostly married men. Seriously, you've never heard of her?' Joe asked, sounding incredulous.

'I don't have time for twenty questions,' I shouted, losing the tenuous grip I had on my temper as I wrapped a napkin around my bleeding fingers. The sting of expensive liquor in the cuts grounded me, turning the emotion churning in my belly into a cold, hard knot of anger. 'How the hell can Edie Spencer be her—the woman I just played can't be more than early twenties…'

Dewy soft skin, artless kisses, wide guileless eyes filled with passion and then devastation. How could all of that have been a lie too?

You didn't play her—she played you…

I sucked in a shattered breath, disgusted by the wave of lust that still accompanied the memory of her. The anger spiked.

'She would barely have been born in the nineties,' I finished, my voice rising as my fevered mind tried to get a grip on the sense of betrayal, the shot of confusion, tangling with the whirlwind of anger and lust still burning in my gut.

'Yeah, I know. She's not *Madeleine* Trouvé. Madeleine died in a helicopter crash four years ago with one of her lovers. Some Spanish nobleman. We think she may be the younger of Madeleine's two daughters. Edie Trouvé.'

'How sure are you?' I asked, the tangle of lust and anger and loss muted by the fierce jolt of determination. I would find Edie and teach her a lesson she wouldn't soon forget about trying to play the wrong guy.

I wasn't some spoilt, pampered, inbred aristocrat like the men her mother had obviously favoured. I had dragged myself up—literally—from the back streets of Naples. I'd run away from a series of foster families and group homes, lived on the streets as a teenager, worked like a dog in a series of dead end jobs to earn my stake, even been left beaten and bloody in an alleyway in Paris at the age of seventeen when I'd made a miscalculation on my rise to the top. No one got the better of me. And certainly not a slip of a girl with big green eyes and a sprinkle of freckles across her pert nose...

'Pretty sure,' Joe replied, thankfully interrupting the renewed wave of longing.

Which made no sense at all.

I didn't want Edie Spencer... No, Edie Trouvé. Not any more. The heat I couldn't seem to control was just the residual effect of temper and too many hours of sexual frustration. Frustration which I could see clearly now Edie had started and then stoked every chance she got. Culminating in that blasted kiss.

Basta.

What was it they said about the apple not falling far from the tree? The girl had learned how to tempt and tantalise men from a woman who had spent a lifetime using sex, and the promise of sex, like a weapon. Her own mother.

A woman who, for all intents and purposes, was no better than my own mother.

I cut off the crippling thought, the dangerous memories.

Don't go there. These two situations are not related. Edie Trouvé means nothing to you.

'Do you know where to find her?' I gritted out the words.

'Not yet, but we're working on it,' Joe replied.

'Good,' I said as a strange kind of calm settled over me and the roaring fury in the pit of my stomach. 'Work faster. I want her found.'

CHAPTER SEVEN

'WHAT DO YOU MEAN, the bank draft I gave Allegri's cashier was fake?' I stared at Carsoni's henchman, the aptly named Brutus, my terror mixing with a bitter sense of outrage. They'd tricked me into defrauding Allegri's casino. Already I had a debt I couldn't pay, but that had been my brother-in-law's debt. This felt worse. So much worse, because this debt was on me.

I'd sat down at that poker table in good faith. I'd played and I'd lost, through my own weaknesses, my own failings. I had very little else left now but my good name. And okay, the name I'd given Allegri had been a false one, but I had never intended to cheat him.

Maybe it was foolish to care about what he thought of me. But somehow it mattered.

'You should thank me, *ma petite*,' Brutus said, the husky tone, the sleazy use of the endearment and the way his beady eyes skimmed over my figure, as they had done a million times before—every time he paid us a visit to collect payment of Carsoni's interest—made me want to vomit. 'You're already into the boss for five million euro—why add another million to the pot?'

'But Allegri will figure it out. He could have me arrested. Fraud is a crime. And then how will I pay back Carsoni?' Weirdly, the thought of being arrested and imprisoned didn't seem as bad as having Allegri despise me.

I locked the thought away because it made no sense. I was never going to see Allegri again. What he thought of me didn't matter; it was what I thought of myself.

Up till now I'd done everything I could to honour the debts Jason had created. Maybe the path I'd chosen had been reckless and foolishly ambitious, and stemmed from a pride in my own abilities that was misplaced, to say the least; I could see that now. But I'd never meant to do something, however inadvertently, that made me a criminal.

'Allegri's not going to figure it out,' Brutus murmured. 'You used a fake ID, remember. I arranged it myself.'

They had suggested the fake ID, in case

Allegri figured out my system and had me banned. And I'd gone along with it. Because I'd been naïve and desperate. Desperate enough to believe a loan shark's bullyboy.

'And Carsoni has other ideas about how you can pay him back now.'

'What?' I scrambled back as he lifted his hand to my face. The sick weight in my stomach—which had been growing ever since I had fled The Inferno early that morning or, rather, ever since Allegri had turned over his winning hand and I'd finally woken up to the terrible mistakes I had made—twisted into something mangled and ugly.

Brutus grabbed a handful of my hair and tugged me back towards him. His breath—stale with tobacco smoke—brushed my lips. I gagged and bit down on my tongue to stop myself from throwing up, my disgust now almost as huge as my terror.

He laughed. 'Stop acting surprised. Carsoni likes you. You're a pretty little thing. And he's bored, waiting for you to pay up.'

My head hurt, my scalp stinging as he dragged me closer, close enough to bury his face against my neck. I struggled, trying to pull away from him, revulsion skittering over my skin like a plague of cockroaches.

He twisted his fist in my hair, his tongue touching my neck. 'Stop acting so high and mighty,' he murmured. 'Your mother was a highly priced whore. Carsoni will forget about the debt if you show him the proper appreciation.'

I wanted to scream, but the scream was locked in my throat. If I screamed, Jude would come to my rescue. I couldn't risk endangering her too. Jude had no idea of the threats I'd already faced from Brutus and his boss, but this was worse. The terror was so huge now, I was almost gagging on it. But I couldn't let him see that. Bullies, in my experience, were only emboldened if you showed them your fear.

I struggled in earnest. He let me go and I fell back a step.

'We're selling the house…' I pleaded. 'It's worth at least the five million we owe.' Or I hoped it was.

I had no idea where we were going to live. But we would survive. I was young and strong and a hard worker. And so was Jude. Maybe we wouldn't have Belle Rivière any more. The small chateau was the only place we had felt safe, or important in our mother's life, growing up. But however beautiful this place was—the meadows and pastures overflowing with wild-flowers, the river running through the bottom of the property where we'd swum as children during those long idyllic summers, the elegance of the eighteenth-century design my mother's grandfather had built as a summer house for his ailing wife—and, however much we loved it, it was just bricks and mortar and fond memories.

My efforts to save it, my refusal to sell it as soon as Jason had incurred the debt, had only got us deeper into trouble. It was way past time I faced reality. And stopped struggling against the inevitable. Or my reality could get a whole lot worse.

The hideous truth of how much worse had my blood running cold as Brutus stepped towards me, the lecherous smirk on his face making my skin crawl.

'Maybe it'll fetch what you owe,' he said, glancing around the empty library, devoid of furniture now and books, because we'd had to sell the lot months ago to service the interest on Jason's debt. 'And maybe it won't,' he added, his gaze landing back on me. 'Either way, money isn't what the boss wants any more.'

Fury rose up like a tidal wave to cover the fear. 'Tough, because money is all he's going to get from me.'

The slap was so sudden, and so shocking, I didn't have a chance to brace.

The pain exploded in my cheekbone, snapping my head back. I slammed into the floor, rapping my elbow on the hard wood as I attempted to break my fall.

'You think?' Brutus said, the casualness of his brutality shocking me almost as much as the pain now ricocheting through my tired body as he stood over me.

I tried to slap his hands away as he grabbed my hair again, but my movements were jerky and uncoordinated, my mind entering another dimension of shock and loss and terror as he lifted me off the ground.

'Let's see how high and mighty you are once you realise what the alternative is,' he said, the calm, conversational tone striking terror into my heart.

I kicked out at him and he hit me again. Even

prepared for the pain this time, the slap exploded on my cheek and released the scream I had tried to keep locked in my throat. The buzzing in my head became louder, like whirring blades.

Swish, swish, swish. As if a helicopter were landing in the library. I thought of Dante, his eyes burning into mine, telling me he wanted me.

I could hear Jude's crying, the door rattling.

'Edie, Edie, open the door. What's happening in there?'

My dazed mind realised that Brutus had locked it when we came in here—to discuss our latest payment. The fear became huge. I kicked at his shins and he let me go. I stumbled and fell, then scrambled up, trying to run, trying to hide from those cruel fists. But the room was bare—where could I go?

I heard shouting outside, a deep voice I recognised.

He's not here... No one can save you but yourself.

'Come here.' Brutus grabbed me again, strong fingers digging into my arm hard enough to bruise.

An almighty crash startled us both. I watched the door smash inwards and fly off its hinges.

Dante Allegri strode into the room like an avenging angel, followed by his casino manager. My mind whirred like the blades of that imaginary helicopter.

Not imaginary—had Dante come to save me?

'Call the police, Joe,' he shouted, reaching us in a few strides.

You're dreaming. It's not him. Why would he come to save you?

Brutus' bruising fingers released me.

'Who the—?' The words cut off as Dante's fist connected with the henchman's jaw. Brutus's big body folded in on itself in slow motion.

I watched him drag himself up as Dante approached him. Then, like all bullies, he raced out of the door, shoving past Joseph Donnelly and my sister.

I skittered back, crouched on the floor now, as I watched my attacker run. His footfalls echoed in my aching head—which had been stuffed full of cotton wool.

Was this really happening or was I imagining it all?

The brief jolt of euphoria turned to turmoil. A

part of me knew I was in shock. But as Dante walked back towards me, flexing his fingers, the knuckles bleeding, the full import of what had happened smacked into me. The fear, the confusion, the panic cracked open like an earthquake inside me. Until all that was left was the pain.

I wrapped my arms around my knees, my whole body trembling so violently I was scared I might shake myself apart.

He knelt down, that handsome face so close to me I could smell him—spicy cologne and cedar soap and man. But still I didn't believe it. Why was he here? Why had he saved me? And then I remembered. I owed him a million euros.

'Bella,' he murmured as gentle fingers touched my cheek.

I flinched, tears leaking out of my eyes. Tears I knew I shouldn't shed. Because they were tears of self-pity.

Jude appeared by my side. 'Edie…he hit you? That bastard…'

I flinched again as she cried, her sobbing making the pain in my head and my heart so much worse. I pressed my bruised face into my knees. I didn't want Dante to see me like this.

Brutalised and terrified and unable to defend myself. I was so ashamed.

But I couldn't run, or hide. I hurt all over now—the pain in my face, and my elbow, and my ribs, no longer dull and indistinct but sharp and throbbing as the adrenaline of my scuffle with Brutus wore off. I was so weary, my bones felt as if they were anchored to the floor.

I shrank into myself, with some childish notion that if I couldn't see him—and the pity on his face—he wouldn't be able to see me.

'Stop crying,' Dante said to Jude, his voice soft but steely. 'And call an ambulance for your sister.'

'Already done,' Joe, the casino manager, interrupted from above me. 'Hey, colleen, come with me; your sister's going to be okay. Dante will take care of her now,' he said.

My sister's crying became muffled and distant, the casino manager's soft Irish brogue comforting her as their footsteps faded away.

Dante will take care of her now.

I stifled the pang of something agonising under my breastbone at the words. How pathetic, to want it to be true. I wasn't Dante's responsibility.

I kept my head buried in my knees and began to rock, even though each movement made the pain increase. The yearning would show on my face and I couldn't bear for him to know how much his kindness meant to me.

'Look at me, *bella*.' The gentle demand reminded me of the night before, the moment when I'd lost everything on the final turn of the cards. Or thought I'd lost everything. Why did this feel so much worse? Perhaps because, even now, I wanted to cling to the kindness he was showing me. Wanted to believe it meant something, other than the obvious thing. That he pitied the pathetic creature I had become.

I shook my head, unable to speak, still unable to look at him.

'How badly did he hurt you?' he asked and I heard the suppressed fury in his voice. 'And who was he?' he added. 'That he dared put his hands on you like that?'

I could hear more than just fury in his voice now. The underlying thread of protectiveness, and outrage, speaking to a place deep inside me which I had kept buried for so long. I couldn't allow those needs to consume me again, the way they had when I was a little girl, or they might very well destroy me.

'I'm okay,' I managed. 'Please could you leave now?'

I heard a rough breath—halfway between a sigh and a curse—and sensed him sitting on the floor beside me.

'Not going to happen, *bella*,' he said, the gruff endearment as painful as the aching pain in my cheekbone where Brutus had struck me. 'You owe me a million euro, remember.'

CHAPTER EIGHT

EDIE LIFTED HER HEAD. That had got her attention.

Rage fired through my body when I saw the red mark on her cheek where that bastard had attacked her. Who was he? A boyfriend? A husband? A pimp?

I dismissed the last possibility instantly, knowing it was beneath me and her. Just because her mother had enjoyed the protection of a string of rich men did not mean Edie was willing to sell herself to the highest bidder.

Dressed in jeans and sneakers and a T-shirt, her face devoid of make-up and her arms clasping her knees as if she were trying to hold herself together, she looked impossibly young and vulnerable. Too vulnerable.

I stifled the renewed pang of sympathy making my chest ache. The medics arriving stopped me from questioning her further about the scene I had interrupted. It was a welcome pause. I needed a chance to get a grip on the emotions rioting through me.

But as I stepped back to let them check her for a concussion and assess her injuries, it was a major struggle to remain calm and focused.

I'd come here in anger to demand she pay the money she owed me. To punish her for cheating me. And running out on me. Instead I'd walked in on a scene that had turned my fury with her—a fury which I knew now had been about a lot more than just the money—into something a great deal more complicated.

Seeing that bastard with his hands on her had ignited not just my natural rage—against any man who would treat a woman in such a way—but something more personal. As my fist had connected with the bastard's jaw and I'd felt the satisfying crunch of bone on bone it hadn't been the instinct to protect a being more vulnerable than myself, but rather the spark of something dark and possessive—a spark that had been ignited the night before, the moment I had touched my lips to hers and felt her livewire response to my kiss—that had been driving me.

I was forced to acknowledge that it was that

possessive instinct too which had propelled me all the way to Northern France from Monaco this afternoon in the first place.

After all, I'd never felt the need to track down a fraudster personally before.

As she answered the paramedic's questions, I struggled to even my breathing and compose myself. The bright afternoon light flooded through dusty windows and I noticed for the first time the complete lack of furniture in the room, which must once have been some sort of library. Paint peeled from the woodwork and the faded wallpaper on the ceiling had old stains where water had leaked through from the floor above. As I studied the rundown state of the room's décor, I recalled the generally dilapidated state of the stonework on the building's exterior and the overgrown gardens which I had noticed when the helicopter had touched down outside.

The place was virtually derelict. The opposite of what I'd expected to find when I'd been obsessing about confronting Edie on her home turf in the helicopter ride from Monaco.

I'd convinced myself, after she'd run out on me and Joe had alerted me to the fraudulent bank draft, that she was a spoilt, indulged young woman who didn't like to pay her dues. It was a picture she'd deliberately helped to create during our evening together. But the sorry state of her mother's chateau told a very different story.

The skirmish I had interrupted between her and a man twice her size had been shocking enough—and I intended to find out exactly what that was about as soon as the medics had given Edie the all-clear. But, from everything I'd seen so far, it was clear to me that, far from being spoilt brats, Edie and her sister were destitute, or close to it.

While her desperation didn't excuse her decision to enter the poker game fraudulently and then flee, I felt strangely vindicated that she was not what she had originally appeared to be. Perhaps this explained my confusing responses to her.

The young female paramedic finally finished assessing Edie. I escorted her and her colleague from the room. When we reached the door I murmured, 'How is she?'

'She's okay. No signs of concussion, just some nasty bruises,' the female paramedic told me in French as she hefted her case back onto her shoulder. 'I'll wait outside for the *gendarmes* and apprise them of her condition when they arrive so they can add it to their report.' The medic glanced over her shoulder at Edie, who sat alone on the room's window seat, staring out at the chateau's overgrown garden. 'I hope they find the bastard who did this.'

Not as much as I do.

'Will she need a follow-up appointment?' I asked, trying to keep my fury under wraps.

The woman shook her head. 'Keep an eye on her for the next few hours. If she becomes lethargic or disorientated call us back immediately. She'll have some impressive bruises tomorrow, but otherwise she should be okay. Apart from the psychological trauma, of course,' she added darkly.

Thanking her again as she left, I returned to Edie, who looked small and frail in the empty room.

She turned towards me as I approached. 'You're still here?' she said, the wistful tone disconcerting me.

'Of course,' I replied, annoyed at the implication that I would leave without ensuring she was all right. 'I need to speak to the *gendarmes*. I intend to give them a detailed description of the man who attacked you.' I glanced at my watch. Joe had called them a good fifteen minutes ago. 'When they finally arrive.'

'Would you consider…?' She hesitated.

'Would I consider what?' I asked, the weariness in her voice and her body language making the pang worse.

'Would you consider not telling them about the bank draft? I'll pay you back every penny, I swear. But I can't do that if you press charges.'

I had absolutely no intention of informing the police about the bank draft, but I decided not to tell her that yet. There were a lot of questions I wanted answered… No, I *needed* answered. And the one million euros she owed me was the only leverage I had.

'*How* will you pay it back?' I asked, giving the empty room a pointed once-over. I didn't give a damn about the money any more, but I wanted to know exactly how bad her circumstances were. 'You don't appear to have much more left to sell.'

She blinked furiously, then looked away in a vain attempt to hide her distress. The pang sharpened in my chest. The sunlight shining through dusty glass illuminated the sheen of anguish she was trying so valiantly to contain.

'I…' She swallowed, the bold determination in the green depths reminding me of the woman who had captivated me so comprehensively at the poker table last night. 'We still own Belle Rivière,' she said. 'Even in its present state, it should fetch just about enough to pay off the mortgage we have on it and what we owe you and Carsoni.'

'Jean-Claude Carsoni?' I snapped. What the hell did that bastard have to do with this situation? 'You owe him money? How much?'

I did a quick calculation. It had to be a substantial sum because her home, however forlorn it might look, would be worth well over ten million euro.

And she'd said 'we'.

So whose debts was she paying off here? Because, from the cautious, clever way she'd played Texas Hold 'Em, right up until that kiss had distracted us both, she hadn't struck me as a problem gambler. Not only that but, after the bank draft had bounced, Joe had wired the picture taken by the security cameras when she'd entered The Inferno to all our competitors to identify her, and not one of them had ever seen or heard of her. I'd dismissed the possibility she might be a novice gambler this morning during the helicopter ride to Chantilly, because I'd been way too busy fuming about her deception.

But now I wasn't so sure. Was it possible she had little or no experience at the tables? My admiration for her—and the way she'd played—increased, which only disturbed me more.

I wasn't usually drawn to vulnerable, needy women—and under that tough cookie shell that was exactly what Edie Trouvé appeared to be—especially if she was up to her eyeballs in debt to a *bastardo* like Carsoni.

'You know Carsoni?' she said, sounding surprised.

'Enough to have him banned from operating his money-lending services anywhere near my casinos.'

Carsoni was a leech who preyed on problem gamblers then charged them criminal levels of interest they couldn't possibly repay.

I flexed my fingers, the slight throbbing in my knuckles reminding me of the creep I'd dispatched. 'Was that one of his men, *bella*?' I asked, my concern for her increasing tenfold.

She wasn't my responsibility. Or shouldn't be. But the slow-burning anger smouldering in my gut—and the desire to take Carsoni by the throat with my bare hands and strangle him for daring to let his goons touch her—was telling me I was not going to be able to walk away from this mess. However much I might want to.

She looked out of the window again. 'I don't see how that's any of your business.'

Maybe she was right on one level, but when the sunlight caught the darkening bruise on her cheekbone, the slow burn flared into something more insistent. Capturing her stubborn chin between my thumb and forefinger, I tugged her head back towards me.

'You made it my business,' I said, 'when you came to my casino.' *And kissed me with an artless fervour I cannot forget.*

My gaze strayed to her lips, the memory of her taste, so sweet and passionate, making hunger fire through me.

Her pupils dilated and a flush flamed over her pale skin, highlighting the bruise on her cheekbone. She tugged her chin out of my grasp, but not before I'd seen the flash of heat and panic.

It is pointless to deny it, bella, *we will have to feed the hunger eventually, if we want this torture to stop.*

But the sprinkle of freckles on her nose that made her look so young, and the purpling bruise that made her look so fragile, made it clear now wasn't the time to pursue the overwhelming physical attraction we shared.

Protecting her from Carsoni and his goons and accounting for her debt to me would have to be handled first.

'I told you, I'll pay you back,' she said, but I could hear the quiver of uncertainty.

'How much do you owe Carsoni?' I asked again.

Defiance sparkled in her emerald eyes. I found it strangely pleasing. 'That's none of your...'

'Stop...' I pressed a finger to her lips, silencing her protest '...being so stubborn. And let me help. You don't want to sell your home, or you would have done it long before it came to this,' I added, letting my thumb skim under the livid bruise blossoming on her cheekbone.

'Why would you even want to help me?' she asked. 'I tried to rob you.'

Shame flickered across her face, and suddenly I knew there was more to the story of that fake bank draft than she was telling me. Had she even known the draft was fake? I wondered. If she had, why would she have stayed at the table so long—when our accounts department could discover the fraud at any time? She was an intelligent woman, however desperate she was. I didn't believe she would have put herself in that situation knowingly.

'How much do you owe Carsoni?' I demanded for the third time, letting my impatience show.

She huffed out a breath but I could see the fight leave her as her shoulders slumped. 'It was only two million to start with, but it's over five million now,' she said, the resignation making me want to do a lot more than just strangle Carsoni. The *bastardo* deserved to be hung, drawn and quartered.

'We got a loan on the property to start with, but we could never pay off enough of it. And the debt just kept getting bigger and bigger.'

I forced myself not to react. But fury tightened around my chest as the desire to eviscerate Carsoni increased.

'How was the debt incurred?' I asked, because I was convinced now that it wasn't her debt to repay.

She stared at me directly. 'Actually it was incurred in The Inferno.'

'How so?' I asked.

She sighed, resignation clear in her voice when she began to talk.

'My brother-in-law Jason and my sister Jude went on holiday to Monaco a year ago. They visited The Inferno. Jude still says she doesn't know what happened to Jason that night. He was winning at first, but then the losses started to pile up. And he wouldn't leave. Eventually he'd lost all their savings. They came back here devastated. I was angry with him, for losing everything and I told him so.' I could hear the tinge of guilt in her voice, and it annoyed me. Why was she taking responsibility for this *idiota*? But I didn't interrupt. The mention of The Inferno's involvement had unsettled me.

We made every effort to spot problem or addicted gamblers and ban them. I prided myself on running an operation where people only parted with money they could afford to lose. It seemed we would need to tighten our regulations.

'I still do not understand how your brother-in-law became indebted to Carsoni. The Inferno does not accept loans secured in his name.'

'All I know,' she continued, her voice dull and lifeless, 'is that a week later Jason got a loan from Carsoni and returned to Monaco. I suppose he didn't lose that money at The Inferno.' Her shoulders bowed as if she were carrying a ten-ton boulder on her back, probably because that is exactly what she had been doing for over a year. 'I guess he wanted to win the money back. We haven't seen or heard from him since. Carsoni turned up a week after Jason disappeared with the credit agreement Jason had signed in Jude's name.'

So the debt was her brother-in-law's and by extension her sister's... And yet she'd had no hesitation in taking it on.

Every one of my assumptions about her had been incorrect. She wasn't spoilt, lazy or a coward. Why that should make my hunger for her more acute wasn't something I wanted to think about—because it also made it more problematic.

The desire to throttle Carsoni and Edie's idiot brother-in-law was much easier to explain. I despised men who preyed on women.

'You should have told me all this when you arrived at The Inferno,' I said, frustrated at the thought that she had come to the casino, and participated in the game, primarily to win back money which had been lost, in the first instance, at my roulette table.

I had no reason to feel guilty. I ran a business—if people chose to play, they had to deal with the consequences. But the qualification wasn't doing a damn thing for the pang spreading across my breastbone and tightening around my ribs like a vice.

She glanced at me then, surprise evident on her face. 'Why would I do that? It's not your problem; it's mine.'

'It is my problem now, as there is a matter of one million euros to repay.'

She flushed. 'Once we sell the chateau I can...'

'No,' I said, startling her, as I became increasingly annoyed with her stubbornness. 'You are not selling your home. I will not allow it.'

'That's not your choice to make,' she said.

I forced myself to dial down on my frustration. She had been brought to the brink of ruin because of her brother-in-law's recklessness, and then roughed up by one of Carsoni's men. She couldn't afford to refuse my help.

But as I opened my mouth to tell her what I planned to do about this situation, I heard the *gendarmes'* sirens.

I swore softly. *About damn time.*

She looked relieved by the interruption.

We spoke to the police together, but when she was questioned about the goon who had been hitting her when I arrived she said she couldn't identify him.

I knew she was lying because she watched me as she spoke to the young *gendarme*, her eyes pleading with me not to intervene—and contradict her.

I remained silent. But only because I knew that informing the *gendarmes* of Carsoni's involvement was not the answer.

As the police left us to question her sister Jude and Joe about the incident, Edie murmured under her breath, 'Thanks, for not saying anything about Carsoni.'

I nodded.

'And for punching that creep for me,' she added. 'I should have said that sooner.'

'No thanks is necessary,' I said, biting down on my irritation at her polite, impersonal tone.

She was clearly exhausted. And I had no inclination to argue with her further.

I knew exactly how to handle a vile parasite like Carsoni. I had refrained from correcting her—and informing the police of her attacker's identity as one of Carsoni's goons—for the simple reason that I knew the police wouldn't be able to touch the money lender. And without Carsoni's help it would be impossible to track down the man who had attacked Edie.

I, on the other hand, intended to make sure both men paid for what they had done to Edie. And, unlike the police, I did not intend to play by the rules.

She pressed a hand to her forehead.

'Have you got a headache?' I asked, concerned by the deathly colour of her skin, which only made the purpling bruise on her cheek more pronounced.

'It's not too bad, considering,' she said, looking ready to keel over.

At last the police left, with promises to start a search for the attacker, who I had no doubt would be long gone by now.

I directed my attention to Jude, who still had Joe hovering over her. I'd never seen my casino manager quite so attentive with a woman before—but then Jude Trouvé was almost as beautiful as Edie. Almost. Which probably explained Joe's attentiveness. He was a man who appreciated beauty as much as I did.

'Edie needs to rest—can you keep an eye on her?' I asked Jude, who looked almost as washed out as her sister. 'The paramedics said to look out for signs of lethargy or disorientation.'

'Yes, of course.' Jude put a gentle arm around Edie's shoulder.

'I don't have time to rest,' Edie said wearily, trying to shrug off Jude's arm. 'We've got to put the house on the market—'

'There's no need to do it today,' I interrupted.

In fact there would be no need to do it at all, once my legal team had contacted Carsoni and informed him of what was going to happen next, if he wanted to stay out of prison. But she had that stubborn look in her eyes again, and I decided to humour her rather than indulge in a pointless argument that would just exhaust her more.

I fully intended to handle this situation, with or without her permission, but I needed to make sure she was being properly taken care of before I could leave.

'Mr Allegri is right, Edie.' Jude tightened her arm on her sister's shoulders before she could argue further. 'We can worry about the money again tomorrow. It's not like the problem's going to disappear if you worry about it more now.'

I said nothing as I watched her sister usher her up the stairs. Edie allowed herself to be led, the last of the fight having drained out of her. The sight of those bowed shoulders and her painful movements made it hard for me to speak round the ball of outrage in my throat.

When they reached the landing, Jude glanced over her shoulder. 'Thank you so much, Mr Allegri.' Her gaze landed on Joe and her skin flushed a becoming shade of pink. 'And you too, Mr Donnelly. I consider you both knights in shining armour. I can't thank you enough for saving Edie from that brute.'

I didn't want her thanks, any more than I had wanted Edie's. And I knew damn well I was the opposite of a knight—in or out of armour. But I nodded anyway.

'Would you be okay to see yourselves out?' she added, her request gentle but firm. I nodded again. I had a job to do before I returned to check on Edie.

As Joe and I left the chateau, it occurred to me that while Edie was the bolder of the two sisters, Jude had a quiet strength that was equally impressive.

'Jude told me that creep Carsoni is at the bottom of this,' Joe growled as we walked down the driveway towards the helicopter. 'Apparently they owe him some astronomical amount of money—and the debt just keeps increasing.'

'I know,' I said as I climbed into the cockpit of the helicopter, my fury at the whole situation flaring again. 'Rest assured, by tomorrow they will owe him nothing.'

CHAPTER NINE

I GROANED AS I rolled over in bed the following morning, awoken by the shaft of sunlight streaming through the old casement window in my bedroom. The pain in my cheekbone and my elbow though didn't hurt as much as the hollow ache in my stomach at the thought that this would be my last summer at Belle Rivière.

I crawled out of bed and walked over to the window seat where I had spent countless lazy hours reading books on everything from geometry to Gauguin to *Green Gables* in those idyllic summer months when our mother had been vivacious and happy, usually because she had a new protector. That state of bliss had never lasted very long—because rich, powerful men had a tendency to get easily bored, especially when the woman they were dating had the sort of emotional baggage my needy, insecure mother carried with her everywhere she went. But in the brief weeks and months of a new affair Jude and I had learned to be as inconspicuous and undemanding as possible, so that my mother could concentrate on the new man in her life. And stay happy. That usually meant boarding schools in England in the winter months and Belle Rivière in the summer, where we would stay with the staff while my mother gallivanted about the country on the arm of her new beau.

The boarding schools would change frequently, according to my mother's whim and what the man she was currently attached to was prepared to pay for our education. But summers in Belle Rivière had been the one constant in our lives. And it was here that I missed her the most.

My mother had been far from perfect, but on her good days she had been a force of nature that could line any dark cloud with dazzling silver sparkles. If she was here now, she would be able to take the worry away—probably with an impromptu picnic or a dress-up party—she'd never been good on finding practical solutions but she had been a master of delightful distractions. When she died, all the light and laughter was sucked out of my life and Jude's. And,

however impractical it was, I would do anything for even a tiny glimmer of those dazzling
sparkles right now.

I sat down and gazed out of the window at
a scene I had come to love over those frenetic
summers. But all I could see was the beauty I
was going to lose.

The forest of oaks and pines and spruce
marked the perimeter of the sixteen-acre property, the ruins of an old stone chapel in the distance overgrown with wild roses. A carpet of
poppies added a splash of vibrant red to the intense greens of the meadow leading down to
the river. I prised open the window latch, forced
open the swollen frame and breathed in the perfume of wild flowers and pine sap I had come
to adore. I could hear the musical tinkle of the
river in the distance which wound its way along
the bottom of the meadow shielded by the val-
ley of trees and reminded me of my mother's
laughter—bright and bubbly and so beguiling.

I swallowed heavily. How was I going to survive without this oasis in my life? After losing
my mother, I wasn't sure I could bear to lose
this too.

I squeezed my fingers to the bridge of my

nose and then wiped away the tear that slid over my sore cheek.

'Edie, at last you're up.'

I turned and winced, my neck muscles protesting at the sudden movement. Jude stood in the doorway, grinning.

'Hi,' I grumbled, massaging the stiffness.

'How are you feeling?' she asked as she rushed across the room, her voice a mixture of concern and something that sounded weirdly like excitement.

'I'm okay,' I said, determined not to worry her any more than I had already. 'I just wish…' I blinked. *Don't cry—it'll only make this situation worse.* 'I wish I could have found a way for us to keep Belle Rivière.'

If only I could burrow into a ball in the centre of my bed and make all the worries disappear, the way I'd sometimes had to do as a little girl, when I could hear my mother's crying, or the feral sounds of lovemaking from her room next door, which had always confused and frightened me.

Jude plopped herself opposite me and took my hand in hers. 'I think we can save Belle Rivière after all, because I've got some news.'

'What news?' I said, wanting to believe her but unable to shift the lump of failure and old grief wedged in my throat.

'Incredible, incredible news,' Jude said, grasping my hands and enjoying the suspense. 'Dante Allegri just called—he's got Carsoni to cancel the debt. We don't owe that bastard another cent.'

'He's...? What?' That got my attention. I stared at her blankly, forcing myself to quash the leap of pure joy in my heart. A hope dashed was so much harder to bear than no hope at all. 'But... How did he manage that?'

'I have no idea,' she said, her smile so bright it hurt my eyes. 'I didn't ask, because I really don't care. All I care about is that no one ever hurts you like that again. If we get to keep Belle Rivière that's even better.' She clasped my arms, but the hope starting to bloom under my breastbone meant I couldn't even feel the bruises. 'But you're the only thing I really care about,' she said. 'I should never have let you take the risks you did.' She glanced around the room—the faded curtains, the moth-eaten rug, the worn bed sheets. 'I love this place too, but nothing's more important to me than you, Edie.'

'He must have paid him off,' I said, the leap of joy in my heart joined by that disturbing feeling of connection I'd tried so hard to ignore the afternoon before—when Allegri had punched Brutus for me. 'It's the only thing that makes any sense.'

'Blimey, do you really think so?' Jude said, her eyes popping wide. 'But we owed Carsoni over five million euros by the last estimate.'

'I know,' I said, my stomach churning with shock.

Nobody had ever done anything like that for me before. But why would he?

The urgency and hunger in his kiss blasted into my memory—and made the churning in my stomach become hot and languid. Was it possible…?

'He must like you an awful lot…' Jude said, her thoughts straying into the same uncharted territory as mine. 'But then, he did beat up Brutus for you.'

I forced myself to contain the leap of excitement at the memory of that punch.

Get a clue, Edie. Dante Allegri can have any woman he wants. For goodness' sake, the man dates supermodels. Why would he want you?

I pressed trembling fingers to my lips, the memory of his tongue commanding the inside of my mouth in greedy strokes sending my senses reeling.

Okay, he had wanted me as much as I had wanted him, during that searing kiss. But even I knew the promise of that kiss wasn't worth five million euros. I was still a virgin. I had zero experience. Then again, he didn't know that.

'Do you think…?' Jude stared at me, her mind still heading in the same insane direction as mine. 'Do you think he'll expect you to become his mistress?'

'I don't know,' I said, not nearly as horrified at the prospect as I probably ought to be.

Inappropriate and unbidden heat flushed through my system. The thought of sleeping with Carsoni for money had disgusted me, but the thought of taking that kiss to its logical conclusion with Allegri didn't disgust me at all. In fact, at the moment the only thing that was really worrying me was the thought that once he found out I was a virgin, and I didn't know the first thing about pleasuring a man, he might ask for his five million euros back.

Which was probably very bad of me. After all, agreeing to become Allegri's mistress because he'd paid off a five-million-euro debt for me would compromise me, the way my mother had always been compromised. Really, I ought to feel trapped and humiliated. But I couldn't seem to muster the required shame or indignation. At all.

Because the prospect of being free of debt was almost as intoxicating as the memory of that turbo-charged kiss… And where it might lead.

'Well, I guess we're going to find out,' Jude said, looking sheepish. 'Because he's coming over later today to check up on you.'

My heartbeat bumped my throat, threatening to gag me, while the heat sunk deep into my abdomen.

I'd entered the game at Allegri's casino and lost—precisely because I had been determined to prove I was not as needy as my mother. But as the heat spread through me, softening my thigh muscles and dampening my panties at the thought of what Dante might want from me, I wasn't even sure of that any more.

CHAPTER TEN

'I CAN'T THANK you enough for helping us, Mr Allegri. My sister and I are completely beholden to you. I'm more than willing to show you my gratitude in any way you think is appropriate. Even though I'm aware that five million euros is a lot more than my gratitude is worth.'

'What five million euros are you talking about, *bella*?' I asked, trying to keep a grip on my temper as my gaze roamed over the livid bruise on Edie Trouvé's cheek, which had spread into a dark circle under her eye overnight.

What insanity was this now? And was there no end of ways this woman could stir both my desire and my exasperation?

She stood before me in the furniture-less room where she had been attacked the day before, sporting the marks that Brutus Severin had inflicted, looking as if a strong wind would blow her down. But, despite her obvious fragility, she seemed not to realise how vulnerable she was, her face open and eager and full of hope, as if I were some kind of saviour. Nothing could be further from the truth.

'Didn't you pay Carsoni the money we owe him?' she asked. 'To get him to cancel the debt?'

'No, I did not.'

She frowned, clearly confused. 'But then, how did you get him to cancel it?'

My exasperation increased at the realisation that my hunger for her had not abated in the least, despite her obvious naiveté.

'I didn't get him to cancel the loan; my legal team did,' I said. 'The credit agreement your brother-in-law signed was invalid.' Or, rather, Carsoni had been persuaded that trying to enforce it would cost him more than the debt was worth, not just in money but also in a lethal blow to what was left of his reputation on the Côte D'Azur. 'Carsoni was only too happy to forego the debt once he realised he would be meeting the might of the Allegri Corporation in court—instead of two penniless women—if he chose to collect any more money from you.'

I had also had my lawyer inform him that he and his organisation would be the subject of a criminal investigation if I chose to inform the police who had employed Severin.

'I… Oh.' She sounded more disconcerted than pleased by this revelation. 'So you didn't pay him five million euros on our behalf?' she asked again.

'No, I most certainly did not.'

'I see. Well, that's good. That's very good.' A blush flared across her chest.

She looked disconcerted, even a little deflated, the vivid blush riding her collarbone and seeping into her cheeks.

It occurred to me she had painted herself into an interesting corner with the suggestion I had paid off Carsoni. A corner I couldn't resist shining a light into.

'What kind of gratitude did you have in mind, *bella*?' I asked. The blush illuminated the freckles on her nose.

'I… Can you forget I said that?' she said.

'No, I think not,' I said, not about to let her off so easily. Seeing her rattled felt like payback. Because she had done nothing but rattle me ever since I had first laid eyes on her. 'I'm just wondering what kind of gratitude would be worth five million euros?'

'It doesn't matter,' she said, busy avoiding eye contact.

My lips quirked. Damn, but she was even cuter when she was mortified.

'Five million euros is a lot of money,' I mused. 'I would expect something very exceptional for that amount,' I added, openly teasing her now.

The strange thought that she would be worth every cent of that amount hit me unawares though, as she raised her head and stared at me.

Her soft skin was flushed with embarrassed heat but her eyes sparkled with a strength of character that reminded me of a battle-weary Valkyrie.

Edie Trouvé might be that very rare thing, a woman as honest and open as she was fearless.

Desire flushed through my system.

What would it be like to have such a woman in my bed, surrendering herself to pleasure?

The stab of longing at the thought disturbed me on a level so visceral, my amusement at the situation faded.

Edie Trouvé wasn't fearless; she was desperate. And on one level she had just insulted me, by offering me her 'gratitude' in payment for five million euros. There was nothing honest or open about what she'd implied. Sex was always a transaction, just like everything else in life, but all she'd done was prove that point.

I'd learnt at a very young age that needs and desires only made you weak. I'd made my fortune, forged a future for myself alone, without relying on or having to trust anyone, knowing that no one gave anything freely. There was always a price, and Edie's offer was no different.

'You're mocking me,' she said, the sparkle of excitement gone from her eyes. 'But I do want to thank you, Mr Allegri, for contacting Carsoni and making this happen. If you let me know what the legal fees are I'll endeavour to repay you that.'

I should have been vindicated by her surrender. But somehow the defeated tone had the exact opposite effect.

Exasperation gave way to annoyance. 'My legal team are on a retainer, so there are no additional fees for this work.'

She nodded. 'Then it's just the matter of repaying the million euros I owe you.'

'That debt is erased too,' I said curtly.

'Are you sure?' she said.

'Tell me honestly,' I said. 'Did you know the bank draft was fraudulent?'

She paused for a moment and then shook her head. 'But I still lost the money at the table. So surely I still owe it to you.'

I nodded. 'Yes, but unfortunately it's very clear you cannot afford to repay it.'

The flush of arousal, the rapid rise and fall of her breathing and the nipples visible against the worn cotton of her T-shirt, were making it hard for me to concentrate on the conversation.

The urge to take her in my arms and kiss that concerned look off her face was not something I could pursue while she was still bruised from yesterday's assault. I had come here with an entirely different purpose. One I needed to focus on now, before I did something I might later regret.

I needed time to properly assess my attraction to this woman. Because, in light of her current circumstances, it made even less sense than it had two nights ago, when I'd believed her to be the spoilt daughter of a rich man.

Pint-sized Valkyries weren't my type any more than spoilt little rich girls.

But I had mulled over her situation and done some Internet research on her and her family during the night I'd spent in a nearby hotel and had decided that offering her a position as part of my team for the upcoming house party at my estate on the Côte D'Azur made even more sense now than before.

She might currently be destitute, but her family had an aristocratic lineage that could be traced back to the Huguenots and the highest echelons of British high society. She was the bastard issue of her mother's affair with the married younger son of a British duke. Her great-grandfather had been a French count and one of her grandfathers that British duke. Maybe her father and her father's family had never acknowledged her. But that blue blood still ran through her veins—while mine was as red and wild as the poppies that grew in abundance in the fields outside the house.

She had, no doubt, gone to the best schools, while I had learned my lessons on the back streets of Naples, scrapping and struggling for every single bite. And, while no one knew the full degradation of my heritage, everyone knew I had come from nothing. I was a gambler, a self-made billionaire, and while I had always been proud of what I had achieved, having her as part of my team at this event would give me a status I could use—a bankable commodity which I was more than happy to pay for.

And her skills at the table would be invaluable if used properly.

In some ways, our circumstances weren't all that dissimilar. She was illegitimate too, and had been at the mercy of forces beyond her control. Like me, she had worked hard to rise above her circumstances, the way I had worked hard to rise above my station and erase the circumstances of my birth.

But my admiration for her ended there. And giving her a chance didn't have to mean anything other than that. As long as she understood that I was not a charitable man, and I didn't do anything out of the goodness of my heart—because I really didn't have a heart. After all, I had been careful to cut it out ever since…

I shut off the thought, the shaft of memory not something I wished to revisit.

The two situations were not the same. I had been a child then. I was a man now. A man who had made himself invulnerable to pain.

'Your sister told me exactly how deep your financial troubles go,' I said. 'I have a possible solution.'

'What is it?' she said, desperation plain on her face.

'Would you consider working for me?' I asked.

'You're... You're offering me a job?'

She sounded so surprised, I found my lips curving in amusement again.

'As it happens, I am hosting an event at my new estate near Nice at the end of the month. I could use your skills as part of the team I'm putting together.'

'What exactly do you need me to do?' she said, her eagerness a sop to my ego.

'The guests I am inviting are some of the world's most powerful businessmen and women.' I outlined the job. 'They have all shown an interest in investing in the expansion of the Allegri brand. The event is a way of assessing their suitability as investors. As part of the week, I will be offering some recreational poker events. These people are highly competitive and they enjoy games of chance. What they don't know is that how they play poker tells me a great deal more about their personalities and their business acumen—and whether we will be compatible—than a simple profit and loss portfolio of their companies. But I find that successful people, no matter how competitive they are, are also smart enough to know that they cannot best me at a poker table. So I need someone who does not intimidate them, but who can observe how they play and make those assessments for me.' I kept my eyes on her reaction, surprised myself by how much I wanted her to say yes.

My attraction to her might be unexpected, but I had spent a lifetime living by my wits and never doubting my instincts. When I had originally considered giving her a hosting position I'd been aware of the possible fringe benefits for both of us and I didn't see why that should change. She had made it very clear she was more than happy to blur the lines between employer and lover, and all her responses made it equally clear she desired me as much as I desired her.

'I'll pay you four thousand euros for the fortnight,' I said, to make her position clear. This was a genuine job, and a job she would be very good at. 'Joe can brief you on each of the participants—and what I need to know about them. If you do a good enough job, and your skills prove as useful as I'm expecting them to be, I would consider offering you a probationary position.'

She blinked several times, her skin now flushed a dark pink. But didn't say anything.

'So do you want the job?' I asked, letting my impatience show, annoyed by the strange feeling of anticipation. Why should it matter to me if she declined my offer?

'Yes, yes,' she said. 'I'll take the job. And thank you.'

Triumph surged up my chest, which seemed out of proportion to what I had actually achieved. Of course she'd said yes—why on earth would I doubt it? And why should I even care that much?

She tugged at her lip. Desire bloomed in my groin and I had my answer. My eagerness to have her in my employ was about physical desire and exceptional chemistry, nothing more or less.

I pulled a card out of my back pocket and

handed it to Edie. 'Joe will contact you with all the necessary details of your employment in a couple of days,' I said. 'If you need to contact me directly, my personal number is on the card.'

She took the card and nodded. Then the strangest thing happened—the line of her lips tipped up on one side. The smile was tentative and shy and self-deprecating, but it lit her eyes, giving them a glow which highlighted the shards of gold in the emerald green of her irises.

The jolt hit my chest unawares as it occurred to me I'd never seen her smile before. It only made her beauty rarer and more exquisite.

She ran her thumb over the card, the sheen of moisture in those stunning eyes making the jolt twist sharply.

'Thank you, Mr Allegri—for everything,' she said, her gratitude genuine and heartfelt and all the more disturbing for it. 'I won't disappoint you, I swear.'

'Then start by calling me Dante,' I said.

'Thank you, Dante,' she said.

I turned and left but as I climbed into my car and drove off the estate the jolt refused to go away, forcing me to consider the possibility that my attraction to Edie Trouvé went beyond the physical... Which would not be good at all.

CHAPTER ELEVEN

As THE HELICOPTER touched down on the cliff-top heliport, I was sure my eyes were literally popping out of their sockets at the sight before me.

Belle Rivière was beautiful, but it had none of the sheer grandeur and elegance of Dante Allegri's estate on the Côte D'Azur. Over ten acres of manicured gardens, arranged in terraces leading down to the sea on three sides, the grounds were peppered with statues and follies, waterfalls and lavish ponds as well as a huge marble swimming pool at the back of the villa with steps leading down to a dock and one of the estate's three private beaches.

Guest houses were nestled among the gardens, but the house itself stood proud as the centrepiece. I estimated the chateau had to have at least twenty or thirty bedrooms as the helicopter circled the building. A summer house originally built for a Portuguese prince, the mansion, with its rococo flourishes, elegant walkways, Belle Époque frontage and lavish plasterwork, had been described by Joseph Donnelly as a villa, but that description seemed far too modest for the palace below me.

I had known Dante Allegri was a rich man, but I'd never really considered how rich.

Two members of staff appeared at the heliport to greet me as I stepped down from the aircraft. Joseph had seen me off in Monaco less than twenty minutes ago.

I had spent the last three days with him and the casino staff being briefed on the guests who would begin arriving in a few days for Dante Allegri's house party. I'd taken copious notes on the names and faces, the businesses they owned and what their preferences were, and how I should address them—I'd also re-searched their finances and how they'd made their money, so I could observe their play and assess their attitudes to risk with more context.

I hadn't seen Allegri while I was staying in the apartment assigned to me at the casino, and I had been grateful for that. I needed as much time as possible to calm my nerves and get a grip on my instinctive reaction to him before I saw him again.

I wanted to make a good impression. I needed to earn the probationary position he'd mentioned, if I was going to have any chance of salvaging not just my pride, but my family's finances and Belle Rivière. Allegri's actions had freed us from Carsoni's threats and the crippling debts, but we still had a sizeable mortgage on the estate and the house itself was rundown and unfurnished. Jude had suggested we turn it into a bed and breakfast inn, so we could make it self-sufficient, but for that we would need to invest in it. And a new job with good prospects could provide the capital we so desperately needed if Dante Allegri offered it to me.

Allegri… No, Dante, I corrected myself, as my skin heated. Dante had given me an opportunity—an opportunity I wanted to make the most of.

Thank goodness he didn't know my experience of these sorts of high society events was precisely zero. My mother had been shunned by polite society in both the UK and France—and my only experience of it was the years I'd spent observing the behaviour of the daughters of the wealthy in boarding school and, more recently, the jobs I'd had cleaning the houses of the rich and privileged.

But, while I might not have a profile in society, I did understand numbers. And probabilities. Joseph Donnelly had told me Dante was a man who preferred cold hard facts. If I could give him a numerical breakdown of exactly how well each person played—what risks they took and didn't take, the bets they made and the bets they won, how often they bluffed, et cetera—I would be able to amass a wealth of data which he could use to his advantage. I'd already worked out several formulas to assist me in compiling the data.

More than anything, I wanted to impress upon him that he hadn't made a mistake in giving me this chance. Which meant not getting ideas above my station, as I had that excruciating morning at Belle Rivière, about what he did and didn't want from me.

'Miss Trouvé, welcome to La Villa Paradis. My name is Collette; I am Mr Allegri's villa manager,' an older woman greeted me in perfect English, before directing a young bellboy to take my carry-on bag. 'Pascal will take your belongings to the guest house Mr Allegri has assigned to you. I hope your flight wasn't too tiring?'

'Not at all,' I said. The flight had been just one more eye-popping experience. I'd never travelled in a helicopter before. 'It was perfect,' I said.

Collette sent me a warm smile. 'Good, then let me show you to your guest villa. I have arranged for a light lunch to be served to you there, but if there is anything else you require just let me know.'

'Thank you.' I nodded, disconcerted by the offer and her manner. I was Dante's employee too, not a guest.

'I thought you might like to rest for an hour before meeting with the stylist,' she added. 'So I have pushed the appointment back until three o'clock, if that is okay?'

'Yes, but… What stylist?' I asked, even more disconcerted.

'Mr Allegri has hired Nina Saint Jus of La Roche to assemble your look,' she said, naming a Parisian designer and fashion house so famous even I'd heard of them.

'My look?' I repeated dully, feeling the blush warm my cheekbones.

Apart from the second-hand ball gown I'd worn to the casino the night I'd first met Dante, my wardrobe wasn't exactly illustrious, being a collection of jeans and T-shirts in various states of disrepair. But Joseph had already arranged an advance on my salary for the event, and I'd managed to find some bargains online that I had hoped would ensure I didn't look like a waif and stray Dante had dragged in off the street.

I knew I needed to look the part, that dress was important. But a stylist? And one of Nina Saint Jus's pedigree? How could I possibly afford to pay for this wardrobe? It would probably cost more than my entire salary.

'Mr Allegri has not mentioned this to you?' Collette asked with a benevolent smile on her face, as if she wasn't the least bit surprised.

'No, he hasn't.'

She sighed and rolled her eyes heavenward. 'Men!' she said and sent me a conspiratorial grin that downgraded my panic a notch. She patted my hand as she led me down a path shaded by palm trees, the flower beds choked with an array of lilies and roses that added a heavy perfume to the fresh sea air. 'Mr Allegri is arriving after lunch,' she said helpfully. 'He has requested that you meet him for dinner after your fitting; you will be able to talk to him then.'

Far from downgrading my panic, Collette's casual comment had it swelling into a ball—and head-butting my tonsils.

Ten hours later, as I was escorted through the mansion's east ballroom and up a staircase to a mezzanine level, worry sat like a boulder wedged in my solar plexus.

I had wanted to make the best possible impression today. But the fitting hadn't gone well. While I had been trying to keep the price down, the stylist and her three assistants had insisted on discarding all the clothes I had brought with me and selecting a whole new wardrobe.

For tonight, I was dressed in a fire-red satin body-con dress picked by the designer from her *prêt a porter* collection. My usually unruly hair was pinned up in a waterfall of curls that draped down my back, my make-up had been professionally done, and it had all been achieved by a team of beauty stylists who had arrived at my villa an hour before my dinner date with Dante.

The expensive satin caressed my skin as I walked. The dress was absolutely exquisite, more beautiful, and a lot more expensive, than anything I'd ever worn before in my life. The designer had referred to it as a simple cocktail dress, while taking my measurements to design a series of more formal gowns for the 'entertainments' Dante had planned for the week ahead.

To say all this activity had intimidated me would be putting it mildly.

What entertainments? I wondered.

As I walked along the balcony that skirted the ballroom, the heeled sandals I was wearing were muffled by the silk carpeting.

The mansion's grand décor—the modern art that lined the walls, the ornate plasterwork and elegant lighting—did nothing to calm my jangling nerves.

I didn't feel like me any more. When I had looked in the mirror after the styling I hadn't recognised myself.

I would have to tell Dante the truth at dinner.

The truth I had hoped to keep hidden. That I really didn't fit into this world. Into his world. That I could easily make a catastrophic mess of the job he'd given me, say something gauche or inappropriate, address someone the wrong way. That it was highly likely some of the guests might have known my mother, or certainly knew of her notoriety. And that I couldn't possibly afford this wardrobe.

My escort, a young man called Gaston with a friendly smile, opened a large door and I stepped into a room that was easily the size of the whole of Belle Rivière's ground floor. Dante was standing on the other end of the huge banqueting hall, silhouetted against a view of the villa's lavish gardens, currently lit by a series of nightlights. The long table which took up most of the space was set at the far end for two people with antique crystal and fine china.

Were we eating alone tonight?

'*Bon appétit*, Mademoiselle Trouvé.' Gaston bowed and left, closing the door behind him before I had a chance to thank him.

My inadequacy started to strangle me, but it was joined by the pulsing deep in my abdomen when Dante turned. He watched me but made no move towards me, so I was forced to walk to him.

'Hi.' My greeting came out on a helium squeak worthy of Minnie Mouse. I cleared my throat, mortified now as well as nervous.

Dante's lips quirked in that knowing smile which only unnerved me more.

His gaze burned down my dress. The silky satin rubbed my sensitised skin like sandpaper.

'I see Nina has done the job I paid her for,' he said. 'You look exquisite, *bella*.'

His voice reverberated through me, making the liquid tug in my abdomen sink into my sex.

'Thank you,' I said, then bit into my bottom lip.

Tell him now, you ninny.

'There is a problem,' he said, and I realised he had noticed my nervousness. 'You don't like the dress?'

'No, I love it,' I said. 'It's just…'

'Just what?' he prompted.

'I can't afford it,' I said. 'Any of it.'

He chuckled. 'I guess it's a good thing I'm paying for it then.'

'But…' My eyes widened again. I had to look like a rabbit in the headlights by now, but I couldn't help it. I was totally overwhelmed. 'Really?'

His lips crinkled in a wry smile. The way they had when he'd teased me before, after I'd made that daft suggestion about showing him five million euros' worth of gratitude.

'Of course, I need you to look the part, Edie. Some people will assume you're my mistress.'

'They will?' The heat flared in my cheeks.

'Is that a problem?' The muscle in his jaw tensed and I had the horrible thought that I might have insulted him with my shocked reaction.

'No, not at all. It's… I just didn't expect you to pay for my clothing. As well as the generous salary you're paying me.'

The muscle relaxed and his smile returned. 'It's all part of the job, *bella*. If you really want to, you can always return the clothes to me once the event is over. But I doubt they will fit me.'

I laughed, and his smile widened.

He stepped closer and his thumb skimmed my cheek. 'Has the bruise healed? Or is that the work of a good make-up artist?'

Something shimmered through me, more than the heat. I tried to pull it back. His concern was nothing out of the ordinary. He was just being a conscientious employer. The only reason I was taking it so much to heart was that I'd never had a man look at me like that before, as if he actually cared that I had been hurt.

'Yes, it's better, thanks,' I said.

'I'm glad,' he murmured. The something shimmered through me again. He dropped his hand—and I felt a strange sense of loss. Holding out his arm, he indicated the table behind us as two serving staff entered the room. 'Let's sit down,' he said. 'This is a working dinner. We have much to discuss about next week.'

My heart lurched into my throat as he seated me and the waiters set out a selection of delicate salads, fresh bread and charcuterie for our starters.

I needed to come clean about my qualifications for this job, or rather the lack of them, I told myself. My panic attack over the clothes was proof of that.

He poured me a glass of wine and I gulped it down as he served me from the terrines on the table.

'Mr Allegri, there's something I…' I began.

'Call me, Dante,' he said. 'You are part of my team, not a waitress.'

I cleared my throat, the colour flushing through my system at the intimacy in the look he sent me. 'Dante, I'm not sure I'm who you think I am.'

'How so?' he asked, leaning back in his chair to sip his wine.

The colour rose to my hairline under that assessing gaze.

I'd never been ashamed of my background. I was illegitimate—I'd never met my father; in fact he'd never even acknowledged me or my sister. Because we'd been the product of an extra-marital affair. But, despite that, I'd never been ashamed of my mother's choices.

She'd been reckless and irresponsible and selfish in a lot of ways, and careless—especially with other women's husbands—but she'd also been loving and vivacious. And she had also been notorious, her exploits, her affairs, her lack of decorum or compunction documented in minute detail and found wanting in the tabloid press. She'd tried to shield us from that as children. But I'd heard all the whispers about her behaviour at the boarding schools I'd attended. That she was a marriage-wrecker, a slut, a whore. I'd got into enough fights over the years defending her honour, even though I knew in some ways she didn't have any. The one time I'd confronted her about one of her 'protectors' when the story had hit the tabloids that she had broken up the marriage of a famous actor—and the girls at school had made my and Jude's life a misery—she had simply laughed and said, 'If his wife wanted to keep him, she should have made more of an effort to entertain him.'

But, here and now, as I sat in front of Dante, it was hard for me to explain my upbringing without wishing it could be different.

'I think you may have got the impression because of Belle Rivière...' I swallowed, trying to alleviate the dryness in my throat '...and my background, that I'm an aristocrat and I know the workings of high society. I don't.'

He didn't seem surprised by this revelation. 'You are the granddaughter of a British duke—is this not true?'

My ribs felt as if they were squeezing my lungs. So he *had* heard the rumours. The few bites of salad I had eaten coalesced in the pit of my stomach.

'My mother always maintained as much,' I said. 'But I never met him or my father. And our father certainly never acknowledged us.' I tried to sound flippant; the circumstances of my birth had never been important to me before. Why would they? My father had chosen not to be a part of my life. But, for the first time ever, instead of feeling belligerent and indifferent about the man who had sired me, I actually wished I could claim the pedigree Dante clearly believed I had.

I didn't want to lose this job, and it wasn't about the money any more. This was the first chance I'd ever had to prove myself. And then there was the thought of being able to spend a whole ten days in his company. I might as well admit it, after his rescue a week ago and the way he had swooped in to give my sister and me a way out of our problems, not to mention the memory of that kiss, I had a massive crush on him. When he'd said that some people might consider me to be his mistress, I'd had the weirdest reaction. Not embarrassment or humiliation, but excitement and pride.

'I was educated in private schools,' I continued, because he was still watching me with that assessing gaze, not giving away his feelings about my revelations. 'But I've never been to an event like the one you're hosting here,' I finished.

His eyes narrowed and the muscle in his jaw tensed again, but I couldn't tell whether he was angry or disappointed with this information.

'Why are you telling me this?' he said at last.

The question confused me. Wasn't it obvious? 'Because I don't want to disappoint you,' I said, forcing myself to admit it. 'Although I didn't recognise any of the names on the guest list...' *Thank God.* 'Some of your guests may still have known my mother, and they may well know *of* me, that I'm...' I breathed in and looked out into the night, not able to look into his eyes any more. It was hard to say the word, because I had always been sure to make certain it did not define me, but I knew I had to be honest with him because it might very well define me now and my ability to do the job he'd given me. He'd bought me an incredible wardrobe, he'd put me up in one of the villa's guest houses, he was giving me a four-figure salary for two weeks' work and treating me with respect—as if I were more than an employee. He was even happy to have people believe we were dating. He'd shown a faith in me that no other man had ever shown, not even my own father—especially my own father—but I didn't want to take what he was offering under false pretences, especially as it might have an adverse effect on what he wanted to achieve here. Or that would make me as complicit as my mother in the many, many marriages she'd destroyed.

'That you're what?' he prodded, forcing me to bring my gaze back to his.

'That I'm a bastard,' I finally managed, pushing out the hateful word on a harsh breath. 'Mr Donnelly said one of the purposes of this event and the new expansion is to increase the public profile of your company and to give the Allegri brand additional status and respect.' I hurried on as his expression remained tense and shadowed. I had angered him with this revelation, I could see that now, even though he was making an effort not to show it. My hopes shattered. He would fire me, of course he would—what had made me think that I could hide who I really was, even for a second?

'I don't want to mess that up with my presence, or tarnish your company's brand, however inadvertently.'

CHAPTER TWELVE

I SAT STUNNED, not just by Edie's revelation—which, of course, was not news to me at all—but by the honesty and openness and genuine anguish on her face as she related her background to me. I gritted my teeth, trying hard not to reveal my reaction. And trying even harder not to feel it.

But, despite my best efforts, the all-consuming anger—towards the bastards who had ever made her think the circumstances of her birth diminished her—was followed by an even more disturbing sense of connection—at the realisation that she had once been subjected to the same petty prejudices and insults, the same cruel judgements that I had suffered so often as a boy.

She pressed her napkin down on the table and stood. 'I should leave,' she said.

Wait... What?

I got up and walked round the table to grab

her before she could run out on me again. 'Where are you going?' I asked.

'Don't you want me to go?'

'Bella...' I tried, but I couldn't seem to stem the sympathy that overwhelmed me at the sight of her distress. 'Why would you think that?'

'I've just told you my mother was a...' She swallowed and I could see her struggle with the ugly word she had no doubt had levelled at her a hundred times. 'She was notorious, Dante. I don't want to...'

'Shh...' I pressed a finger to her lips. 'My mother was a street whore in Naples, Edie,' I said, breaking a silence I had kept since I was a child. 'She picked up men for pennies, screwed them in alleyways. Or brought them back to the room where we lived. My earliest memory is hearing the sounds of sexual intercourse from my crib.'

Shock widened her eyes, but I couldn't seem to stop myself from exorcising the bitter truth. Stupid that I should feel safe giving her this information. I hardly knew her, but something about the way she had confided in me, not to gain my pity or my empathy but simply to protect my company's reputation, touched a part of me I thought was incapable of being touched.

'Do you really think whatever your mother did or didn't do with the men in her life could be worse than that?'

I cupped her cheek, the softness of her skin, the brutal flush igniting her cheeks making me want to capture her mouth again and devour it.

She wasn't innocent—how could she be with a background like hers? She had grown up in the school of hard knocks, just like I had. Maybe her life had had the cushion of gentility that mine had comprehensively lacked, but we had both suffered, thanks to the weaknesses—and arbitrary prejudices—of others. It connected us in a way I might not like, but I could no longer fail to acknowledge.

'I'm so sorry, Dante,' she said, covering my hand with hers. The consoling words and the warmth in her eyes confused me—who exactly was comforting whom here? 'That must have been so traumatic for you as a young boy,' she added.

I drew my hand away, appalled by her pity, but appalled more by the way it made me feel. Not angry, or even irritated, but moved.

'And for your mother—what a terrible life for her too,' she added, and I recoiled.

Was she serious? I had hated my mother for so long—the life she had given me, the way she had discarded me like so much rubbish, I couldn't quite comprehend what Edie was saying. I didn't want her pity, but I couldn't even understand her pity for the woman who had given birth to me.

'It was a very long time ago, *bella*,' I said, forcing an indifference into my tone that I didn't feel. I had exposed myself by confiding the details of my childhood. Why the hell had I done that? Perhaps because I wanted this woman more than I had ever wanted any woman. 'My childhood gave me the tools to become the man I am today.'

'I understand,' she said, but the sympathy still shone in her eyes. And I knew she didn't understand.

I had meant that my childhood had made me ruthless and driven, prepared to do just about anything to get away from where I had started to arrive at where I was now.

'You've worked so hard for your business,'

she continued. 'But that's why I wanted you to know about…'

'I already knew,' I said, to cut off her illogical confession and the way it was making me feel. The connection I had felt to her was not something I should encourage, so why had I, with that ill-advised confession about my background?

'Bella,' I added, 'I did an Internet search on your background before I hired you.' I could see I'd surprised her, so I continued. 'Your social connections or the lack of them are of no interest to me.'

'But aren't they important if I'm to represent the Allegri Corporation at this—'

'Absolutely not.' I cut off the argument. 'And Joe Donnelly was wrong to give you that impression.' I was going to be having words with my friend to find out exactly what he'd said to Edie to give her the impression her background mattered—although I suspected Edie had simply got the wrong end of the stick; after all, Joe was as much of a mongrel as I was.

'What I'm interested in is your intellect and your ability to assess my guests' attitude to risk,' I reiterated. 'That's why I hired you and that's what I'm paying you for. And, believe me, I intend to get my money's worth. We'll meet each evening for a debrief with the rest of my management team after the guests have gone to bed—which will sometimes be at two or three in the morning. I'll expect you to be alert and informative and articulate about every aspect of your interactions—I'm a night owl and I tend to conduct most of my business at night. I'll also want a written analysis in the mornings before the next day's activities begin. And as much useful data as you can give me. I'll expect you to be my eyes and my ears at the tables whenever I'm not there. Believe me, your role here will not be easy. But pedigree means absolutely nothing to me. What I look for in an employee is results. And, more importantly, if you in any way think that someone is judging you I want you to tell me. As I have already explained...' I wished once again I hadn't blurted that information out, because she was looking at me now with a sort of hero-worship '...no one's as much of a mongrel as I am. And anyone who judges you for it would also judge me, so they're not someone I would want to do business with.'

'I won't disappoint you,' she said breathlessly. And I knew she wouldn't. I'd never seen someone so eager to please.

But the thought sent an unwelcome shaft of unease through me.

Her intellect, her data skills and her ability to read the play on the poker table weren't the only reasons I'd hired her. My gaze raked over the silky dress, which hugged her curves like a lover, and the heat in my groin became intense and insistent.

'But that's not the only reason I offered you this job,' I said, determined to be as open and honest with her as she had been with me—so that I could crush this foolish sense of connection once and for all. 'There's another reason I wanted you at my beck and call for the next ten days...'

I watched the pulse in her collarbone flutter.

'What's that?' she said, her voice coming out on a husky croak as her pupils darkened, and those expressive eyes became huge.

She had to know what I was referring to. She'd initiated that damn kiss. The kiss that had been firing my imagination and keeping me awake every night since. Perhaps she was being coy. I almost wished she was, but somehow I doubted it. There was something about her that seemed so fresh and young and forthright. And to think I'd once believed she was hard to read. At the moment she seemed far too easy to read.

'I think you know the reason,' I said.

Unable to quell the desire to touch her a moment longer, I lifted my hand and teased the lock of hair the stylist had left dangling. The temptation to feast on that damn mouth and finally ease the hunger in my groin was immense, but I resisted it.

I wanted her to come to me. No, I *needed* her to come to me. Then there would be no confusion—no blurring of the lines between her employment and her decision to spend time in my bed. So I dropped my hand.

Her breath gushed out, the pulse in her collarbone fluttering alarmingly as her breasts rose and fell in a staggered rhythm against the bodice of her dress.

'The chemistry between us is off the charts, *bella*,' I said, stating the obvious. 'I think we would be foolish not to enjoy it while we're here, in whatever down time we have.'

Her tongue darted out to lick her lips. My gaze fixed on her mouth. Damn, but I wanted to taste those lips again so badly.

'But anything that happens between us would be entirely your choice,' I continued, my voice now a husky croak. 'And would have absolutely no bearing on your employment with me. Is that understood?'

She nodded, her eyes still wide. The emotions that crossed her face—astonishment, confusion, arousal—would have been amusing if the erection now pounding in my pants wasn't getting all my attention. The important thing was that I could see no fear. And I'd take that.

The serving staff chose that moment to reenter the room with our entrées. I directed her to sit down. 'I'm glad we got that settled. Now, do you want to join me for the next course and we can talk about what we're actually here to talk about?'

She nodded again, and regained her seat.

The remainder of the meal was predictably excruciating, for both of us. Every time she placed a morsel of food into that too kissable mouth, or leaned forward, allowing the candlelight to flicker over the hint of cleavage, my groin tightened, the pounding in my pants becoming unbearable. But I forced myself to focus on laying the groundwork for our professional relationship.

The only consolation was I could see her struggling to maintain her side of the conversation too. Somehow or other, we got through the meal without jumping each other.

I quickly discovered she was every bit as bright and intuitive as I had believed, and she, I hoped, discovered that I wouldn't pounce on her until she was ready.

But as I bid her goodnight I couldn't help bringing her trembling fingers to my lips. I kissed her knuckles, satisfied by the flare of heat she couldn't disguise.

'I'll be back in two days' time,' I said, a little disconcerted when I saw her shoulders slump with relief. Perhaps I hadn't been quite as unthreatening as I'd hoped. I would have to work on it. 'The guests arrive that afternoon so we can meet for lunch that day.'

'Okay, I'll work out the formulas we talked about,' she said breathlessly.

I had to give her points for remembering the discussion, which had slipped my mind already.

'Excellent, I look forward to it,' I said. 'Good night, *bella*,' I added, giving her permission to leave.

She nodded but, before she could hurry out of the room, I added, 'And remember, you are a free agent when it comes to anything other than work.'

'I know, Dante,' she said, the glow of pleasure in her eyes having a strange effect on me.

I realised it wasn't just my groin that was throbbing painfully as I watched her rush from the room. My heart felt as if it had expanded to twice its normal size and was thundering against my ribcage.

Dammit man, chill out.

I returned to my seat to nurse the last of my wine—to cool off and get this insatiable hunger into perspective. It occurred to me that it was probably a good thing I would be gone for the next two days, and once I returned there would be no time, for the first few days at least, for me to pursue Edie, because I would be far too busy—and so would she.

I hadn't lied, this week-long house party was important to my business—and I was not about to allow my desire for Edie Trouvé to get in the way of achieving everything I wanted to achieve. I'd been planning this event for months. I was on the verge of expanding the Allegri Corporation. I needed investors I could trust, and deciding who I did and did not want to invite into financial partnerships was crucial. I couldn't afford to get distracted from those goals.

But after those initial impressions had been made, and assuming Edie was as adept at what I was hiring her to do as she seemed, there would be time at the end of the week to indulge ourselves.

Assuming she chose to do so.

I stroked my thumb over the crystal, watched the red wine sparkle in the candlelight. The pounding in my groin increased as something raw clawed at me.

What would I do if she chose not to come to me?

I took a fortifying gulp of the expensive vintage, let the fruity flavours burst on my tongue—the moment of uncertainty reminding me unpleasantly of the boy I'd once been.

I swallowed and coughed out a rough laugh,

realising how ludicrous the direction of my thoughts was.

The throaty sound—arrogant and assured—echoed off the antique furniture which had once belonged to a Portuguese prince. But which now belonged to me.

Don't be a damn fool, Dante. She wants you, just as much as you want her—you're not that feral kid any more.

This attraction was all about sex—and chemistry—I'd told her so myself.

I finished the wine.

All I had to do now was wait. And, luckily, I had something much more important to focus on than satisfying my libido—namely taking Allegri to the next level—to keep me busy in the meantime.

CHAPTER THIRTEEN

I BLINKED INTO the crisp morning light as it shone through the huge picture window in the guest villa's bedroom and checked the brand new, state-of-the-art smartphone I had been given a week ago by Joseph Donnelly as part of my employee package.

Pleasure rippled through me at the thought of another day working as part of Dante's elite management team. We'd been up till two o'clock last night, going through the individual reports by each member of the team. Dante had presided over the meeting in his office and even though it had been the middle of the night, the energy and enthusiasm in the room had been addictive.

I'd come to love those late-night meetings, when the guests had retired to their villas and we would gather—two other women and three men, all several years older than me—to pore over our individual reports and observations of everything that had gone on during the day and evening. Yesterday, Dante's events manager had arranged a flotilla of yachts and sailing boats to take the guests and the team to a picnic on a private island off the coast. There had been a lavish lunch arranged, not what I'd call a picnic, then water skiing and snorkelling safaris—and, for the less athletically inclined, sunbathing—in the afternoon, followed by an evening barbecue and then a night sail back to base for the evening rounds of poker and *vingt-et-un*. Dante had rather cleverly subbed all the guests a hundred thousand dollars' worth of chips for the week, with the promise that any profits they made by the end of the week would be theirs and any losses written off as a gesture of goodwill.

Last night's poker session had been my first chance to really shine. Everyone had been much more relaxed than the first night and, as a result, had bet more freely. I'd been able to gather much more data on their attitudes to risk. And when I'd detailed it all during our nightly round-up, in front of the other members of the team, and Dante, I'd felt Dante's encouragement—and his approval.

I was proving myself. Showing that his investment in me was worth it. I felt like a valued member of his team and it was intoxicating.

Pulling back the covers, I raced into the adjoining walk-in wardrobe and found the selection of swimsuits Nina had picked out for me. So far I'd only worn the one-piece ones, too shy to be seen by Dante wearing anything as skimpy as the bikinis she had selected.

My skin flushed.

Yesterday, Dante had asked me to join his crew for the evening sail back to La Villa Paradis and I'd imagined he'd had his eyes on me the whole time. Of course, he hadn't; that was just my overactive imagination. Since our dinner four days ago, he'd been nothing but professional with me. But it had still been a heady feeling—remembering the way he had looked at me that night at supper and the things he'd said.

I pulled the tiny triangles of blue Lycra out of the drawer and slipped them on. I'd never worn a bikini before which, considering I was half-French, was probably sacrilege.

I wasn't ashamed of my body; I'd inherited my mother's physique, slim but curvaceous.

But I'd never worn anything so revealing before. Instead of feeling over-exposed though, awareness shimmered over my skin. And I imagined Dante looking at me, and liking what he saw, my breasts cupped by the stretchy fabric, my round hips and flat stomach displayed to their best advantage. I'd never felt so young and alive and carefree. And Dante was responsible for that, for freeing me and my sister from our debts and bringing me here and showing me he had faith in my abilities. I hadn't realised until these last few days of working with Dante and his team, and not having to worry about the basics—such as where the next meal was coming from—how much the last year, and even the years before that, had dragged me down with worry. I was only twenty-one years old, but I'd been burdened with so much grief and responsibility ever since our mother had died that I hadn't felt young in a long, long time.

I took a deep breath and flung the pashmina away which I had planned to wrap around my shoulders. I slipped on a pair of sandals and grabbed a towel from the pile in the bathroom.

There were three private beaches on the estate, with steps leading down to them from the extensive gardens. Two were large stretches of open sand well stocked with loungers, a beach bar where staff served a range of food and drink from 11:00 a.m. onwards, and hot showers so the guests could rinse off before returning to their accommodation. But two days ago I had found a tiny cove at the far end of the headland. The beach was a small crescent of white sand and there was an outdoor shower to rinse off and an unstaffed beach shelter furnished with lounging couches and a fridge stocked with delicacies. Despite those amenities, it was obviously too low-key for the guests because no one seemed to use it. I'd been there several times for a morning swim and had yet to meet anyone else there.

As a result, I had come to consider it my own private beach. I headed through the gardens for the entrance to the steps down to the cove, breathing in the fragrant scent of flowers, listening to the tinkle of the water fountains, admiring the view across the headland of the pastel-coloured houses of Villefranche on the other side of the bay.

My spirits were high, buzzing at the thought

of taking an early morning swim in the cool blue ocean in my revealing bikini.

No one would see me but me. No one else would be up yet; our team didn't have to assemble for the morning briefing about today's activities—and the rundown of who to concentrate on and who Dante had already eliminated from his roster of possible investors—for another two hours. And none of the guests usually emerged until at least noon. But still, wearing the skimpy swimwear and going for a swim alone felt reckless, exciting, exhilarating.

I found the partially hidden entrance to the steps behind one of the garden follies—a Japanese pagoda with a pond full of koi carp. I rushed down the steps hewn into the rock-face, then stopped dead as I came to the platform above the cove.

Someone else was here, swimming across the inlet. His broad shoulders and dark head sliced through the waves in smooth, purposeful strokes.

Dante.

I recognised him instantly because of the way he moved, eating up the water, his powerful body forging its own path regardless of surf or tide.

I noticed the small pile of clothes on the sand. Was he swimming naked?

My breathing stopped at the errant thought, my heart thundering so hard against my ribs I became light-headed. I shrunk back against the warm rock-face, behind a lavender bush that grew out of the crevice, so that I could see him clearly but he could not see me.

I devoured the sight of him, those strong steady strokes echoing in my abdomen and making my breasts feel swollen and heavy, barely confined by my bikini.

At last he swam back towards the shore. And walked out of the surf, slicking his hair back. His body emerged from the sea and my breathing speeded up. The pounding in my chest plunged deep into my abdomen.

His torso was hard and contoured like a work of art; the water shining on his bronze skin shimmered in the sunlight and made him look like some sort of god. A sea king like Poseidon, powerful and indomitable. I was less than fifteen feet away from him but thankfully, because of the sound of the waves buffeting the shore, he couldn't hear my ragged breathing, which was becoming heavier by the second as I waited for him to emerge the rest of the way. From this distance I could see the white marks of scars that marred his skin and the dark ink of a tattoo that covered his left shoulder then looped around his neck. My heart hit my chest as I recalled his devastating revelations about his childhood four nights ago, and the guarded, wary way he had responded to my sympathy for that traumatised child. As if he had regretted revealing so much.

I swallowed down the thickening in my throat as I revisited the emotions that had bombarded me that night—horror for what that little boy must have endured, and huge admiration for the man he had become.

But then all coherent thought fled as Dante walked the rest of the way out of the water.

He *was* naked. And he looked utterly magnificent. I knew I should look away—I was spying on him—but I couldn't seem to detach my gaze from the masculine beauty of his nude body. The lean waist, the narrow hips, the muscular thighs and long legs, the bunch and flex of his abdominal muscles as he moved in sinuous motion. Adrenaline surged through me in a heady wave of arousal so fierce I felt giddy. My mouth dried to parchment as my gaze finally arrowed down through the magnificent V of his hip flexors to the nest of dark hair at his groin.

Mon Dieu.

He was very large. And long.

Weren't men supposed to shrink in the cold water?

Excitement and arousal warred with panic in the centre of my chest, but did nothing to counteract the deep throbbing in my sex at the sight of his naked penis.

My mind screamed at me to move, to flee, to scurry back up the beach steps before he caught me.

If I stayed, if he became aware of my presence, I knew that all bets would be off. I would be incapable of protecting myself from this rush of need. I would be forced to make the choice he had given me four days ago—and finally feed the hunger which had been building inside me for weeks, ever since our first and only kiss.

I tried to debate the pros and cons of taking

that step, as he lifted a towel from the pile of clothing and dried himself in rough efficient strokes.

I still had a chance here. To escape this need, this longing.

But the insistent pulse in my sex refused to be silenced. And suddenly all I could think about was discovering what it would be like to become Dante's lover. Would I be totally overwhelmed again by the hunger that had thrilled me and frightened me ever since I had met him? Did I even care any more if I was?

This was not the man I had run from in Monaco. Back then he had been a distant, frightening figure. A man who could destroy me with a click of his fingers. But he had chosen not to do that; instead he'd given me a chance, a way out, when he didn't have to. He'd told me more than once that he wasn't a kind man, or a nice man, and on some levels I knew he wasn't kidding about that. He could be ruthless, he was ambitious and driven, because he'd had to be. He would be a difficult man to love, if not impossible. But this wasn't about love, I told myself staunchly as my heart all but choked me. This was about feeding the hunger, allowing myself to take something for myself. And I knew, whatever else happened, I trusted him. He would make this exciting, special, important—he'd promised me that much and I believed him.

No, he wasn't a nice man, or a kind man, but I sensed, beneath the scars and the tattoos, the rough upbringing and the dogged pursuit of power and status, and wealth, he was a good man.

And that was all I really needed him to be. He couldn't hurt me if I didn't let him.

When would I ever have a chance like this again? To take a man as hot and magnificent as Dante Allegri to be my lover? My first lover?

I was by nature a cautious person. I'd had to be. But as I stood there in the warming sunlight, my whole body alive with sensation and gripped by the deep visceral tug of longing, I knew I didn't want to be cautious any longer. Not about this. Because of my upbringing, because of spending so much of my childhood watching my mother falling in and out of love with powerful men, I was sure I could keep my heart safe while my body reached out to this man. And took everything it wanted. Everything he had promised me.

He had tugged on his shorts and was busy running the towel over his hair as I stepped out of my hiding place. As if he sensed me, his head rose suddenly and his movements stilled.

I could feel his gaze burning over every inch of my exposed skin—and there was a lot of it—as I walked down the last of the steps to the beach on shaky legs.

He didn't stop looking at me, his gaze roaming over me as his hand fell to his side and the towel dropped to the sand.

The adrenaline rioting through my system gave me the strength to walk the rest of the way across the warm sand towards him. I knew somehow that he wouldn't take a single step towards me. It was all part of the promise he'd made me. That this was my choice.

But, as I approached him, I could see the arousal burning in his eyes, inching out the blue of his irises and turning them to black as his pupils dilated. His breathing was as heavy as my own and that matching need somehow calmed the last of the nerves knotting in my belly.

'Bella...' The endearment which I had come to adore issued from those sensual lips on a husky croak of need as I finally reached him. 'What the hell are you doing here?'

Satisfaction surged through me at the dark frown, the confusion matched by the hunger in his gaze.

I might be woefully inexperienced sexually, but I felt bold, brazen even, in my excuse for a bikini. He'd given me the choice and I was making it. No regrets, no excuses, no turning back.

'Spying on you,' I said on a tortured huff of breath. Unafraid. And unashamed.

I let my gaze drift over him in return, and let every ounce of my excitement show as the muscles of his six-pack rippled with tension, and the thick ridge stretching his boxer briefs lengthened.

The erection looked enormous, but I didn't care. I wasn't scared. I knew it would hurt but my sex had melted, the liquid tug between my thighs throbbing painfully now with the desire to feel that thick ridge thrusting inside me.

A cold knuckle tucked under my chin and he lifted my face to his.

'You're playing with fire, Edie. Unless you want me to make love to you in the next five seconds, you need to leave now.'

Make love to you.

They were only words, I knew that, to describe a basic, elemental desire. But they pierced my heart as I forced a smile to my lips, trying to appear assured and uninhibited.

I knew instinctively that I needed to keep exactly how inexperienced I was hidden from him. Or this affair would be over before it had begun.

Dante wasn't looking for intimacy—his horrified reaction to my sympathy four nights ago had told me that much. And neither was I, despite the heavy thuds of my heartbeat. I might be a virgin, but I had always known the vast difference between lust and love—unlike my mother... Perhaps because of my mother and all the heartache I'd watched her suffer over men who had wanted her body but never her heart. Her mistake had been to think that by giving one she would get the other. I though, was a realist who would never make that mistake.

'I'm not going anywhere,' I said.

I saw his control snap, and the surge of adrenaline flowed through my veins as he swore softly and then grasped my upper arms to yank me into his embrace.

He cupped my bottom, pressing the hard ridge of his erection into my belly. I reached up and sunk my fingers into the wet silk of his hair as his lips sucked on my collarbone, finding the place where my pulse pounded and throbbed.

His chilly fingers sunk beneath the scrap of blue Lycra and I bucked against him, shocked by the intimacy of his touch as the heel of his hand pressed against my vulva and then he found the hot nub of my clitoris.

'*Bella*, you're so wet for me already,' he murmured against my neck, stroking, circling, caressing and making my whole body dance to his tune.

He dragged off the bikini top, snapping the strap, and covered my swollen breast with his mouth, while continuing to play with his thumb, devious strokes that thrust me into a maelstrom of needs.

Part of me panicked at the speed and intensity of the feelings engulfing me, but as the waves rose up to batter my body, the arrow of sensation in my breast as he suckled hard at the nipple reverberated in my sex. The sobs of my fulfilment echoed off the surrounding rocks, drowning out the sound of the sea, the surf and the thundering beating of my heart.

'Come for me now,' he demanded.

I hung suspended for what felt like for ever but could only have been a few seconds, then flew over, my fingers tugging at his hair, my body bucking furiously as I ground my sex against his hand, his thumb having located the perfect spot to force me over that high wide ledge.

I crashed down, my besieged body shuddering from an orgasm so sudden and intense I felt as if I'd survived a war.

I had barely come back to my senses when I felt the sand shift beneath my feet.

He had scooped me into his arms, I realised. My eyelids fluttered open and my gaze fixed on his chin, and the small crescent-shaped scar that cut through the morning stubble on his top lip.

'Thank you,' I muttered.

'You're welcome.' He gave a throaty chuckle. 'We're not finished yet though,' he said as he carried me into the beach shelter and placed me gently on one of the long cushioned couches.

He touched his thumb to my reddened nipple, played with the pebbled peak. I felt the flush of colour spread up to my hairline, knowing what a spectacle I made, lying there, all languid and sated, the bikini bra hanging off my shoulder.

He grinned, then plucked the strings that still held the garment on and drew it away. As I laid on my back topless, I shivered, seeing the feral light in his eyes. His grin died as he made quick work of the two bows that tied on the bikini bottom and tugged that off too.

Leaning over me, he swirled his tongue around my already tender nipples. I gasped, shaken by the swift return of arousal. I had thought I was sated. I was wrong.

I could hear the rush of the ocean in my ears, feel the warm breeze flowing over my over-sensitised skin, every part of me becoming an erogenous zone—throbbing with life and passion as he kissed and nipped, licked and caressed every inch of my skin.

I was writhing, the desire so intense it was almost pain when he finally parted the slick folds of my sex and lapped at the very heart of me. How could I be wild for him again so soon?

I moaned, about to go over again from the tantalising caresses, the wet suction of his lips on that swollen nub, when he rose over me. His broad shoulders cut out the sun as he stood up.

'Hold that thought, *bella*,' he said, his voice so low I could barely make out the words over the persistent thud of my pulse in my ears.

He shucked his shorts and the giant erection sprang free. Long and thick, it bowed up towards his belly button. I had a momentary fear that something so large and hard would never fit inside me, but I couldn't take my eyes away.

'I don't have protection with me,' he said as he grasped the base of the erection and stroked it absently. 'But I want so badly to feel you come apart around me,' he added, becoming even bigger and harder as I watched. 'I promise I am clean, and I will pull out in time.'

A shiny drop of moisture appeared at the tip. I was so fascinated and so turned-on I could hardly talk, let alone think. The juices between my thighs flowed freely, the desire to feel that thick length inside me unbearable. I licked my lips, fixated on the sight of him, and gloried in the thought that I had done that to him.

'*Bella*, look at me,' he ordered and my head jerked up to meet his gaze. He looked amused. 'Is that okay?'

It took me a moment to register what he was asking. The blush intensified as I realised he'd caught me gawping at his erection like a child in a sweet factory.

'Yes, I'm clean,' I said. 'And I'm on the Pill,' I said, for once impossibly grateful that I had started taking the medication to regulate my periods—which had become erratic, my doctor had insisted, because of stress. But I didn't feel stressed now; I felt languid and exhilarated all at the same time. 'And I want you inside me too,' I said, just in case there was any doubt in his mind.

'*Grazie Dio,*' he murmured, the muffled curse full of the strain it was taking him to go slowly, hold back until he had my consent.

Somehow the thought of that had my heart beating double time in my chest as I watched him climb onto the lounger. His body looked so wonderful, the many imperfections as beautiful as the sleek muscles, the deeply tanned skin, the sprinkle of hair that brushed against my trembling legs and my reddened nipples. He kissed me, his tongue tangling with mine as he lifted my leg and hooked it over his. I tasted sea salt and the musty scent of my own arousal as the kiss deepened and became hungrier. The huge head of his erection nudged at the swollen folds he had primed so perfectly.

Then he thrust hard and deep. The pinching pain shocked me, the stretched feeling becoming unbearable as he plunged through the barrier of my virginity.

I bit down on my lip, swallowing the whimper of distress, as my tender flesh adjusted to the immense weight inside me. I felt impaled, conquered, overpowered.

He stilled and stared down at me. I saw shock, then confusion, then suspicion cross his face, before he masked it. For several torturous seconds I lay there shivering, waiting for him to pull out. I thought he had figured out that I was a virgin and he was angry. But as the blush fired back across my cheeks, that assured smile returned to his lips and all he said was, 'You're incredibly tight, *bella*. Am I hurting you?'

I shook my head, the muscles of my sex relaxing at last. He was still too big, too overwhelming, the intrusion still sore, still too much, but I didn't want him to stop. And I definitely didn't want him to figure out my secret—that I had no experience of sex at all. That I was a fraud.

'I can make it better—just relax,' he said, still lodged so deep inside me I was sure I could feel him in my throat. He placed a tender kiss on my lips. Then focused all his attention on my nipple again, licking and sucking the responsive flesh. He stayed inside me without moving, allowing me to adjust to his size, his girth. The darts of pleasure began to build again, and the muscles of my sex released him a little more.

At last he found the tender nub of my clitoris with that clever thumb again, and began to circle it. My sex softened, allowing him to move, rocking out, pressing back in slow, careful thrusts.

'How does that feel?' he said as he pressed deeper, but there was no pain now, only the exquisite waves of pleasure, building, breaking.

'Good,' I managed around the thickness in my throat, at the care he'd taken with me.

He pulled me under him completely and gripped my thighs, positioning me, and angling my hips, until I was wide open to him. The slow, sure, steady strokes, became harder, faster, deeper. His fingers dug into my buttocks as he forced me to take the full measure of him, butting a place that had the waves building with staggering speed.

My hands grasped his sweat-slicked shoulders, trying to cling onto my sanity as the titanic climax raced towards me.

It hit me hard, crashing into me with the force and fury of a tsunami. I cried out, swept away by the conflagration of sensation charging through my body. He grunted as I massaged his thick length, then reared back, the hoarse shout echoing off the cliffs above us as his hot seed spurted against my belly and he collapsed on top of me.

I held onto him, the shelf of his tattooed shoulder pressed me into the cushions as his jagged breathing matched my own. The haze of afterglow covered me like a golden cloak full of sparkling lights, twinkling around me and sprinkling fairy dust over my skin. I tried to suppress the fanciful thought, but the intensity of my orgasm was working against me. Everywhere we touched I could feel him, imprinted on my flesh for ever.

As I stared at the blue sky above me, the sunlight warmed my skin and my heart expanded against my ribs as his hard length finally began to soften against my belly. But as much as I tried to dismiss the overly romantic images still flickering through my brain, and that compelling feeling of contentment and security—and concentrate on the small aches and pains brought about by the primitive fury of our lovemaking—I couldn't seem to qualify it, or even acknowledge the truth, that everything I was thinking and feeling in this moment was simply the intense physical aftermath of my first multiple orgasm.

Any more than I could ignore the clenching sensation in my chest and the desire to lie there for ever—safe and secure in his arms.

CHAPTER FOURTEEN

SHE WAS A VIRGIN, you idiot. She tricked you. And now she'll expect more from you than you can ever give. Or would want to give, I added swiftly, as my mind tried to engage with what had just happened.

The recriminations swirled around in my brain, but the ripples of afterglow still pulsing through my body made it hard for me to regret what I had done.

Her belly twitched against my softening erection and I felt the tingle of arousal at the base of my spine as I began to harden again.

What the...? This was madness. How could I possibly want her again so soon?

The realisation shocked me, enough to have me lifting up and rolling away from her. I lay on my back beside her and covered my eyes with my forearm.

I had felt her flinch as I drew out, but she said nothing as we lay there together, getting our breath back. Shame hung over me, not just because I had taken her with so little finesse, ploughing into her tight flesh like a battering ram, but at the knowledge that I could want to ravage her again so soon when she must be sore as hell.

I struggled to control my desire and willed my breathing to even out. She lay next to me on the lounger. I should move. I should offer to wash off my seed and the blood that had to be there. Thank God I had pulled out before I ejaculated, despite her assurances she was on the Pill. Surely that could have been a lie too, just like the pretence of sexual experience.

Dammit, why had she given herself to me so easily, so freely? Hadn't I told her exactly how much I was prepared to offer? I felt like a bastard now and I didn't like it. But what I liked even less was the urge to take her sweet, succulent and now no doubt bruised body back into my arms and apologise for what I'd done.

It wasn't my fault she'd remained silent. I'd given her ample chances to stop me, but she hadn't. Why hadn't she? What exactly was she expecting to happen now?

But instead of the emotional manipulations I

expected to hear, instead of the muffled tears maybe because I had deflowered her with so little care or attention, I felt her fingers touch my arm. Tentative and halting.

I lifted my forearm to find her leaning over me, her face a picture of flushed arousal. Still. What was up with that? She couldn't possibly still desire me.

'Is everything okay, Dante?' she asked and I could hear the concern in her voice.

I huffed out a laugh that sounded strained and forced, but I could see her concern for me was genuine.

What on earth was going on? She was looking at me as if I were the injured party, instead of the other way around.

'Everything's terrific,' I said, still waiting for the other shoe to drop, or rather the axe to fall on my head, but instead of railing at me or demanding to know what my intentions were now, the sweet, unbearably sexy smile that I had only seen once before curved her lips.

I tried to quash the answering smile that wanted to curve my lips in response but there was no help for it. She wasn't going to mention her virginity, or the ruthless way I had plunged into her or the fact that I hadn't stopped when I should have done, or apologised even, like the heartless bastard I was. She wasn't even going to mention my loss of control and the fact I had carried on making love to her.

Could she actually be that guileless? That sweet? That innocent? Because it seemed that she was, and I couldn't seem to decide what I felt about that.

On the one hand it was going to let me off this hook very nicely indeed—because if she wasn't about to draw attention to her virginity, I certainly was not... But it also made her seem even more vulnerable than she had before—when I'd walked in on her being beaten by Carsoni's goon. But now the man hurting her and treating her without the proper care was me.

'You enjoyed it?' she said, but I could hear the question.

I rolled back towards her and stroked the side of her face with my thumb; the grinding feeling of inadequacy and shame and futile temper I hadn't wanted to acknowledge released in my chest.

'*Bella*, couldn't you tell?' I said.

The blush, which I had found so fascinating when I'd first met her, lit up her cheeks again. But now I knew exactly where that blush originated, from an openness and honesty far greater than I had already realised, it didn't just fascinate me, it captivated me. And although I knew I shouldn't, I had the strangest feeling of satisfaction that, for whatever reason, she had chosen me to be her first.

Maybe it wasn't that significant for her, that was why she hadn't mentioned it. And why she clearly didn't want me to mention it either—which was fine by me. But that didn't stop me from knowing. And wondering why on earth she would have chosen me. I hoped to hell it wasn't some foolish notion that I would give her more but it seemed so far as if my deeply cynical reaction to her virginity had been an overreaction, to say the least.

With that in mind, I needed to be casual now. Not to make a big deal of any of this. I forced myself to relax and smile back at her, even though the tightening in my chest felt far too significant.

'I… Yes, of course I could tell,' she said, feigning an experience I knew she didn't have.

Why her little pretence should suddenly seem appealing instead of threatening or suspicious I had no idea but I decided to go with it.

'I should...' She thrust her thumb over her shoulder, pointing towards the shower at the bottom of the cliff steps. 'I should go and shower...' She smiled. 'I have an important meeting with my boss in an hour and a half.'

She grabbed a towel from the pile by the lounger and wrapped it around that luscious body. I grabbed one too, to cover myself, because I could feel myself getting hard again and I didn't want to scare her off.

Although she didn't seem scared. Which I decided was good. Once wasn't going to be enough for either one of us, but we needed to establish some parameters for this...hook-up. Because that's all this could ever be. She seemed to already realise that, which was also good, I supposed. And while I knew her attempts to appear blasé and urbane about what we'd done were really just an act, I didn't have a problem with that either. But not to the point that I was going to allow her to rush off now—or pretend that nothing had happened when I saw her again at the team briefing at eleven.

I had never slept with an employee before and certainly not one of my engagement team. But I didn't see why it should be a problem. We were all adults. Consenting adults. And everyone knew I didn't play favourites in a business situation. Every single person on my team had earned their place there. And Edie more than most. Her work so far had been exemplary. She was observant, erudite and incredibly sharp and that was before you even factored in her exceptional analytical abilities and her creative use of data to rationalise and assess the investment potential of each of the candidates we were considering. Not only had she worked hard over the last week and a half, she had impressed every member of the team and earned her place. And I knew how much that meant to her, after our conversation over dinner four nights ago. After the abuse she had clearly suffered because of her mother's behaviour, Edie had wrongly believed she had a lot to prove.

Considering that abuse, I would hazard a guess that was why she didn't want anyone knowing that we were an item. Because the professionalism she had done so much to achieve might be compromised.

Unfortunately though, keeping our liaison a secret wasn't going to work for me.

So when she went to leave, I grasped her wrist. 'Not so fast, Edie.'

She sat down on the lounger, her hands twisting on the towel she had wrapped around that delectable body.

'At the meeting today, and during the rest of this week,' I said, 'the guests and the team are going to know we have been intimate.'

She blinked, the blush exploding on her cheeks again. 'How?'

I had to resist the urge to laugh at the gaucheness of the question. Did she have any idea how she looked right now—like a woman who had been well and truly...? I cut off the crude word before I could even think it. She wasn't a whore, like my mother had been, like her own mother had been. In fact she was exactly the opposite. She didn't deserve to be thought of in that way. But that didn't mean I was going to avoid stating the obvious. If she wanted to pretend she was experienced, I was entitled to treat her as if she were.

'Because I plan to sleep with you again. And I'm not about to keep it a secret. In fact,'

I added, thinking of the practicalities, because from the look of stunned disbelief on her face she was clearly incapable of doing so. 'I would like to have your belongings moved into my suite of rooms. It seems pointless us staying at opposite ends of the estate. Logistically speaking. There's going to be little enough downtime given the roster of events Evan has planned for the remainder of the week. If we're going to make the most of the time we have available it makes sense for us to stay in the same place. And my suite is a great deal bigger than yours.'

'But...' she actually sputtered, her blush now radioactive, which I found ridiculously charming. It shouldn't matter to me, but it felt oddly exhilarating knowing I was the first man, the only man, she had ever been in a relationship with. 'Won't that compromise my position with the team?' she said, confirming my suspicions about her insecurities.

'Absolutely not. What you do in your spare time... What we both do in our spare time, for that matter... With each other. Is no one else's business. Believe me, you have more than proved yourself with every member of the team, including me, and no one is going to question that.' A flush of pleasure lit her eyes at the praise and the strange clenching in my chest increased. I forced it down. It wasn't as if I was complimenting her for any other reason than she had earned it. 'Plus, I've seen how some of the male guests have been sniffing around you,' I added, because now we had slept together it didn't seem inappropriate to admit to the jealousy that had gripped me every time one of the bastards even glanced at her. 'I don't like it. As long as they know you're now with me, they'll back off, which will save me the trouble of having to punch anyone. Which could get awkward, let's face it, if they turn out to be one of the people we choose as an investor,' I finished, only half joking.

'You would punch one of the guests?' She sounded both horrified and astonished. But the flush of colour told a slightly different story—which I suspected she was wholly unaware of—that having a man prepared to fight for her was a novel, but not entirely unwelcome, experience. I thought of the father who had refused to acknowledge her and couldn't help the sudden desire to punch him too.

'If a man got too familiar with you, yes, I'd

punch him in a minute,' I confirmed as I tucked a tendril of hair behind her ear. I let my thumb glide down the side of her neck, to caress the pulse which hammered her collarbone. I could see the beginnings of beard burn where I had devoured the soft flesh earlier. I would have to be more careful with her, I noted; her skin was so delicate. 'I don't share,' I added, which was true. I insisted all relationships I had were mutually exclusive, no matter how short. But the strange surge of possessiveness at the thought of any other man touching her, or even looking at her, was something entirely new.

I dismissed the thought. It was only because she was so young and so inexperienced, and she was also in my employ, that I felt protective towards her. It would fade, along with my hunger for her. But, until it did, I didn't see a problem with indulging myself. And her.

'So how do you feel about having your belongings moved into my suite?' I asked.

She hesitated, tugging that lush bottom lip with her teeth as she considered my request, and for a split second my pulse rate sped up—at the insane thought that she might refuse me. Of course she would not; she had enjoyed the sex as much as I had after that initial discomfort, I was sure about that now. And anyway, if she refused I was more than capable of persuading her. But weirdly, despite all my qualifications, my pulse remained elevated and erratic until she stopped biting her lip and nodded.

'Okay,' she said, the eager smile and the flicker of excitement in her eyes captivating me as much as that damn blush. 'If you insist,' she said.

'I do,' I murmured, unable to prevent an equally eager smile—at the thought of all the pleasure we would have after hours. I gave her a friendly pat on the butt. 'Now, you'd better go shower,' I said. 'Or you'll be late for work, and I know what a hard taskmaster your boss is.'

She laughed, the sound so light and sweet and carefree, my pulse rate spiked again, for an entirely different reason. But as she stood, with the towel still wrapped tightly around her lush curves, she looked down at me, her smile turning sultry and sexy and remarkably bold for a young woman who had only just been initiated into the joys of sex. An odd sense of pride gripped me at yet more evidence that my Edie was an exceptionally fast learner.

'Are you sure you don't want to join me?' she said, flicking her gaze provocatively towards the open shower used to rinse off the sea salt.

Blood surged into my groin at the image of her wet and dripping, those lush curves covered in soap suds as my hands teased her nipples and explored her warm flesh.

Whoa, ragazzo.

I shifted on the lounger, but kept the towel pressed firmly over my growing erection to hide my reaction to her bold suggestion.

As much as I would love to take her up on her offer, I knew she had to be sore and I didn't want to risk hurting her by taking things too far. Too soon.

While her flesh might be willing, mine was far too weak. Or, rather, not nearly weak enough.

'I think I will stay here and enjoy the view instead,' I said, with as casual a tone as I could muster, knowing it was going to be torture. 'You have exhausted me, *bella,*' I lied, but I was glad I had when she laughed with obvious pleasure, like the fledging man-eater she was. 'And we don't want to both be late for work.'

She nodded, again revealing that artless smile.

I watched her walk to the shower, unable to

detach my gaze as she dropped the towel and put on a display worthy of a seasoned courtesan as she washed her beautiful body—a display which was all the more arousing for being entirely unconscious.

I waved to her as she left the beach, having slipped into one of the towelling robes left for the guests. I finally managed to drag my gaze off her as she disappeared up the beach steps. I would need to get my reaction to her under ruthless control before our morning team briefing, I realised, or all the promises I'd made to maintain our professional relationship in the professional spaces we shared would be shot to hell.

I gathered the triangles of blue fabric I had ripped off her earlier, intending to dispose of them for her and order her another bikini— because I was already anticipating the sight of those lush curves so temptingly confined again. But as I climbed off the lounger I noticed the spots of blood she had also left behind. Along with her innocence.

Not that I had needed any confirmation of her virginity after our encounter, but the sight had my heartbeat stuttering. And, although I knew it was a little disingenuous, I couldn't help making a silent vow as I stared at the evidence of her trust in me.

No woman had ever given me such a gift. And, while I hadn't asked for it, and did not intend to acknowledge it, I felt a strange sense of responsibility towards her because of it.

This liaison wouldn't last. I would soon grow bored and restless, as I always did, and she would eventually discover I was a dangerous man to become too attached to. Luckily Edie was a smart, intuitive woman, however inexperienced, and she would soon figure out the truth about me, if she hadn't already.

But as I stood under the shower myself and took my erection in hand to give myself some necessary relief, I made Edie one promise. Whatever happened, I would endeavour to make this liaison as fun and pleasurable for her as it was for me.

Given my appetite for her—and the intensity of our sexual chemistry—I was liable to make a lot of demands in the next days as we enjoyed each other. But I would be careful to gauge her reaction and make sure that I never asked too much. I would take nothing for granted and I would also attempt to smooth out at least a few of my rough edges. And, most importantly of all, I would let her down gently when this liaison reached its inevitable conclusion. Because, however bold and brave and intelligent Edie was, she was still entirely new to this—and she certainly hadn't picked the most tender, or refined, or gentle of men to initiate her.

And, if nothing else, I didn't want her to ever regret that.

CHAPTER FIFTEEN

I STOOD ON the balcony of Dante's suite, watching the guests mingle below me in the torchlit gardens in their designer ball gowns and tuxedos—like exotic peacocks displaying their wealth and status in the summer night. *Cordon bleu* canapés and vintage champagne were being served on sterling silver platters, and I could hear the strains of the orchestra in the ballroom below me playing the opening bars of a Viennese waltz for those people elegant enough, or merry enough, to brave the dance floor.

The night was perfect, and a little surreal, and I was a part of it. An essential part of it.

Nerves and excitement tangled in the pit of my stomach, going some way to alleviate the bubble of regret that had been lodged in my throat all day.

I'd had such an amazing time in the last five days, ever since Dante and I had started sleeping together. The sex had been… Well, nothing short of a revelation. I'd never felt more alive or present, more hungry and yet sated all at the same time. Dante had kept to his word, and been absolutely incredible—making me feel both cherished and desired, while also keeping a clear separation between my work responsibilities and the things we did after hours. Despite agreeing to allow our affair to become public knowledge, I had been unbearably nervous that first day. Surely the other team members would resent my involvement with Dante, would judge me for it. And in some ways I'd been prepared for it, had even understood it.

But no such problems had arisen. If anything, most of the team had found it amusing and kind of sweet. Collette had even whispered to me that first day, while she was supervising having my belongings moved to Dante's quarters, 'You are good for him. He has been much less of a taskmaster this week than usual.'

I knew she was joking. Dante wasn't a taskmaster at all; he was focused, yes, and he had high expectations which he expected to be met by every one of his employees. But he was also fair and very good at communicating those expectations, so there was no confusion.

But still, I had basked in Collette's approval and laughed with Jenny Caldwell, the middle-aged woman who ran his accounts department, when she had winked at me after Dante had grabbed my hand and dragged me out of the office when last night's final briefing had finished.

Of course, the attitude of the staff had had a lot to do with how Dante had handled the whole situation. Not only had he been forthright and pragmatic about our 'arrangement', but he'd also made a point of showing me no favouritism within the team. He'd been equally frank with the guests—making a point of treating me with respect in front of them, but also making no bones about claiming me as his during the leisure time we had together, when he never missed an opportunity to touch me or caress me.

And he simply hadn't given me a chance to be ashamed of how much I enjoyed his attentiveness.

There had only been one small moment of unpleasantness, with a woman called Elise

Durand, the CEO of a large French hospitality firm, who had approached me yesterday. In the few interactions I had had with the woman at the poker table, my assessment of her business acumen and her approach to risk had been favourable and I knew she was one of the front runners for investor status. It was quite possible Dante and his two top financiers were offering her a stake in the new expansion right now. A chill ran up my spine as I recalled what she had said to me the night before, as I was rushing through the gardens, already anticipating the rendezvous at our private cove which I had arranged with Dante for a late-night swim.

'You remind me a great deal of your mother, Edie. She also had a taste for powerful men and knew how to use it to her best advantage.'

I watched the moon glow over the bay, the lights of Villefranche in the distance twinkling, and forced myself to ignore the feeling of inadequacy that had assailed me. How stupid, to let something so innocuous ruin my happy buzz. It had been a throwaway comment, which I had taken far too much to heart, because I was over-sensitive about my mother's reputation.

I hadn't mentioned the comment to Dante. Or

anyone else. Because I didn't want to appear unprofessional, and I certainly didn't want to prejudice Dante's decision about whom he invited to invest in his company because of our fling and my own insecurities.

The bubble of regret expanded another inch. The fling that was going to end tonight.

I swallowed, trying not to let the feeling of ennui—of sadness—get the better of me. I'd always known this would be a few days of bliss. Dante hadn't promised more than a quick fling and I hadn't asked him for more. Which was for the best, I now realised. Because, even after only five days as his lover, I knew I was sinking too deep into this relationship. Wanting things from it that I knew I could never have.

Already, I was consumed with anticipation every time I saw him. I reacted with complete abandon to even the slightest show of affection or attention from him. And I had become utterly addicted to his lovemaking.

A blush warmed my cheeks despite the sea breeze, as I recalled the shameless way I had responded the night before. To be fair, that wasn't entirely my fault, I added to myself. Dante, I had discovered, could be an absolute devil.

Last night, on the beach, almost as if he had sensed my loss of confidence after my encounter with Elise, he had worked me into a frenzy of need and longing, until all I could focus on, and all I could think about, was him.

Using his tongue and his teeth in ways he already knew would drive me wild, he had given me mini-orgasm after mini-orgasm without ever giving me enough relief to completely satisfy me. Eventually I had been a quivering bundle of raw nerves and desperate needs. I had cried myself hoarse, literally begging him to thrust deep enough and hard enough to release me from the sensual torture—and, when he finally had, the orgasm had been so powerful I was pretty sure I had actually passed out.

But it was the way he had washed me so tenderly afterwards, and insisted on carrying me back through the gardens and all the way into our suite of rooms, that had all but destroyed me.

I'd fallen into a deep sleep—the dreams of belonging, of safety and security all the more devastating when I had woken this morning with his strong body wrapped around me and he'd made love to me again with a ruthless tenderness which I had convinced myself for one bright shining moment meant much more than it did.

I heard the outer door to our suite open and Dante's footsteps on the carpeting.

My heart leapt into my throat on cue as I turned and watched him walk towards me. He looked dashing and debonair in the tailored tuxedo, reminding me of the man I'd met that first night who had terrified me on some visceral level.

He terrified me even more now, I realised, because I couldn't seem to control the erratic beat of my heart as he gathered me into his arms.

'At last, the work is finally finished, the investors are in place and we can celebrate,' he murmured, nuzzling my neck, raising goosebumps that rioted over my collarbone and arrowed into my sex—which had already begun to melt at the sight of him, readying itself for the erection that pressed insistently against my belly.

'That's wonderful,' I said, trying to smile, and swallow down the bubble that only got larger at the thought that we only had tonight now, before this affair would be over.

He drew back and held out my arms, his gaze becoming dark and intense as it roamed over the satin ball gown Nina had had made for me especially for tonight's occasion. 'You look absolutely stunning,' he said.

The familiar blush flared across my cleavage. He never forgot to compliment me, to make his appreciation and his approval known. And I realised I had become completely addicted to that too. My skin burned at the reminder that Nina had insisted I wear nothing under the gown.

'So do you,' I said, letting my gaze roam over him in turn. He really did look magnificent in the dark evening wear. I imagined the scars that lurked beneath it, which I had explored with my fingers and lips countless times now. They were a testament, just as the suit was, to how hard he'd worked to escape the degradation of his upbringing. A stupid spurt of pride at his achievements worked its way up my torso, even though I'd had nothing whatsoever to do with them.

'Hey?' He lifted my chin and met my gaze. 'Is something wrong?'

'No, nothing,' I lied easily enough. I didn't want to mar our last night together with my ridiculous emotions. 'I just wish we could stay and celebrate here,' I said boldly, which wasn't a lie.

He let out a hoarse chuckle. 'You and me both.'

He gripped my fingers and gave them a squeeze. 'But I'm afraid we're going to have to make an appearance. I wouldn't want that beautiful gown to go to waste...' His pupils darkened as he led me towards the door, his thumb rubbing my palm possessively. 'Before I rip it off you,' he added, sending the familiar shiver of anticipation through me.

I let out a strained laugh as we walked down the wide sweeping staircase towards the ballroom. People turned to stare, and I had the weirdest sensation of being like a princess at a ball—young and desperately in lust with the handsome prince every other woman here wanted but couldn't have, because he had chosen me.

The sensation of acceptance, of belonging, was fanciful and fleeting for sure, but still I rejoiced in the renewed leap in my heartbeat.

Why not enjoy tonight, and worry about the struggle to keep my emotions in check tomorrow, when I returned to Belle Rivière—and reality intruded again?

'Who did you decide to offer investor status to in the end?' I asked, as Dante took a glass of champagne off the tray of a passing waiter and handed it to me.

'Devon O'Reilly and the consortium from Le Grange,' Dante said, mentioning an Irish race-horse owner and a group of hedge fund managers, both of whom I'd recommended. There was only one other person I'd recommended.

'Not Elise Durand?' I asked, surprised but also stupidly pleased. I tried to quell the trickle of pleasure that she hadn't been invited to invest after all, because it made me feel petty and insecure.

'No, not Elise,' he said, his brows lowering as he watched me over his glass. 'Although it might have been nice if I had found out about her unsuitability from you, instead of Collette.'

'I… I don't understand.'

I lowered my glass from my lips, scared to take another sip in case I choked on the emotion currently rising up my torso.

Had he found out about Elise's comment to me from Collette? And if he had, why was he so angry about it, because I could see the temper swirling in his eyes?

'She insulted you, Edie,' he said, giving me the answer to a question I had been too scared to ask. 'Do you really think I would want to do business with her after that? I had her escorted off the estate as soon as I found out. And I intend to make it known that I refused to do business with her or her company.'

'I'm not sure she meant it as an insult,' I said, not sure why I was defending her. Because it seemed very obvious to me now that's exactly what she had intended—to undermine and belittle me. And of course she had succeeded, tapping into my insecurities, my feelings of inadequacy with a simple offhand remark. But what seemed so much more dangerous now was Dante's reaction. Because he hadn't just spotted the insult before me, he had jumped to my defence. And was clearly furious on my behalf. Enough to base an important business decision on it. It suddenly felt like too much. Not just his decision to defend me and protect me, and do something as extreme as having Elise Durand kicked off the estate, but also my reaction to that response.

I had tried so hard not to fall in love with this man. And I'd succeeded, despite the violent intensity of his lovemaking, despite the respect he showed me at every turn, despite the way he had cherished and complimented me. But I could feel myself slipping—no, crashing—over the edge as he stared back at me now with outrage and annoyance, at me as much as Elise, etched on his face.

His emotions were rarely so unguarded, and that unsettled me too. That he would let me see how much Elise's insult had angered him.

'Don't ever apologise for or excuse other people's prejudices again,' he said, or rather commanded, and just like that I felt my heart drop like a stone. Wow, I really was a hopeless case, I realised vaguely, as I tumbled into the abyss—unsure of where I would land but unable to break my fall.

How could I be falling in love with this man, not because of his sensitive nurturing qualities, not because of his protectiveness, or even his epic skills in the sack, but because of his quick-fire temper, his possessiveness and his overbearing arrogance? It would be utterly tragic... If it weren't so... I took a shuddering breath, trying to collect myself and fight back the tears threatening to spill over my lids... If it weren't so wonderful.

'You're not your mother,' he continued, still lecturing me and clearly completely oblivious to the emotions I was struggling to get a grip on. 'And no one gets to judge you or insult you because of the mistakes she made. You're worth so much more than that. Do you understand?'

I nodded, because my heart was too swollen and rammed too far up my throat to attempt coherent speech.

He paused, finally realising that he was browbeating me. 'All right, then. Let's forget about it now,' he said, sounding disconcerted for the first time since I'd met him. Was he as stunned by his impassioned defence of me as I was?

I thought of his own background, the horrors of his childhood which he had outlined to me in such stark, unemotional terms. As if they'd happened to another man, as if he'd come to terms with them years ago and got over them. And now I wondered—was that really the case? Perhaps he believed he had been unaffected, that he had risen above those traumas and moved on. But surely he hadn't, if he could hear about the fairly minor slight Elise had subjected me to—which, I would hazard a guess, was nothing like the kind of insults he had probably suffered—and be so enraged on my behalf.

'She's gone and she's not coming back,' he added.

He tossed the last of the champagne back, and I wondered if his mouth was now as dry as mine.

'Do you want the rest of that?' he asked, nodding at my full glass as he dumped his own empty glass on a waiter's tray.

I shook my head, still not sure of my ability to speak coherently with so many wants and needs and desires swirling inside me.

'Bene,' he said lapsing into Italian, which I knew he only did when his emotions were too close to the surface. He grabbed my glass and dumped it on the waiter's tray too, then grasped my hand. 'Because I want to get my hands on you,' he said, marching through the crowd as he hauled me towards the ballroom and the sound of the orchestra playing another waltz. 'And the only way I'm going to be able to do that for the next few hours is to dance with you.'

He spun me into his arms, his steps assured and confident, his arms holding me tight. I clung to his wide shoulders as the kaleidoscope of lights whirled around us.

My heart expanded another inch, threatening to choke me. The dangerous emotions surging through me were so strong and so real I knew they would hurt immeasurably tomorrow when we parted—and this affair was over. But tonight all I was capable of doing was following his lead and letting those glorious, overwhelming feelings take hold. Because it was far too late to stop them.

The evening drifted past in a daze, his body wrapped around me as we danced, his hand never letting go of mine even when the music paused and he was forced to release me. He even gripped my hand during the speech he had to give and the final toasts.

The clock was ticking towards midnight, the applause still ringing in my ears when he dragged me through the crowd to charge up the staircase towards our suite.

Perhaps I should have been embarrassed. I could see the knowing looks on some of the guests' faces, the lascivious smiles on others.

Every single person had to know exactly where we were going and why we were leaving the ball so abruptly. But after his passionate defence of me, the petty judgements of people like Elise Durand no longer had the power to hurt me.

I wanted him with a hunger that had been consuming me too—and I refused to be ashamed of it.

Even so, my breath caught in my lungs, my thighs quivering with anticipation, my nipples so hard they hurt when he slammed shut the door of our suite and pressed me back against the wood.

'I thought tonight would never end,' he growled, his irritation sending darts of pleasure through my system as he fumbled with the fastening of my gown. 'To hell with it,' he said, before the sound of rending fabric tore through the air.

Shock and excitement careered through my body as the exquisite gown slid to the floor, leaving me naked.

'*Dio?* Seriously?' he groaned, the feral grunt filled with outrage. 'All this time you've been wearing no underwear beneath this thing?'

'I couldn't,' I said, moaning as he captured one yearning nipple between his lips and plunged thick fingers between the slick folds of my sex. 'Nina insisted it would ruin the line of the dress.'

'I'm going to kill Nina next time I see her,' he said as I arched into his caresses. 'But first I'm going to punish you,' he added, but the teasing tone was hoarse and not remotely convincing.

'Please…' I said, circling my hips, thrusting against his hand, as his thumb found the swollen nub of my clitoris—the diabolical touch too much, and yet not nearly enough.

'Tell me what you need, *bella*,' he demanded.

'I need you,' I said, blurting out the truth, the emotion which had been holding me hostage all evening starting to strangle me.

'Anch'io ho bisogno di te…' he murmured, his voice as raw as my own now. *I need you too.*

I'd barely had time to translate the words, to grasp hold of what they might mean, before he released his erection and lifted me.

Suddenly, the immense weight of him was plunging heavily inside me, his hands gripping my buttocks to hold me up, to hold me open for him. My back thudded the door as he began to rock his hips and drive into me. My body welcomed the deep thrusts, the huge erection filling up the empty spaces inside me, sending me higher and higher. I sobbed as the orgasm raced towards me.

At last I soared on the rolling wave of pleasure pushing away all my doubts and fears until all that was left was the sweet, sublime joy of our lovemaking. As the orgasm broke over me and I heard his harsh shout of release echoing in my ear, I clung to him, wishing the moment could last for ever…

But knowing if tonight was all I could have, I would take it.

As I floated in afterglow, giddy and dazed and a little sore, stupidly close to tears, he carried me to the bed, then stripped off his clothing.

I needed to protect myself, I knew that, but I couldn't seem to find the energy or the will to do so as he gathered me against him, our naked bodies slick with sweat from the fury of our coupling.

'Are you okay?' he asked, his fingers brushing my hair back as he stared down at me with a tenderness that broke my heart. 'I didn't hurt you, did I?'

'No, of course not,' I said, confused by the edge in his voice.

'Are you sure?' he said. 'I just took you like a...' The remark was cut off, but I could hear what he hadn't said.

Like a whore.

But the edge in his voice was aimed at him, not me, I realised. I remembered the way he had talked about his mother, the bitterness and anger in his voice when he had told me she was a prostitute. But all I could hear now was regret. Then I remembered the way he had jumped to my defence earlier in the evening. And what he had said.

You're not your mother. And no one gets to judge you or insult you because of the mistakes she made. You're worth so much more than that. Do you understand?

And I wondered again why he had defended me so passionately. Was it just me he was trying to defend, or himself?

I lifted up on my elbow, to see his face in the darkness—and the wariness and tension

I saw had the emotion flooding back which I had been trying so hard to qualify, and control.

'I love it when you take me like that,' I said, desperate to reassure him. *With such need, such urgency.*

I wanted to add the words but held back, scared to burden him with my feelings—when I could see he was struggling with his own.

'Okay, good,' he murmured, then swept his hand down my hair. 'Go to sleep,' he said, pressing me down until my head rested against his shoulder.

I kissed his chest, grinning at his huff of breath.

'Don't do that or I'm going to want you again,' he said, his voice strained. 'And then neither of us is going to get any sleep.'

His appetite for me sent a thrill through my body, but the feeling of closeness thrilled me more.

'Dante, can I ask you a question?' I said, the darkness, the intimacy making me bolder than I had ever been.

'Sure,' he grunted, stroking my hair. 'As long as you promise to go to sleep afterwards.'

'What did your mother do that made you hate her so?'

His breathing stilled as he tensed and I regretted the probing question, knowing I had no right to ask it. But before I could take it back he answered me.

'I told you. She was a prostitute,' he murmured, but he didn't sound bitter now, or angry; he simply sounded guarded.

'I know,' I said. 'And that must have been terrible for both of you,' I continued, wanting to understand; the life he had described to me sounded traumatic. 'But...'

'Why would it be terrible for her?' he interrupted me. 'She *chose* that life.'

'How do you know that?' I asked. 'Surely very few people choose to be prostitutes,' I added when he remained silent. 'They do it out of desperation or addiction or coercion. Are you sure she wasn't forced to make that choice?' I said, wanting to ease his pain, because, beneath the harsh words, I could hear the ripple of insecurity.

He had given me so much in the past five days, by showing faith in me, by making me feel special and valued and important. And

I wanted to do the same for him. Obviously his feelings for his mother were complex and their circumstances when he was growing up something I knew very little about. I couldn't right the wrongs she may have done him. But being a prostitute, being forced to sell yourself for money didn't make you a bad person; it didn't mean his mother hadn't loved him, any more than my mother's search for love in all the wrong places meant she hadn't loved me. People were complex, they could be weak and fickle, foolish and selfish, but there was almost always goodness in them too. And I had the strangest feeling when he spoke about his mother, he was also speaking about himself. I couldn't tell him how I felt about him. It was too soon. Too much. But I wanted him to know how special he was, regardless.

'How about we stop talking about her?' he said at last, his open palm stroking my hair in an absent caress—but I could hear the edge in his voice again, and knew I'd gone too far, I'd overstepped the mark. 'It's a real buzzkill,' he added. 'And the truth is, I don't hate her; I don't even remember her that well.'

'Okay,' I said.

'Hey?' He shifted, his knuckle nudging my chin up. 'Don't look so sad. What happened to me as a kid is so long ago it doesn't matter now.' But I could hear the hollow tone, and the deafening thunder of his heartbeat beneath my ear, and I wondered if he was lying.

But then he rolled on top of me and the stiff weight of his erection brushed my thigh. The inevitable surge of blood rushed to my core.

'And I've got something much more important to discuss,' he said, his tone husky and assured again.

He was distracting me with sex, putting emotional distance between us, the way he had done right from the start. But as his lips captured mine in a demanding kiss and he angled my hips to slide the thick erection home, I gave myself up to the physical pleasure to stem the foolish wave of sadness.

My feelings were my own to handle and control—and, however much it might hurt in the long run, I would always be grateful for these brief, beautiful moments of connection. I had the vague realisation my mother had made the same brutal bargain—to trade sex for intimacy–but, before the disturbing thought could take root, he rocked his hips and surged deep. I cried out as the muscles of my sex clamped around his thick length, milking him in the throes of another earth-shattering orgasm.

I drifted moments later on the edges of a dream, his arm tight around my shoulder as he lulled me to sleep, and for one foolish moment a wish flickered in my consciousness. If only I could find a way past the demanding, cynical, indomitable man he had become and reach the little boy beneath, then I could tell him how much he was loved, by me at least.

CHAPTER SIXTEEN

I LAY IN the darkness, staring at the ceiling cornice above my bed, and felt the weight of Edie's head on my shoulder. My sweat-soaked skin felt clammy as it dried.

She was exhausted; I'd exhausted her. We'd exhausted each other. But I wouldn't be sleeping any time soon, the adrenaline powering through my system like one of Alexi's damn racing cars, speeding around and around in circles with nowhere to go.

I'd pounded into her like a madman until I heard her sobs of release and felt her swollen flesh hold me in the grip of her orgasm. Not once, but twice.

But far worse had been what came in between, her quiet words, whispered in the darkness.

'What did your mother do that made you hate her so?'

'Surely few people choose to be prostitutes.'

Words that were just like Edie. Sweet, naïve, romantic… And sadly idealistic.

But, as much as I wanted to disregard what Edie had said, deny her defence of a woman who didn't deserve an ounce of my sympathy or hers, the conversation had left me feeling raw and exposed. And scared, dammit.

It was midnight. I needed to sleep too. It was going to be a long day tomorrow. I had to say goodbye to the guests, brief my finance team about the decisions made over the week and get the next stage of the expansion plan in motion now the new investors had been chosen.

Then I was supposed to be catching a flight to Las Vegas tomorrow night. I had a new hotel and casino complex opening there in two weeks and I wanted to oversee the inauguration.

But, as Edie shifted beside me, the events of the night kept tumbling over and over in my head.

I had planned to take her with me to Vegas. I'd already asked Nina to design a new wardrobe for the trip, had included Edie's name on the flight roster and informed my PA in Vegas that she would be joining me for all the events we had planned.

I was supposed to be telling her in a few hours' time.

But I couldn't ask her now. Because of that innocuous question, that should have been easily answered.

I didn't remember my mother, not really; I'd made sure of it. But Edie was right. I still hated her for what she had done to me.

But what I hated more was that Edie knew. That she had exposed my weakness so easily.

It shouldn't matter what Edie thought of me or didn't think of me. It shouldn't matter that she cared, but somehow it did. Because she already mattered to me more than she should.

Seeing the moisture in Edie's eyes when I had told her how furious I had been with Elise Durand on her behalf had all but crippled me.

Gratitude, affection, perhaps even love for me had shone clearly in her expression and for one agonising second I had wanted desperately to be worthy of it.

That desire had only escalated during the evening.

The dancing, when I couldn't let her out of my arms, the intensity of our lovemaking afterwards, had all been a pathetic attempt to redirect the feelings I had developed for Edie. But now as I lay in the darkness, the pearly light of a midsummer night illuminating the bedroom's furnishings, and felt the need still pulsing in my groin as I listened to her soft breathing, I knew I was kidding myself.

Just like all the lies I'd been telling myself for days about the reasons why I wanted to take her to Vegas with me. It wasn't for her bright, brilliant mind, or her sweet, lively companionship, or even the incredible way she responded to my touch, even though I had become addicted to all those things. No, it was far, far worse than that. I wanted her to come to Vegas with me because I didn't want this affair to end. Because, after only five days of having her in my bed and only a few weeks of having her in my life, I couldn't imagine what I would do without her.

I didn't want to let her go. Which was precisely why I had to.

I couldn't open myself up to those needs again, those wants.

I shuddered, despite the warmth of the room in the sultry night. The memory of cold stone, rain spattering my bare arms and legs, hands holding me, voices whispering strange words as I screamed and kicked and cried. The nightmares that had come again and again, waking me in strange beds, reminding me I was alone. I wasn't enough. I could never be enough.

I couldn't go back there again. Not ever. Not for any woman. I'd spent years getting over that night, burying that broken child so deep no one could find him, not even me. But somehow Edie had brought him out of hiding.

Which made her a threat I had to protect myself against.

As much as I hated the thought of letting Edie go, I hated the thought of being dependent on her touch, her laughter or her kindness a great deal more.

Edie was fierce and sweet, but also an innocent. She might believe she loved me but, once she discovered how cynical and disillusioned I really was, she would realise I could never love her back... And then her feelings would sour. Maybe not now, maybe not even in the next few weeks or months, but it would happen eventually, and it would hurt me... I could not afford to give her a chance to break me—the way my mother had broken that little boy.

Edie's hand unfurled against my chest as she

slept. She snuggled closer, resting her palm on my sternum, gravitating towards me even in sleep. The possessive, unconscious touch sent a shaft of longing through me and my heart slammed into my ribs.

I tried to calm the heavy erratic rhythm as I listened to the soft murmur of her breathing… And considered how to end our affair swiftly and irrevocably tomorrow while I waited for the dawn.

CHAPTER SEVENTEEN

Take a week off at Belle Rivière. You've earned it. Joe will be expecting you in Monaco on the eighteenth. Contact him if you have any concerns.
Buon viaggio!
D

I STARED AT the note from Dante that had been delivered to the suite as I packed, my hands shaking, and gulped down the ball of confusion and anguish in my throat.

Something was wrong. Very wrong. And now I was being forced to confront it.

I'd known something wasn't right as soon as I'd woken up this morning, my body aching from the intensity of Dante's lovemaking, with Dante nowhere in sight. It was the first time in five days I'd woken up without Dante's arms around me.

When I'd joined him in the breakfast room,

he'd been in the middle of a phone call and had barely glanced at me. And I hadn't had a chance to speak to him since. Not properly. Not even during my private team interview after the guests had departed.

He'd informed me I was getting a two-thousand-euro bonus along with the rest of the team. I'd been hopelessly flattered and so proud. He hadn't mentioned us—I'd assumed as part of his efforts to keep our affair out of the work environment—so I'd made an effort not to mention anything personal too.

But before he'd dismissed me he'd told me he was offering me the probationary position he'd spoken about. I'd be working alongside Joseph Donnelly in the landmark casino in Monaco as a player strategy consultant—to observe the play and spot the systems the high stakes players were developing or using to gain an unfair advantage against the house. The salary was more than I had ever dreamed of earning—enough to support both me and Jude, to pay off the mortgage on Belle Rivière and undertake the estate's much needed renovations. We'd even be able to hire a small staff to help keep the place clean and well-maintained again—if

I could persuade him I could do a better job of spotting the cheats than his current team.

It was more than I could have imagined in my wildest dreams. And I had been absolutely thrilled to accept the position.

But as soon as he'd outlined the job offer, in that impersonal, pragmatic tone, and the excitement had built under my breastbone, I'd known the primary reason I was so thrilled wasn't because of the amazing benefits and salary, or even the exciting challenges and opportunities the work would represent, but because he had shown such faith in me. And also because working in an important executive position in Dante's organisation would give me the chance not just to see him again, but maybe even for us to continue our affair. Or at least that's what I'd hoped.

Somewhere, deep down, I had even managed to convince myself that was one of the other reasons he had offered me the job. Because he wanted to keep me close too.

In the hours after I'd accepted the job and signed the contract though, there had still been no chance to talk to Dante privately. I'd tried to convince myself it was because he was busy.

After the last of the guests had left and the team interviews had been completed, Dante had hosted a final lunch for the team out on the terrace, with everyone laughing and toasting each other on a job well done. I'd left a seat for him next to me, but he'd walked past it and taken a seat at the far end of the table with Joseph Donnelly and his events manager, Evan Jones. I'd been stupidly hurt at first and then realised how ridiculous I was being.

What was I, five? He probably still had work to discuss with Joe and Evan.

But after the meal he'd disappeared again. And my insecurities had begun to mount.

Why had he hardly spoken to me? Was he avoiding me? Was it because of what I'd said to him about his mother the night before? Why had I probed like that?

I'd tried to keep a lid on my fears and anxieties by keeping busy myself. Surely he would talk to me in time, explain what was happening, where we stood.

After saying goodbye to the other team members as they climbed into their various cars and taxis, I had headed up to our suite of rooms. The vague hope I'd had that he might be up there packing had been dashed when I'd walked in on a maid busy folding all his clothes into a series of suitcases.

I'd duly packed my own stuff. At last there had been nothing else left to do, I could hear the staff being ordered about by Collette, who was making the final preparations to clear the chateau and close it up for the next few weeks. As I sat in the bedroom alone, my own suitcases stacked ready to leave, I began to feel as if I had been totally forgotten. Should I go downstairs, find Dante? Where was he? Was it possible he'd already left, without even telling me?

And that's when one of Dante's assistants had come to inform me Dante had arranged for the company helicopter to return me to Belle Rivière. And handed me the note, written in Dante's bold cursive script.

I read it again as my head started to pound.

Had he dismissed me? The chill that had been working its way over my skin all day seemed to wrap around my heart.

Had I done something wrong? Was it because of the liberties I'd taken last night? Was he angry about that conversation? What had happened to the man who had been prepared to fight for my honour over a single snide comment? Who had danced with me and then made love to me—bringing me to two mind-blowing orgasms. And then held me in his arms while I fell asleep.

I didn't understand; my confusion became almost as huge as the deep well of hurt at his actions.

Was this how my mother had always felt? When she'd been discarded by the men she had loved.

I'd tried to tell myself my affair with Dante was not the same, because I was working for him. Because we were equals. Because I hadn't become too invested in our relationship. But as the empty space in my belly grew, seeming to consume me, I knew that was a lie.

Something fundamental had changed for me last night. And it hadn't changed for him. Or he wouldn't have ignored me today.

I wanted to feel outraged, but all I felt was devastated.

I folded the note.

'Do you want to leave now?' the young man

who had delivered the note said. 'I believe the helicopter is ready whenever you want to go.'

'Is Dant… I mean, is Mr Allegri still here?' I asked.

I should leave—a part of me knew it would only hurt more to confront him about my dismissal. I wouldn't make a scene, I promised myself, remembering all those times I'd heard my mother plead, or seen her cling to a lover as he'd left her. Remembering the times my sister and I had crept into her bed and tried to comfort her tears, tried to stave off the black mood we knew would come until she found a new 'protector'. I wouldn't do that. I couldn't.

My heart wasn't broken. I couldn't let it be. I couldn't afford to lose the job he'd offered me.

He owed me nothing; I understood that. I'd entered into this affair with my eyes open. Or at least I had tried to. And, while things had changed for me, it wasn't his fault that they hadn't changed for him. It had only been five days after all. Five glorious, intense days. But I couldn't live with myself if I didn't at least get to say goodbye.

Before I saw him again in a work situation I needed to have closure. To know that there was no chance for us, or I might become delusional again.

The young man smiled. 'Yes, he's still here; he's in his office.'

'Do you know if he's with anyone?' I asked. I wanted to be brave and bold, the way he'd made me feel this past week, but I wasn't quite bold or brave enough to interrupt him while he was in a meeting.

'No, everyone else has left except you and the skeleton staff who are locking up the villa.'

I nodded and stood up. 'If you could have the luggage taken to the helicopter, that would be great. I'll meet you down there.' I would need to make a quick getaway once I'd said my good-byes. I couldn't afford to linger, or the boulder pressing against my larynx might start to choke me.

The young man nodded and left to get some of the staff to help him.

I tucked the curt, businesslike note into the back pocket of my jeans, brushed sweaty palms on the denim and headed in the opposite direction. As I approached Dante's office, my throat started to ache with unshed tears. I'd been such a naïve fool.

I didn't knock. I didn't have to; his office door was ajar and I could see him sitting at his desk, tapping on his laptop. He was wearing the same shirt and tailored trousers combo he'd worn when I'd come in here for my interview.

His head jerked up as I stepped into the room, reminding me painfully of the first time we'd made love—the way he'd sensed my presence while he'd stood on the beach.

His eyes narrowed. 'Edie, hello—is there a problem with the travel arrangements?' he asked. 'I thought you would have left by now.'

So polite. So distant. So businesslike. How could this be the same man who had plunged into me over and over again—as if he wanted to brand me as his?

'I wanted to say goodbye before I left,' I said. 'I thought...' The words jammed in my throat as he continued to look at me as if I were just another employee.

He closed his laptop and leaned back in his chair. 'You thought what?' he said, not unkindly, but the whisper of impatience in his tone destroyed me.

'I thought... I didn't think it would end like this.'

'How did you think it would end?' he said, confirming my worst fears—that this was it, that he had tired of me, that I had been discarded.

The man in front of me looked like Dante Allegri. He had the same striking bone structure, the same muscular physique. I could see the tattoo that looped around his shoulder peeking through the open collar of his shirt. I noticed the small scar on his top lip. But this wasn't the man who had held me last night. Because that man had been arrogant, yes, and more than a little domineering, but he hadn't been cruel.

'I thought you would have told me...' I said, trying to keep my voice firm, so as not to give away how devastated I was.

'I was busy today, Edie,' he said, and it occurred to me that he hadn't once called me *bella*, not since last night. Not since the last time we had made love. 'I simply didn't have time.'

'You didn't have time to even speak to me?' I said, incredulous now as well as devastated.

'We did speak—I offered you a very lucrative contract and you accepted it, as I recall.'

'Is it because of what I said about your

mother? I know it was none of my business and I'm so sorry…' I began realising I was begging after all when he held up his hand.

'Of course not,' he said. 'If you're going to make an emotional scene now though, I may have to reconsider my offer. I know you're young and naïve but I got the impression you understood exactly where this was leading.'

The chill spread through me at the curt tone. He was talking to me as if I were a child.

'But I…'

'*You* came to *me*, Edie, if you recall. You made it clear you wanted me as a lover. If you now feel you gave away your virginity too cheaply, I'm afraid it's too late to change your mind.'

I trembled, the blood exploding in my ears, the caustic, casual tone almost as agonising as the contempt on his face.

'You… You knew?' I gasped, shock warring with devastation.

He leaned forward. 'Of course I knew. I'm not quite as inexperienced as you are.'

'But you didn't say anything?' I said, still unable to grasp why he seemed angry about it.

'Why would I? It was none of my concern,'

he said, but I could still hear it in his voice, that edge of steel, the accusation. And then the rest of his comment came back to me, hitting me in the solar plexus with the force of a sledge-hammer.

If you now feel you gave away your virginity too cheaply.

And I realised what he was accusing me of. Of trying to trick him, to deceive him, to make him feel beholden to me, to barter my body for money. When I had never once put any demands on him. Even now all I'd asked for was a proper goodbye.

'I didn't expect anything in return,' I said. 'I gave myself to you freely. I wanted you to be my first.' I tried to explain, the words tumbling over themselves, struggling to get out of my mouth in the face of his cynicism. 'Why would you even think that?' I asked, horrified anew at the accusation and the cool scepticism on his face.

'All sex is a transaction,' he said. 'Of one form or another. Your mother knew it, and so did mine.'

'That's not true. My mother always loved the men she slept with…' I said, my heart shattering in my chest. This wasn't just scepticism; this was damage. How could he believe the things he was saying? What had happened to him that would make him so hard, so cold, so uncaring and so cynical? He'd said he didn't hate his mother, but now I could see he'd lied.

'How convenient then, that she only ever fell in love with rich men,' he said, the mockery in his voice reminding me of all the times I had been teased or insulted, made to feel less than, an outcast, because of the way people judged my mother.

But this was so much worse.

Tears stung the backs of my eyes, tears I knew I couldn't shed. I'd thought he'd understood. That he'd been on my side. But he was worse than any of them.

'You bastard,' I whispered, trying to locate the anger I should be feeling to cover the misery.

'We're both bastards, Edie. I thought we already established that.'

'I'm not talking about the circumstances of your birth. You... You used me,' I said, still not able to believe it.

'We used each other. You amused me this

week, and I gave you the chance to discover what a sensual person you are. Something that you've clearly been denying, or you wouldn't have remained a virgin so long.'

I nodded. 'Well, thanks for that,' I said, trying to sound flippant, trying to wound him the way he'd wounded me. 'I'll be sure to use the lessons you taught me about how to pleasure a man when I take my next lover.'

His jaw tightened, his brows lowering in a thunderous frown as I turned and fled.

It wasn't until I was sitting in the helicopter, the blades whirring, the sun dipping towards the horizon as the huge black machine lifted into the sky, that I finally let the tears fall. Tears of anguish, and grief. And humiliation at my own stupidity. But, most of all, tears of heartache—which only made the humiliation worse.

How could I ever have been young enough or naïve enough to be fooled by Dante Allegri—to have believed that, buried beneath the ambition and the ruthlessness, the magnetism and the overpowering sexuality and the horrors he had obviously suffered as a child, there lay a kindred spirit, a man who, despite everything, had a good heart?

I gulped down my sobs and scrubbed the tears off my cheeks, forcing my gaze away from the villa and towards the horizon.

I would survive and I would prosper. I would be the best employee he'd ever had. And I would be grateful for the important lesson he had taught me. A lesson I thought I had learned during the years of my childhood.

Never to fall in love with a man who valued money and power and ambition—for whatever reason—over love.

CHAPTER EIGHTEEN

'IS THAT EDIE, talking to Alexi Galanti?' I barked at Joe Donnelly who had greeted me at the entrance to The Inferno as I spotted Edie's slim figure displayed in a wisp of blue silk standing beside the Formula One owner on the far corner of the casino floor.

Anxiety and anger sliced through my gut. I'd stayed away from Monaco for three weeks. Three long torturous weeks. As memories of Edie and what we'd shared tormented me daily.

Her face, determined and tense on our first night together, as she played poker. Her lips, trembling but eager, as I kissed her in the moonlight. Her breasts, full and yearning, in that excuse for a bikini. Her arms soft and secure as we danced together at the investors' ball. Her eyes, the deep green sheened with tears, as I forced her to accept the reality of who I was and how little I could offer her.

Every one of those memories slammed into

me now as I stared at her like a starving man. Memories that had turned my temper into gel-ignite, ready to explode at a moment's notice. Memories that bombarded me every time I closed my eyes. Then woke me up, hard and aching and empty inside. Memories which were the real reason I'd arrived in Monaco unannounced. Because after three weeks of staying away, of trying and failing to forget about her, I hadn't. And now this is what I found.

The woman I'd initiated, looking at another man the way she'd once looked at me.

'Yeah, Edie's hosting the Millionaire Club game tonight; Alexi's playing.' Joe's voice murmured beside me but I could barely hear it through the buzzing in my brain.

Why was she smiling at Alexi like that? Was there something between them? Why hadn't I listened to my instincts and returned sooner? She was an innocent and I'd let her loose among a sea of sharks. My friend—or, rather, my former friend—being the most voracious and ruthless of the lot.

'Nice to see you too, by the way,' Joe said, curtly enough to distract me for a second. 'We weren't expecting to see you for another week.'

'My plans changed,' I said, turning back to stare at the woman who had haunted my dreams. Alexi was standing too damn close to her. I didn't like it. Any more than I liked the low neckline on her dress. He could probably see right down to her navel in that thing.

Joe's fingers clicked in my face. 'Snap out of it, Dante.'

'What?' I forced my eyes away.

'You're staring at her as if you want to devour her in a few quick greedy bites.'

Because I do.

I wetted my lips, trying to deny the errant thought as blood surged heavily into my groin.

'Alexi's got no damn business hovering around her like that. She's an employee here.'

'I know that,' Joe said, searching my face in a way I didn't like. 'But do you?'

'What's that supposed to mean?'

'You know damn well what it means,' he shot back, only increasing my irritation. Joe was a friend, probably my best friend. He'd been my wingman since we were little more than kids. But no one got to speak to me like that, not even him. Before I could point this out though, he cut me off.

'You've been ringing me every day to check up on her. And now you're here, when you're supposed to be in Paris. What the hell is going on between you two, because I thought you broke up with her?'

'Alexi's flirting with my employee and I'm not supposed to be pissed about that?' I said, raising my voice as my gaze locked on Edie again across the casino.

Damn, but I had missed her. The sight of her, the smell of her, the feel of her body curled around me in sleep. When was this longing going to end? Why couldn't I get a handle on it? And why did seeing her again only make all the memories worse, not better, the way I'd hoped?

'Alexi flirts with everyone,' Joe said, raising his voice too. 'It never bothered you before.'

We were starting to attract attention. But then Alexi lifted his finger to tuck a lock of hair behind Edie's ear. And Edie smiled at him, that sweet smile that had only ever been meant for me.

Rage exploded inside me, the same rage I had kept so carefully at bay... Ever since Edie had thrown her parting words at me.

I'll be sure to use the lessons you taught me about how to pleasure a man when I take my next lover.

Those words had tortured me every night since. But I'd stayed away, determined not to give in to the need, the jealousy, the longing.

Big mistake.

'*Bastardo!*' I shouted and several people turned towards me.

'Dante, wait!' Joe said, trying to grab my arm, I shook it off as I strode through the crowd.

This ended here and now. Edie needed to protect herself against guys like Alexi Galanti. She was too innocent and naïve—what the hell had I been thinking, giving her a job that would expose her to bastards like him? And then left her alone. She needed my protection, now more than ever. Even if we weren't together, I had a responsibility to keep her safe.

As I approached, Edie's head swung round as if she had sensed my approach. The deep emerald gaze which had always captivated me locked with mine. My stride faltered, the jolt of awareness hitting me like a bolt of lightning as our eyes met.

'Dante?' Her lips slicked with gloss whispered my name—and I heard it in my soul.

'Galanti, you're banned,' I snarled at Alexi without taking my gaze off Edie.

I shoved him aside, grasped Edie's arm and carried on walking, marching her towards the security booth at the back of the casino. Her skin felt so soft, so fragile beneath my fingertips. Her biceps tensed and I loosened my fingers, scared to hurt her, but kept my grip firm, knowing I never wanted to let her go.

Alexi shouted something after us—mocking or annoyed—I couldn't tell because of the blood rushing in my ears. But I didn't care because all I could see was Edie, and all I could feel was the surge of heat shooting up my arm and the rage threatening to blow the top of my head off.

'Why are you here?' she said, confused, wary, wounded, but she didn't resist me as I dragged her into the booth. 'Have I done something wrong?'

'We need to talk,' I said, struggling to keep my voice firm and even. 'Everyone out,' I shouted at the three guys in the booth.

The security personnel scurried out, leaving

us alone as I forced myself to release her arm and kicked the door shut. The blue light from the monitors illuminated her face. How could I have forgotten how exquisite she was? With her hair gathered in some kind of up-do, the tendrils caressed her neck. Her full breasts rose and fell in staggered rhythm against the revealing bodice of that excuse for a gown. The desire to bury my face against her neck and breathe in her fresh, sultry scent, to lick her collarbone and gather her taste on my tongue, to tear off her gown so I could free those ripe orbs, capture her nipples in my teeth and…

Focus, Dante. Dio!

I shook my head, trying to clear the erotic fog that descended whenever I was near her. I wasn't here to slake my own hunger. I was here to protect her from guys like Alexi Galanti… And myself.

'Are you sleeping with him?' I asked, the words coming out on a hoarse rasp of breath as a sense of loss and injustice wrapped around my heart. I'd given her up to save her from me. And she'd immediately been seduced by a man who was just as jaded and cynical as I was. If not more so.

I should have come to check up on her in person a lot sooner. I'd given her this position to keep her safe, to keep her secure, to keep an eye on her. And then I'd stayed away from her. What a damn fool I'd been.

But I was here now, and I wasn't leaving again until she understood I would do whatever I had to do to protect her. Even if it meant protecting her from her own naiveté.

'Because he's not worthy of you, *bella*,' I added. 'Any more than I am.'

She was staring at me, her face flaming with the delectable blush which marked out her innocence. She might think she was experienced, worldly, because of what we'd shared, but she wasn't. She was far too gullible, too innocent, too idealistic to ever understand the way men's minds worked.

'Answer me, *bella*,' I said, steeling myself against her answer as I cupped her cheek. She jerked away from my touch and the knife twisted in my gut. 'Are you sleeping with Alexi?'

CHAPTER NINETEEN

'WHY DO YOU want to know that?' I whispered at the man in front of me as emotions I'd struggled to keep in check for weeks threatened to destroy me all over again.

The giddy rush of love I still couldn't control had risen up as soon as I'd spotted him striding towards me—even in black jeans and a dark polo shirt he had looked indomitable, overwhelming, as the casino patrons in tuxedos and evening gowns scattered to let him pass— but right behind that rush of love had been the shattering pain he'd caused.

I clasped my arms around my waist, trying to hold in the violent trembling as conflicting emotions swelled and surged inside me. Shock, panic, confusion, desire, love, longing, but most of all the deep, dark well of hurt that had dogged me ever since the last time I'd seen him.

I stared at him now, trying to understand.

But he looked like a madman—his breathing ragged, his chest heaving, his eyes wild with something I didn't understand.

And while a million questions swirled in my head, about what he was doing here, why he was behaving like this and what any of it had to do with Mr Galanti, the only one I could grasp was one I had asked myself a thousand times since the last time I'd seen him.

How could he look at me with such longing when he had discarded me so easily? It had taken me three weeks to convince myself it hadn't been my fault. I shouldn't have spoken to him about his mother, I could see that, but I hadn't meant to upset him. Maybe what I'd said had been misguided, inappropriate, but it had come from a place of love.

'I need to know if Alexi has seduced you?' he said, his voice surprisingly firm for someone who appeared to be talking in tongues. 'Because if he has I'm going to kill him.'

'Stop it,' I hissed, my lungs tight with all those conflicting emotions now. 'Stop asking me about Mr Galanti—are you mad?'

'Mr Galanti? Not Alexi. *Grazie a Dio.*' He let out a relieved chuckle, the self-satisfied slash of white in his tanned face making him look like a marauding pirate to my confused mind. 'So you haven't slept with him.'

His blue eyes lit with determination and danger as he lifted his hand and touched his thumb to the rampaging pulse in my collarbone.

'This is good news, *bella*. I am proud of you.'

The tidal wave of longing hit me hard, spreading heat throughout my body. The desire to lean in to the caress, to accept his praise, his protection, almost more than I could bear. Hadn't I dreamt about this happening every night since I'd left La Villa Paradis? That he would come back, that he would claim me, that he would tell me he still cared about me, that one day he might take me back. That he hadn't meant to destroy me the way he had.

But what hit me harder was the tidal wave of fury. The fury I'd tried so hard to locate three weeks ago when he'd dumped me—because his behaviour then hadn't been a mistake. It had been callous and deliberate and unnecessarily brutal.

Fury spread through my body like wildfire, torching everything in its wake—the yearning, the confusion, the anguish, the hollow empty loneliness, the weeks of soul-searching and re-criminations—until all that was left was the burning desire to hurt him the way he'd hurt me.

I slapped at his hand, hard enough to make him grunt.

'Don't you dare touch me,' I yelled. 'How dare you ask me about my sex life...? You...' I was so furious I could barely speak. 'You have no right.'

'I have every right,' he barked back, but I could see my outburst had shocked him—almost as much as it had shocked me. 'You're my employee,' he said, but for once he didn't sound sure or indomitable. Instead he sounded tense and wary. 'And I was your first lover. I'm trying to protect you. Alexi is a notorious playboy. He uses women and then he discards them, he...'

'This has nothing to do with Mr Galanti,' I interrupted him, finally finding the words I should have found three weeks ago. 'And don't you dare throw my virginity back in my face again. If I was ever innocent I'm certainly not any more. And if you wanted to protect me, why didn't you protect me from you, Dante?'

I pointed out, just in case he'd forgotten that salient point.

Tears rolled down my cheeks and I scrubbed them away, but I wasn't ashamed of them any more and I wasn't afraid to let him see them.

'*Bella*, please don't cry,' he said in an agonised whisper and reached for me again. But I stepped back.

'No,' I said, firmly and succinctly, even though my heart was ripping open inside my chest. 'You *left* me, Dante. Which means you don't get to come storming back into my life three weeks later, telling me who I can and cannot sleep with. You don't get to call me *bella*, or touch me as if you own me, or look at me as if you care about me when we both know you don't. You *hurt* me,' I said, my breath shuddering out as the tears mercifully stopped. 'I know it was only five days. I know I overreacted, probably romanticised it too much. That it was too soon. But those feelings were still real. I was falling in love with you and you knew... And still you treated me like nothing.'

'You were an innocent. I only discarded you to protect you,' he said, his voice raw with emotion now too, and I could see he actually believed it—which only made the heartache worse.

'No, you didn't,' I said, the tears still lodged in my throat as I realised how hopeless this situation was and had always been. He still wanted me and I still wanted him—we could have had so much, could have built on those five glorious days together—but it wasn't my insecurities that had held us back, as a part of me had always believed—it was his. 'You did it to protect yourself,' I said.

I clasped my arms around my waist to control the trembles threatening to tear me apart.

'I don't know what your mother did to you, Dante,' I said and he stiffened, his eyes becoming shadowed and distant, as I hit the raw nerve I knew would always lie between us. 'But, whatever it is,' I said, 'I hope one day you can get over it.'

I walked past him. I had to get out of here, to get away from him. It had been a mistake taking this job. I'd done it for all the wrong reasons. I'd wanted to be able to see him again, to be near him, even if he didn't want me any more. I'd wanted the chance to impress him, to soak up his approval. I had convinced myself in the last three weeks my susceptibility to Dante's charms had been a result of the skewed legacy of being my mother's daughter, being fatherless—that I had an unconscious need for male attention I had never acknowledged before. But I realised now it was more personal than that… And the mistakes made had been his as much as mine. He was right, I had been innocent and naïve and maybe too gullible. He'd been my first lover and my first love— and he was an overpowering man. But he had used me, and it was way past time I protected myself against him and the overwhelming effect he had on me.

'Where are you going?' he demanded. 'You're still my employee.'

'Not any more,' I said. 'I quit.'

CHAPTER TWENTY

'YOU NEED TO go get her back, Dante. Apologise, grovel, do whatever you have to do, but we need her here.'

'No,' I said calmly to Joe, even though calm was the last thing I felt.

'Why not?' My casino manager leaned forward in the chair on the other side of my desk, about to launch into the diatribe I'd been hearing for three days now, ever since Edie had walked out of the casino, still wearing the dress I'd bought her. The dress had been returned a day later, along with the rest of the wardrobe I'd ordered from Nina Saint Jus—but she hadn't.

The grinding pain in the pit of my stomach, that deep well of emptiness and guilt which had only got bigger since our showdown in the booth, grew another few centimetres.

'Because there's no point in apologising,' I said.

'Of course there is,' Joe said. 'You behaved like a dick. If you…'

'It's not that I *won't* apologise; it's that it would do no good,' I clarified, feeling unbearably weary. I'd had three more sleepless nights since Edie had walked away from me. But this time, instead of hot, sweaty dreams of Edie, my nights had been filled with cold, rain-spattered nightmares—the same nightmares that had haunted me throughout my childhood. My mother's face, sad and pleading. My childish terror as it had dawned on me that she was never coming back.

The questions that had tormented me then had woken me in a cold sweat in the middle of the night.

Why wasn't I enough? Why hadn't she loved me? Why had she abandoned me?

But this time the answer had been all too obvious.

Edie had abandoned me because I was a selfish coward. I'd been too scared to reach for the golden ring, had refused to trust my feelings and hers, because of something that had happened over twenty years ago. Edie had called it exactly right. I had discarded her to protect myself and this was the inevitable result. I'd destroyed what we might have had, only to realise what it was I'd lost when it was way too late to get it back.

'That's nuts!' Joe said. 'She needs this job—she's got a mortgage to pay. And she's brilliant at it. If you just tell her you'll never behave like a dick again she...'

'I can't do that either,' I said, the hopelessness of the situation suffocating me as I met Joe's accusing gaze. 'Because I can't guarantee I won't act like that again. I can't be rational where she's concerned. Seeing her with Alexi made me behave like a crazy person. Just thinking about her with another man is tying my guts in knots right now.' Yet another cross I was going to have to bear for a long time to come.

Joe's eyes widened. He swore softly in Irish. 'I had no idea you'd fallen in love with her.' He slumped in his chair, finally realising the hopelessness of the situation too. 'In less than a week. That's a hell of a thing.'

I let out a humourless laugh. *'Precisamente.'*

How ironic that it didn't even freak me out to admit how far gone I was over Edie.

Less than a month ago—hell, only three days ago—I would have laughed in Joe's face if he'd suggested such a thing to me. I would have called him a romantic fool. A gullible, naïve idiot—which is what I'd accused Edie of being.

I hadn't believed in love, then. Hadn't believed it really existed. And, if it did, I had considered it a weakness, a foolish sentimental emotion to be avoided and denied until it went away.

'I can't believe she walked out of here after you told her,' Joe said. 'I could have sworn she felt the same way. She was gutted after you broke up with her at the Villa, even though she was doing her best to hide it, poor kid.'

The shaft of guilt, fuelled by the memory of the tears streaming down her cheeks in the booth, combined with the hole in the pit of my stomach to make it a yawning chasm.

I know it was only five days. I know I overreacted, probably romanticised it too much. That it was too soon. But those feelings were still real. I was falling in love with you and you knew... And still you treated me like nothing.

'I didn't tell her,' I corrected Joe as the evidence of exactly how badly I'd treated her echoed in my head.

'Why not?' Joe looked dumbfounded.

'Because I'd already hurt her too much.'

What would be the point of telling her I loved her when she would never be able to forgive me? When I couldn't even forgive myself?

'That sounds like an excuse to me,' Joe said. 'How do you know what she'd do if you didn't even tell her how you feel about her? Isn't that making the choice for her?'

Something built under my breastbone, fuelled by the conviction in Joe's tone.

'I don't want to hurt her any more than I already have,' I said, but my reasoning sounding weak even to me.

Could Joe be right? Was there still a chance?

'I don't see how telling her you love her is gonna hurt her,' he said bluntly.

But what if she decides she doesn't want me?

The real reason I was reluctant to go to her, to lay my feelings bare, reverberated in my head. It was the same fear that had haunted me my whole life. What if I took this chance, risked everything, and she rejected me? Edie had the power to wound me in ways no other woman had—since my mother.

Except Edie wasn't my mother. She hadn't abandoned me. Until I'd abandoned her.

Images of her—in her second-hand ballgown playing poker to save her home, with a bruise blossoming on her cheek as she defended herself against a thug, with tears streaming down her cheeks as she stood up to me—shimmered across my consciousness.

Edie was brave and tough, passionate and resourceful and strong. She'd taken terrible risks, defied impossible odds to protect her family and her home. Perhaps it was time I did the same... If I wanted to be worthy of her.

CHAPTER TWENTY-ONE

'Edie, at last you're back. Didn't you get any of my texts?' my sister greeted me as I dumped my bag of cleaning supplies on the hall floor.

'I had a job to do, Jude,' I said, stretching my back to work out the kinks that had set in after scrubbing what felt like an acre of parquet flooring. 'I can't answer my phone while I'm working. If anyone catches me, they think I'm slacking.'

Walking out of my job at the casino had been the right thing to do. I would never get a handle on my feelings for Dante if I remained in his orbit. But having to return to scrubbing floors for a living had felt like an additional punishment I didn't deserve.

'There's someone here to see you. He's waiting in the library,' Jude said.

'Who?'

'Mr Allegri,' she said, triggering the myriad emotions I'd been trying to suppress. 'I think he wants to offer you your job back.' She sounded so pleased and eager I didn't have the heart to tell her the truth.

I hadn't explained any of it to Jude. That I'd fallen in love with a man as damaged and ruthless as the men our mother had always gravitated towards.

'I don't want to see him.' I couldn't speak to him now, whatever he had to say to me. It would hurt too much to hash over it all again. And I couldn't be sure that I would stick to my guns. That I had the strength to walk away a second time.

But Jude had already grasped my arm and was tugging me towards the library. 'Don't be daft, Edie. You have to see him. He came all the way here in his helicopter. And he looks... I don't know...he looks a little desperate.'

Before I could muster the strength to tell her the truth, she had propelled me into the room, run out and slammed the door shut behind her.

'Edie?' Dante appeared out of the shadows in the room, which was lit by a single lamp in the corner.

The sight of his tall frame and broad shoulders had a predictable effect on me. I tried to stifle it, to stay strong. I'd thought it all through. I'd fallen into the same trap as my mother by falling for this man. But if I could just stay away from him, I'd get over it eventually.

'You have to leave, Dante,' I said. 'I can't come back to the casino, if that's why you're here.' I'd done a good job, I knew that—which was probably why he had come. He was a practical, pragmatic businessman, and I'd managed to spot three cheats at the high stakes game in as many weeks.

'I'm not here about the job. I have one simple question to ask you.' He walked towards me. 'Do you love me? If you do, it is not too late.'

Desperation assailed me at the intensity in his gaze. I shook my head. I wanted to tell him no. I wanted for it not to be true. How could I still be so besotted with a man who had hurt me? But I couldn't say the words and I saw the spark of hope light his eyes.

'Tell me you don't still love me and I will go, *bella*,' he said. 'And we will never speak of this again.'

A part of me hated him in that moment. Because I knew he would see right through the lie if I tried to deny my feelings for him. But it was so grossly unfair, that I should be bound by my emotions, tricked into giving in to him when it would make me so vulnerable again.

Unable to speak, I turned to flee from the room.

But he followed me, flattening his palm against the door as I tried to open it. I stood in the cage of his arms, pressing my forehead to the worn wood, feeling my body succumb to desire—as it always did when he was near me. I could smell him, the tempting scent of salt and cedar and musk assaulting my nostrils as he stood too close behind me.

'You cannot say it, *bella*, because it is true,' he whispered against my neck. 'You love me and you still want me, you know you do. Let me make it better. Let me fix this.'

I swung round and flattened my palms against his chest. He was going to kiss me. He wanted to kiss me. I could see the yearning in his face because it matched my own. But I found the strength from somewhere to hold him off.

'Don't you see it isn't enough?' I said. To my surprise, instead of taking advantage of my weakness, he let his arms fall and stepped back.

'It doesn't matter if I love you,' I added, suddenly weary to the bone. 'It doesn't matter if I still want you. If I let you kiss me now, make love to me again, after the way you treated me, I'd simply be inviting you to do it again. I saw my mother eventually become a shadow of herself that way. Each time a new love affair started she would kid herself that this man would be different. She did everything in her power to make those men love her, but of course they didn't because she was too compliant, too undemanding, too accommodating. She never asked for a commitment, for an equal stake in those relationships and, because she didn't, they eventually grew bored of her, the way you grew bored of me.'

'I never grew bored of you...' he interrupted, his voice breaking now too. 'I wanted you so much. I still do.' His gaze roamed over me, the look of need in his eyes open and unguarded for the first time since I'd met him.

'You're just talking about sex,' I said, despairing.

'No, that isn't it,' he said, the fervour in his voice fierce and uninhibited. 'I didn't just want you in my bed. I wanted you to be a part of my life.' He sighed. 'Your wit, your joy, your kindness, your intelligence—everything about you turns me on, not just your delectable body.'

He lifted his hand as if to touch me, but then dropped it when I flinched.

'It's why I couldn't stay away from you. Why I went insane when I saw you talking to Alexi. I am in love with you too, *bella*. Please tell me it's not too late to make this right.'

His words crucified me, because I could hear the truth in them. He was serious. But I forced myself to stifle the hope that wanted to surge through me. Because it still wasn't enough. In fact it was almost worse.

If he had fallen for me too, how could he have hurt me the way he had? And what was going to stop him from doing it again?

'How could you treat me that way if you loved me?' I asked.

He let out a heavy sigh and I could see the turmoil in his face, but I couldn't let it go. I deserved an answer.

'Because loving you terrified me,' he murmured.

The clouds passed over the moon as he said it and the silvery light shone through the library window, illuminating his face which had been thrown into shadow by the lamp behind him. For the first time, I saw circles under his eyes and the tight lines around his mouth. He was exhausted, I realised.

I wanted to cradle his cheeks in my palms, to hold him close and promise him that whatever demons were chasing him, I would scare them away... But I fisted my fingers and kept my hands by my sides. If I gave in to the urge to soothe and comfort him, I might never know why he had reacted the way he had, and then I would be the one who was scared—scared it could happen again.

'What were you terrified of?' I asked.

His gaze flashed with emotions so real and vulnerable my heart contracted in my chest, my breath squeezing out of my lungs.

'That you would leave me,' he said, the words so low I could barely hear them above the ambient sounds of the night outside the library window, the hum of the crickets and the rustle of the forest leaves. 'The way she did.'

'Is this your mother?' I asked.

I saw his Adam's apple bob. Then he nodded. 'When you asked me about her, I lied. I said

I didn't remember her. But the truth is, when I began to have feelings for you…it all came back to me. What happened that day. And I was scared it would happen again,' he said.

He looked away, but I had seen the naked pain in his face. My heart lurched in my chest. He had pushed me away because he was scared of losing me. As mad as that sounded on one level, it made complete sense to me on another.

I cupped his cheek, drew his head round to mine, unable to hold back a moment longer. I felt the muscles in his jaw bunch as I kissed him softly. His breath brushed my cheek as he sighed.

'Can you tell me what happened?' I asked.

He touched his forehead to mine, placed his hands on my hips to draw me into his arms, but I could hear the hopelessness in his voice when he said, 'Yes.'

CHAPTER TWENTY-TWO

IF ONLY I could avoid this conversation. I'd spent so much of my life denying what had happened to me. How could the wounds still be so raw, so fresh? But I knew I owed it to Edie. How would she ever be able to trust me again after what I had done, if I didn't explain why I had done it?

I'd tried to dodge and avoid, but she'd been brave and determined. And now I needed to be brave too.

'I was maybe five, six, I can't remember.' I started to talk as I clung to her, breathing in her scent to give me strength, and balance— as I tumbled into the black hole of memory. 'The night before, there had been…violence. Her pimp had beaten her. I had tried to intervene and he had beaten me too…'

Edie shuddered with reaction, her hands settling on my lower back, keeping me upright. 'It's okay,' she said. 'I'm here.'

It was exactly the right thing to say. It grounded me, reminded me that I wasn't that little boy any more, so scared, so brutalised. I was a grown man, and Edie would never hurt me the way my mother had.

'I think maybe that was the reason she wanted to get rid of me. She cried a lot the next morning. Then she made me dress in my best clothes and took me to the steps of the church where we went to Mass each Sunday.' I huffed out a bitter laugh. 'Ironic, no? That a prostitute would go to church?'

'Go on,' Edie said.

'She told me to wait for her, that she would be back soon. She told me that she loved me before she left me there.' The bitterness sharpened as I recalled her exact words, and the quiver of emotion in her voice as she whispered the lie in my ear.

'Coraggio, Dante. Ti voglio bene assai.'

Be a brave boy, Dante. I love you very much.

'I waited, as people came and went. The priest tried to talk to me and then a policeman and a social worker came. It had begun to rain and they wanted me to come inside the church. I went wild. I told them I couldn't go inside, that I mustn't leave. I was sure that she would come back because she had promised me she would. And I was scared that if I left that step she would never find me.' I shook, remembering the tears again, the screams, the rain cold and clammy on my skin, the grunts of the policeman as I kicked against his hold.

'Oh, Dante, I'm so sorry.' Edie's arms closed around me and she held me tight, burying her head against my chest. I could feel her tears dampening my shirt. But her anguish didn't feel like pity any more; it felt like compassion. 'It must have been so agonising for you,' she said, her words muffled, 'and for her.'

The last part of her sentence struck me and I drew back, all the emotion I had locked away for so long coalescing in the pit of my stomach and plunging into the black hole.

'Why would it be hard for her?' I asked, but the emotion welling in my throat felt strange and different this time, not jagged and ugly, just weary and tense. 'She didn't love me. She abandoned me.'

Edie lifted her face from my chest. 'Do you really think so?'

'Of course,' I said, but the doubt in her voice gave me pause.

'What happened to you afterwards? After she left you?' Edie asked.

'I went into the foster system in Naples. I found it hard to settle. I was so lonely. I wanted my mother. And then I became angry. That she had left me.'

'But were you ever hit again? Or abused?' she asked.

'No,' I said. If anything, I was the one who had been abusive, I realised, as I remembered the many families who had taken me in. Hard-working, good people, who had only wanted to help me and whose help I had rejected.

'Do you think it's possible that she left you there not because she didn't love you, but because she loved you very much? And she didn't want to see you hurt again? Her lifestyle sounds as if it was very chaotic; maybe she was trying to protect you?' Her voice was coaxing and gentle and devoid of criticism—but still I could hear the truth in it when she said, 'You said she had a pimp who was violent. Isn't it possible she thought she had to give you up to keep you safe?'

Something snapped open deep inside me at Edie's comment. And suddenly all the memories I had kept locked away in my subconscious for years burst out.

'Ti voglio bene assai.'

How often had my mother said those words to me? Not just that one time, but a hundred times. A thousand? How often had she hugged me and kissed me—tickled my belly and made me laugh? How often had she told me stories late at night, after the men had gone, to help me sleep? I could see her face clearly now in my mind's eye, the way it had come to me in nightmares, but for the first time I realised how young she looked. She must have been a teenager when she had me. No more than her early twenties when she left me.

The soreness in my throat began to choke me.

'Dio!' I swore softly against Edie's hair as I clung to her. 'How could I not have seen this before?' I said, but I knew why. Because I had been determined not to see it, not to trust, not to love, so I could protect myself at all costs. It's why I had always rejected the truth about my mother, and why I had treated Edie so appallingly. 'I have been blaming my selfishness

and my cowardice on her when the person who is truly responsible is me.'

Edie grasped my cheeks and forced my gaze to meet hers, until she was staring me straight in the eyes. The love I saw there humbled me.

'That's rubbish, Dante,' she said. And I almost laughed at the fierceness in her tone. 'You're a good man.'

No, I wasn't. But if she believed it, it was enough. At this point, I really didn't care if I deserved her or not. I would take anything I could get. Anything that she would give me and thank God for it always.

'You were scared and, after what happened with your mum,' she added, still fierce, still determined to see the best in me, 'it makes sense you would push me away.'

'Are you saying you forgive me, *bella*?' I asked, ready to believe in miracles.

The torment of the last few minutes, the last few hours and days and weeks melted away as her lips curved into the sweet smile I had become addicted to.

Warmth spread through me. She was going to give me a second chance. I could see it in her eyes. *Dio*, but she was utterly adorable. What on earth had I done to deserve her? And what wouldn't I do to keep her?

'What do you think?' she said as she wrapped her arms around my neck and lifted her lips to mine.

I didn't need another invitation.

I grasped her hips and captured her mouth, thrusting my tongue deep, determined to claim her, to brand her as mine for all eternity.

CHAPTER TWENTY-THREE

DANTE'S MOUTH CRUSHED mine as hope and excitement and a deep welling tenderness blossomed inside my heart.

He'd come to me, he'd told me he loved me, he'd even told me about his mother—a subject I knew it was very difficult for him to discuss. We were equals. We had a chance now to make this something good and strong, solid and lasting. And I intended to grab that chance with both hands.

I sank into the kiss, need arrowing through me as the prominent outline of his erection pressed against my belly. Even through our clothing, the thick ridge felt powerful and potent. My sex softened, ready to receive it.

'You will come back to work at The Inferno? And live with me at La Villa Paradis?' he murmured as his lips caressed my neck and his hands cupped my bottom.

'Yes, yes...' Joy surged through me at his

offer. I wanted to be with him more than any-thing in the world. And I loved the work I had been doing at the casino. 'But…' I tore myself away from him to look into his eyes '…you must promise never to freak out like that again when I'm working.'

'Of course, I would never freak out at *you*, *bella*,' he said instantly. A flush of heat—and stunned pleasure—spread up my torso and into my cheeks at his easy capitulation and the evi-dence that he respected me, professionally as well as personally. But then he added, 'But Galanti is a dead man if he ever smiles at you like that again.'

'Dante, that's mad,' I said, because I could see he wasn't entirely joking. 'You can't kill Mr Galanti for smiling at me. It would be very bad for business.'

But, before I could argue further, he captured the pulse point in my collarbone with his lips and suckled strongly. Arousal shot through me as the liquid tug in my abdomen became a def-inite yank. And my mind blurred on my last coherent thought.

Welcome to The Inferno, indeed!

EPILOGUE

'THAT WAS JOE. We've finalised the training course,' I clicked off my smartphone and shouted to Dante above the hum of the helicopter blades as the big black bird came in to land on La Villa Paradis's heliport. 'By the end of this year we should have all the casino staff trained on how to stop the different systems I've uncovered,' I added proudly, pleased with everything I'd achieved in my role as Allegri's Head of Gaming Systems and Security.

'Excellent work, *bella*,' Dante said as he unclipped his seat belt and mine while the helicopter's blades swished to a stop. But then he scooped my phone out of my hands and tucked it in his back pocket. 'But there is to be no more shop talk now for the rest of the weekend,' he said as he hauled me out of my seat and into his arms. 'Or I will have to fire you.'

'Go ahead,' I teased back as I banded my arms around his lean waist. 'I know several other casino owners who would hire me in a second.'

'Then they would have to die,' he said before leaning down to cover my lips in a possessive kiss.

The kiss went from amused to carnal in seconds—as it always did with Dante—but just as I became desperate, the heat burning up my torso like wildfire, he pulled away from me, ducked down and hefted me onto his shoulder in a fireman's lift.

'What are you doing?' I demanded, suddenly staring at the tight muscles of his backside outlined in worn denim—as he hauled me off the helicopter like a sack of potatoes. 'Put me down,' I added, but my protests lacked heat, thanks to the laughter bubbling out of my mouth.

'Be still, woman,' he said, giving me a playful pat on my bottom. 'Or I'll drop you.'

Ignoring my struggles, Dante marched past the pilot and Collette and her staff, who were watching our antics with amusement. But, instead of heading into the house and straight up to our suite, as I had expected, he walked in the opposite direction, around the side of the chateau, then through the grounds, past the fountains and the follies and the Japanese pagoda. I had to stop struggling, scared he might drop me for real, as he carried me down the steps to our private beach.

The sun heated my skin and my heart swelled in my chest as I finally landed on my feet again—in our special place.

It was over a year since we'd first made love in this cove and we always found time to christen it again whenever we escaped to La Villa Paradis from our work in Monaco. It had been a year filled with love and light and laughter, and the occasional passionate argument, because Dante was still the most infuriating man I'd ever met. As well as the most wonderful.

'You're a menace,' I said, with no heat whatsoever. 'I can't believe you just carried me off like that in front of the staff. As if you were a pirate and I was your captive! They'll never take me seriously again.'

'The staff adore you, as you well know,' he chastised me, the twinkle of mischief in his eyes suggesting my punishment wasn't over yet. A giddy thrill careered through my system. 'And if you don't want to be treated like a captive then don't threaten to leave me.'

My cheeks flushed as he captured my face in his palms, his fingers caressing my neck and sending erotic shivers to the rest of my body.

'You know it makes me crazy,' he murmured and I realised the playful spark had disappeared.

'You know I'd never leave you,' I said. Surely he knew I had only been joking?

A sensual smile spread across his lips and relief flooded through my system.

'I know,' he said. 'But I think it is time we made that official. And I wanted to bring you here to make that happen.'

Huh?

My eyes widened as he reached into the front pocket of his jeans and produced a small velvet box. He flipped it open to reveal a ring nestled in black velvet—a white gold band studded with tiny emeralds which sparkled in the sunlight.

My sight blurred and my heart bounced up to bump my tonsils as he sunk to one knee on the sand in front of me.

'My love, my life, my *bella*,' he said, his voice

gruff and deadly serious now. 'Will you become my wife?'

I covered my mouth with quivering fingers as tears of joy seeped over my lids to course down my cheeks—so shocked and moved I could barely speak. 'Oh, Dante, I... I... I can't...'

'All you have to do is say yes, *bella*,' he said gently, the tiny quiver of uncertainty as his gaze met mine making me love him all the more.

'Oh, Dante...' I said again. And then I flew at him, throwing my arms around his shoulders and knocking him over. 'Yes, yes, yes!' I shouted, so the whole world could hear me. And him most of all. 'Absolutely yes!'

His deep chuckles joined my joyous laughter as we rolled over together.

The sun shone on his waves of dark hair as he rose over me. 'Damn, I think I've lost the ring,' he said as he glanced at the now empty ring box still clutched in his fist.

'It doesn't matter,' I said, flinging my arms around his neck to pull him down towards me. 'We'll find it, together.'

He smiled at me, the cool blue of his irises hot with the promise of all the years to come. 'Yes,' he said, his voice rich and full of confidence—like my heart. 'We will find it, together.'

Then he kissed me, and his lips tasted of safety and security, and love, and sunshine, and happiness... And sand!

* * * * *

LET'S TALK

Romance

For exclusive extracts, competitions
and special offers, find us online:

f facebook.com/millsandboon

◎ @millsandboonuk

𝕏 @millsandboon

Or get in touch on 0844 844 1351*

For all the latest titles coming soon,
visit millsandboon.co.uk/nextmonth

*Calls cost 7p per minute plus your phone company's price per
minute access charge